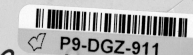

Archie at RIVERDALE HIGH®

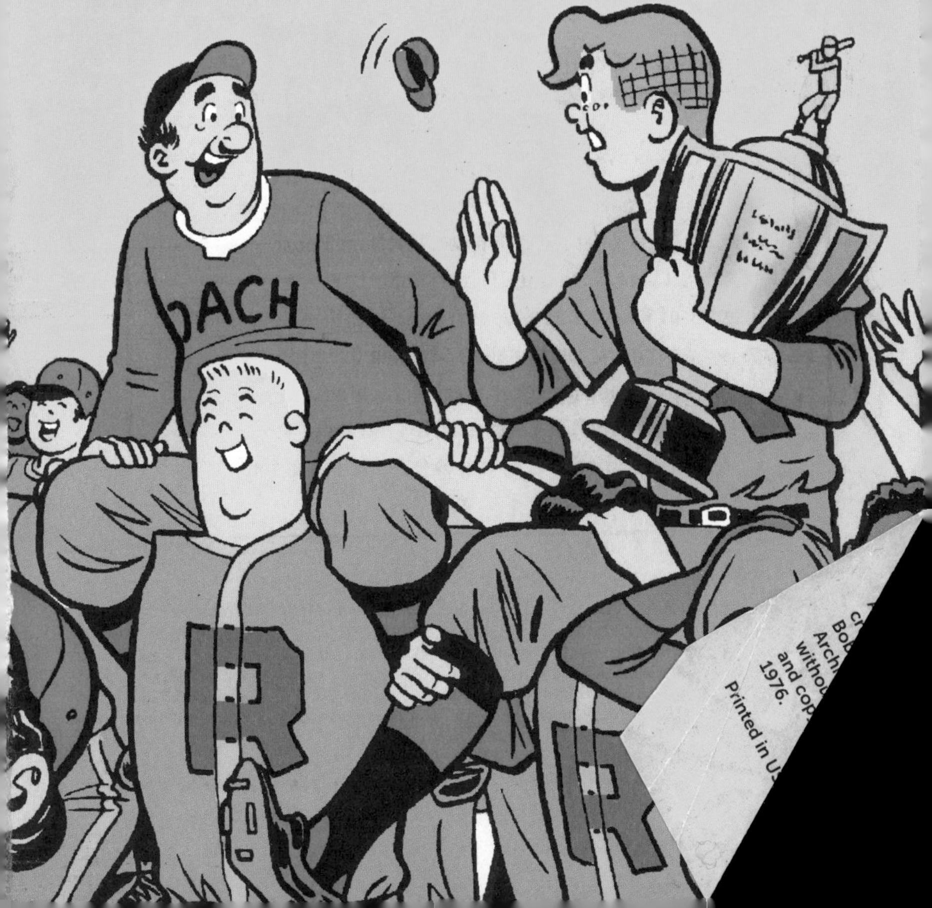

Archie at RIVERDALE HIGH

Publisher / Co-CEO: Jon Goldwater
Co-CEO: Nancy Silberkleit
Co-President / Editor-In-Chief: Victor Gorelick
Co-President: Mike Pellerito
Co-President: Alex Segura
Chief Creative Officer: Roberto Aguirre-Sacasa
Chief Operating Officer: William Mooar
Chief Financial Officer: Robert Wintle
Director of Book Sales & Operations: Jonathan Betancourt
Production Manager: Stephen Oswald
Lead Designer: Kari McLachlan
Associate Editor: Carlos Antunes
Assistant Editor / Proofreader: Jamie Lee Rotante

USA. First Printing. ISBN: 978-1-68255-897-3

WRITTEN BY

Frank Doyle, George Gladir,
& Bob Bolling

ART BY

Harry Lucey, Dan DeCarlo, Stan Goldberg, Bob Bolling,
Jon D'Agostino, Rudy Lapick, Chic Stone, Henry Scarpelli,
Jim DeCarlo, Mike Esposito, Barry Grossman & Bill Yoshida

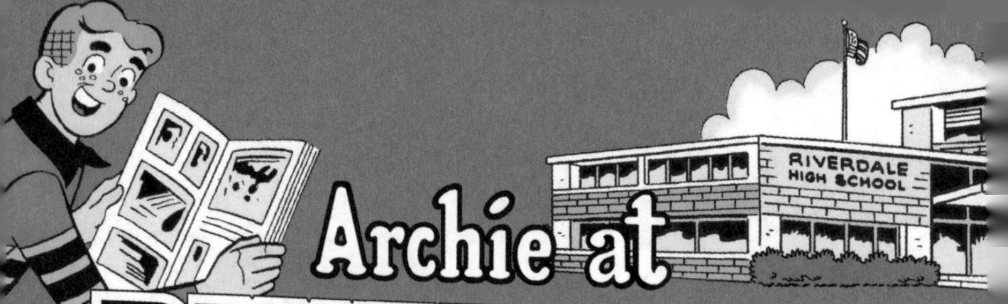
RIVERDALE
HIGH SCHOOL

Archie at RIVERDALE HIGH®

TABLE OF CONTENTS

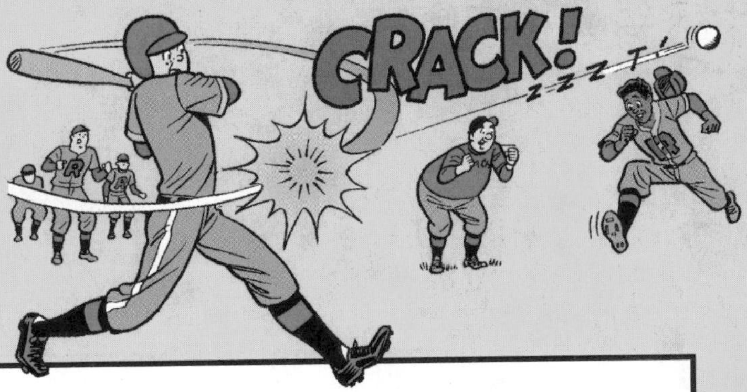
CRACK!

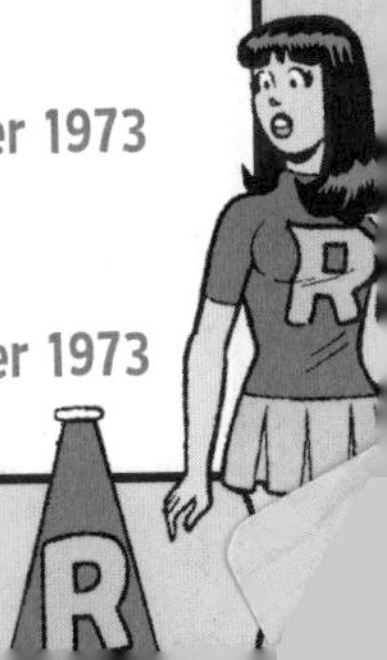

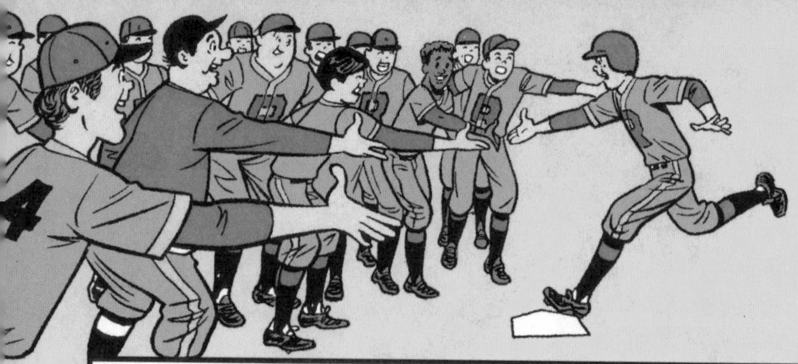

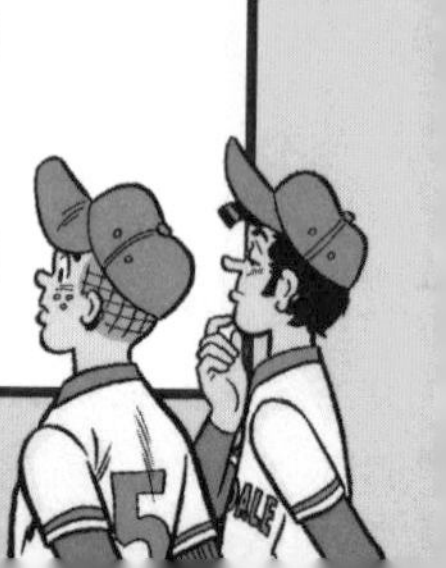

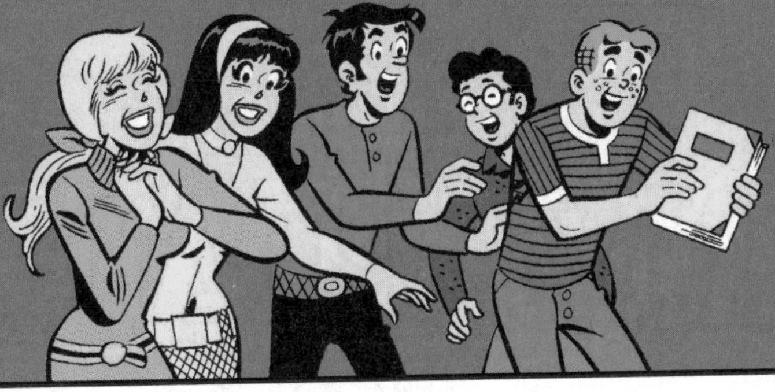

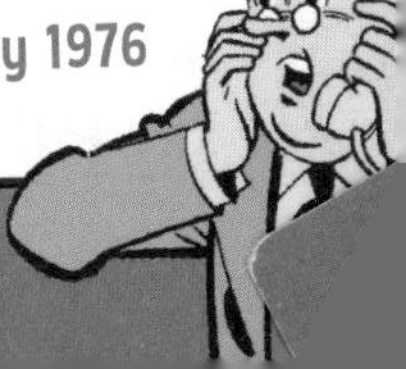

Archie at RIVERDALE HIGH®

Archie fans—and TV fans around the world—are very familiar with the hallowed halls of Riverdale High. It's not just the local educational institution of Archie and his pals 'n' gals, it's the center of their universe! And that's certainly true for this classic 1970s series that focuses not only on the adventures of Archie, Jughead, Moose, Reggie, Betty, Veronica and the rest of the gang at their alma mater, Riverdale High—Mr. Weatherbee, Riverdale's long-suffering principal, also takes center stage, along with the various teachers, coaches, secretaries, lunchroom ladies, and other familiar faculty of the high school.

Archie at Riverdale High was a unique series in that it wasn't always the usual 5- 6-page funny story; it also features longer-form tales that dive into the mysterious, the dramatic, the action-packed and even the downright chilling!

Grab your backpack and join us for class... things are going to get interesting!

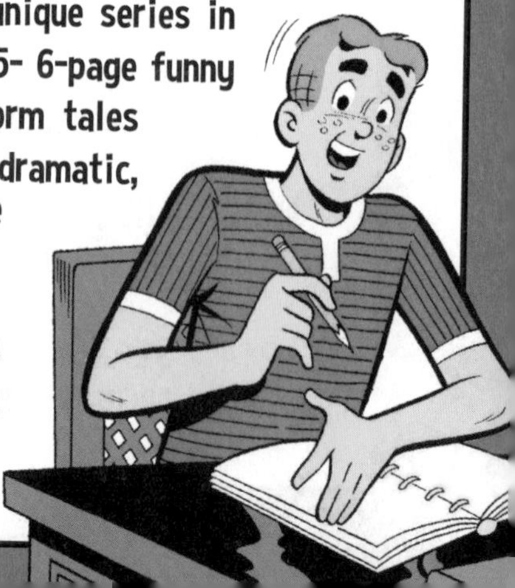

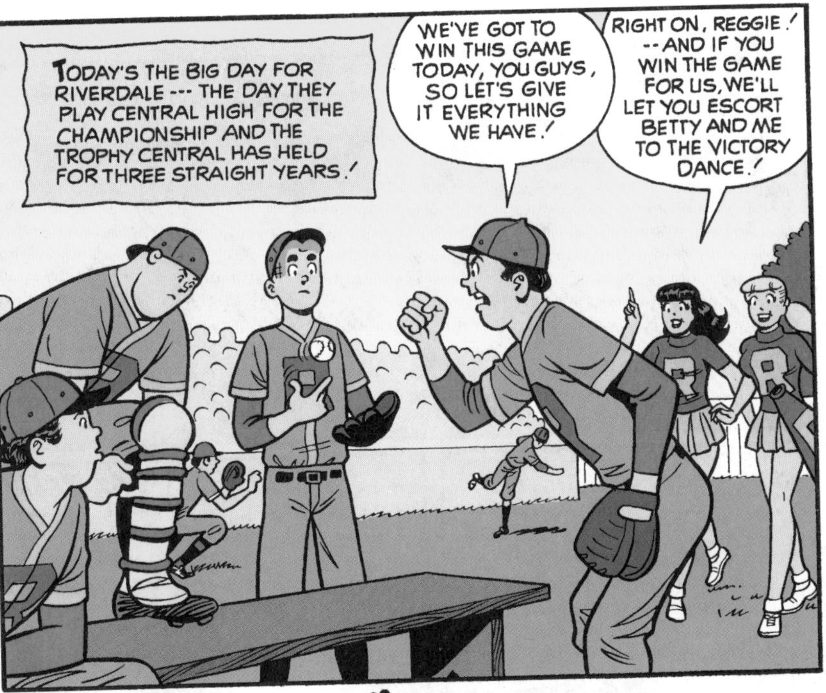
TODAY'S THE BIG DAY FOR RIVERDALE --- THE DAY THEY PLAY CENTRAL HIGH FOR THE CHAMPIONSHIP AND THE TROPHY CENTRAL HAS HELD FOR THREE STRAIGHT YEARS!
WE'VE GOT TO WIN THIS GAME TODAY, YOU GUYS, SO LET'S GIVE IT EVERYTHING WE HAVE!
RIGHT ON, REGGIE! -- AND IF YOU WIN THE GAME FOR US, WE'LL LET YOU ESCORT BETTY AND ME TO THE VICTORY DANCE!

Archie

"YOU CAN'T WIN 'EM ALL"

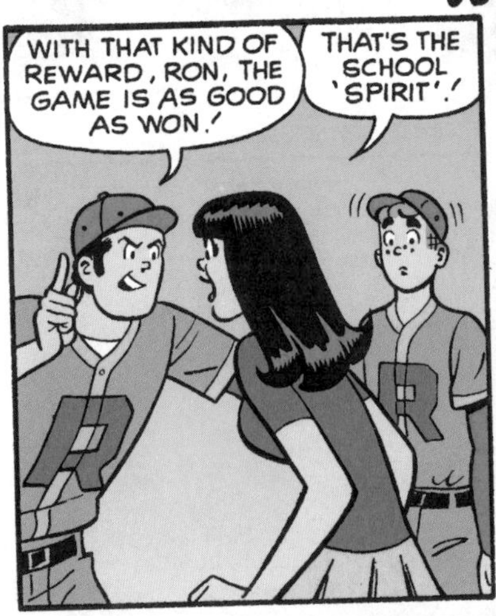
WITH THAT KIND OF REWARD, RON, THE GAME IS AS GOOD AS WON!
THAT'S THE SCHOOL 'SPIRIT'!

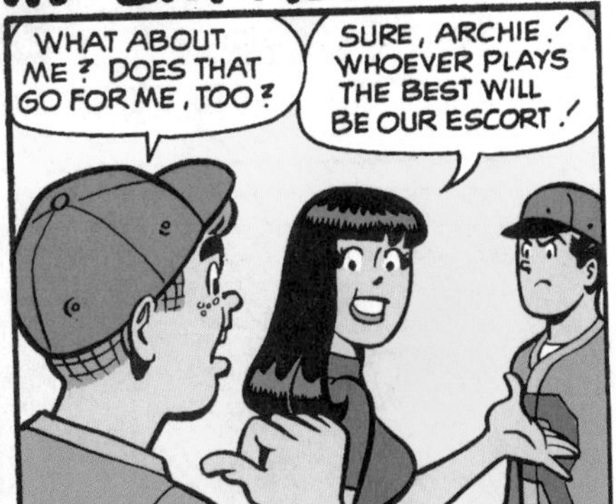
WHAT ABOUT ME? DOES THAT GO FOR ME, TOO?
SURE, ARCHIE! WHOEVER PLAYS THE BEST WILL BE OUR ESCORT!

Story: Frank Doyle   Art: Harry Lucey

Originally printed in ARCHIE AT RIVERDALE HIGH #1, AUGUST 1972

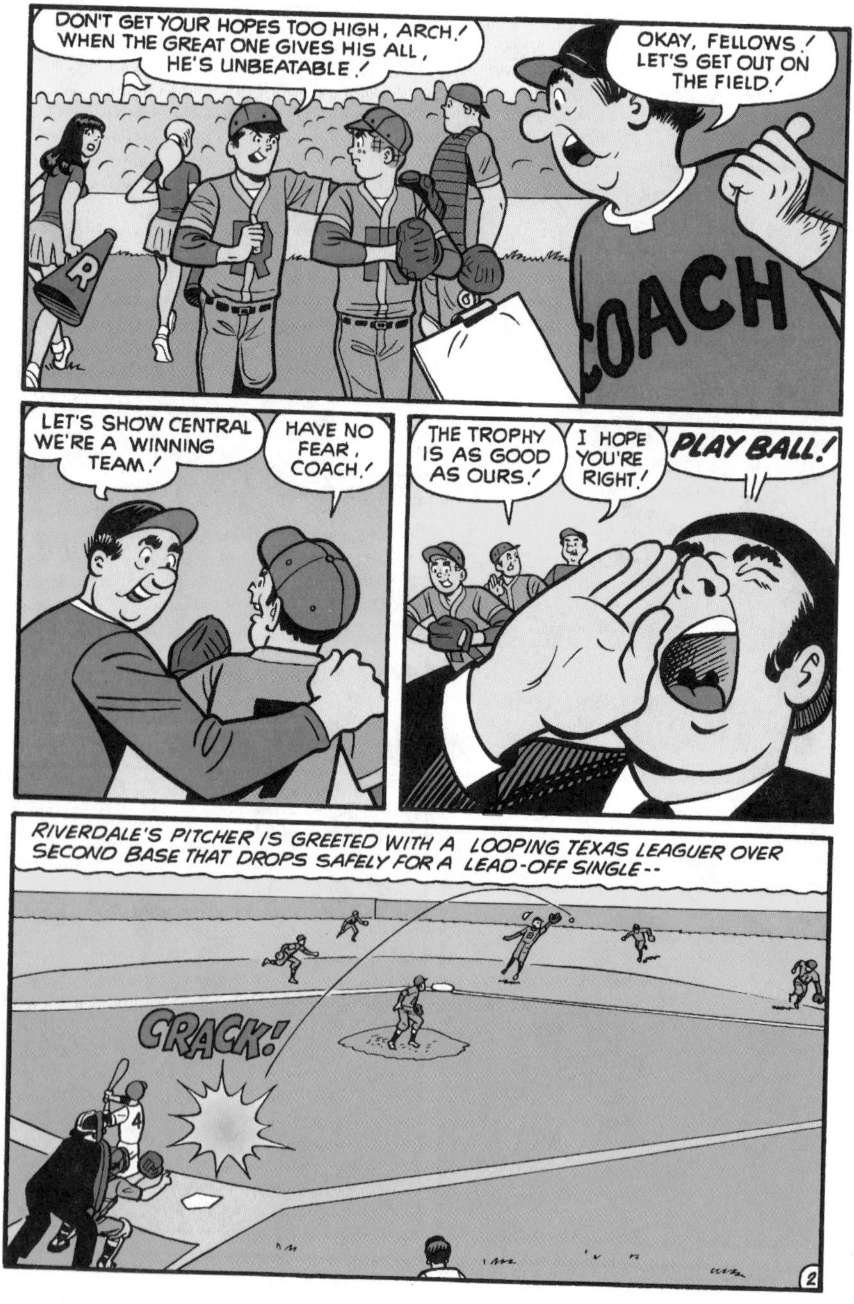
DON'T GET YOUR HOPES TOO HIGH, ARCH! WHEN THE GREAT ONE GIVES HIS ALL, HE'S UNBEATABLE!
OKAY, FELLOWS! LET'S GET OUT ON THE FIELD!
COACH
LET'S SHOW CENTRAL WE'RE A WINNING TEAM!
HAVE NO FEAR, COACH!
THE TROPHY IS AS GOOD AS OURS!
I HOPE YOU'RE RIGHT!
PLAY BALL!
RIVERDALE'S PITCHER IS GREETED WITH A LOOPING TEXAS LEAGUER OVER SECOND BASE THAT DROPS SAFELY FOR A LEAD-OFF SINGLE--
CRACK!
2

THE NEXT MAN MOVES THE RUNNER ALONG WITH A PERFECT SACRIFICE!

FACING THE HEAVY PART OF THE BATTING ORDER, RIVERDALE'S PITCHER WORKS CAREFULLY AND THE COUNT GOES TO 3-2!

BALL FOUR!

SHAKEN BY THE CLOSE CALL, HE HANGS A CURVE BALL TO CENTRAL'S CLEANUP HITTER WHO EXPLODES A HOME RUN!

POW!

FINALLY SETTLING DOWN HE GETS THE NEXT TWO BATTERS ON A STRIKE-OUT AND AN EASY FLY BALL, BUT CENTRAL IS ON THE SCOREBOARD EARLY WITH THREE BIG RUNS!

	1	2	3	4
VISITORS	3			
RIVERDALE				

AT BAT 6 BALL 2 STRIKE 2

OKAY, BOYS! LET'S GET A RALLY GOING AND GET THOSE RUNS BACK!

RIGHT, COACH! JUST WATCH!

OUT!

PLOP!

AND SO IT GOES-- THROUGH SEVEN INNINGS CENTRAL'S PITCHER BAFFLES RIVERDALE'S BATTERS--

PIP!

EVEN MOOSE FLAILS FUTILELY AT THE ELUSIVE HORSEHIDE!

STRIKE THREE!

SWISH!

PLOP!

WHILE RIVERDALE IS FORCED TO MAKE SENSATIONAL FIELDING PLAYS TO KEEP CENTRAL FROM ADDING MORE RUNS TO ITS EARLY SCORE!

PLOP!

OUT!

PLOP!

PLOP!

	1	2	3	4
VISITORS	3	0	0	0
RIVERDALE	0	0	0	0

AT BAT 5   BALL 2   STRIKE

④

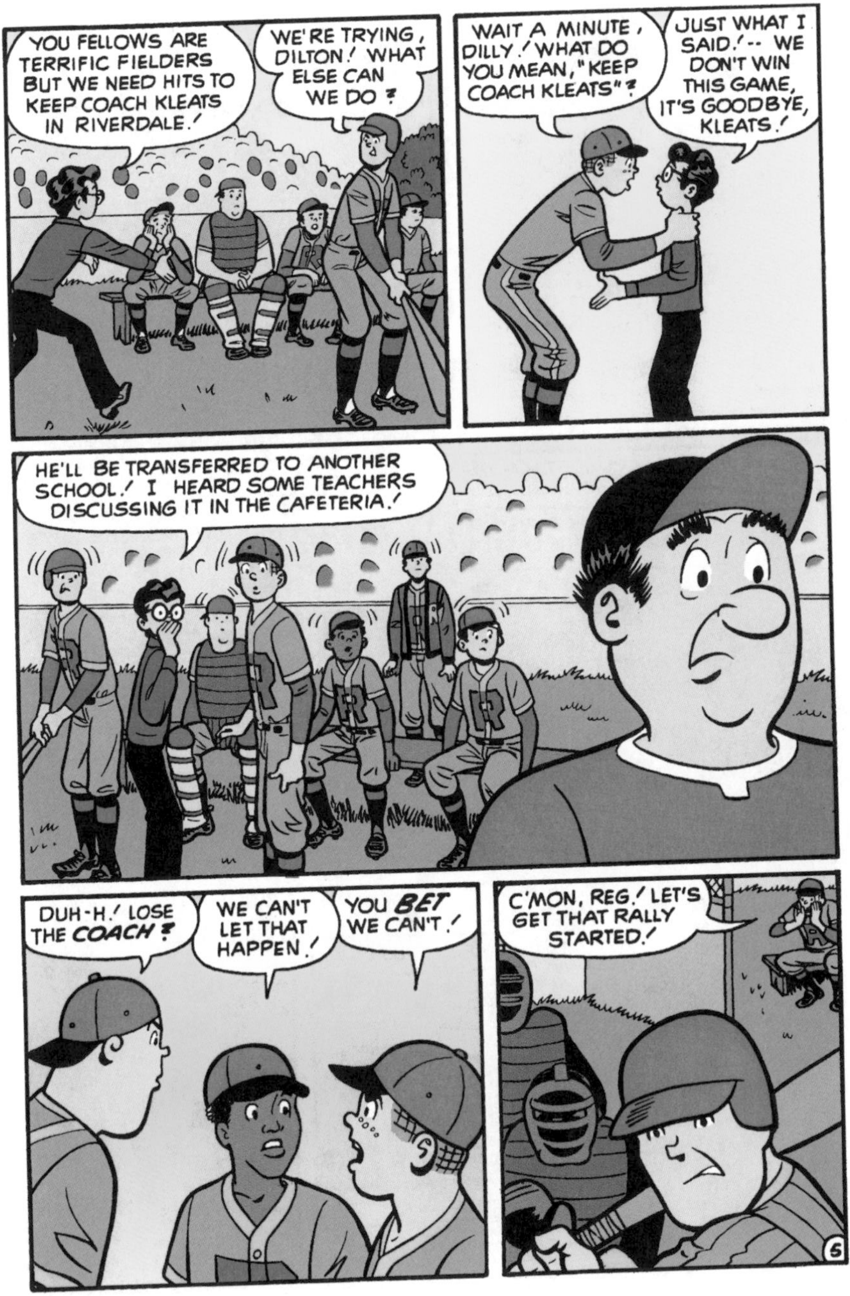
YOU FELLOWS ARE TERRIFIC FIELDERS BUT WE NEED HITS TO KEEP COACH KLEATS IN RIVERDALE!
WE'RE TRYING, DILTON! WHAT ELSE CAN WE DO?
WAIT A MINUTE, DILLY! WHAT DO YOU MEAN, "KEEP COACH KLEATS"?
JUST WHAT I SAID! -- WE DON'T WIN THIS GAME, IT'S GOODBYE, KLEATS!
HE'LL BE TRANSFERRED TO ANOTHER SCHOOL! I HEARD SOME TEACHERS DISCUSSING IT IN THE CAFETERIA!
DUH-H! LOSE THE *COACH*?
WE CAN'T LET THAT HAPPEN!
YOU *BET* WE CAN'T!
C'MON, REG! LET'S GET THAT RALLY STARTED!
6

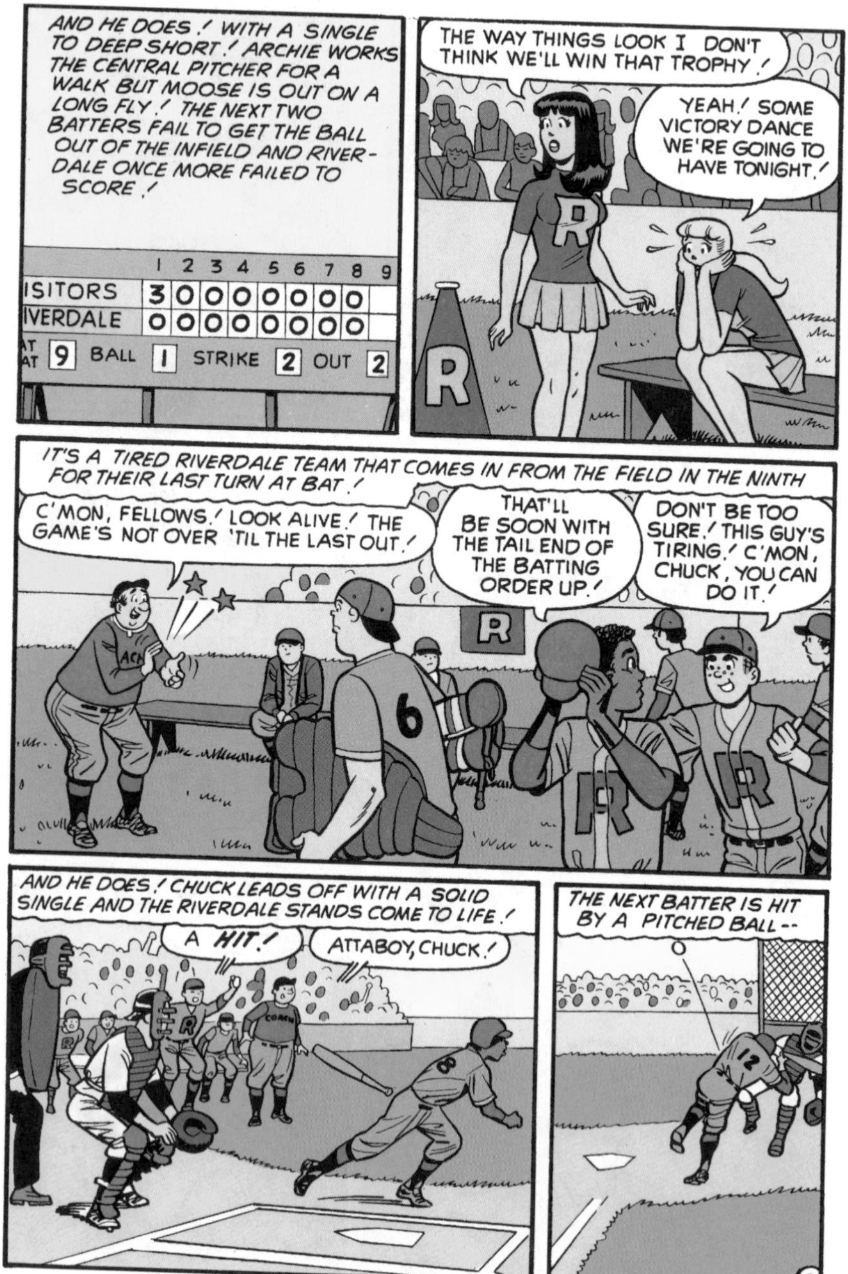
AND HE DOES! WITH A SINGLE TO DEEP SHORT! ARCHIE WORKS THE CENTRAL PITCHER FOR A WALK BUT MOOSE IS OUT ON A LONG FLY! THE NEXT TWO BATTERS FAIL TO GET THE BALL OUT OF THE INFIELD AND RIVER-DALE ONCE MORE FAILED TO SCORE!
1 2 3 4 5 6 7 8 9
ISITORS 3 0 0 0 0 0 0 0 0
IVERDALE 0 0 0 0 0 0 0 0 0
9 BALL 1 STRIKE 2 OUT 2
THE WAY THINGS LOOK I DON'T THINK WE'LL WIN THAT TROPHY!
YEAH! SOME VICTORY DANCE WE'RE GOING TO HAVE TONIGHT!
R
R
IT'S A TIRED RIVERDALE TEAM THAT COMES IN FROM THE FIELD IN THE NINTH FOR THEIR LAST TURN AT BAT!
C'MON, FELLOWS! LOOK ALIVE! THE GAME'S NOT OVER 'TIL THE LAST OUT!
THAT'LL BE SOON WITH THE TAIL END OF THE BATTING ORDER UP!
DON'T BE TOO SURE! THIS GUY'S TIRING! C'MON, CHUCK, YOU CAN DO IT!
R
6
AND HE DOES! CHUCK LEADS OFF WITH A SOLID SINGLE AND THE RIVERDALE STANDS COME TO LIFE!
A HIT!
ATTABOY, CHUCK!
THE NEXT BATTER IS HIT BY A PITCHED BALL--
12
6

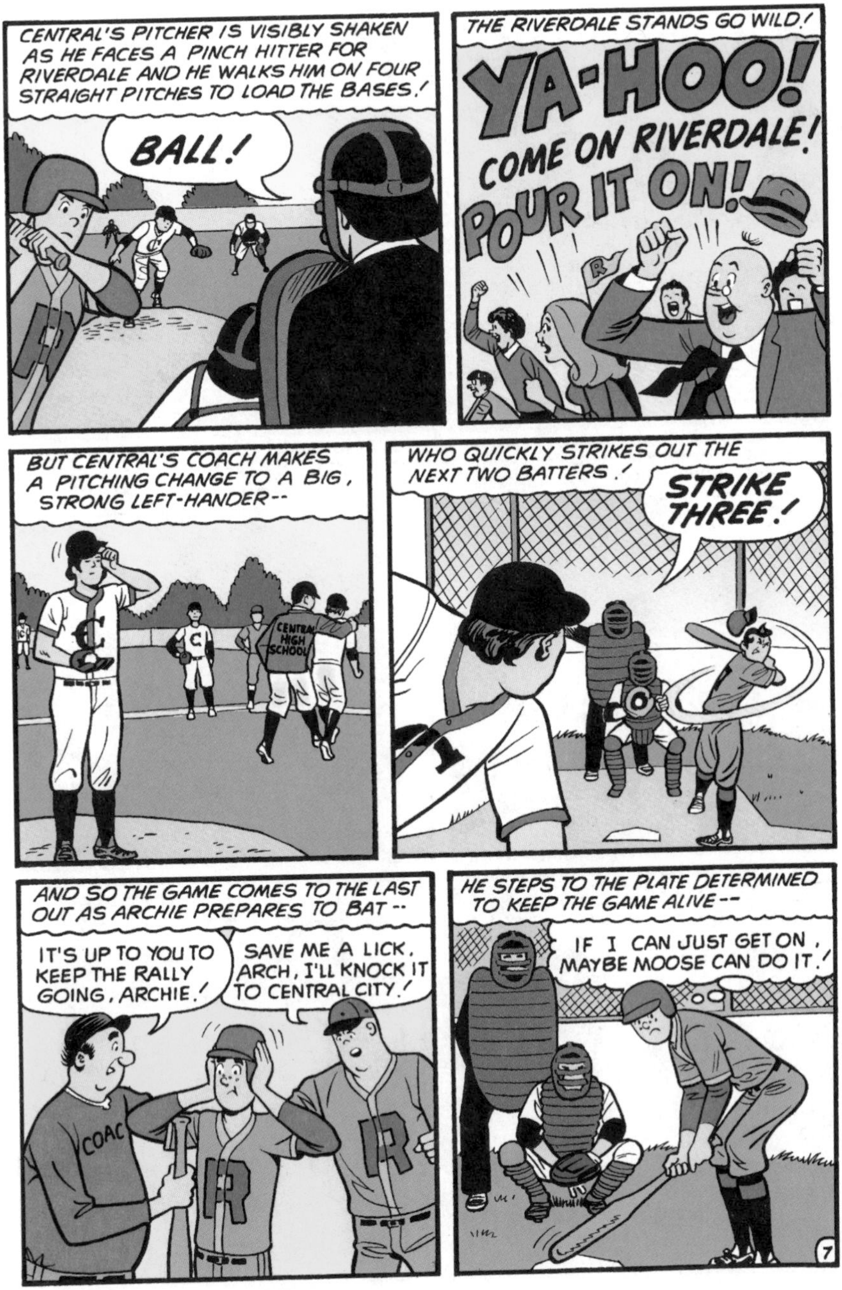
CENTRAL'S PITCHER IS VISIBLY SHAKEN AS HE FACES A PINCH HITTER FOR RIVERDALE AND HE WALKS HIM ON FOUR STRAIGHT PITCHES TO LOAD THE BASES.!
BALL!
THE RIVERDALE STANDS GO WILD!
YA-HOO!
COME ON RIVERDALE!
POUR IT ON!
BUT CENTRAL'S COACH MAKES A PITCHING CHANGE TO A BIG, STRONG LEFT-HANDER--
CENTRAL HIGH SCHOOL
WHO QUICKLY STRIKES OUT THE NEXT TWO BATTERS!
STRIKE THREE!
AND SO THE GAME COMES TO THE LAST OUT AS ARCHIE PREPARES TO BAT--
IT'S UP TO YOU TO KEEP THE RALLY GOING, ARCHIE!
SAVE ME A LICK, ARCH, I'LL KNOCK IT TO CENTRAL CITY!
COAC
HE STEPS TO THE PLATE DETERMINED TO KEEP THE GAME ALIVE--
IF I CAN JUST GET ON, MAYBE MOOSE CAN DO IT!
7

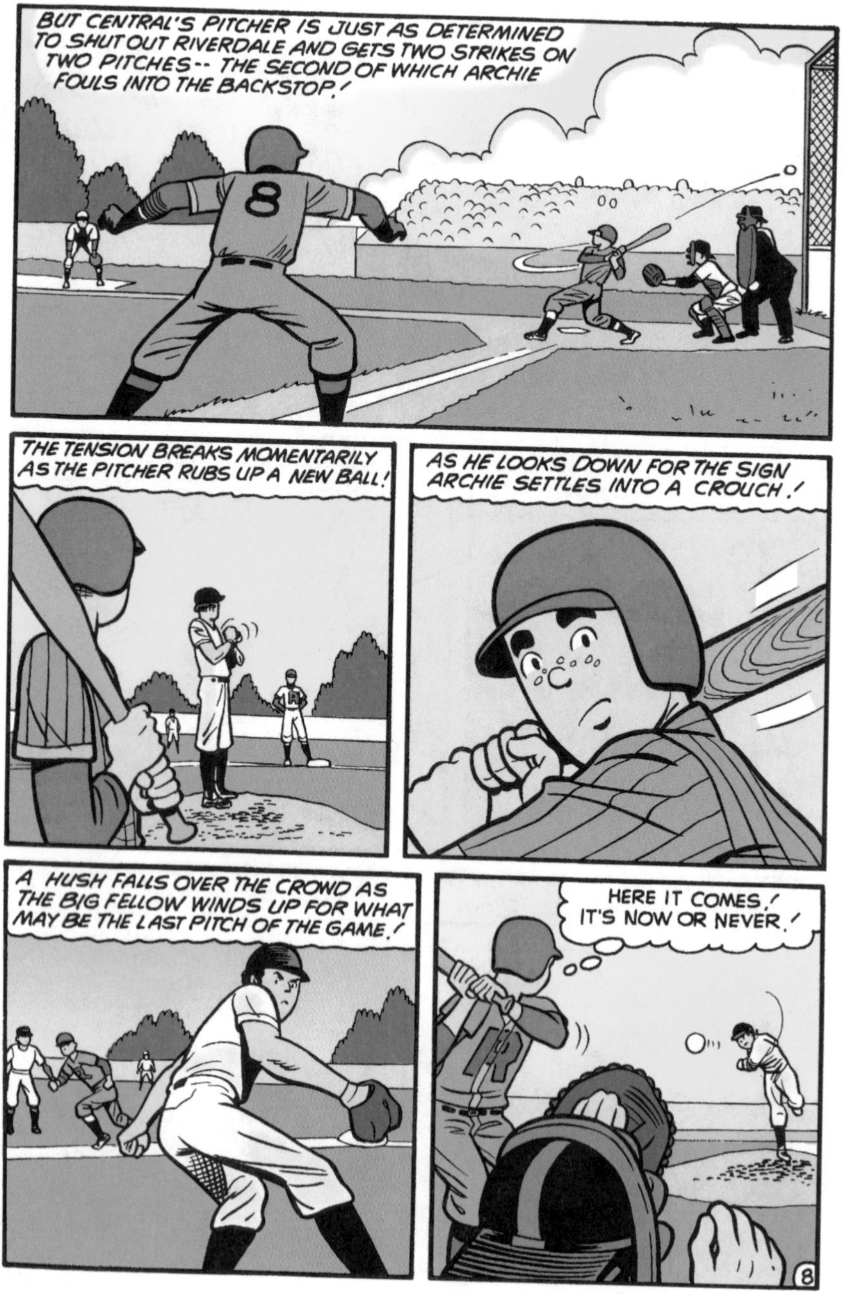
BUT CENTRAL'S PITCHER IS JUST AS DETERMINED TO SHUT OUT RIVERDALE AND GETS TWO STRIKES ON TWO PITCHES-- THE SECOND OF WHICH ARCHIE FOULS INTO THE BACKSTOP!
THE TENSION BREAKS MOMENTARILY AS THE PITCHER RUBS UP A NEW BALL!
AS HE LOOKS DOWN FOR THE SIGN ARCHIE SETTLES INTO A CROUCH!
A HUSH FALLS OVER THE CROWD AS THE BIG FELLOW WINDS UP FOR WHAT MAY BE THE LAST PITCH OF THE GAME!
HERE IT COMES! IT'S NOW OR NEVER!
8

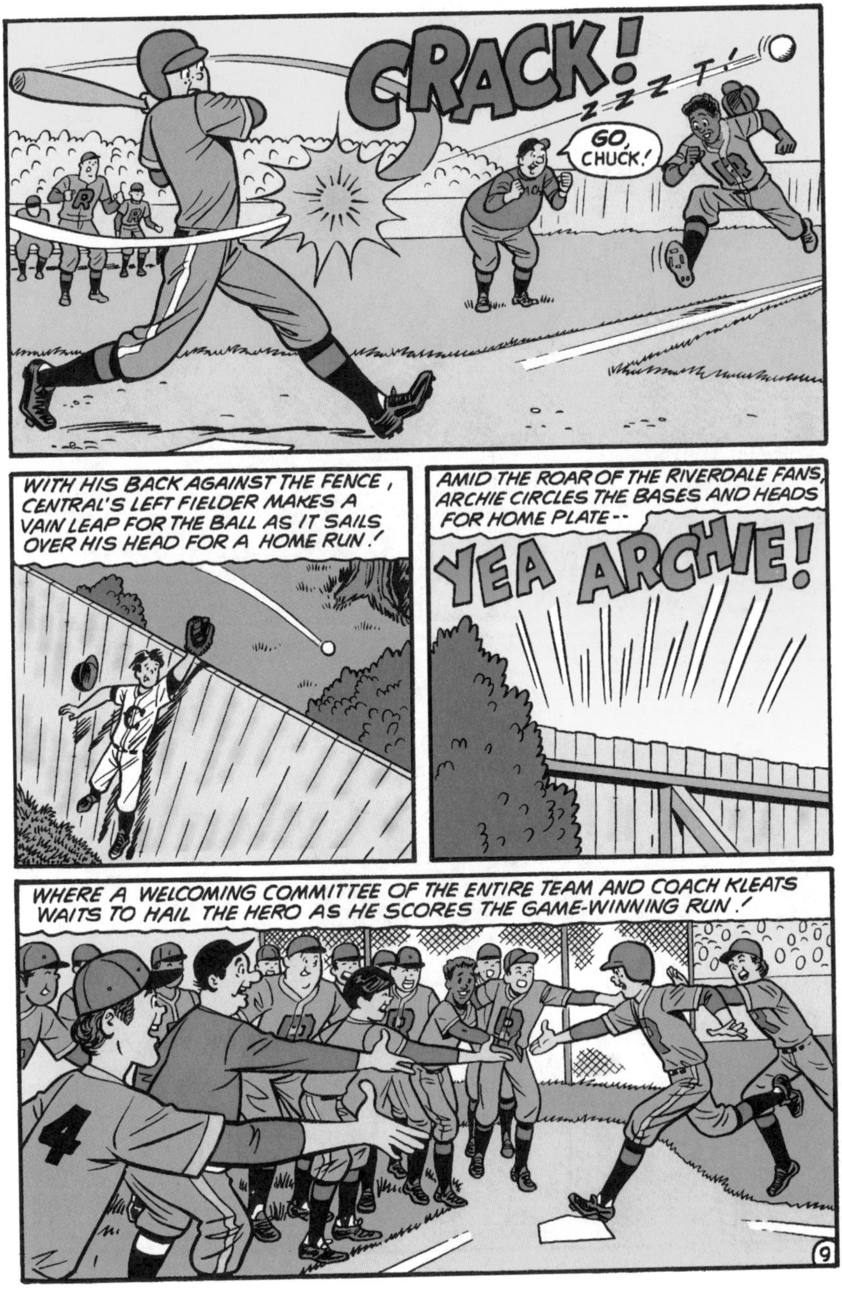
CRACK!
ZZZZZT!
GO, CHUCK!
WITH HIS BACK AGAINST THE FENCE, CENTRAL'S LEFT FIELDER MAKES A VAIN LEAP FOR THE BALL AS IT SAILS OVER HIS HEAD FOR A HOME RUN!
AMID THE ROAR OF THE RIVERDALE FANS, ARCHIE CIRCLES THE BASES AND HEADS FOR HOME PLATE--
YEA ARCHIE!
WHERE A WELCOMING COMMITTEE OF THE ENTIRE TEAM AND COACH KLEATS WAITS TO HAIL THE HERO AS HE SCORES THE GAME-WINNING RUN!
4
9

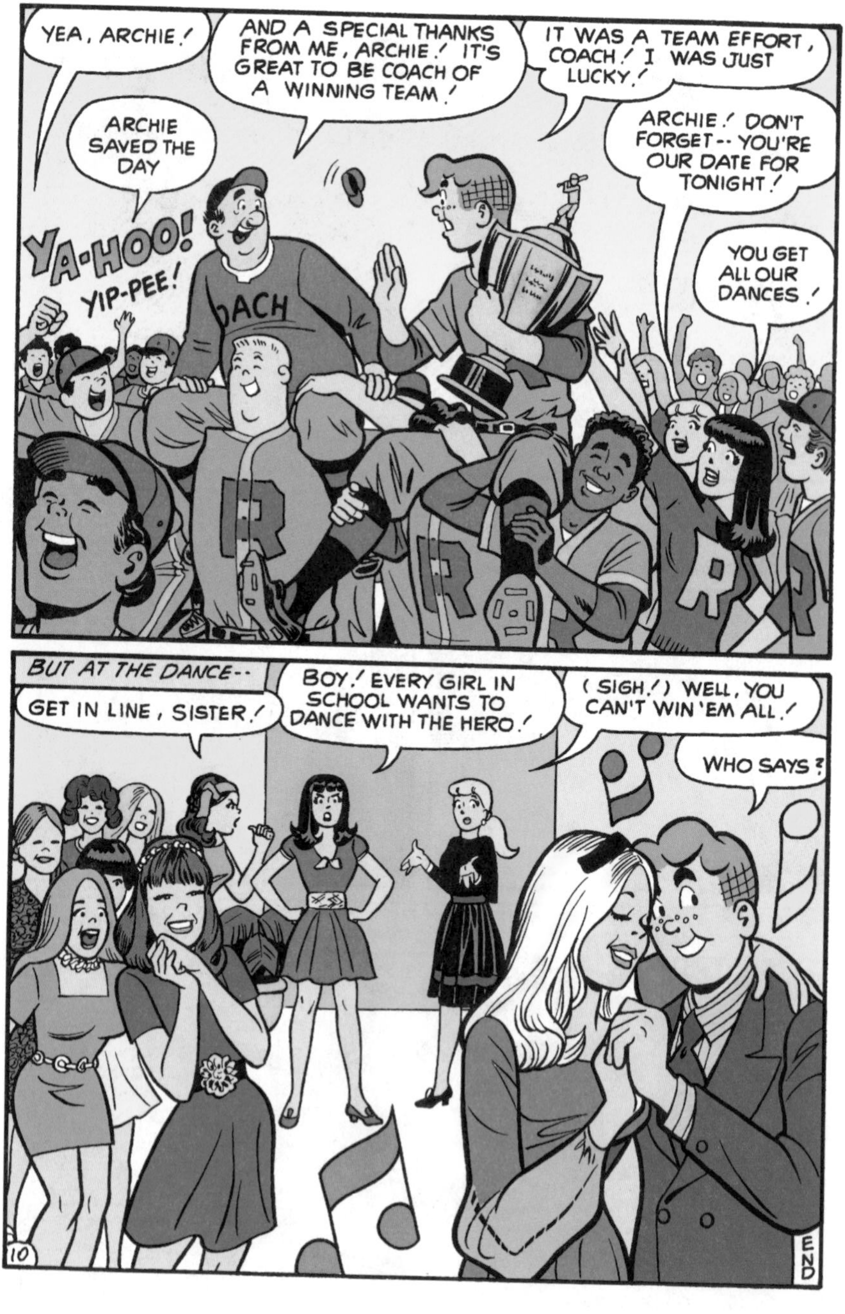
YEA, ARCHIE!
AND A SPECIAL THANKS FROM ME, ARCHIE! IT'S GREAT TO BE COACH OF A WINNING TEAM!
IT WAS A TEAM EFFORT, COACH! I WAS JUST LUCKY!
ARCHIE SAVED THE DAY
ARCHIE! DON'T FORGET-- YOU'RE OUR DATE FOR TONIGHT!
YA-HOO!
YIP-PEE!
YOU GET ALL OUR DANCES!
BUT AT THE DANCE--
GET IN LINE, SISTER!
BOY! EVERY GIRL IN SCHOOL WANTS TO DANCE WITH THE HERO!
(SIGH!) WELL, YOU CAN'T WIN 'EM ALL!
WHO SAYS?
10
END

Archie at Riverdale High "Second Chance"

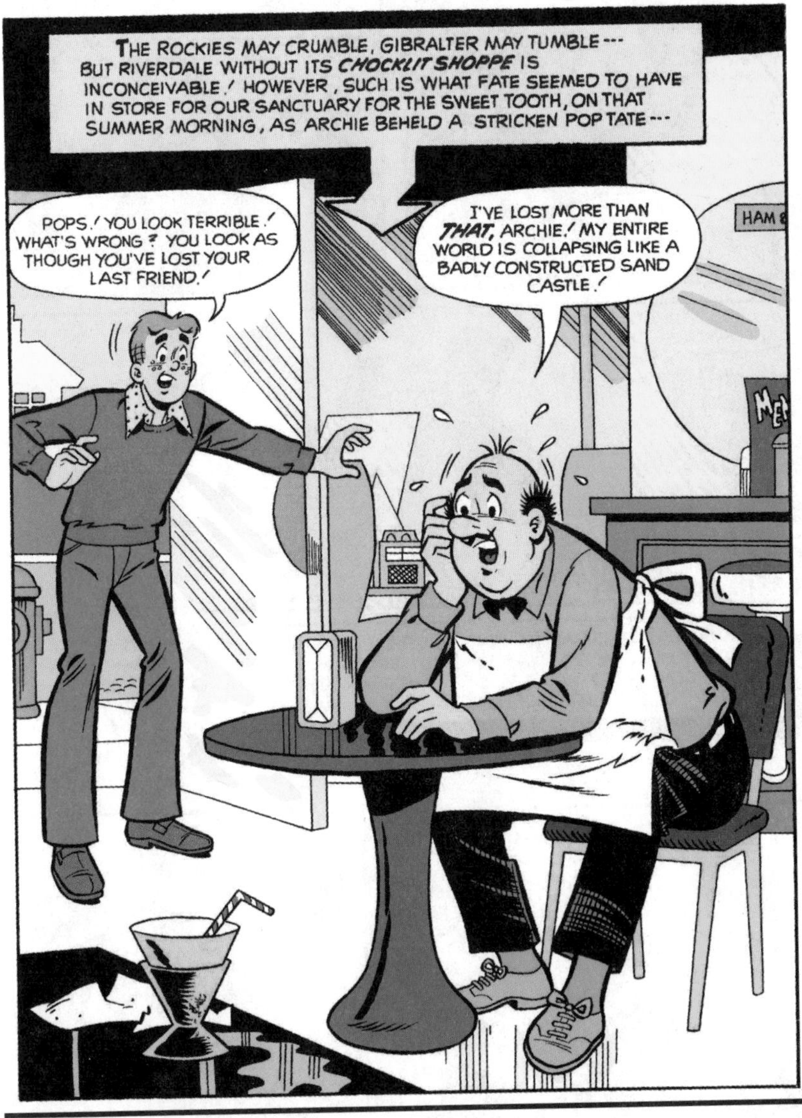
THE ROCKIES MAY CRUMBLE, GIBRALTER MAY TUMBLE--- BUT RIVERDALE WITHOUT ITS CHOCKLIT SHOPPE IS INCONCEIVABLE! HOWEVER, SUCH IS WHAT FATE SEEMED TO HAVE IN STORE FOR OUR SANCTUARY FOR THE SWEET TOOTH, ON THAT SUMMER MORNING, AS ARCHIE BEHELD A STRICKEN POP TATE---
POPS! YOU LOOK TERRIBLE! WHAT'S WRONG? YOU LOOK AS THOUGH YOU'VE LOST YOUR LAST FRIEND!
I'VE LOST MORE THAN THAT, ARCHIE! MY ENTIRE WORLD IS COLLAPSING LIKE A BADLY CONSTRUCTED SAND CASTLE!

Story: Frank Doyle   Pencils: Stan Goldberg
Inks: Jon D'Agostino   Letters: Bill Yoshida

Originally printed in ARCHIE AT RIVERDALE HIGH #1, AUGUST 1972

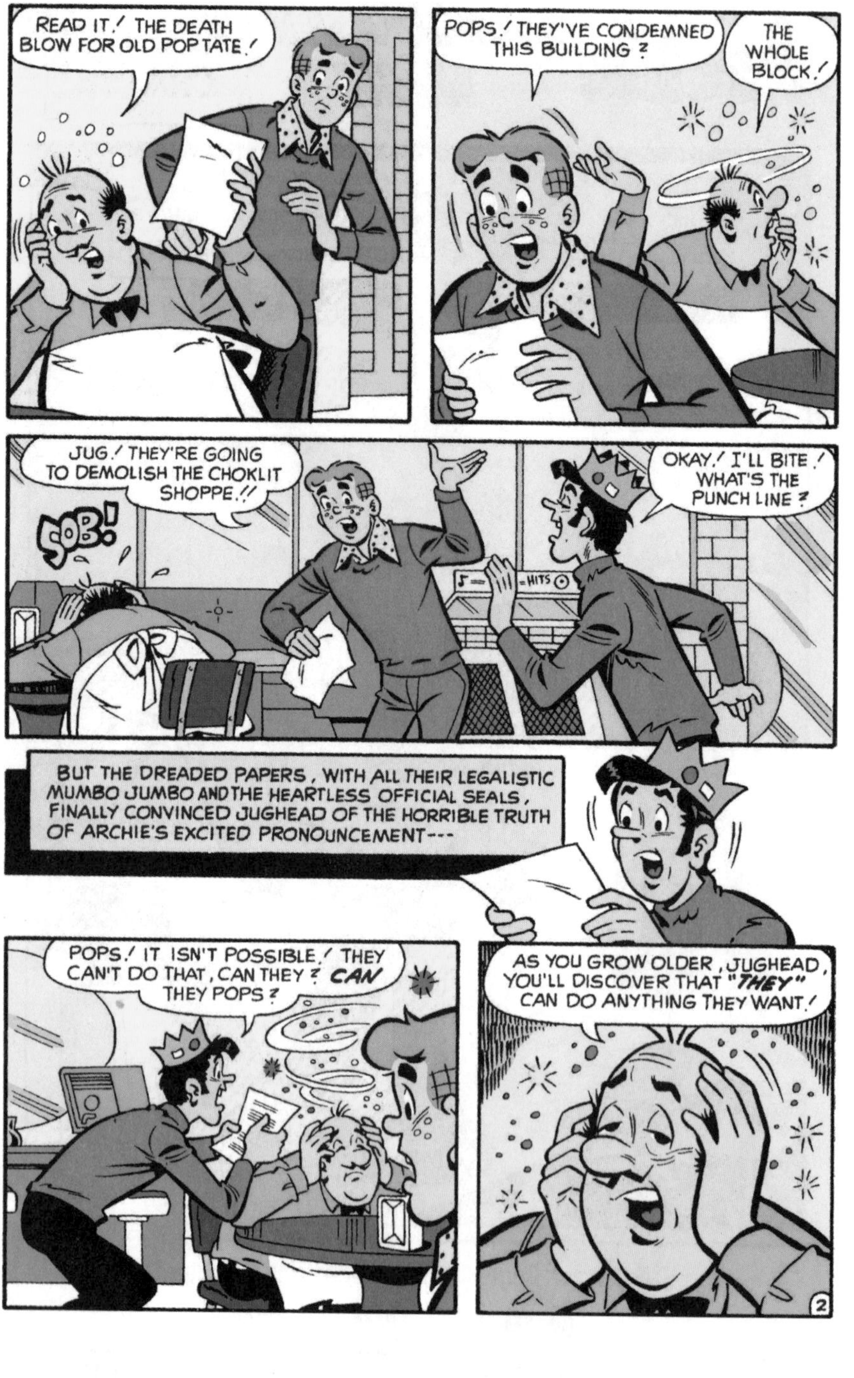
READ IT! THE DEATH BLOW FOR OLD POP TATE!
POPS! THEY'VE CONDEMNED THIS BUILDING?
THE WHOLE BLOCK!
JUG! THEY'RE GOING TO DEMOLISH THE CHOKLIT SHOPPE!!
SOB!
OKAY! I'LL BITE! WHAT'S THE PUNCH LINE?
=HITS
BUT THE DREADED PAPERS, WITH ALL THEIR LEGALISTIC MUMBO JUMBO AND THE HEARTLESS OFFICIAL SEALS, FINALLY CONVINCED JUGHEAD OF THE HORRIBLE TRUTH OF ARCHIE'S EXCITED PRONOUNCEMENT---
POPS! IT ISN'T POSSIBLE! THEY CAN'T DO THAT, CAN THEY? CAN THEY POPS?
AS YOU GROW OLDER, JUGHEAD, YOU'LL DISCOVER THAT "THEY" CAN DO ANYTHING THEY WANT!
2

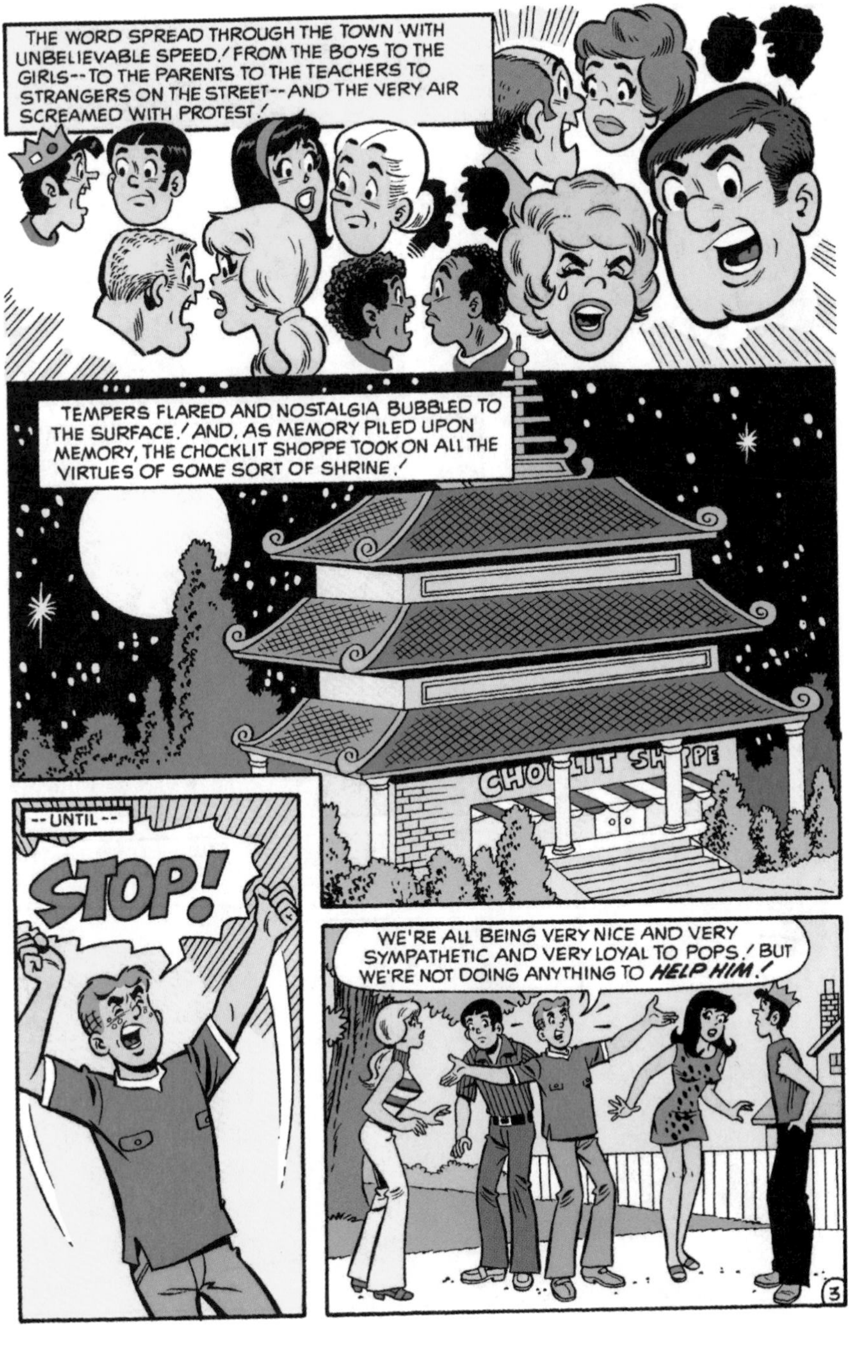
THE WORD SPREAD THROUGH THE TOWN WITH UNBELIEVABLE SPEED! FROM THE BOYS TO THE GIRLS--TO THE PARENTS TO THE TEACHERS TO STRANGERS ON THE STREET--AND THE VERY AIR SCREAMED WITH PROTEST!
TEMPERS FLARED AND NOSTALGIA BUBBLED TO THE SURFACE! AND, AS MEMORY PILED UPON MEMORY, THE CHOCKLIT SHOPPE TOOK ON ALL THE VIRTUES OF SOME SORT OF SHRINE!
--UNTIL--
STOP!
WE'RE ALL BEING VERY NICE AND VERY SYMPATHETIC AND VERY LOYAL TO POPS! BUT WE'RE NOT DOING ANYTHING TO HELP HIM!
3

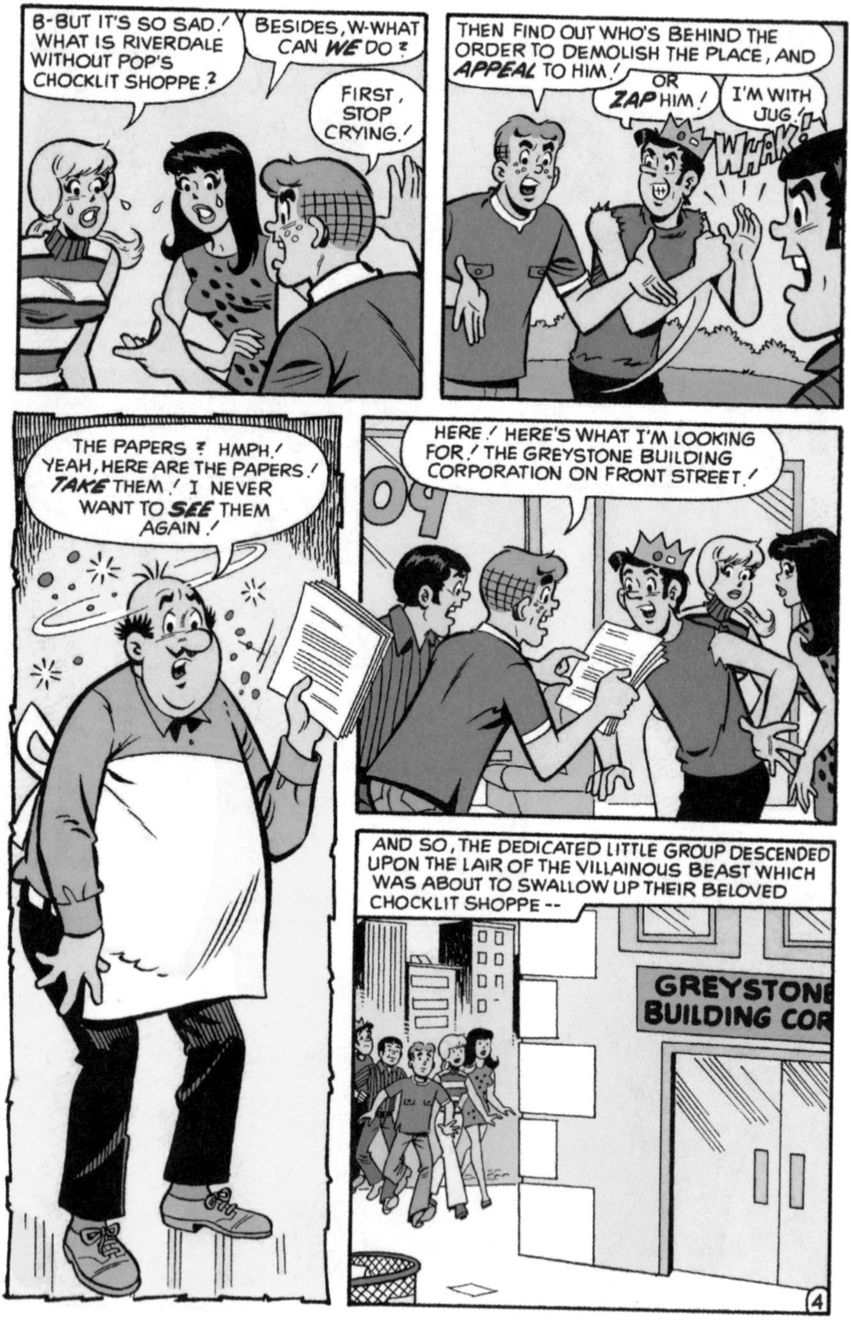

B-BUT IT'S SO SAD! WHAT IS RIVERDALE WITHOUT POP'S CHOCKLIT SHOPPE?
BESIDES, W-WHAT CAN WE DO?
FIRST, STOP CRYING!
THEN FIND OUT WHO'S BEHIND THE ORDER TO DEMOLISH THE PLACE, AND APPEAL TO HIM!
OR ZAP HIM!
I'M WITH JUG!
WHAK!
THE PAPERS? HMPH! YEAH, HERE ARE THE PAPERS! TAKE THEM! I NEVER WANT TO SEE THEM AGAIN!
HERE! HERE'S WHAT I'M LOOKING FOR! THE GREYSTONE BUILDING CORPORATION ON FRONT STREET!
AND SO, THE DEDICATED LITTLE GROUP DESCENDED UPON THE LAIR OF THE VILLAINOUS BEAST WHICH WAS ABOUT TO SWALLOW UP THEIR BELOVED CHOCKLIT SHOPPE --
GREYSTONE BUILDING COR
4

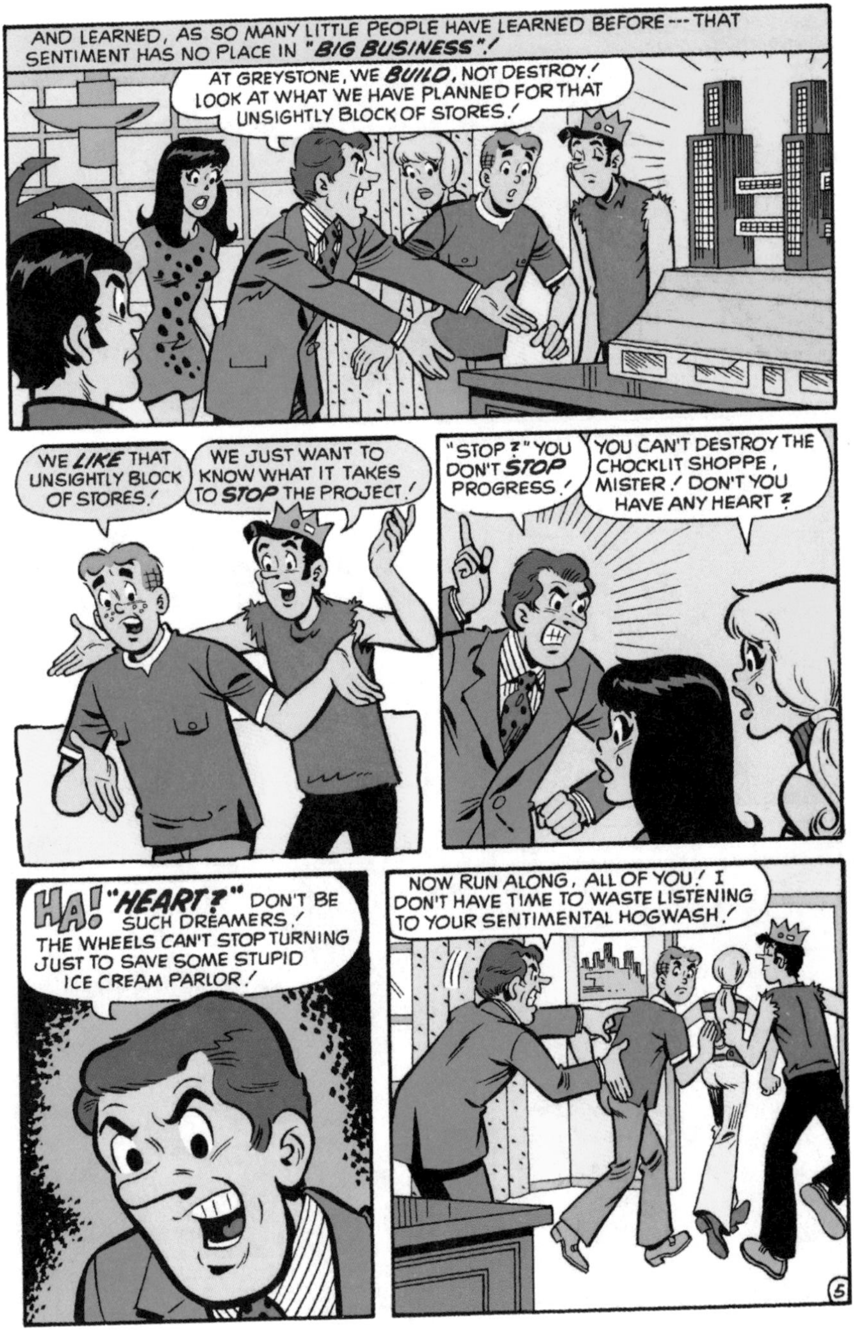
AND LEARNED, AS SO MANY LITTLE PEOPLE HAVE LEARNED BEFORE --- THAT SENTIMENT HAS NO PLACE IN "BIG BUSINESS"!
AT GREYSTONE, WE BUILD, NOT DESTROY! LOOK AT WHAT WE HAVE PLANNED FOR THAT UNSIGHTLY BLOCK OF STORES!
WE LIKE THAT UNSIGHTLY BLOCK OF STORES!
WE JUST WANT TO KNOW WHAT IT TAKES TO STOP THE PROJECT!
"STOP?" YOU DON'T STOP PROGRESS!
YOU CAN'T DESTROY THE CHOCKLIT SHOPPE, MISTER! DON'T YOU HAVE ANY HEART?
HA! "HEART?" DON'T BE SUCH DREAMERS! THE WHEELS CAN'T STOP TURNING JUST TO SAVE SOME STUPID ICE CREAM PARLOR!
NOW RUN ALONG, ALL OF YOU! I DON'T HAVE TIME TO WASTE LISTENING TO YOUR SENTIMENTAL HOGWASH!
5

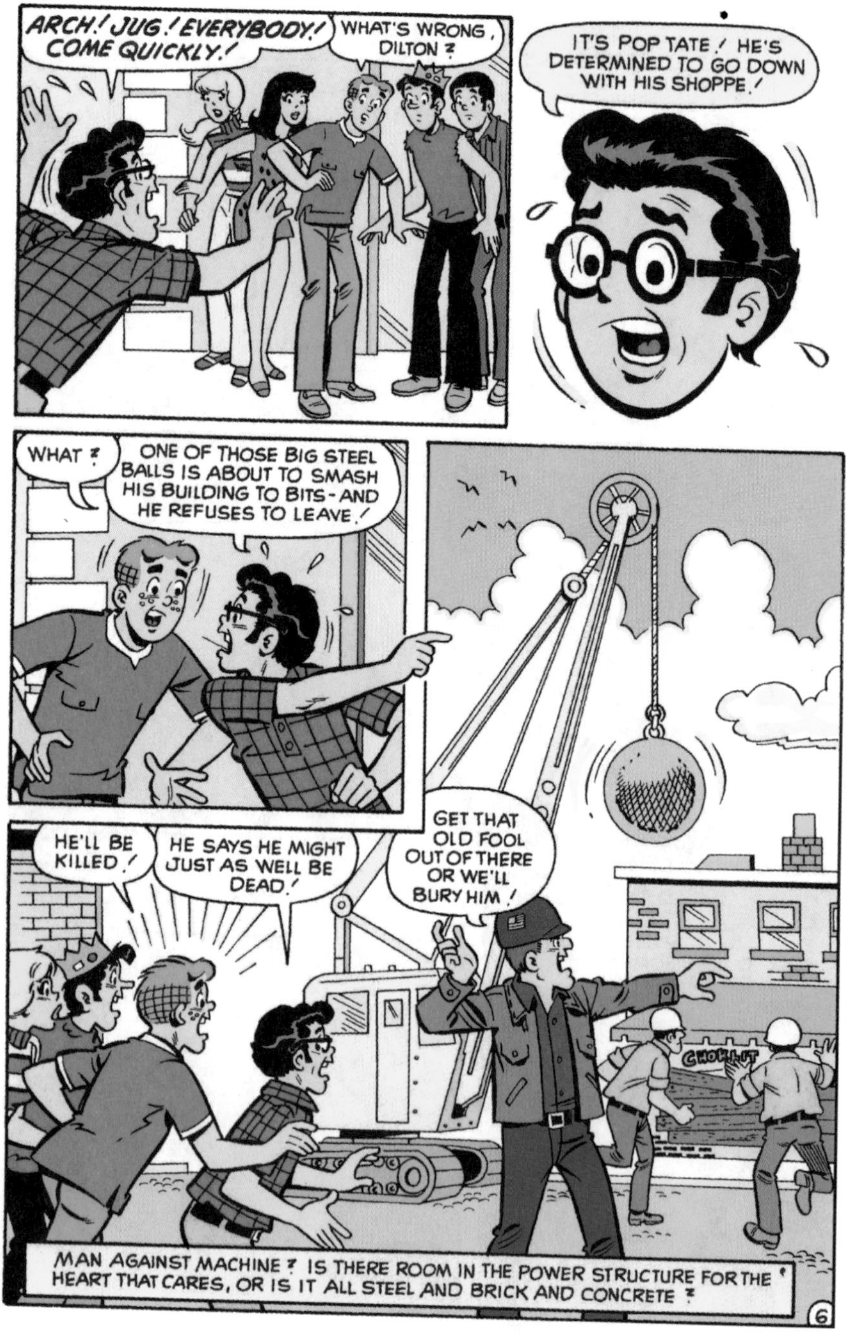
ARCH! JUG! EVERYBODY! COME QUICKLY!
WHAT'S WRONG, DILTON?
IT'S POP TATE! HE'S DETERMINED TO GO DOWN WITH HIS SHOPPE!
WHAT?
ONE OF THOSE BIG STEEL BALLS IS ABOUT TO SMASH HIS BUILDING TO BITS - AND HE REFUSES TO LEAVE!
HE'LL BE KILLED!
HE SAYS HE MIGHT JUST AS WELL BE DEAD!
GET THAT OLD FOOL OUT OF THERE OR WE'LL BURY HIM!
CHOKLIT
MAN AGAINST MACHINE? IS THERE ROOM IN THE POWER STRUCTURE FOR THE HEART THAT CARES, OR IS IT ALL STEEL AND BRICK AND CONCRETE?
6

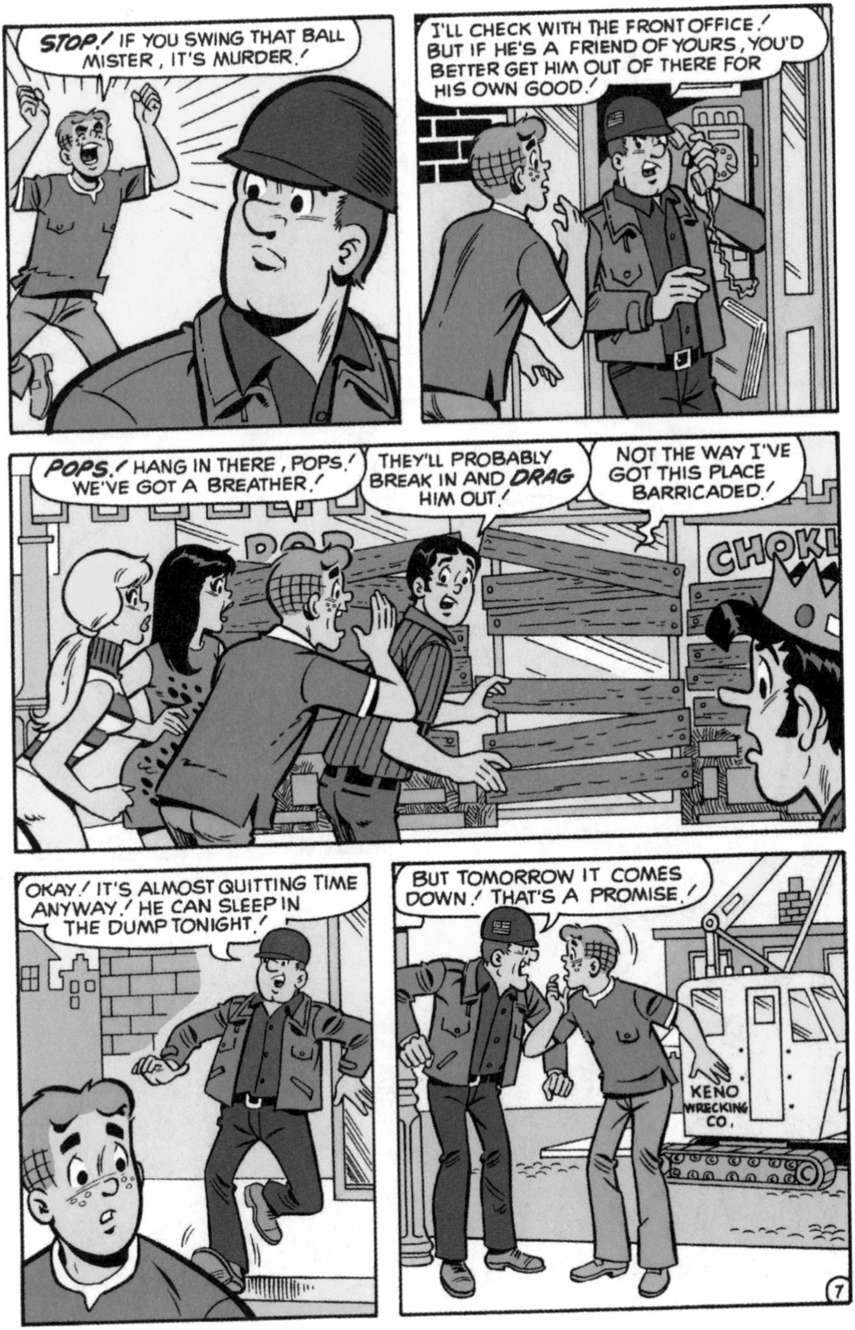
STOP! IF YOU SWING THAT BALL MISTER, IT'S MURDER!
I'LL CHECK WITH THE FRONT OFFICE! BUT IF HE'S A FRIEND OF YOURS, YOU'D BETTER GET HIM OUT OF THERE FOR HIS OWN GOOD!
POPS! HANG IN THERE, POPS! WE'VE GOT A BREATHER!
THEY'LL PROBABLY BREAK IN AND DRAG HIM OUT!
NOT THE WAY I'VE GOT THIS PLACE BARRICADED!
CHOKL
OKAY! IT'S ALMOST QUITTING TIME ANYWAY! HE CAN SLEEP IN THE DUMP TONIGHT!
BUT TOMORROW IT COMES DOWN! THAT'S A PROMISE!
KENO WRECKING CO.
7

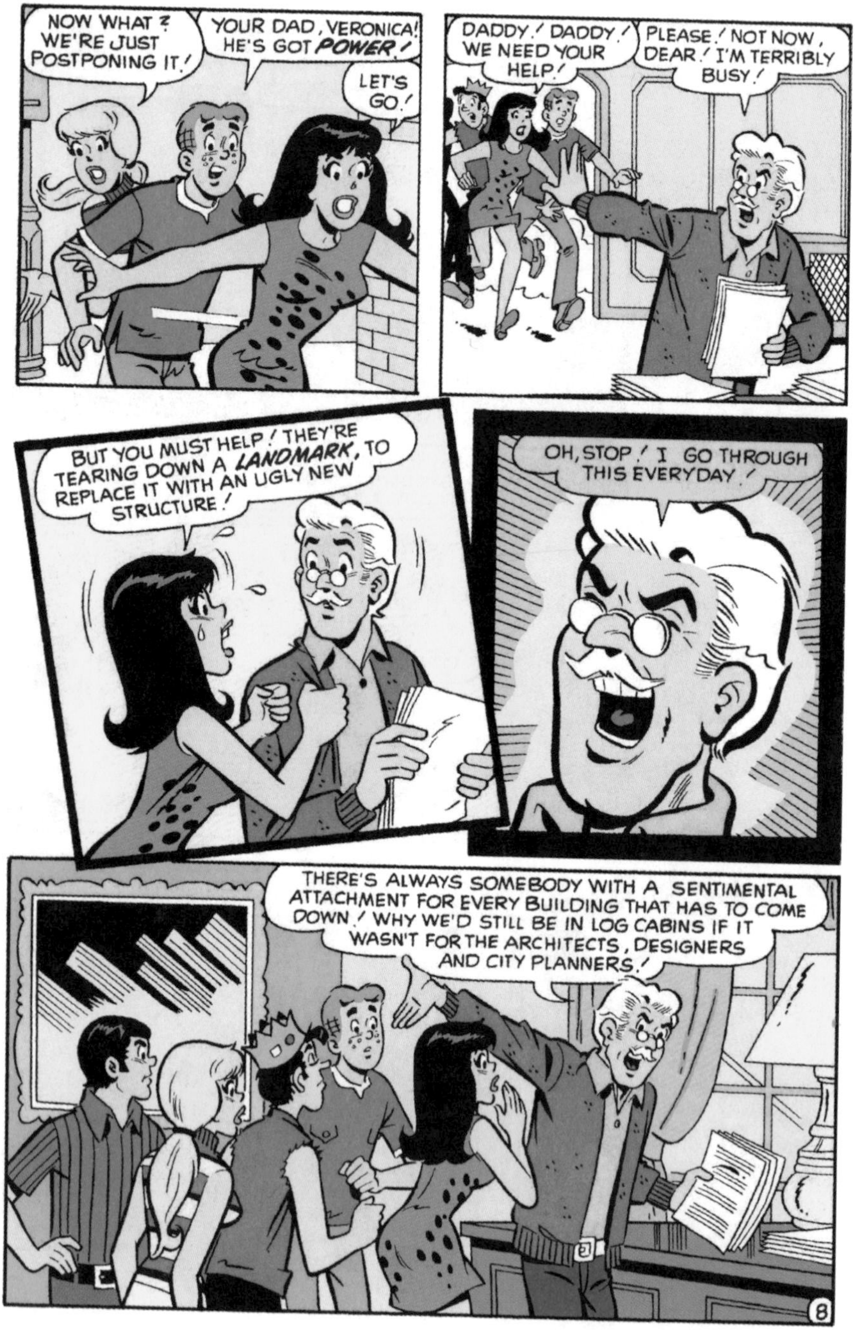
NOW WHAT? WE'RE JUST POSTPONING IT!
YOUR DAD, VERONICA! HE'S GOT POWER!
LET'S GO!
DADDY! DADDY! WE NEED YOUR HELP!
PLEASE! NOT NOW, DEAR! I'M TERRIBLY BUSY!
BUT YOU MUST HELP! THEY'RE TEARING DOWN A LANDMARK, TO REPLACE IT WITH AN UGLY NEW STRUCTURE!
OH, STOP! I GO THROUGH THIS EVERYDAY!
THERE'S ALWAYS SOMEBODY WITH A SENTIMENTAL ATTACHMENT FOR EVERY BUILDING THAT HAS TO COME DOWN! WHY WE'D STILL BE IN LOG CABINS IF IT WASN'T FOR THE ARCHITECTS, DESIGNERS AND CITY PLANNERS!
8

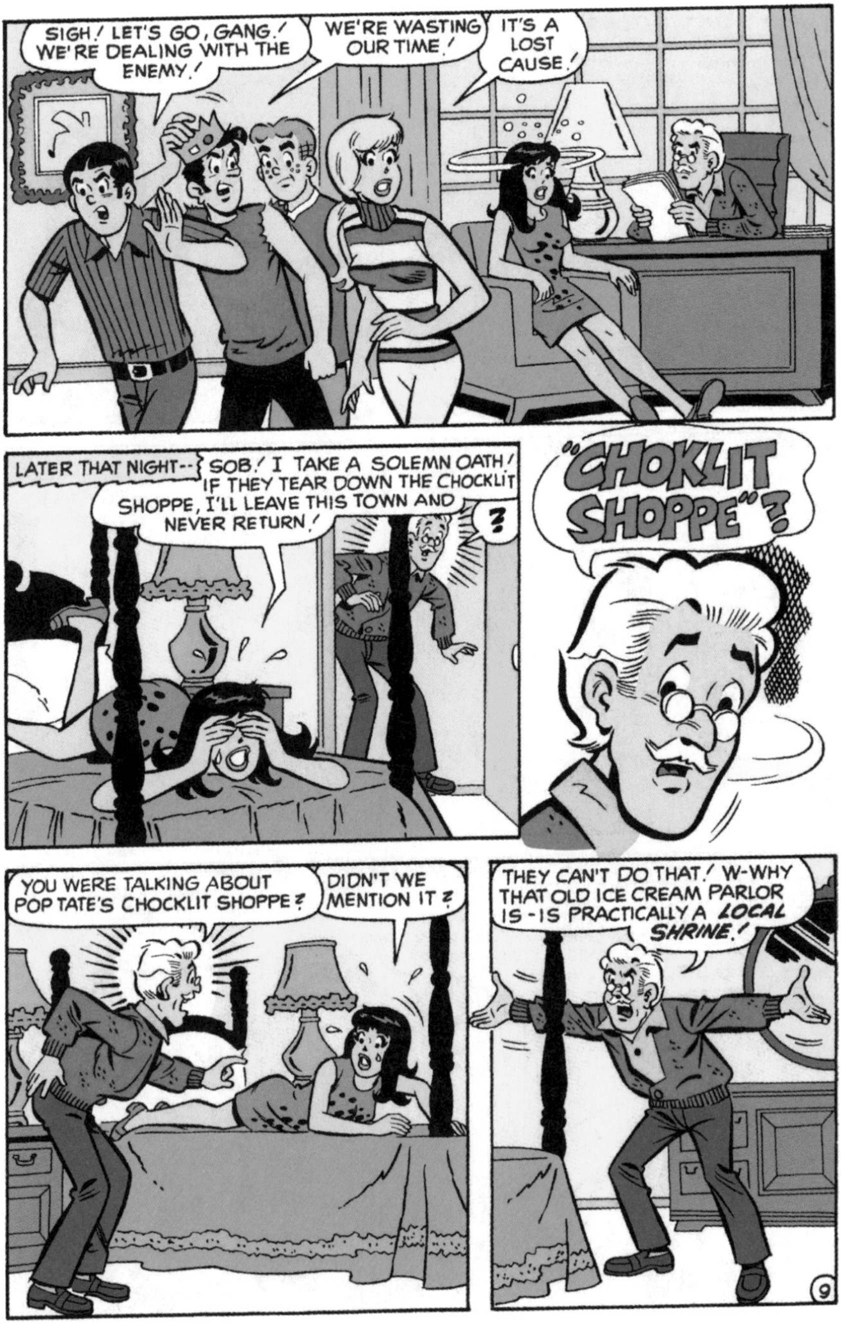
SIGH! LET'S GO, GANG! WE'RE DEALING WITH THE ENEMY!
WE'RE WASTING OUR TIME!
IT'S A LOST CAUSE!
LATER THAT NIGHT--
SOB! I TAKE A SOLEMN OATH! IF THEY TEAR DOWN THE CHOCKLIT SHOPPE, I'LL LEAVE THIS TOWN AND NEVER RETURN!
?
"CHOKLIT SHOPPE"?
YOU WERE TALKING ABOUT POP TATE'S CHOCKLIT SHOPPE?
DIDN'T WE MENTION IT?
THEY CAN'T DO THAT! W-WHY THAT OLD ICE CREAM PARLOR IS-IS PRACTICALLY A LOCAL SHRINE!
9

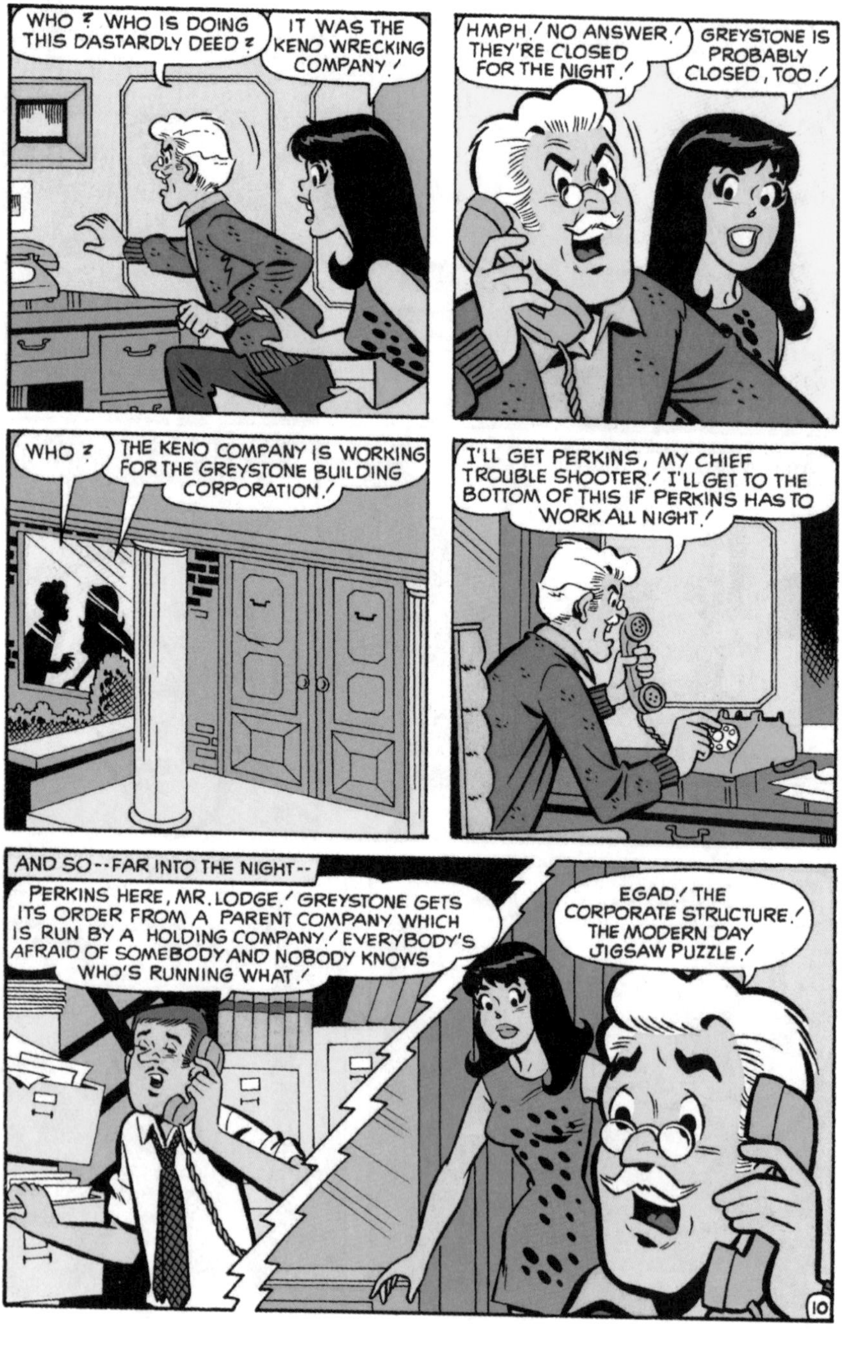
WHO ? WHO IS DOING THIS DASTARDLY DEED ?
IT WAS THE KENO WRECKING COMPANY !
HMPH ! NO ANSWER ! THEY'RE CLOSED FOR THE NIGHT !
GREYSTONE IS PROBABLY CLOSED, TOO !
WHO ?
THE KENO COMPANY IS WORKING FOR THE GREYSTONE BUILDING CORPORATION !
I'LL GET PERKINS, MY CHIEF TROUBLE SHOOTER ! I'LL GET TO THE BOTTOM OF THIS IF PERKINS HAS TO WORK ALL NIGHT !
AND SO--FAR INTO THE NIGHT--
PERKINS HERE, MR. LODGE ! GREYSTONE GETS ITS ORDER FROM A PARENT COMPANY WHICH IS RUN BY A HOLDING COMPANY ! EVERYBODY'S AFRAID OF SOMEBODY AND NOBODY KNOWS WHO'S RUNNING WHAT !
EGAD ! THE CORPORATE STRUCTURE ! THE MODERN DAY JIGSAW PUZZLE !
10

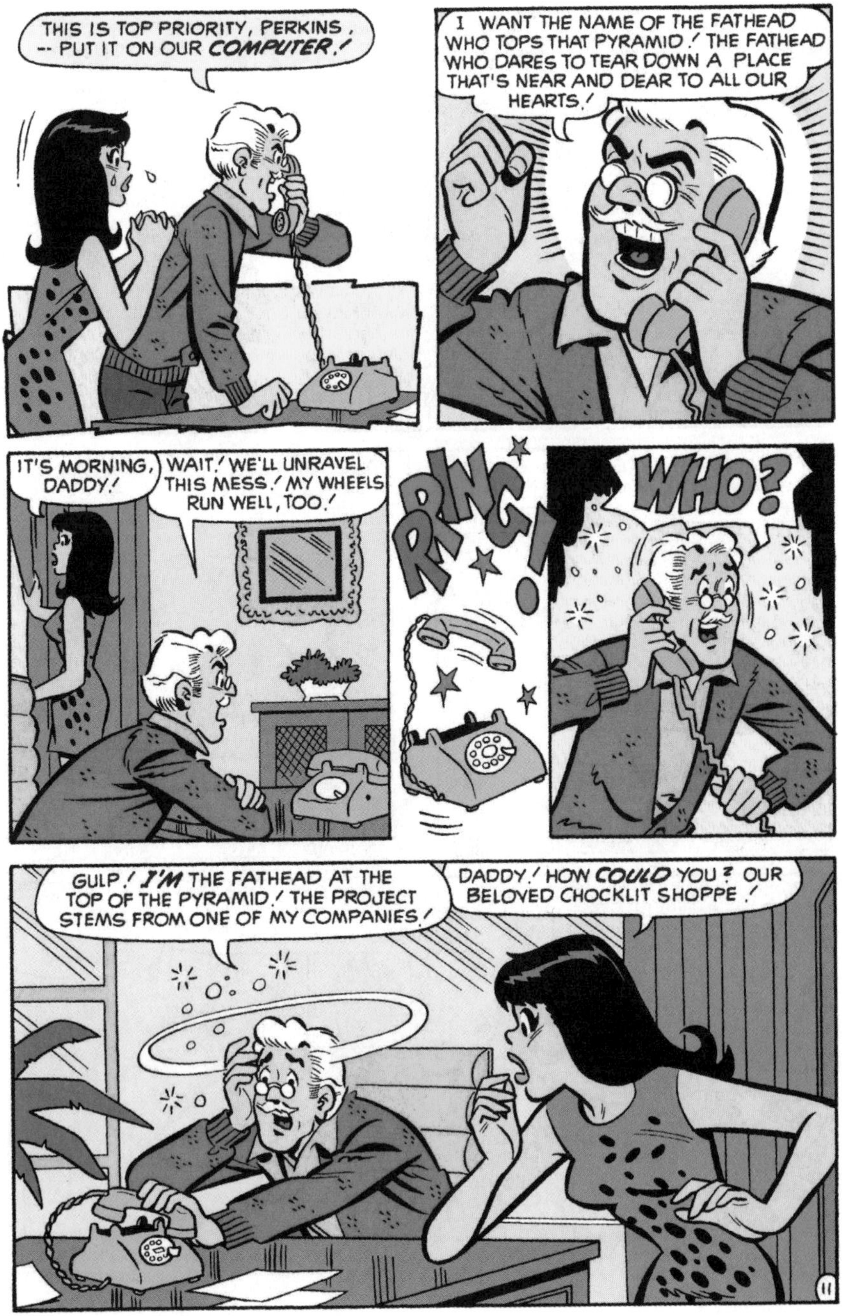
THIS IS TOP PRIORITY, PERKINS, -- PUT IT ON OUR COMPUTER!
I WANT THE NAME OF THE FATHEAD WHO TOPS THAT PYRAMID! THE FATHEAD WHO DARES TO TEAR DOWN A PLACE THAT'S NEAR AND DEAR TO ALL OUR HEARTS!
IT'S MORNING, DADDY!
WAIT! WE'LL UNRAVEL THIS MESS! MY WHEELS RUN WELL, TOO!
RRING!
WHO?
GULP! I'M THE FATHEAD AT THE TOP OF THE PYRAMID! THE PROJECT STEMS FROM ONE OF MY COMPANIES!
DADDY! HOW COULD YOU? OUR BELOVED CHOCKLIT SHOPPE!
11

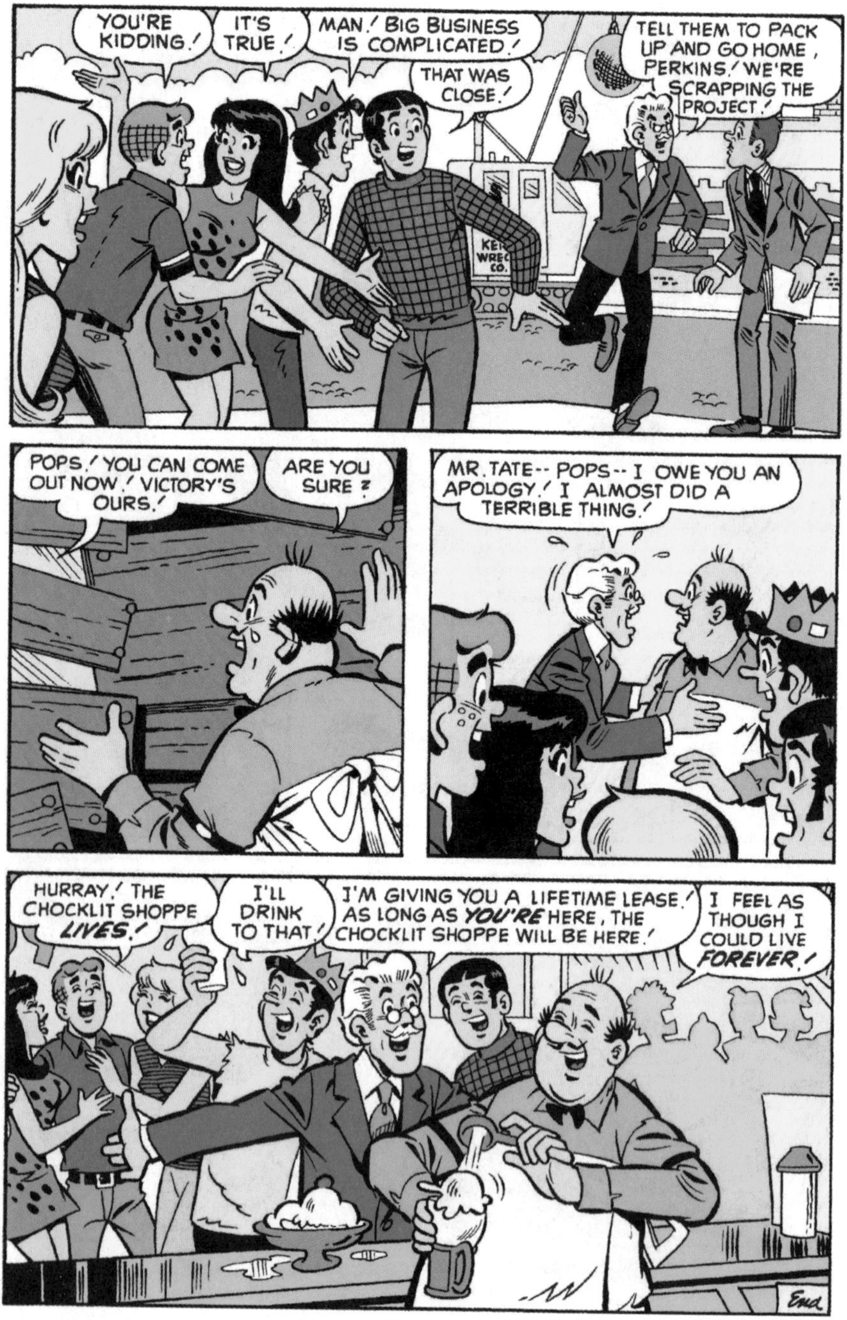
YOU'RE KIDDING!
IT'S TRUE!
MAN! BIG BUSINESS IS COMPLICATED!
THAT WAS CLOSE!
TELL THEM TO PACK UP AND GO HOME, PERKINS! WE'RE SCRAPPING THE PROJECT!
POPS! YOU CAN COME OUT NOW! VICTORY'S OURS!
ARE YOU SURE?
MR. TATE-- POPS-- I OWE YOU AN APOLOGY! I ALMOST DID A TERRIBLE THING!
HURRAY! THE CHOCKLIT SHOPPE *LIVES!*
I'LL DRINK TO THAT!
I'M GIVING YOU A LIFETIME LEASE! AS LONG AS *YOU'RE* HERE, THE CHOCKLIT SHOPPE WILL BE HERE!
I FEEL AS THOUGH I COULD LIVE *FOREVER!*
End

Archie in "First in Friendship"

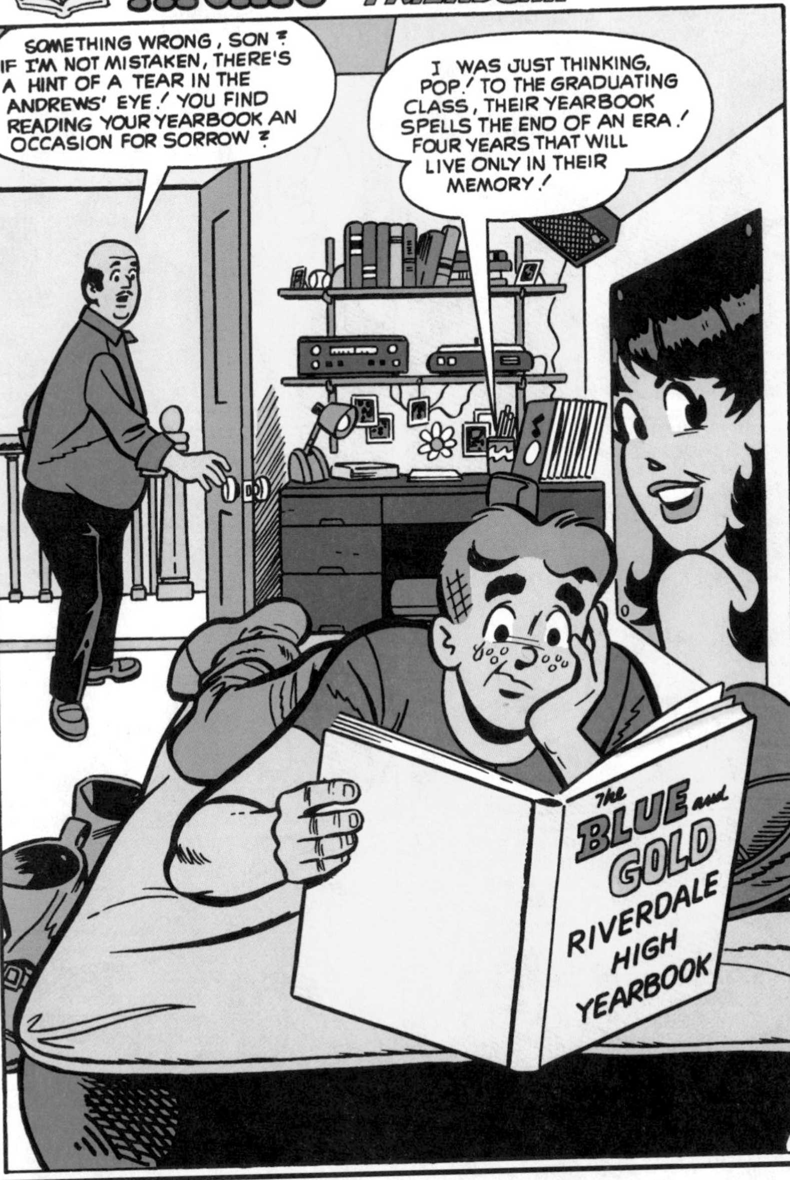
SOMETHING WRONG, SON? IF I'M NOT MISTAKEN, THERE'S A HINT OF A TEAR IN THE ANDREWS' EYE! YOU FIND READING YOUR YEARBOOK AN OCCASION FOR SORROW?
I WAS JUST THINKING, POP! TO THE GRADUATING CLASS, THEIR YEARBOOK SPELLS THE END OF AN ERA! FOUR YEARS THAT WILL LIVE ONLY IN THEIR MEMORY!
The BLUE and GOLD
RIVERDALE HIGH YEARBOOK

Story: Frank Doyle   Pencils: Dan DeCarlo

Inks: Rudy Lapick   Letters: Bill Yoshida   Colors: Barry Grossman

Originally printed in ARCHIE AT RIVERDALE HIGH #2, September 1972

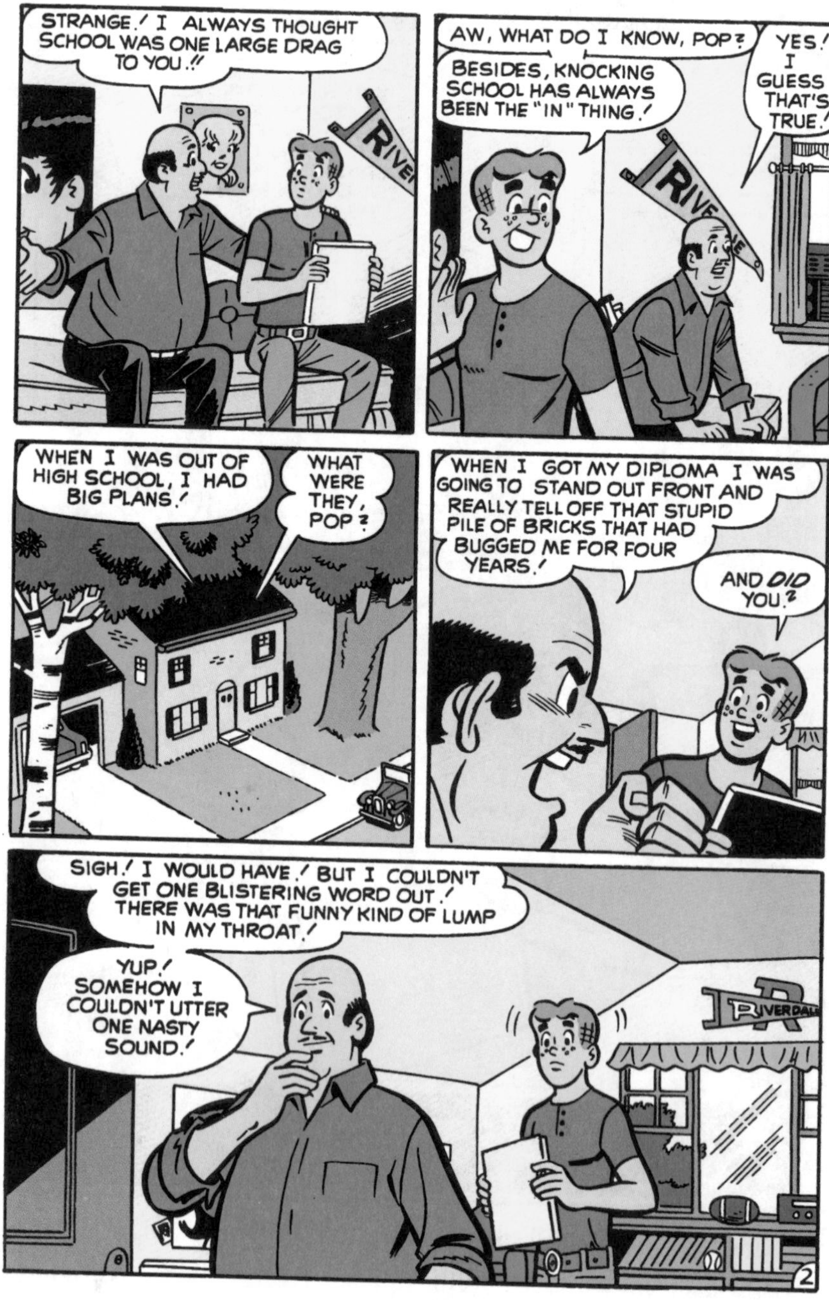
STRANGE! I ALWAYS THOUGHT SCHOOL WAS ONE LARGE DRAG TO YOU!!
AW, WHAT DO I KNOW, POP?
BESIDES, KNOCKING SCHOOL HAS ALWAYS BEEN THE "IN" THING!
YES! I GUESS THAT'S TRUE!
WHEN I WAS OUT OF HIGH SCHOOL, I HAD BIG PLANS!
WHAT WERE THEY, POP?
WHEN I GOT MY DIPLOMA I WAS GOING TO STAND OUT FRONT AND REALLY TELL OFF THAT STUPID PILE OF BRICKS THAT HAD BUGGED ME FOR FOUR YEARS!
AND DID YOU?
SIGH! I WOULD HAVE! BUT I COULDN'T GET ONE BLISTERING WORD OUT! THERE WAS THAT FUNNY KIND OF LUMP IN MY THROAT!
YUP! SOMEHOW I COULDN'T UTTER ONE NASTY SOUND!
2

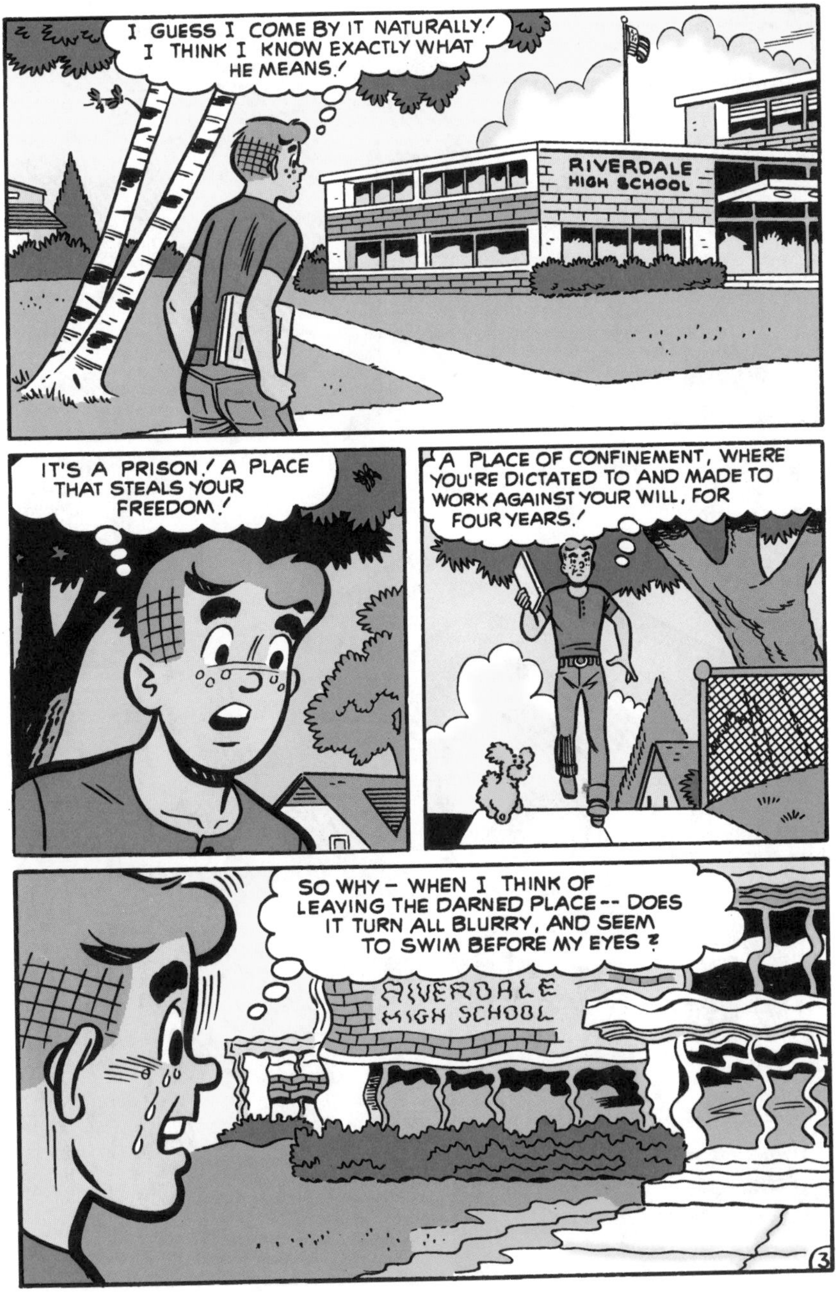
I GUESS I COME BY IT NATURALLY! I THINK I KNOW EXACTLY WHAT HE MEANS!
RIVERDALE HIGH SCHOOL
IT'S A PRISON! A PLACE THAT STEALS YOUR FREEDOM!
A PLACE OF CONFINEMENT, WHERE YOU'RE DICTATED TO AND MADE TO WORK AGAINST YOUR WILL, FOR FOUR YEARS!
SO WHY - WHEN I THINK OF LEAVING THE DARNED PLACE -- DOES IT TURN ALL BLURRY, AND SEEM TO SWIM BEFORE MY EYES ?
RIVERDALE HIGH SCHOOL
3

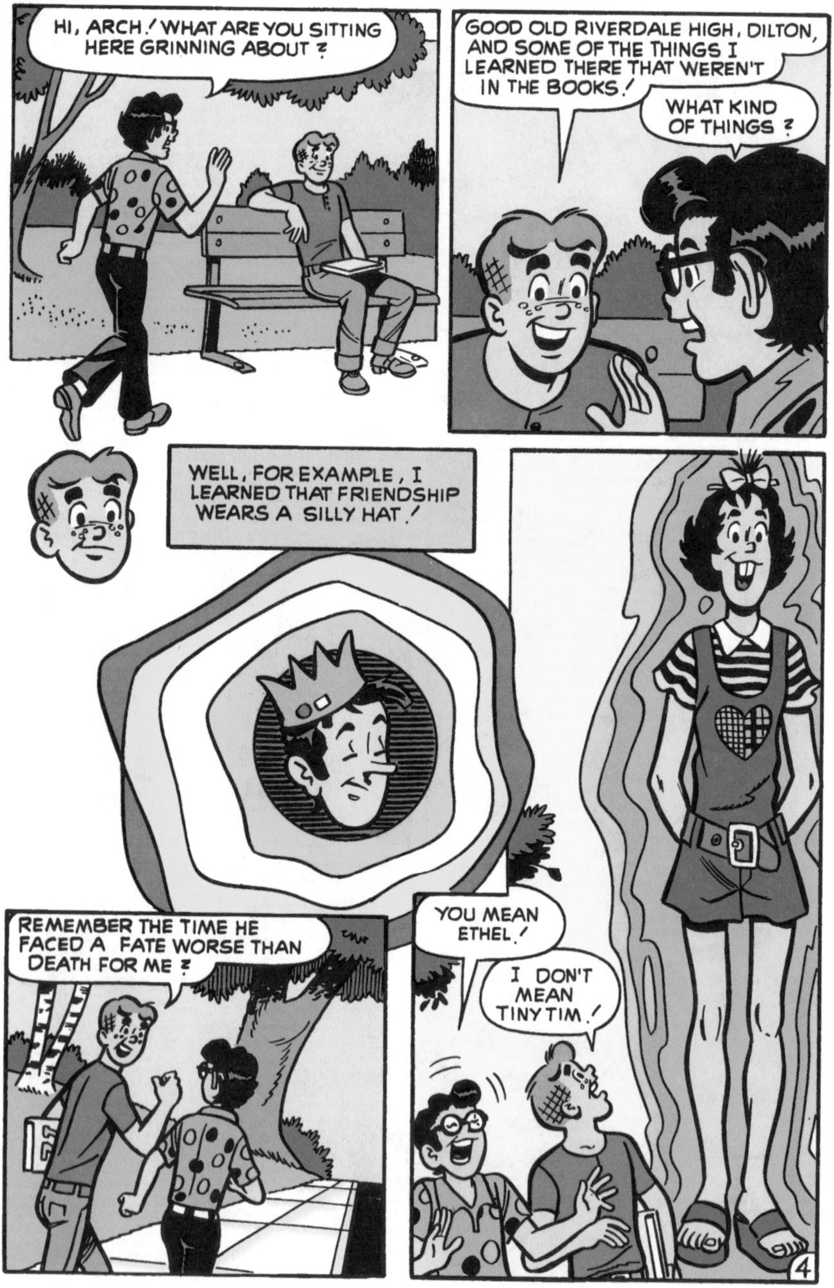
HI, ARCH! WHAT ARE YOU SITTING HERE GRINNING ABOUT ?
GOOD OLD RIVERDALE HIGH, DILTON, AND SOME OF THE THINGS I LEARNED THERE THAT WEREN'T IN THE BOOKS!
WHAT KIND OF THINGS ?
WELL, FOR EXAMPLE, I LEARNED THAT FRIENDSHIP WEARS A SILLY HAT!
REMEMBER THE TIME HE FACED A FATE WORSE THAN DEATH FOR ME ?
YOU MEAN ETHEL!
I DON'T MEAN TINY TIM!
4

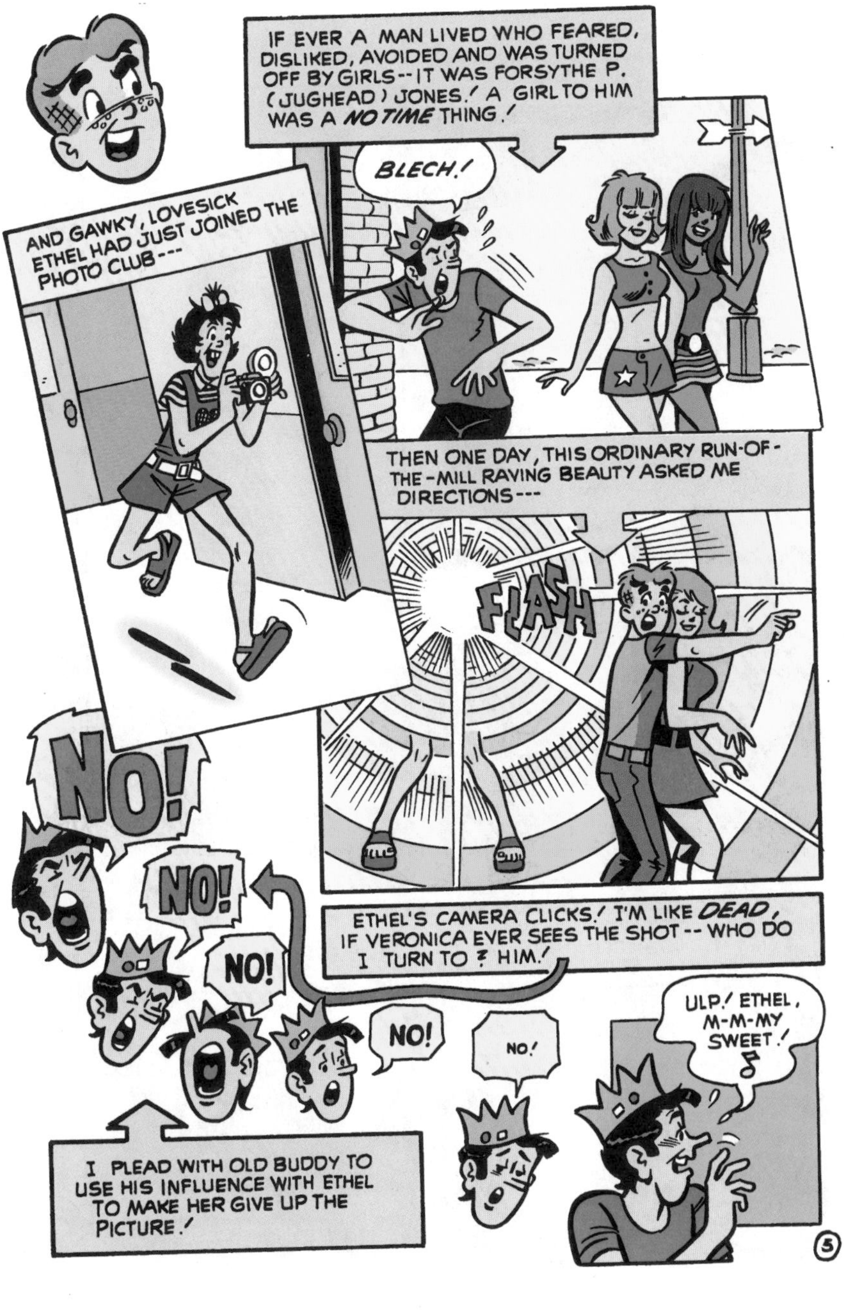

IF EVER A MAN LIVED WHO FEARED, DISLIKED, AVOIDED AND WAS TURNED OFF BY GIRLS -- IT WAS FORSYTHE P. (JUGHEAD) JONES.! A GIRL TO HIM WAS A NO TIME THING.!
BLECH.!
AND GAWKY, LOVESICK ETHEL HAD JUST JOINED THE PHOTO CLUB---
THEN ONE DAY, THIS ORDINARY RUN-OF-THE-MILL RAVING BEAUTY ASKED ME DIRECTIONS---
FLASH
ETHEL'S CAMERA CLICKS.! I'M LIKE DEAD, IF VERONICA EVER SEES THE SHOT -- WHO DO I TURN TO ? HIM.!
NO!
NO!
NO!
NO!
I PLEAD WITH OLD BUDDY TO USE HIS INFLUENCE WITH ETHEL TO MAKE HER GIVE UP THE PICTURE.!
NO.!
ULP.! ETHEL, M-M-MY SWEET.!
5

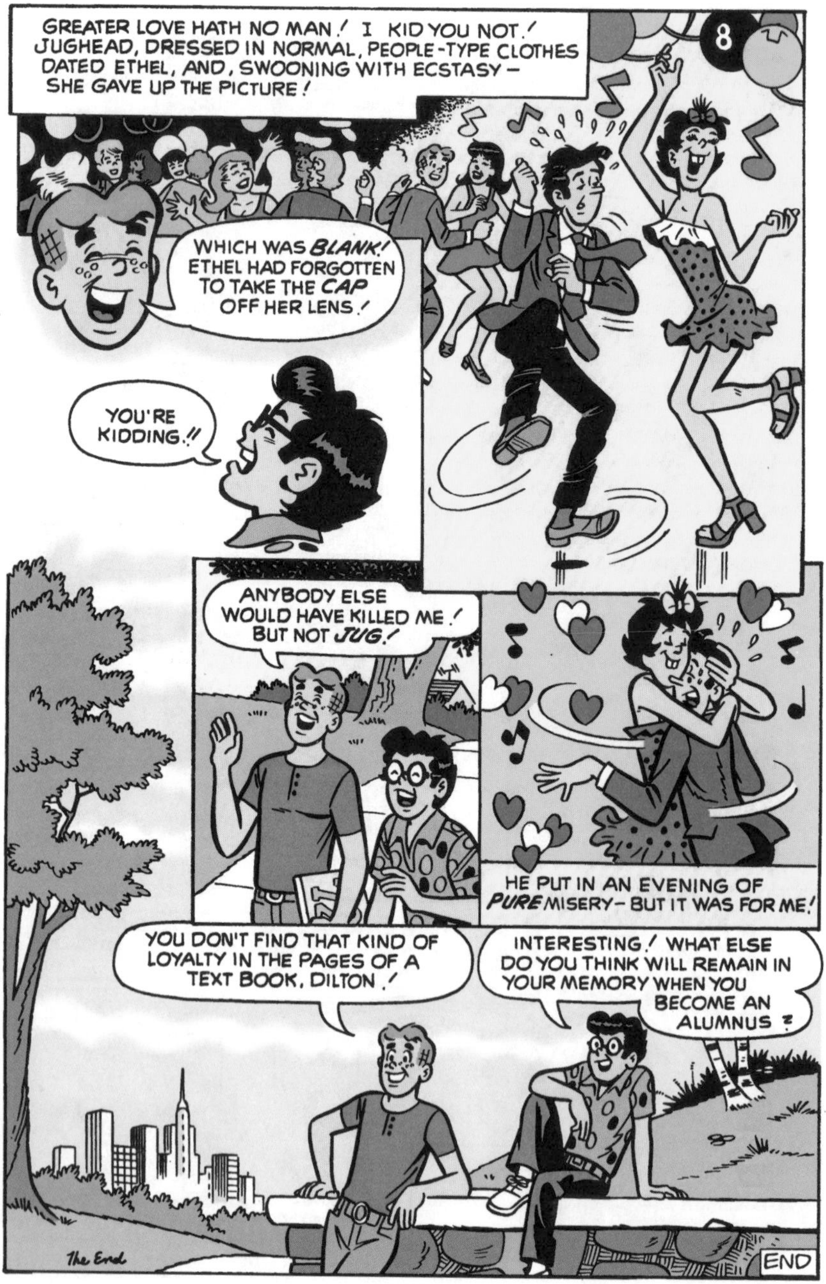
GREATER LOVE HATH NO MAN! I KID YOU NOT! JUGHEAD, DRESSED IN NORMAL, PEOPLE-TYPE CLOTHES DATED ETHEL, AND, SWOONING WITH ECSTASY — SHE GAVE UP THE PICTURE!
8
WHICH WAS BLANK! ETHEL HAD FORGOTTEN TO TAKE THE CAP OFF HER LENS!
YOU'RE KIDDING.!!
ANYBODY ELSE WOULD HAVE KILLED ME! BUT NOT JUG!
HE PUT IN AN EVENING OF PURE MISERY — BUT IT WAS FOR ME!
YOU DON'T FIND THAT KIND OF LOYALTY IN THE PAGES OF A TEXT BOOK, DILTON!
INTERESTING! WHAT ELSE DO YOU THINK WILL REMAIN IN YOUR MEMORY WHEN YOU BECOME AN ALUMNUS?
The End
END

Archie in "NEVER KID A KIDDER"

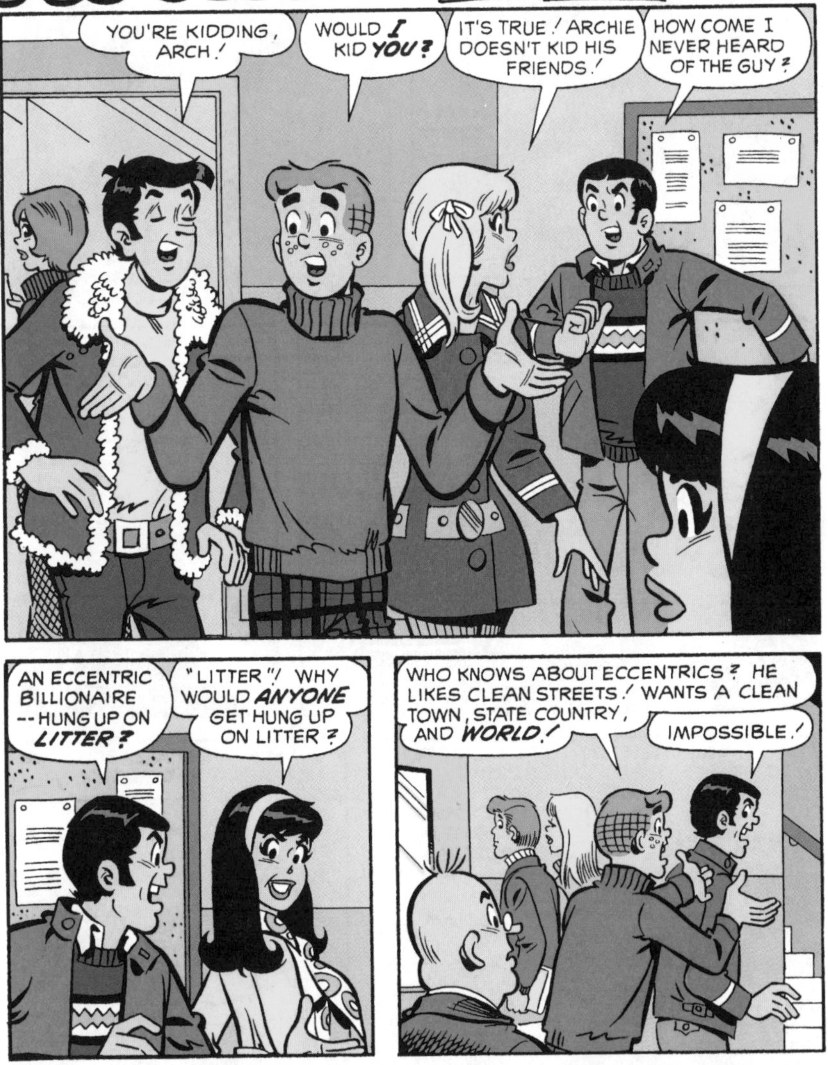
YOU'RE KIDDING, ARCH!
WOULD I KID YOU?
IT'S TRUE! ARCHIE DOESN'T KID HIS FRIENDS!
HOW COME I NEVER HEARD OF THE GUY?
AN ECCENTRIC BILLIONAIRE --HUNG UP ON LITTER?
"LITTER"! WHY WOULD ANYONE GET HUNG UP ON LITTER?
WHO KNOWS ABOUT ECCENTRICS? HE LIKES CLEAN STREETS! WANTS A CLEAN TOWN, STATE COUNTRY, AND WORLD!
IMPOSSIBLE!

Story: Frank Doyle   Pencils: Stan Goldberg

Inks: Jon D'Agostino   Letters: Bill Yoshida   Colors: Barry Grossman

Originally printed in ARCHIE AT RIVERDALE HIGH #5, February 1973

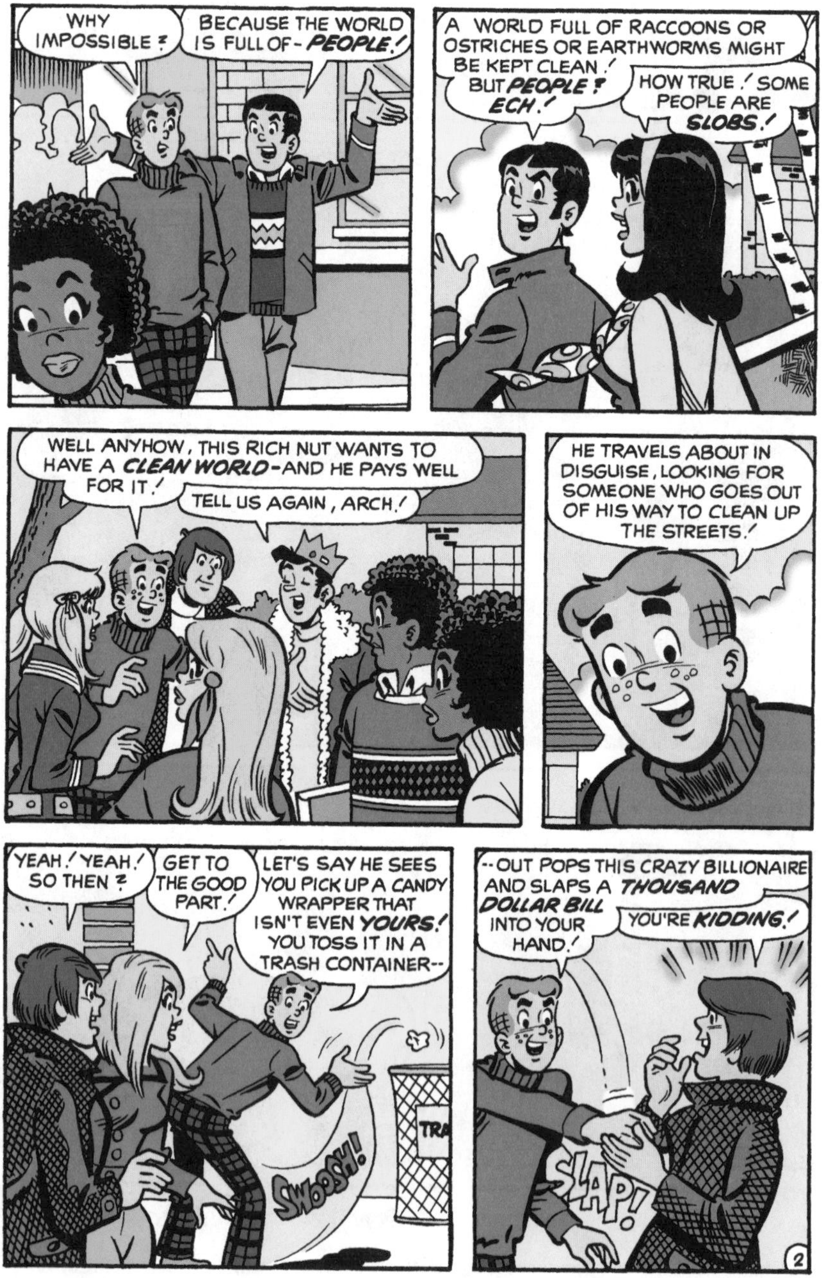
WHY IMPOSSIBLE ?
BECAUSE THE WORLD IS FULL OF - PEOPLE!
A WORLD FULL OF RACCOONS OR OSTRICHES OR EARTHWORMS MIGHT BE KEPT CLEAN! BUT PEOPLE? ECH!
HOW TRUE! SOME PEOPLE ARE SLOBS!
WELL ANYHOW, THIS RICH NUT WANTS TO HAVE A CLEAN WORLD - AND HE PAYS WELL FOR IT!
TELL US AGAIN, ARCH!
HE TRAVELS ABOUT IN DISGUISE, LOOKING FOR SOMEONE WHO GOES OUT OF HIS WAY TO CLEAN UP THE STREETS!
YEAH! YEAH! SO THEN ?
GET TO THE GOOD PART!
LET'S SAY HE SEES YOU PICK UP A CANDY WRAPPER THAT ISN'T EVEN YOURS! YOU TOSS IT IN A TRASH CONTAINER--
SWOOSH!
--OUT POPS THIS CRAZY BILLIONAIRE AND SLAPS A THOUSAND DOLLAR BILL INTO YOUR HAND!
YOU'RE KIDDING!
SLAP!
2

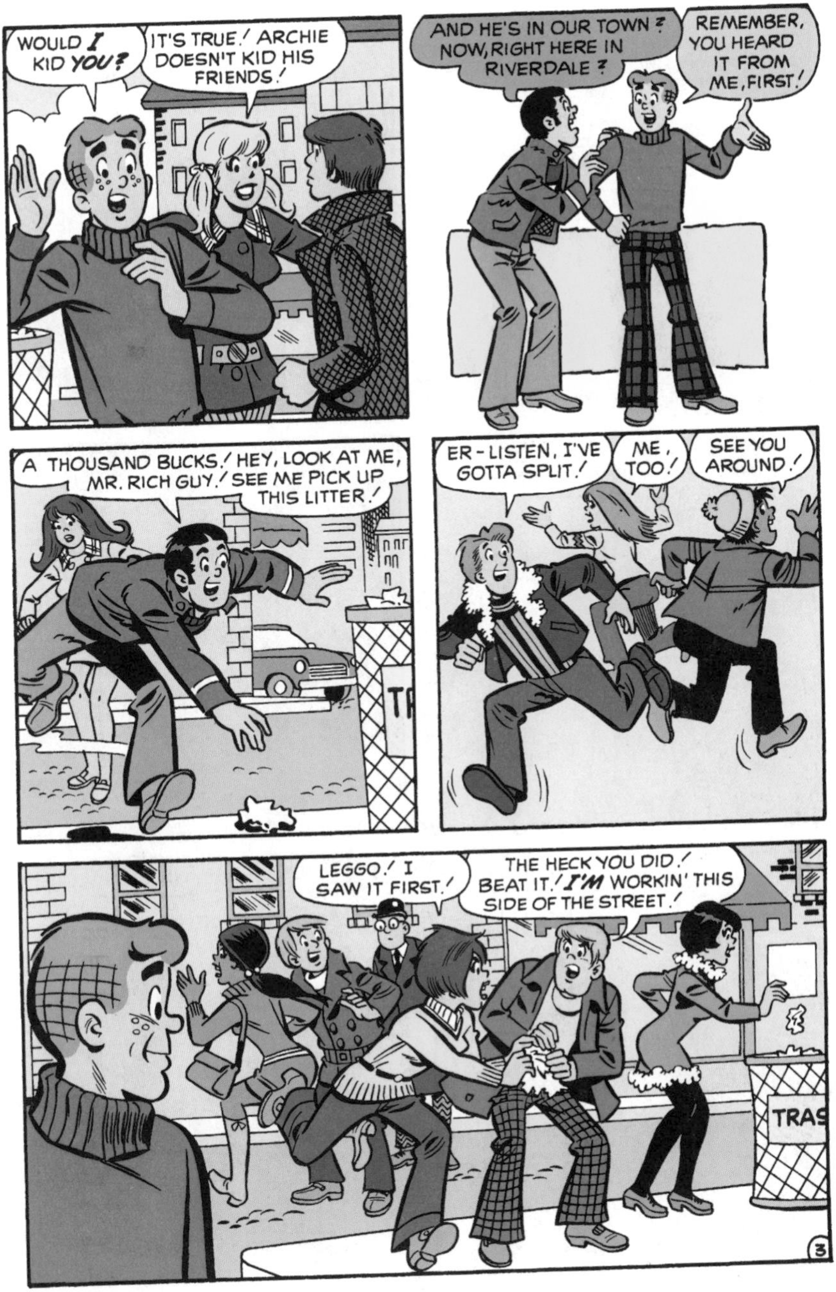
WOULD I KID YOU?
IT'S TRUE! ARCHIE DOESN'T KID HIS FRIENDS!
AND HE'S IN OUR TOWN? NOW, RIGHT HERE IN RIVERDALE?
REMEMBER, YOU HEARD IT FROM ME, FIRST!
A THOUSAND BUCKS! HEY, LOOK AT ME, MR. RICH GUY! SEE ME PICK UP THIS LITTER!
ER-LISTEN, I'VE GOTTA SPLIT!
ME, TOO!
SEE YOU AROUND!
LEGGO! I SAW IT FIRST!
THE HECK YOU DID! BEAT IT! I'M WORKIN' THIS SIDE OF THE STREET!
TRAS
3

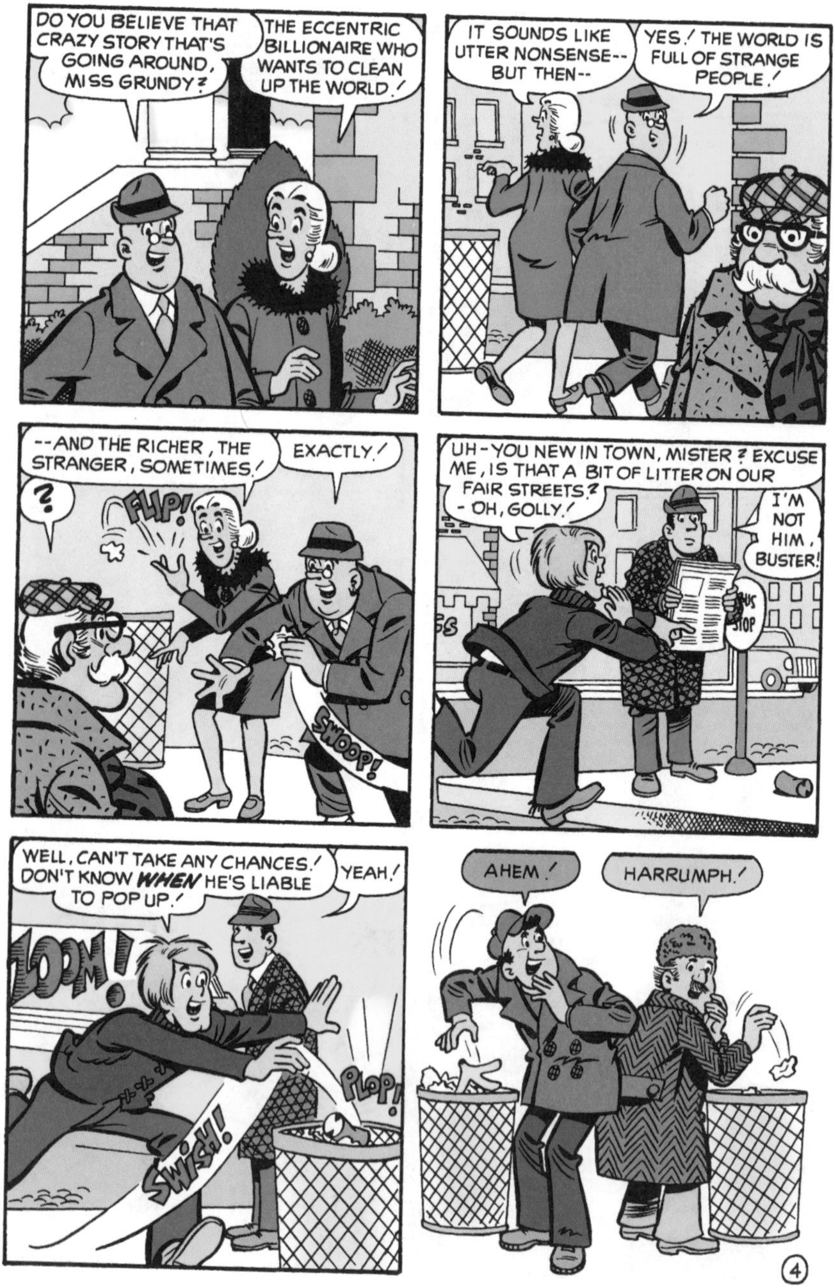
DO YOU BELIEVE THAT CRAZY STORY THAT'S GOING AROUND, MISS GRUNDY?
THE ECCENTRIC BILLIONAIRE WHO WANTS TO CLEAN UP THE WORLD!
IT SOUNDS LIKE UTTER NONSENSE-- BUT THEN--
YES! THE WORLD IS FULL OF STRANGE PEOPLE!
--AND THE RICHER, THE STRANGER, SOMETIMES!
EXACTLY!
?
FLIP!
SWOOP!
UH-YOU NEW IN TOWN, MISTER? EXCUSE ME, IS THAT A BIT OF LITTER ON OUR FAIR STREETS? - OH, GOLLY!
I'M NOT HIM, BUSTER!
BUS STOP
WELL, CAN'T TAKE ANY CHANCES! DON'T KNOW WHEN HE'S LIABLE TO POP UP!
YEAH!
ZOOM!
PLOP!
SWISH!
AHEM!
HARRUMPH!
4

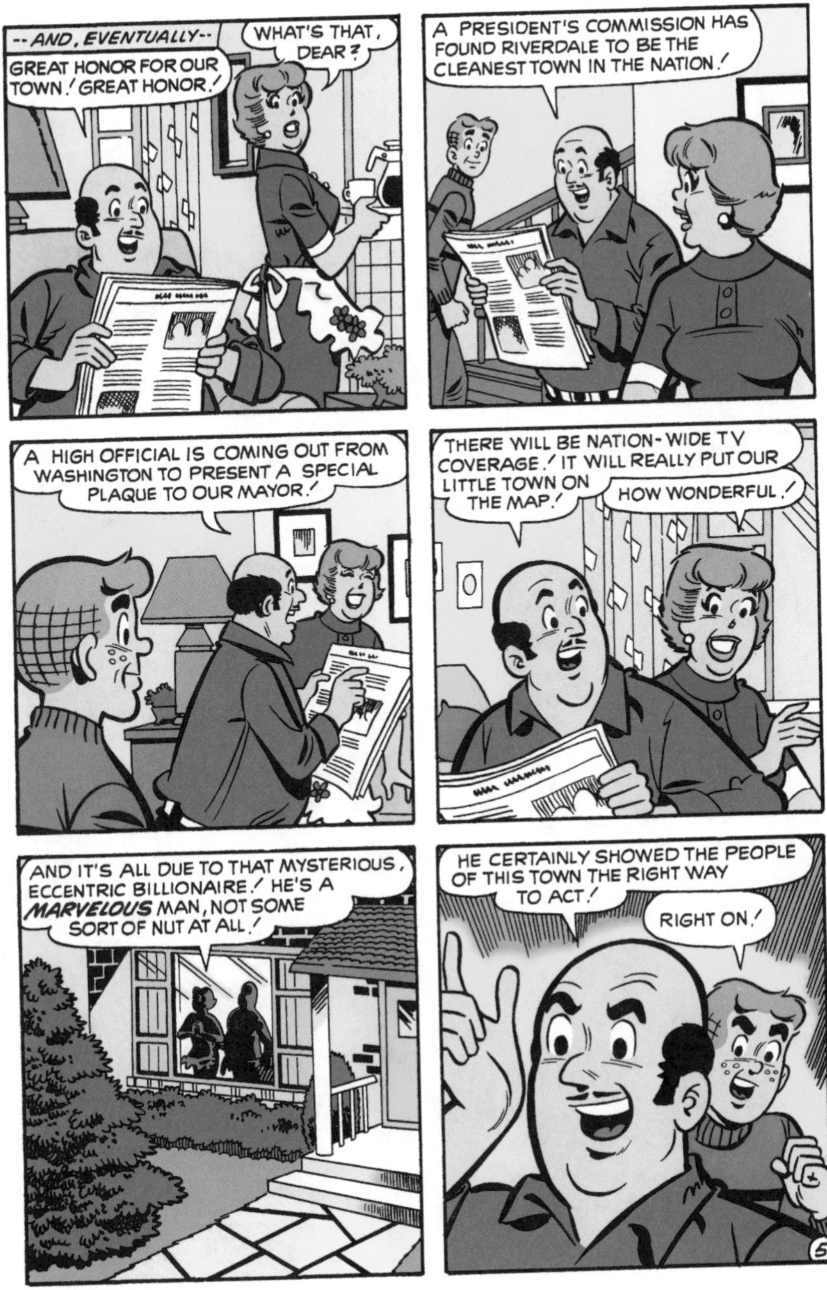
-- AND, EVENTUALLY --
GREAT HONOR FOR OUR TOWN! GREAT HONOR!
WHAT'S THAT, DEAR?
A PRESIDENT'S COMMISSION HAS FOUND RIVERDALE TO BE THE CLEANEST TOWN IN THE NATION!
A HIGH OFFICIAL IS COMING OUT FROM WASHINGTON TO PRESENT A SPECIAL PLAQUE TO OUR MAYOR!
THERE WILL BE NATION-WIDE TV COVERAGE! IT WILL REALLY PUT OUR LITTLE TOWN ON THE MAP!
HOW WONDERFUL!
AND IT'S ALL DUE TO THAT MYSTERIOUS, ECCENTRIC BILLIONAIRE! HE'S A MARVELOUS MAN, NOT SOME SORT OF NUT AT ALL!
HE CERTAINLY SHOWED THE PEOPLE OF THIS TOWN THE RIGHT WAY TO ACT!
RIGHT ON!
5

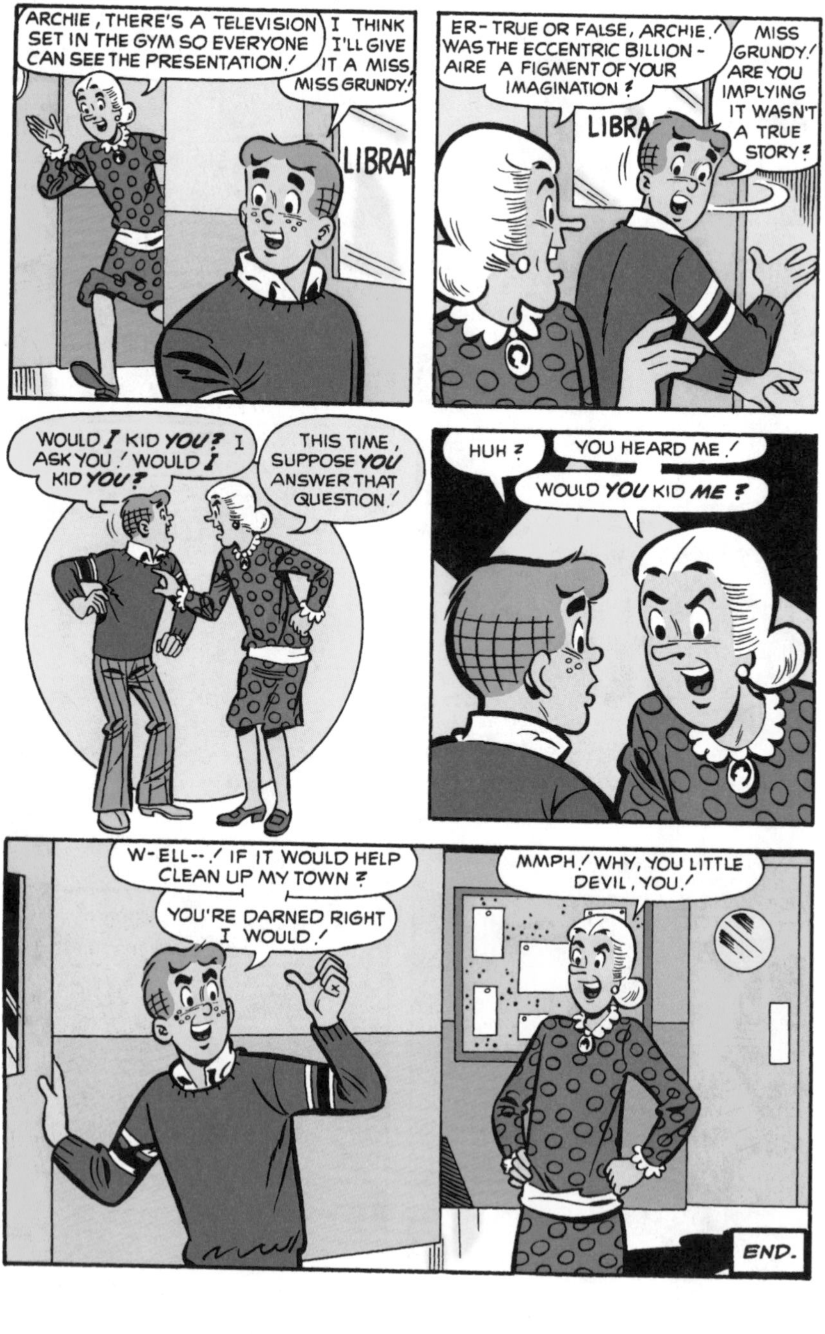
ARCHIE, THERE'S A TELEVISION SET IN THE GYM SO EVERYONE CAN SEE THE PRESENTATION!
I THINK I'LL GIVE IT A MISS, MISS GRUNDY!
LIBRAR
ER-TRUE OR FALSE, ARCHIE! WAS THE ECCENTRIC BILLION-AIRE A FIGMENT OF YOUR IMAGINATION?
MISS GRUNDY! ARE YOU IMPLYING IT WASN'T A TRUE STORY?
LIBRA
WOULD I KID YOU? I ASK YOU! WOULD I KID YOU?
THIS TIME, SUPPOSE YOU ANSWER THAT QUESTION!
HUH?
YOU HEARD ME!
WOULD YOU KID ME?
W-ELL--! IF IT WOULD HELP CLEAN UP MY TOWN?
YOU'RE DARNED RIGHT I WOULD!
MMPH! WHY, YOU LITTLE DEVIL, YOU!
END.

Archie at Riverdale in "Blackout"

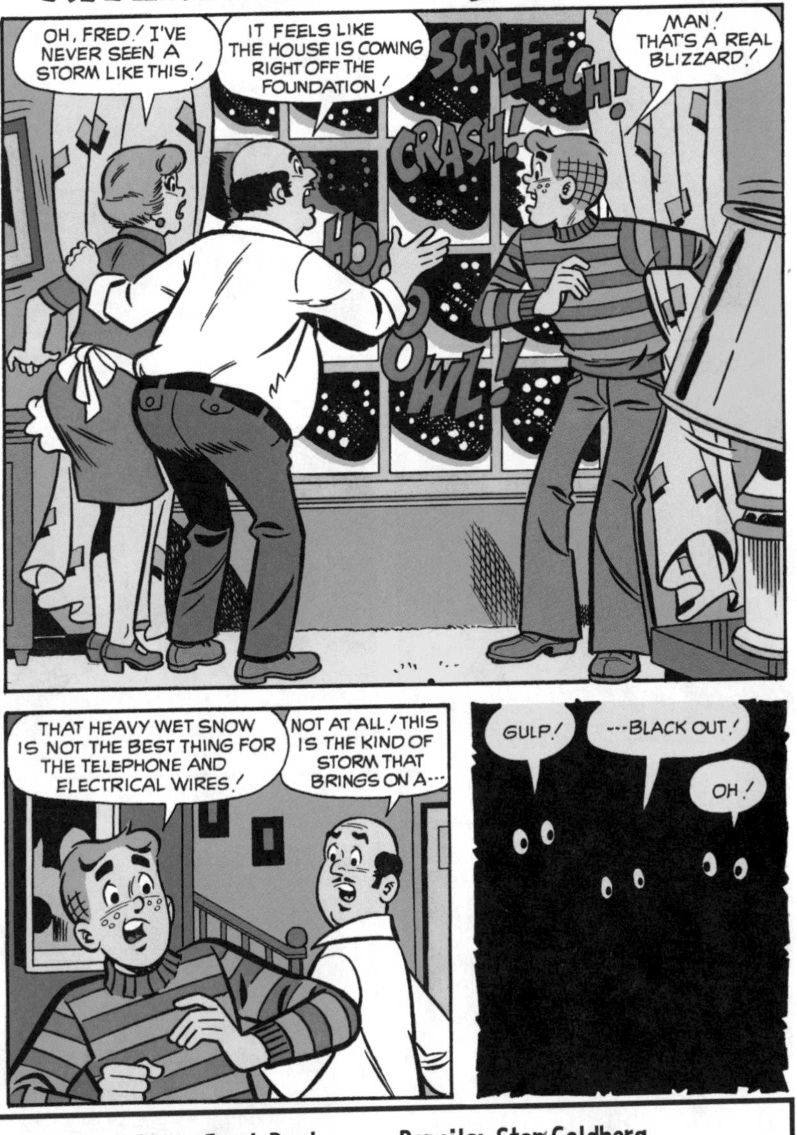
OH, FRED! I'VE NEVER SEEN A STORM LIKE THIS!
IT FEELS LIKE THE HOUSE IS COMING RIGHT OFF THE FOUNDATION!
SCREEEECH!
CRASH!
HOOOOWL!
MAN! THAT'S A REAL BLIZZARD!
THAT HEAVY WET SNOW IS NOT THE BEST THING FOR THE TELEPHONE AND ELECTRICAL WIRES!
NOT AT ALL! THIS IS THE KIND OF STORM THAT BRINGS ON A---
GULP!
---BLACK OUT!
OH!

Story: Frank Doyle Pencils: Stan Goldberg

Inks: Jon D'Agostino Letters: Bill Yoshida Colors: Barry Grossman

Originally printed in ARCHIE AT RIVERDALE HIGH #5, February 1973

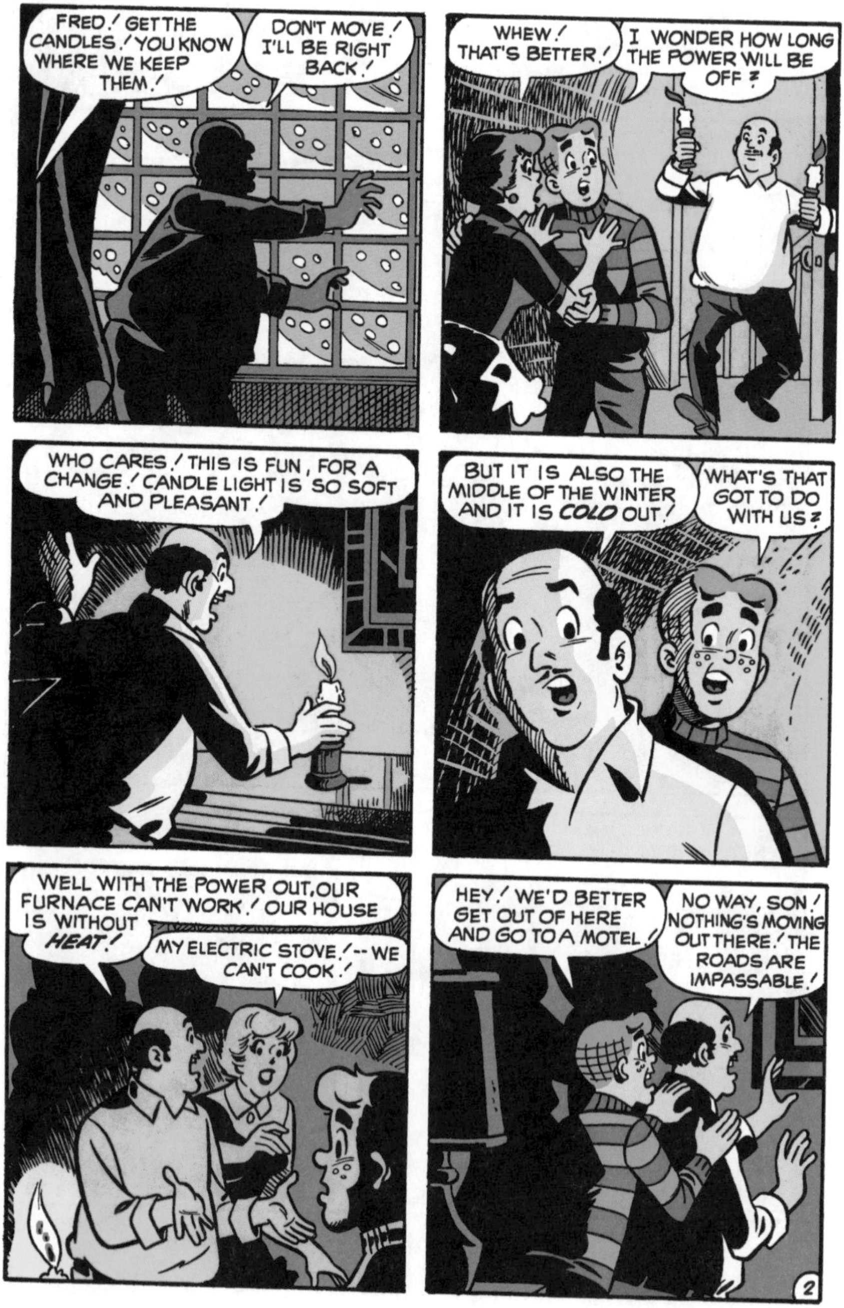
FRED! GET THE CANDLES! YOU KNOW WHERE WE KEEP THEM!
DON'T MOVE! I'LL BE RIGHT BACK!
WHEW! THAT'S BETTER!
I WONDER HOW LONG THE POWER WILL BE OFF?
WHO CARES! THIS IS FUN, FOR A CHANGE! CANDLE LIGHT IS SO SOFT AND PLEASANT!
BUT IT IS ALSO THE MIDDLE OF THE WINTER AND IT IS COLD OUT!
WHAT'S THAT GOT TO DO WITH US?
WELL WITH THE POWER OUT, OUR FURNACE CAN'T WORK! OUR HOUSE IS WITHOUT HEAT!
MY ELECTRIC STOVE! -- WE CAN'T COOK!
HEY! WE'D BETTER GET OUT OF HERE AND GO TO A MOTEL!
NO WAY, SON! NOTHING'S MOVING OUT THERE! THE ROADS ARE IMPASSABLE!
2

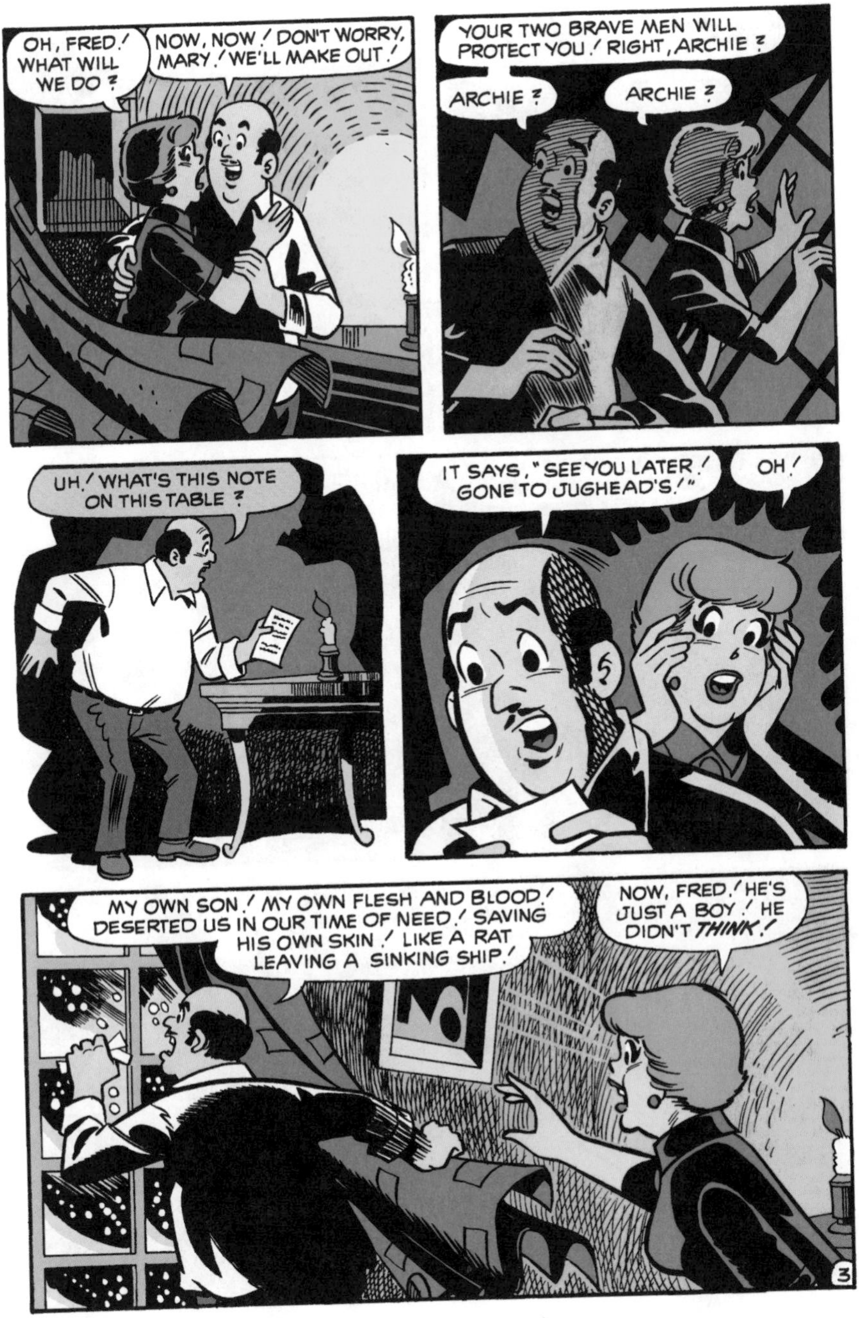
OH, FRED! WHAT WILL WE DO?
NOW, NOW! DON'T WORRY, MARY! WE'LL MAKE OUT!
YOUR TWO BRAVE MEN WILL PROTECT YOU! RIGHT, ARCHIE?
ARCHIE?
ARCHIE?
UH! WHAT'S THIS NOTE ON THIS TABLE?
IT SAYS, "SEE YOU LATER! GONE TO JUGHEAD'S!"
OH!
MY OWN SON! MY OWN FLESH AND BLOOD! DESERTED US IN OUR TIME OF NEED! SAVING HIS OWN SKIN! LIKE A RAT LEAVING A SINKING SHIP!
NOW, FRED! HE'S JUST A BOY! HE DIDN'T THINK!
3

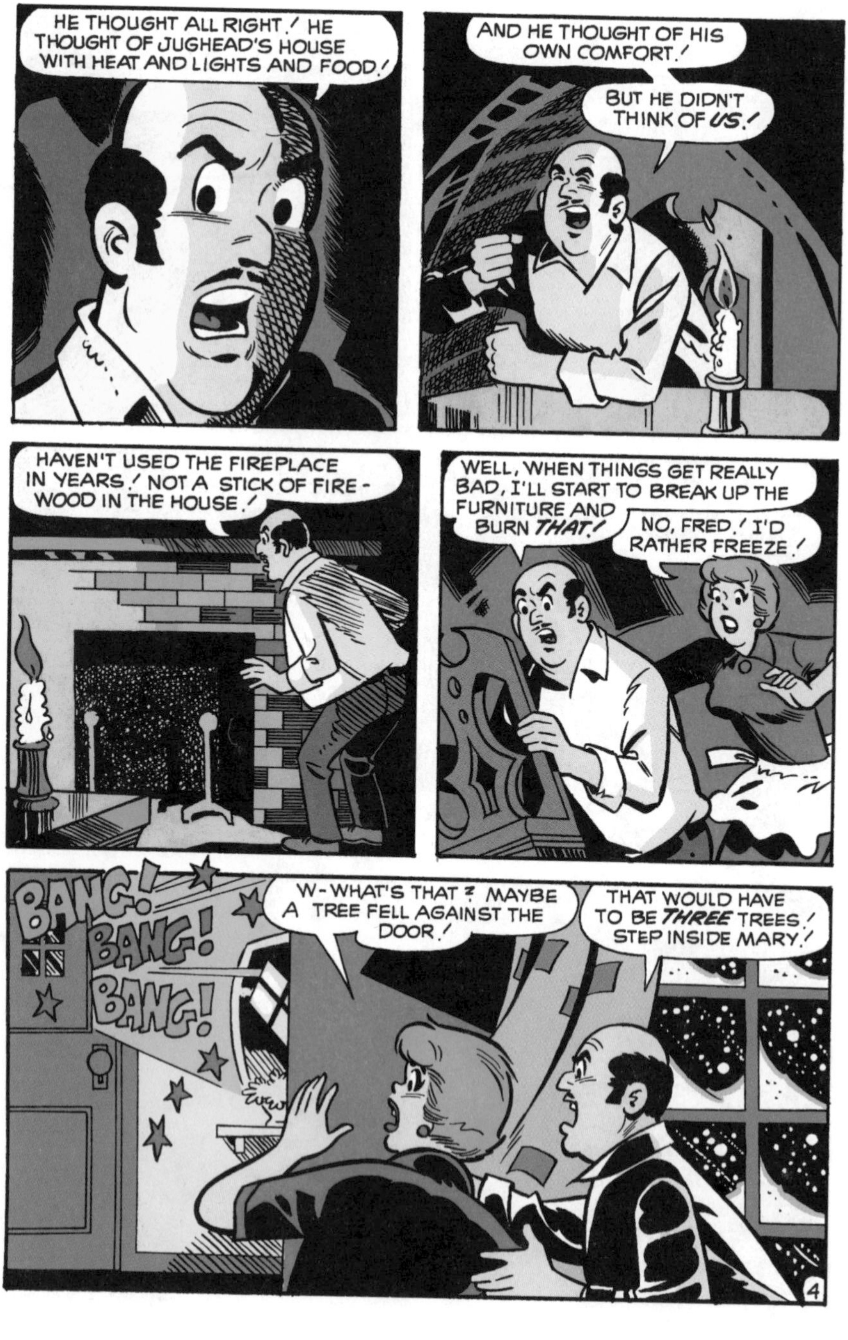
HE THOUGHT ALL RIGHT! HE THOUGHT OF JUGHEAD'S HOUSE WITH HEAT AND LIGHTS AND FOOD!
AND HE THOUGHT OF HIS OWN COMFORT!
BUT HE DIDN'T THINK OF US!
HAVEN'T USED THE FIREPLACE IN YEARS! NOT A STICK OF FIRE-WOOD IN THE HOUSE!
WELL, WHEN THINGS GET REALLY BAD, I'LL START TO BREAK UP THE FURNITURE AND BURN THAT!
NO, FRED! I'D RATHER FREEZE!
BANG! BANG! BANG!
W-WHAT'S THAT? MAYBE A TREE FELL AGAINST THE DOOR!
THAT WOULD HAVE TO BE THREE TREES! STEP INSIDE MARY!
4

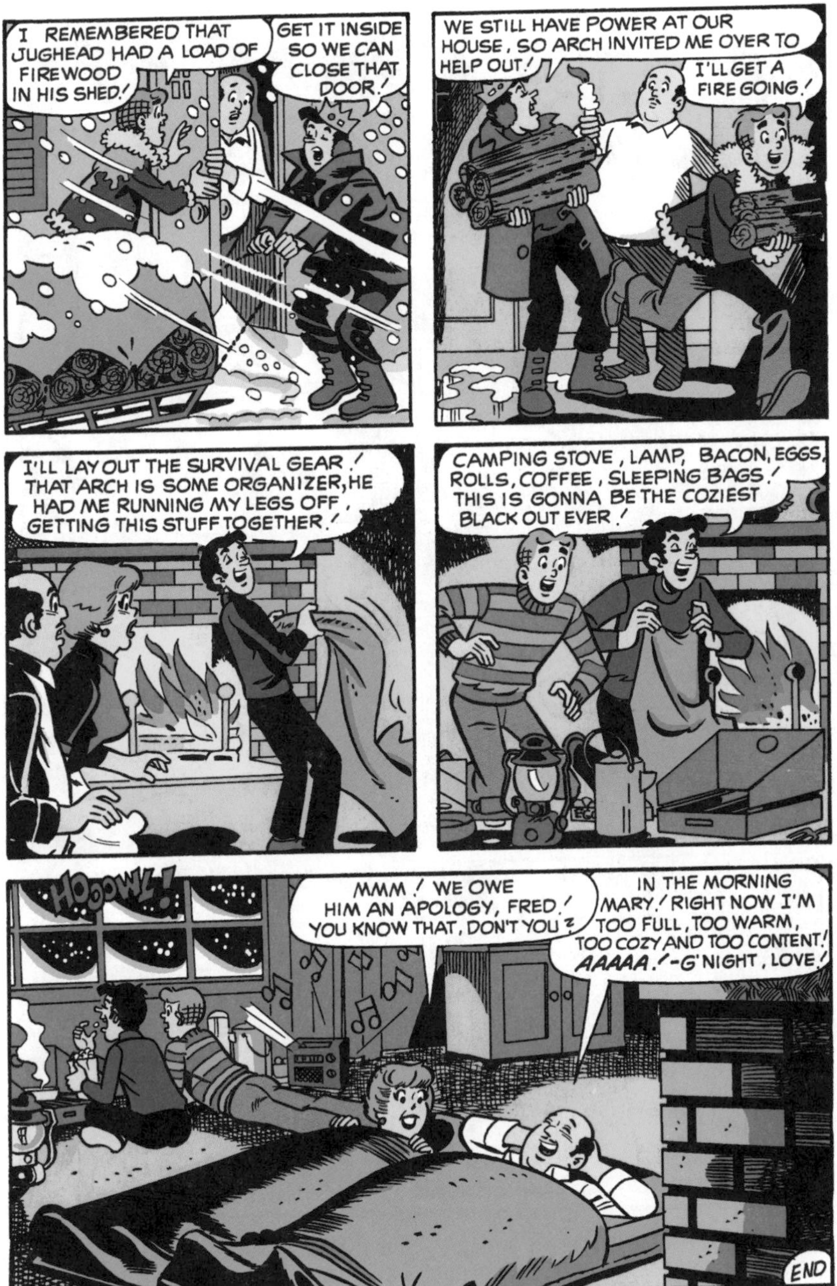
I REMEMBERED THAT JUGHEAD HAD A LOAD OF FIREWOOD IN HIS SHED!
GET IT INSIDE SO WE CAN CLOSE THAT DOOR!
WE STILL HAVE POWER AT OUR HOUSE, SO ARCH INVITED ME OVER TO HELP OUT!
I'LL GET A FIRE GOING!
I'LL LAY OUT THE SURVIVAL GEAR! THAT ARCH IS SOME ORGANIZER, HE HAD ME RUNNING MY LEGS OFF GETTING THIS STUFF TOGETHER!
CAMPING STOVE, LAMP, BACON, EGGS, ROLLS, COFFEE, SLEEPING BAGS! THIS IS GONNA BE THE COZIEST BLACK OUT EVER!
HOOOWL!
MMM! WE OWE HIM AN APOLOGY, FRED! YOU KNOW THAT, DON'T YOU?
IN THE MORNING MARY! RIGHT NOW I'M TOO FULL, TOO WARM, TOO COZY AND TOO CONTENT! AAAAA! -G'NIGHT, LOVE!
END

Archie in "Paint by Numbers"

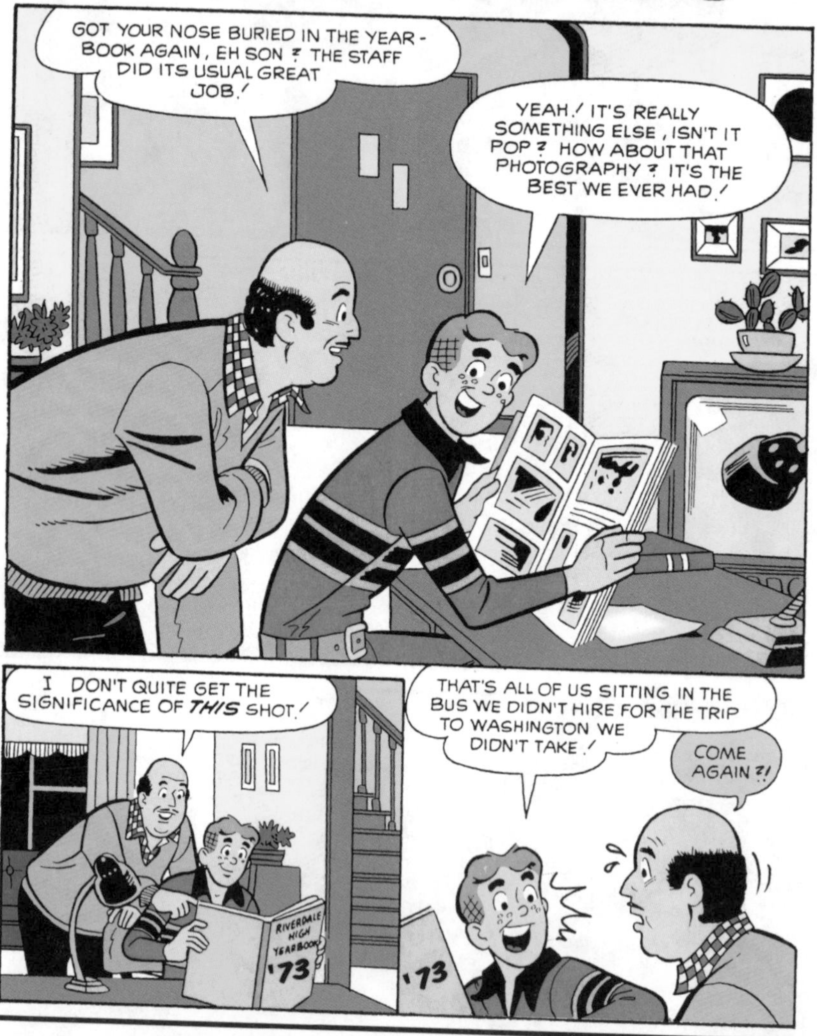
GOT YOUR NOSE BURIED IN THE YEAR-BOOK AGAIN, EH SON? THE STAFF DID ITS USUAL GREAT JOB!
YEAH! IT'S REALLY SOMETHING ELSE, ISN'T IT POP? HOW ABOUT THAT PHOTOGRAPHY? IT'S THE BEST WE EVER HAD!
I DON'T QUITE GET THE SIGNIFICANCE OF THIS SHOT!
RIVERDALE HIGH YEARBOOK '73
THAT'S ALL OF US SITTING IN THE BUS WE DIDN'T HIRE FOR THE TRIP TO WASHINGTON WE DIDN'T TAKE!
COME AGAIN?!
'73

Story: Frank Doyle **Pencils:** Dan DeCarlo

Inks: Jim DeCarlo **Letters:** Bill Yoshida

Originally printed in ARCHIE AT RIVERDALE HIGH #6, April 1973

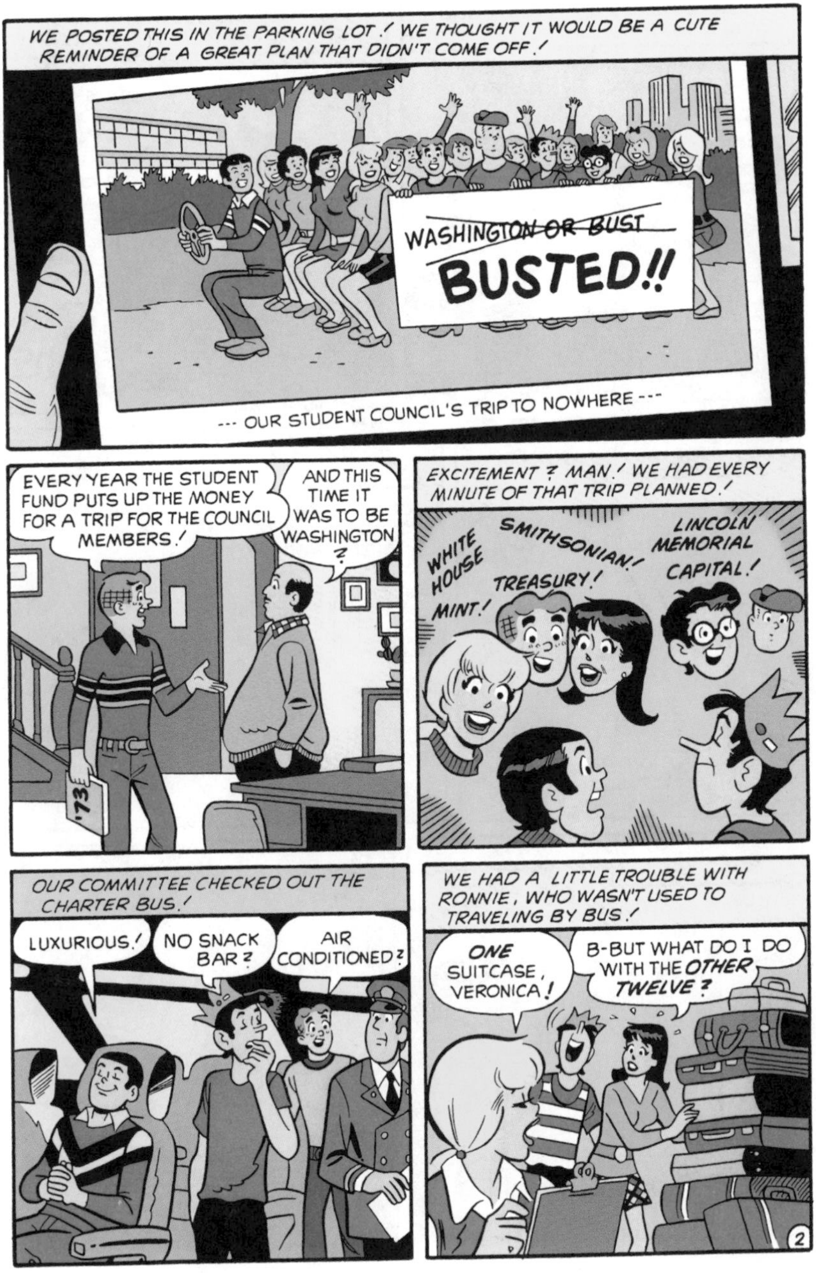
WE POSTED THIS IN THE PARKING LOT! WE THOUGHT IT WOULD BE A CUTE REMINDER OF A GREAT PLAN THAT DIDN'T COME OFF!
WASHINGTON OR BUST
BUSTED!!
--- OUR STUDENT COUNCIL'S TRIP TO NOWHERE ---
EVERY YEAR THE STUDENT FUND PUTS UP THE MONEY FOR A TRIP FOR THE COUNCIL MEMBERS!
AND THIS TIME IT WAS TO BE WASHINGTON?
'73
EXCITEMENT? MAN! WE HAD EVERY MINUTE OF THAT TRIP PLANNED!
WHITE HOUSE
SMITHSONIAN!
LINCOLN MEMORIAL
TREASURY!
CAPITAL!
MINT!
OUR COMMITTEE CHECKED OUT THE CHARTER BUS!
LUXURIOUS!
NO SNACK BAR?
AIR CONDITIONED?
WE HAD A LITTLE TROUBLE WITH RONNIE, WHO WASN'T USED TO TRAVELING BY BUS!
ONE SUITCASE, VERONICA!
B-BUT WHAT DO I DO WITH THE OTHER TWELVE?
2

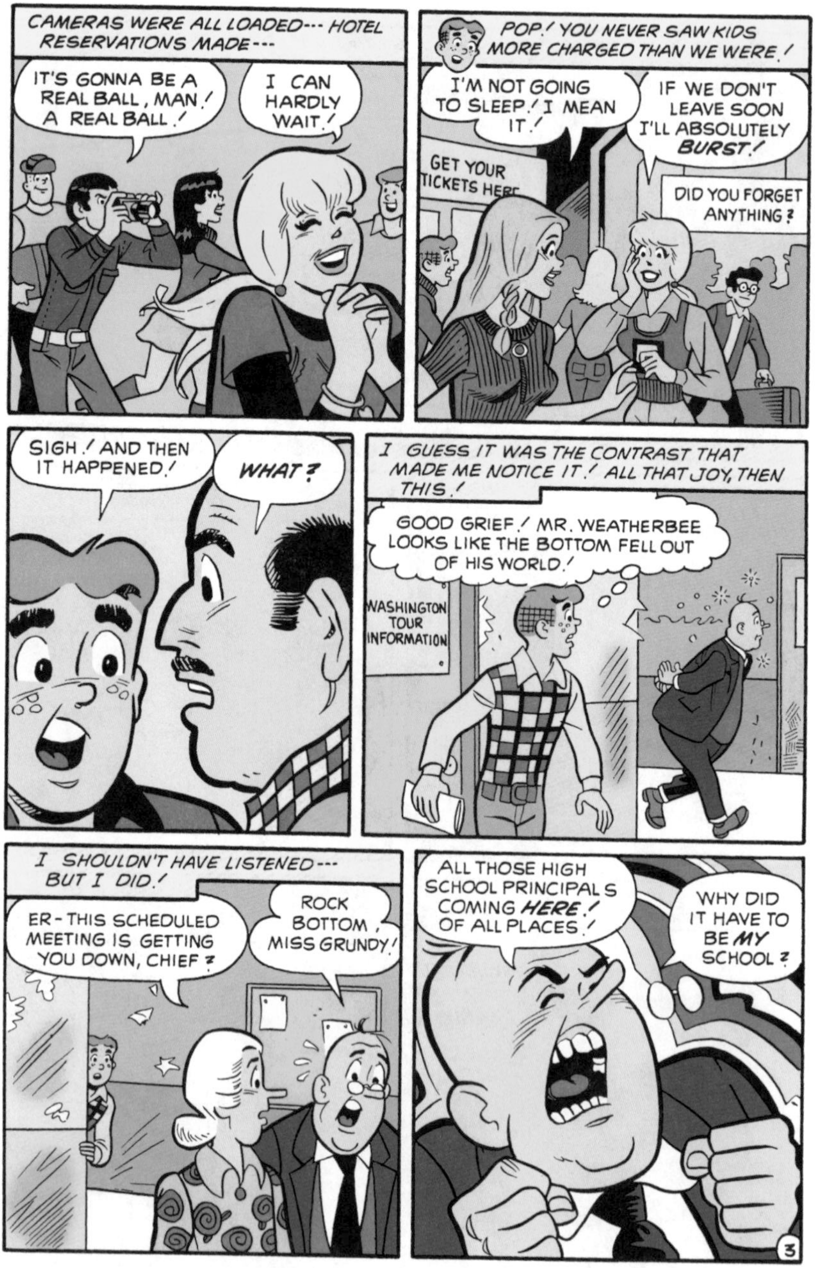
CAMERAS WERE ALL LOADED--- HOTEL RESERVATIONS MADE---
IT'S GONNA BE A REAL BALL, MAN! A REAL BALL!
I CAN HARDLY WAIT!
POP! YOU NEVER SAW KIDS MORE CHARGED THAN WE WERE!
I'M NOT GOING TO SLEEP! I MEAN IT!
IF WE DON'T LEAVE SOON I'LL ABSOLUTELY BURST!
GET YOUR TICKETS HERE
DID YOU FORGET ANYTHING?
SIGH! AND THEN IT HAPPENED!
WHAT?
I GUESS IT WAS THE CONTRAST THAT MADE ME NOTICE IT! ALL THAT JOY, THEN THIS!
GOOD GRIEF! MR. WEATHERBEE LOOKS LIKE THE BOTTOM FELL OUT OF HIS WORLD!
WASHINGTON TOUR INFORMATION
I SHOULDN'T HAVE LISTENED--- BUT I DID!
ER-THIS SCHEDULED MEETING IS GETTING YOU DOWN, CHIEF?
ROCK BOTTOM, MISS GRUNDY!
ALL THOSE HIGH SCHOOL PRINCIPALS COMING HERE! OF ALL PLACES!
WHY DID IT HAVE TO BE MY SCHOOL?
3

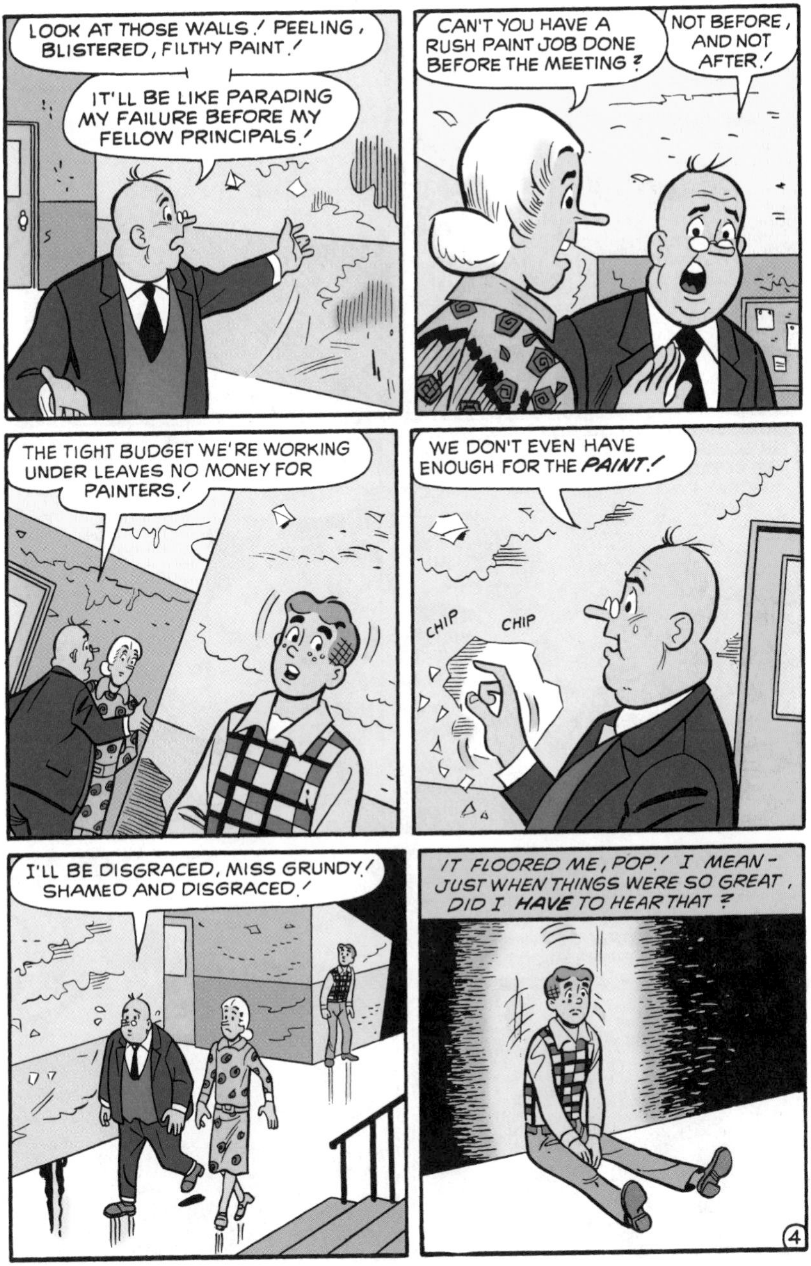
LOOK AT THOSE WALLS! PEELING, BLISTERED, FILTHY PAINT!
IT'LL BE LIKE PARADING MY FAILURE BEFORE MY FELLOW PRINCIPALS!
CAN'T YOU HAVE A RUSH PAINT JOB DONE BEFORE THE MEETING?
NOT BEFORE, AND NOT AFTER!
THE TIGHT BUDGET WE'RE WORKING UNDER LEAVES NO MONEY FOR PAINTERS!
WE DON'T EVEN HAVE ENOUGH FOR THE *PAINT*!
CHIP
CHIP
I'LL BE DISGRACED, MISS GRUNDY! SHAMED AND DISGRACED!
*IT FLOORED ME, POP! I MEAN- JUST WHEN THINGS WERE SO GREAT, DID I **HAVE** TO HEAR THAT?*
4

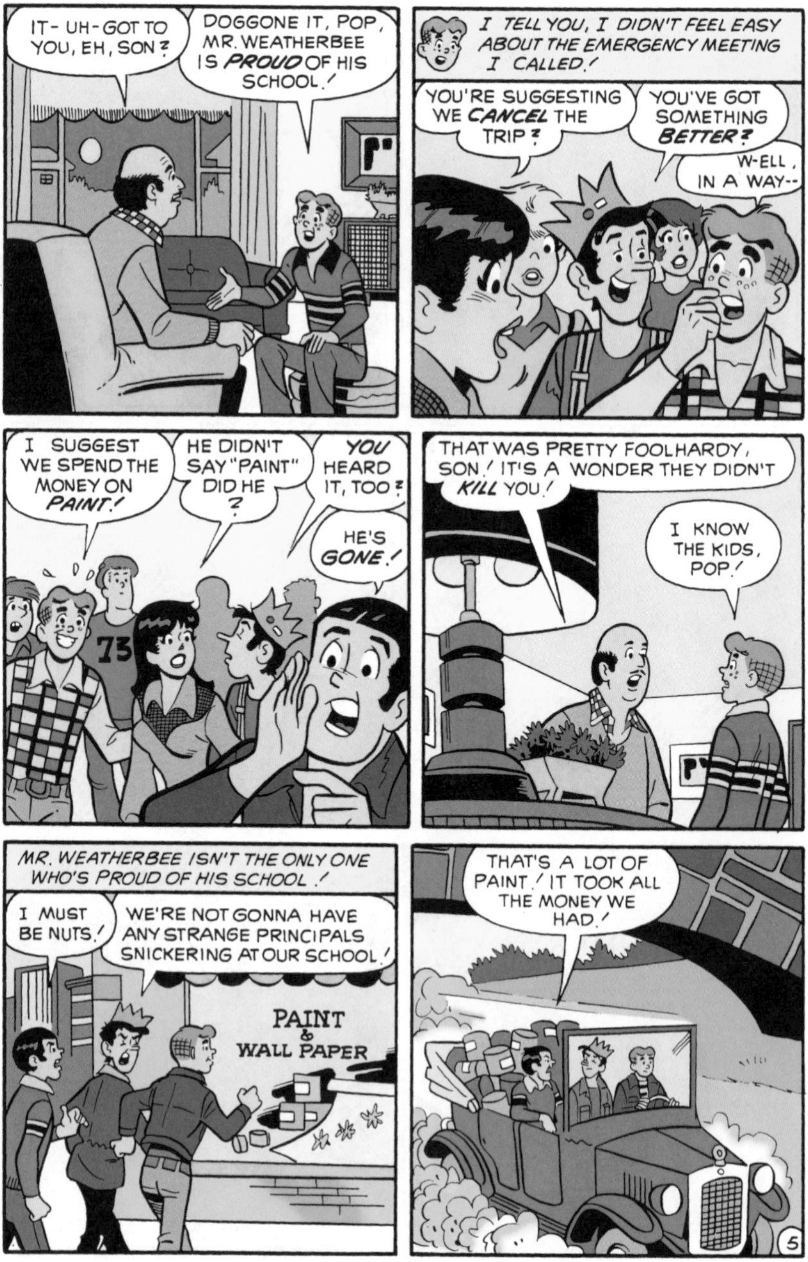
IT- UH- GOT TO YOU, EH, SON?
DOGGONE IT, POP, MR. WEATHERBEE IS PROUD OF HIS SCHOOL!
I TELL YOU, I DIDN'T FEEL EASY ABOUT THE EMERGENCY MEETING I CALLED!
YOU'RE SUGGESTING WE CANCEL THE TRIP?
YOU'VE GOT SOMETHING BETTER?
W-ELL, IN A WAY--
I SUGGEST WE SPEND THE MONEY ON PAINT!
HE DIDN'T SAY "PAINT" DID HE?
YOU HEARD IT, TOO?
HE'S GONE!
73
THAT WAS PRETTY FOOLHARDY, SON! IT'S A WONDER THEY DIDN'T KILL YOU!
I KNOW THE KIDS, POP!
MR. WEATHERBEE ISN'T THE ONLY ONE WHO'S PROUD OF HIS SCHOOL!
I MUST BE NUTS!
WE'RE NOT GONNA HAVE ANY STRANGE PRINCIPALS SNICKERING AT OUR SCHOOL!
PAINT & WALL PAPER
THAT'S A LOT OF PAINT! IT TOOK ALL THE MONEY WE HAD!
5

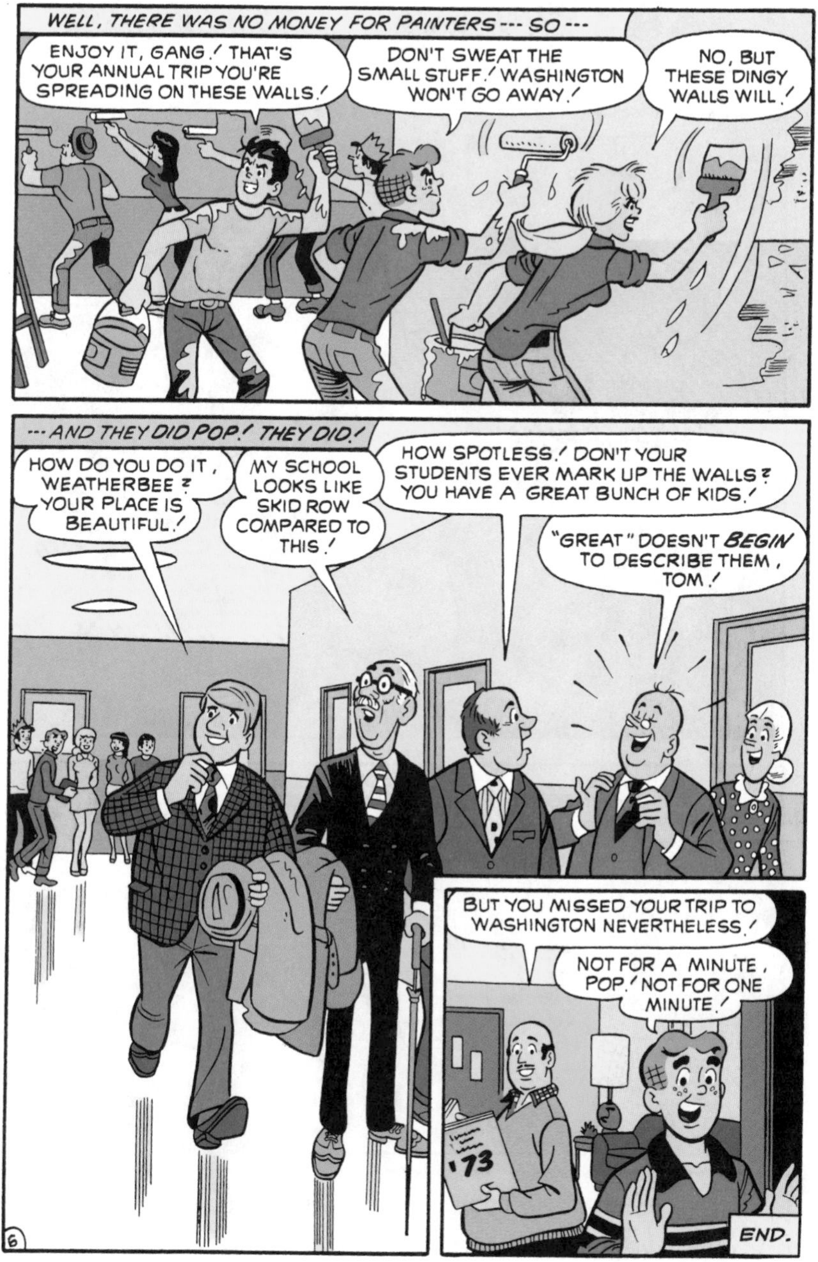
WELL, THERE WAS NO MONEY FOR PAINTERS --- SO ---
ENJOY IT, GANG! THAT'S YOUR ANNUAL TRIP YOU'RE SPREADING ON THESE WALLS!
DON'T SWEAT THE SMALL STUFF! WASHINGTON WON'T GO AWAY!
NO, BUT THESE DINGY WALLS WILL!
--- AND THEY DID POP! THEY DID!
HOW DO YOU DO IT, WEATHERBEE? YOUR PLACE IS BEAUTIFUL!
MY SCHOOL LOOKS LIKE SKID ROW COMPARED TO THIS!
HOW SPOTLESS! DON'T YOUR STUDENTS EVER MARK UP THE WALLS? YOU HAVE A GREAT BUNCH OF KIDS!
"GREAT" DOESN'T *BEGIN* TO DESCRIBE THEM, TOM!
6
BUT YOU MISSED YOUR TRIP TO WASHINGTON NEVERTHELESS!
NOT FOR A MINUTE, POP! NOT FOR ONE MINUTE!
'73
END.

Archie in "Short Cut to Success"

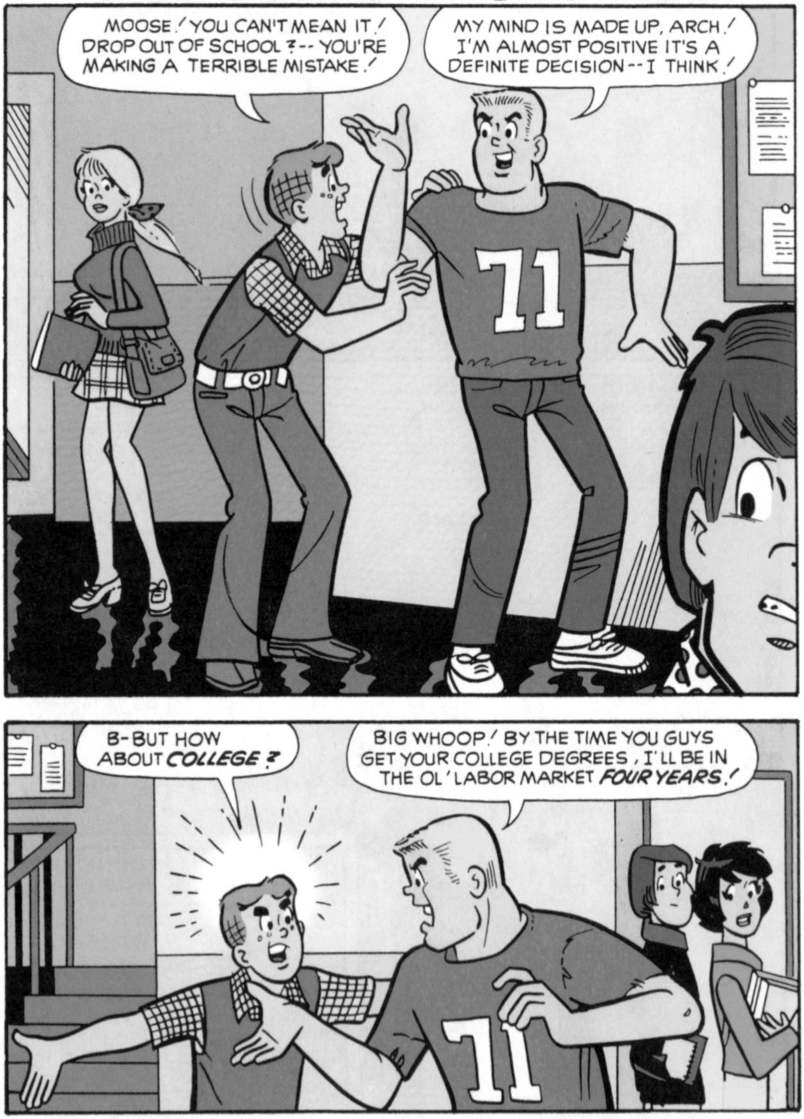
MOOSE! YOU CAN'T MEAN IT! DROP OUT OF SCHOOL ?-- YOU'RE MAKING A TERRIBLE MISTAKE!
MY MIND IS MADE UP, ARCH! I'M ALMOST POSITIVE IT'S A DEFINITE DECISION -- I THINK!
71
B-BUT HOW ABOUT *COLLEGE* ?
BIG WHOOP! BY THE TIME YOU GUYS GET YOUR COLLEGE DEGREES, I'LL BE IN THE OL' LABOR MARKET *FOUR YEARS*!
71

Story: Frank Doyle | Pencils: Stan Goldberg
Inks: Henry Scarpelli | Letters: Bill Yoshida

Originally printed in ARCHIE AT RIVERDALE HIGH #6, April 1973

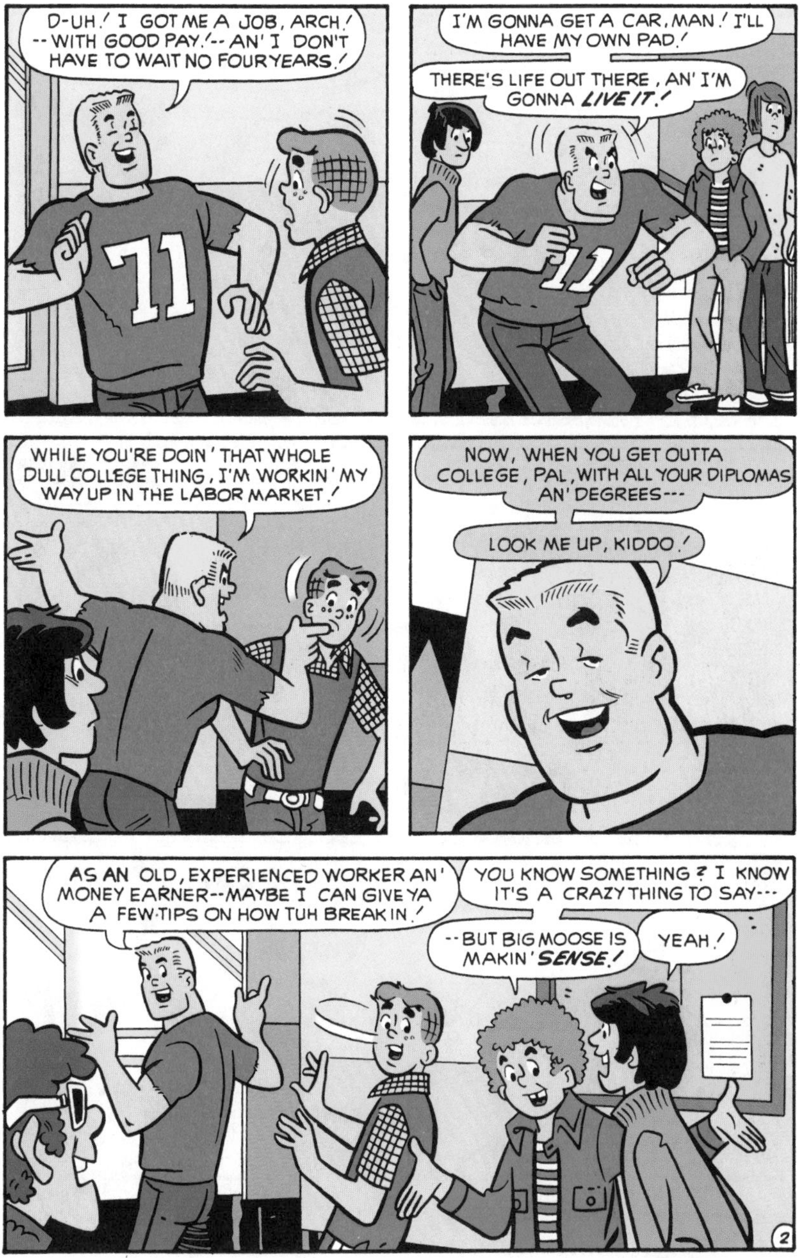
D-UH.! I GOT ME A JOB, ARCH.! --WITH GOOD PAY.!-- AN' I DON'T HAVE TO WAIT NO FOUR YEARS.!
I'M GONNA GET A CAR, MAN.! I'LL HAVE MY OWN PAD.!
THERE'S LIFE OUT THERE, AN' I'M GONNA *LIVE IT*.!
WHILE YOU'RE DOIN' THAT WHOLE DULL COLLEGE THING, I'M WORKIN' MY WAY UP IN THE LABOR MARKET.!
NOW, WHEN YOU GET OUTTA COLLEGE, PAL, WITH ALL YOUR DIPLOMAS AN' DEGREES---
LOOK ME UP, KIDDO.!
AS AN OLD, EXPERIENCED WORKER AN' MONEY EARNER--MAYBE I CAN GIVE YA A FEW TIPS ON HOW TUH BREAK IN.!
YOU KNOW SOMETHING? I KNOW IT'S A CRAZY THING TO SAY---
--BUT BIG MOOSE IS MAKIN' *SENSE*.!
YEAH.!
2

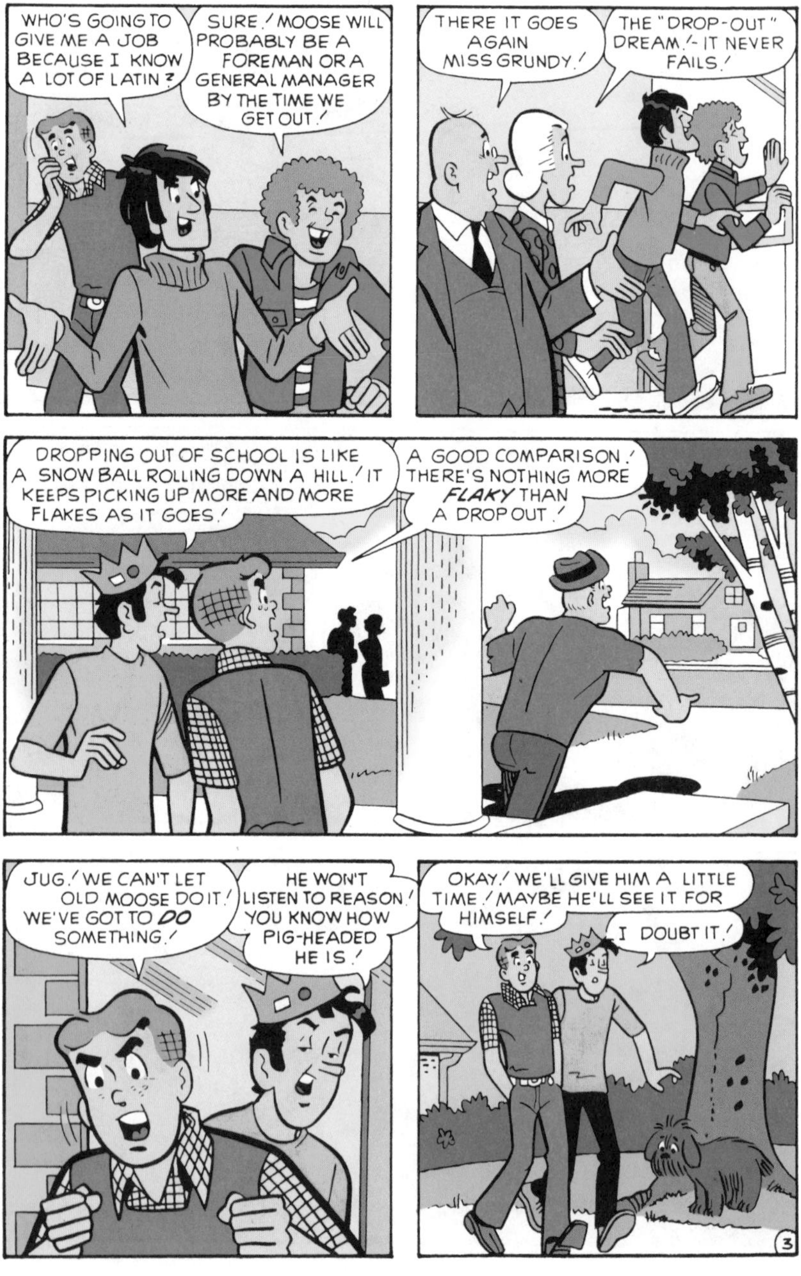
WHO'S GOING TO GIVE ME A JOB BECAUSE I KNOW A LOT OF LATIN?
SURE! MOOSE WILL PROBABLY BE A FOREMAN OR A GENERAL MANAGER BY THE TIME WE GET OUT!
THERE IT GOES AGAIN MISS GRUNDY!
THE "DROP-OUT" DREAM!- IT NEVER FAILS!
DROPPING OUT OF SCHOOL IS LIKE A SNOW BALL ROLLING DOWN A HILL! IT KEEPS PICKING UP MORE AND MORE FLAKES AS IT GOES!
A GOOD COMPARISON! THERE'S NOTHING MORE FLAKY THAN A DROP OUT!
JUG! WE CAN'T LET OLD MOOSE DO IT! WE'VE GOT TO DO SOMETHING!
HE WON'T LISTEN TO REASON! YOU KNOW HOW PIG-HEADED HE IS!
OKAY! WE'LL GIVE HIM A LITTLE TIME! MAYBE HE'LL SEE IT FOR HIMSELF!
I DOUBT IT!
3

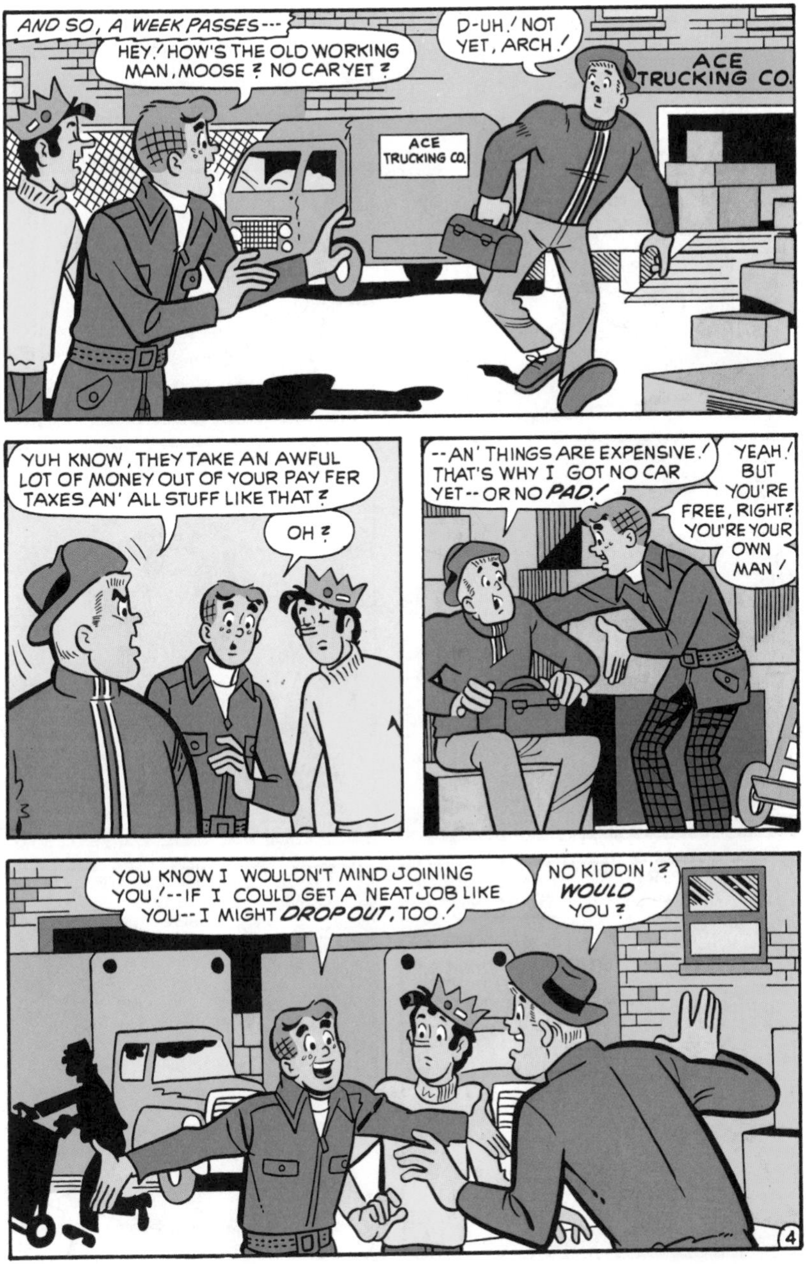
AND SO, A WEEK PASSES---
HEY! HOW'S THE OLD WORKING MAN, MOOSE? NO CAR YET?
D-UH! NOT YET, ARCH!
ACE TRUCKING CO.
ACE TRUCKING CO.
YUH KNOW, THEY TAKE AN AWFUL LOT OF MONEY OUT OF YOUR PAY FER TAXES AN' ALL STUFF LIKE THAT?
OH?
--AN' THINGS ARE EXPENSIVE! THAT'S WHY I GOT NO CAR YET--OR NO PAD!
YEAH! BUT YOU'RE FREE, RIGHT? YOU'RE YOUR OWN MAN!
YOU KNOW I WOULDN'T MIND JOINING YOU!--IF I COULD GET A NEAT JOB LIKE YOU--I MIGHT DROP OUT, TOO!
NO KIDDIN'? WOULD YOU?
4

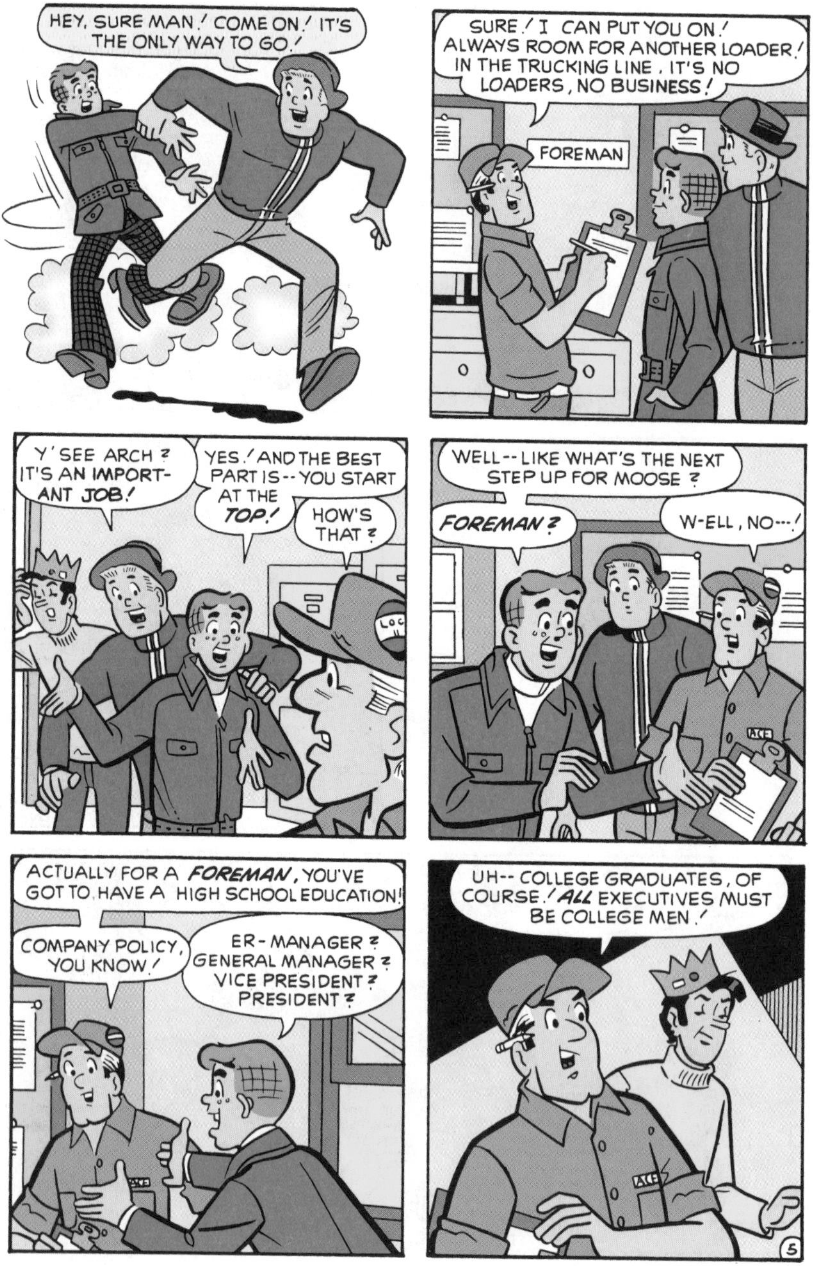
HEY, SURE MAN! COME ON! IT'S THE ONLY WAY TO GO!
SURE! I CAN PUT YOU ON! ALWAYS ROOM FOR ANOTHER LOADER! IN THE TRUCKING LINE. IT'S NO LOADERS, NO BUSINESS!
FOREMAN
Y' SEE ARCH? IT'S AN IMPORTANT JOB!
YES! AND THE BEST PART IS--YOU START AT THE TOP!
HOW'S THAT?
WELL--LIKE WHAT'S THE NEXT STEP UP FOR MOOSE?
FOREMAN?
W-ELL, NO---!
ACTUALLY FOR A FOREMAN, YOU'VE GOT TO HAVE A HIGH SCHOOL EDUCATION!
COMPANY POLICY, YOU KNOW!
ER-MANAGER? GENERAL MANAGER? VICE PRESIDENT? PRESIDENT?
UH--COLLEGE GRADUATES, OF COURSE! ALL EXECUTIVES MUST BE COLLEGE MEN!
5

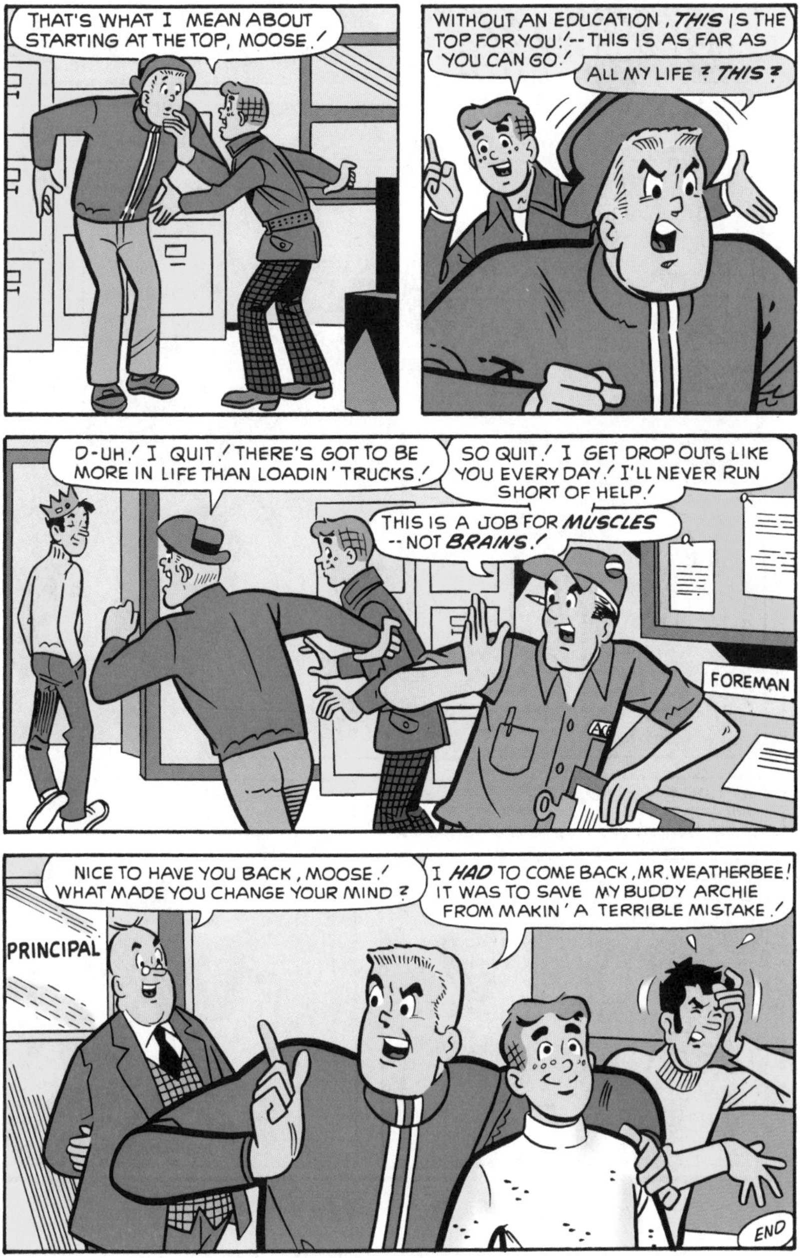
THAT'S WHAT I MEAN ABOUT STARTING AT THE TOP, MOOSE!
WITHOUT AN EDUCATION, THIS IS THE TOP FOR YOU!--THIS IS AS FAR AS YOU CAN GO!
ALL MY LIFE? THIS?
D-UH! I QUIT! THERE'S GOT TO BE MORE IN LIFE THAN LOADIN' TRUCKS!
SO QUIT! I GET DROP OUTS LIKE YOU EVERY DAY! I'LL NEVER RUN SHORT OF HELP!
THIS IS A JOB FOR MUSCLES --NOT BRAINS!
FOREMAN
NICE TO HAVE YOU BACK, MOOSE! WHAT MADE YOU CHANGE YOUR MIND?
I HAD TO COME BACK, MR. WEATHERBEE! IT WAS TO SAVE MY BUDDY ARCHIE FROM MAKIN' A TERRIBLE MISTAKE!
PRINCIPAL
END

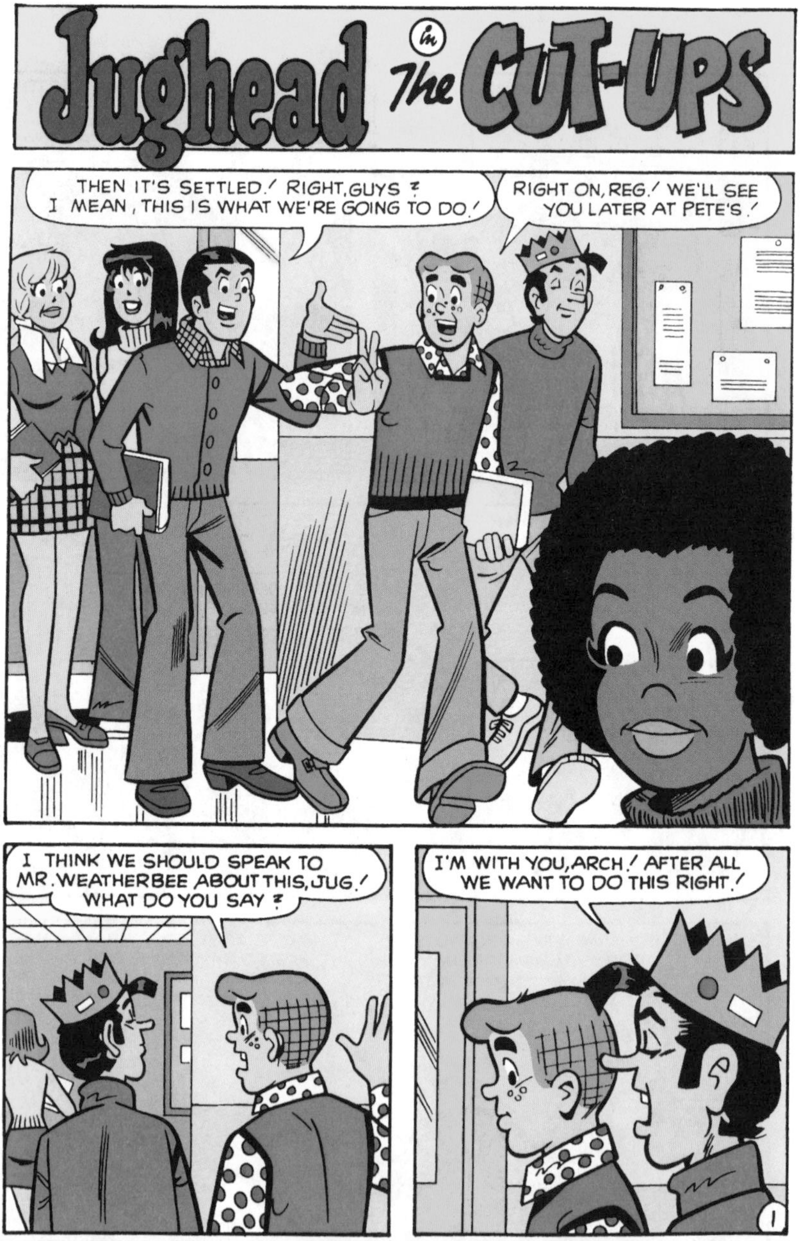
Jughead in The CUT-UPS
THEN IT'S SETTLED! RIGHT, GUYS? I MEAN, THIS IS WHAT WE'RE GOING TO DO!
RIGHT ON, REG.! WE'LL SEE YOU LATER AT PETE'S!
I THINK WE SHOULD SPEAK TO MR. WEATHERBEE ABOUT THIS, JUG.! WHAT DO YOU SAY?
I'M WITH YOU, ARCH! AFTER ALL WE WANT TO DO THIS RIGHT!
1

Story: George Gladir Pencils: Stan Goldberg

Inks: Jon D'Agostino Letters: Bill Yoshida Colors: Barry Grossman

Originally printed in ARCHIE AT RIVERDALE HIGH #6, April 1973

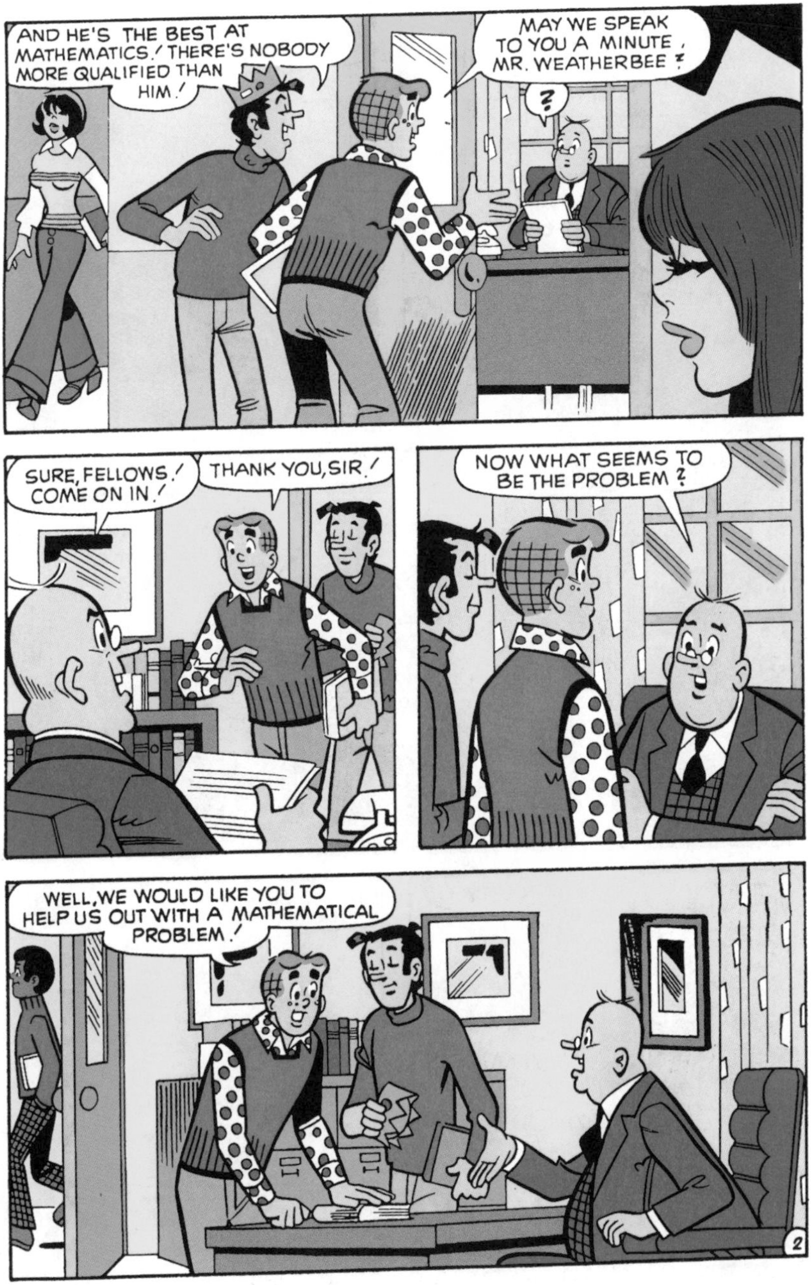
AND HE'S THE BEST AT MATHEMATICS! THERE'S NOBODY MORE QUALIFIED THAN HIM!
MAY WE SPEAK TO YOU A MINUTE, MR. WEATHERBEE?
?
SURE, FELLOWS! COME ON IN!
THANK YOU, SIR!
NOW WHAT SEEMS TO BE THE PROBLEM?
WELL, WE WOULD LIKE YOU TO HELP US OUT WITH A MATHEMATICAL PROBLEM!
2

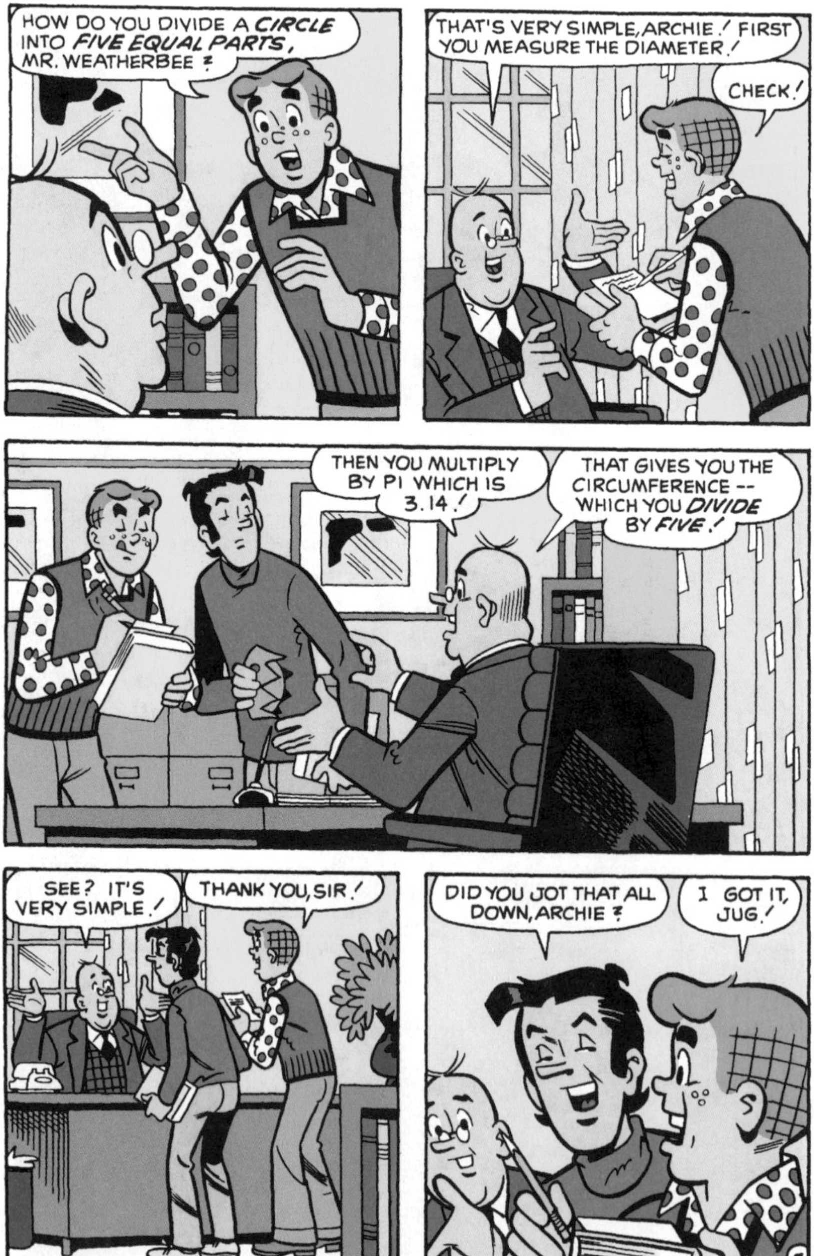
HOW DO YOU DIVIDE A *CIRCLE* INTO *FIVE EQUAL PARTS*, MR. WEATHERBEE ?
THAT'S VERY SIMPLE, ARCHIE! FIRST YOU MEASURE THE DIAMETER!
CHECK!
THEN YOU MULTIPLY BY PI WHICH IS 3.14!
THAT GIVES YOU THE CIRCUMFERENCE -- WHICH YOU *DIVIDE* BY *FIVE*!
SEE? IT'S VERY SIMPLE!
THANK YOU, SIR!
DID YOU JOT THAT ALL DOWN, ARCHIE ?
I GOT IT, JUG!
3

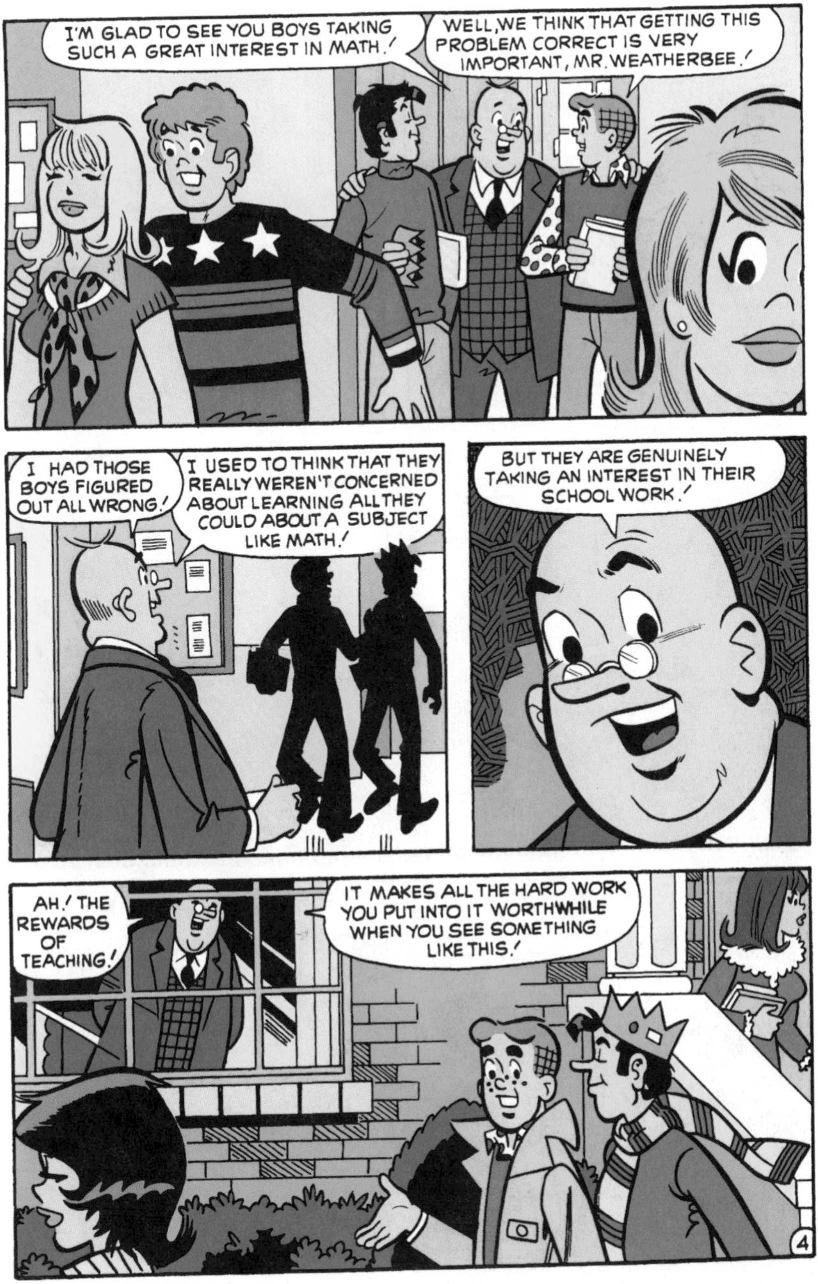
I'M GLAD TO SEE YOU BOYS TAKING SUCH A GREAT INTEREST IN MATH!
WELL, WE THINK THAT GETTING THIS PROBLEM CORRECT IS VERY IMPORTANT, MR. WEATHERBEE!
I HAD THOSE BOYS FIGURED OUT ALL WRONG!
I USED TO THINK THAT THEY REALLY WEREN'T CONCERNED ABOUT LEARNING ALL THEY COULD ABOUT A SUBJECT LIKE MATH!
BUT THEY ARE GENUINELY TAKING AN INTEREST IN THEIR SCHOOL WORK!
AH! THE REWARDS OF TEACHING!
IT MAKES ALL THE HARD WORK YOU PUT INTO IT WORTHWHILE WHEN YOU SEE SOMETHING LIKE THIS!
4

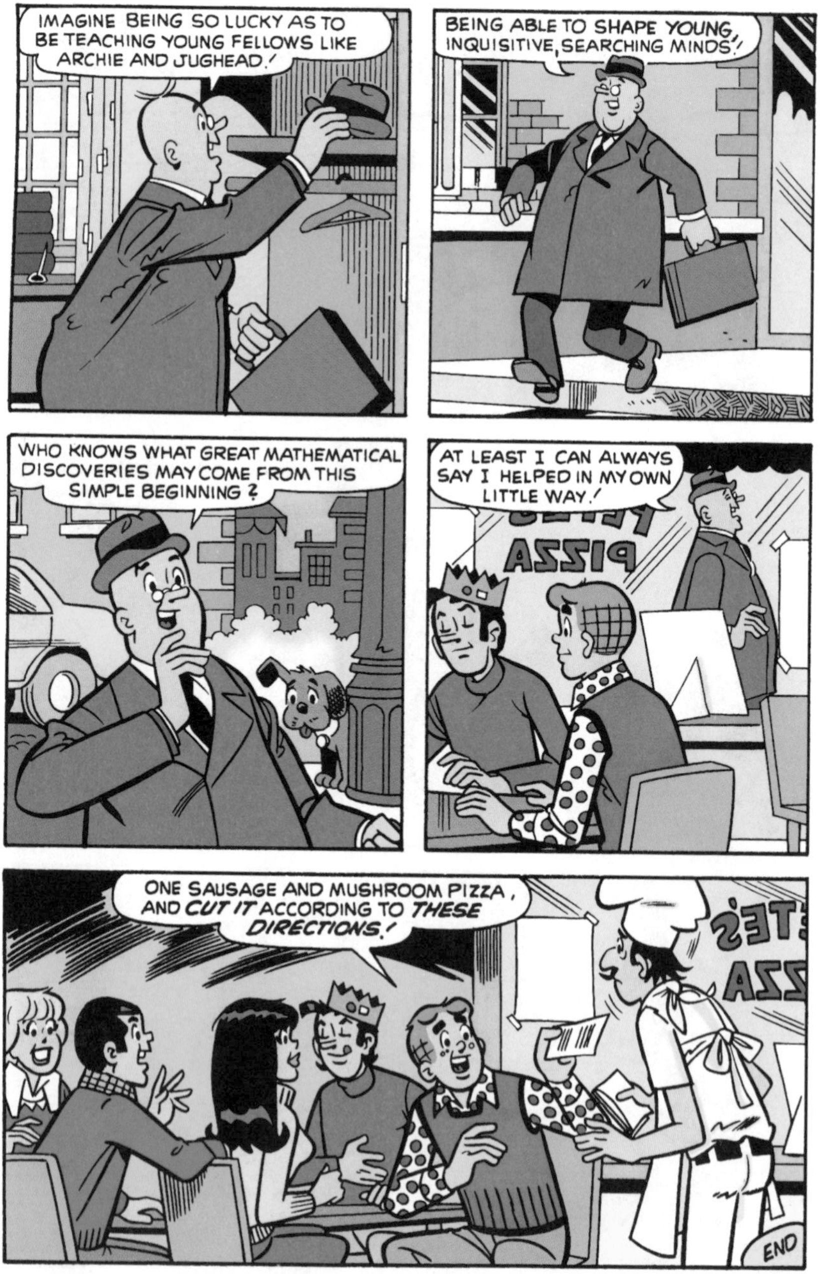
IMAGINE BEING SO LUCKY AS TO BE TEACHING YOUNG FELLOWS LIKE ARCHIE AND JUGHEAD!
BEING ABLE TO SHAPE YOUNG, INQUISITIVE, SEARCHING MINDS!
WHO KNOWS WHAT GREAT MATHEMATICAL DISCOVERIES MAY COME FROM THIS SIMPLE BEGINNING?
AT LEAST I CAN ALWAYS SAY I HELPED IN MY OWN LITTLE WAY!
PIZZA
ONE SAUSAGE AND MUSHROOM PIZZA, AND CUT IT ACCORDING TO THESE DIRECTIONS!
END

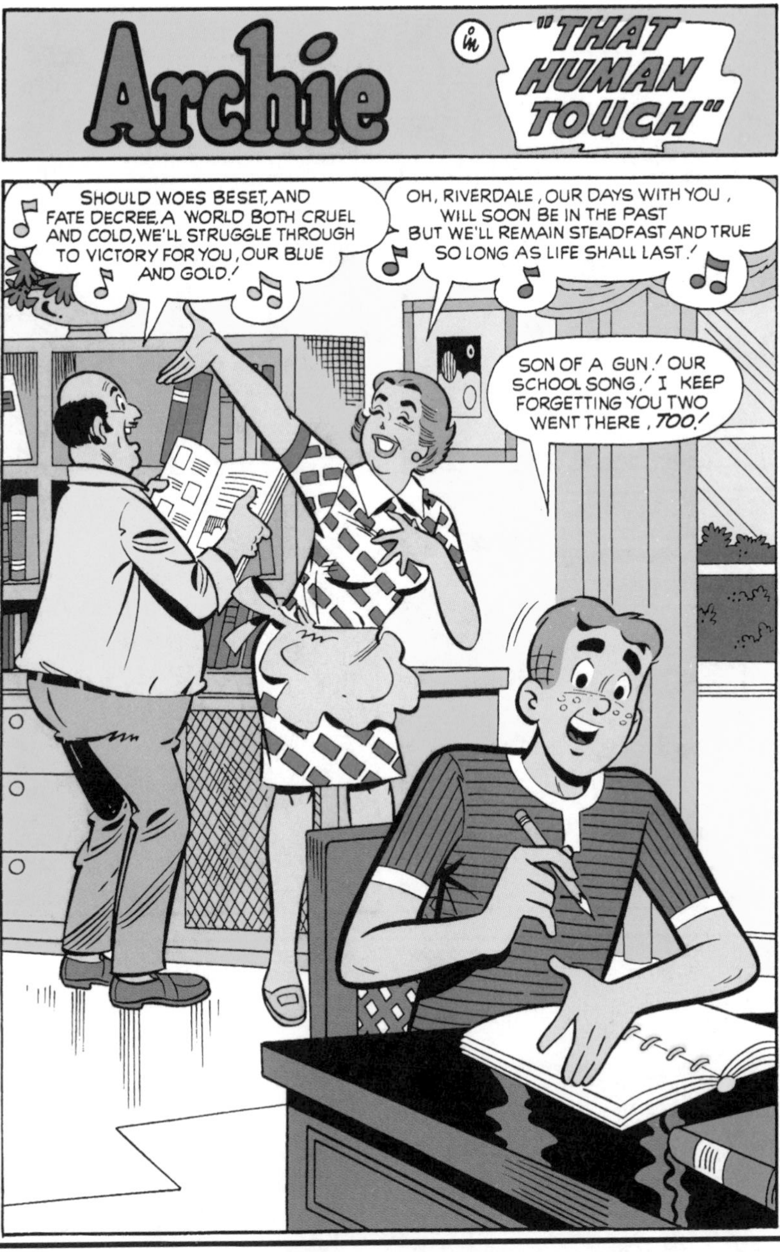
Archie in "THAT HUMAN TOUCH"
SHOULD WOES BESET, AND FATE DECREE, A WORLD BOTH CRUEL AND COLD, WE'LL STRUGGLE THROUGH TO VICTORY FOR YOU, OUR BLUE AND GOLD!
OH, RIVERDALE, OUR DAYS WITH YOU, WILL SOON BE IN THE PAST BUT WE'LL REMAIN STEADFAST AND TRUE SO LONG AS LIFE SHALL LAST!
SON OF A GUN! OUR SCHOOL SONG! I KEEP FORGETTING YOU TWO WENT THERE, TOO!

Story: Frank Doyle   Pencils: Stan Goldberg

Inks: Jon D'Agostino   Letters: Bill Yoshida   Colors: Barry Grossman

Originally printed in ARCHIE AT RIVERDALE HIGH #6, April 1973

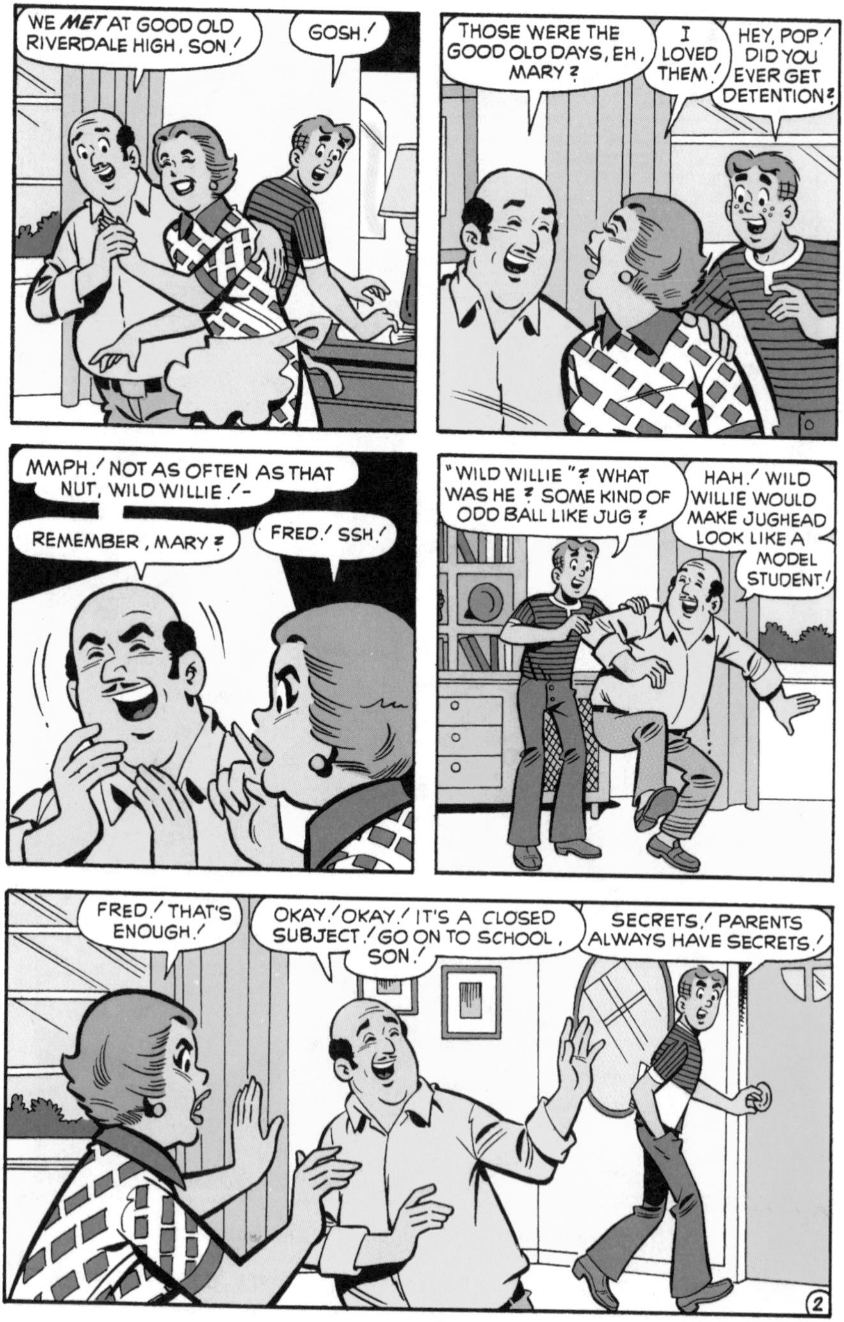
WE MET AT GOOD OLD RIVERDALE HIGH, SON!
GOSH!
THOSE WERE THE GOOD OLD DAYS, EH, MARY?
I LOVED THEM!
HEY, POP! DID YOU EVER GET DETENTION?
MMPH! NOT AS OFTEN AS THAT NUT, WILD WILLIE!-
REMEMBER, MARY?
FRED! SSH!
"WILD WILLIE"? WHAT WAS HE? SOME KIND OF ODD BALL LIKE JUG?
HAH! WILD WILLIE WOULD MAKE JUGHEAD LOOK LIKE A MODEL STUDENT!
FRED! THAT'S ENOUGH!
OKAY! OKAY! IT'S A CLOSED SUBJECT! GO ON TO SCHOOL, SON!
SECRETS! PARENTS ALWAYS HAVE SECRETS!
2

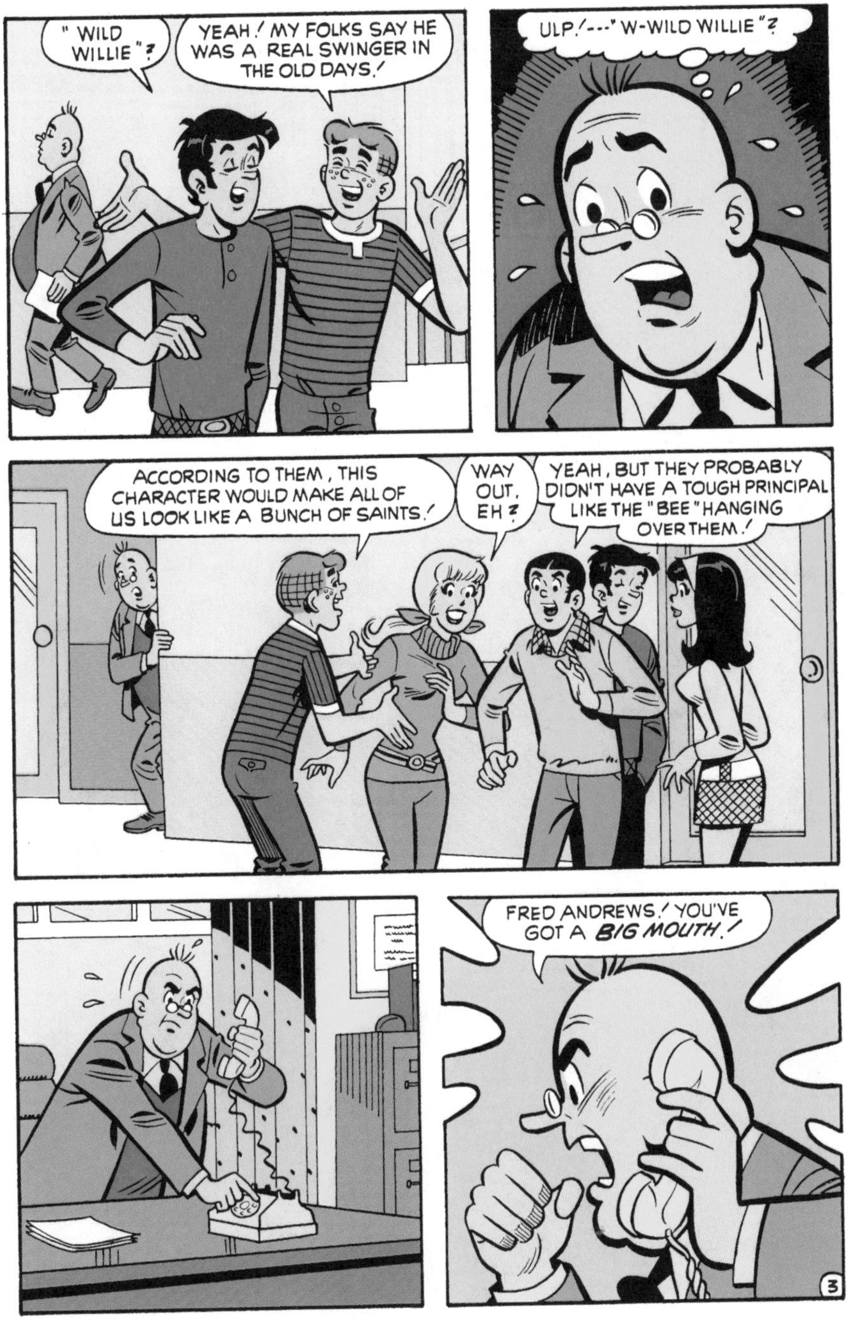
" WILD WILLIE "?
YEAH! MY FOLKS SAY HE WAS A REAL SWINGER IN THE OLD DAYS!
ULP!---" W-WILD WILLIE "?
ACCORDING TO THEM, THIS CHARACTER WOULD MAKE ALL OF US LOOK LIKE A BUNCH OF SAINTS!
WAY OUT, EH?
YEAH, BUT THEY PROBABLY DIDN'T HAVE A TOUGH PRINCIPAL LIKE THE "BEE" HANGING OVER THEM!
FRED ANDREWS! YOU'VE GOT A ***BIG MOUTH***!
3

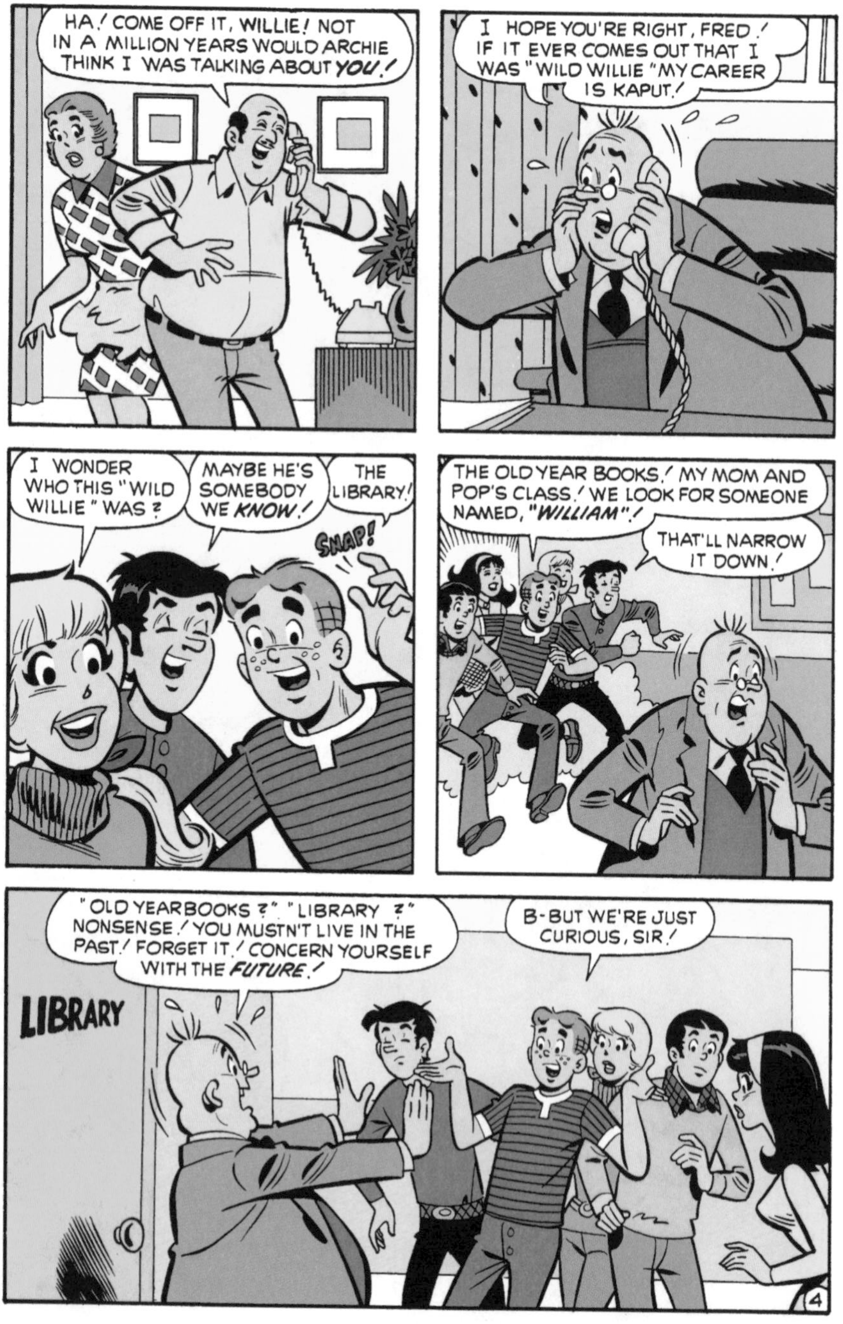
HA! COME OFF IT, WILLIE! NOT IN A MILLION YEARS WOULD ARCHIE THINK I WAS TALKING ABOUT YOU!
I HOPE YOU'RE RIGHT, FRED! IF IT EVER COMES OUT THAT I WAS "WILD WILLIE" MY CAREER
IS KAPUT!
I WONDER WHO THIS "WILD WILLIE" WAS?
MAYBE HE'S SOMEBODY WE KNOW!
THE LIBRARY!
SNAP!
THE OLD YEAR BOOKS! MY MOM AND POP'S CLASS! WE LOOK FOR SOMEONE NAMED, "WILLIAM"!
THAT'LL NARROW IT DOWN!
"OLD YEARBOOKS?" "LIBRARY?" NONSENSE! YOU MUSTN'T LIVE IN THE PAST! FORGET IT! CONCERN YOURSELF WITH THE FUTURE!
B-BUT WE'RE JUST CURIOUS, SIR!
LIBRARY
4

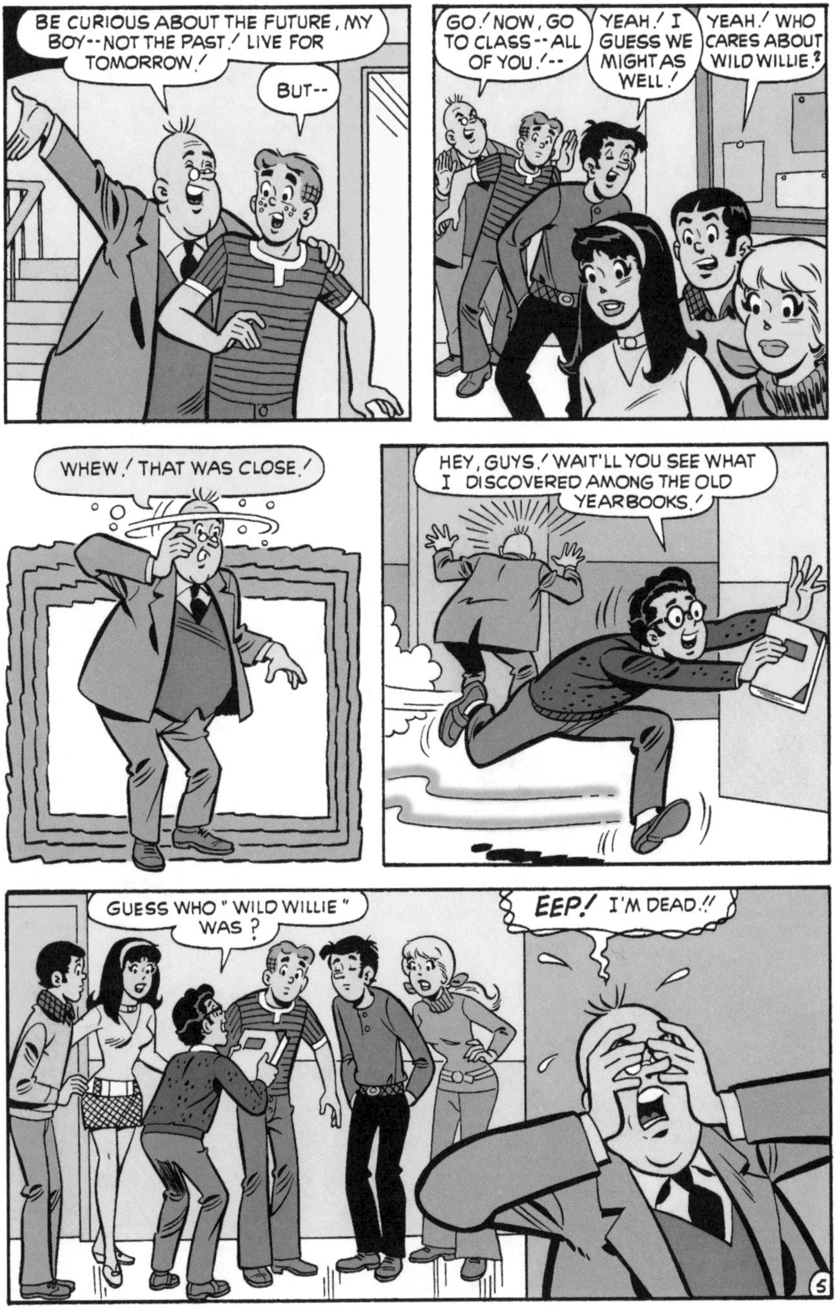
BE CURIOUS ABOUT THE FUTURE, MY BOY--NOT THE PAST! LIVE FOR TOMORROW!
BUT--
GO! NOW, GO TO CLASS--ALL OF YOU!--
YEAH! I GUESS WE MIGHT AS WELL!
YEAH! WHO CARES ABOUT WILD WILLIE?
WHEW! THAT WAS CLOSE!
HEY, GUYS! WAIT'LL YOU SEE WHAT I DISCOVERED AMONG THE OLD YEARBOOKS!
GUESS WHO "WILD WILLIE" WAS?
EEP! I'M DEAD!!
5

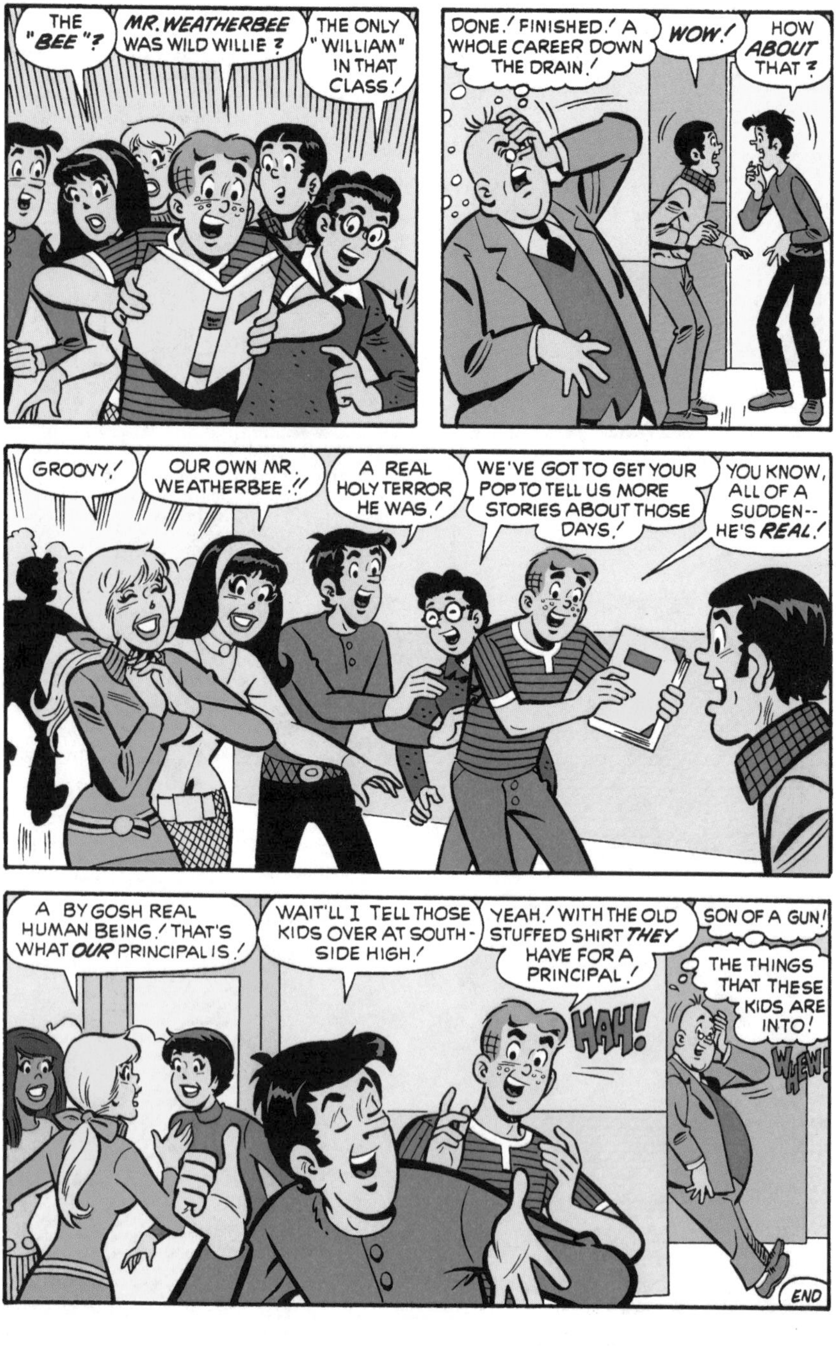
THE "BEE"?
MR. WEATHERBEE WAS WILD WILLIE?
THE ONLY "WILLIAM" IN THAT CLASS!
DONE! FINISHED! A WHOLE CAREER DOWN THE DRAIN!
WOW!
HOW ABOUT THAT?
GROOVY!
OUR OWN MR. WEATHERBEE!!
A REAL HOLY TERROR HE WAS!
WE'VE GOT TO GET YOUR POP TO TELL US MORE STORIES ABOUT THOSE DAYS!
YOU KNOW, ALL OF A SUDDEN-- HE'S REAL!
A BY GOSH REAL HUMAN BEING! THAT'S WHAT OUR PRINCIPAL IS!
WAIT'LL I TELL THOSE KIDS OVER AT SOUTH-SIDE HIGH!
YEAH! WITH THE OLD STUFFED SHIRT THEY HAVE FOR A PRINCIPAL!
HAH!
SON OF A GUN!
THE THINGS THAT THESE KIDS ARE INTO!
WHEW!
END

Archie at Riverdale "The Hard Ones"

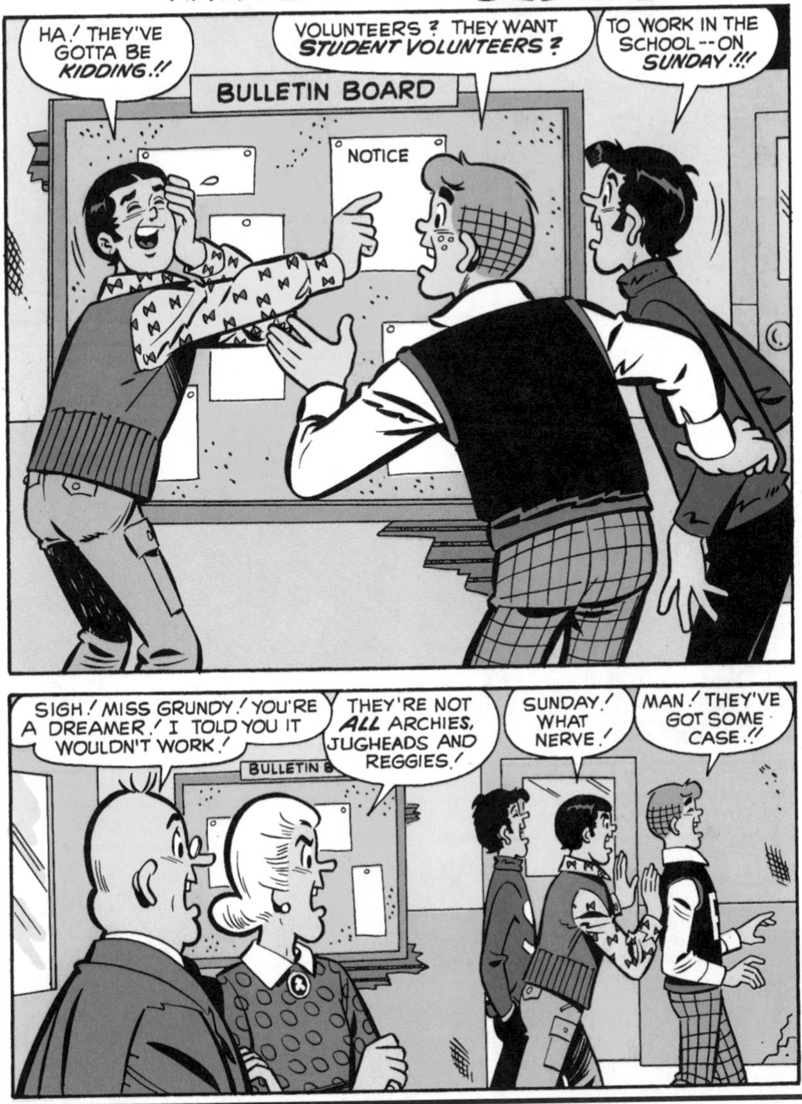
HA! THEY'VE GOTTA BE KIDDING!!
VOLUNTEERS? THEY WANT STUDENT VOLUNTEERS?
TO WORK IN THE SCHOOL--ON SUNDAY!!!
BULLETIN BOARD
NOTICE
SIGH! MISS GRUNDY! YOU'RE A DREAMER! I TOLD YOU IT WOULDN'T WORK!
THEY'RE NOT ALL ARCHIES, JUGHEADS AND REGGIES!
SUNDAY! WHAT NERVE!
MAN! THEY'VE GOT SOME CASE!!

Story: Frank Doyle Pencils: Stan Goldberg

Inks: Jon D'Agostino Letters: Bill Yoshida Colors: Barry Grossman

Originally printed in ARCHIE AT RIVERDALE HIGH #7, June 1973

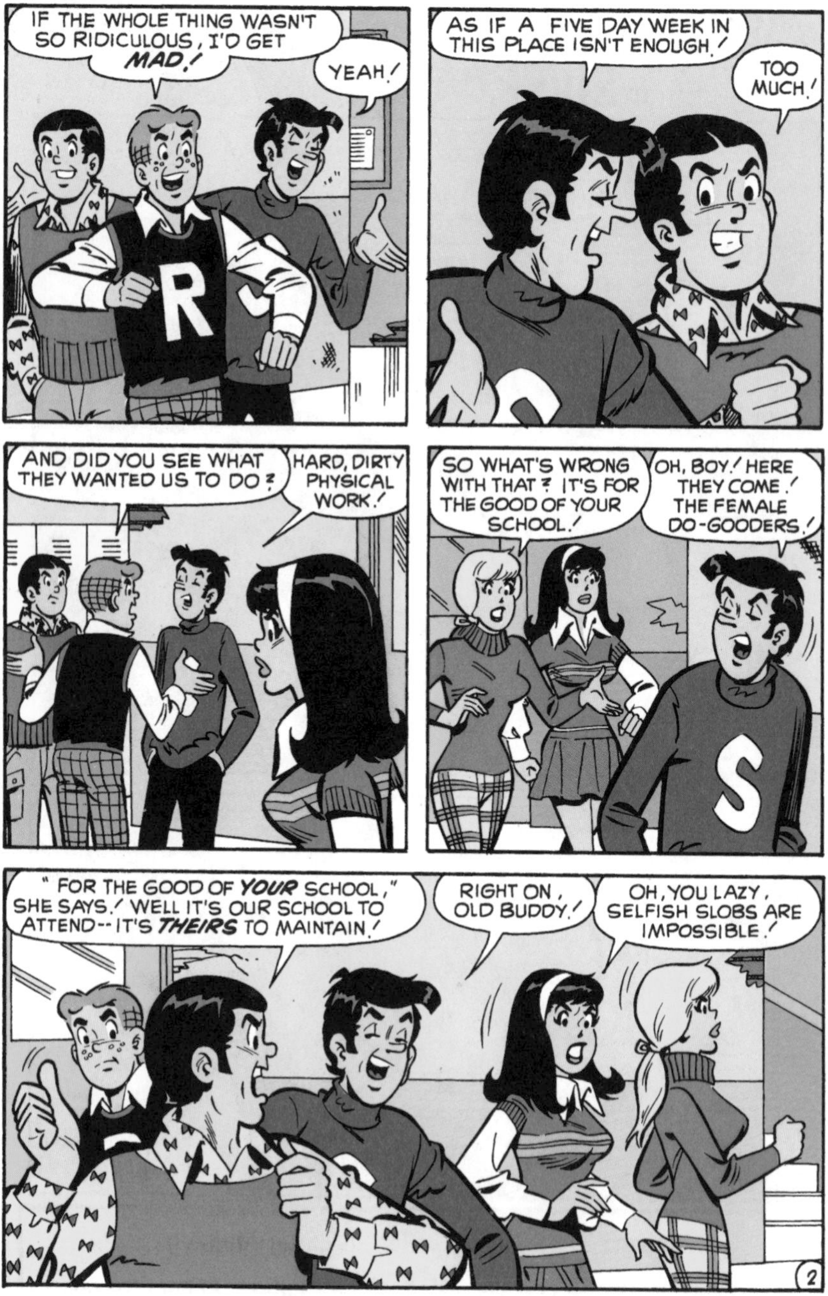
IF THE WHOLE THING WASN'T SO RIDICULOUS, I'D GET MAD!
YEAH!
AS IF A FIVE DAY WEEK IN THIS PLACE ISN'T ENOUGH!
TOO MUCH!
AND DID YOU SEE WHAT THEY WANTED US TO DO?
HARD, DIRTY PHYSICAL WORK!
SO WHAT'S WRONG WITH THAT? IT'S FOR THE GOOD OF YOUR SCHOOL!
OH, BOY! HERE THEY COME! THE FEMALE DO-GOODERS!
"FOR THE GOOD OF YOUR SCHOOL," SHE SAYS! WELL IT'S OUR SCHOOL TO ATTEND--IT'S THEIRS TO MAINTAIN!
RIGHT ON, OLD BUDDY!
OH, YOU LAZY, SELFISH SLOBS ARE IMPOSSIBLE!
2

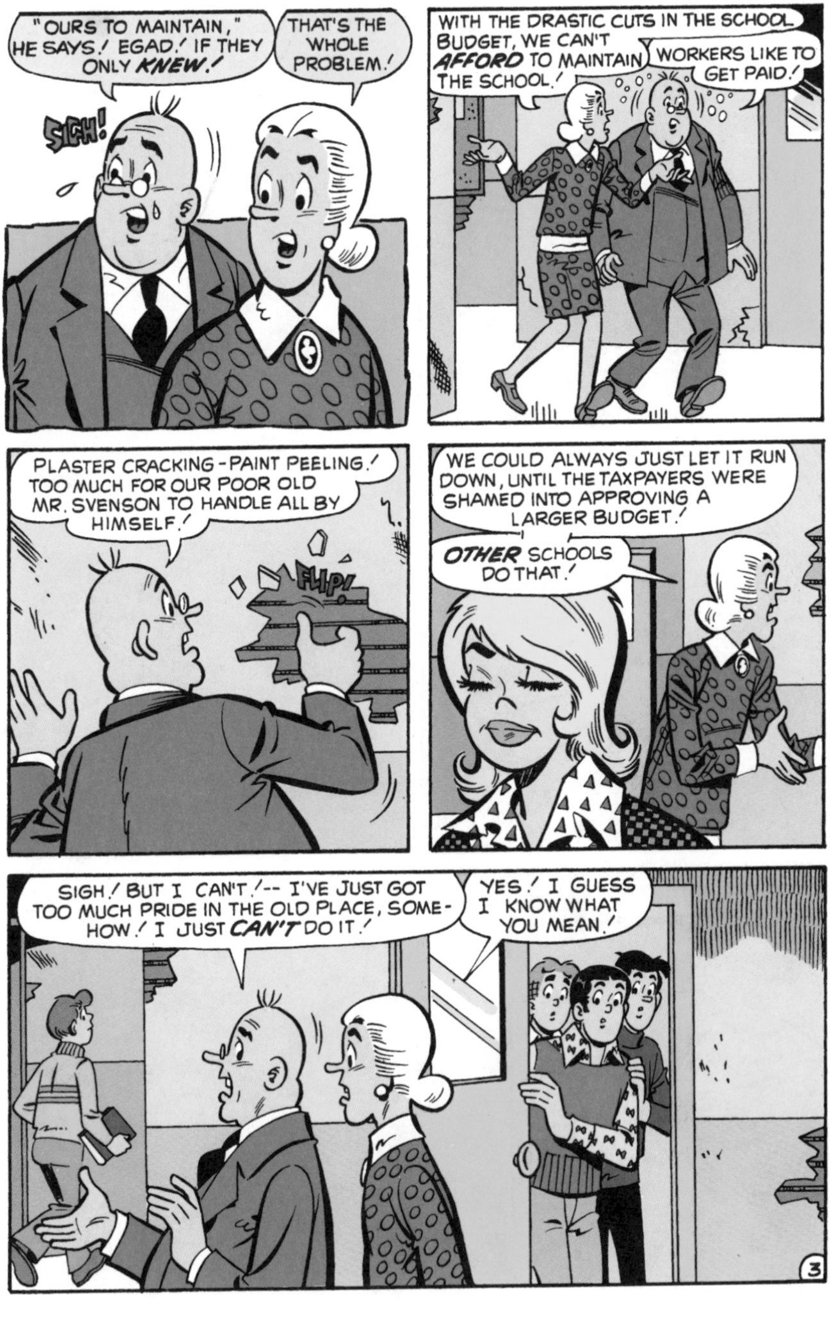
"OURS TO MAINTAIN," HE SAYS! EGAD! IF THEY ONLY KNEW!
THAT'S THE WHOLE PROBLEM!
SIGH!
WITH THE DRASTIC CUTS IN THE SCHOOL BUDGET, WE CAN'T AFFORD TO MAINTAIN THE SCHOOL!
WORKERS LIKE TO GET PAID!
PLASTER CRACKING-PAINT PEELING! TOO MUCH FOR OUR POOR OLD MR. SVENSON TO HANDLE ALL BY HIMSELF!
FLIP!
WE COULD ALWAYS JUST LET IT RUN DOWN, UNTIL THE TAXPAYERS WERE SHAMED INTO APPROVING A LARGER BUDGET!
OTHER SCHOOLS DO THAT!
SIGH! BUT I CAN'T!-- I'VE JUST GOT TOO MUCH PRIDE IN THE OLD PLACE, SOME-HOW! I JUST CAN'T DO IT!
YES! I GUESS I KNOW WHAT YOU MEAN!
3

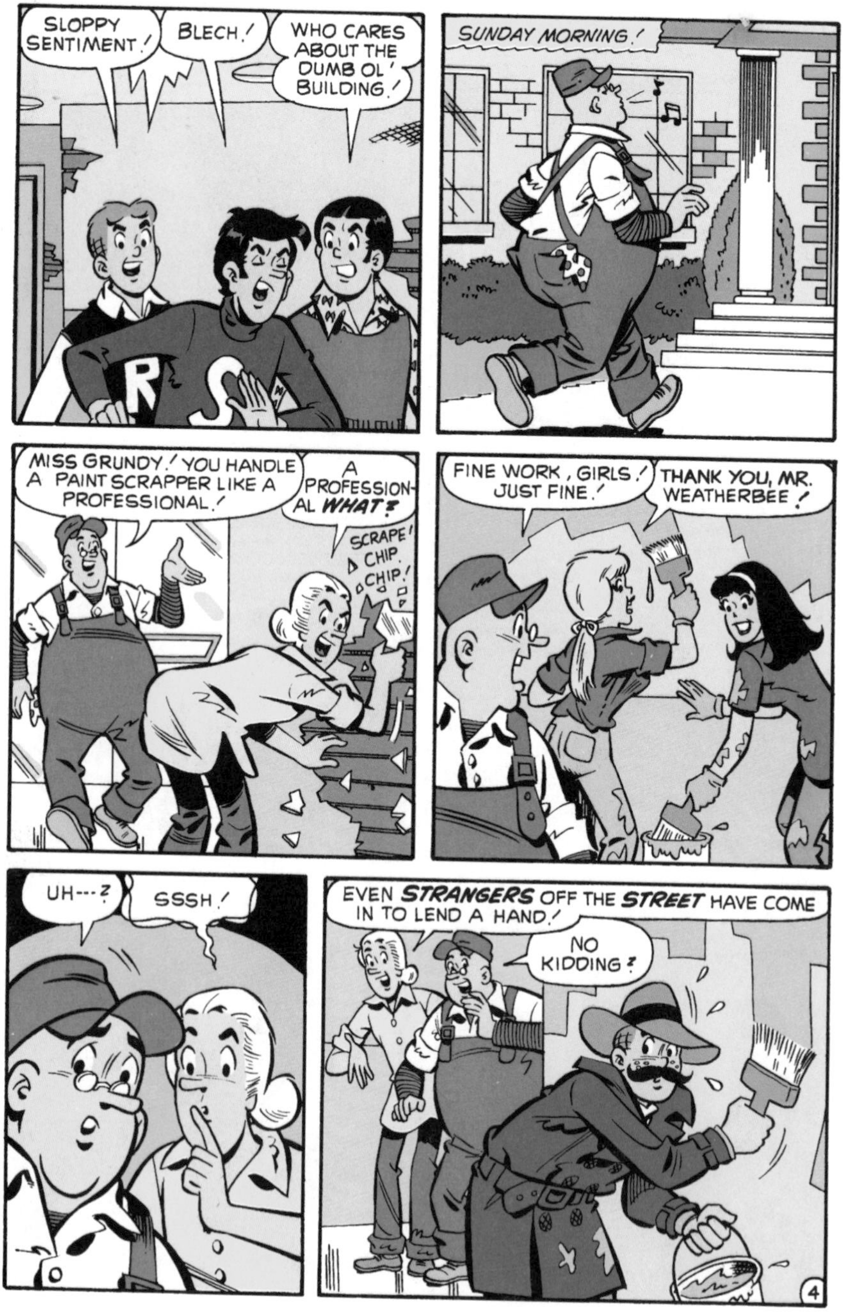
SLOPPY SENTIMENT!
BLECH!
WHO CARES ABOUT THE DUMB OL' BUILDING!
SUNDAY MORNING!
MISS GRUNDY! YOU HANDLE A PAINT SCRAPPER LIKE A PROFESSIONAL!
A PROFESSION-AL WHAT?
SCRAPE!
CHIP
CHIP!
FINE WORK, GIRLS! JUST FINE!
THANK YOU, MR. WEATHERBEE!
UH---?
SSSH!
EVEN STRANGERS OFF THE STREET HAVE COME IN TO LEND A HAND!
NO KIDDING?
4

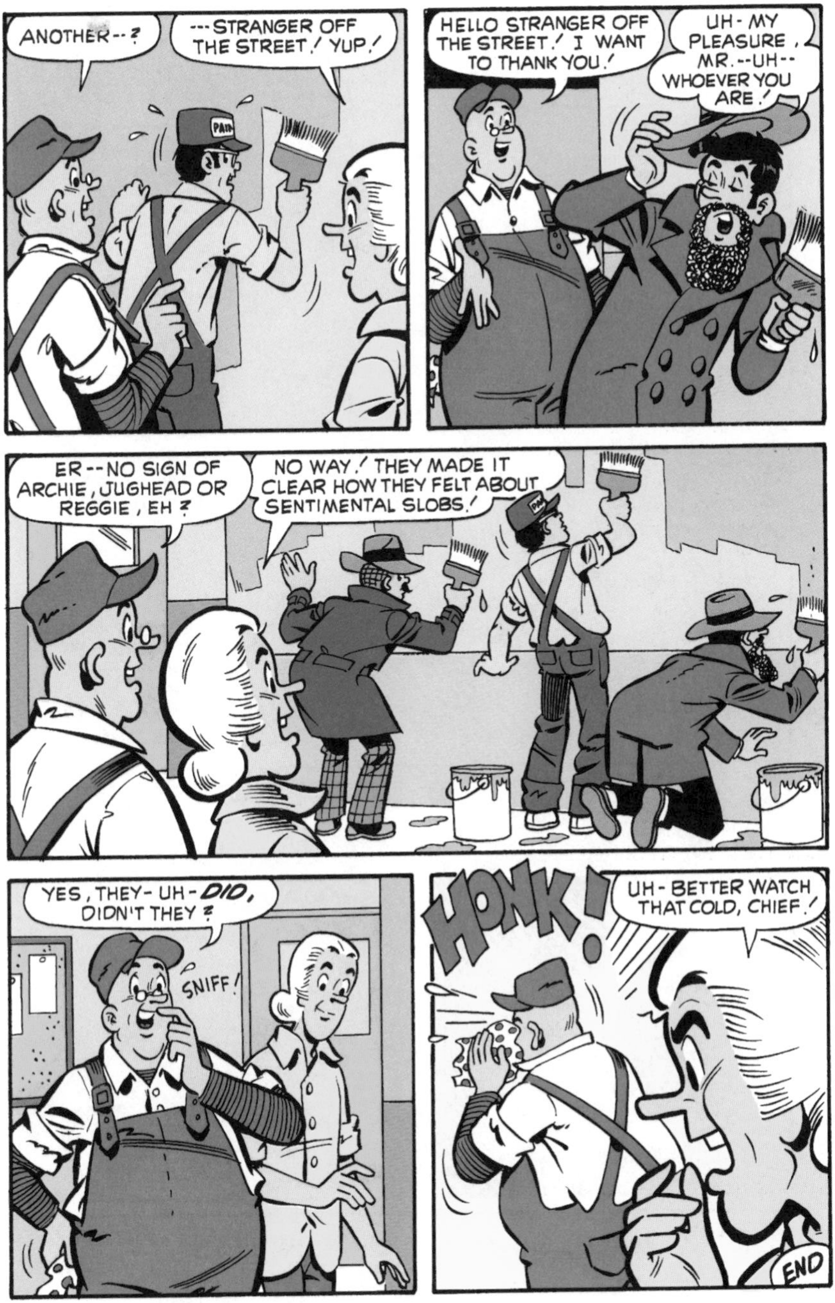
ANOTHER--?
---STRANGER OFF THE STREET! YUP!
PAI
HELLO STRANGER OFF THE STREET! I WANT TO THANK YOU!
UH-MY PLEASURE, MR.--UH-- WHOEVER YOU ARE!
ER--NO SIGN OF ARCHIE, JUGHEAD OR REGGIE, EH?
NO WAY! THEY MADE IT CLEAR HOW THEY FELT ABOUT SENTIMENTAL SLOBS!
YES, THEY-UH-*DID*, DIDN'T THEY?
SNIFF!
HONK!
UH-BETTER WATCH THAT COLD, CHIEF!
END

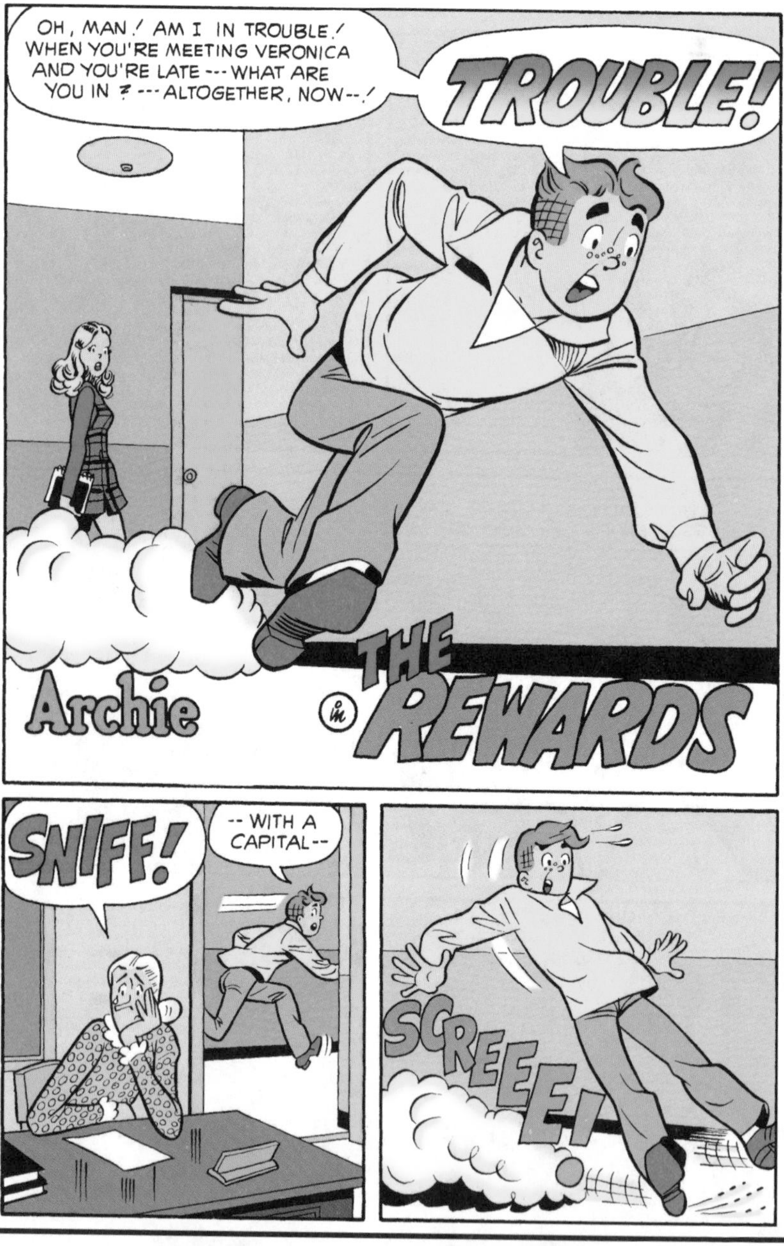
OH, MAN! AM I IN TROUBLE! WHEN YOU'RE MEETING VERONICA AND YOU'RE LATE --- WHAT ARE YOU IN ? --- ALTOGETHER, NOW--!
TROUBLE!
Archie in THE REWARDS
SNIFF!
-- WITH A CAPITAL --
SCREEE!

Story: Frank Doyle   Pencils: Harry Lucey
Inks: Chic Stone   Letters: Bill Yoshida

Originally printed in ARCHIE AT RIVERDALE HIGH #7, June 1973

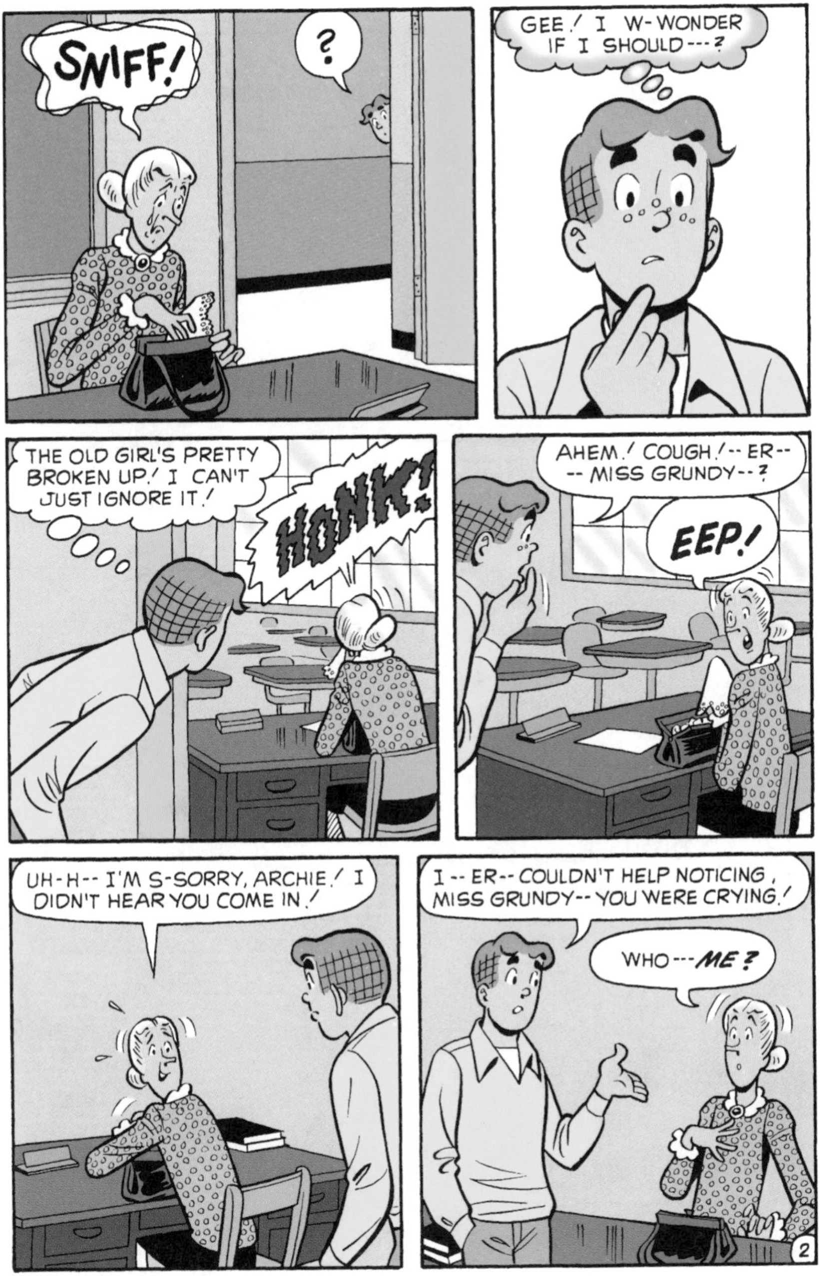
SNIFF!
?
GEE! I W-WONDER IF I SHOULD---?
THE OLD GIRL'S PRETTY BROKEN UP! I CAN'T JUST IGNORE IT!
HONK!
AHEM! COUGH! -- ER -- -- MISS GRUNDY--?
EEP!
UH-H-- I'M S-SORRY, ARCHIE! I DIDN'T HEAR YOU COME IN!
I -- ER-- COULDN'T HELP NOTICING, MISS GRUNDY-- YOU WERE CRYING!
WHO---ME?
2

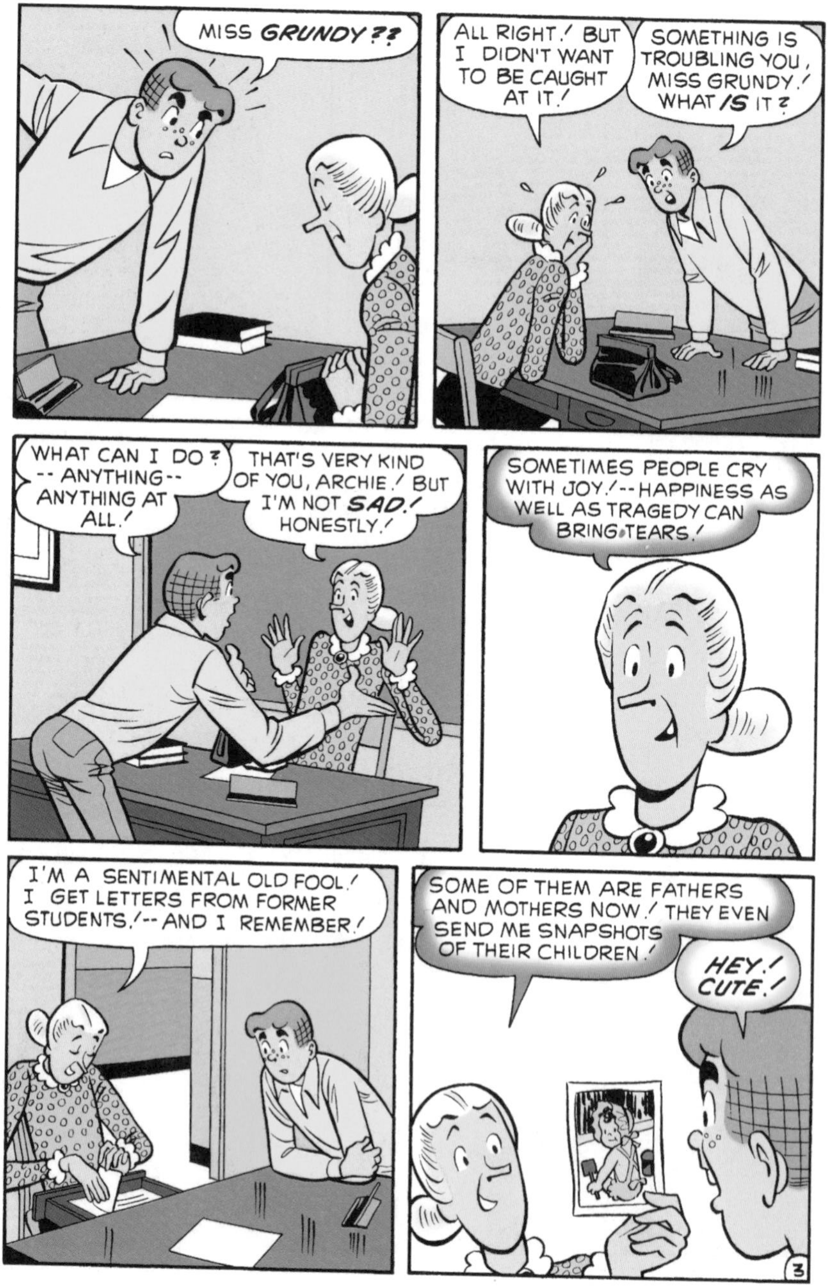
MISS GRUNDY??
ALL RIGHT! BUT I DIDN'T WANT TO BE CAUGHT AT IT!
SOMETHING IS TROUBLING YOU, MISS GRUNDY! WHAT IS IT?
WHAT CAN I DO? -- ANYTHING -- ANYTHING AT ALL!
THAT'S VERY KIND OF YOU, ARCHIE! BUT I'M NOT SAD! HONESTLY!
SOMETIMES PEOPLE CRY WITH JOY!--HAPPINESS AS WELL AS TRAGEDY CAN BRING TEARS!
I'M A SENTIMENTAL OLD FOOL! I GET LETTERS FROM FORMER STUDENTS!--AND I REMEMBER!
SOME OF THEM ARE FATHERS AND MOTHERS NOW! THEY EVEN SEND ME SNAPSHOTS OF THEIR CHILDREN!
HEY! CUTE!
3

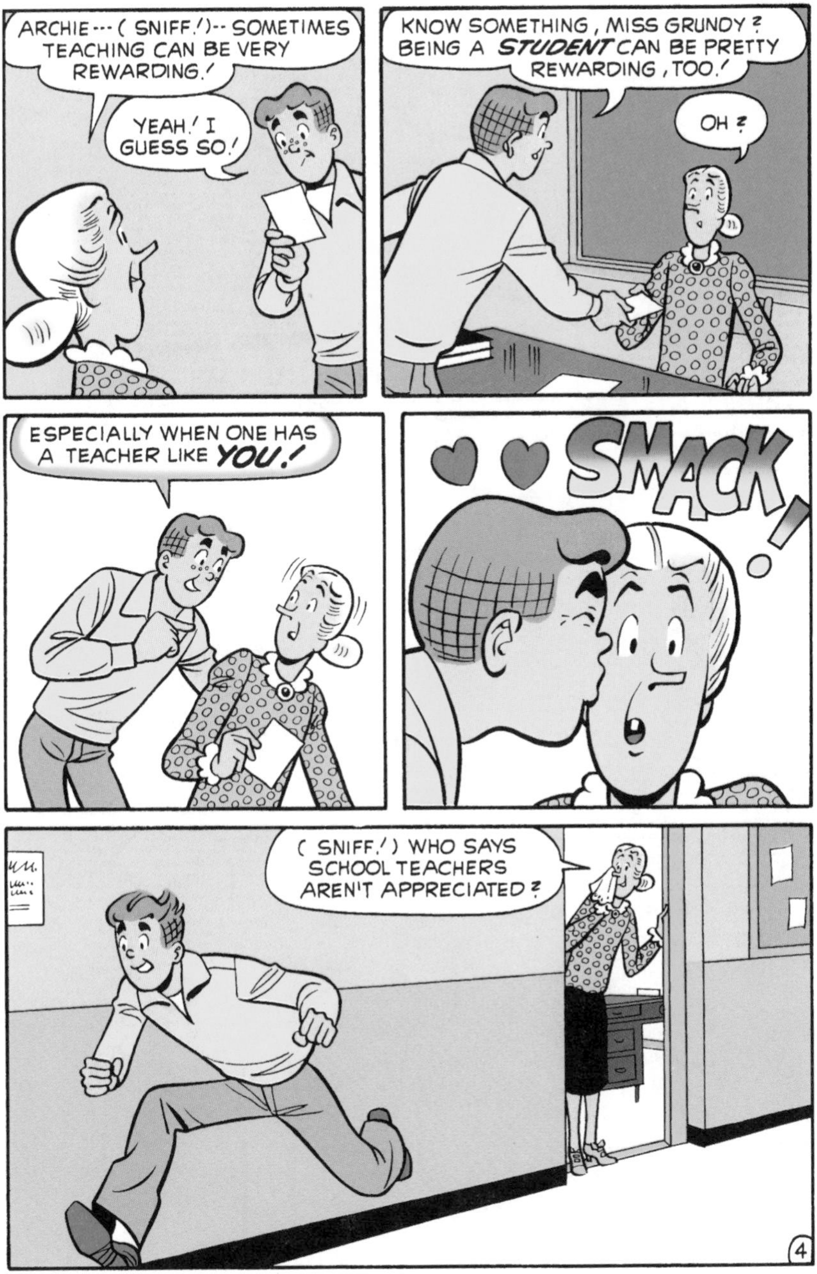
ARCHIE --- (SNIFF.'!)-- SOMETIMES TEACHING CAN BE VERY REWARDING!
YEAH! I GUESS SO!
KNOW SOMETHING, MISS GRUNDY? BEING A STUDENT CAN BE PRETTY REWARDING, TOO!
OH?
ESPECIALLY WHEN ONE HAS A TEACHER LIKE YOU!
SMACK!
(SNIFF!) WHO SAYS SCHOOL TEACHERS AREN'T APPRECIATED?
4

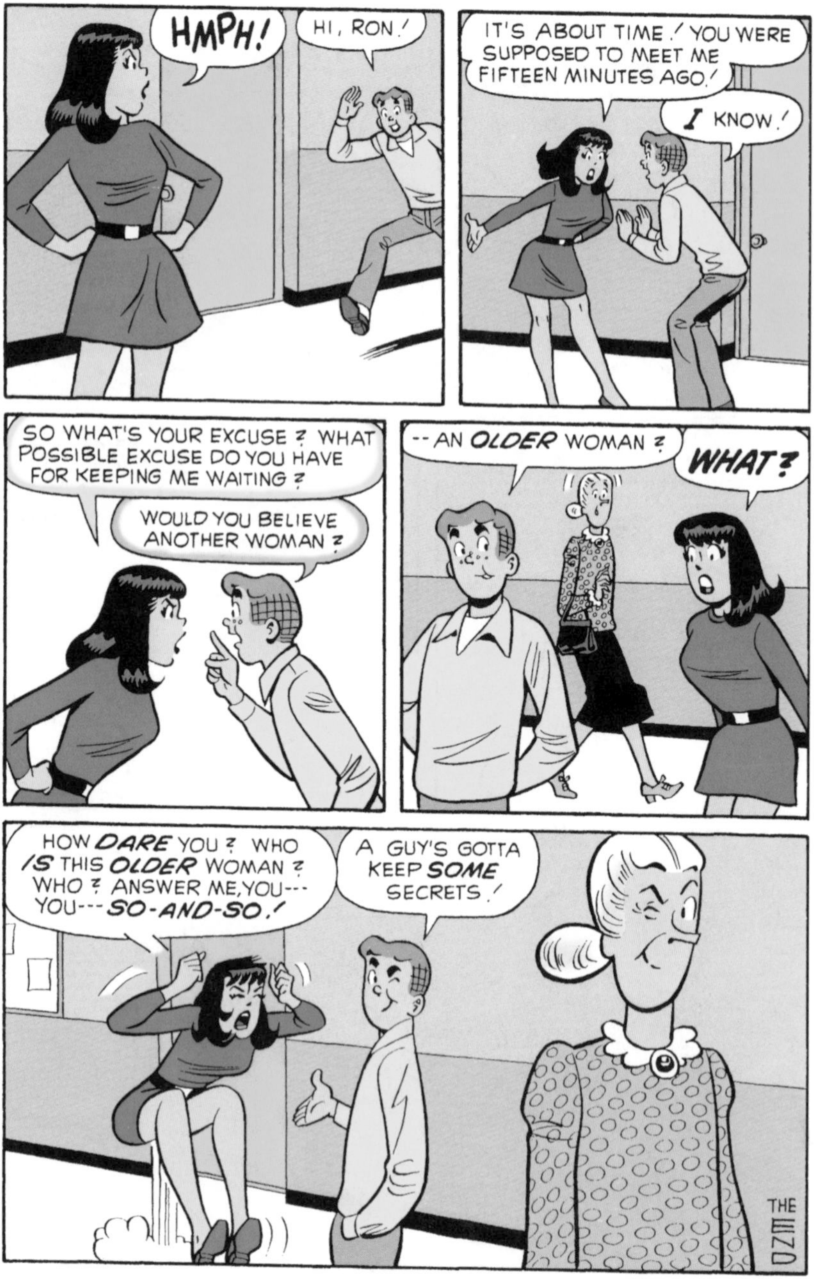
HMPH!
HI, RON!
IT'S ABOUT TIME! YOU WERE SUPPOSED TO MEET ME FIFTEEN MINUTES AGO!
I KNOW!
SO WHAT'S YOUR EXCUSE? WHAT POSSIBLE EXCUSE DO YOU HAVE FOR KEEPING ME WAITING?
WOULD YOU BELIEVE ANOTHER WOMAN?
--AN OLDER WOMAN?
WHAT?
HOW DARE YOU? WHO IS THIS OLDER WOMAN? WHO? ANSWER ME, YOU--- YOU---SO-AND-SO!
A GUY'S GOTTA KEEP SOME SECRETS!
THE END

Archie Memories ARE MADE of THIS!

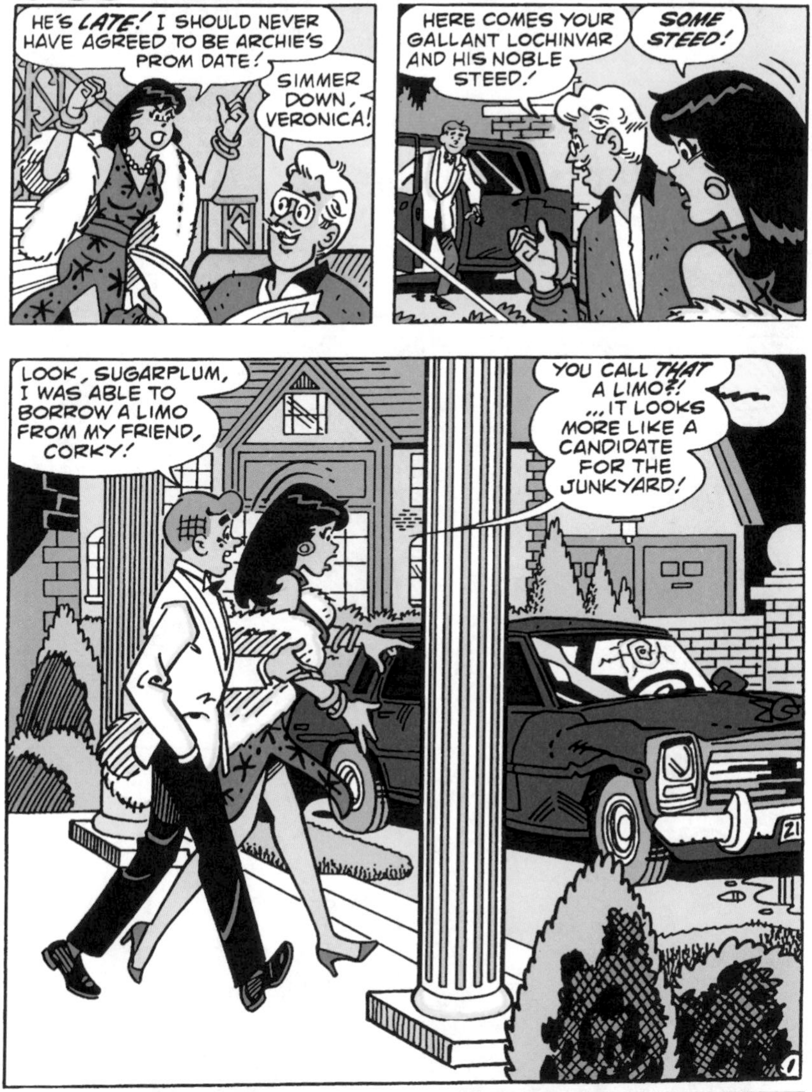
HE'S LATE! I SHOULD NEVER HAVE AGREED TO BE ARCHIE'S PROM DATE!
SIMMER DOWN, VERONICA!
HERE COMES YOUR GALLANT LOCHINVAR AND HIS NOBLE STEED!
SOME STEED!
LOOK, SUGARPLUM, I WAS ABLE TO BORROW A LIMO FROM MY FRIEND, CORKY!
YOU CALL THAT A LIMO?! ...IT LOOKS MORE LIKE A CANDIDATE FOR THE JUNKYARD!
21
1

Story: George Gladir Pencils: Stan Goldberg

Inks: Mike Esposito Letters: Bill Yoshida Colors: Barry Grossman

Originally printed in ARCHIE AT RIVERDALE HIGH #8, July 1973

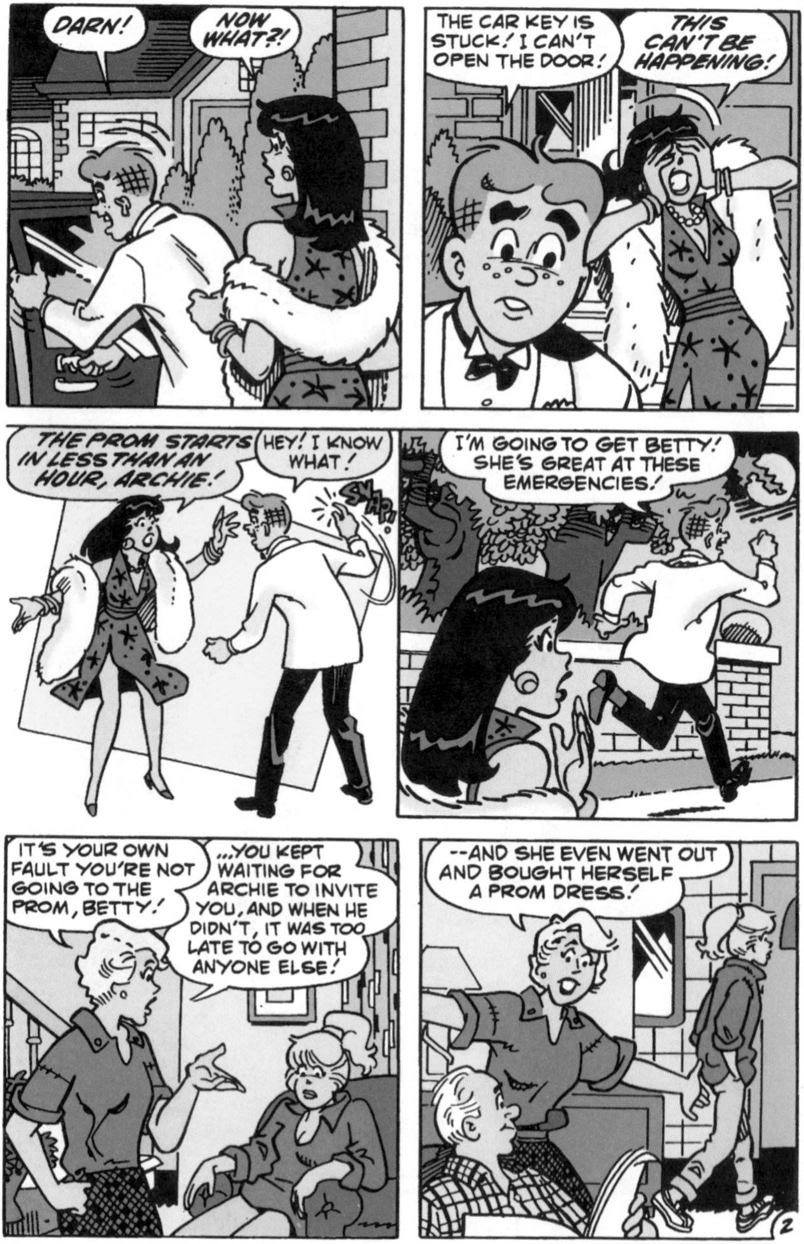
DARN!
NOW WHAT?!
THE CAR KEY IS STUCK! I CAN'T OPEN THE DOOR!
THIS CAN'T BE HAPPENING!
THE PROM STARTS IN LESS THAN AN HOUR, ARCHIE!
HEY! I KNOW WHAT!
SNAP!
I'M GOING TO GET BETTY! SHE'S GREAT AT THESE EMERGENCIES!
IT'S YOUR OWN FAULT YOU'RE NOT GOING TO THE PROM, BETTY!
...YOU KEPT WAITING FOR ARCHIE TO INVITE YOU, AND WHEN HE DIDN'T, IT WAS TOO LATE TO GO WITH ANYONE ELSE!
--AND SHE EVEN WENT OUT AND BOUGHT HERSELF A PROM DRESS!
2

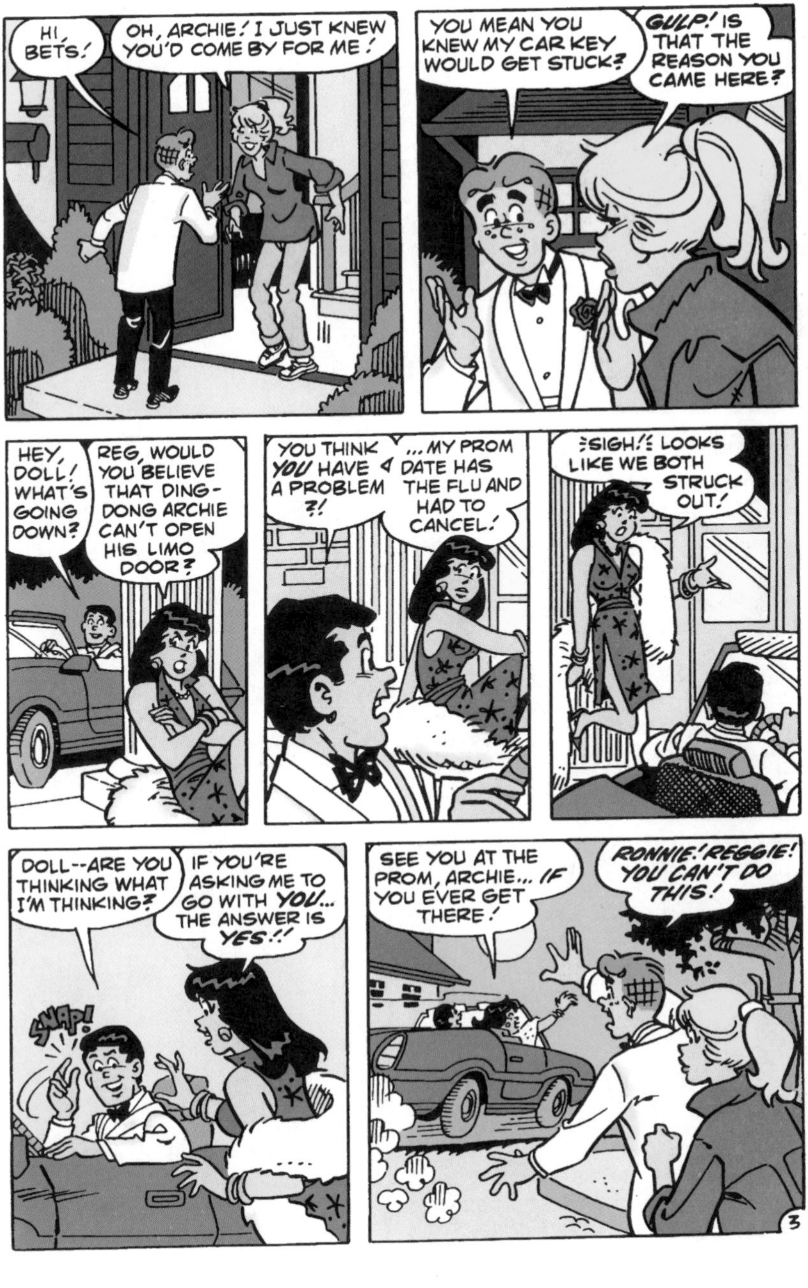
HI, BETS!
OH, ARCHIE! I JUST KNEW YOU'D COME BY FOR ME!
YOU MEAN YOU KNEW MY CAR KEY WOULD GET STUCK?
GULP! IS THAT THE REASON YOU CAME HERE?
HEY, DOLL! WHAT'S GOING DOWN?
REG, WOULD YOU BELIEVE THAT DING-DONG ARCHIE CAN'T OPEN HIS LIMO DOOR?
YOU THINK YOU HAVE A PROBLEM?!
...MY PROM DATE HAS THE FLU AND HAD TO CANCEL!
SIGH! LOOKS LIKE WE BOTH STRUCK OUT!
DOLL--ARE YOU THINKING WHAT I'M THINKING?
IF YOU'RE ASKING ME TO GO WITH YOU... THE ANSWER IS YES!!
SNAP!
SEE YOU AT THE PROM, ARCHIE... IF YOU EVER GET THERE!
RONNIE! REGGIE! YOU CAN'T DO THIS!
3

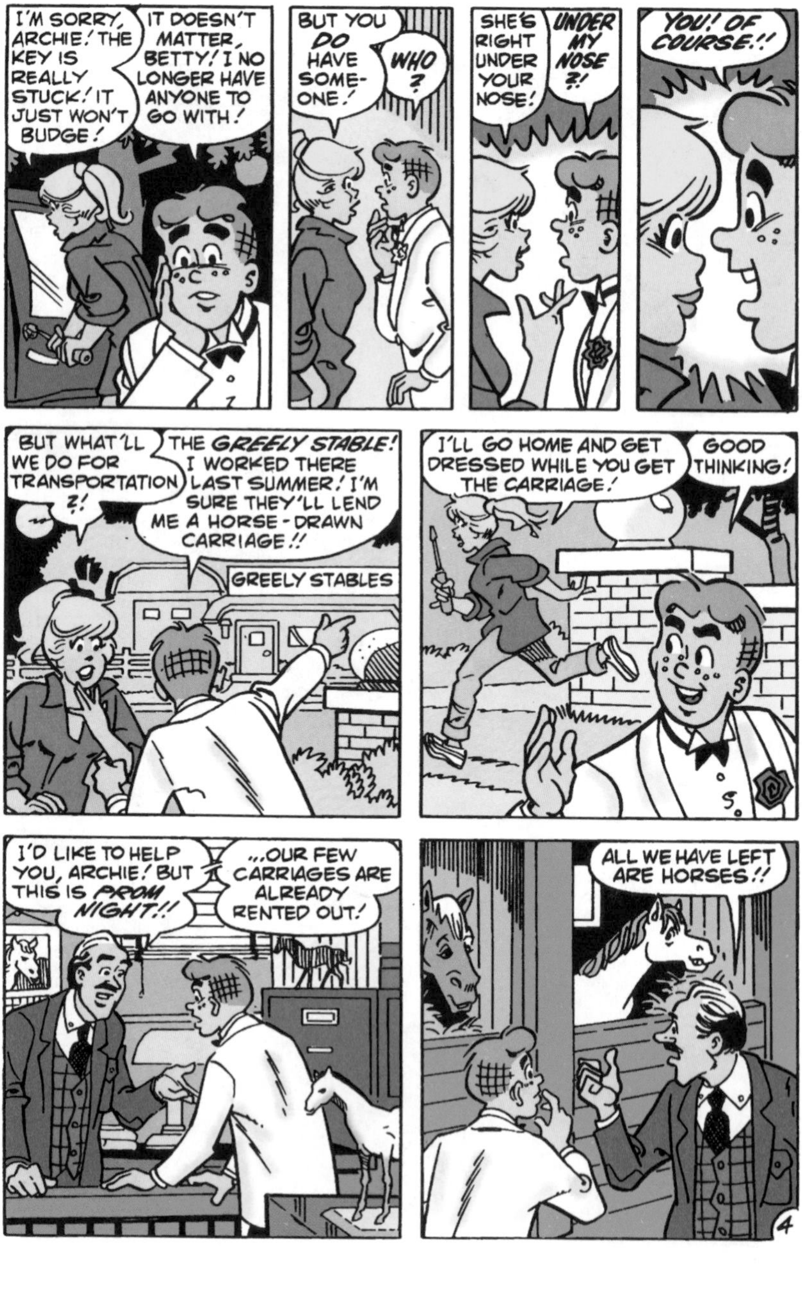
I'M SORRY, ARCHIE! THE KEY IS REALLY STUCK! IT JUST WON'T BUDGE!
IT DOESN'T MATTER, BETTY! I NO LONGER HAVE ANYONE TO GO WITH!
BUT YOU DO HAVE SOMEONE!
WHO ?
SHE'S RIGHT UNDER YOUR NOSE!
UNDER MY NOSE ?!
YOU! OF COURSE!!
BUT WHAT'LL WE DO FOR TRANSPORTATION ?!
THE GREELY STABLE! I WORKED THERE LAST SUMMER! I'M SURE THEY'LL LEND ME A HORSE-DRAWN CARRIAGE!!
GREELY STABLES
I'LL GO HOME AND GET DRESSED WHILE YOU GET THE CARRIAGE!
GOOD THINKING!
I'D LIKE TO HELP YOU, ARCHIE! BUT THIS IS PROM NIGHT!!
...OUR FEW CARRIAGES ARE ALREADY RENTED OUT!
ALL WE HAVE LEFT ARE HORSES!!
4

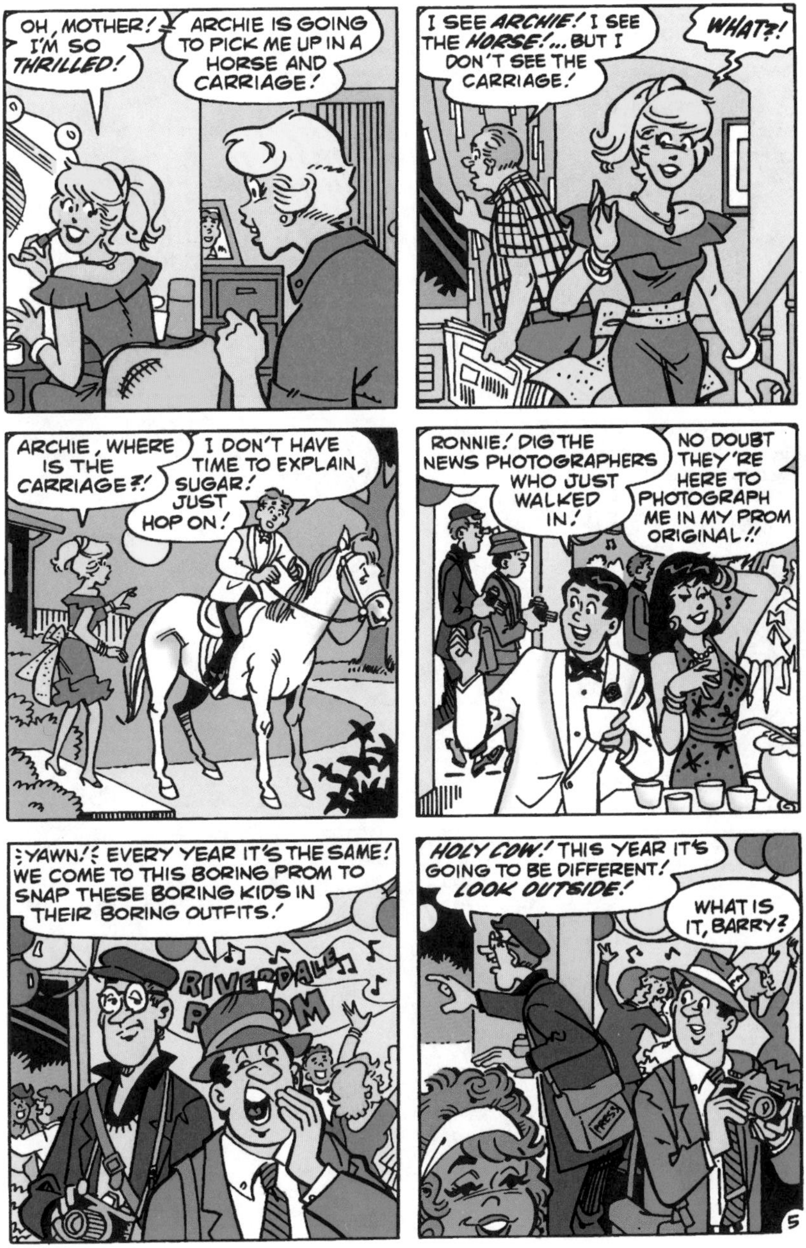
OH, MOTHER! I'M SO THRILLED!
ARCHIE IS GOING TO PICK ME UP IN A HORSE AND CARRIAGE!
I SEE ARCHIE! I SEE THE HORSE!... BUT I DON'T SEE THE CARRIAGE!
WHAT?!
ARCHIE, WHERE IS THE CARRIAGE?!
I DON'T HAVE TIME TO EXPLAIN, SUGAR! JUST HOP ON!
RONNIE! DIG THE NEWS PHOTOGRAPHERS WHO JUST WALKED IN!
NO DOUBT THEY'RE HERE TO PHOTOGRAPH ME IN MY PROM ORIGINAL!!
YAWN! EVERY YEAR IT'S THE SAME! WE COME TO THIS BORING PROM TO SNAP THESE BORING KIDS IN THEIR BORING OUTFITS!
RIVERDALE PROM
HOLY COW! THIS YEAR IT'S GOING TO BE DIFFERENT! LOOK OUTSIDE!
WHAT IS IT, BARRY?
PRESS
5

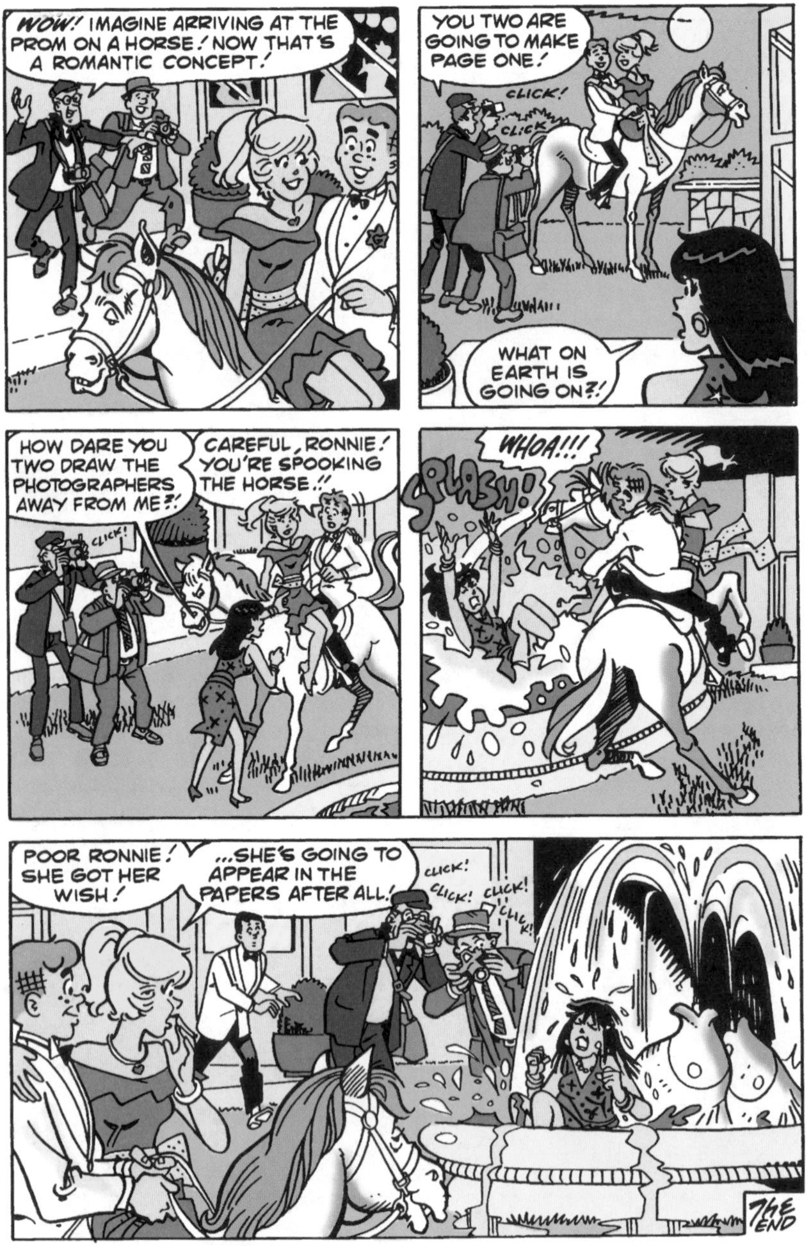
WOW! IMAGINE ARRIVING AT THE PROM ON A HORSE! NOW THAT'S A ROMANTIC CONCEPT!
YOU TWO ARE GOING TO MAKE PAGE ONE!
CLICK!
CLICK
WHAT ON EARTH IS GOING ON?!
HOW DARE YOU TWO DRAW THE PHOTOGRAPHERS AWAY FROM ME?!
CAREFUL, RONNIE! YOU'RE SPOOKING THE HORSE!!
CLICK!
WHOA!!!
SPLASH!
POOR RONNIE! SHE GOT HER WISH!
...SHE'S GOING TO APPEAR IN THE PAPERS AFTER ALL!
CLICK!
CLICK!
CLICK!
CLICK!
THE END

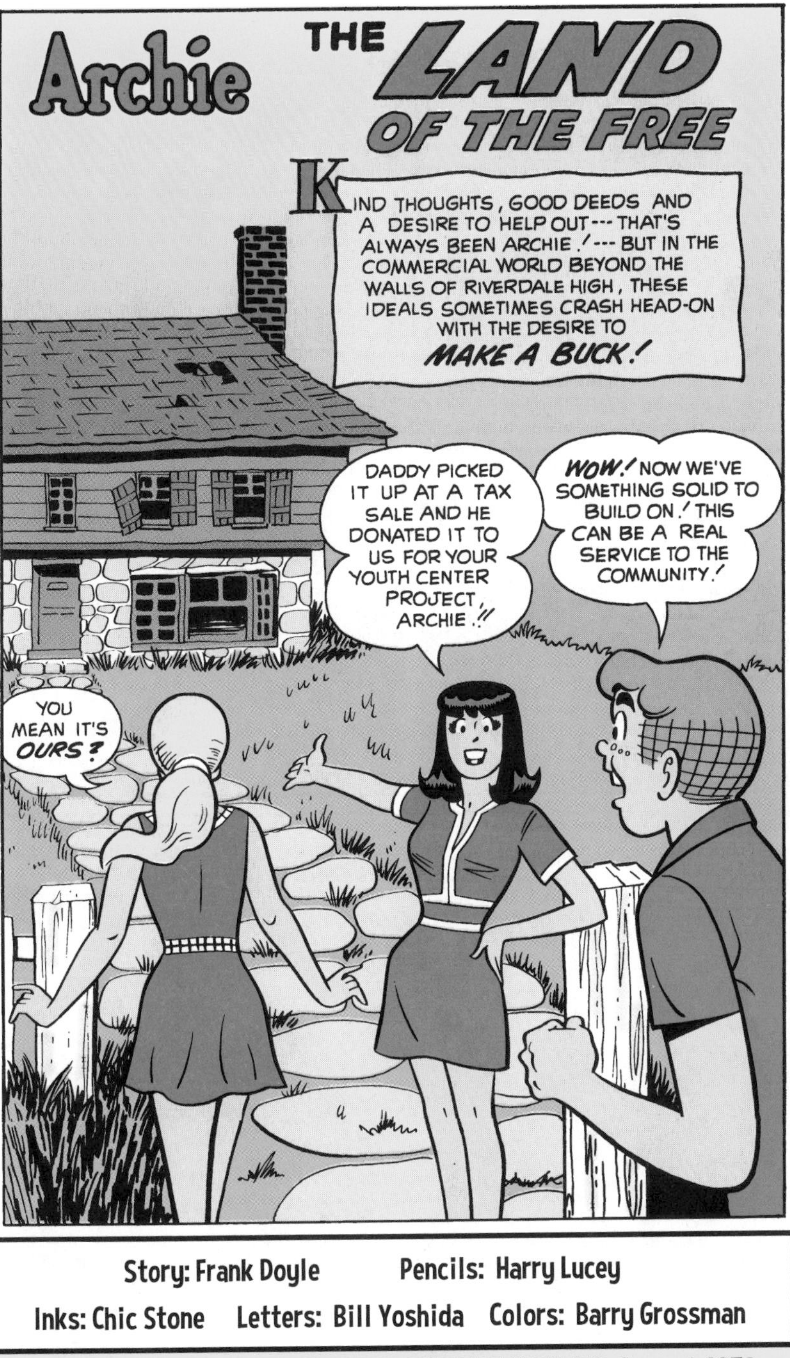
Archie
THE LAND OF THE FREE
KIND THOUGHTS, GOOD DEEDS AND A DESIRE TO HELP OUT--- THAT'S ALWAYS BEEN ARCHIE.!--- BUT IN THE COMMERCIAL WORLD BEYOND THE WALLS OF RIVERDALE HIGH, THESE IDEALS SOMETIMES CRASH HEAD-ON WITH THE DESIRE TO MAKE A BUCK!
DADDY PICKED IT UP AT A TAX SALE AND HE DONATED IT TO US FOR YOUR YOUTH CENTER PROJECT, ARCHIE.!!
WOW! NOW WE'VE SOMETHING SOLID TO BUILD ON! THIS CAN BE A REAL SERVICE TO THE COMMUNITY!
YOU MEAN IT'S OURS?

Story: Frank Doyle Pencils: Harry Lucey

Inks: Chic Stone Letters: Bill Yoshida Colors: Barry Grossman

Originally printed in ARCHIE AT RIVERDALE HIGH #9, August 1973

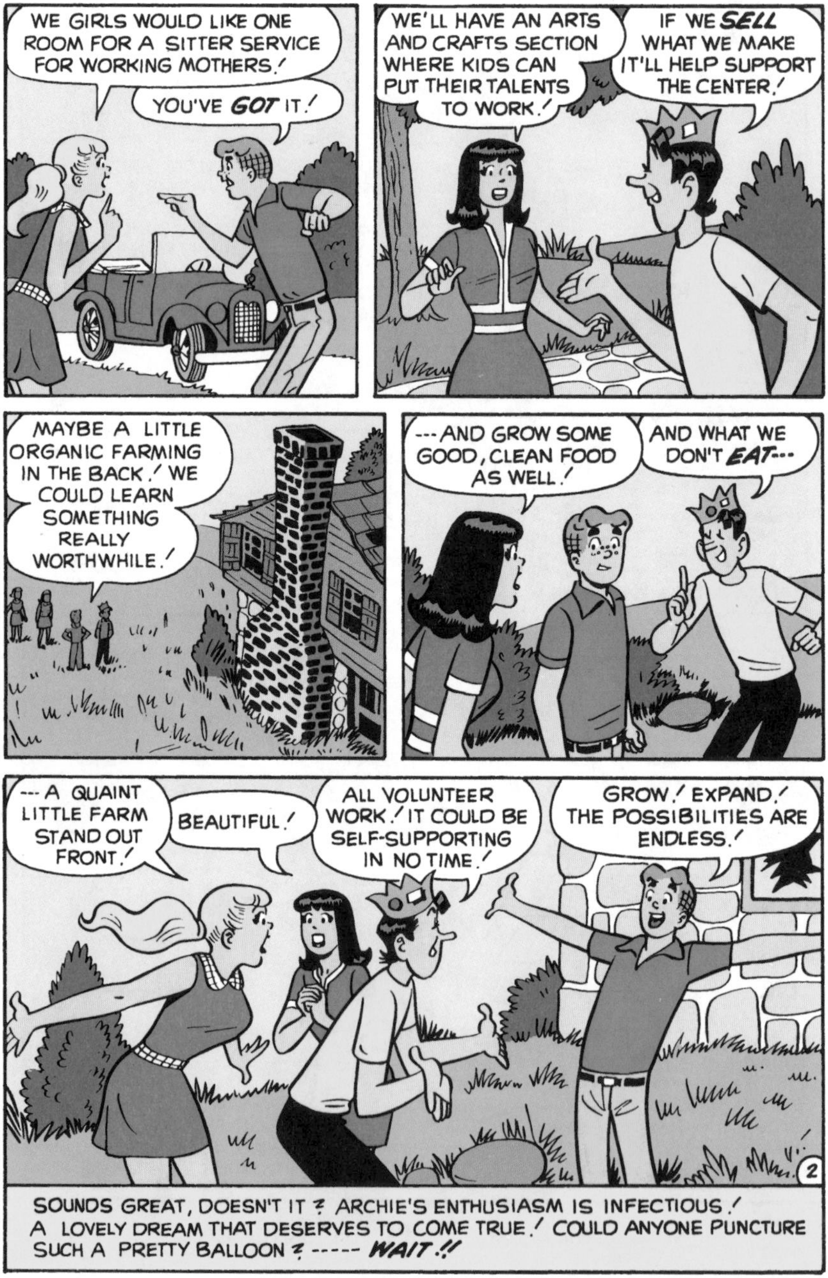
WE GIRLS WOULD LIKE ONE ROOM FOR A SITTER SERVICE FOR WORKING MOTHERS!
YOU'VE GOT IT!
WE'LL HAVE AN ARTS AND CRAFTS SECTION WHERE KIDS CAN PUT THEIR TALENTS TO WORK!
IF WE SELL WHAT WE MAKE IT'LL HELP SUPPORT THE CENTER!
MAYBE A LITTLE ORGANIC FARMING IN THE BACK! WE COULD LEARN SOMETHING REALLY WORTHWHILE!
---AND GROW SOME GOOD, CLEAN FOOD AS WELL!
AND WHAT WE DON'T EAT---
---A QUAINT LITTLE FARM STAND OUT FRONT!
BEAUTIFUL!
ALL VOLUNTEER WORK! IT COULD BE SELF-SUPPORTING IN NO TIME!
GROW! EXPAND! THE POSSIBILITIES ARE ENDLESS!
2
SOUNDS GREAT, DOESN'T IT? ARCHIE'S ENTHUSIASM IS INFECTIOUS! A LOVELY DREAM THAT DESERVES TO COME TRUE! COULD ANYONE PUNCTURE SUCH A PRETTY BALLOON? ----- WAIT!!

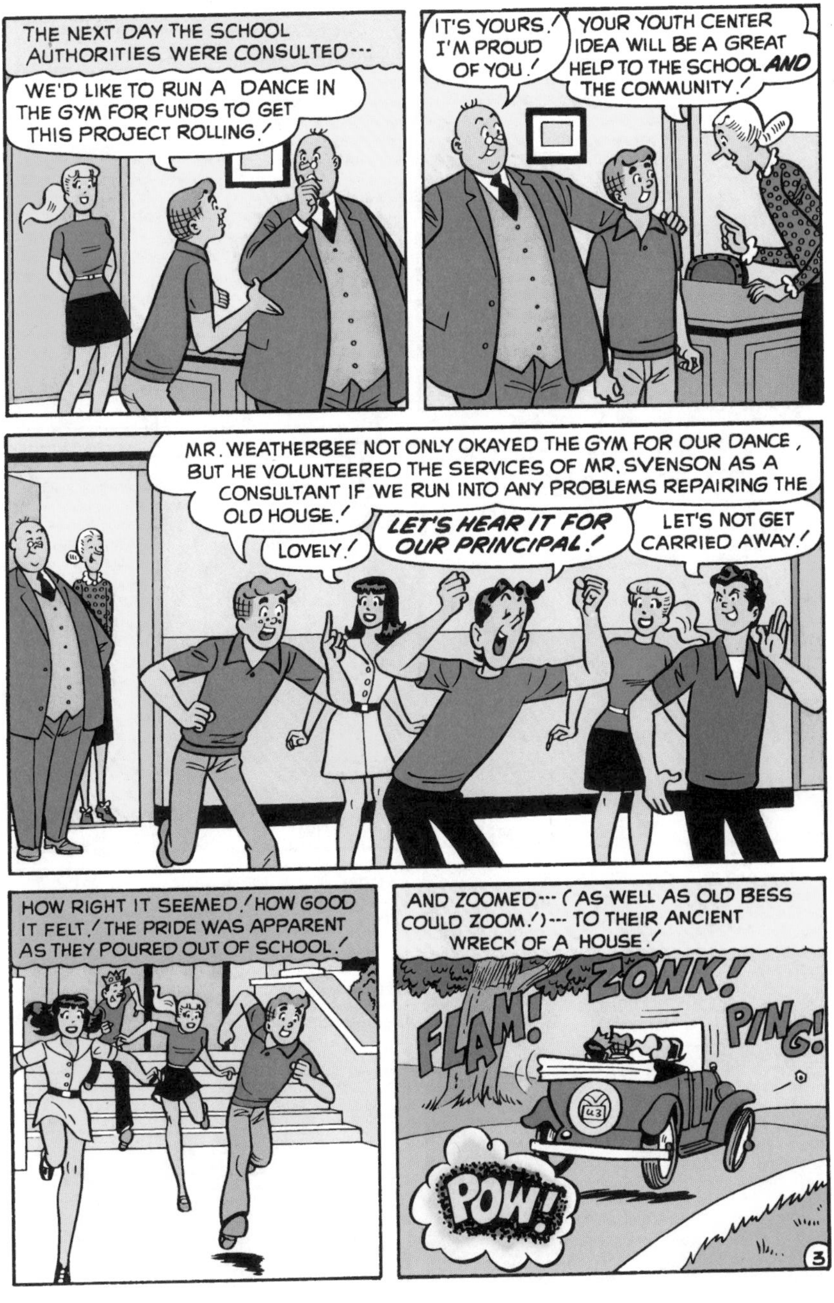
THE NEXT DAY THE SCHOOL AUTHORITIES WERE CONSULTED---
WE'D LIKE TO RUN A DANCE IN THE GYM FOR FUNDS TO GET THIS PROJECT ROLLING!
IT'S YOURS! I'M PROUD OF YOU!
YOUR YOUTH CENTER IDEA WILL BE A GREAT HELP TO THE SCHOOL AND THE COMMUNITY!
MR. WEATHERBEE NOT ONLY OKAYED THE GYM FOR OUR DANCE, BUT HE VOLUNTEERED THE SERVICES OF MR. SVENSON AS A CONSULTANT IF WE RUN INTO ANY PROBLEMS REPAIRING THE OLD HOUSE!
LOVELY!
LET'S HEAR IT FOR OUR PRINCIPAL!
LET'S NOT GET CARRIED AWAY!
HOW RIGHT IT SEEMED! HOW GOOD IT FELT! THE PRIDE WAS APPARENT AS THEY POURED OUT OF SCHOOL!
AND ZOOMED--- (AS WELL AS OLD BESS COULD ZOOM!)--- TO THEIR ANCIENT WRECK OF A HOUSE!
ZONK!
FLAM!
PING!
POW!
3

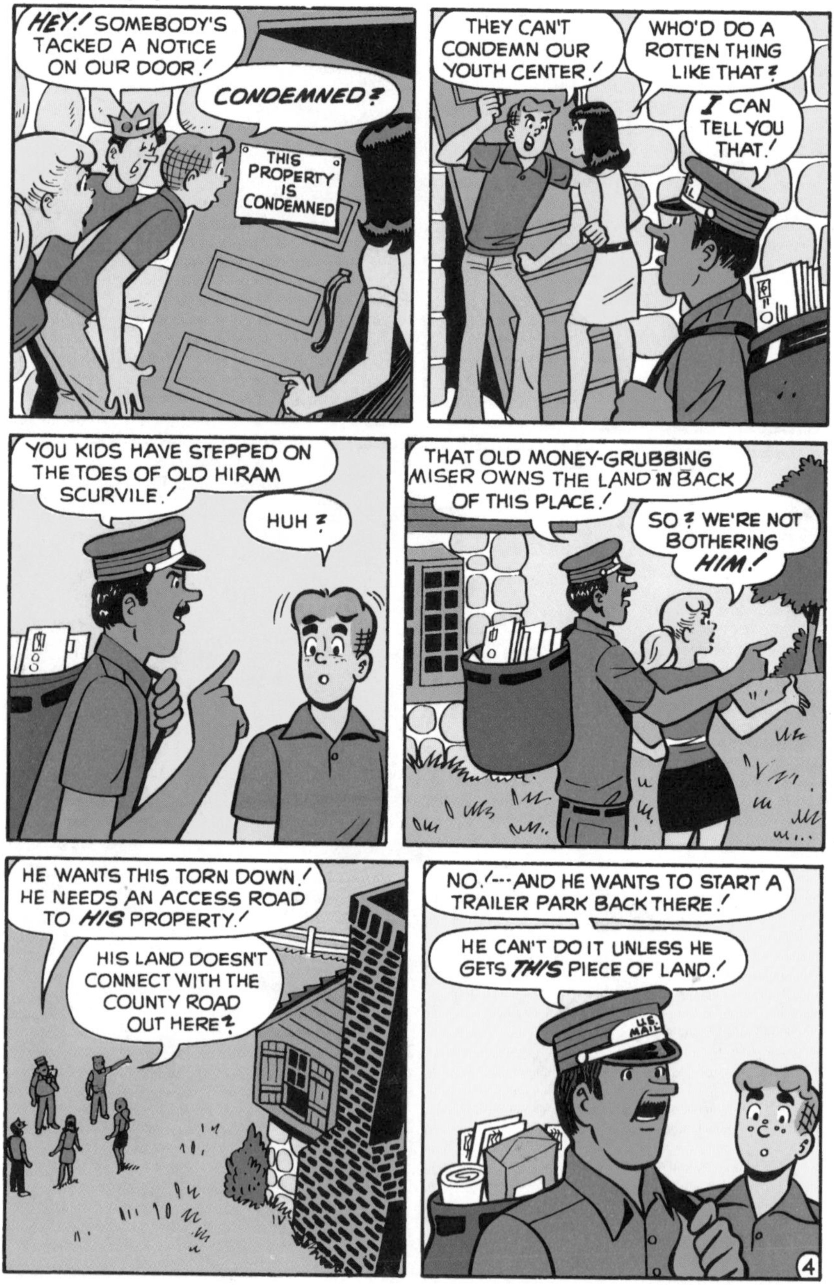
HEY! SOMEBODY'S TACKED A NOTICE ON OUR DOOR!
CONDEMNED?
THIS PROPERTY IS CONDEMNED
THEY CAN'T CONDEMN OUR YOUTH CENTER!
WHO'D DO A ROTTEN THING LIKE THAT?
I CAN TELL YOU THAT!
YOU KIDS HAVE STEPPED ON THE TOES OF OLD HIRAM SCURVILE!
HUH?
THAT OLD MONEY-GRUBBING MISER OWNS THE LAND IN BACK OF THIS PLACE!
SO? WE'RE NOT BOTHERING HIM!
HE WANTS THIS TORN DOWN! HE NEEDS AN ACCESS ROAD TO HIS PROPERTY!
HIS LAND DOESN'T CONNECT WITH THE COUNTY ROAD OUT HERE?
NO!---AND HE WANTS TO START A TRAILER PARK BACK THERE!
HE CAN'T DO IT UNLESS HE GETS THIS PIECE OF LAND!
U.S. MAIL
4

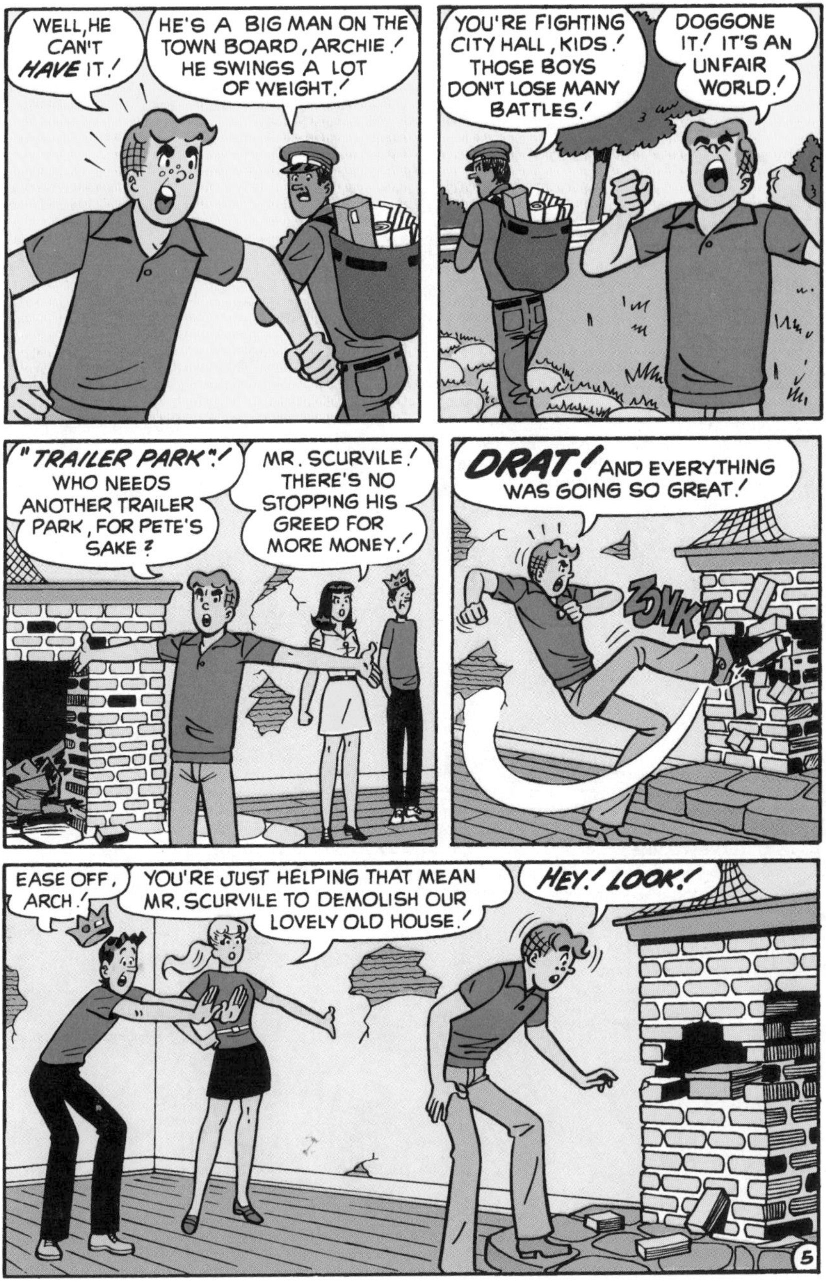
WELL, HE CAN'T HAVE IT!
HE'S A BIG MAN ON THE TOWN BOARD, ARCHIE! HE SWINGS A LOT OF WEIGHT!
YOU'RE FIGHTING CITY HALL, KIDS! THOSE BOYS DON'T LOSE MANY BATTLES!
DOGGONE IT! IT'S AN UNFAIR WORLD!
"TRAILER PARK"! WHO NEEDS ANOTHER TRAILER PARK, FOR PETE'S SAKE?
MR. SCURVILE! THERE'S NO STOPPING HIS GREED FOR MORE MONEY!
DRAT! AND EVERYTHING WAS GOING SO GREAT!
ZONK!
EASE OFF, ARCH!
YOU'RE JUST HELPING THAT MEAN MR. SCURVILE TO DEMOLISH OUR LOVELY OLD HOUSE!
HEY! LOOK!
5

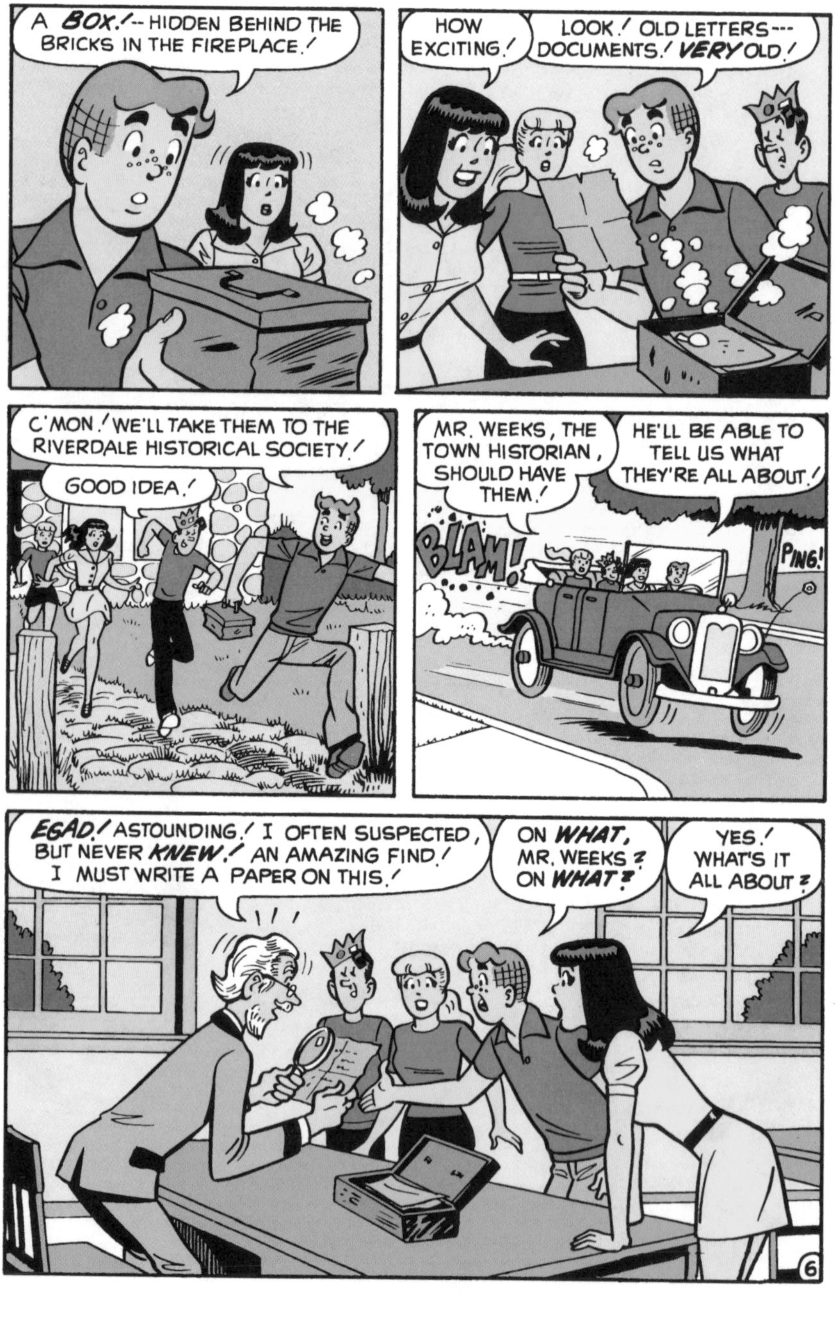
A BOX!-- HIDDEN BEHIND THE BRICKS IN THE FIREPLACE!
HOW EXCITING!
LOOK! OLD LETTERS--- DOCUMENTS! VERY OLD!
C'MON! WE'LL TAKE THEM TO THE RIVERDALE HISTORICAL SOCIETY!
GOOD IDEA!
MR. WEEKS, THE TOWN HISTORIAN, SHOULD HAVE THEM!
HE'LL BE ABLE TO TELL US WHAT THEY'RE ALL ABOUT!
BLAM!
PING!
EGAD! ASTOUNDING! I OFTEN SUSPECTED, BUT NEVER KNEW! AN AMAZING FIND! I MUST WRITE A PAPER ON THIS!
ON WHAT, MR. WEEKS? ON WHAT?
YES! WHAT'S IT ALL ABOUT?
6

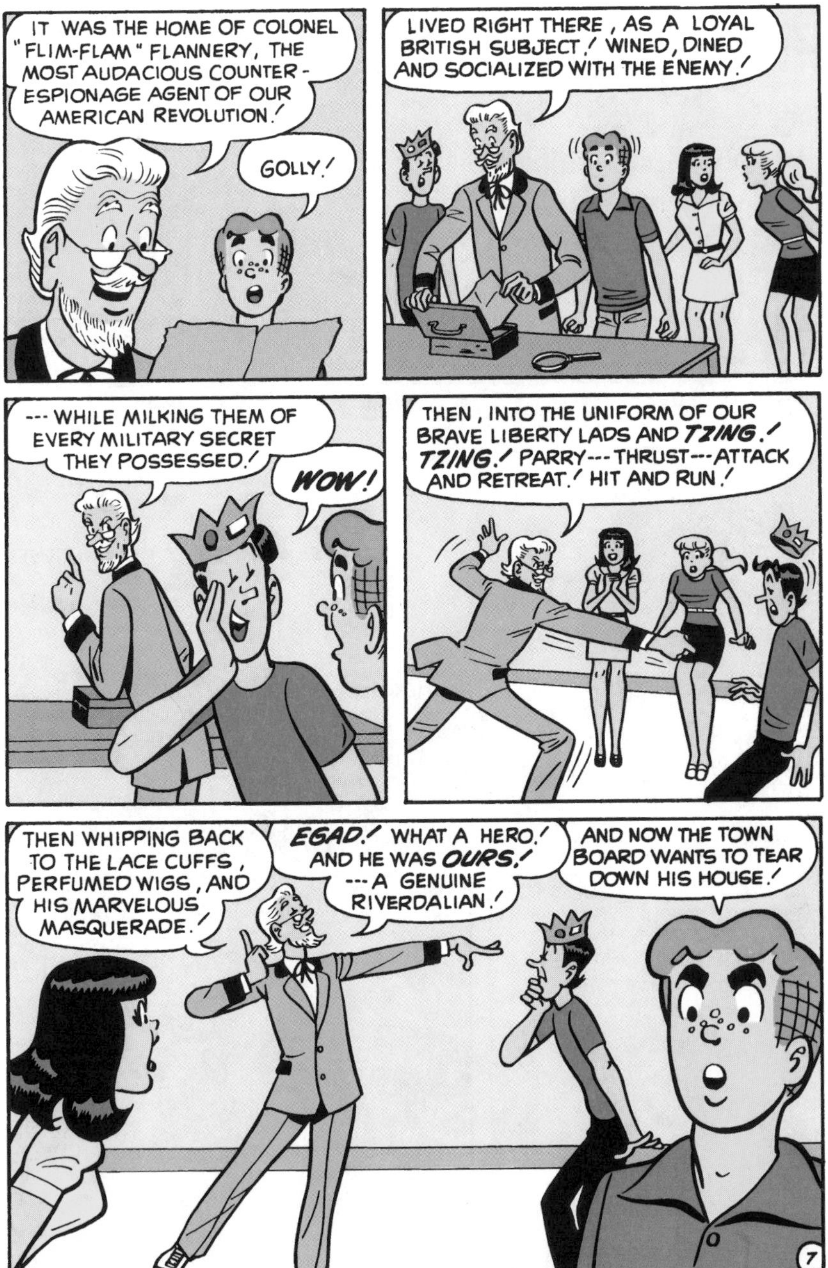
IT WAS THE HOME OF COLONEL "FLIM-FLAM" FLANNERY, THE MOST AUDACIOUS COUNTER-ESPIONAGE AGENT OF OUR AMERICAN REVOLUTION!
GOLLY!
LIVED RIGHT THERE, AS A LOYAL BRITISH SUBJECT! WINED, DINED AND SOCIALIZED WITH THE ENEMY!
--- WHILE MILKING THEM OF EVERY MILITARY SECRET THEY POSSESSED!
WOW!
THEN, INTO THE UNIFORM OF OUR BRAVE LIBERTY LADS AND TZING! TZING! PARRY--- THRUST--- ATTACK AND RETREAT! HIT AND RUN!
THEN WHIPPING BACK TO THE LACE CUFFS, PERFUMED WIGS, AND HIS MARVELOUS MASQUERADE!
EGAD! WHAT A HERO! AND HE WAS OURS! --- A GENUINE RIVERDALIAN!
AND NOW THE TOWN BOARD WANTS TO TEAR DOWN HIS HOUSE!
7

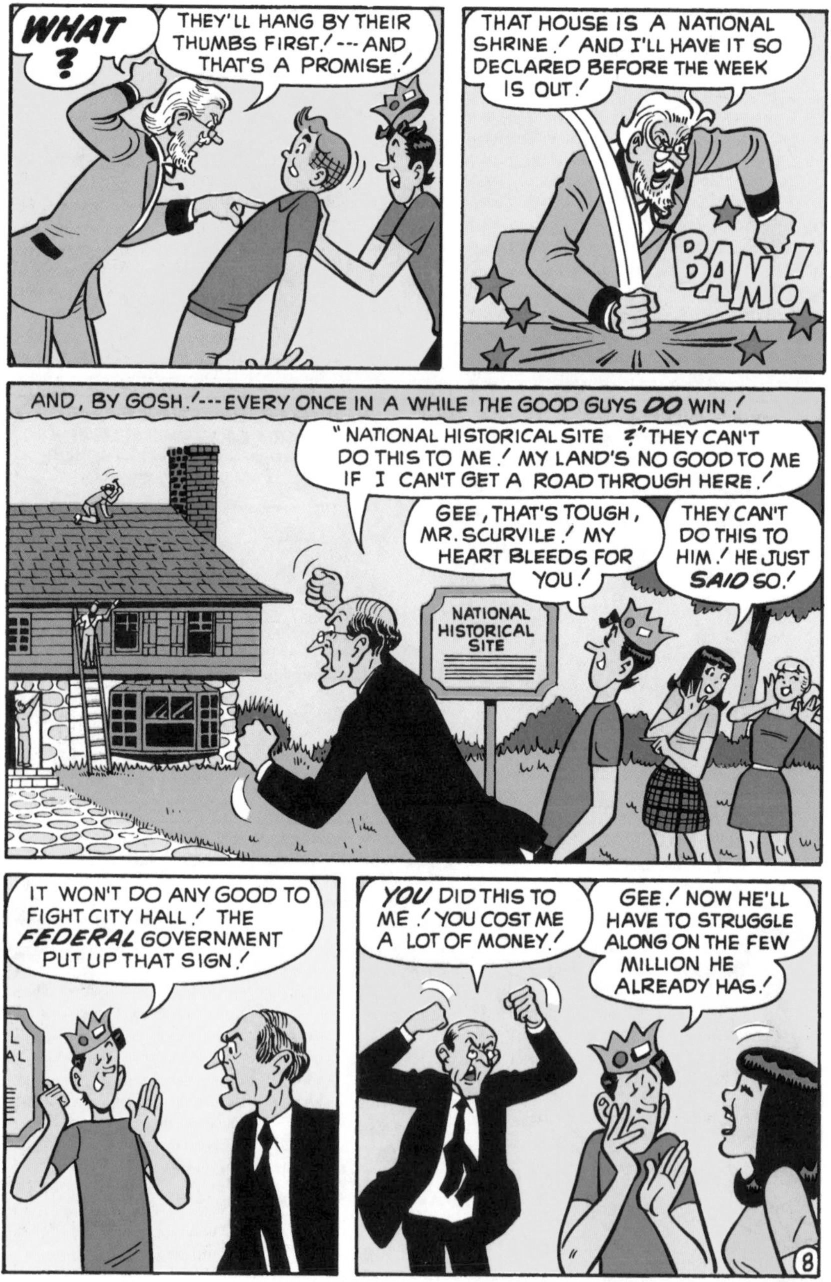
WHAT ?
THEY'LL HANG BY THEIR THUMBS FIRST! --- AND THAT'S A PROMISE!
THAT HOUSE IS A NATIONAL SHRINE! AND I'LL HAVE IT SO DECLARED BEFORE THE WEEK IS OUT!
BAM!
AND, BY GOSH! --- EVERY ONCE IN A WHILE THE GOOD GUYS DO WIN!
"NATIONAL HISTORICAL SITE ?" THEY CAN'T DO THIS TO ME! MY LAND'S NO GOOD TO ME IF I CAN'T GET A ROAD THROUGH HERE!
GEE, THAT'S TOUGH, MR. SCURVILE! MY HEART BLEEDS FOR YOU!
THEY CAN'T DO THIS TO HIM! HE JUST SAID SO!
NATIONAL HISTORICAL SITE
IT WON'T DO ANY GOOD TO FIGHT CITY HALL! THE FEDERAL GOVERNMENT PUT UP THAT SIGN!
YOU DID THIS TO ME! YOU COST ME A LOT OF MONEY!
GEE! NOW HE'LL HAVE TO STRUGGLE ALONG ON THE FEW MILLION HE ALREADY HAS!
8

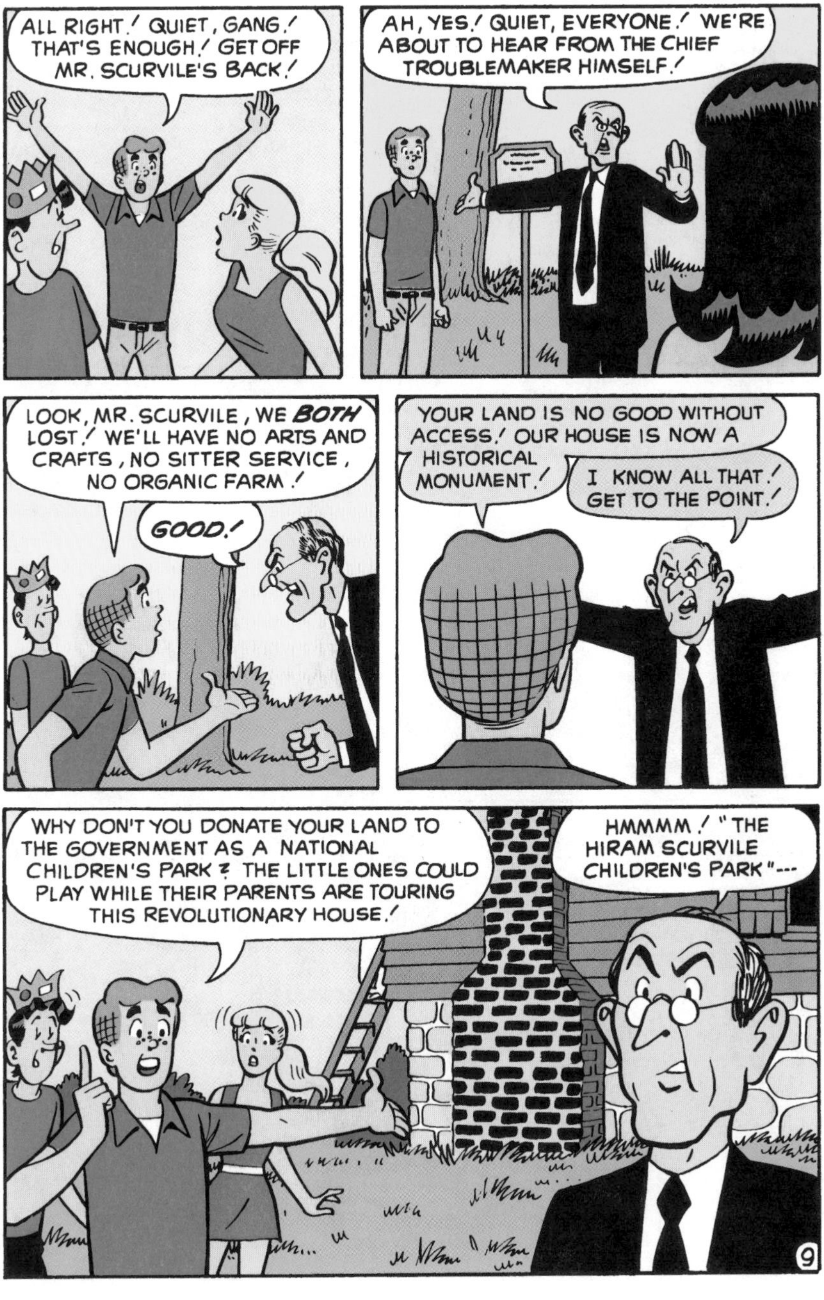
ALL RIGHT! QUIET, GANG! THAT'S ENOUGH! GET OFF MR. SCURVILE'S BACK!
AH, YES! QUIET, EVERYONE! WE'RE ABOUT TO HEAR FROM THE CHIEF TROUBLEMAKER HIMSELF!
LOOK, MR. SCURVILE, WE BOTH LOST! WE'LL HAVE NO ARTS AND CRAFTS, NO SITTER SERVICE, NO ORGANIC FARM!
GOOD!
YOUR LAND IS NO GOOD WITHOUT ACCESS! OUR HOUSE IS NOW A HISTORICAL MONUMENT!
I KNOW ALL THAT! GET TO THE POINT!
WHY DON'T YOU DONATE YOUR LAND TO THE GOVERNMENT AS A NATIONAL CHILDREN'S PARK? THE LITTLE ONES COULD PLAY WHILE THEIR PARENTS ARE TOURING THIS REVOLUTIONARY HOUSE!
HMMMM! "THE HIRAM SCURVILE CHILDREN'S PARK"---
9

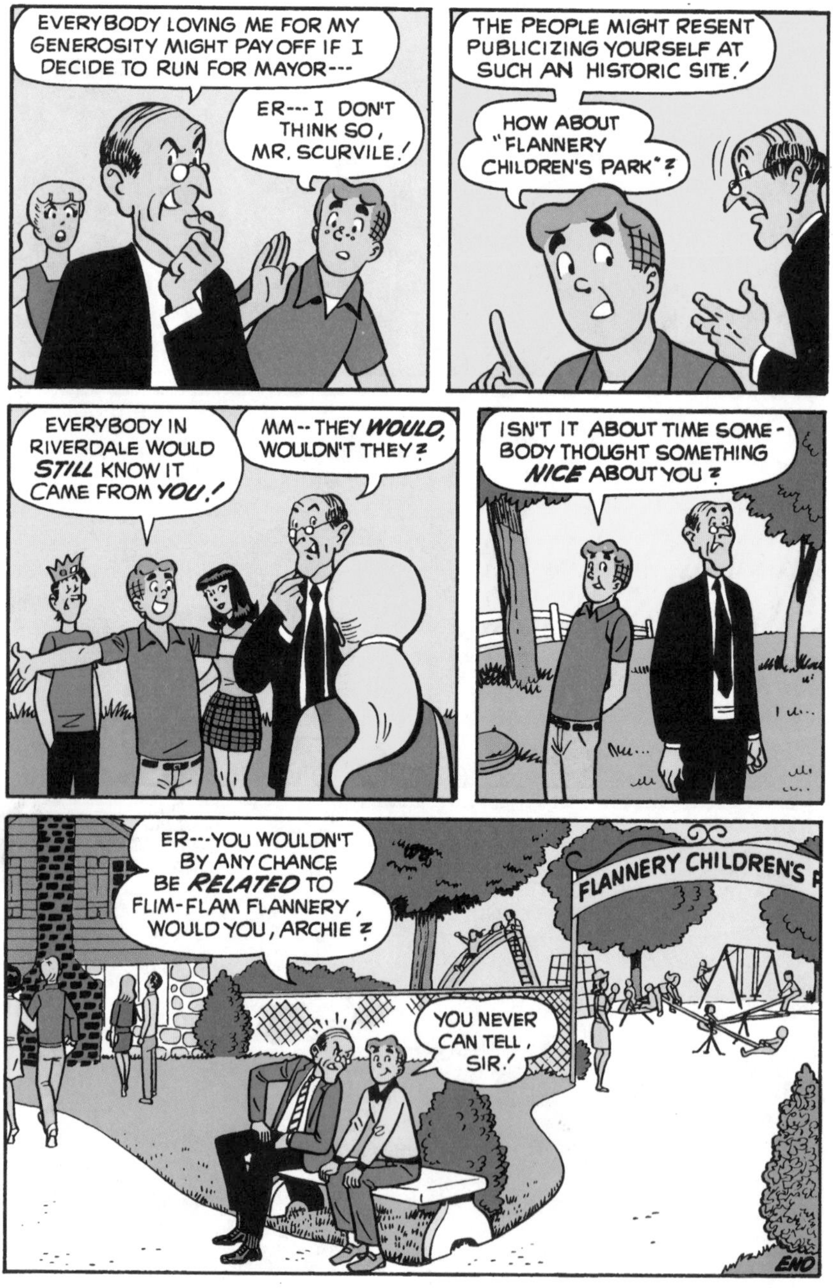
EVERYBODY LOVING ME FOR MY GENEROSITY MIGHT PAY OFF IF I DECIDE TO RUN FOR MAYOR---
ER--- I DON'T THINK SO, MR. SCURVILE!
THE PEOPLE MIGHT RESENT PUBLICIZING YOURSELF AT SUCH AN HISTORIC SITE!
HOW ABOUT "FLANNERY CHILDREN'S PARK"?
EVERYBODY IN RIVERDALE WOULD STILL KNOW IT CAME FROM YOU!
MM-- THEY WOULD, WOULDN'T THEY?
ISN'T IT ABOUT TIME SOMEBODY THOUGHT SOMETHING NICE ABOUT YOU?
ER---YOU WOULDN'T BY ANY CHANCE BE RELATED TO FLIM-FLAM FLANNERY, WOULD YOU, ARCHIE?
FLANNERY CHILDREN'S
YOU NEVER CAN TELL, SIR!
ENO

Archie at Riverdale in Loyalville U.S.A.

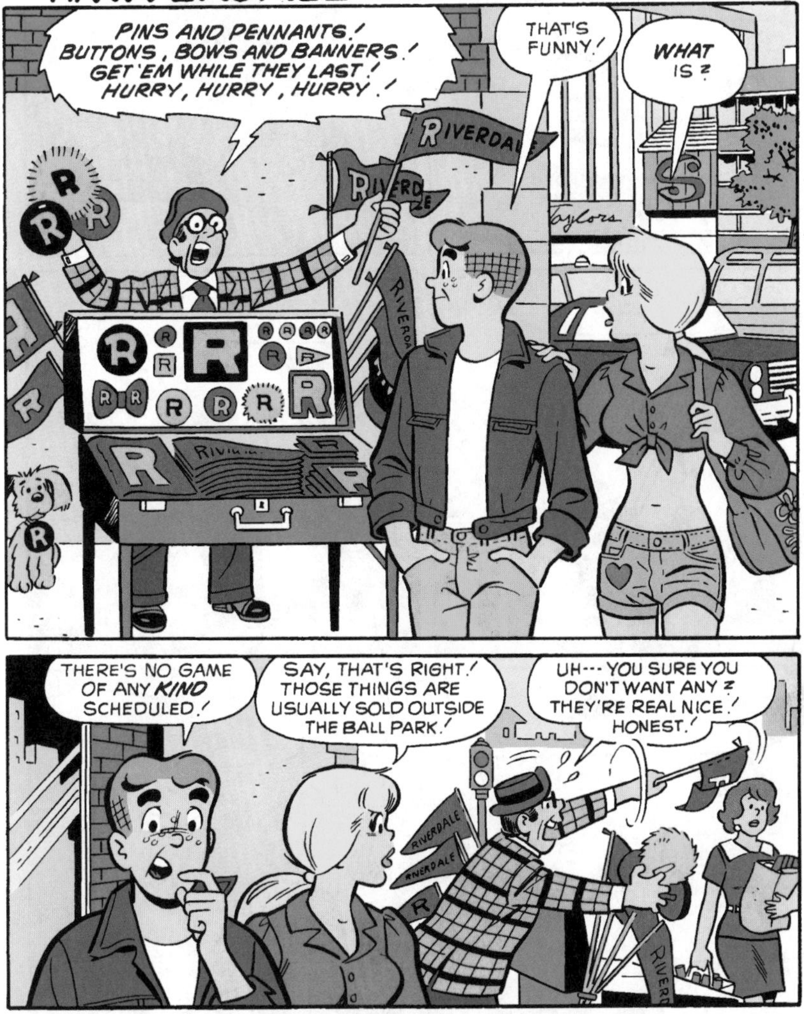
PINS AND PENNANTS! BUTTONS, BOWS AND BANNERS! GET 'EM WHILE THEY LAST! HURRY, HURRY, HURRY!
THAT'S FUNNY!
WHAT IS?
RIVERDALE
Taylors
THERE'S NO GAME OF ANY KIND SCHEDULED!
SAY, THAT'S RIGHT! THOSE THINGS ARE USUALLY SOLD OUTSIDE THE BALL PARK!
UH--- YOU SURE YOU DON'T WANT ANY? THEY'RE REAL NICE! HONEST!
RIVERDALE
RIVERDALE

Story: Frank Doyle Pencils: Dan DeCarlo

Inks: Rudy Lapick Letters: Bill Yoshida Colors: Barry Grossman

Originally printed in ARCHIE AT RIVERDALE HIGH #12, December 1973

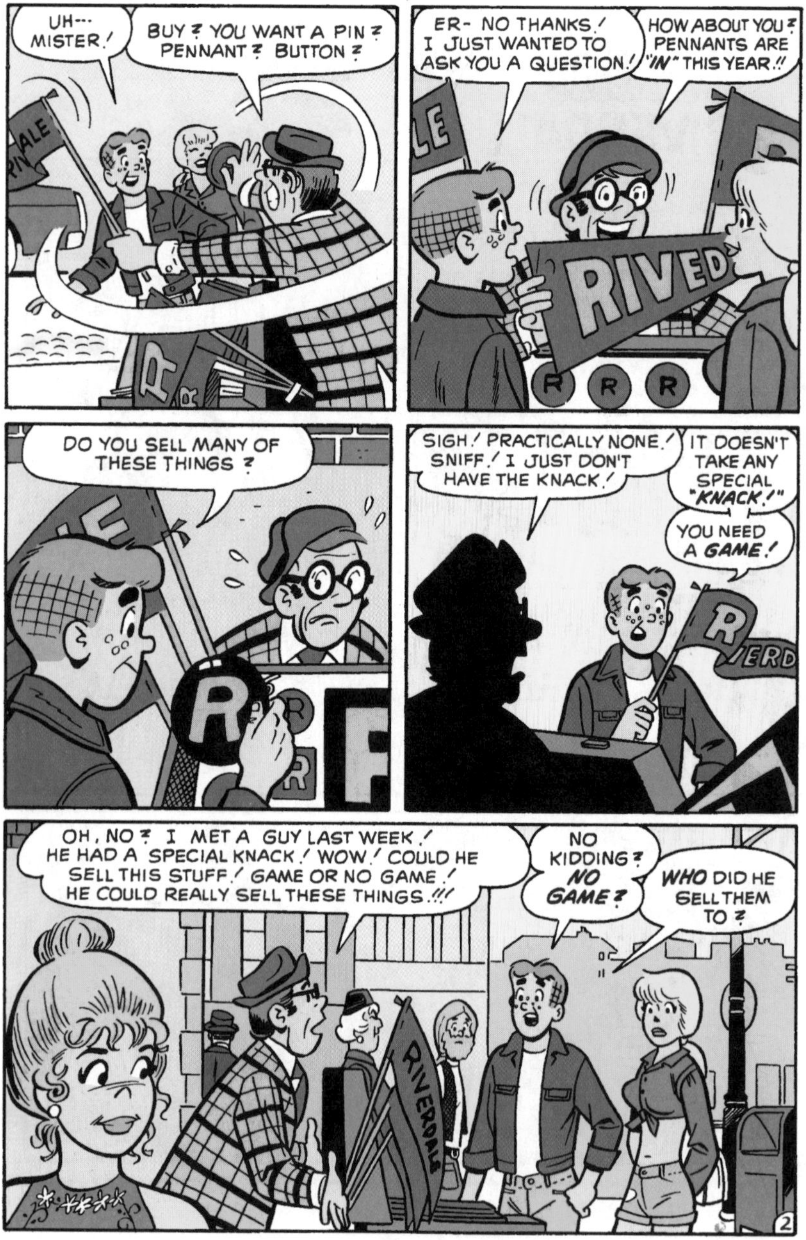
UH--- MISTER!
BUY? YOU WANT A PIN? PENNANT? BUTTON?
ALE
ER- NO THANKS! I JUST WANTED TO ASK YOU A QUESTION!
HOW ABOUT YOU? PENNANTS ARE "IN" THIS YEAR!!
RIVED
DO YOU SELL MANY OF THESE THINGS?
SIGH! PRACTICALLY NONE! SNIFF! I JUST DON'T HAVE THE KNACK!
IT DOESN'T TAKE ANY SPECIAL "KNACK!"
YOU NEED A GAME!
OH, NO? I MET A GUY LAST WEEK! HE HAD A SPECIAL KNACK! WOW! COULD HE SELL THIS STUFF! GAME OR NO GAME! HE COULD REALLY SELL THESE THINGS!!!
NO KIDDING? NO GAME?
WHO DID HE SELL THEM TO?
RIVERDALE
2

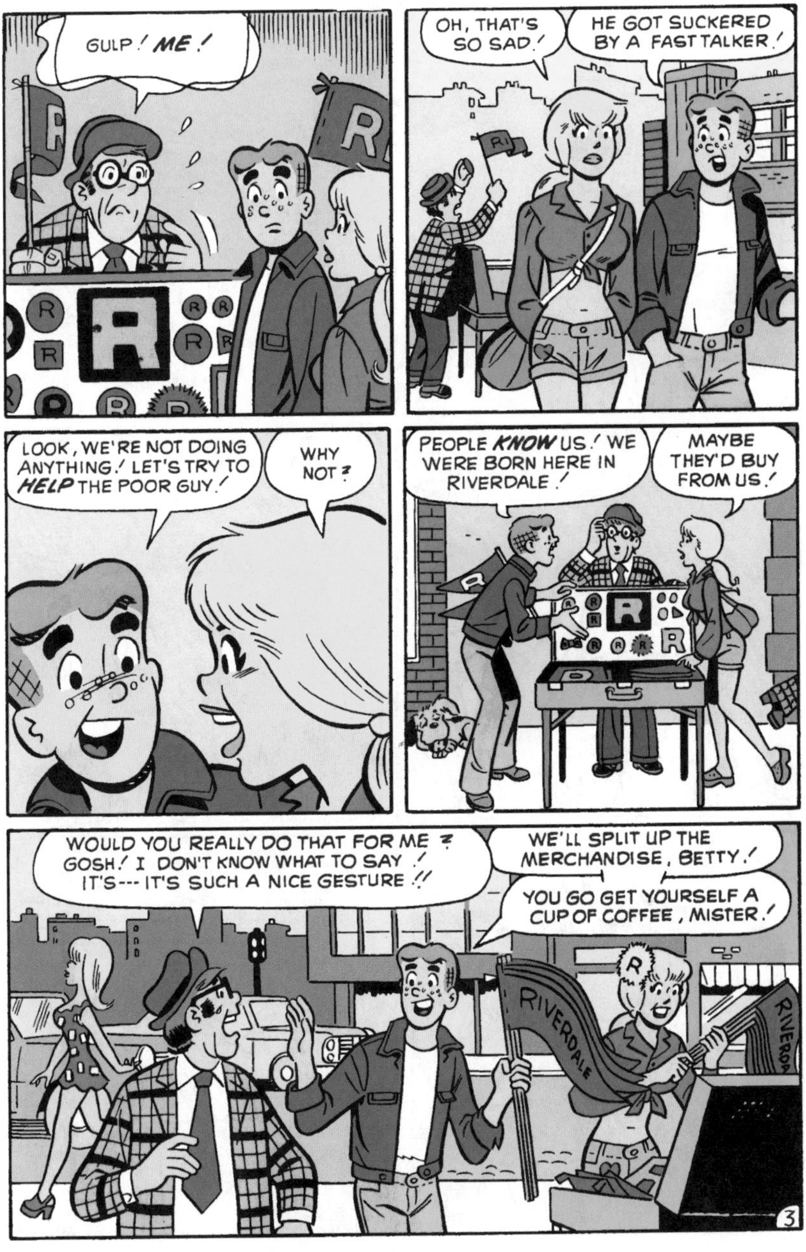
GULP! ME!
OH, THAT'S SO SAD!
HE GOT SUCKERED BY A FAST TALKER!
LOOK, WE'RE NOT DOING ANYTHING! LET'S TRY TO HELP THE POOR GUY!
WHY NOT?
PEOPLE KNOW US! WE WERE BORN HERE IN RIVERDALE!
MAYBE THEY'D BUY FROM US!
WOULD YOU REALLY DO THAT FOR ME? GOSH! I DON'T KNOW WHAT TO SAY! IT'S--- IT'S SUCH A NICE GESTURE!!
WE'LL SPLIT UP THE MERCHANDISE, BETTY!
YOU GO GET YOURSELF A CUP OF COFFEE, MISTER!
RIVERDALE
3

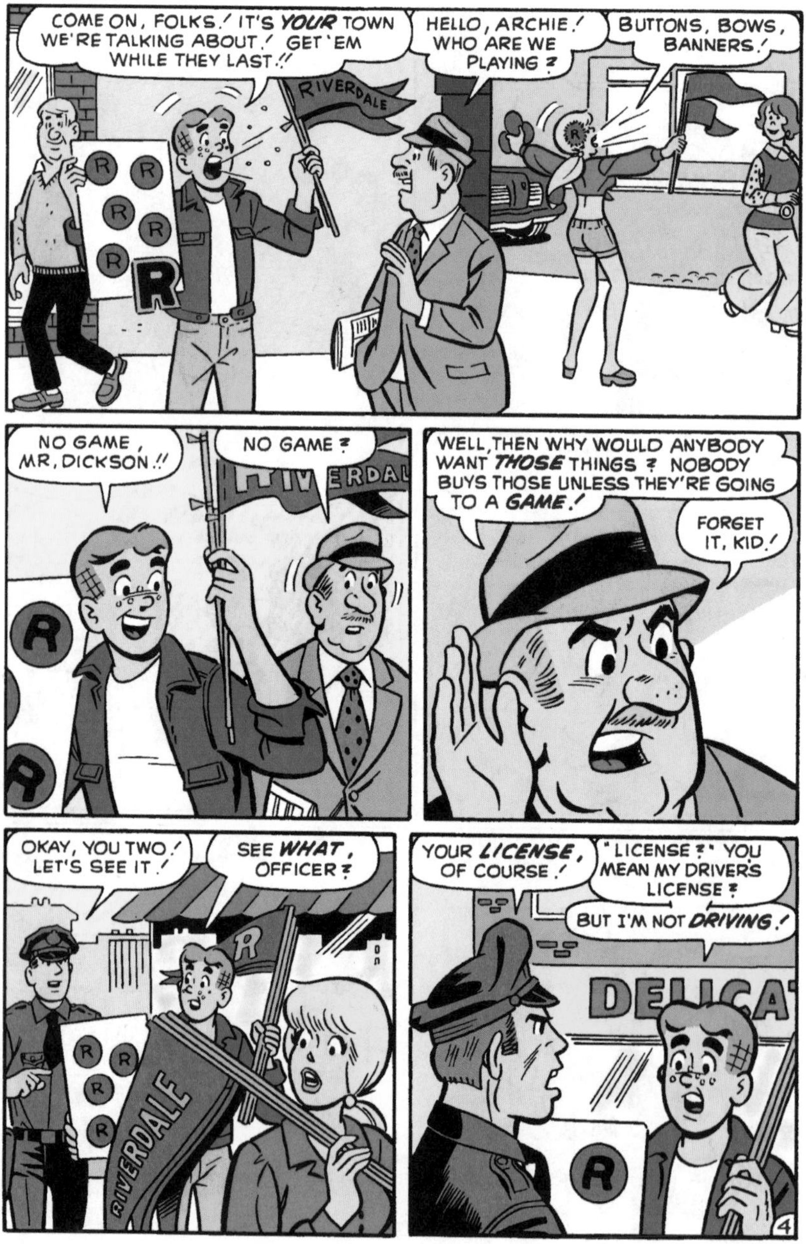
COME ON, FOLKS! IT'S YOUR TOWN WE'RE TALKING ABOUT! GET 'EM WHILE THEY LAST!!
RIVERDALE
HELLO, ARCHIE! WHO ARE WE PLAYING?
BUTTONS, BOWS, BANNERS!
NO GAME, MR. DICKSON!!
NO GAME?
WELL, THEN WHY WOULD ANYBODY WANT THOSE THINGS? NOBODY BUYS THOSE UNLESS THEY'RE GOING TO A GAME!
FORGET IT, KID!
OKAY, YOU TWO! LET'S SEE IT!
SEE WHAT, OFFICER?
RIVERDALE
YOUR LICENSE, OF COURSE!
"LICENSE?" YOU MEAN MY DRIVER'S LICENSE?
BUT I'M NOT DRIVING!
4

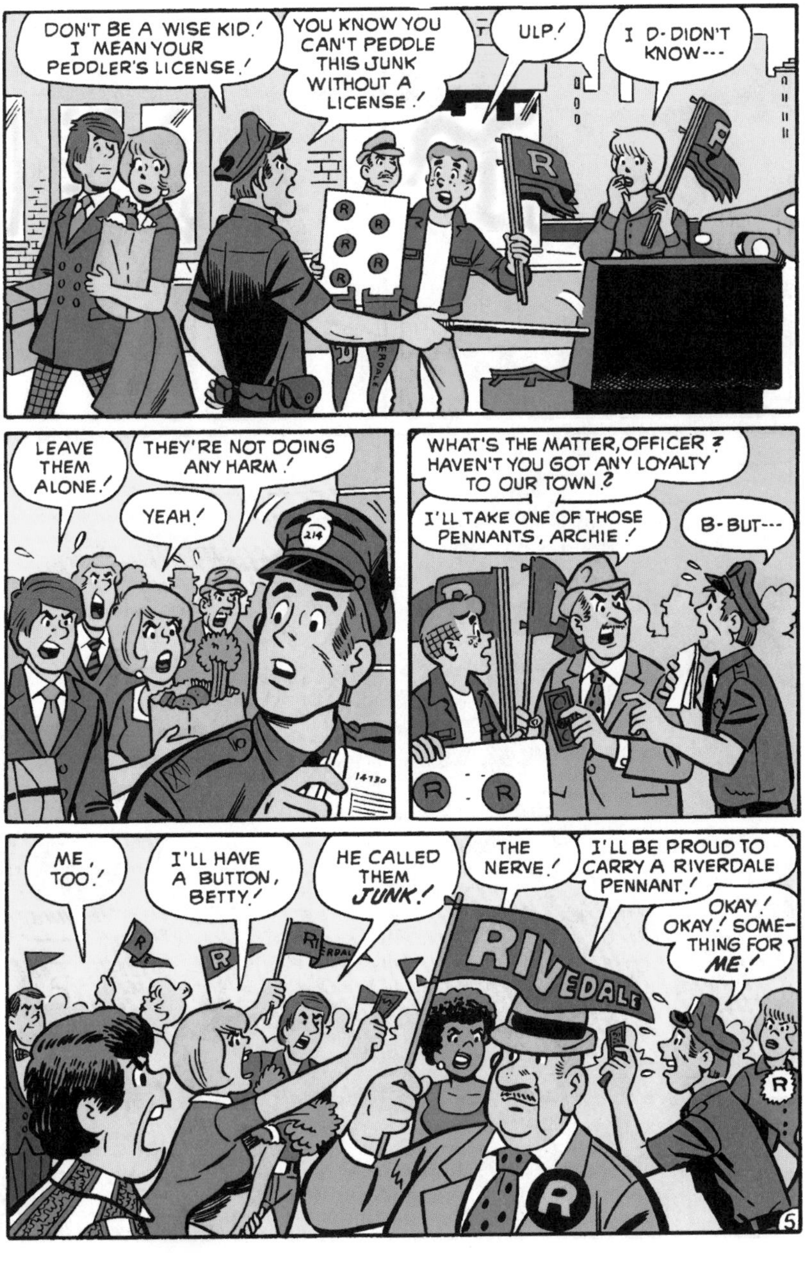
DON'T BE A WISE KID! I MEAN YOUR PEDDLER'S LICENSE!
YOU KNOW YOU CAN'T PEDDLE THIS JUNK WITHOUT A LICENSE!
ULP!
I D-DIDN'T KNOW---
LEAVE THEM ALONE!
THEY'RE NOT DOING ANY HARM!
YEAH!
WHAT'S THE MATTER, OFFICER? HAVEN'T YOU GOT ANY LOYALTY TO OUR TOWN?
I'LL TAKE ONE OF THOSE PENNANTS, ARCHIE!
B-BUT---
ME, TOO!
I'LL HAVE A BUTTON, BETTY!
HE CALLED THEM *JUNK*!
THE NERVE!
I'LL BE PROUD TO CARRY A RIVERDALE PENNANT!
OKAY! OKAY! SOMETHING FOR *ME*!
RIVEDALE
5

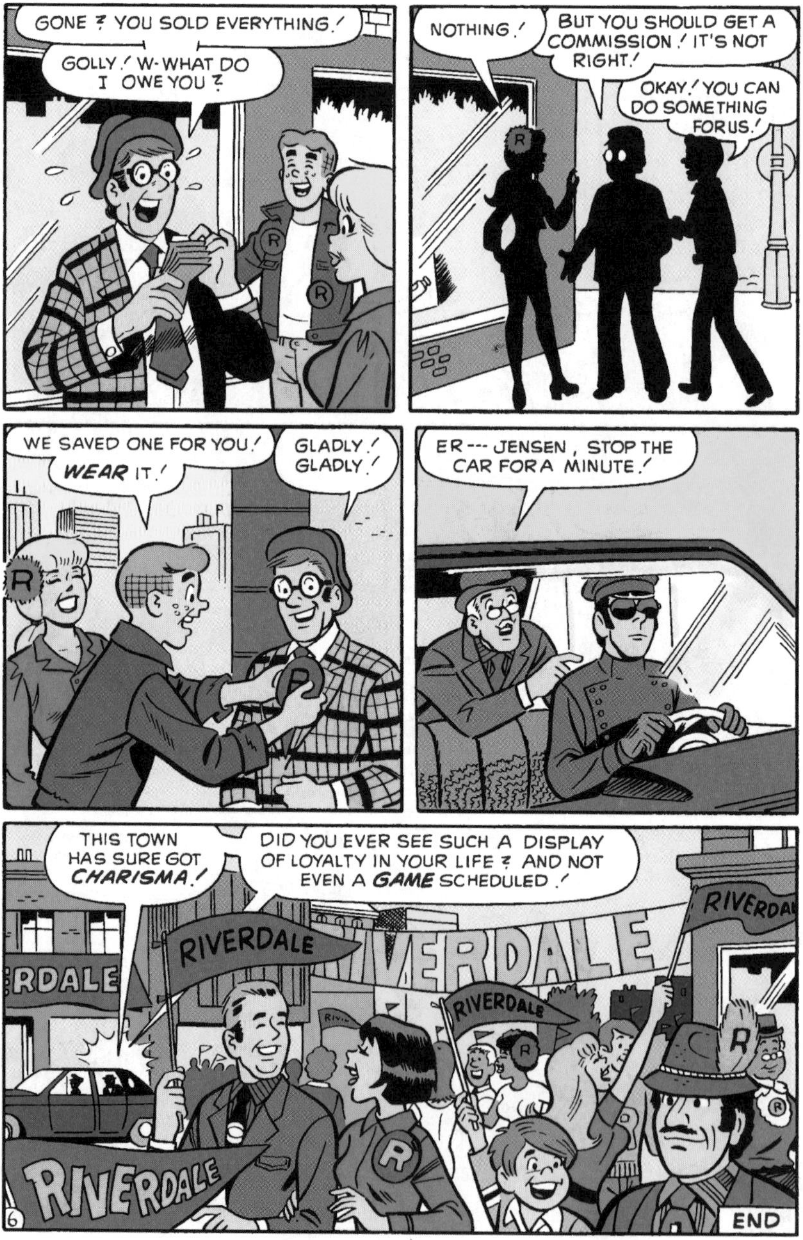
GONE ? YOU SOLD EVERYTHING!
GOLLY! W-WHAT DO I OWE YOU ?
NOTHING!
BUT YOU SHOULD GET A COMMISSION! IT'S NOT RIGHT!
OKAY! YOU CAN DO SOMETHING FOR US!
WE SAVED ONE FOR YOU! WEAR IT!
GLADLY! GLADLY!
ER--- JENSEN, STOP THE CAR FOR A MINUTE!
THIS TOWN HAS SURE GOT CHARISMA!
DID YOU EVER SEE SUCH A DISPLAY OF LOYALTY IN YOUR LIFE ? AND NOT EVEN A GAME SCHEDULED!
RIVERDALE
RIVERDALE
RIVERDALE
RIVERDALE
6
END

Archie in "The RESISTANCE MOVEMENT"

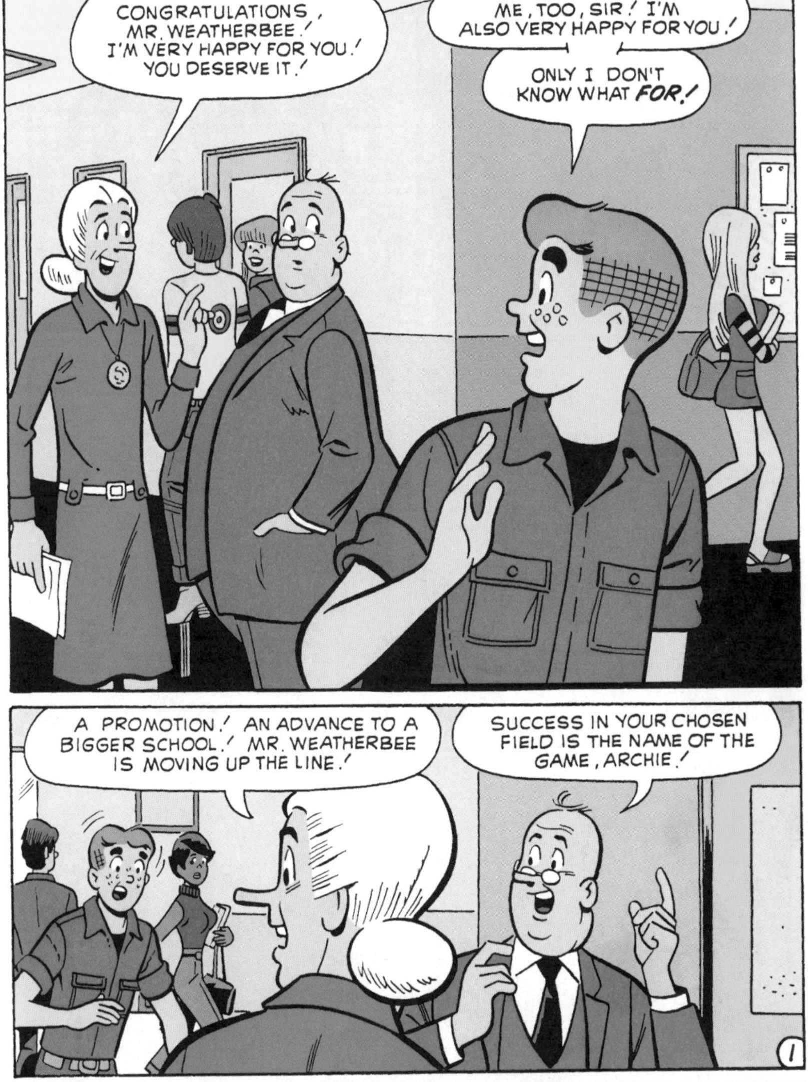
CONGRATULATIONS, MR. WEATHERBEE! I'M VERY HAPPY FOR YOU! YOU DESERVE IT!
ME, TOO, SIR! I'M ALSO VERY HAPPY FOR YOU!
ONLY I DON'T KNOW WHAT **FOR!**
A PROMOTION! AN ADVANCE TO A BIGGER SCHOOL! MR. WEATHERBEE IS MOVING UP THE LINE!
SUCCESS IN YOUR CHOSEN FIELD IS THE NAME OF THE GAME, ARCHIE!
1

Story: Frank Doyle **Pencils:** Dan DeCarlo

Inks: Rudy Lapick **Letters:** Bill Yoshida **Colors:** Barry Grossman

Originally printed in ARCHIE AT RIVERDALE HIGH #12, December 1973

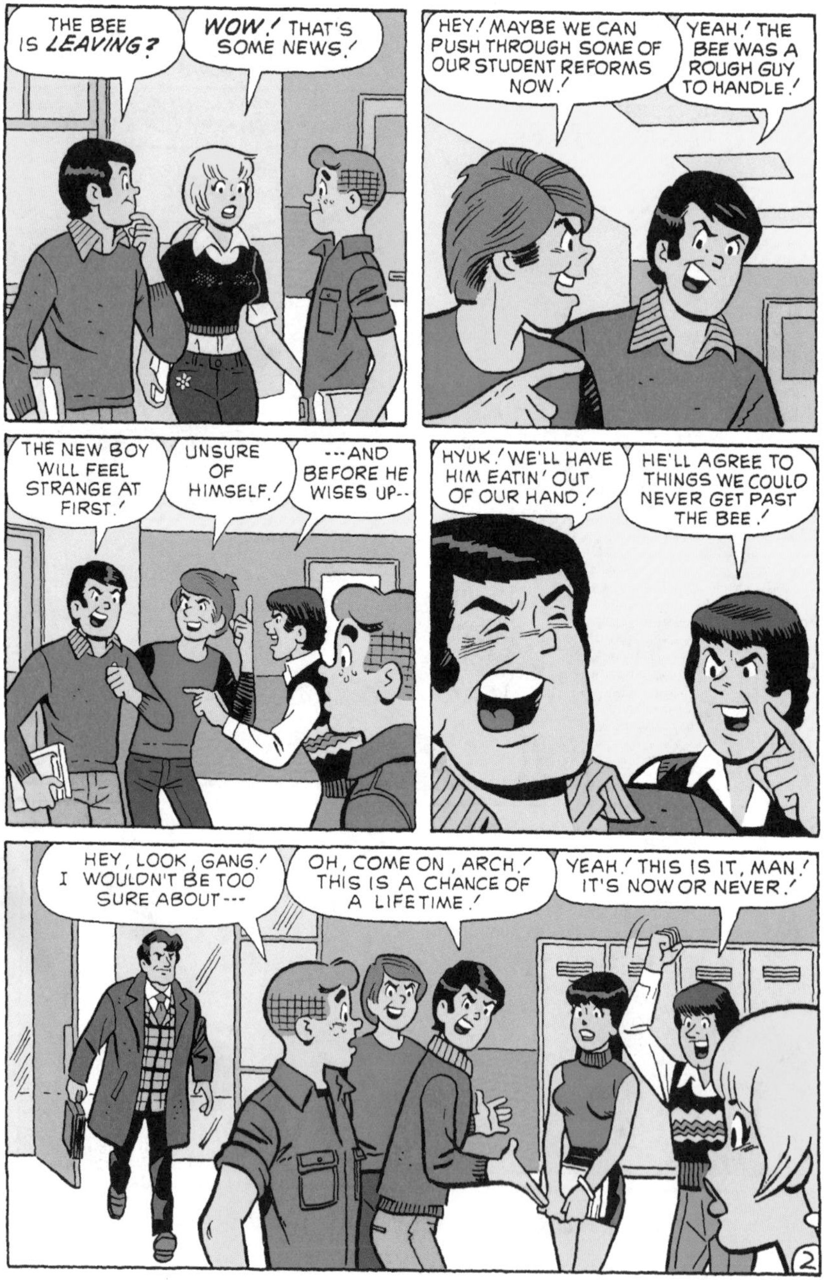
THE BEE IS LEAVING?
WOW! THAT'S SOME NEWS!
HEY! MAYBE WE CAN PUSH THROUGH SOME OF OUR STUDENT REFORMS NOW!
YEAH! THE BEE WAS A ROUGH GUY TO HANDLE!
THE NEW BOY WILL FEEL STRANGE AT FIRST!
UNSURE OF HIMSELF!
---AND BEFORE HE WISES UP--
HYUK! WE'LL HAVE HIM EATIN' OUT OF OUR HAND!
HE'LL AGREE TO THINGS WE COULD NEVER GET PAST THE BEE!
HEY, LOOK, GANG! I WOULDN'T BE TOO SURE ABOUT---
OH, COME ON, ARCH! THIS IS A CHANCE OF A LIFETIME!
YEAH! THIS IS IT, MAN! IT'S NOW OR NEVER!
2

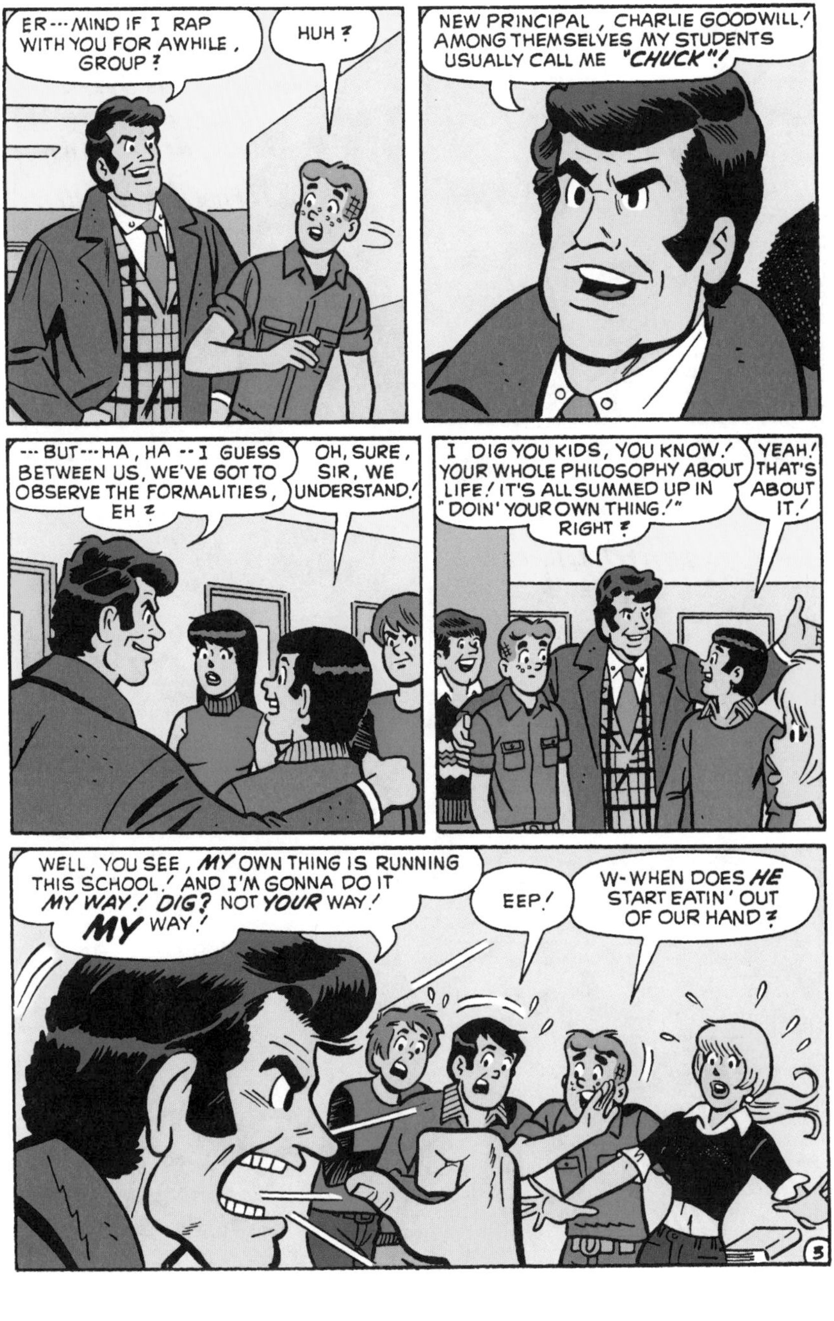
ER--- MIND IF I RAP WITH YOU FOR AWHILE, GROUP?
HUH?
NEW PRINCIPAL, CHARLIE GOODWILL! AMONG THEMSELVES MY STUDENTS USUALLY CALL ME "CHUCK"!
--- BUT --- HA, HA -- I GUESS BETWEEN US, WE'VE GOT TO OBSERVE THE FORMALITIES, EH?
OH, SURE, SIR, WE UNDERSTAND!
I DIG YOU KIDS, YOU KNOW! YOUR WHOLE PHILOSOPHY ABOUT LIFE! IT'S ALL SUMMED UP IN "DOIN' YOUR OWN THING!" RIGHT?
YEAH! THAT'S ABOUT IT!
WELL, YOU SEE, MY OWN THING IS RUNNING THIS SCHOOL! AND I'M GONNA DO IT MY WAY! DIG? NOT YOUR WAY! MY WAY!
EEP!
W-WHEN DOES HE START EATIN' OUT OF OUR HAND?
3

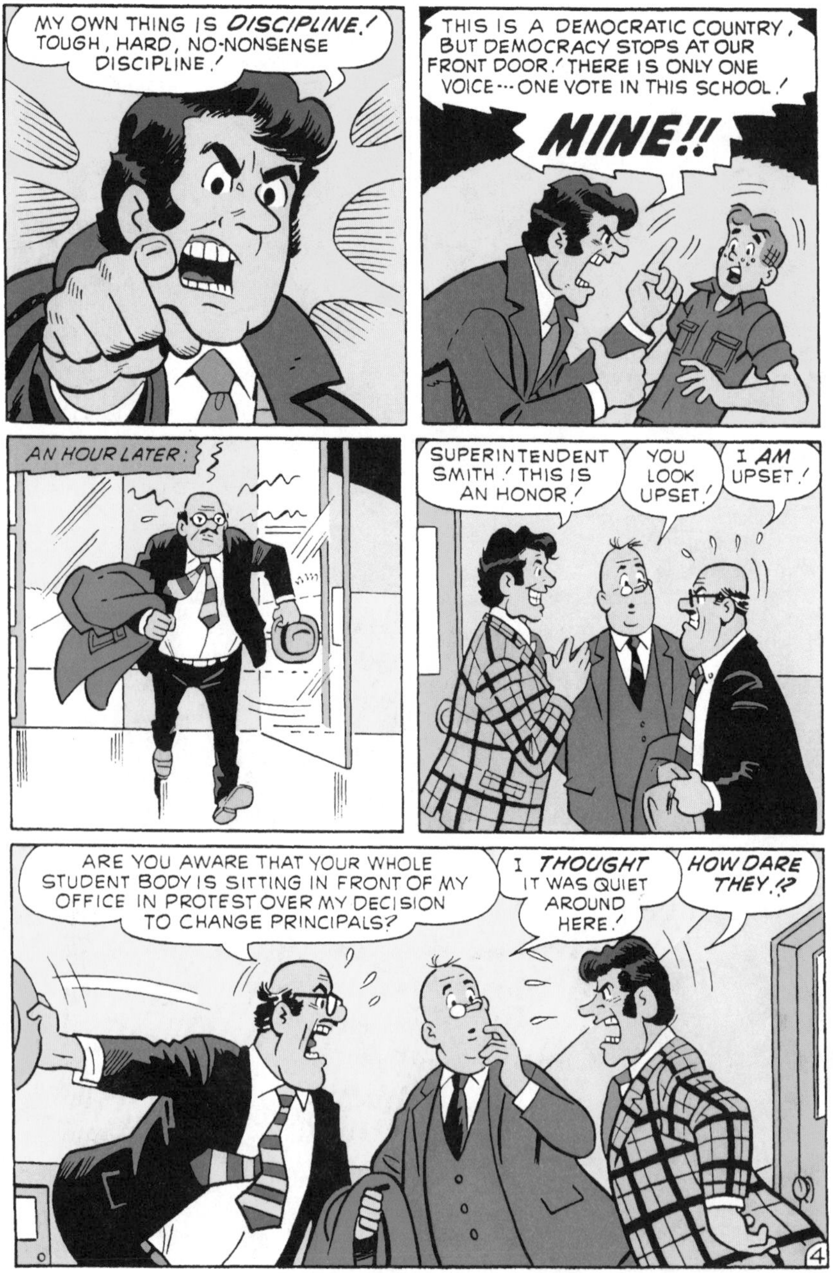
MY OWN THING IS DISCIPLINE! TOUGH, HARD, NO-NONSENSE DISCIPLINE!
THIS IS A DEMOCRATIC COUNTRY, BUT DEMOCRACY STOPS AT OUR FRONT DOOR! THERE IS ONLY ONE VOICE--- ONE VOTE IN THIS SCHOOL!
MINE!!
AN HOUR LATER:
SUPERINTENDENT SMITH! THIS IS AN HONOR!
YOU LOOK UPSET!
I AM UPSET!
ARE YOU AWARE THAT YOUR WHOLE STUDENT BODY IS SITTING IN FRONT OF MY OFFICE IN PROTEST OVER MY DECISION TO CHANGE PRINCIPALS?
I THOUGHT IT WAS QUIET AROUND HERE!
HOW DARE THEY!?
4

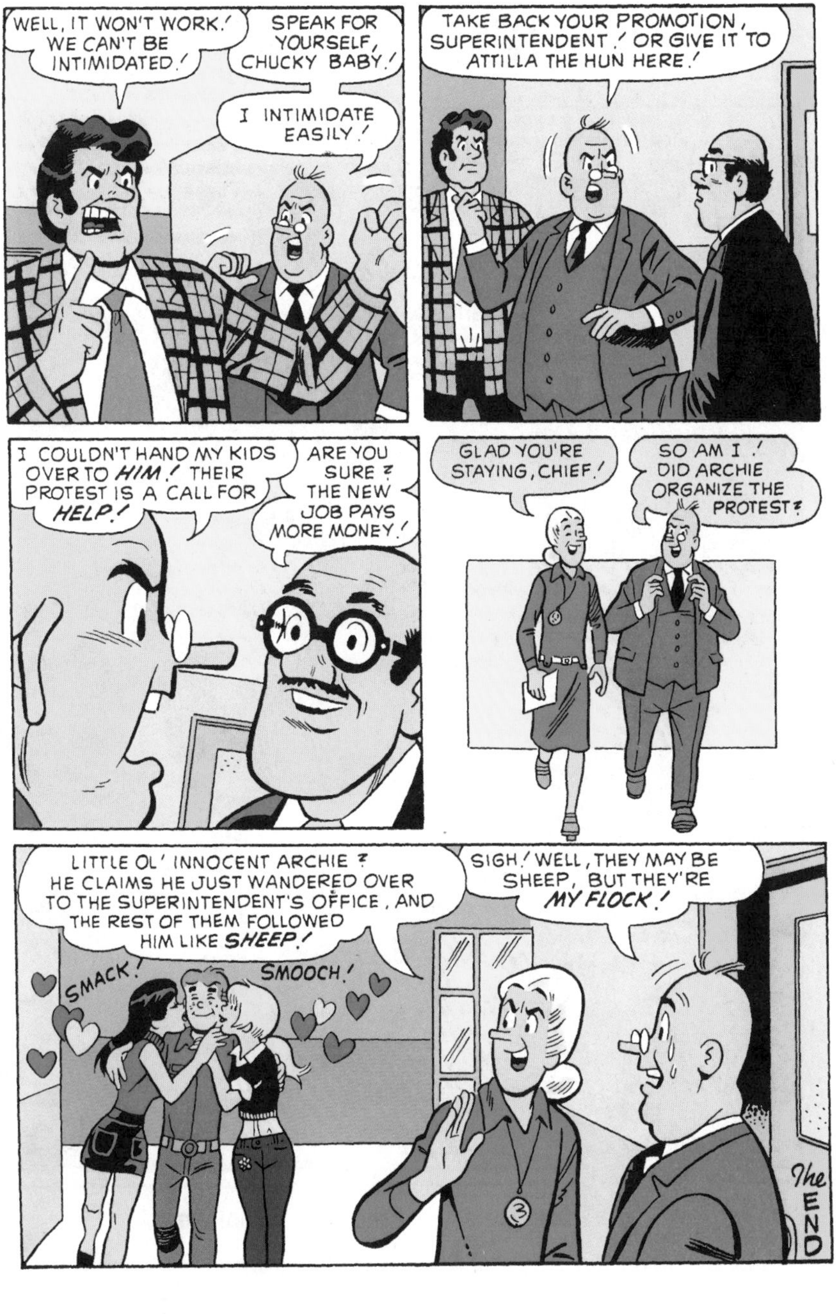
WELL, IT WON'T WORK.! WE CAN'T BE INTIMIDATED.!
SPEAK FOR YOURSELF, CHUCKY BABY.!
I INTIMIDATE EASILY.!
TAKE BACK YOUR PROMOTION, SUPERINTENDENT.! OR GIVE IT TO ATTILLA THE HUN HERE.!
I COULDN'T HAND MY KIDS OVER TO HIM.! THEIR PROTEST IS A CALL FOR HELP.!
ARE YOU SURE? THE NEW JOB PAYS MORE MONEY.!
GLAD YOU'RE STAYING, CHIEF.!
SO AM I.! DID ARCHIE ORGANIZE THE PROTEST?
LITTLE OL' INNOCENT ARCHIE? HE CLAIMS HE JUST WANDERED OVER TO THE SUPERINTENDENT'S OFFICE, AND THE REST OF THEM FOLLOWED HIM LIKE SHEEP!
SMACK!
SMOOCH!
SIGH! WELL, THEY MAY BE SHEEP, BUT THEY'RE MY FLOCK!
The END

Archie in "Still Water"

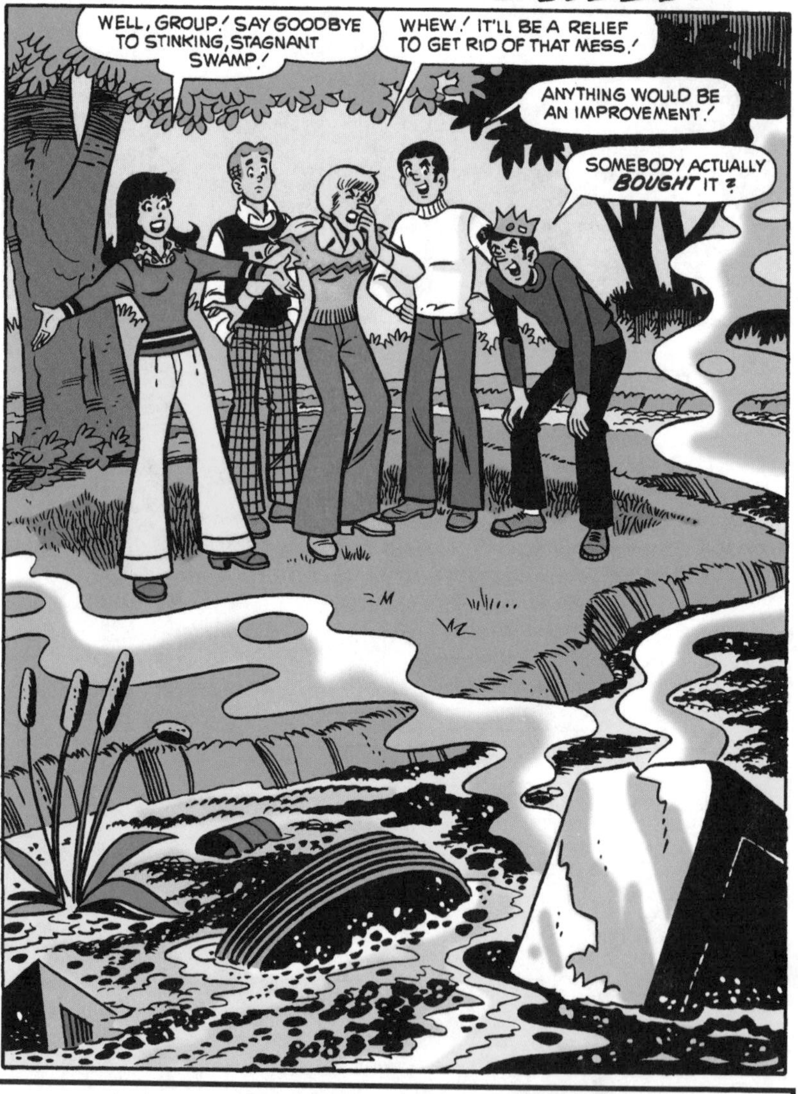
WELL, GROUP! SAY GOODBYE TO STINKING, STAGNANT SWAMP!
WHEW! IT'LL BE A RELIEF TO GET RID OF THAT MESS!
ANYTHING WOULD BE AN IMPROVEMENT!
SOMEBODY ACTUALLY *BOUGHT* IT ?

Story: Frank Doyle   Pencils: Stan Goldberg

Inks: Jon D'Agostino   Letters: Bill Yoshida   Colors: Barry Grossman

Originally printed in ARCHIE AT RIVERDALE HIGH #13, February 1974

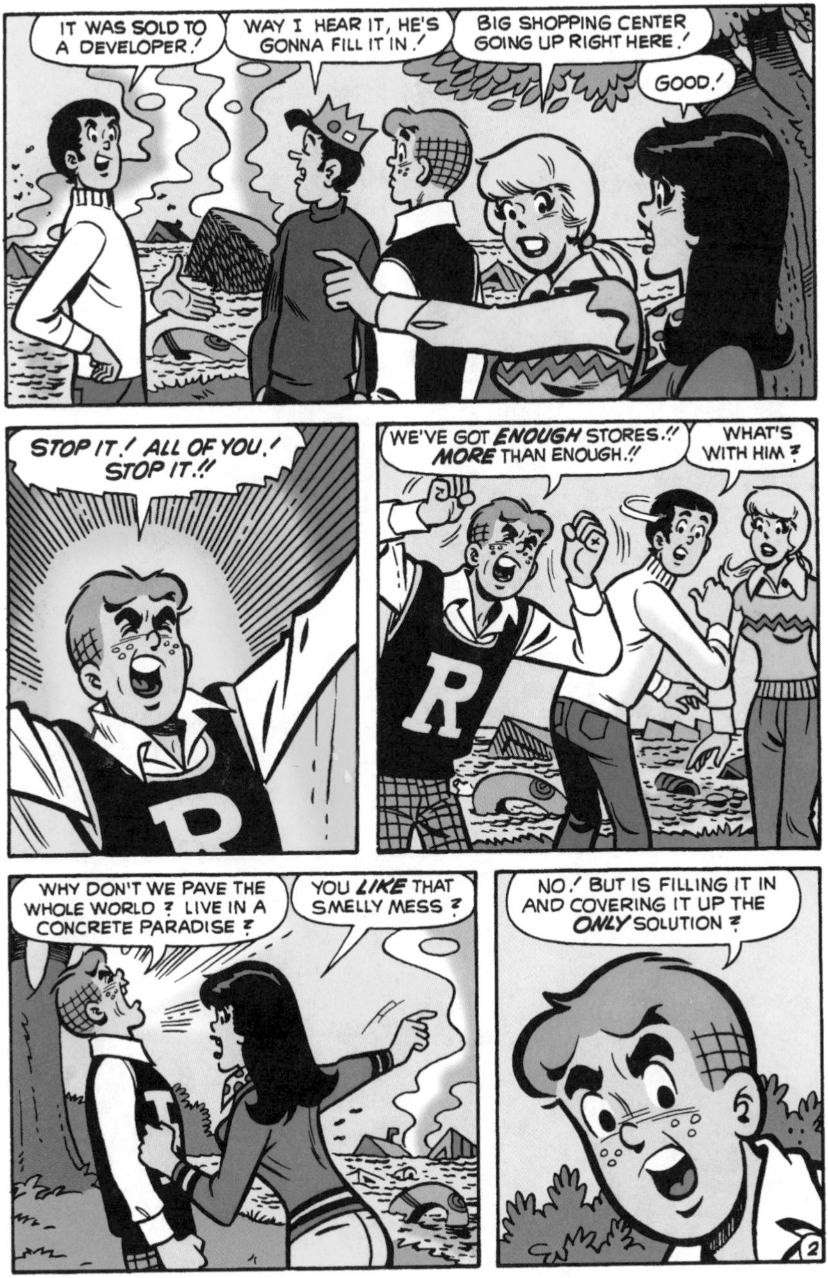
IT WAS SOLD TO A DEVELOPER!
WAY I HEAR IT, HE'S GONNA FILL IT IN!
BIG SHOPPING CENTER GOING UP RIGHT HERE!
GOOD!
STOP IT! ALL OF YOU! STOP IT!!
WE'VE GOT ENOUGH STORES!! MORE THAN ENOUGH!!
WHAT'S WITH HIM?
WHY DON'T WE PAVE THE WHOLE WORLD? LIVE IN A CONCRETE PARADISE?
YOU LIKE THAT SMELLY MESS?
NO! BUT IS FILLING IT IN AND COVERING IT UP THE ONLY SOLUTION?
2

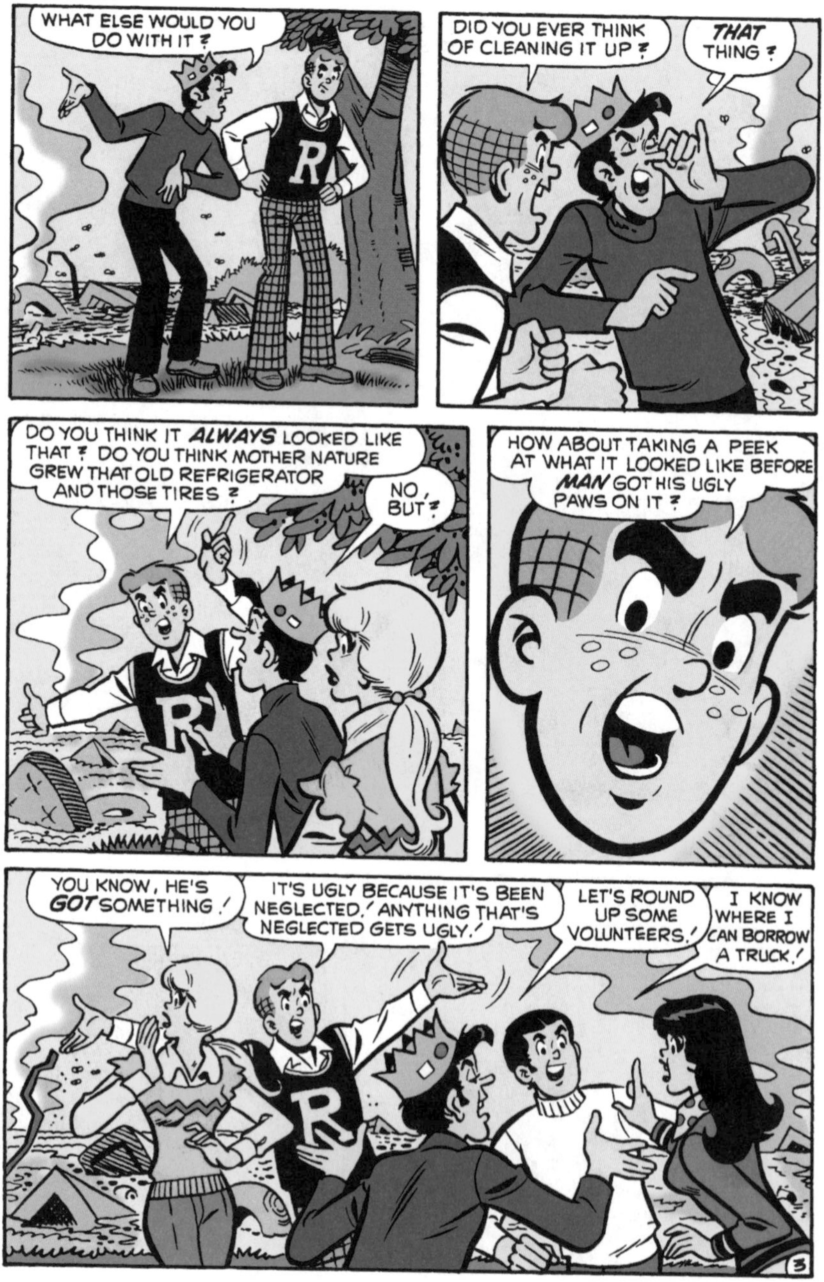
WHAT ELSE WOULD YOU DO WITH IT?
DID YOU EVER THINK OF CLEANING IT UP?
THAT THING?
DO YOU THINK IT ALWAYS LOOKED LIKE THAT? DO YOU THINK MOTHER NATURE GREW THAT OLD REFRIGERATOR AND THOSE TIRES?
NO, BUT?
HOW ABOUT TAKING A PEEK AT WHAT IT LOOKED LIKE BEFORE MAN GOT HIS UGLY PAWS ON IT?
YOU KNOW, HE'S GOT SOMETHING!
IT'S UGLY BECAUSE IT'S BEEN NEGLECTED! ANYTHING THAT'S NEGLECTED GETS UGLY!
LET'S ROUND UP SOME VOLUNTEERS!
I KNOW WHERE I CAN BORROW A TRUCK!
3

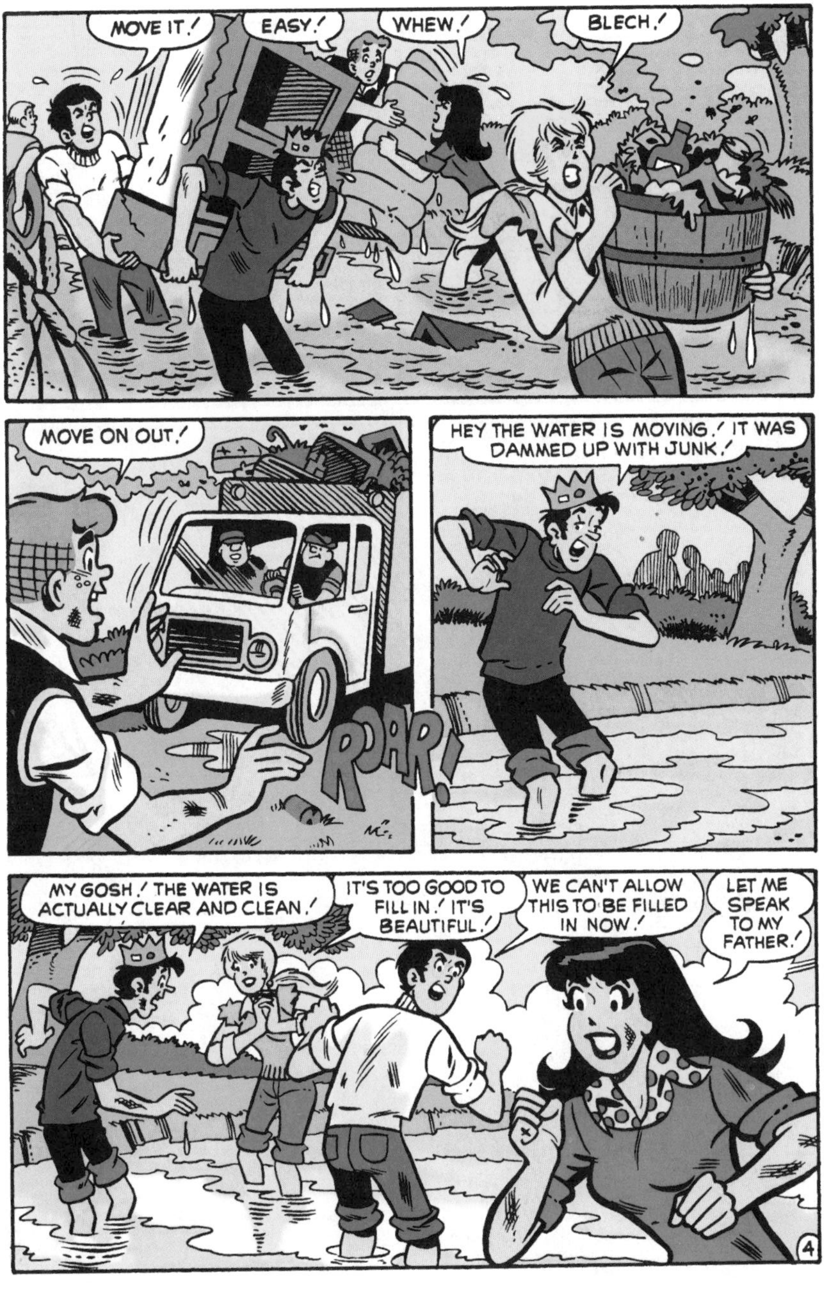
MOVE IT!
EASY!
WHEW!
BLECH!
MOVE ON OUT!
ROAR!
HEY THE WATER IS MOVING! IT WAS DAMMED UP WITH JUNK!
MY GOSH! THE WATER IS ACTUALLY CLEAR AND CLEAN!
IT'S TOO GOOD TO FILL IN! IT'S BEAUTIFUL!
WE CAN'T ALLOW THIS TO BE FILLED IN NOW!
LET ME SPEAK TO MY FATHER!
4

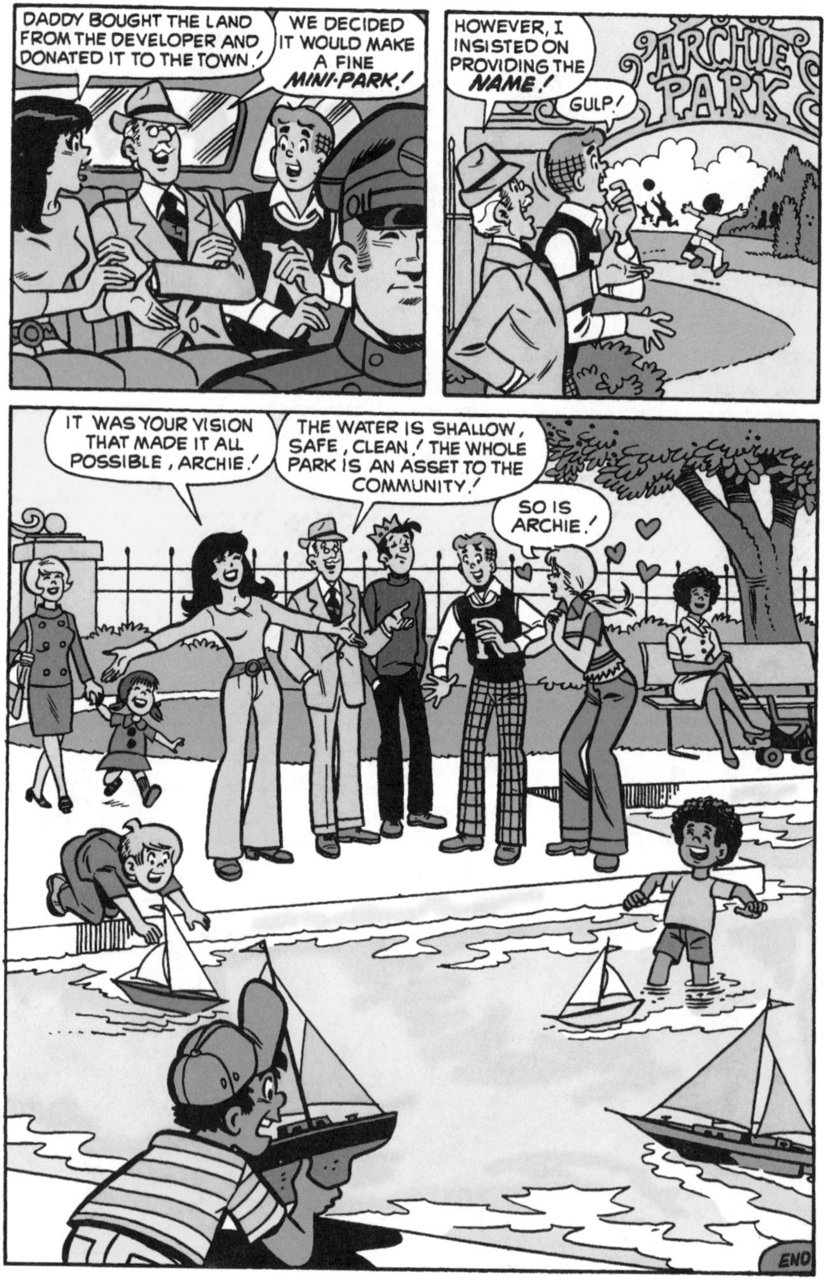
DADDY BOUGHT THE LAND FROM THE DEVELOPER AND DONATED IT TO THE TOWN!
WE DECIDED IT WOULD MAKE A FINE MINI-PARK!
HOWEVER, I INSISTED ON PROVIDING THE NAME!
GULP!
ARCHIE PARK
IT WAS YOUR VISION THAT MADE IT ALL POSSIBLE, ARCHIE!
THE WATER IS SHALLOW, SAFE, CLEAN! THE WHOLE PARK IS AN ASSET TO THE COMMUNITY!
SO IS ARCHIE!
END

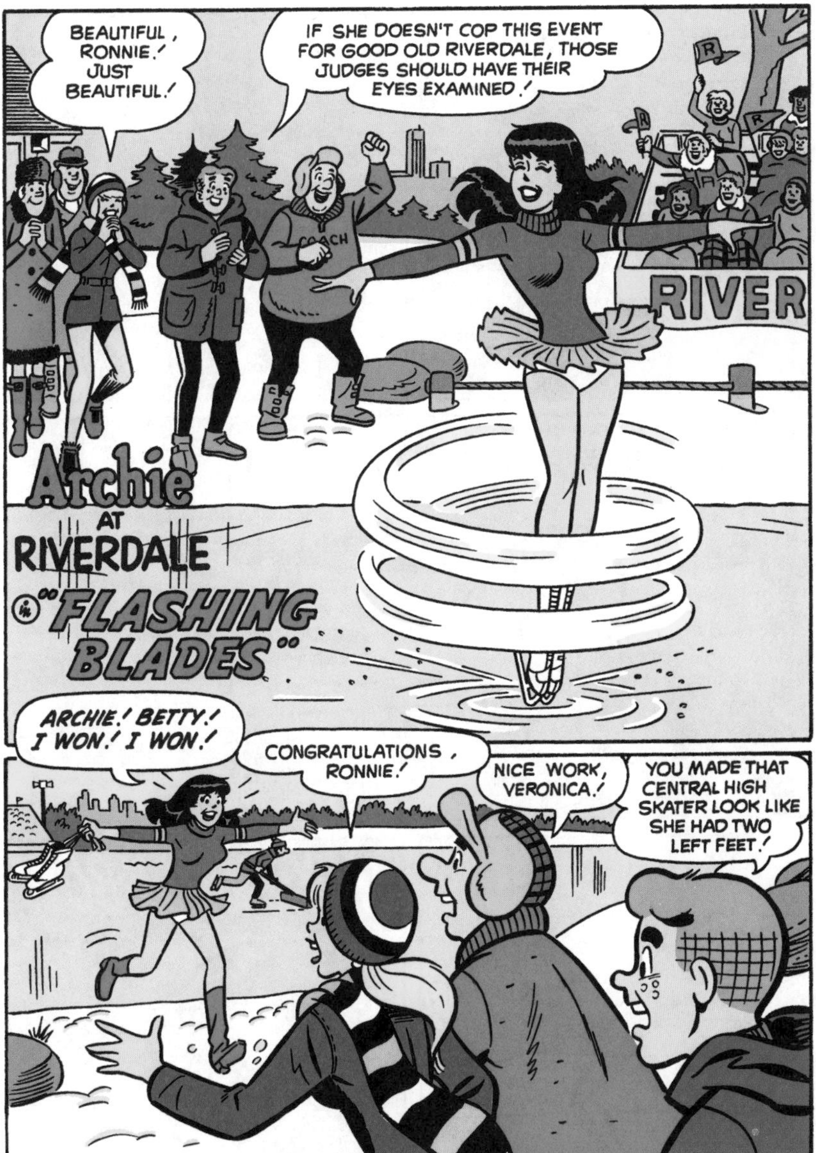
BEAUTIFUL, RONNIE.! JUST BEAUTIFUL.!
IF SHE DOESN'T COP THIS EVENT FOR GOOD OLD RIVERDALE, THOSE JUDGES SHOULD HAVE THEIR EYES EXAMINED.!
RIVER
Archie AT RIVERDALE in "FLASHING BLADES"
ARCHIE.! BETTY.! I WON.! I WON.!
CONGRATULATIONS, RONNIE.!
NICE WORK, VERONICA.!
YOU MADE THAT CENTRAL HIGH SKATER LOOK LIKE SHE HAD TWO LEFT FEET.!

Story: George Gladir Pencils: Dan DeCarlo
Inks: Rudy Lapick Letters: Bill Yoshida Colors: Barry Grossman

Originally printed in ARCHIE AT RIVERDALE HIGH #14, March 1974

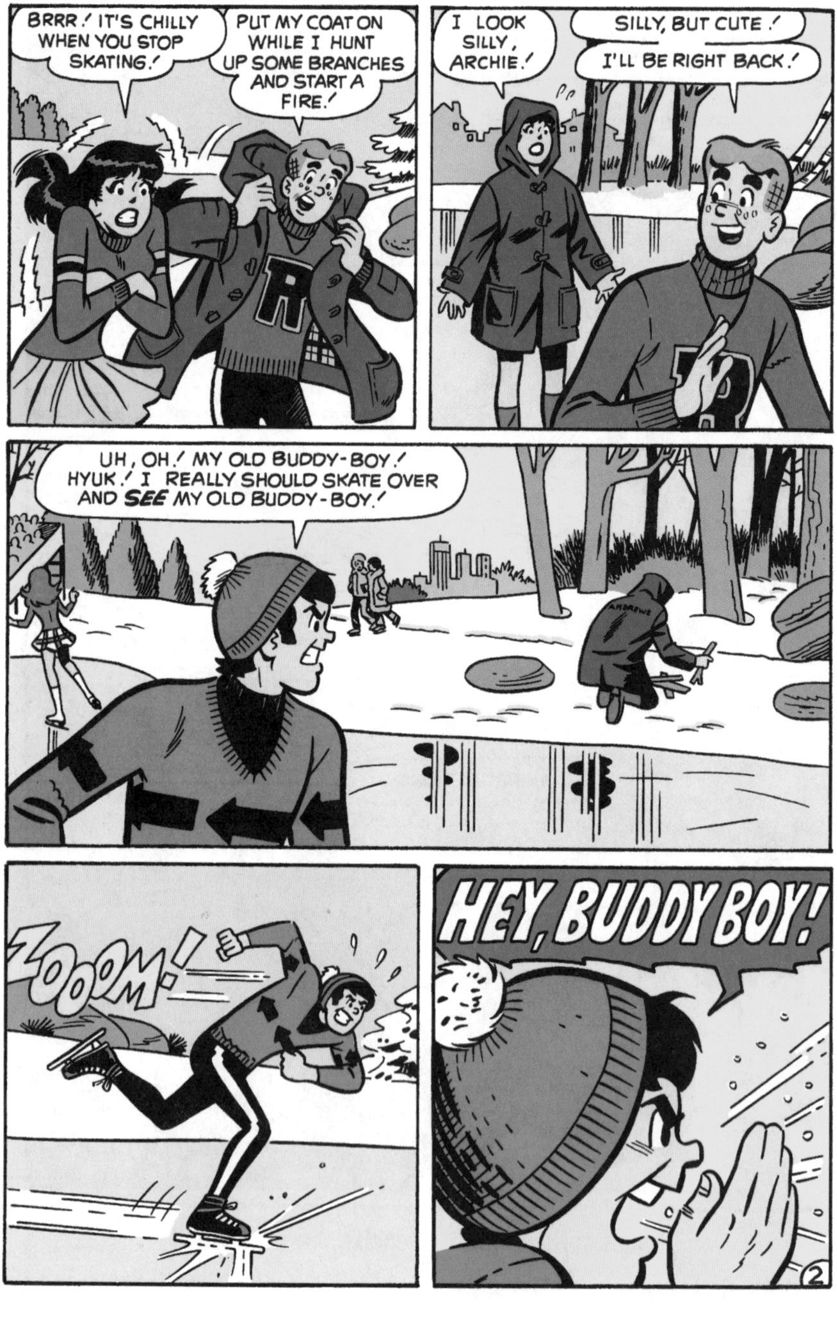
BRRR! IT'S CHILLY WHEN YOU STOP SKATING!
PUT MY COAT ON WHILE I HUNT UP SOME BRANCHES AND START A FIRE!
I LOOK SILLY, ARCHIE!
SILLY, BUT CUTE!
I'LL BE RIGHT BACK!
UH, OH! MY OLD BUDDY-BOY! HYUK! I REALLY SHOULD SKATE OVER AND SEE MY OLD BUDDY-BOY!
ANDREWS
ZOOOM!
HEY, BUDDY BOY!
2

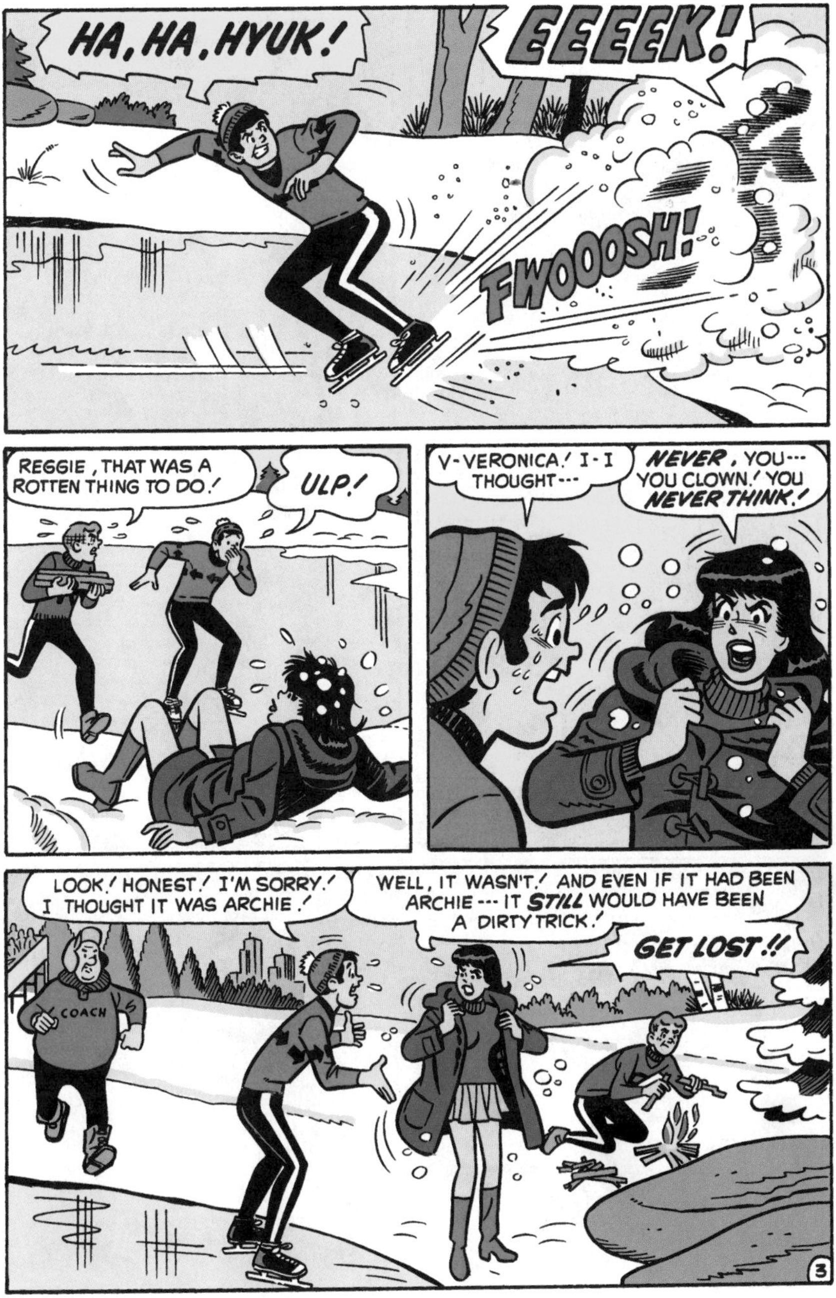
HA, HA, HYUK!
EEEEK!
FWOOOSH!
REGGIE, THAT WAS A ROTTEN THING TO DO!
ULP!
V-VERONICA! I-I THOUGHT---
NEVER, YOU--- YOU CLOWN! YOU NEVER THINK!
LOOK! HONEST! I'M SORRY! I THOUGHT IT WAS ARCHIE!
WELL, IT WASN'T! AND EVEN IF IT HAD BEEN ARCHIE --- IT STILL WOULD HAVE BEEN A DIRTY TRICK!
GET LOST!!
COACH
3

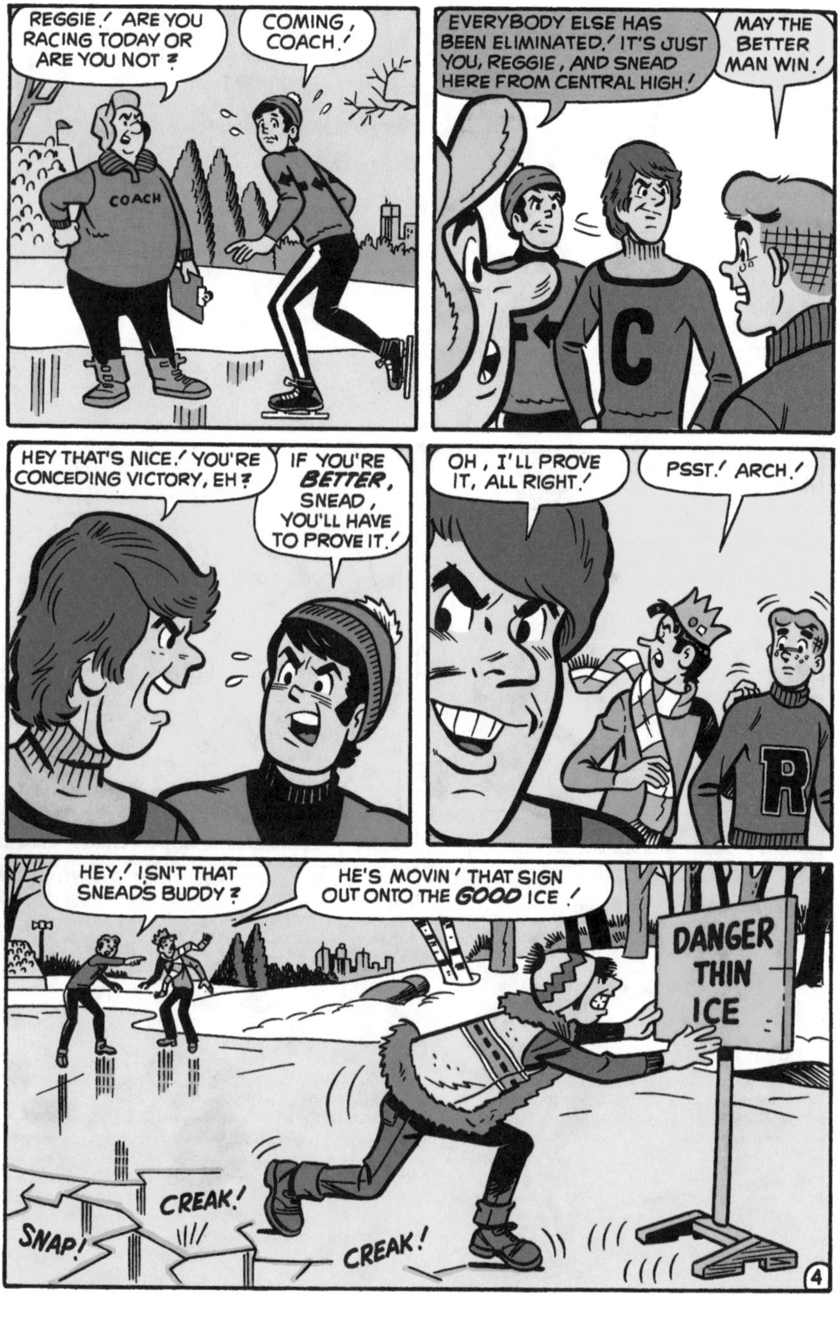
REGGIE! ARE YOU RACING TODAY OR ARE YOU NOT?
COMING, COACH!
COACH
EVERYBODY ELSE HAS BEEN ELIMINATED! IT'S JUST YOU, REGGIE, AND SNEAD HERE FROM CENTRAL HIGH!
MAY THE BETTER MAN WIN!
HEY THAT'S NICE! YOU'RE CONCEDING VICTORY, EH?
IF YOU'RE BETTER, SNEAD, YOU'LL HAVE TO PROVE IT!
OH, I'LL PROVE IT, ALL RIGHT!
PSST! ARCH!
HEY! ISN'T THAT SNEAD'S BUDDY?
HE'S MOVIN' THAT SIGN OUT ONTO THE GOOD ICE!
DANGER THIN ICE
CREAK!
SNAP!
CREAK!
4

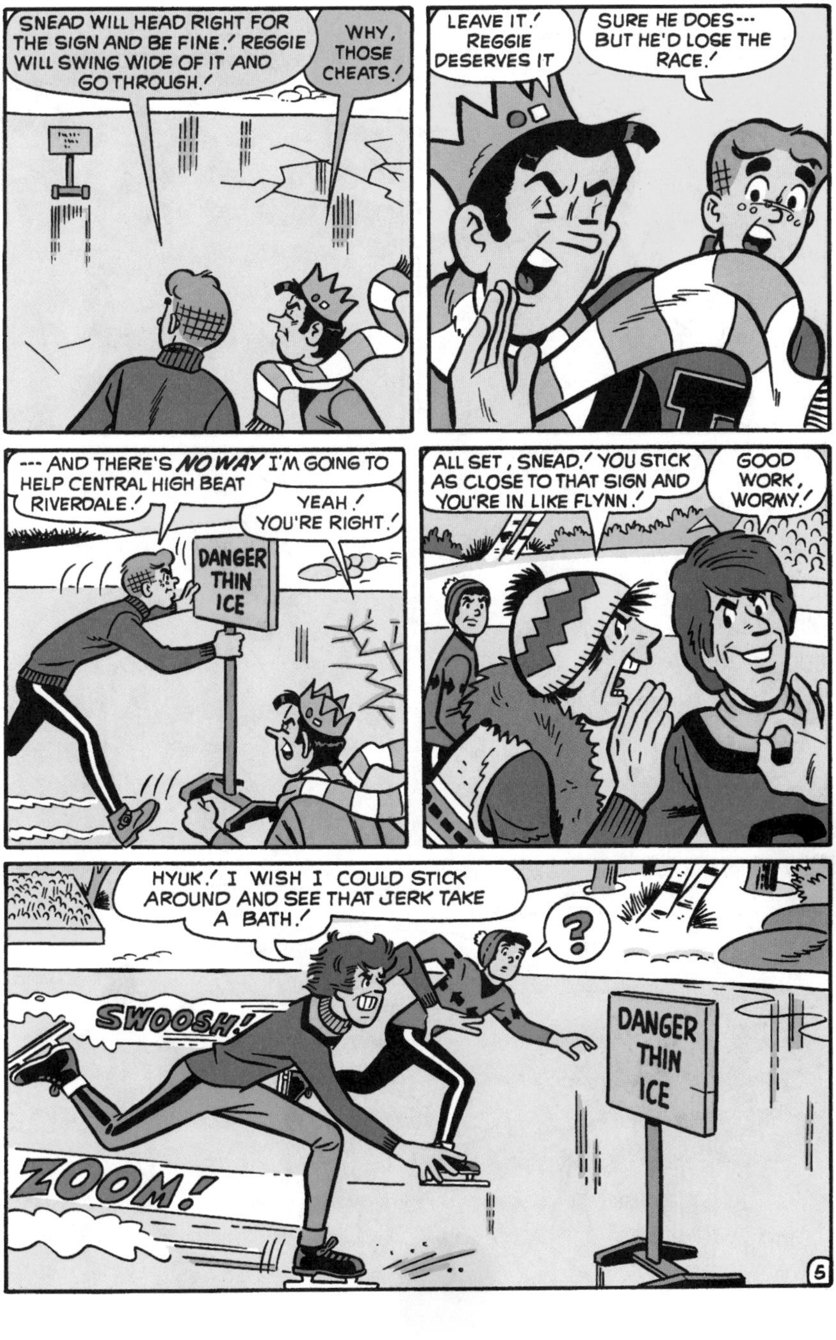
SNEAD WILL HEAD RIGHT FOR THE SIGN AND BE FINE! REGGIE WILL SWING WIDE OF IT AND GO THROUGH!
WHY, THOSE CHEATS!
LEAVE IT! REGGIE DESERVES IT
SURE HE DOES--- BUT HE'D LOSE THE RACE!
--- AND THERE'S NO WAY I'M GOING TO HELP CENTRAL HIGH BEAT RIVERDALE!
YEAH! YOU'RE RIGHT!
DANGER THIN ICE
ALL SET, SNEAD! YOU STICK AS CLOSE TO THAT SIGN AND YOU'RE IN LIKE FLYNN!
GOOD WORK, WORMY!
HYUK! I WISH I COULD STICK AROUND AND SEE THAT JERK TAKE A BATH!
?
SWOOSH!
ZOOM!
DANGER THIN ICE
5

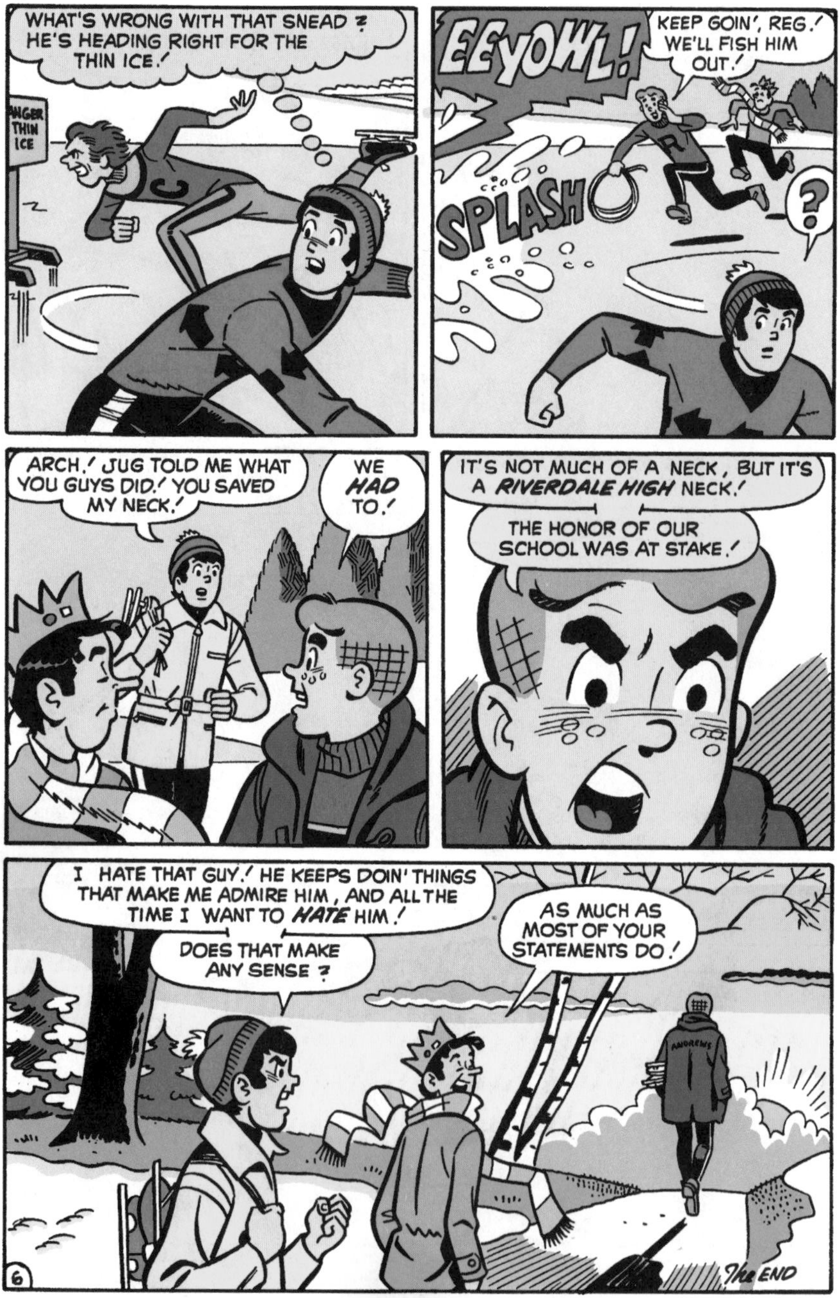
WHAT'S WRONG WITH THAT SNEAD ? HE'S HEADING RIGHT FOR THE THIN ICE!
NGER THIN ICE
EEYOWL!
KEEP GOIN', REG.! WE'LL FISH HIM OUT!
SPLASH
?
ARCH.! JUG TOLD ME WHAT YOU GUYS DID! YOU SAVED MY NECK!
WE HAD TO!
IT'S NOT MUCH OF A NECK, BUT IT'S A RIVERDALE HIGH NECK!
THE HONOR OF OUR SCHOOL WAS AT STAKE!
I HATE THAT GUY! HE KEEPS DOIN' THINGS THAT MAKE ME ADMIRE HIM, AND ALL THE TIME I WANT TO HATE HIM!
DOES THAT MAKE ANY SENSE ?
AS MUCH AS MOST OF YOUR STATEMENTS DO!
6
The END

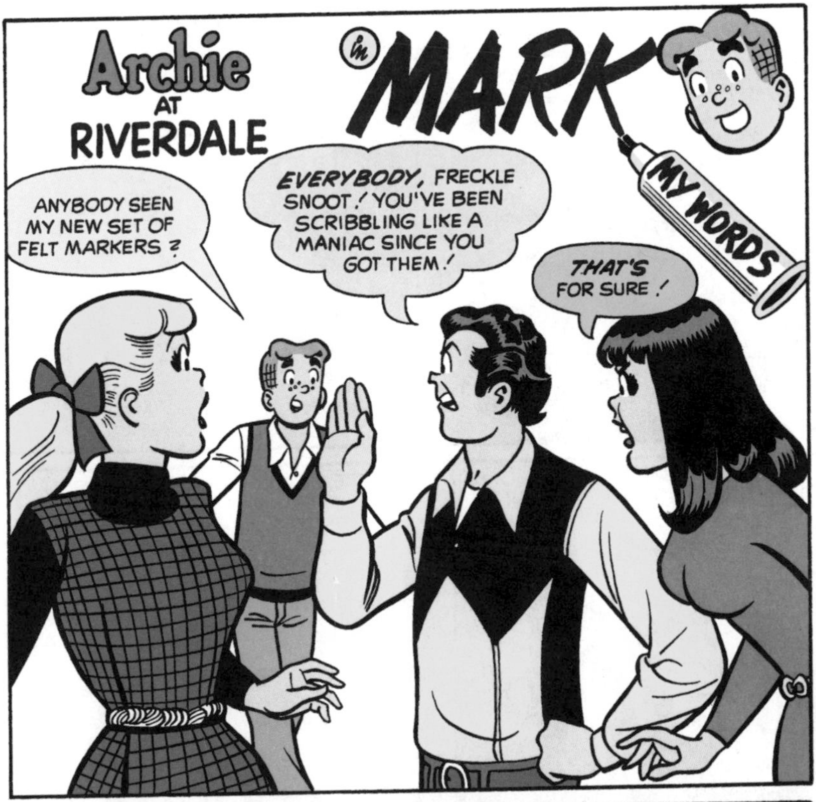
Archie AT RIVERDALE
in MARK MY WORDS
ANYBODY SEEN MY NEW SET OF FELT MARKERS ?
EVERYBODY, FRECKLE SNOOT! YOU'VE BEEN SCRIBBLING LIKE A MANIAC SINCE YOU GOT THEM!
THAT'S FOR SURE!

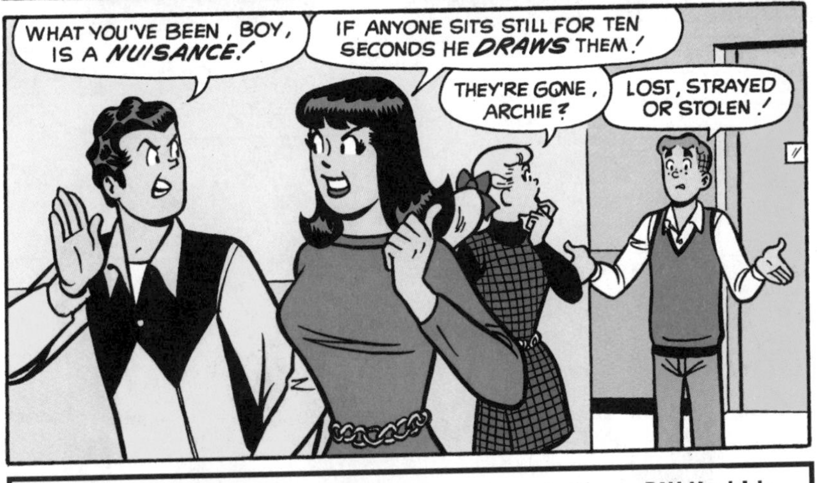
WHAT YOU'VE BEEN, BOY, IS A NUISANCE!
IF ANYONE SITS STILL FOR TEN SECONDS HE DRAWS THEM!
THEY'RE GONE, ARCHIE ?
LOST, STRAYED OR STOLEN!

Story: Frank Doyle Art: Harry Lucey Letters: Bill Yoshida

Originally printed in ARCHIE AT RIVERDALE HIGH #14, February 1974

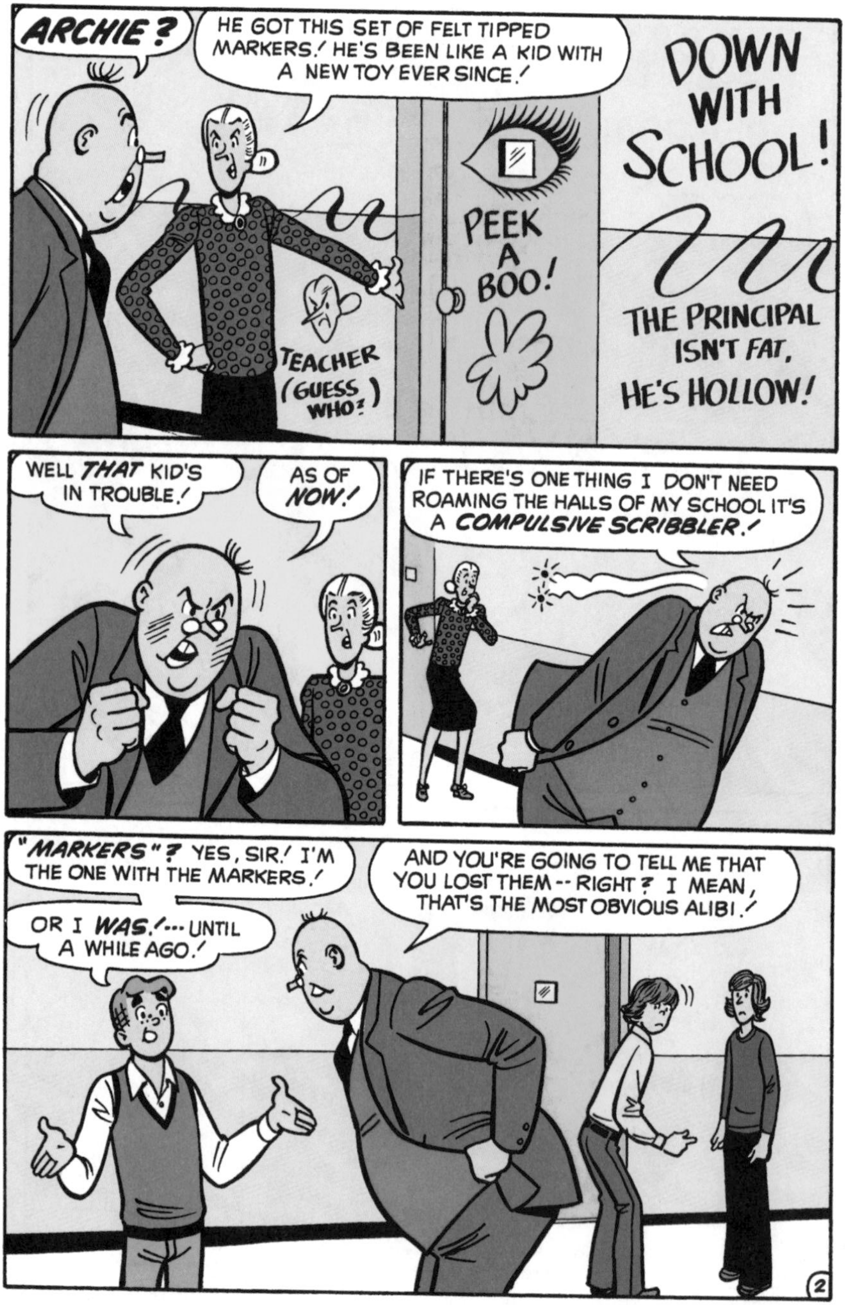
ARCHIE?
HE GOT THIS SET OF FELT TIPPED MARKERS! HE'S BEEN LIKE A KID WITH A NEW TOY EVER SINCE!
DOWN WITH SCHOOL!
PEEK A BOO!
TEACHER (GUESS WHO?)
THE PRINCIPAL ISN'T FAT, HE'S HOLLOW!
WELL THAT KID'S IN TROUBLE!
AS OF NOW!
IF THERE'S ONE THING I DON'T NEED ROAMING THE HALLS OF MY SCHOOL IT'S A COMPULSIVE SCRIBBLER!
"MARKERS"? YES, SIR! I'M THE ONE WITH THE MARKERS!
OR I WAS!... UNTIL A WHILE AGO!
AND YOU'RE GOING TO TELL ME THAT YOU LOST THEM -- RIGHT? I MEAN, THAT'S THE MOST OBVIOUS ALIBI!
2

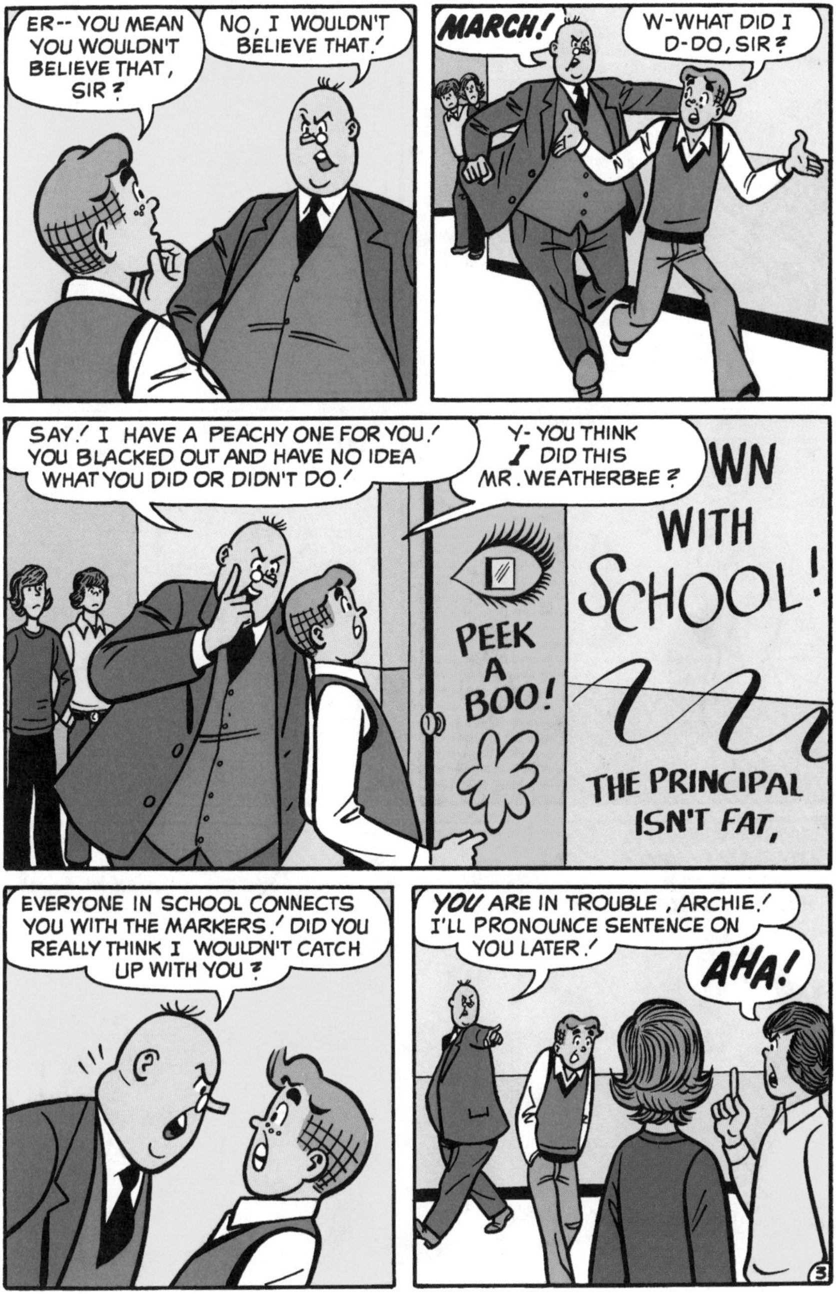
ER-- YOU MEAN YOU WOULDN'T BELIEVE THAT, SIR?
NO, I WOULDN'T BELIEVE THAT!
MARCH!
W-WHAT DID I D-DO, SIR?
SAY! I HAVE A PEACHY ONE FOR YOU! YOU BLACKED OUT AND HAVE NO IDEA WHAT YOU DID OR DIDN'T DO!
Y- YOU THINK I DID THIS MR. WEATHERBEE?
WN
WITH
SCHOOL!
PEEK
A
BOO!
THE PRINCIPAL
ISN'T FAT,
EVERYONE IN SCHOOL CONNECTS YOU WITH THE MARKERS! DID YOU REALLY THINK I WOULDN'T CATCH UP WITH YOU?
YOU ARE IN TROUBLE, ARCHIE! I'LL PRONOUNCE SENTENCE ON YOU LATER!
AHA!
3

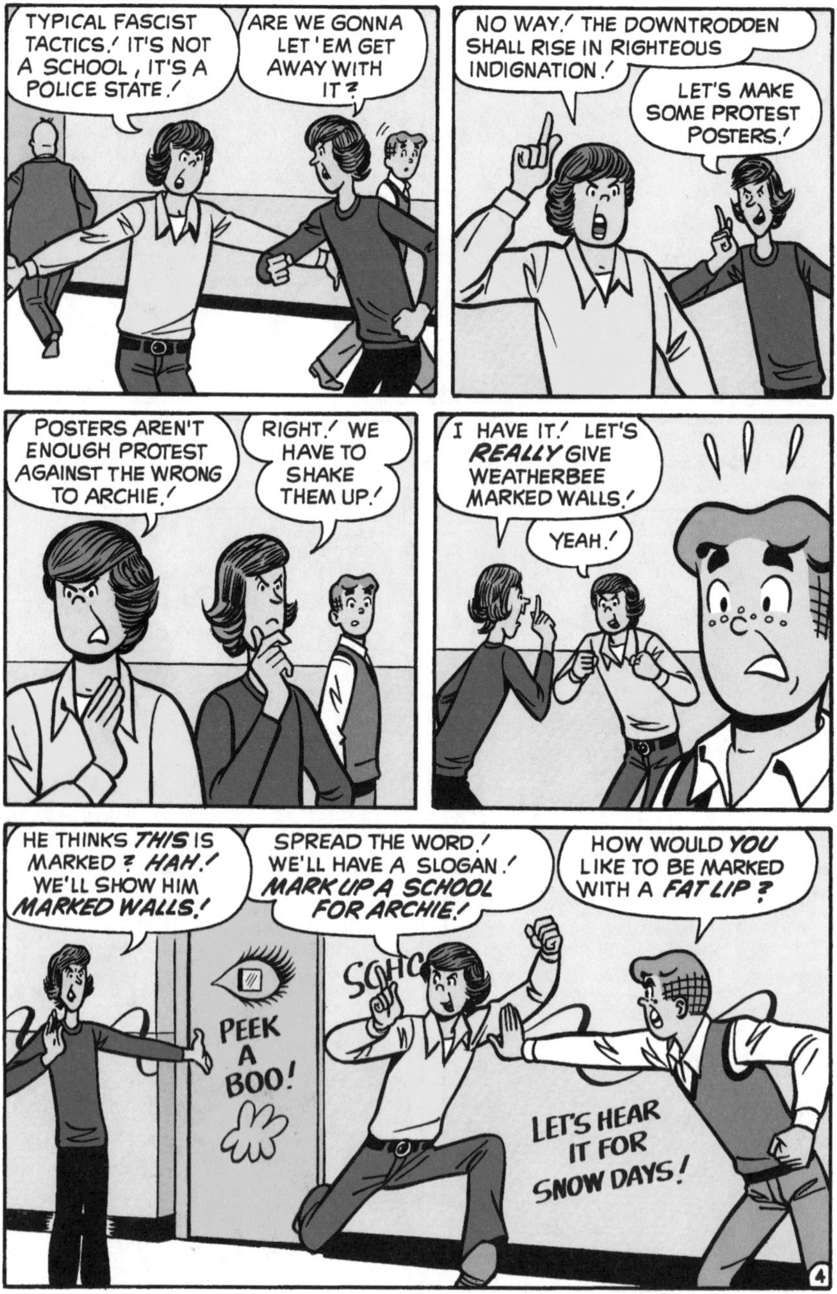
TYPICAL FASCIST TACTICS! IT'S NOT A SCHOOL, IT'S A POLICE STATE!
ARE WE GONNA LET 'EM GET AWAY WITH IT?
NO WAY! THE DOWNTRODDEN SHALL RISE IN RIGHTEOUS INDIGNATION!
LET'S MAKE SOME PROTEST POSTERS!
POSTERS AREN'T ENOUGH PROTEST AGAINST THE WRONG TO ARCHIE!
RIGHT! WE HAVE TO SHAKE THEM UP!
I HAVE IT! LET'S REALLY GIVE WEATHERBEE MARKED WALLS!
YEAH!
HE THINKS THIS IS MARKED? HAH! WE'LL SHOW HIM MARKED WALLS!
SPREAD THE WORD! WE'LL HAVE A SLOGAN! MARK UP A SCHOOL FOR ARCHIE!
HOW WOULD YOU LIKE TO BE MARKED WITH A FAT LIP?
PEEK A BOO!
SCHO
LET'S HEAR IT FOR SNOW DAYS!
4

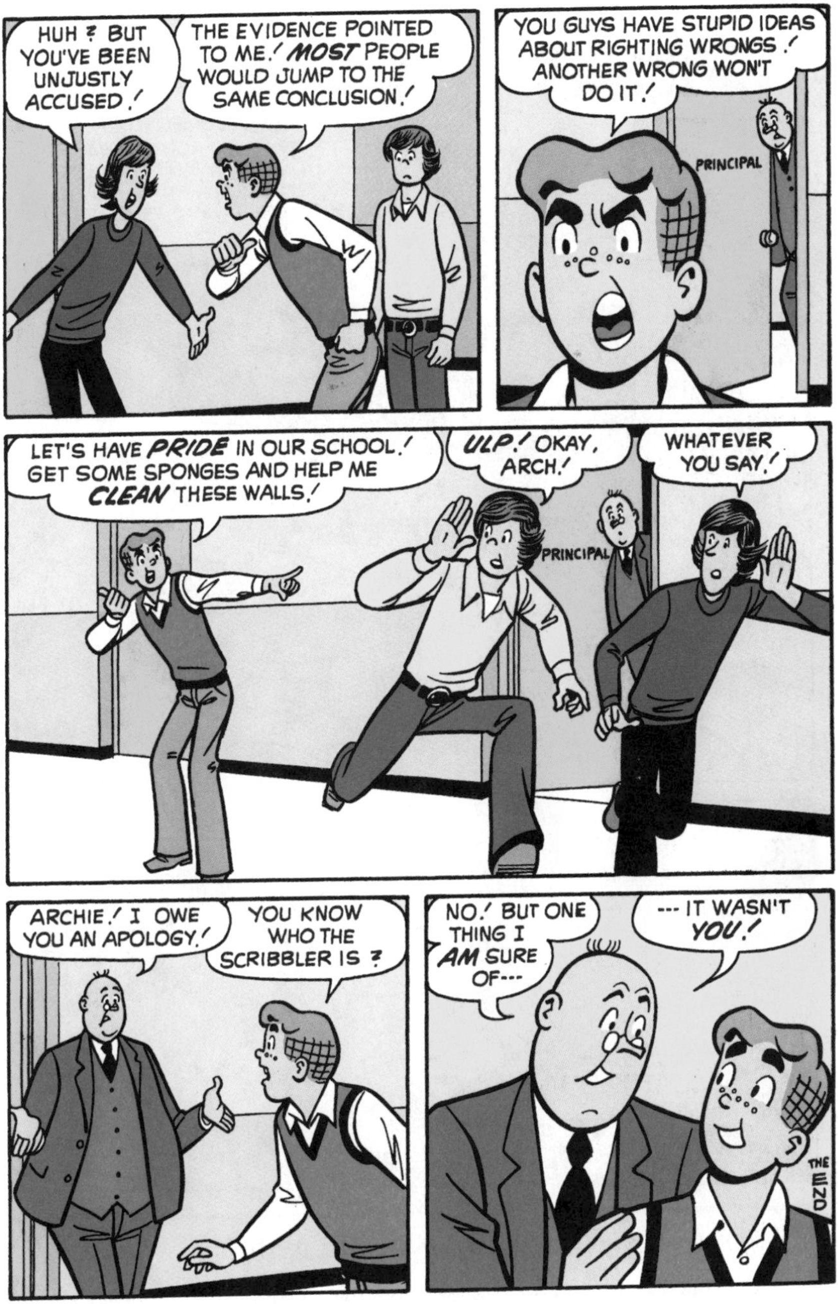
HUH ? BUT YOU'VE BEEN UNJUSTLY ACCUSED !
THE EVIDENCE POINTED TO ME ! MOST PEOPLE WOULD JUMP TO THE SAME CONCLUSION !
YOU GUYS HAVE STUPID IDEAS ABOUT RIGHTING WRONGS ! ANOTHER WRONG WON'T DO IT !
PRINCIPAL
LET'S HAVE PRIDE IN OUR SCHOOL ! GET SOME SPONGES AND HELP ME CLEAN THESE WALLS !
ULP ! OKAY, ARCH !
WHATEVER YOU SAY !
PRINCIPAL
ARCHIE ! I OWE YOU AN APOLOGY !
YOU KNOW WHO THE SCRIBBLER IS ?
NO ! BUT ONE THING I AM SURE OF---
--- IT WASN'T YOU !
THE END

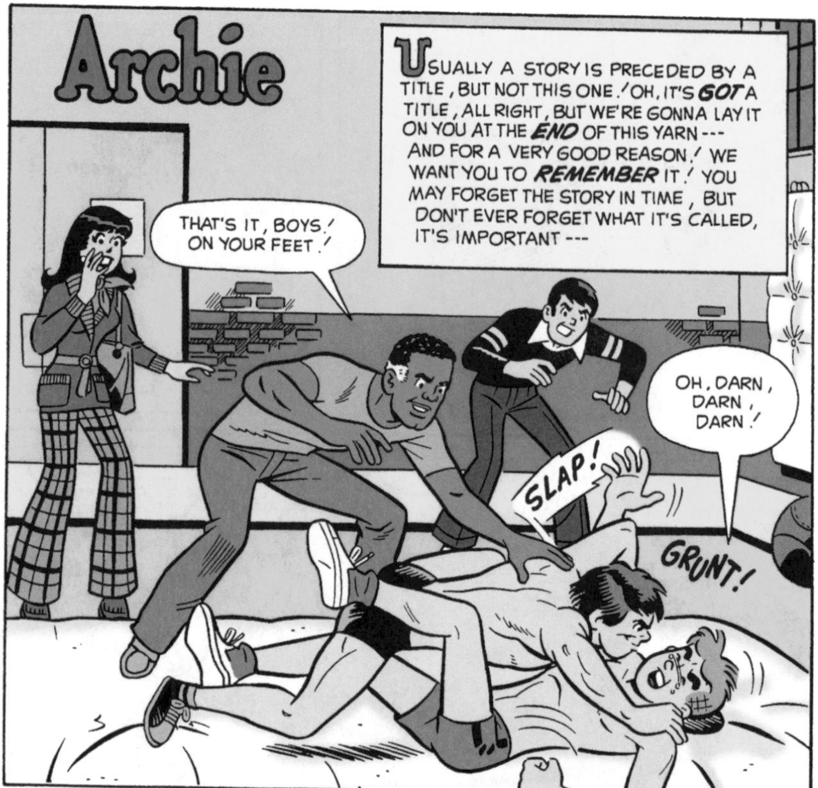
Archie
USUALLY A STORY IS PRECEDED BY A TITLE, BUT NOT THIS ONE.! OH, IT'S GOT A TITLE, ALL RIGHT, BUT WE'RE GONNA LAY IT ON YOU AT THE END OF THIS YARN --- AND FOR A VERY GOOD REASON! WE WANT YOU TO REMEMBER IT! YOU MAY FORGET THE STORY IN TIME, BUT DON'T EVER FORGET WHAT IT'S CALLED, IT'S IMPORTANT ---
THAT'S IT, BOYS! ON YOUR FEET!
OH, DARN, DARN, DARN!
SLAP!
GRUNT!

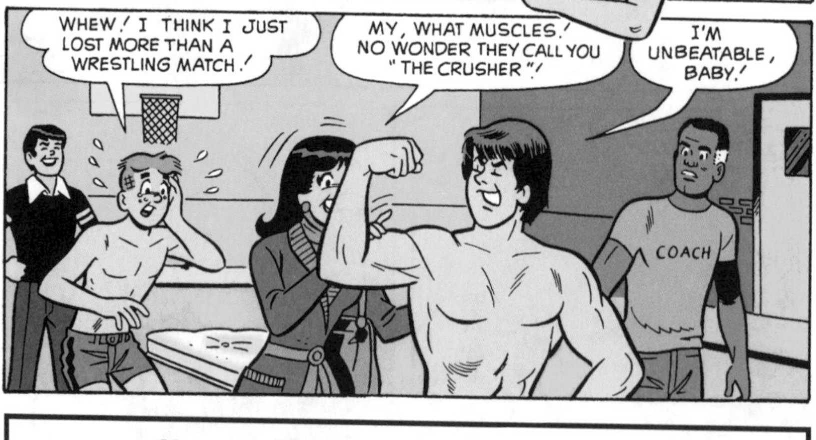
WHEW! I THINK I JUST LOST MORE THAN A WRESTLING MATCH!
MY, WHAT MUSCLES! NO WONDER THEY CALL YOU "THE CRUSHER"!
I'M UNBEATABLE, BABY!
COACH

Story: Frank Doyle Pencils: Dan DeCarlo

Inks: Rudy Lapick Letters: Bill Yoshida Colors: Barry Grossman

Originally printed in ARCHIE AT RIVERDALE HIGH #15, March 1974

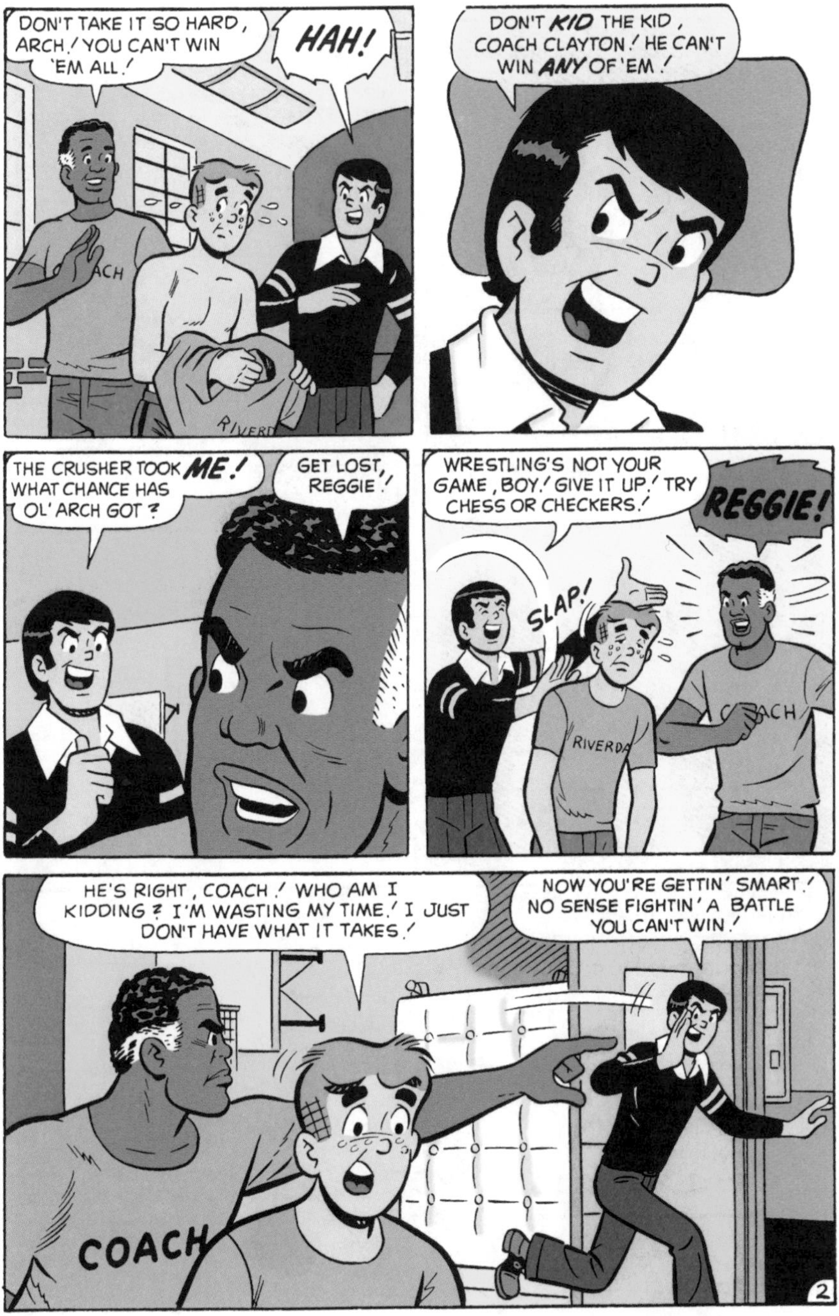
DON'T TAKE IT SO HARD, ARCH! YOU CAN'T WIN 'EM ALL!
HAH!
DON'T KID THE KID, COACH CLAYTON! HE CAN'T WIN ANY OF 'EM!
THE CRUSHER TOOK ME! WHAT CHANCE HAS OL' ARCH GOT?
GET LOST, REGGIE!
WRESTLING'S NOT YOUR GAME, BOY! GIVE IT UP! TRY CHESS OR CHECKERS!
REGGIE!
SLAP!
HE'S RIGHT, COACH! WHO AM I KIDDING? I'M WASTING MY TIME! I JUST DON'T HAVE WHAT IT TAKES!
NOW YOU'RE GETTIN' SMART! NO SENSE FIGHTIN' A BATTLE YOU CAN'T WIN!
2

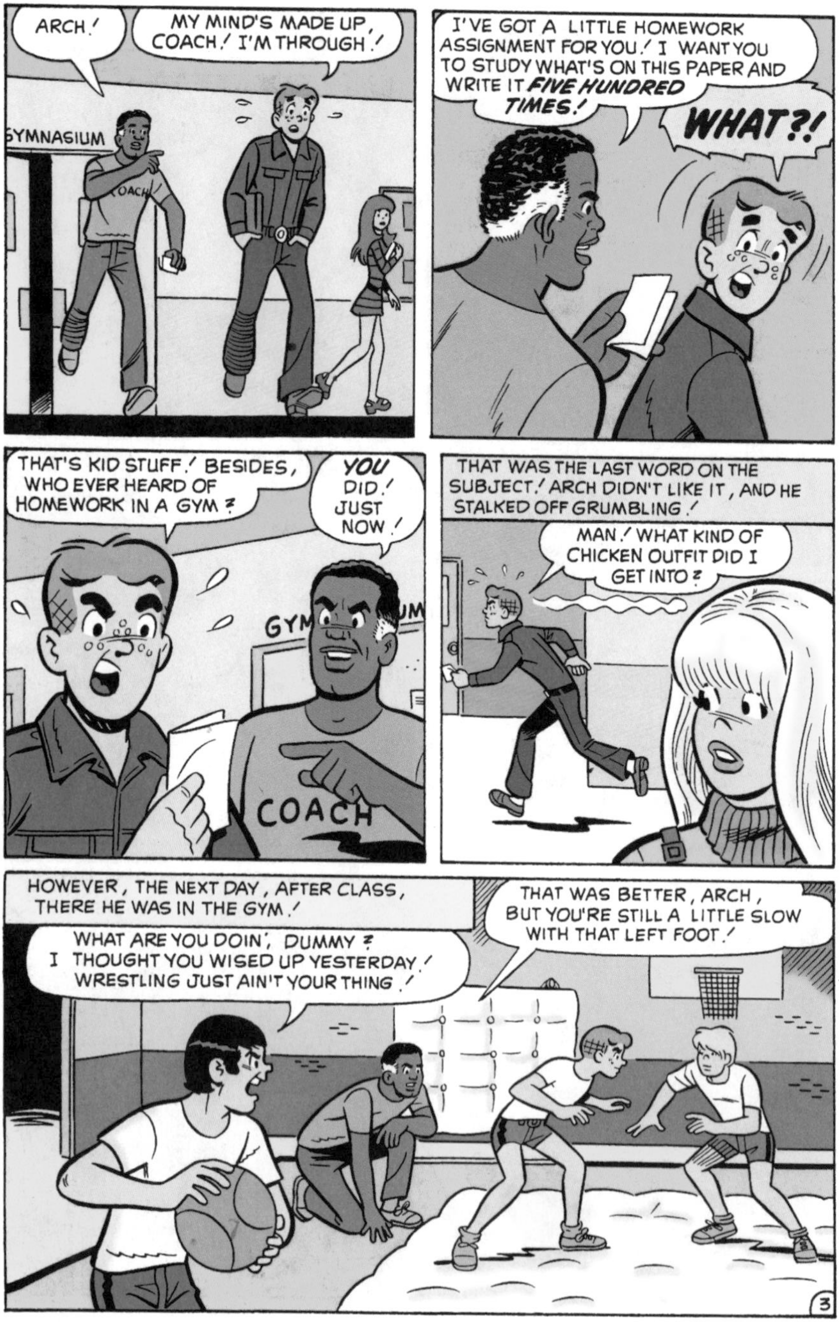
ARCH!
MY MIND'S MADE UP, COACH! I'M THROUGH!
GYMNASIUM
COACH
I'VE GOT A LITTLE HOMEWORK ASSIGNMENT FOR YOU! I WANT YOU TO STUDY WHAT'S ON THIS PAPER AND WRITE IT FIVE HUNDRED TIMES!
WHAT?!
THAT'S KID STUFF! BESIDES, WHO EVER HEARD OF HOMEWORK IN A GYM?
YOU DID! JUST NOW!
COACH
THAT WAS THE LAST WORD ON THE SUBJECT! ARCH DIDN'T LIKE IT, AND HE STALKED OFF GRUMBLING!
MAN! WHAT KIND OF CHICKEN OUTFIT DID I GET INTO?
HOWEVER, THE NEXT DAY, AFTER CLASS, THERE HE WAS IN THE GYM!
WHAT ARE YOU DOIN', DUMMY? I THOUGHT YOU WISED UP YESTERDAY! WRESTLING JUST AIN'T YOUR THING!
THAT WAS BETTER, ARCH, BUT YOU'RE STILL A LITTLE SLOW WITH THAT LEFT FOOT!
3

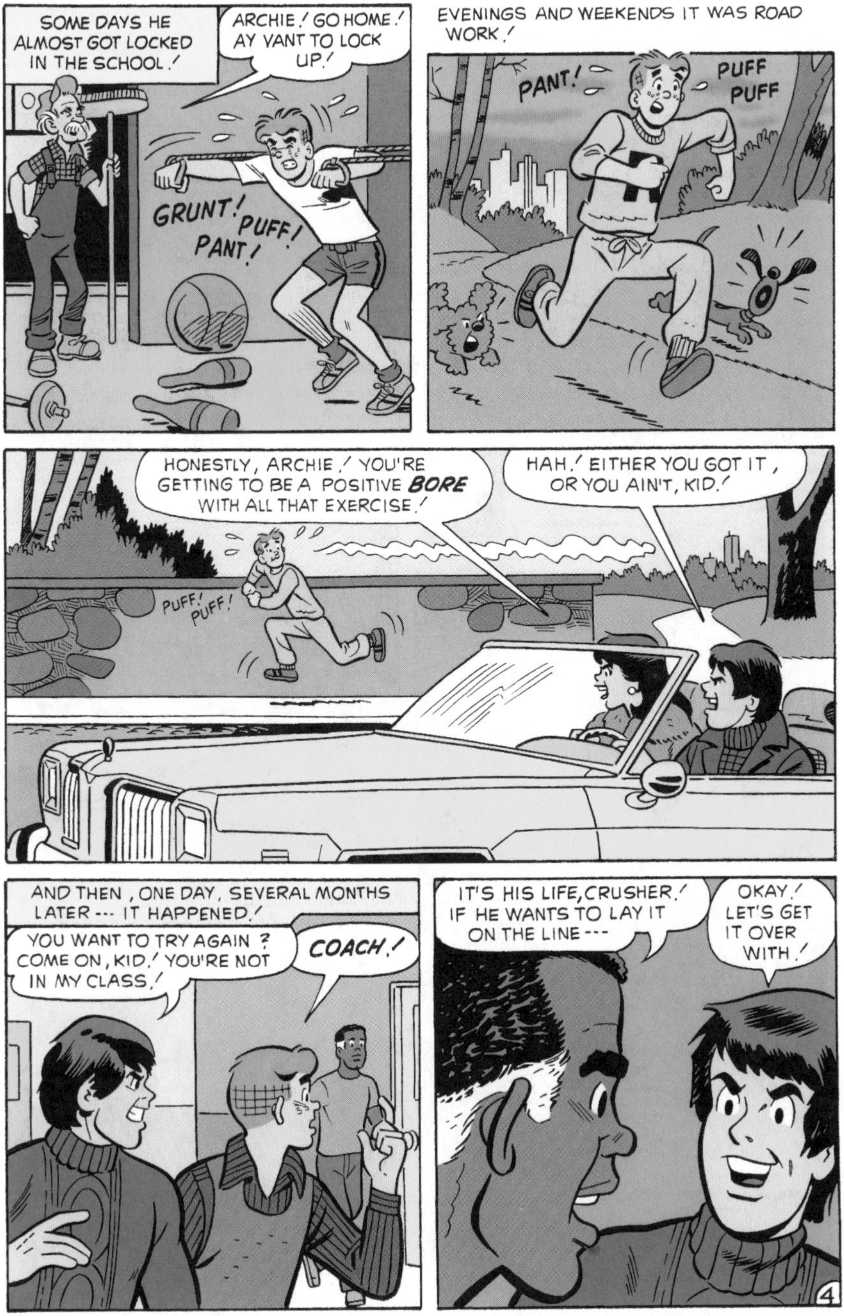
SOME DAYS HE ALMOST GOT LOCKED IN THE SCHOOL!
ARCHIE! GO HOME! AY VANT TO LOCK UP!
GRUNT! PUFF! PANT!
EVENINGS AND WEEKENDS IT WAS ROAD WORK!
PANT!
PUFF PUFF
HONESTLY, ARCHIE! YOU'RE GETTING TO BE A POSITIVE BORE WITH ALL THAT EXERCISE!
HAH! EITHER YOU GOT IT, OR YOU AIN'T, KID!
PUFF! PUFF!
AND THEN, ONE DAY, SEVERAL MONTHS LATER --- IT HAPPENED!
YOU WANT TO TRY AGAIN? COME ON, KID! YOU'RE NOT IN MY CLASS!
COACH!
IT'S HIS LIFE, CRUSHER! IF HE WANTS TO LAY IT ON THE LINE ---
OKAY! LET'S GET IT OVER WITH!
4

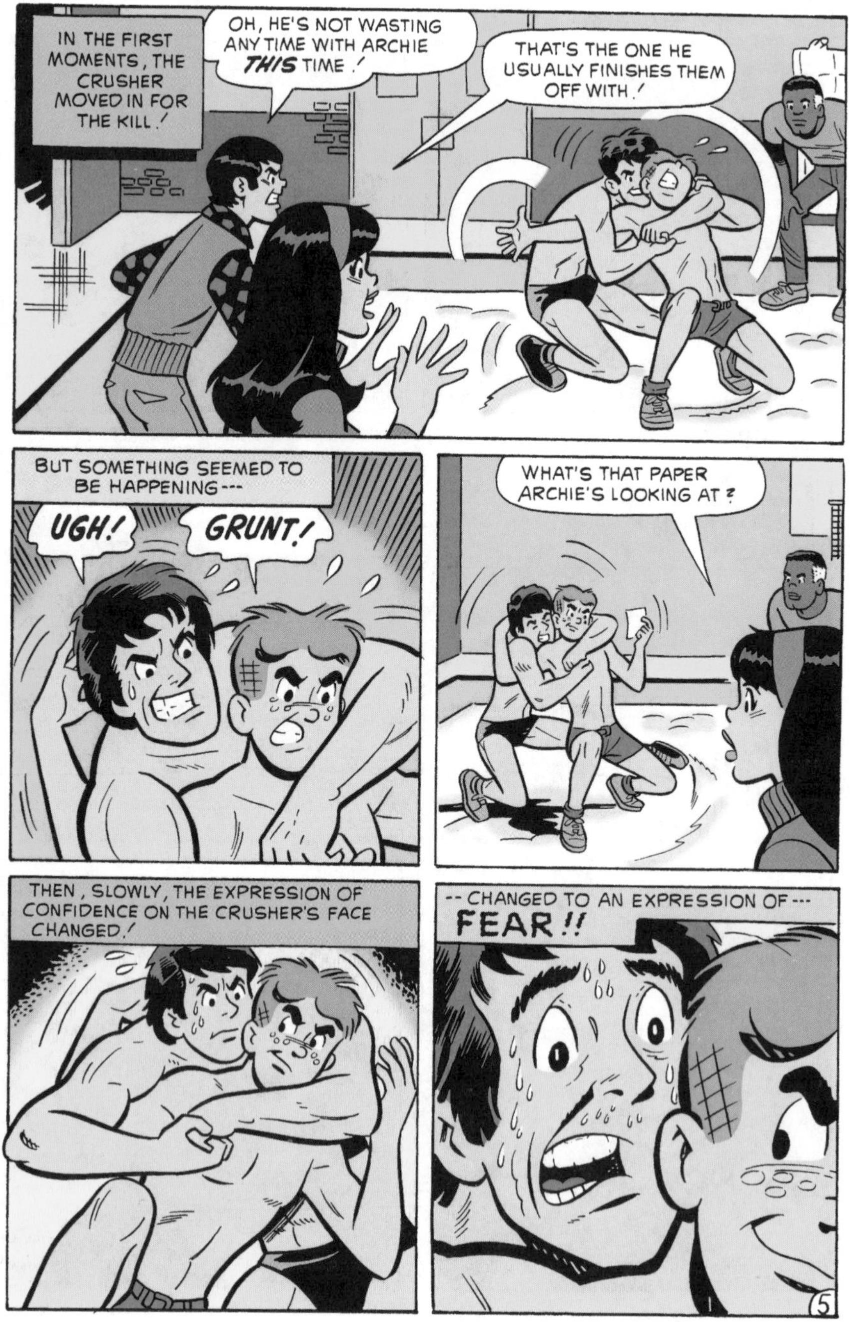
IN THE FIRST MOMENTS, THE CRUSHER MOVED IN FOR THE KILL!
OH, HE'S NOT WASTING ANY TIME WITH ARCHIE THIS TIME!
THAT'S THE ONE HE USUALLY FINISHES THEM OFF WITH!
BUT SOMETHING SEEMED TO BE HAPPENING---
UGH!
GRUNT!
WHAT'S THAT PAPER ARCHIE'S LOOKING AT?
THEN, SLOWLY, THE EXPRESSION OF CONFIDENCE ON THE CRUSHER'S FACE CHANGED!
--CHANGED TO AN EXPRESSION OF--- FEAR!!
5

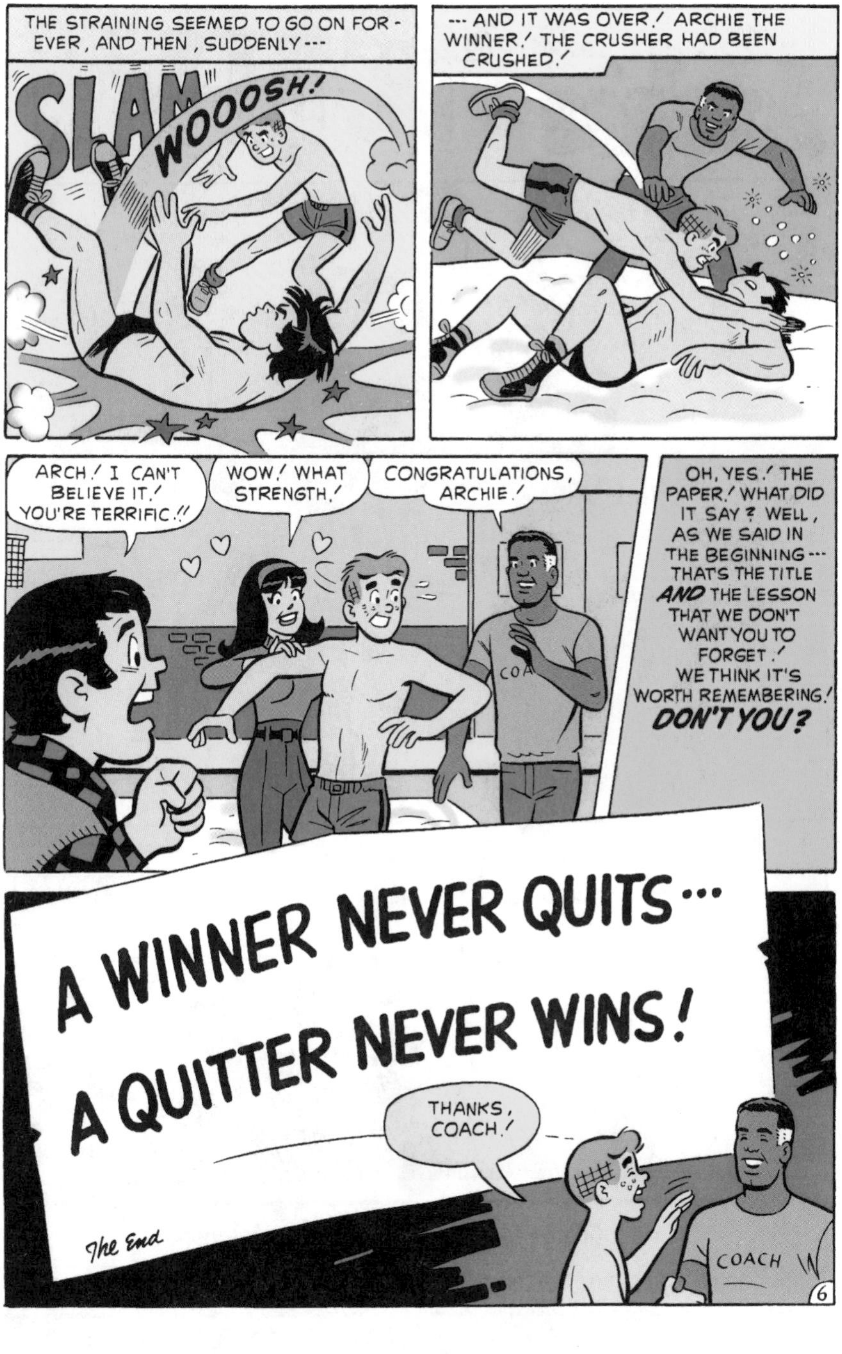
THE STRAINING SEEMED TO GO ON FOREVER, AND THEN, SUDDENLY---
SLAM
WOOOSH!
--- AND IT WAS OVER! ARCHIE THE WINNER! THE CRUSHER HAD BEEN CRUSHED!
ARCH! I CAN'T BELIEVE IT! YOU'RE TERRIFIC!!
WOW! WHAT STRENGTH!
CONGRATULATIONS, ARCHIE!
COA
OH, YES! THE PAPER! WHAT DID IT SAY? WELL, AS WE SAID IN THE BEGINNING--- THAT'S THE TITLE AND THE LESSON THAT WE DON'T WANT YOU TO FORGET! WE THINK IT'S WORTH REMEMBERING! DON'T YOU?
A WINNER NEVER QUITS...
A QUITTER NEVER WINS!
THANKS, COACH!
COACH
The End
6

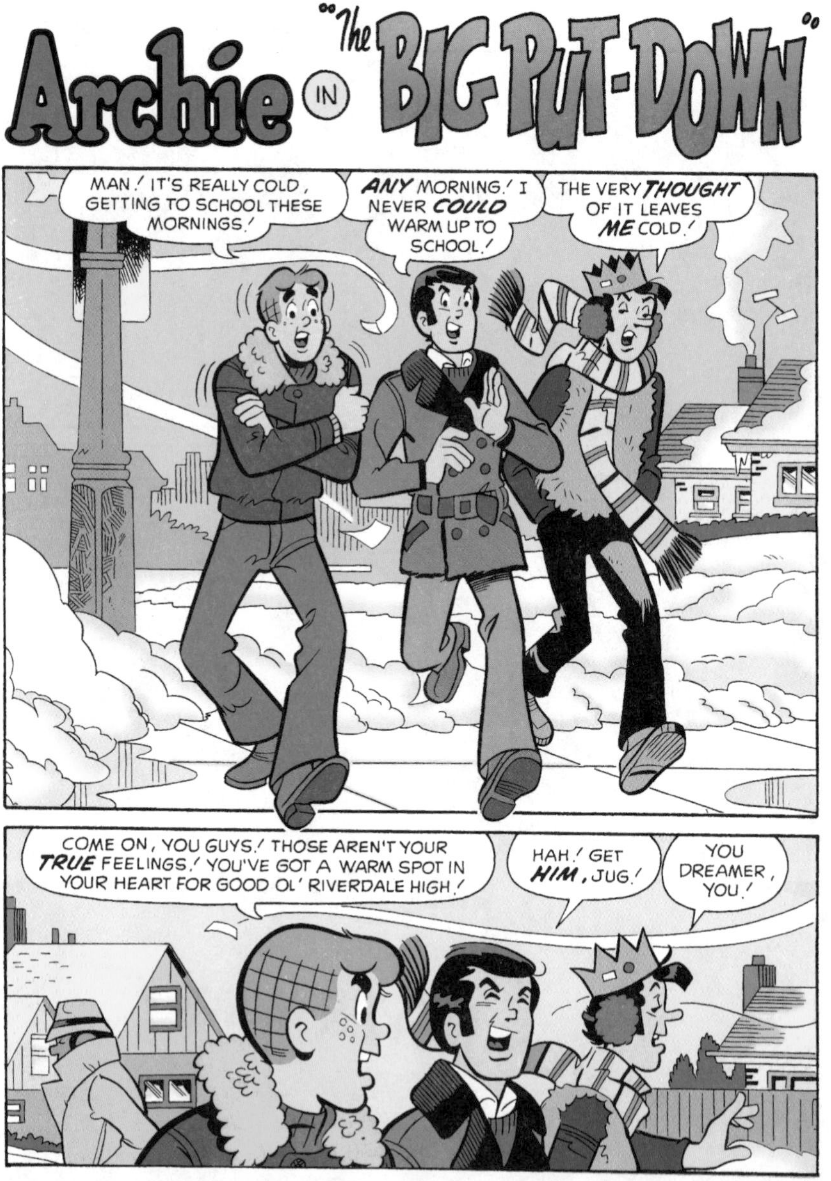
Archie in "The BIG PUT-DOWN"
MAN! IT'S REALLY COLD, GETTING TO SCHOOL THESE MORNINGS!
ANY MORNING! I NEVER COULD WARM UP TO SCHOOL!
THE VERY THOUGHT OF IT LEAVES ME COLD!
COME ON, YOU GUYS! THOSE AREN'T YOUR TRUE FEELINGS! YOU'VE GOT A WARM SPOT IN YOUR HEART FOR GOOD OL' RIVERDALE HIGH!
HAH! GET HIM, JUG!
YOU DREAMER, YOU!

Story: George Gladir Pencils: Stan Goldberg

Inks: Jon D'Agostino Letters: Bill Yoshida Colors: Barry Grossman

Originally printed in ARCHIE AT RIVERDALE HIGH #13, February 1974

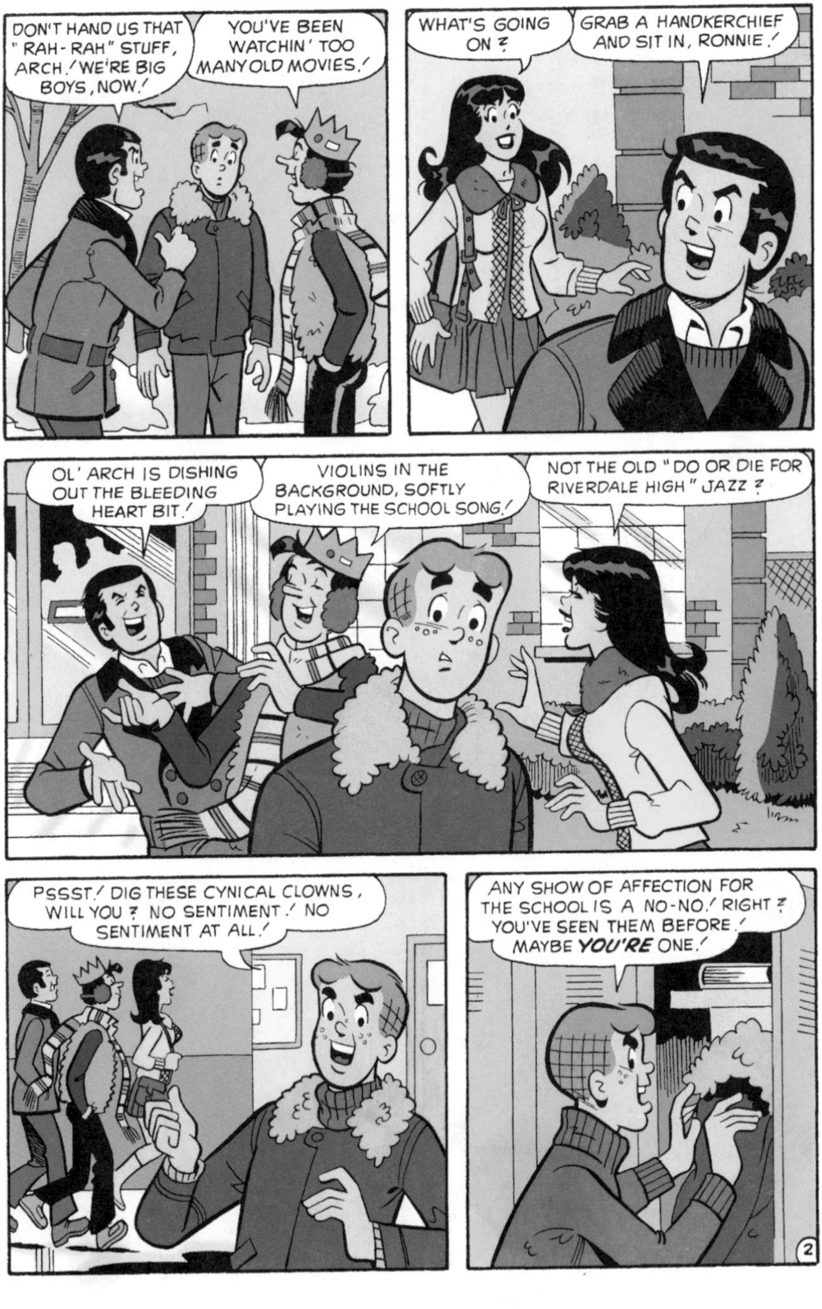
DON'T HAND US THAT "RAH-RAH" STUFF, ARCH.! WE'RE BIG BOYS, NOW.!
YOU'VE BEEN WATCHIN' TOO MANY OLD MOVIES.!
WHAT'S GOING ON ?
GRAB A HANDKERCHIEF AND SIT IN, RONNIE.!
OL' ARCH IS DISHING OUT THE BLEEDING HEART BIT.!
VIOLINS IN THE BACKGROUND, SOFTLY PLAYING THE SCHOOL SONG.!
NOT THE OLD "DO OR DIE FOR RIVERDALE HIGH" JAZZ ?
PSSST.! DIG THESE CYNICAL CLOWNS, WILL YOU ? NO SENTIMENT.! NO SENTIMENT AT ALL.!
ANY SHOW OF AFFECTION FOR THE SCHOOL IS A NO-NO.! RIGHT ? YOU'VE SEEN THEM BEFORE.! MAYBE ***YOU'RE*** ONE.!
2

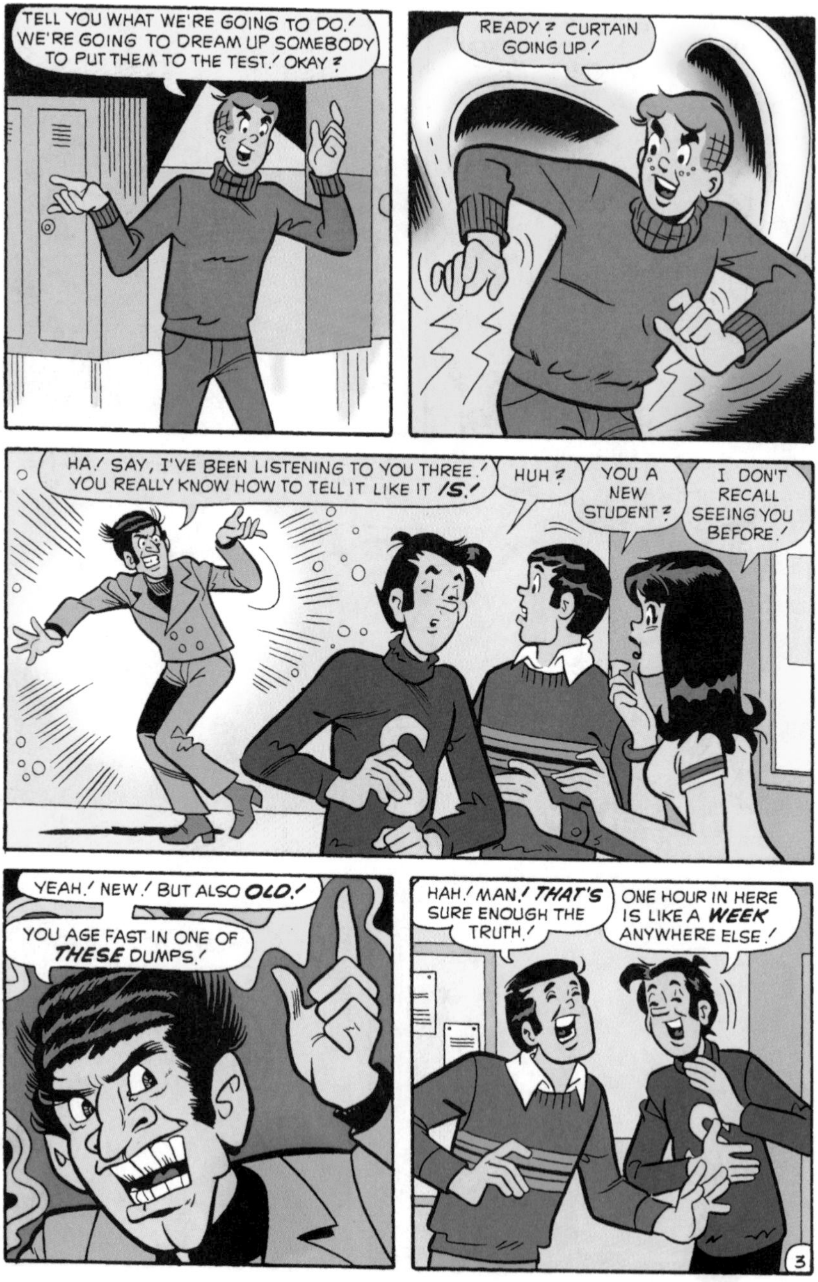
TELL YOU WHAT WE'RE GOING TO DO! WE'RE GOING TO DREAM UP SOMEBODY TO PUT THEM TO THE TEST! OKAY?
READY? CURTAIN GOING UP!
HA! SAY, I'VE BEEN LISTENING TO YOU THREE! YOU REALLY KNOW HOW TO TELL IT LIKE IT *IS!*
HUH?
YOU A NEW STUDENT?
I DON'T RECALL SEEING YOU BEFORE!
YEAH! NEW! BUT ALSO **OLD!**
YOU AGE FAST IN ONE OF **THESE** DUMPS!
HAH! MAN! **THAT'S** SURE ENOUGH THE TRUTH!
ONE HOUR IN HERE IS LIKE A **WEEK** ANYWHERE ELSE!
3

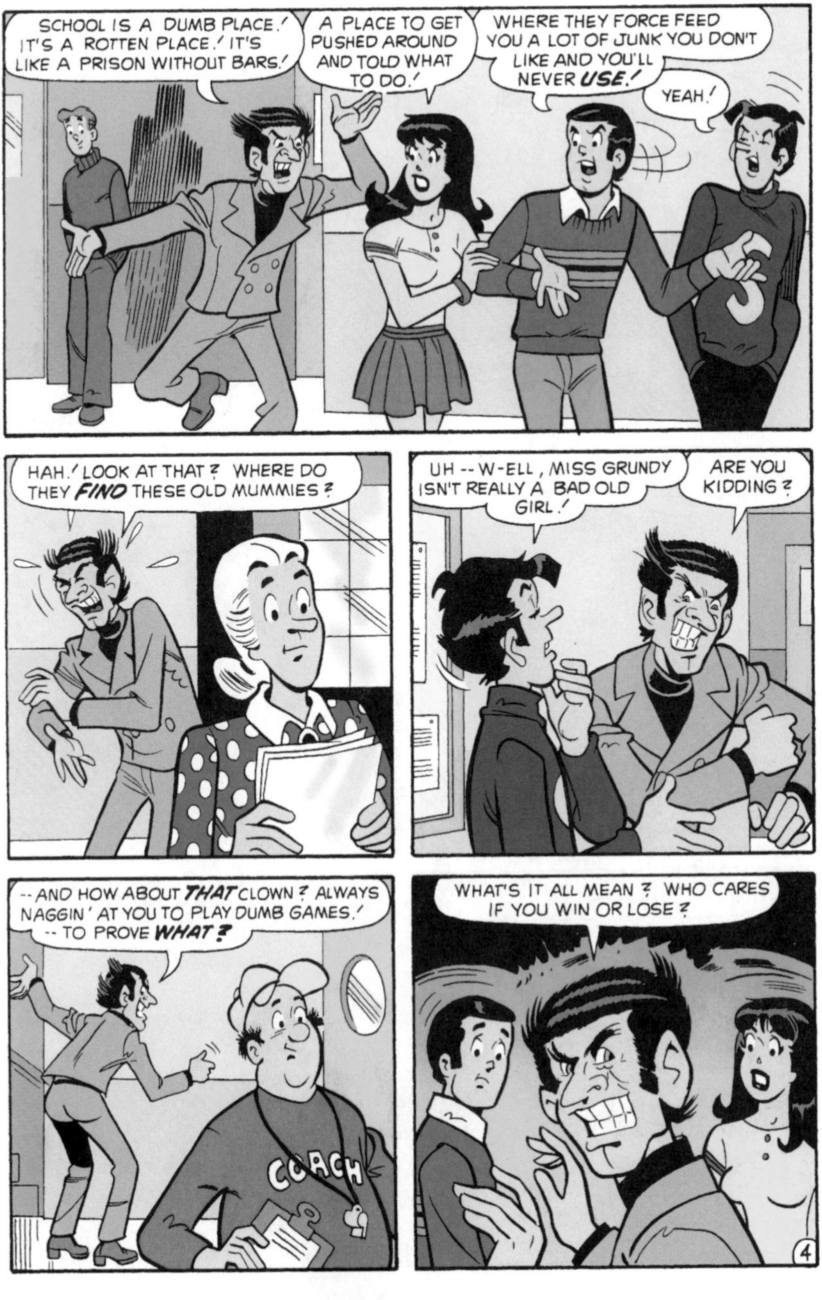
SCHOOL IS A DUMB PLACE! IT'S A ROTTEN PLACE! IT'S LIKE A PRISON WITHOUT BARS!
A PLACE TO GET PUSHED AROUND AND TOLD WHAT TO DO!
WHERE THEY FORCE FEED YOU A LOT OF JUNK YOU DON'T LIKE AND YOU'LL NEVER USE!
YEAH!
HAH! LOOK AT THAT? WHERE DO THEY FIND THESE OLD MUMMIES?
UH -- W-ELL, MISS GRUNDY ISN'T REALLY A BAD OLD GIRL!
ARE YOU KIDDING?
4
-- AND HOW ABOUT THAT CLOWN? ALWAYS NAGGIN' AT YOU TO PLAY DUMB GAMES! -- TO PROVE WHAT?
COACH
WHAT'S IT ALL MEAN? WHO CARES IF YOU WIN OR LOSE?
4

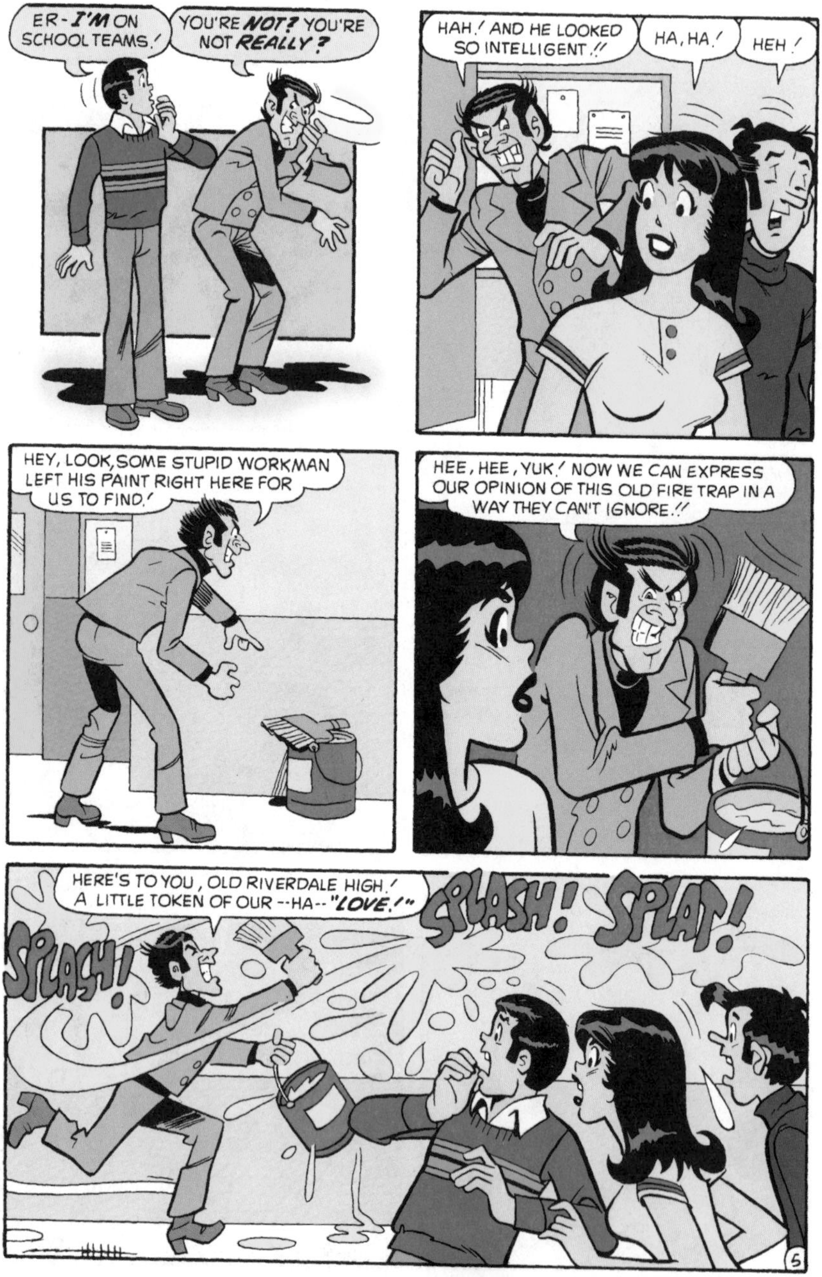
ER-I'M ON SCHOOL TEAMS!
YOU'RE NOT? YOU'RE NOT REALLY?
HAH! AND HE LOOKED SO INTELLIGENT!!
HA, HA!
HEH!
HEY, LOOK, SOME STUPID WORKMAN LEFT HIS PAINT RIGHT HERE FOR US TO FIND!
HEE, HEE, YUK! NOW WE CAN EXPRESS OUR OPINION OF THIS OLD FIRE TRAP IN A WAY THEY CAN'T IGNORE!!
HERE'S TO YOU, OLD RIVERDALE HIGH! A LITTLE TOKEN OF OUR --HA-- "LOVE!"
SPLASH!
SPLASH!
SPLAT!
5

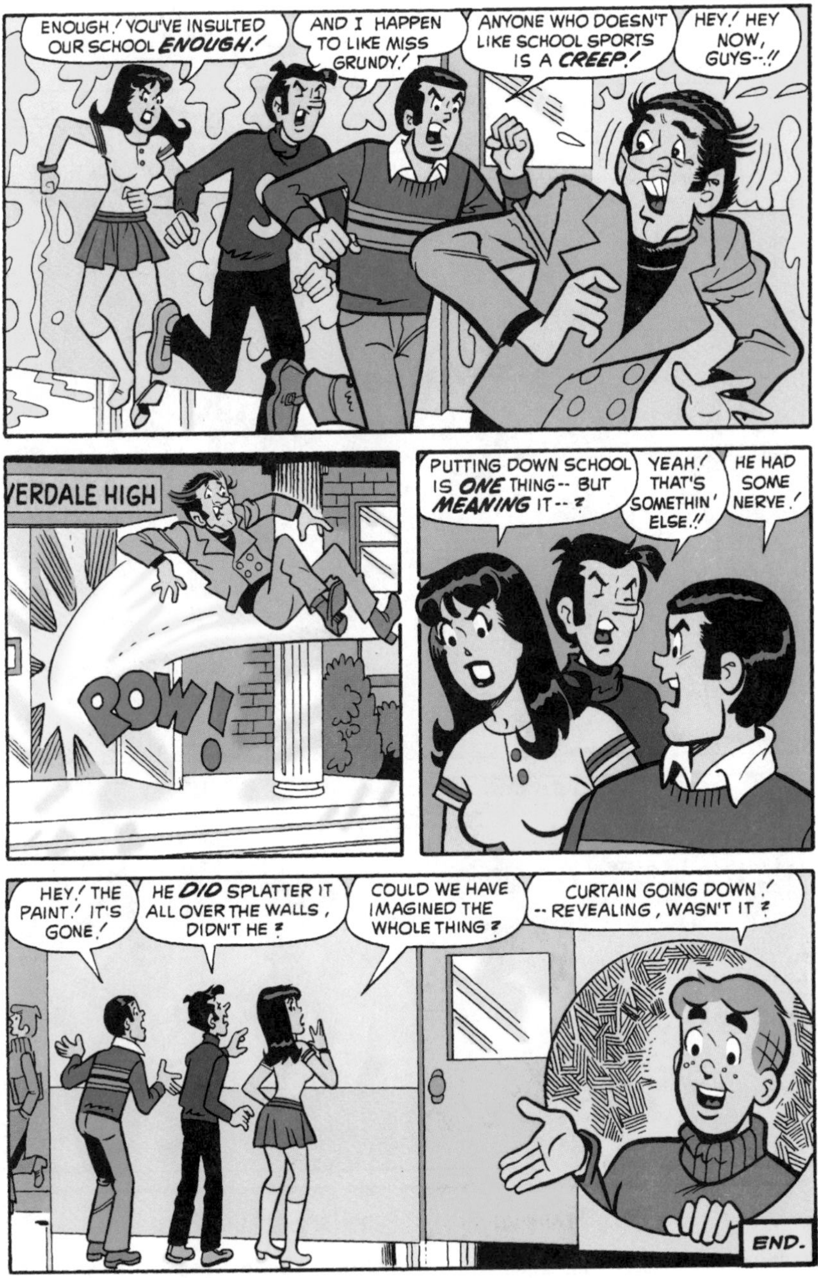
ENOUGH! YOU'VE INSULTED OUR SCHOOL ENOUGH!
AND I HAPPEN TO LIKE MISS GRUNDY!
ANYONE WHO DOESN'T LIKE SCHOOL SPORTS IS A CREEP!
HEY! HEY NOW, GUYS--!!
VERDALE HIGH
POW!
PUTTING DOWN SCHOOL IS ONE THING-- BUT MEANING IT--?
YEAH! THAT'S SOMETHIN' ELSE!!
HE HAD SOME NERVE!
HEY! THE PAINT! IT'S GONE!
HE DID SPLATTER IT ALL OVER THE WALLS, DIDN'T HE?
COULD WE HAVE IMAGINED THE WHOLE THING?
CURTAIN GOING DOWN! -- REVEALING, WASN'T IT?
END.

Archie at RIVERDALE in "The RIVAL"

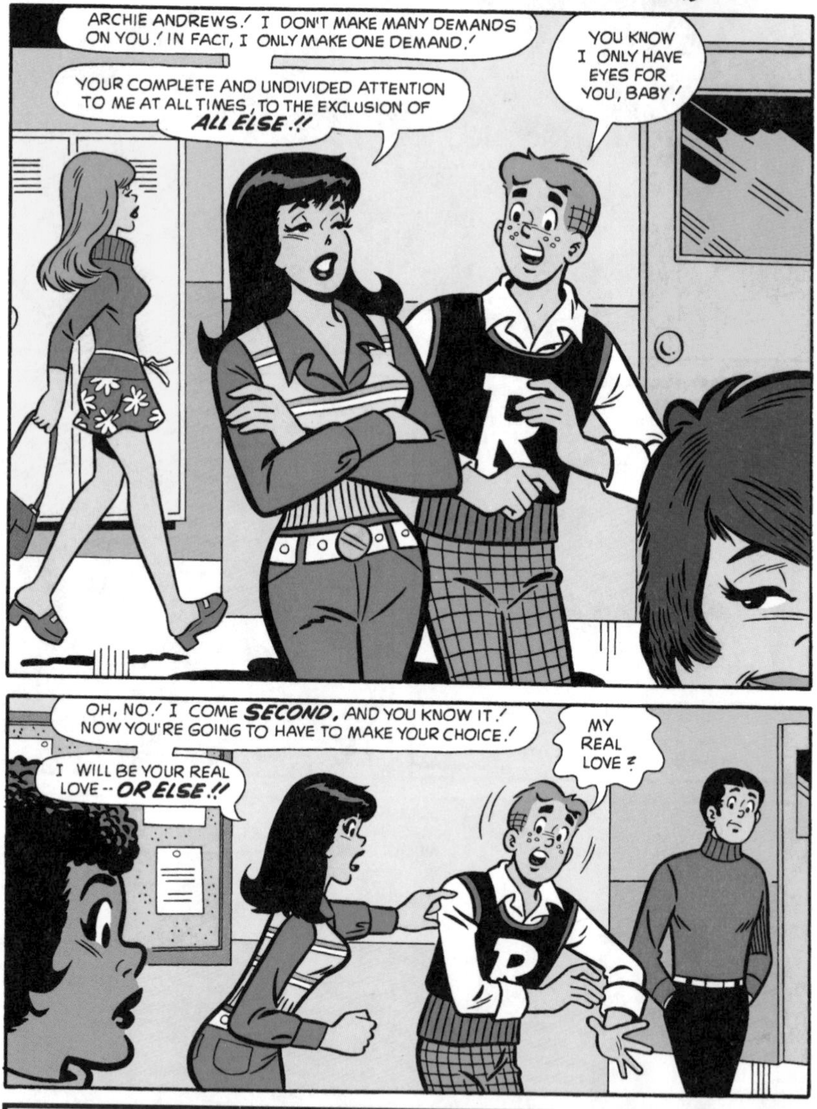
ARCHIE ANDREWS! I DON'T MAKE MANY DEMANDS ON YOU! IN FACT, I ONLY MAKE ONE DEMAND!
YOUR COMPLETE AND UNDIVIDED ATTENTION TO ME AT ALL TIMES, TO THE EXCLUSION OF ALL ELSE!!
YOU KNOW I ONLY HAVE EYES FOR YOU, BABY!
OH, NO! I COME SECOND, AND YOU KNOW IT! NOW YOU'RE GOING TO HAVE TO MAKE YOUR CHOICE!
I WILL BE YOUR REAL LOVE -- OR ELSE!!
MY REAL LOVE?

Story: Frank Doyle Pencils: Stan Goldberg

Inks: Jon D'Agostino Letters: Bill Yoshida Colors: Barry Grossman

Originally printed in ARCHIE AT RIVERDALE HIGH #16, June 1974

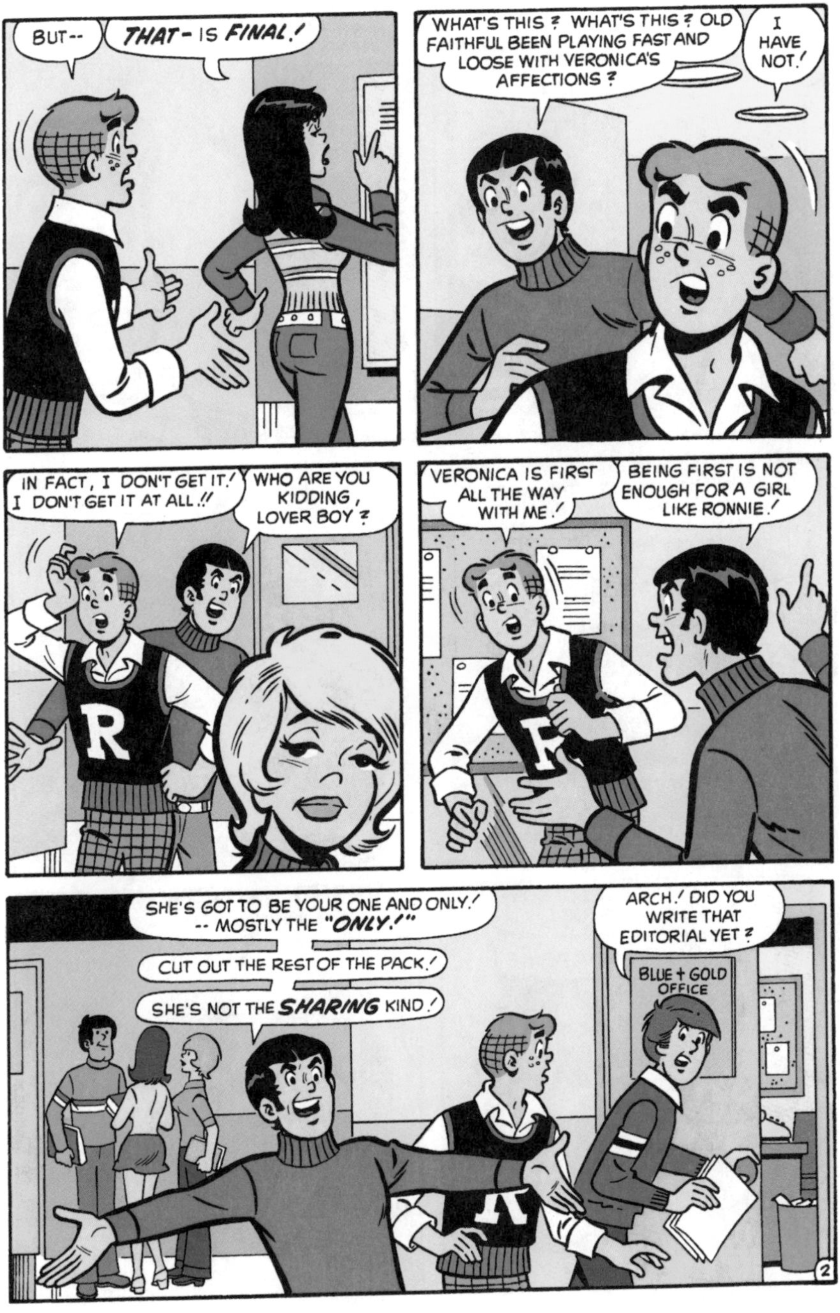
BUT--
THAT- IS FINAL!
WHAT'S THIS? WHAT'S THIS? OLD FAITHFUL BEEN PLAYING FAST AND LOOSE WITH VERONICA'S AFFECTIONS?
I HAVE NOT!
IN FACT, I DON'T GET IT! I DON'T GET IT AT ALL!!
WHO ARE YOU KIDDING, LOVER BOY?
VERONICA IS FIRST ALL THE WAY WITH ME!
BEING FIRST IS NOT ENOUGH FOR A GIRL LIKE RONNIE!
SHE'S GOT TO BE YOUR ONE AND ONLY! -- MOSTLY THE "ONLY!"
CUT OUT THE REST OF THE PACK!
SHE'S NOT THE SHARING KIND!
ARCH! DID YOU WRITE THAT EDITORIAL YET?
BLUE + GOLD OFFICE
2

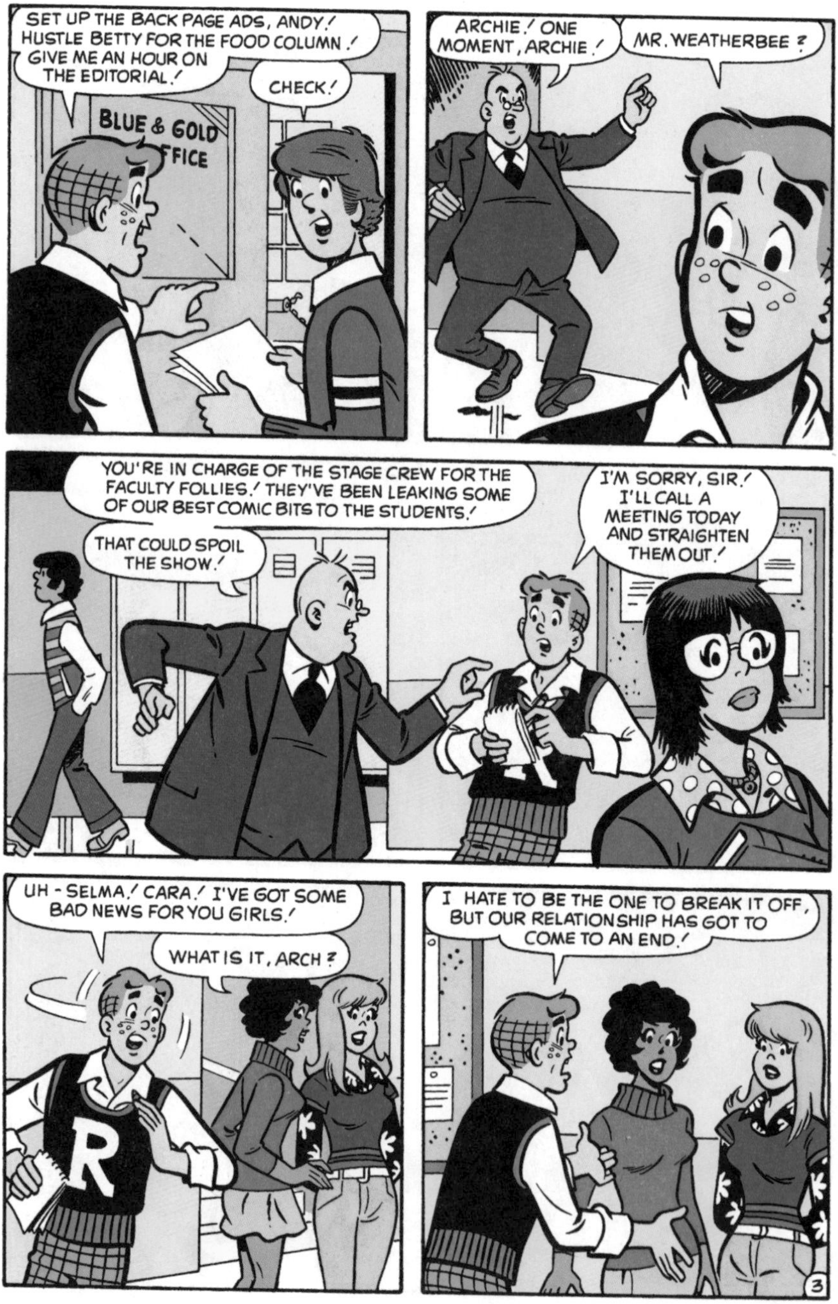
SET UP THE BACK PAGE ADS, ANDY! HUSTLE BETTY FOR THE FOOD COLUMN! GIVE ME AN HOUR ON THE EDITORIAL!
CHECK!
BLUE & GOLD
FFICE
ARCHIE! ONE MOMENT, ARCHIE!
MR. WEATHERBEE?
YOU'RE IN CHARGE OF THE STAGE CREW FOR THE FACULTY FOLLIES! THEY'VE BEEN LEAKING SOME OF OUR BEST COMIC BITS TO THE STUDENTS!
THAT COULD SPOIL THE SHOW!
I'M SORRY, SIR! I'LL CALL A MEETING TODAY AND STRAIGHTEN THEM OUT!
UH - SELMA! CARA! I'VE GOT SOME BAD NEWS FOR YOU GIRLS!
WHAT IS IT, ARCH?
R
I HATE TO BE THE ONE TO BREAK IT OFF, BUT OUR RELATIONSHIP HAS GOT TO COME TO AN END!
3

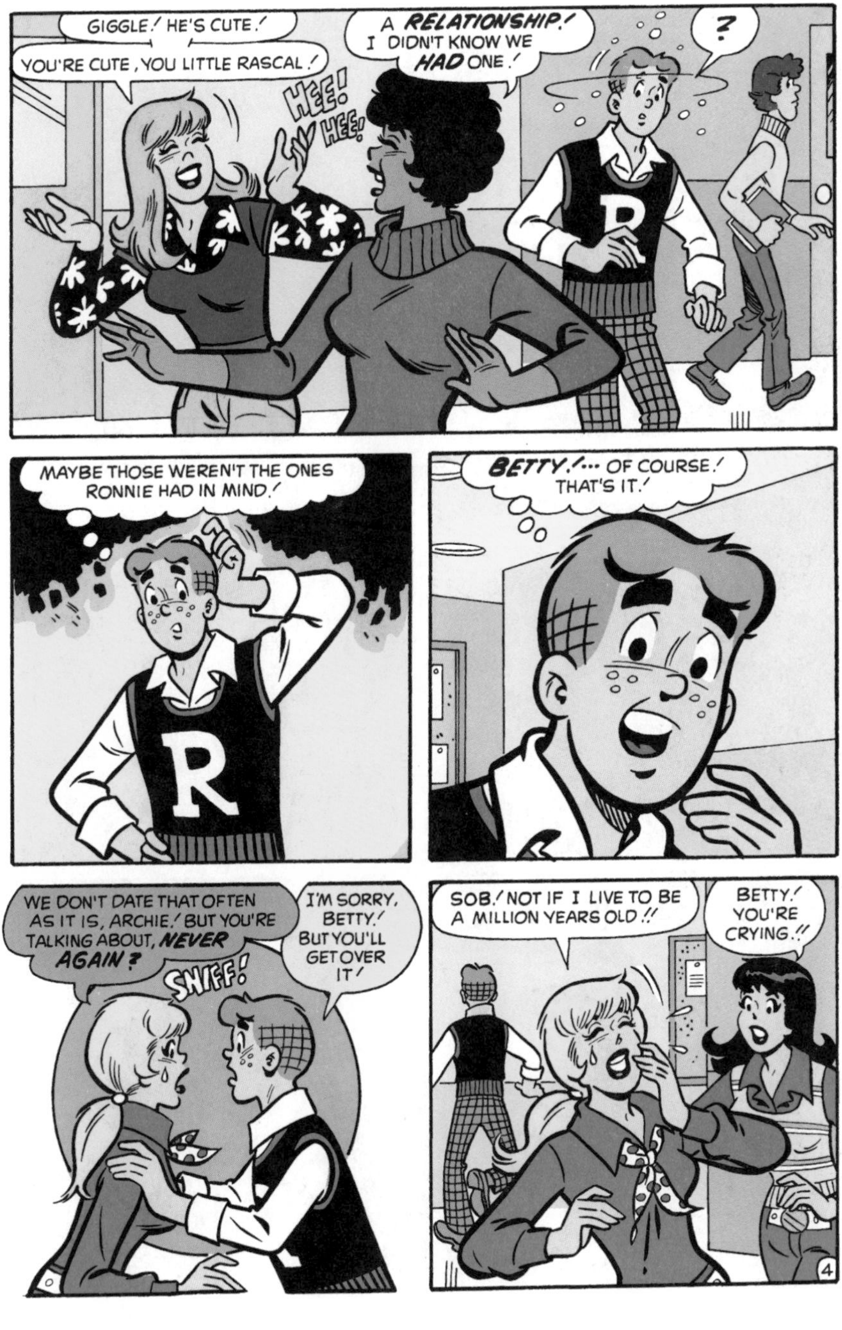
GIGGLE! HE'S CUTE!
YOU'RE CUTE, YOU LITTLE RASCAL!
HEE! HEE!
A RELATIONSHIP! I DIDN'T KNOW WE HAD ONE!
?
MAYBE THOSE WEREN'T THE ONES RONNIE HAD IN MIND!
BETTY!... OF COURSE! THAT'S IT!
WE DON'T DATE THAT OFTEN AS IT IS, ARCHIE! BUT YOU'RE TALKING ABOUT, NEVER AGAIN?
SNIFF!
I'M SORRY, BETTY! BUT YOU'LL GET OVER IT!
SOB! NOT IF I LIVE TO BE A MILLION YEARS OLD!!
BETTY! YOU'RE CRYING!!
4

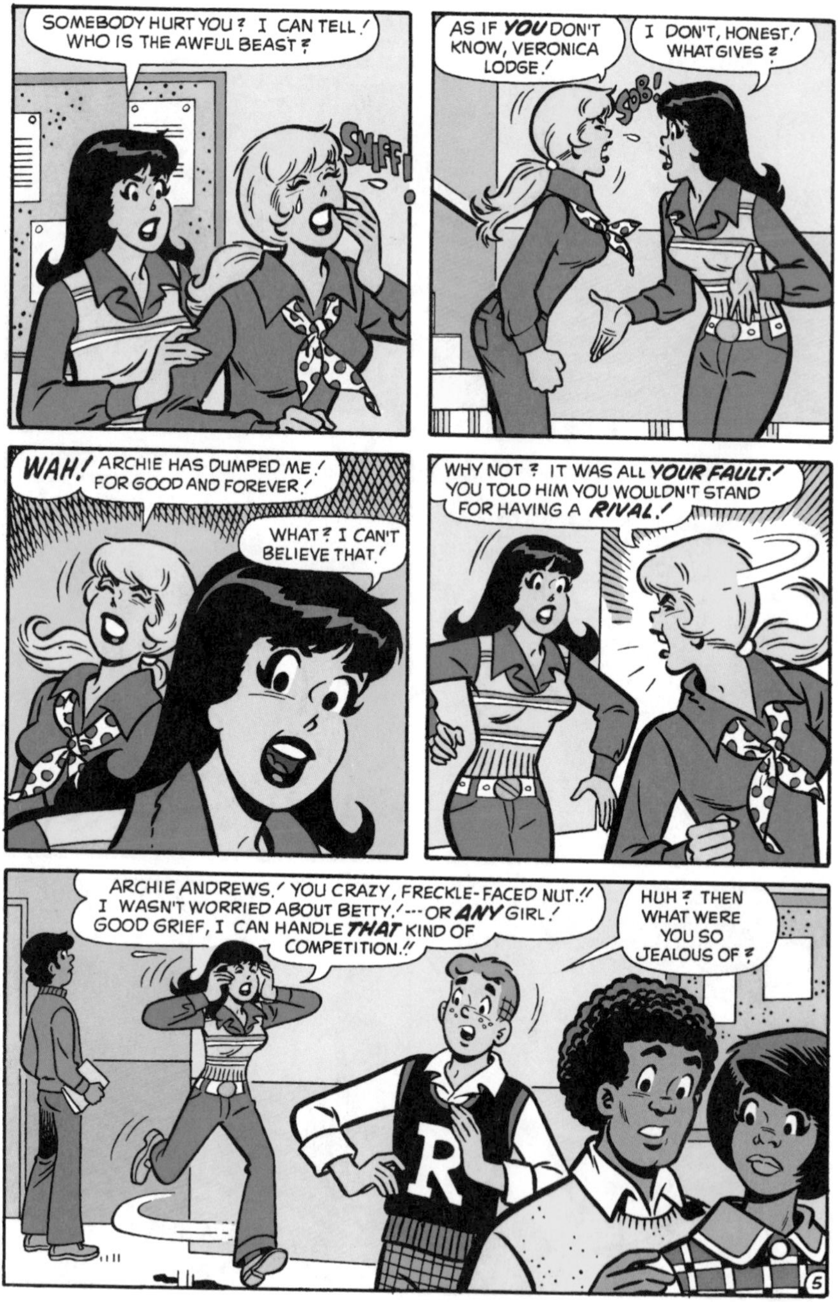
SOMEBODY HURT YOU? I CAN TELL! WHO IS THE AWFUL BEAST?
SNIFF!
AS IF YOU DON'T KNOW, VERONICA LODGE!
SOB!
I DON'T, HONEST! WHAT GIVES?
WAH! ARCHIE HAS DUMPED ME! FOR GOOD AND FOREVER!
WHAT? I CAN'T BELIEVE THAT!
WHY NOT? IT WAS ALL YOUR FAULT! YOU TOLD HIM YOU WOULDN'T STAND FOR HAVING A RIVAL!
ARCHIE ANDREWS! YOU CRAZY, FRECKLE-FACED NUT!! I WASN'T WORRIED ABOUT BETTY!---OR ANY GIRL! GOOD GRIEF, I CAN HANDLE THAT KIND OF COMPETITION!!
HUH? THEN WHAT WERE YOU SO JEALOUS OF?
5

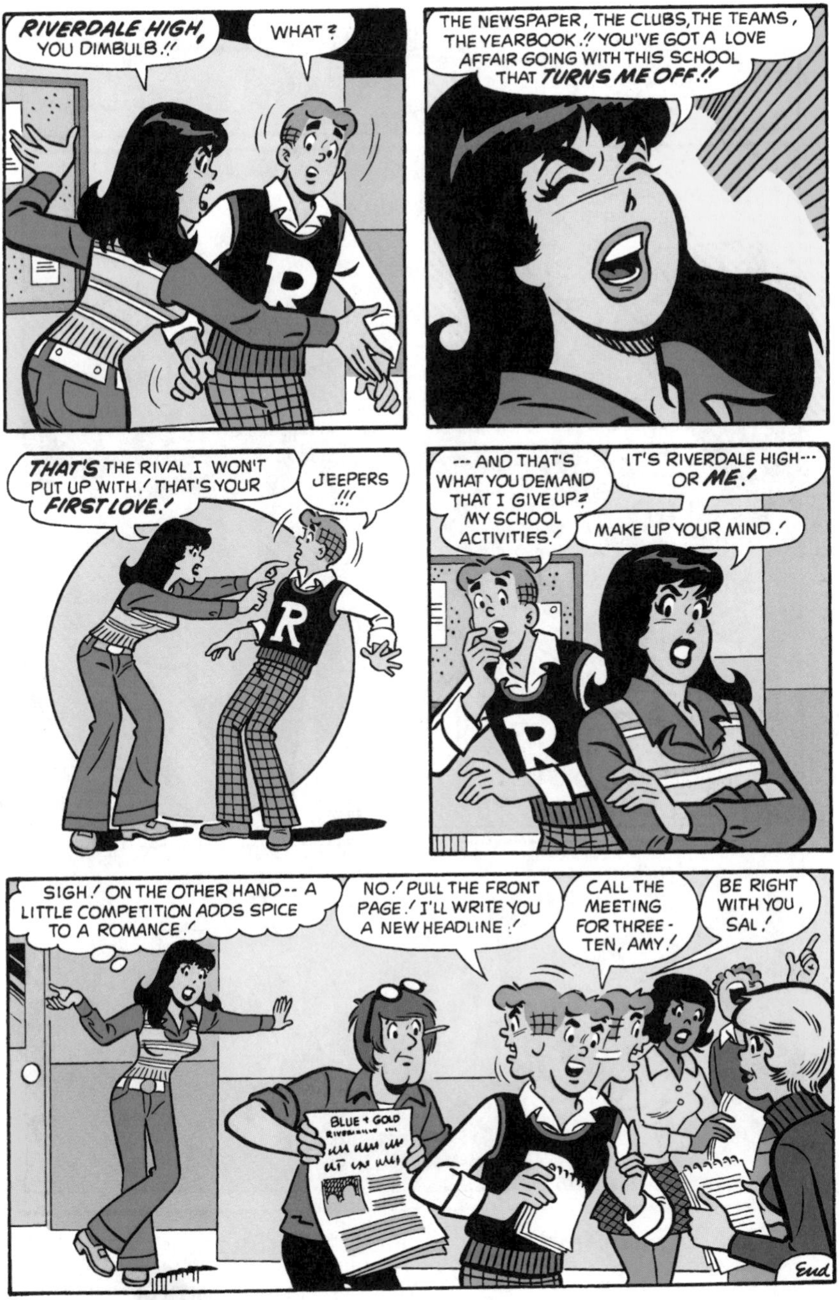
RIVERDALE HIGH, YOU DIMBULB.!!
WHAT?
THE NEWSPAPER, THE CLUBS, THE TEAMS, THE YEARBOOK.!! YOU'VE GOT A LOVE AFFAIR GOING WITH THIS SCHOOL THAT TURNS ME OFF.!!
THAT'S THE RIVAL I WON'T PUT UP WITH.! THAT'S YOUR FIRST LOVE.!
JEEPERS !!!
--- AND THAT'S WHAT YOU DEMAND THAT I GIVE UP? MY SCHOOL ACTIVITIES.!
IT'S RIVERDALE HIGH--- OR ME.!
MAKE UP YOUR MIND.!
SIGH.! ON THE OTHER HAND-- A LITTLE COMPETITION ADDS SPICE TO A ROMANCE.!
NO.! PULL THE FRONT PAGE.! I'LL WRITE YOU A NEW HEADLINE.!
CALL THE MEETING FOR THREE-TEN, AMY.!
BE RIGHT WITH YOU, SAL.!
BLUE + GOLD
End

Archie at Riverdale in "What's in a Name"

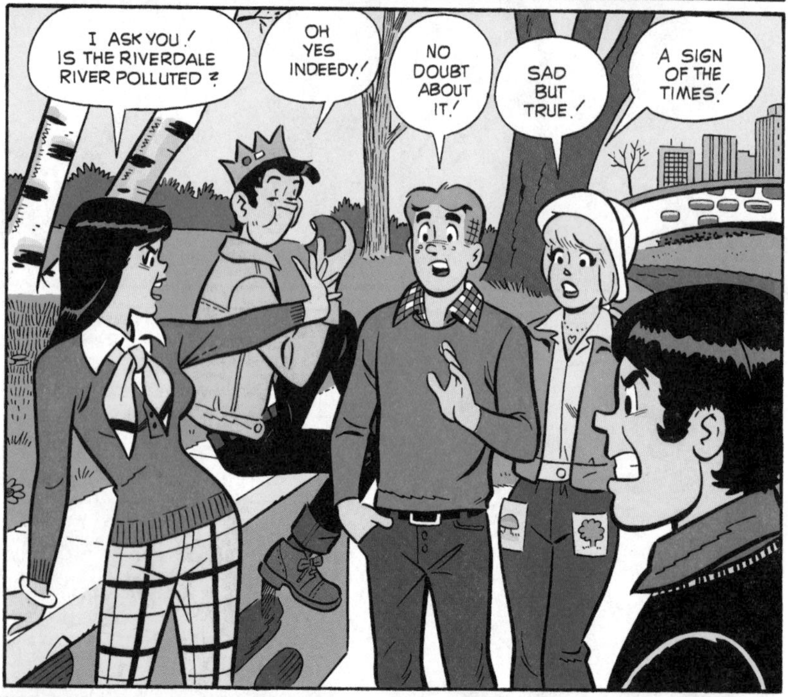
I ASK YOU! IS THE RIVERDALE RIVER POLLUTED?
OH YES INDEEDY!
NO DOUBT ABOUT IT!
SAD BUT TRUE!
A SIGN OF THE TIMES!

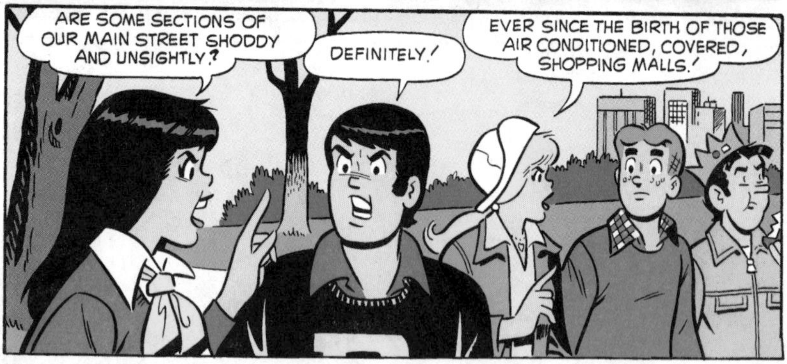
ARE SOME SECTIONS OF OUR MAIN STREET SHODDY AND UNSIGHTLY?
DEFINITELY!
EVER SINCE THE BIRTH OF THOSE AIR CONDITIONED, COVERED, SHOPPING MALLS!

Story: Frank Doyle Pencils: Dan DeCarlo

Inks: Rudy Lapick Letters: Bill Yoshida Colors: Barry Grossman

Originally printed in ARCHIE AT RIVERDALE HIGH #16, June 1974

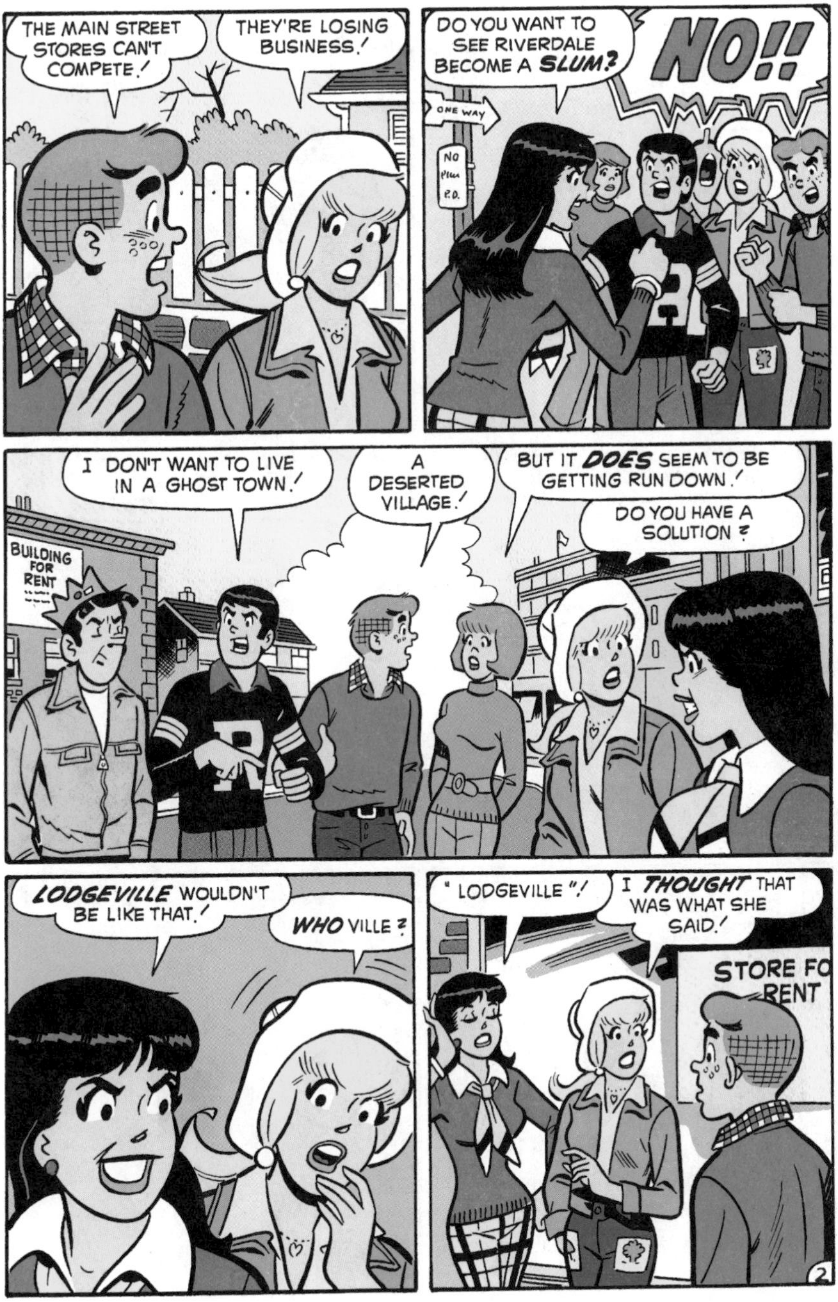
THE MAIN STREET STORES CAN'T COMPETE!
THEY'RE LOSING BUSINESS!
DO YOU WANT TO SEE RIVERDALE BECOME A SLUM?
NO!!
ONE WAY
I DON'T WANT TO LIVE IN A GHOST TOWN!
A DESERTED VILLAGE!
BUT IT DOES SEEM TO BE GETTING RUN DOWN!
DO YOU HAVE A SOLUTION?
BUILDING FOR RENT
LODGEVILLE WOULDN'T BE LIKE THAT!
WHO VILLE?
"LODGEVILLE"!
I THOUGHT THAT WAS WHAT SHE SAID!
STORE FO RENT
2

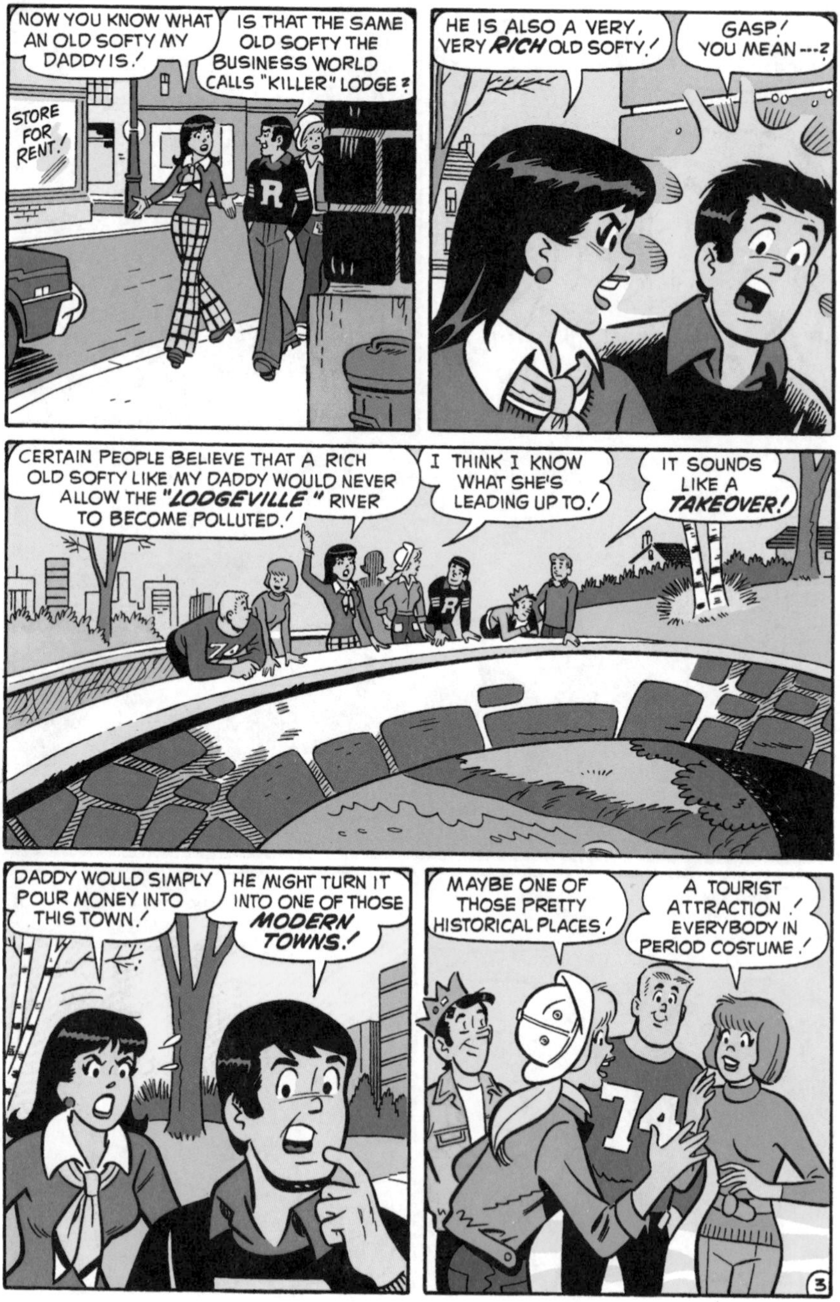
NOW YOU KNOW WHAT AN OLD SOFTY MY DADDY IS!
IS THAT THE SAME OLD SOFTY THE BUSINESS WORLD CALLS "KILLER" LODGE?
STORE FOR RENT!
HE IS ALSO A VERY, VERY RICH OLD SOFTY!
GASP! YOU MEAN ---?
CERTAIN PEOPLE BELIEVE THAT A RICH OLD SOFTY LIKE MY DADDY WOULD NEVER ALLOW THE "LODGEVILLE" RIVER TO BECOME POLLUTED!
I THINK I KNOW WHAT SHE'S LEADING UP TO!
IT SOUNDS LIKE A TAKEOVER!
DADDY WOULD SIMPLY POUR MONEY INTO THIS TOWN!
HE MIGHT TURN IT INTO ONE OF THOSE MODERN TOWNS!
MAYBE ONE OF THOSE PRETTY HISTORICAL PLACES!
A TOURIST ATTRACTION! EVERYBODY IN PERIOD COSTUME!
3

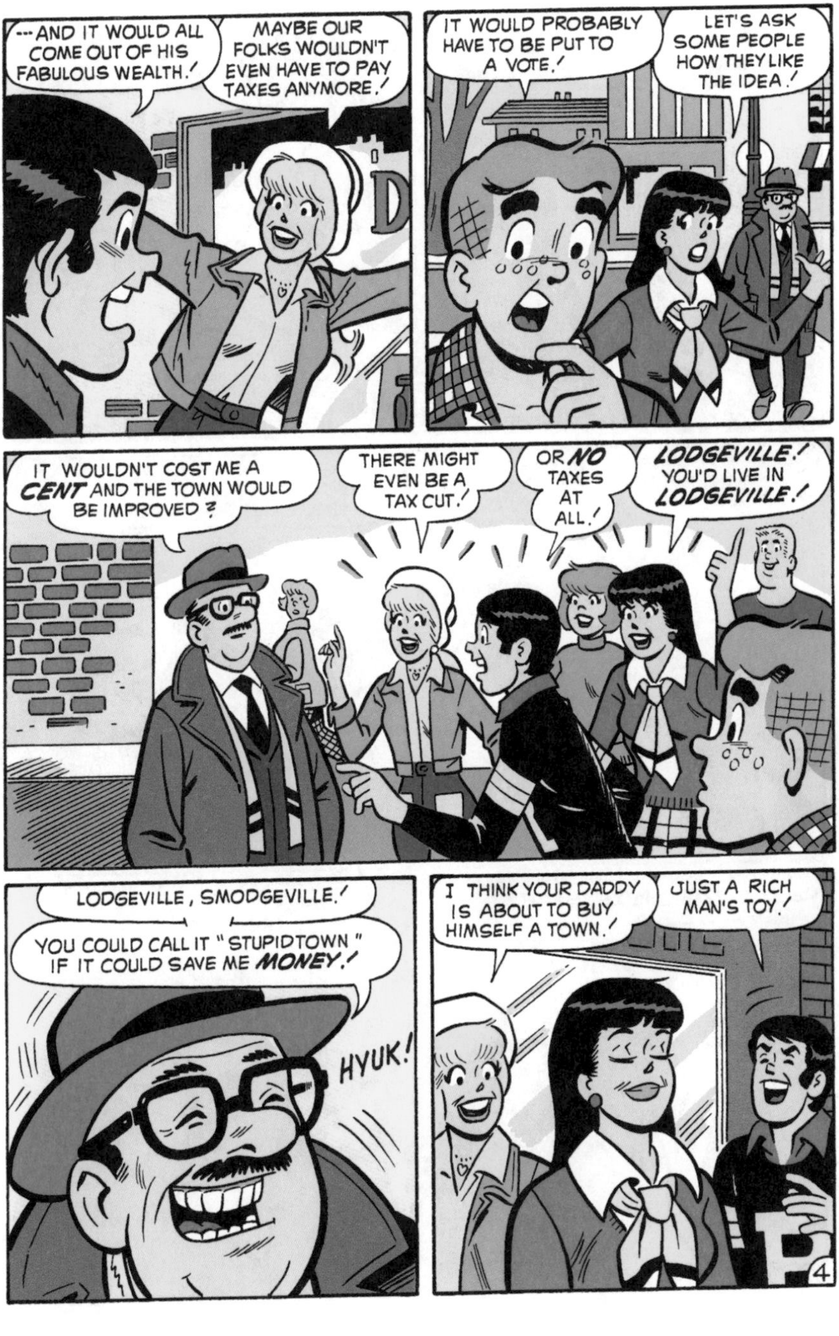
---AND IT WOULD ALL COME OUT OF HIS FABULOUS WEALTH.!
MAYBE OUR FOLKS WOULDN'T EVEN HAVE TO PAY TAXES ANYMORE.!
IT WOULD PROBABLY HAVE TO BE PUT TO A VOTE.!
LET'S ASK SOME PEOPLE HOW THEY LIKE THE IDEA.!
IT WOULDN'T COST ME A CENT AND THE TOWN WOULD BE IMPROVED ?
THERE MIGHT EVEN BE A TAX CUT.!
OR NO TAXES AT ALL.!
LODGEVILLE.! YOU'D LIVE IN LODGEVILLE.!
LODGEVILLE, SMODGEVILLE.!
YOU COULD CALL IT "STUPIDTOWN" IF IT COULD SAVE ME MONEY.!
HYUK!
I THINK YOUR DADDY IS ABOUT TO BUY HIMSELF A TOWN.!
JUST A RICH MAN'S TOY.!
4

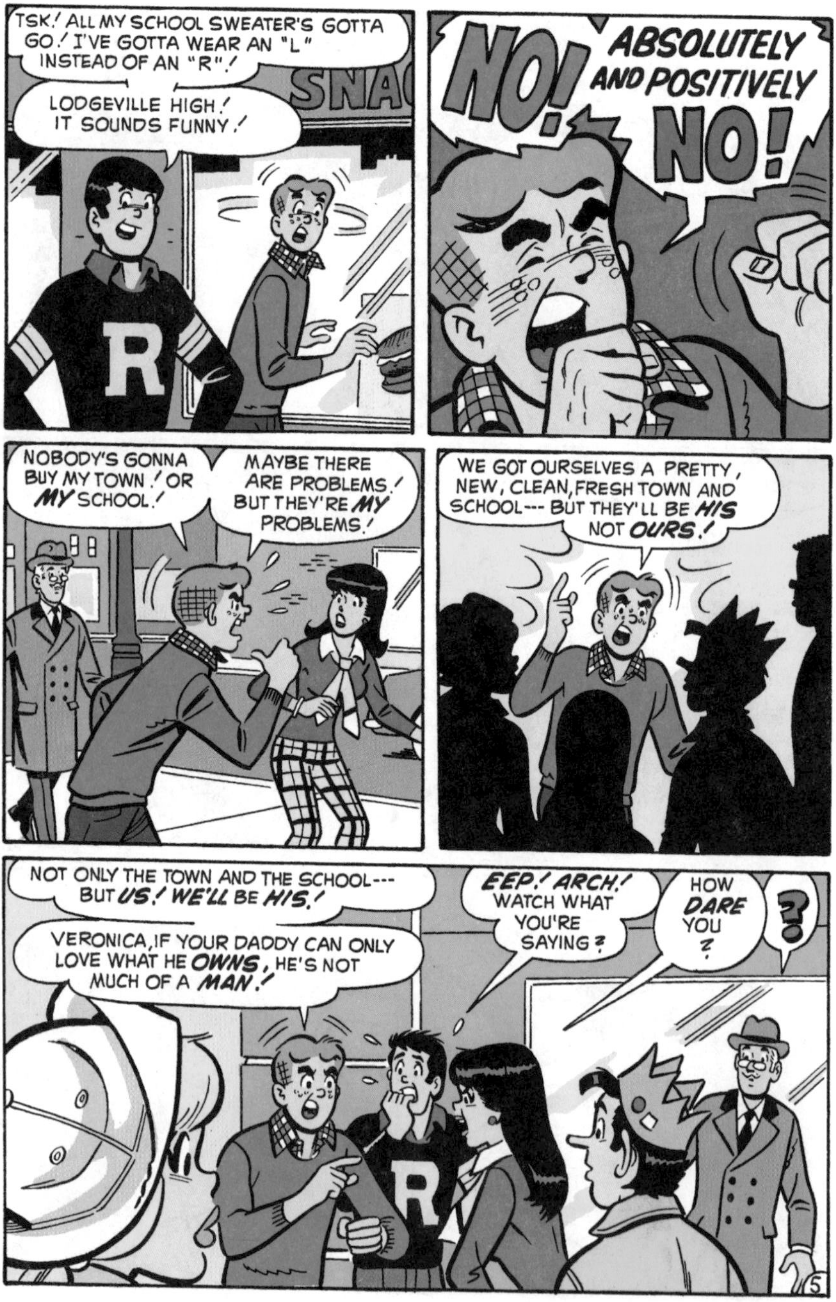
TSK! ALL MY SCHOOL SWEATER'S GOTTA GO! I'VE GOTTA WEAR AN "L" INSTEAD OF AN "R"!
LODGEVILLE HIGH! IT SOUNDS FUNNY!
SNA
NO!
ABSOLUTELY AND POSITIVELY NO!
NOBODY'S GONNA BUY MY TOWN! OR MY SCHOOL!
MAYBE THERE ARE PROBLEMS! BUT THEY'RE MY PROBLEMS!
WE GOT OURSELVES A PRETTY, NEW, CLEAN, FRESH TOWN AND SCHOOL--- BUT THEY'LL BE HIS NOT OURS!
NOT ONLY THE TOWN AND THE SCHOOL--- BUT US! WE'LL BE HIS!
VERONICA, IF YOUR DADDY CAN ONLY LOVE WHAT HE OWNS, HE'S NOT MUCH OF A MAN!
EEP! ARCH! WATCH WHAT YOU'RE SAYING?
HOW DARE YOU?
?
R
R
5

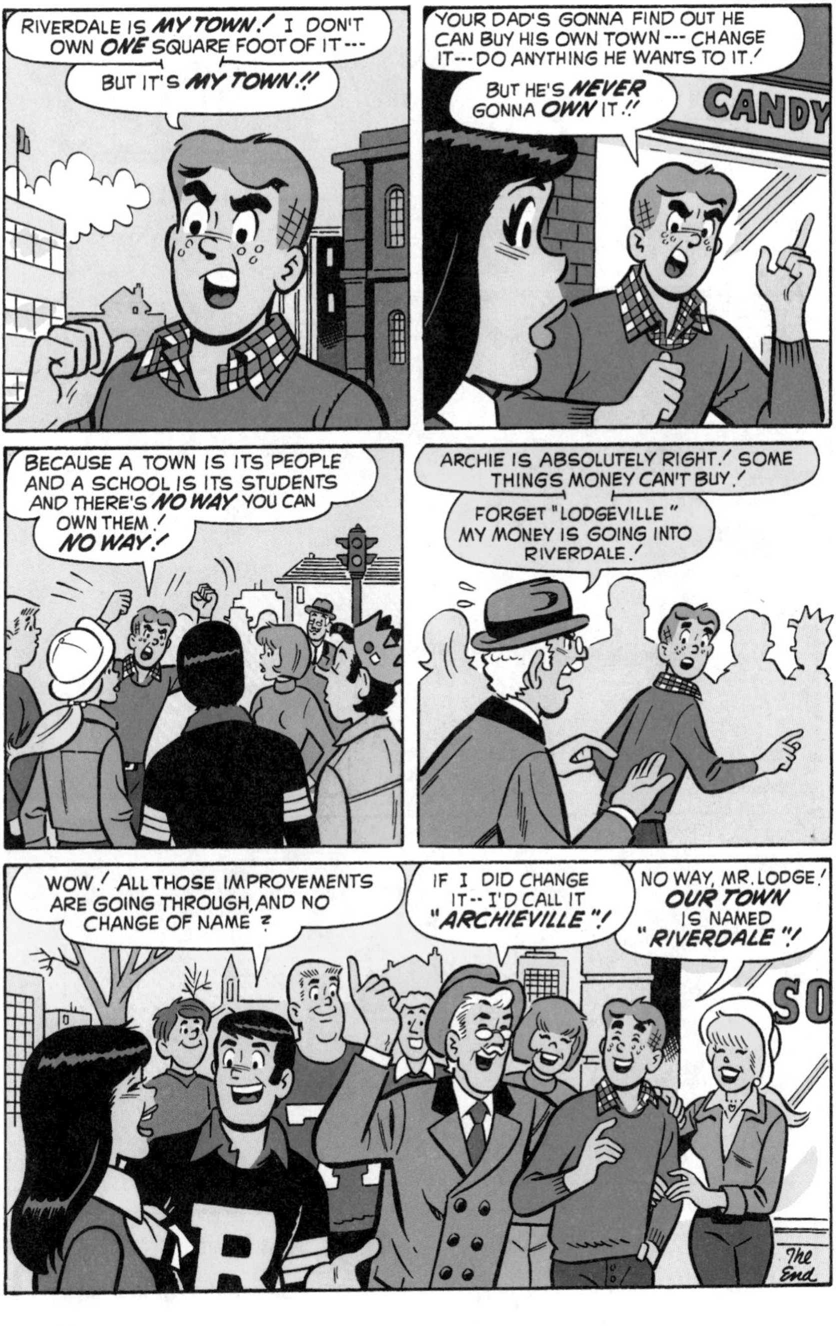
RIVERDALE IS MY TOWN! I DON'T OWN ONE SQUARE FOOT OF IT---
BUT IT'S MY TOWN!!
YOUR DAD'S GONNA FIND OUT HE CAN BUY HIS OWN TOWN --- CHANGE IT--- DO ANYTHING HE WANTS TO IT!
BUT HE'S NEVER GONNA OWN IT!!
CANDY
BECAUSE A TOWN IS ITS PEOPLE AND A SCHOOL IS ITS STUDENTS AND THERE'S NO WAY YOU CAN OWN THEM! NO WAY!
ARCHIE IS ABSOLUTELY RIGHT! SOME THINGS MONEY CAN'T BUY!
FORGET "LODGEVILLE" MY MONEY IS GOING INTO RIVERDALE!
WOW! ALL THOSE IMPROVEMENTS ARE GOING THROUGH, AND NO CHANGE OF NAME ?
IF I DID CHANGE IT-- I'D CALL IT "ARCHIEVILLE"!
NO WAY, MR. LODGE! OUR TOWN IS NAMED "RIVERDALE"!
The End

Archie at Riverdale in "The Quitter"

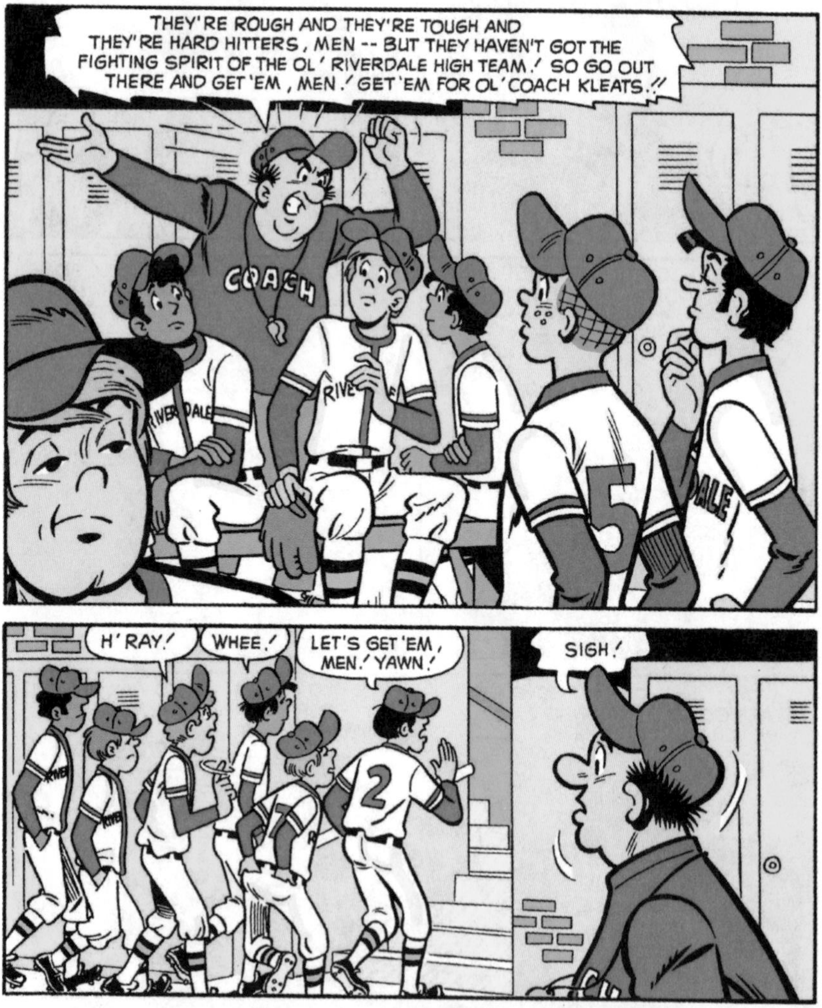
THEY'RE ROUGH AND THEY'RE TOUGH AND THEY'RE HARD HITTERS, MEN -- BUT THEY HAVEN'T GOT THE FIGHTING SPIRIT OF THE OL' RIVERDALE HIGH TEAM! SO GO OUT THERE AND GET 'EM, MEN! GET 'EM FOR OL' COACH KLEATS!!
COACH
RIVERDALE
H'RAY!
WHEE!
LET'S GET 'EM, MEN! YAWN!
SIGH!

Story: Frank Doyle Pencils: Stan Goldberg

Inks: Jon D'Agostino Letters: Bill Yoshida Colors: Barry Grossman

Originally printed in ARCHIE AT RIVERDALE HIGH #18, August 1974

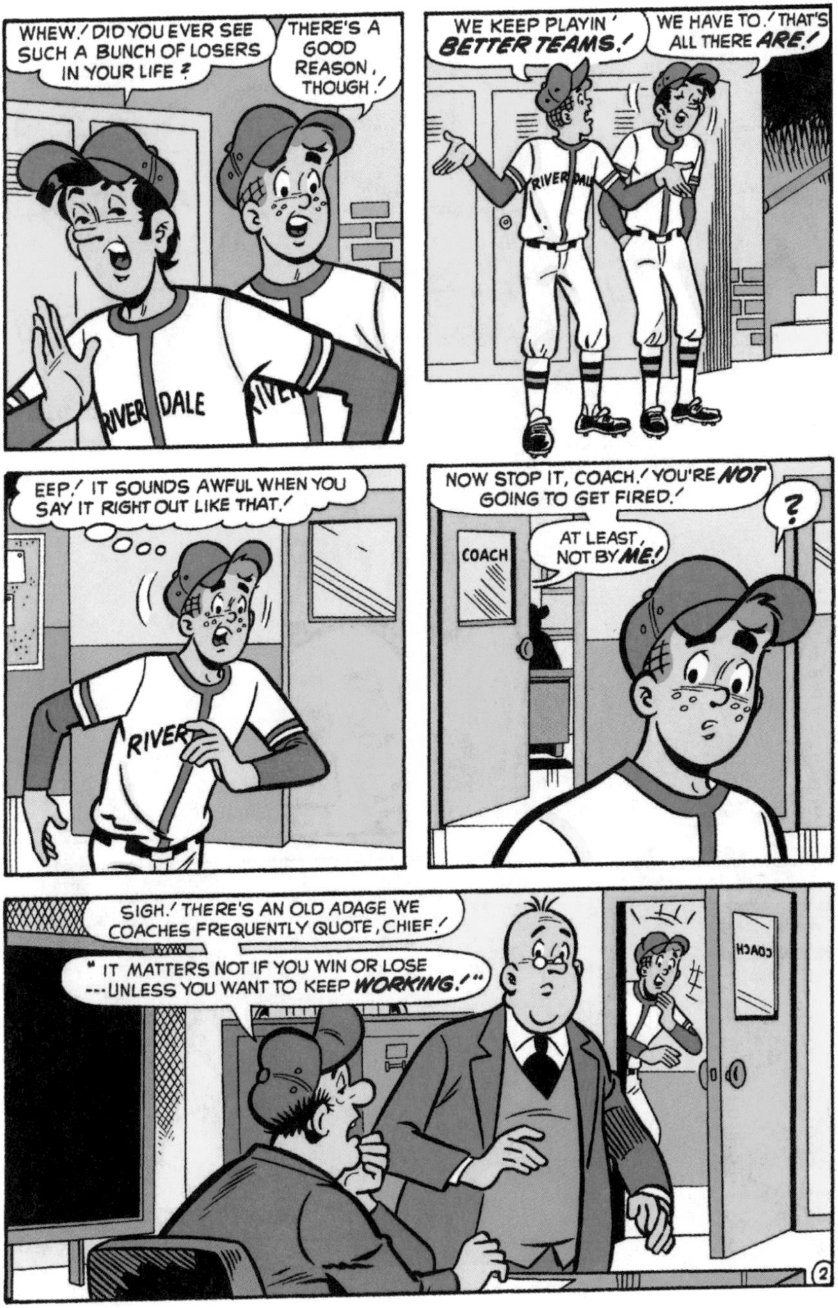
WHEW! DID YOU EVER SEE SUCH A BUNCH OF LOSERS IN YOUR LIFE?
THERE'S A GOOD REASON, THOUGH!
RIVERDALE
WE KEEP PLAYIN' BETTER TEAMS!
WE HAVE TO! THAT'S ALL THERE ARE!
RIVERDALE
EEP! IT SOUNDS AWFUL WHEN YOU SAY IT RIGHT OUT LIKE THAT!
RIVER
NOW STOP IT, COACH! YOU'RE NOT GOING TO GET FIRED!
AT LEAST, NOT BY ME!
?
COACH
SIGH! THERE'S AN OLD ADAGE WE COACHES FREQUENTLY QUOTE, CHIEF!
"IT MATTERS NOT IF YOU WIN OR LOSE ---UNLESS YOU WANT TO KEEP WORKING!"
2

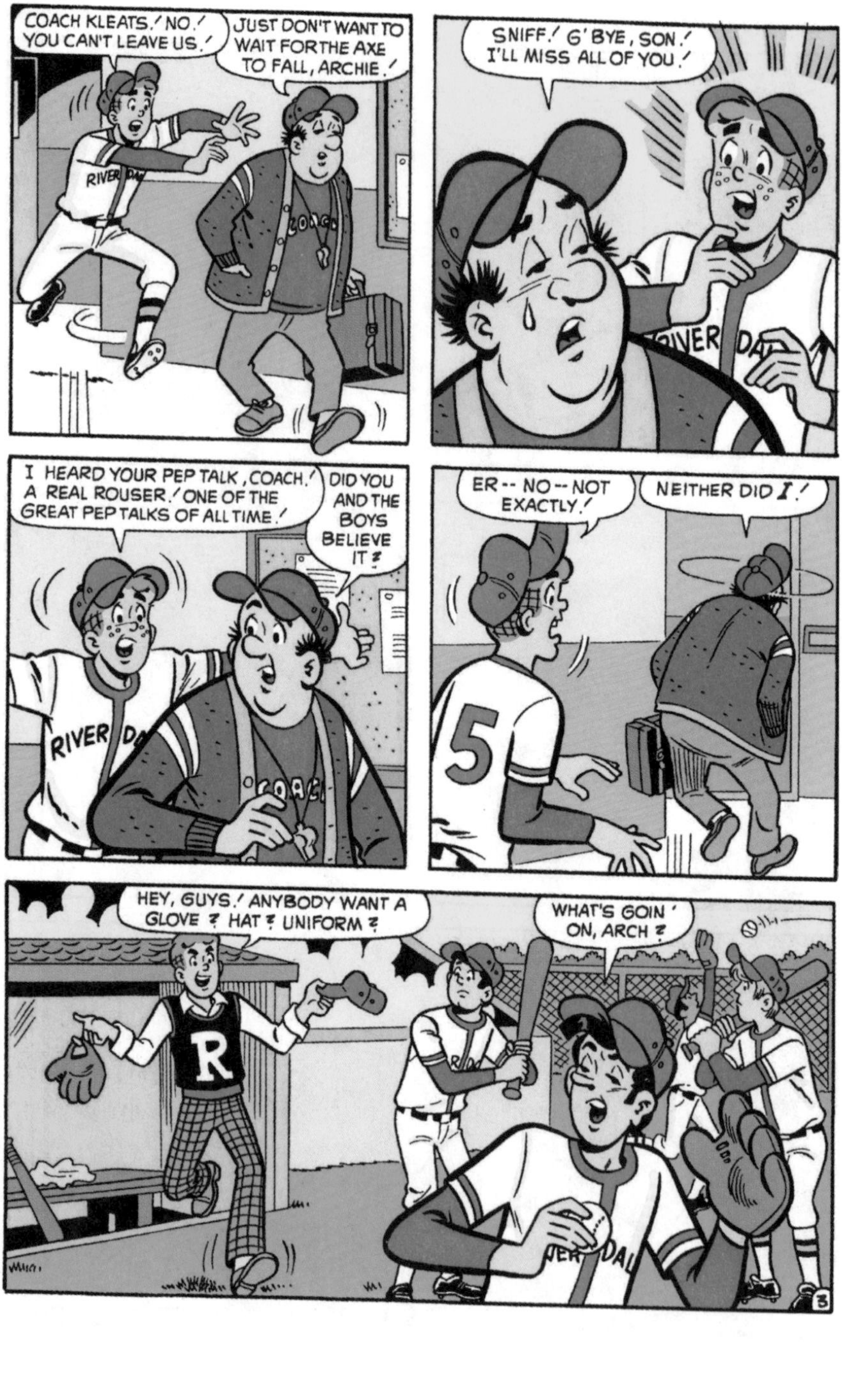
COACH KLEATS! NO! YOU CAN'T LEAVE US!
JUST DON'T WANT TO WAIT FOR THE AXE TO FALL, ARCHIE!
SNIFF! G'BYE, SON! I'LL MISS ALL OF YOU!
I HEARD YOUR PEP TALK, COACH! A REAL ROUSER! ONE OF THE GREAT PEP TALKS OF ALL TIME!
DID YOU AND THE BOYS BELIEVE IT?
ER -- NO -- NOT EXACTLY!
NEITHER DID I!
HEY, GUYS! ANYBODY WANT A GLOVE? HAT? UNIFORM?
WHAT'S GOIN' ON, ARCH?
3

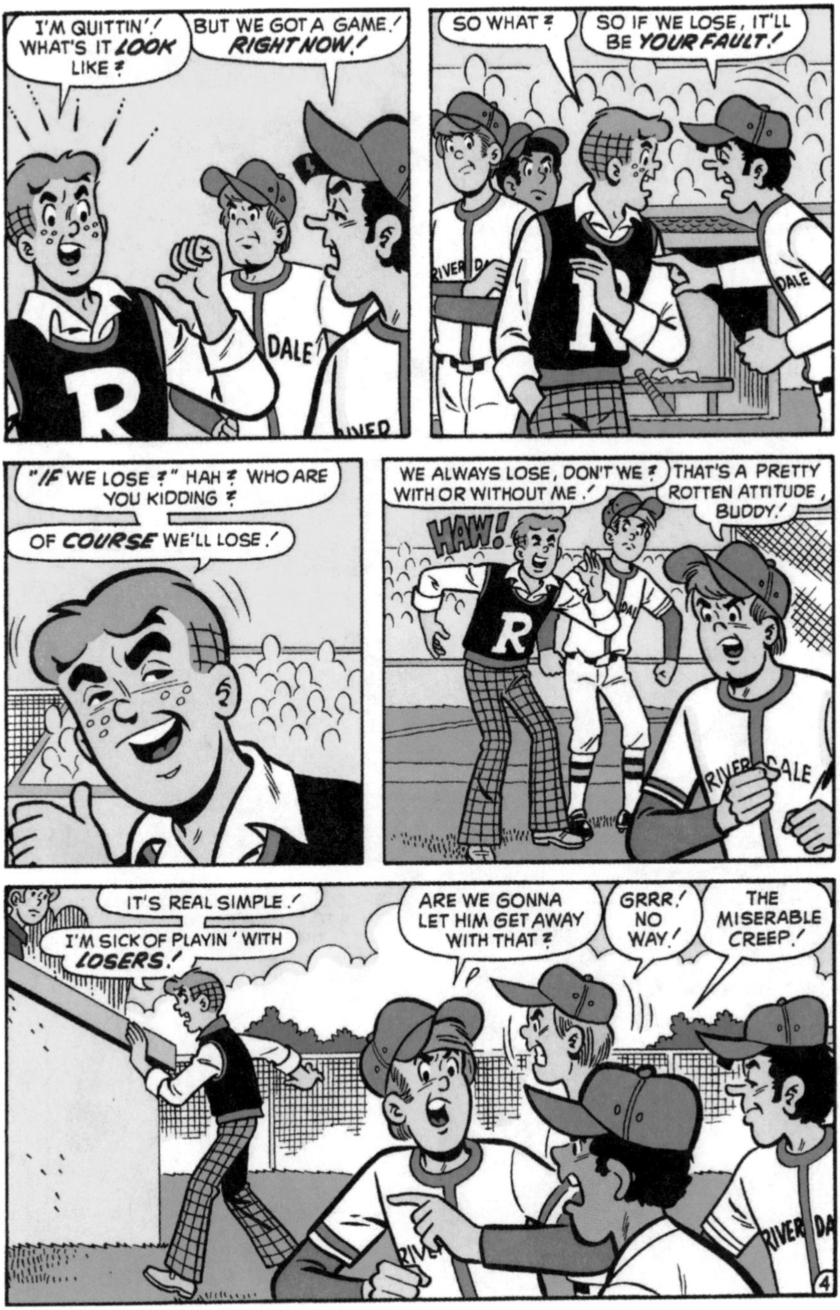
I'M QUITTIN'! WHAT'S IT LOOK LIKE?
BUT WE GOT A GAME! RIGHT NOW!
SO WHAT?
SO IF WE LOSE, IT'LL BE YOUR FAULT!
"IF WE LOSE?" HAH? WHO ARE YOU KIDDING?
OF COURSE WE'LL LOSE!
WE ALWAYS LOSE, DON'T WE? WITH OR WITHOUT ME!
HAW!
THAT'S A PRETTY ROTTEN ATTITUDE, BUDDY!
IT'S REAL SIMPLE!
I'M SICK OF PLAYIN' WITH LOSERS!
ARE WE GONNA LET HIM GET AWAY WITH THAT?
GRRR! NO WAY!
THE MISERABLE CREEP!
4

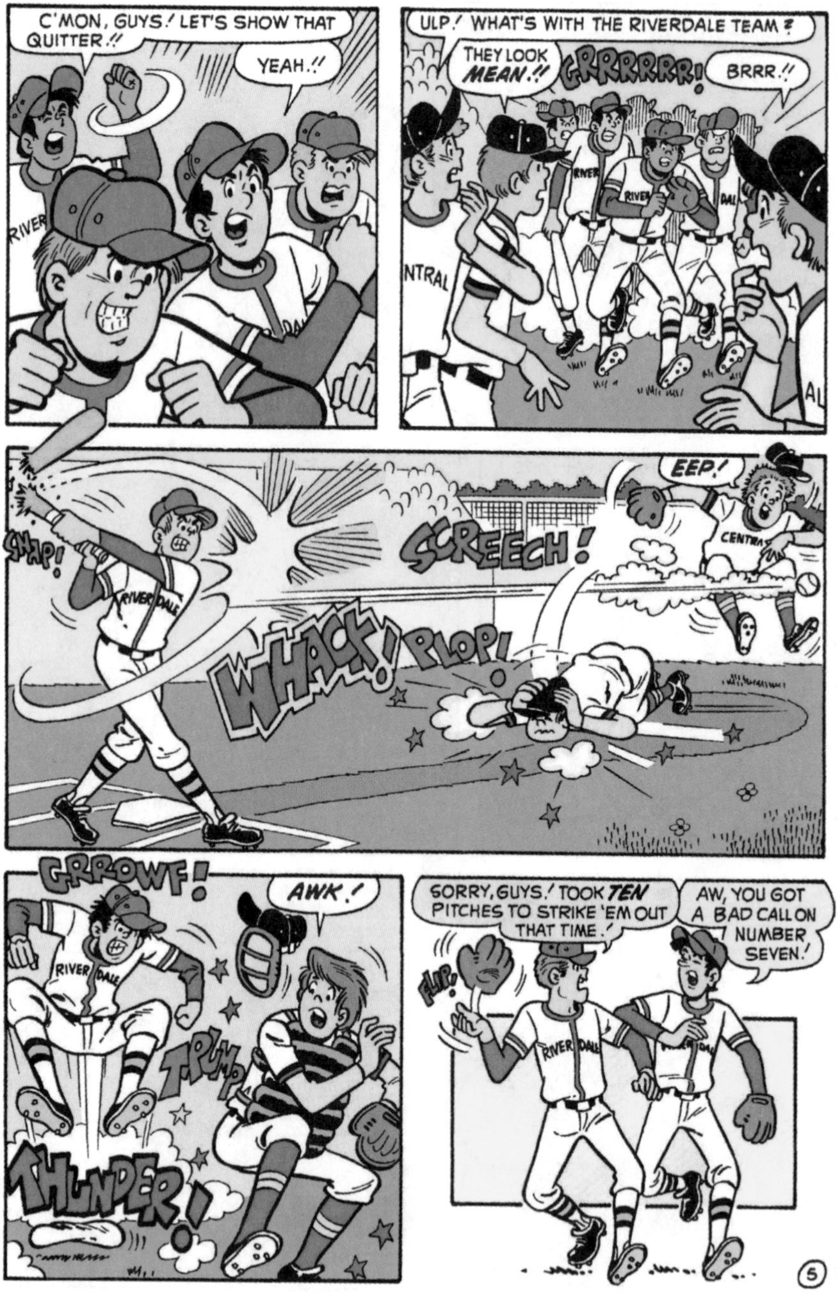
C'MON, GUYS! LET'S SHOW THAT QUITTER!!
YEAH!!
ULP! WHAT'S WITH THE RIVERDALE TEAM?
THEY LOOK MEAN!!
GRRRRRRR!
BRRR!!
SNAP!
SCREECH!
EEP!
WHACK!
PLOP!
GRROWF!
AWK!
TRUMP
THUNDER!
SORRY, GUYS! TOOK TEN PITCHES TO STRIKE 'EM OUT THAT TIME!
AW, YOU GOT A BAD CALL ON NUMBER SEVEN!

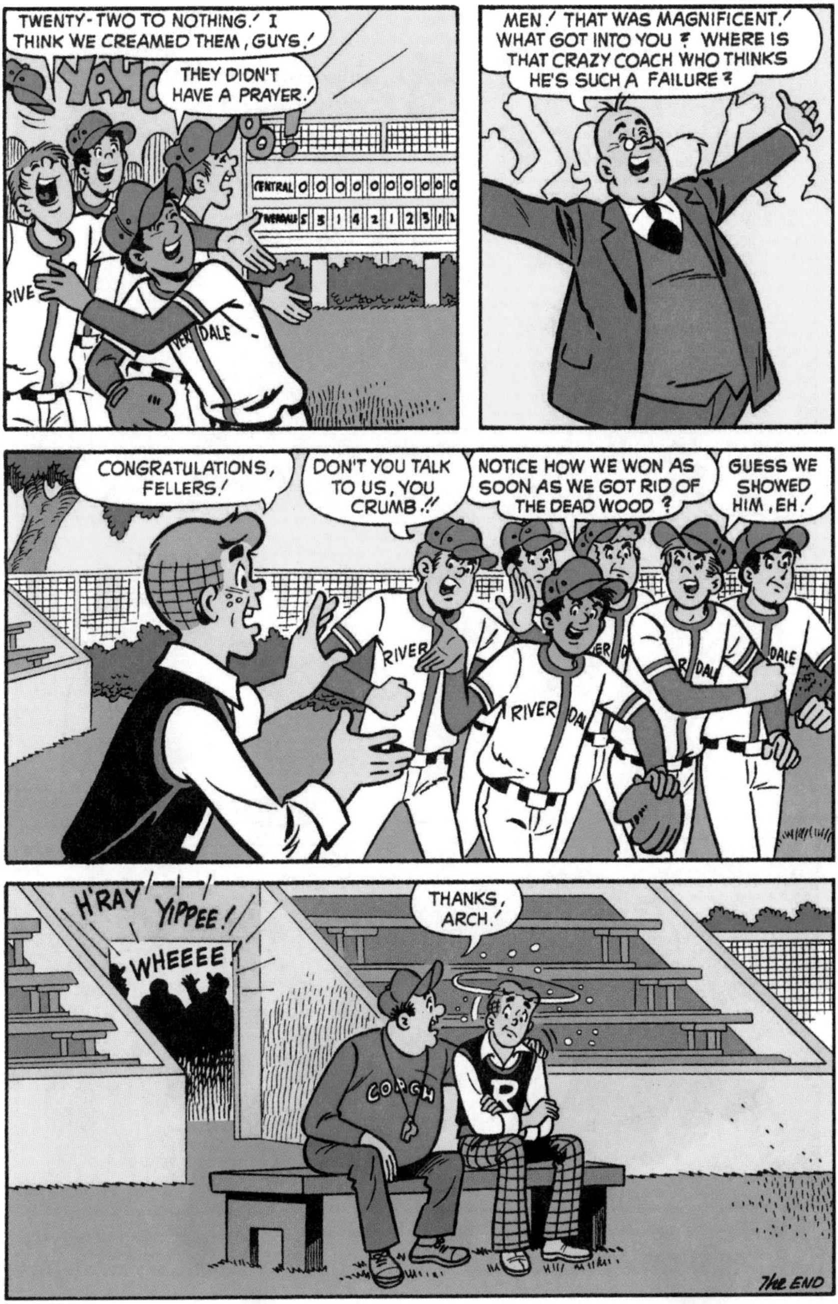
TWENTY-TWO TO NOTHING! I THINK WE CREAMED THEM, GUYS!
YAHOO!
THEY DIDN'T HAVE A PRAYER!
MEN! THAT WAS MAGNIFICENT! WHAT GOT INTO YOU? WHERE IS THAT CRAZY COACH WHO THINKS HE'S SUCH A FAILURE?
CONGRATULATIONS, FELLERS!
DON'T YOU TALK TO US, YOU CRUMB!!
NOTICE HOW WE WON AS SOON AS WE GOT RID OF THE DEAD WOOD?
GUESS WE SHOWED HIM, EH!
H'RAY
YIPPEE!
WHEEEE!
THANKS, ARCH!
COACH
The END

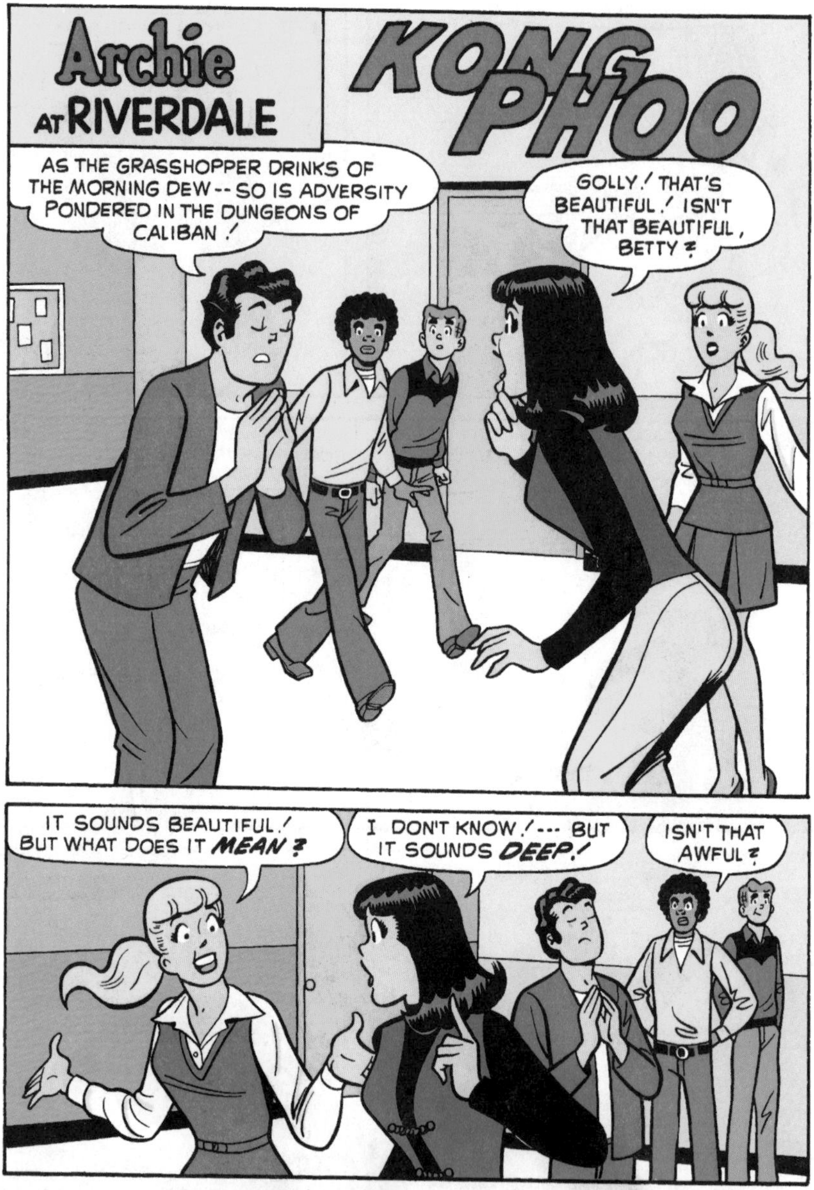
Archie
AT RIVERDALE
KONG PHOO
AS THE GRASSHOPPER DRINKS OF THE MORNING DEW -- SO IS ADVERSITY PONDERED IN THE DUNGEONS OF CALIBAN!
GOLLY! THAT'S BEAUTIFUL! ISN'T THAT BEAUTIFUL, BETTY?
IT SOUNDS BEAUTIFUL! BUT WHAT DOES IT MEAN?
I DON'T KNOW! --- BUT IT SOUNDS DEEP!
ISN'T THAT AWFUL?

Story: Frank Doyle Pencils: Harry Lucey

Inks: Chic Stone Letters: Bill Yoshida

Originally printed in ARCHIE AT RIVERDALE HIGH #18, August 1974

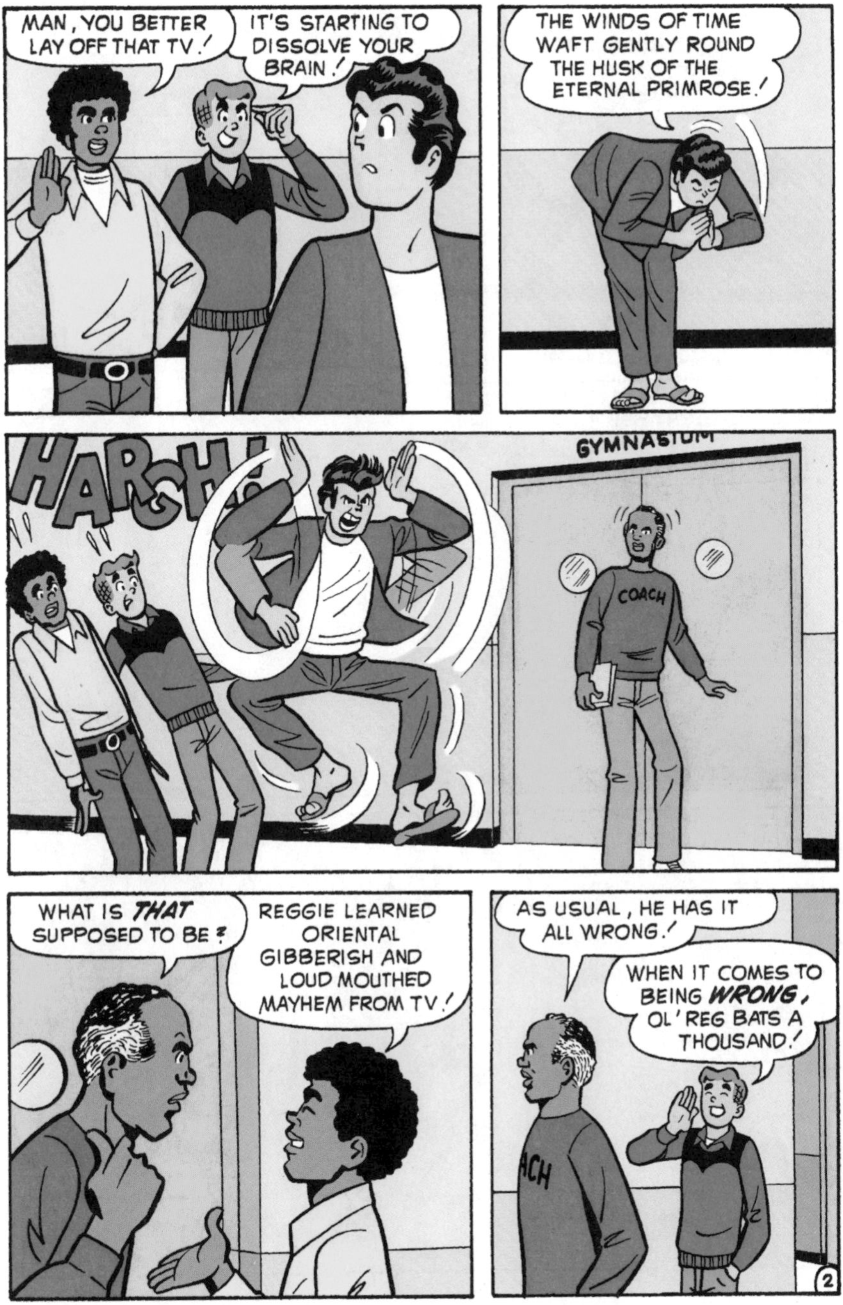
MAN, YOU BETTER LAY OFF THAT TV!
IT'S STARTING TO DISSOLVE YOUR BRAIN!
THE WINDS OF TIME WAFT GENTLY ROUND THE HUSK OF THE ETERNAL PRIMROSE!
GYMNASIUM
COACH
WHAT IS *THAT* SUPPOSED TO BE?
REGGIE LEARNED ORIENTAL GIBBERISH AND LOUD MOUTHED MAYHEM FROM TV!
AS USUAL, HE HAS IT ALL WRONG!
WHEN IT COMES TO BEING *WRONG*, OL' REG BATS A THOUSAND!
2

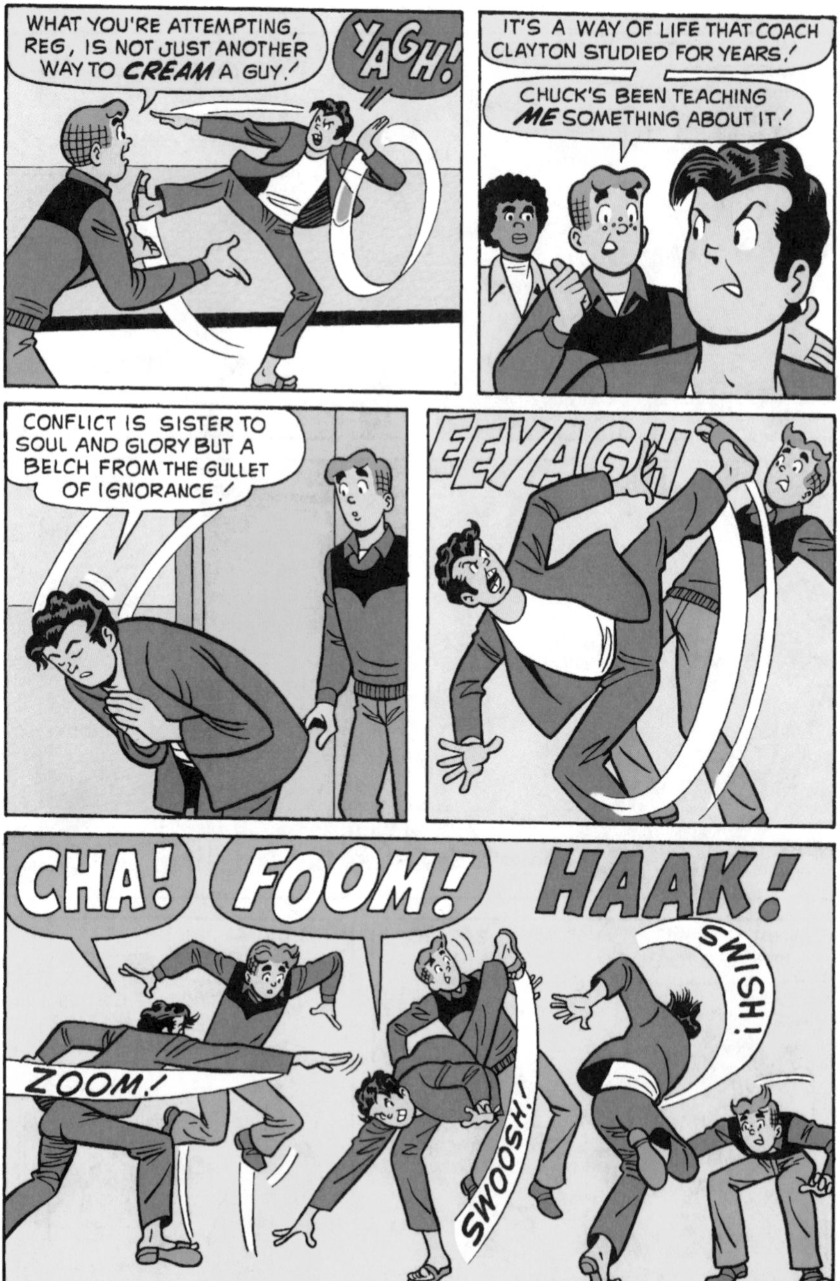
WHAT YOU'RE ATTEMPTING, REG, IS NOT JUST ANOTHER WAY TO CREAM A GUY!
YAGH!
IT'S A WAY OF LIFE THAT COACH CLAYTON STUDIED FOR YEARS!
CHUCK'S BEEN TEACHING ME SOMETHING ABOUT IT!
CONFLICT IS SISTER TO SOUL AND GLORY BUT A BELCH FROM THE GULLET OF IGNORANCE!
EEYAGH
CHA!
FOOM!
HAAK!
SWISH!
ZOOM!
SWOOSH!
3

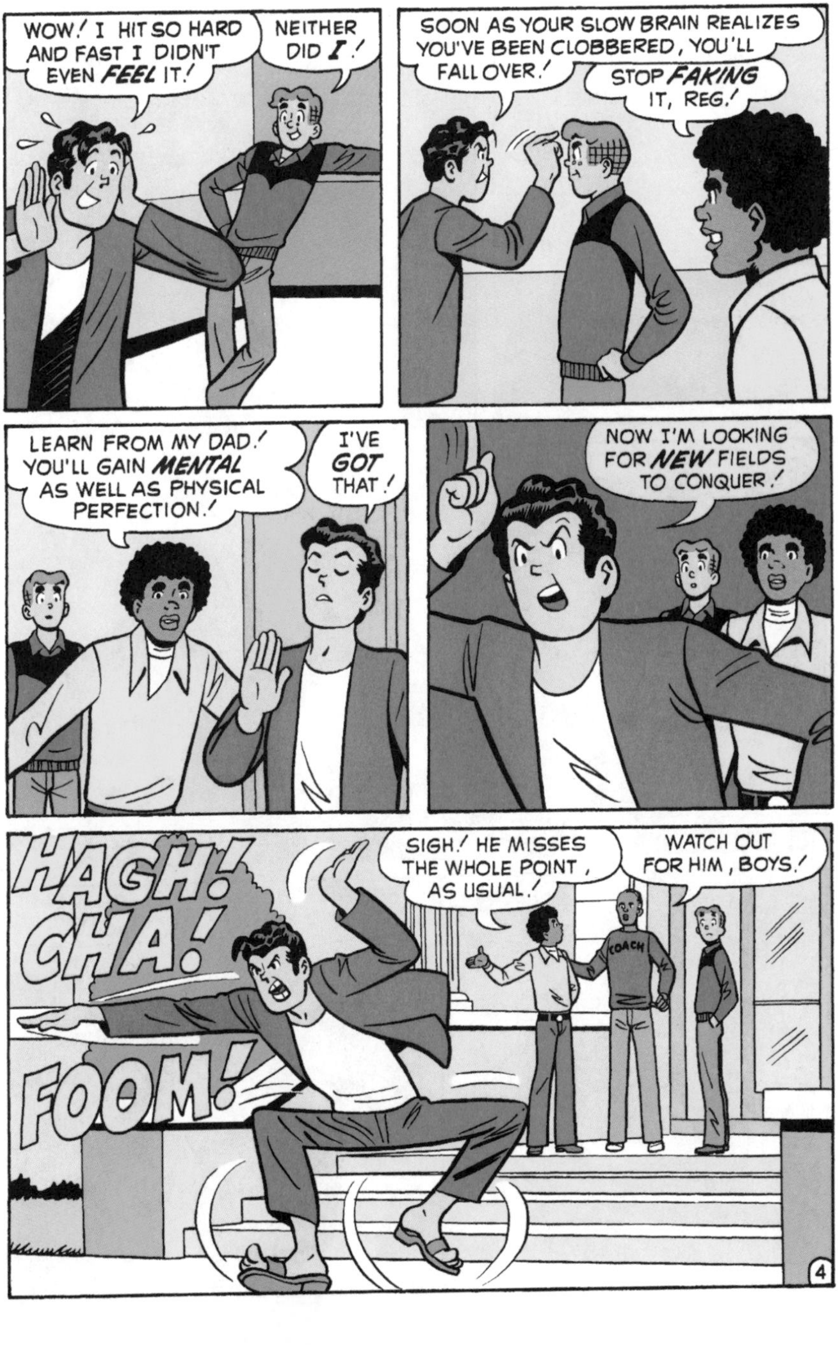
WOW! I HIT SO HARD AND FAST I DIDN'T EVEN FEEL IT!
NEITHER DID I!
SOON AS YOUR SLOW BRAIN REALIZES YOU'VE BEEN CLOBBERED, YOU'LL FALL OVER!
STOP FAKING IT, REG!
LEARN FROM MY DAD! YOU'LL GAIN MENTAL AS WELL AS PHYSICAL PERFECTION!
I'VE GOT THAT!
NOW I'M LOOKING FOR NEW FIELDS TO CONQUER!
HAGH! CHA!
FOOM!
SIGH! HE MISSES THE WHOLE POINT, AS USUAL!
WATCH OUT FOR HIM, BOYS!
COACH
4

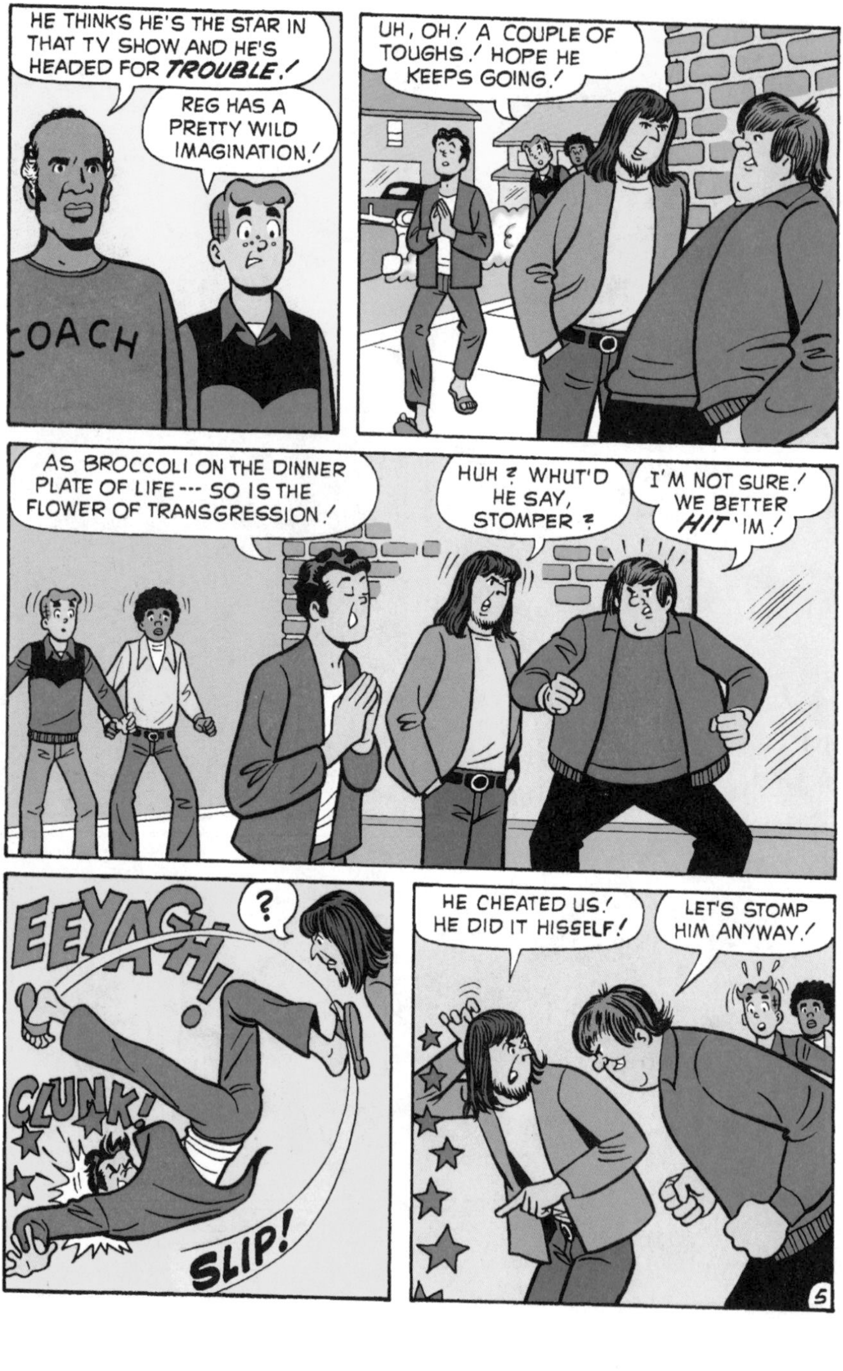

HE THINKS HE'S THE STAR IN THAT TV SHOW AND HE'S HEADED FOR TROUBLE!
REG HAS A PRETTY WILD IMAGINATION!
UH, OH! A COUPLE OF TOUGHS! HOPE HE KEEPS GOING!
COACH
AS BROCCOLI ON THE DINNER PLATE OF LIFE --- SO IS THE FLOWER OF TRANSGRESSION!
HUH? WHUT'D HE SAY, STOMPER?
I'M NOT SURE! WE BETTER HIT 'IM!
EEYAGH!
?
CLUNK!
SLIP!
HE CHEATED US! HE DID IT HISSELF!
LET'S STOMP HIM ANYWAY!
5

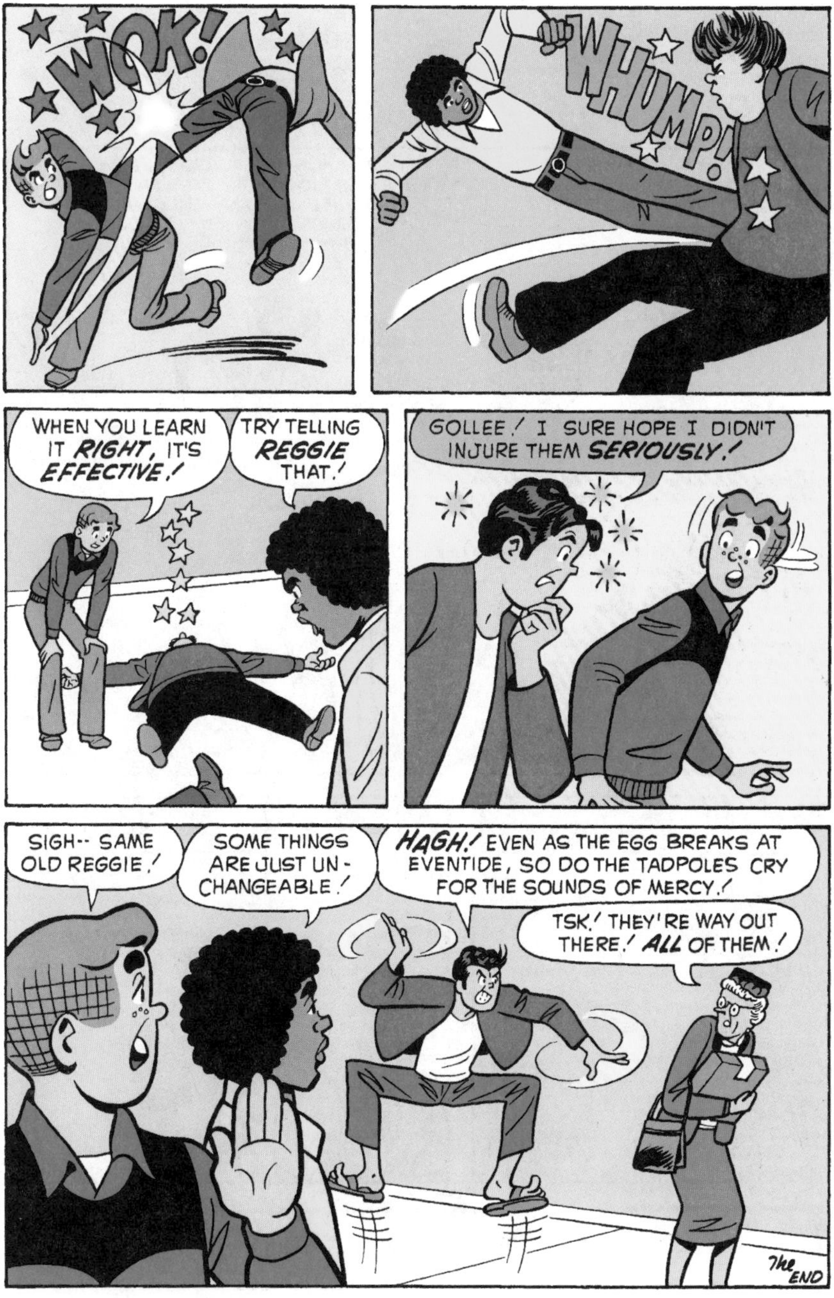
WOK!
WHUMP!
WHEN YOU LEARN IT RIGHT, IT'S EFFECTIVE!
TRY TELLING REGGIE THAT!
GOLLEE! I SURE HOPE I DIDN'T INJURE THEM SERIOUSLY!
SIGH-- SAME OLD REGGIE!
SOME THINGS ARE JUST UN-CHANGEABLE!
HAGH! EVEN AS THE EGG BREAKS AT EVENTIDE, SO DO THE TADPOLES CRY FOR THE SOUNDS OF MERCY!
TSK! THEY'RE WAY OUT THERE! ALL OF THEM!
The END

Archie at Riverdale in "Clean Up Campaign"

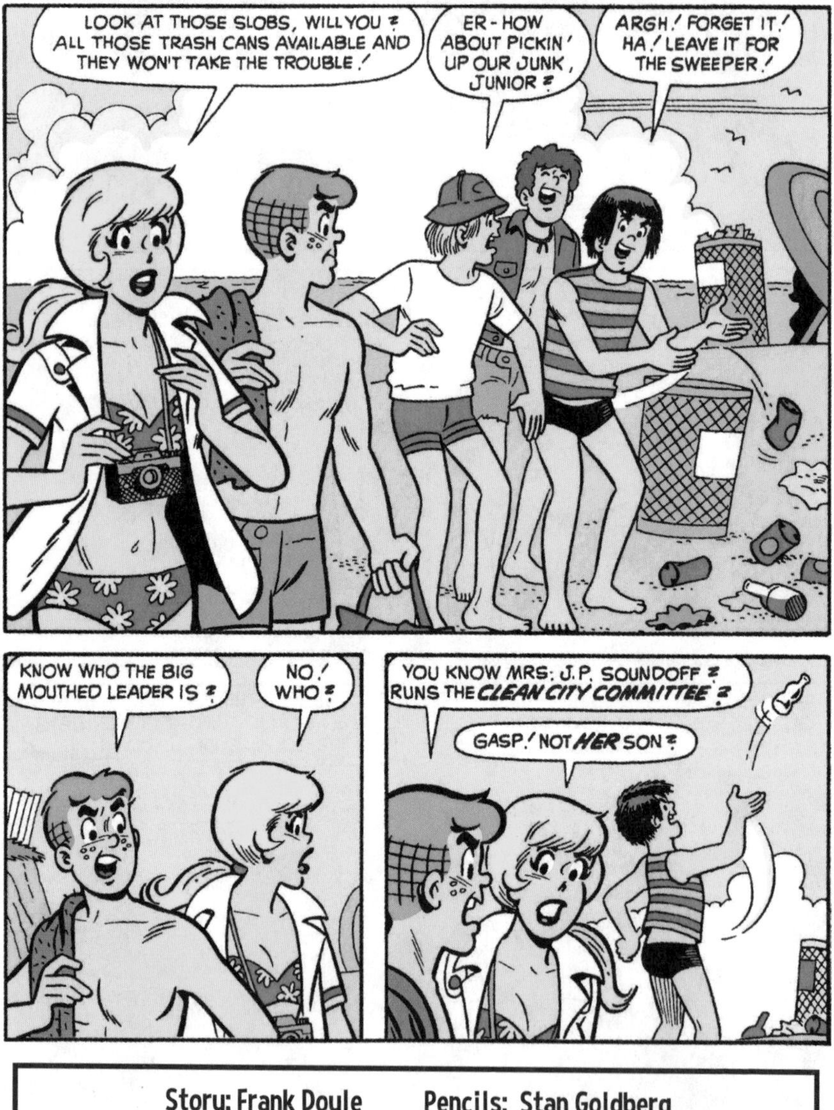
LOOK AT THOSE SLOBS, WILL YOU ? ALL THOSE TRASH CANS AVAILABLE AND THEY WON'T TAKE THE TROUBLE !
ER - HOW ABOUT PICKIN' UP OUR JUNK, JUNIOR ?
ARGH ! FORGET IT ! HA ! LEAVE IT FOR THE SWEEPER !
KNOW WHO THE BIG MOUTHED LEADER IS ?
NO ! WHO ?
YOU KNOW MRS. J.P. SOUNDOFF ? RUNS THE CLEAN CITY COMMITTEE ?
GASP ! NOT HER SON ?

Story: Frank Doyle Pencils: Stan Goldberg

Inks: Jon D'Agostino Letters: Bill Yoshida Colors: Barry Grossman

Originally printed in ARCHIE AT RIVERDALE HIGH #20, October 1974

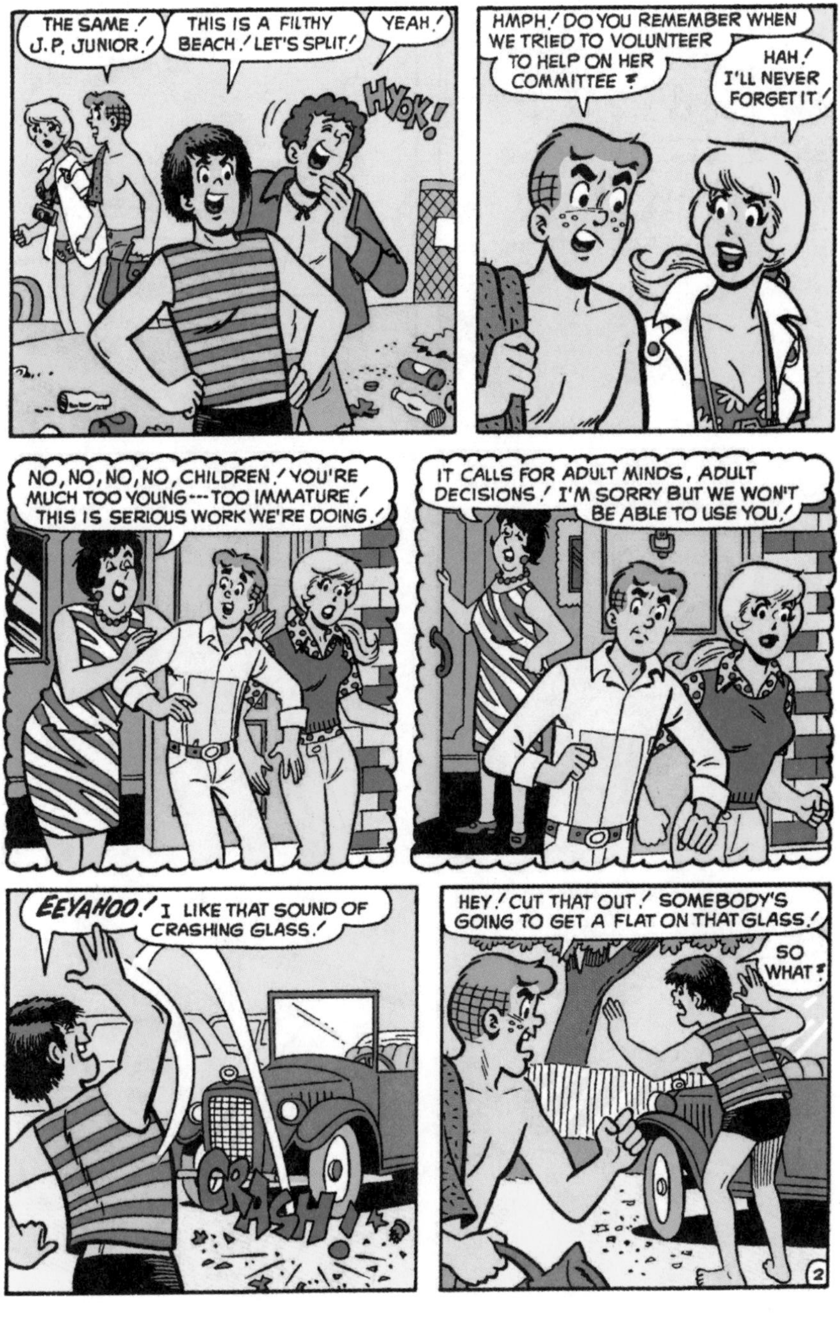
THE SAME! J.P. JUNIOR!
THIS IS A FILTHY BEACH! LET'S SPLIT!
YEAH!
HYOK!
HMPH! DO YOU REMEMBER WHEN WE TRIED TO VOLUNTEER TO HELP ON HER COMMITTEE?
HAH! I'LL NEVER FORGET IT!
NO, NO, NO, NO, CHILDREN! YOU'RE MUCH TOO YOUNG---TOO IMMATURE! THIS IS SERIOUS WORK WE'RE DOING!
IT CALLS FOR ADULT MINDS, ADULT DECISIONS! I'M SORRY BUT WE WON'T BE ABLE TO USE YOU!
EEYAHOO! I LIKE THAT SOUND OF CRASHING GLASS!
CRASH!
HEY! CUT THAT OUT! SOMEBODY'S GOING TO GET A FLAT ON THAT GLASS!
SO WHAT?
2

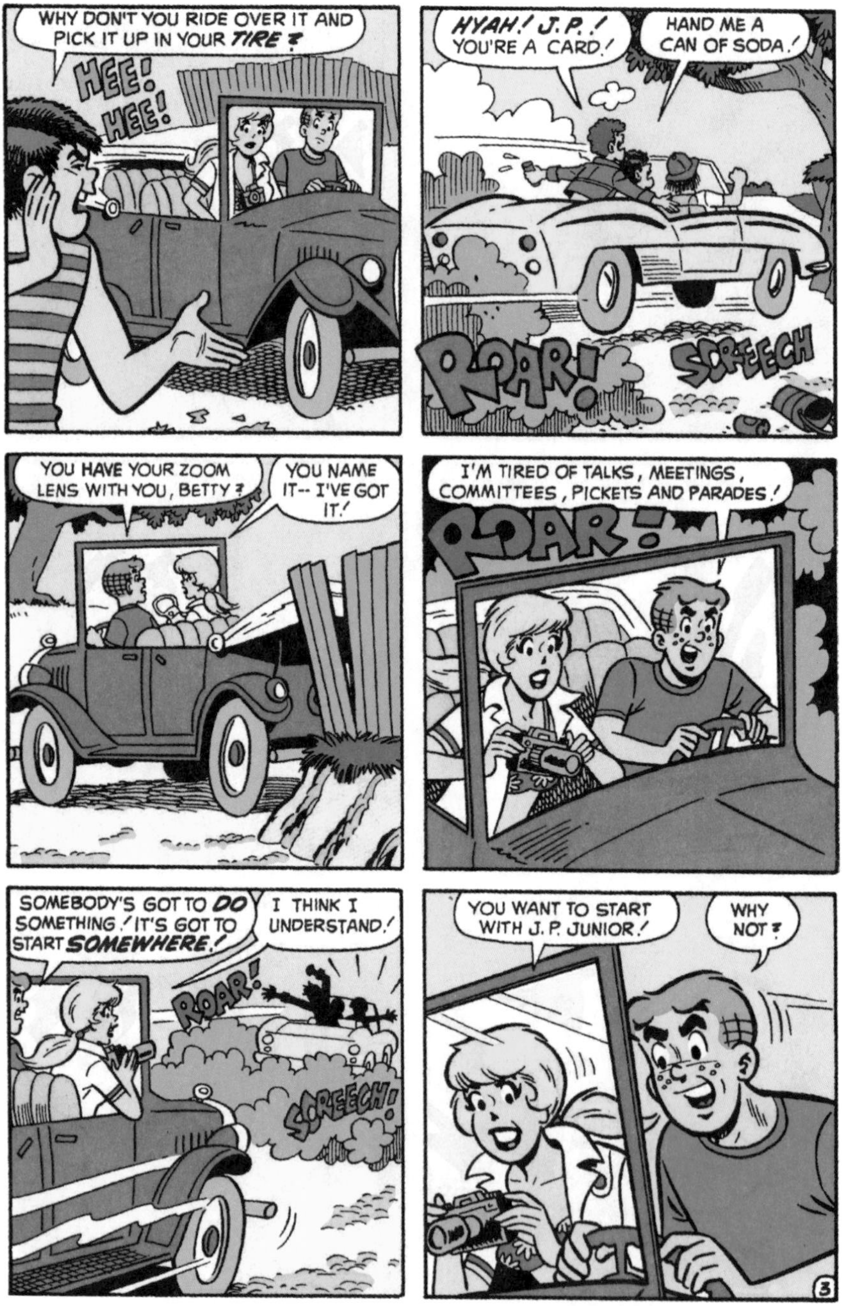
WHY DON'T YOU RIDE OVER IT AND PICK IT UP IN YOUR *TIRE* ?
HEE! HEE!
HYAH! J.P.! YOU'RE A CARD!
HAND ME A CAN OF SODA!
ROAR!
SCREECH
YOU HAVE YOUR ZOOM LENS WITH YOU, BETTY ?
YOU NAME IT-- I'VE GOT IT!
I'M TIRED OF TALKS, MEETINGS, COMMITTEES, PICKETS AND PARADES!
ROAR!
SOMEBODY'S GOT TO *DO* SOMETHING! IT'S GOT TO START *SOMEWHERE*!
I THINK I UNDERSTAND!
ROAR!
SCREECH!
YOU WANT TO START WITH J. P. JUNIOR!
WHY NOT ?
3

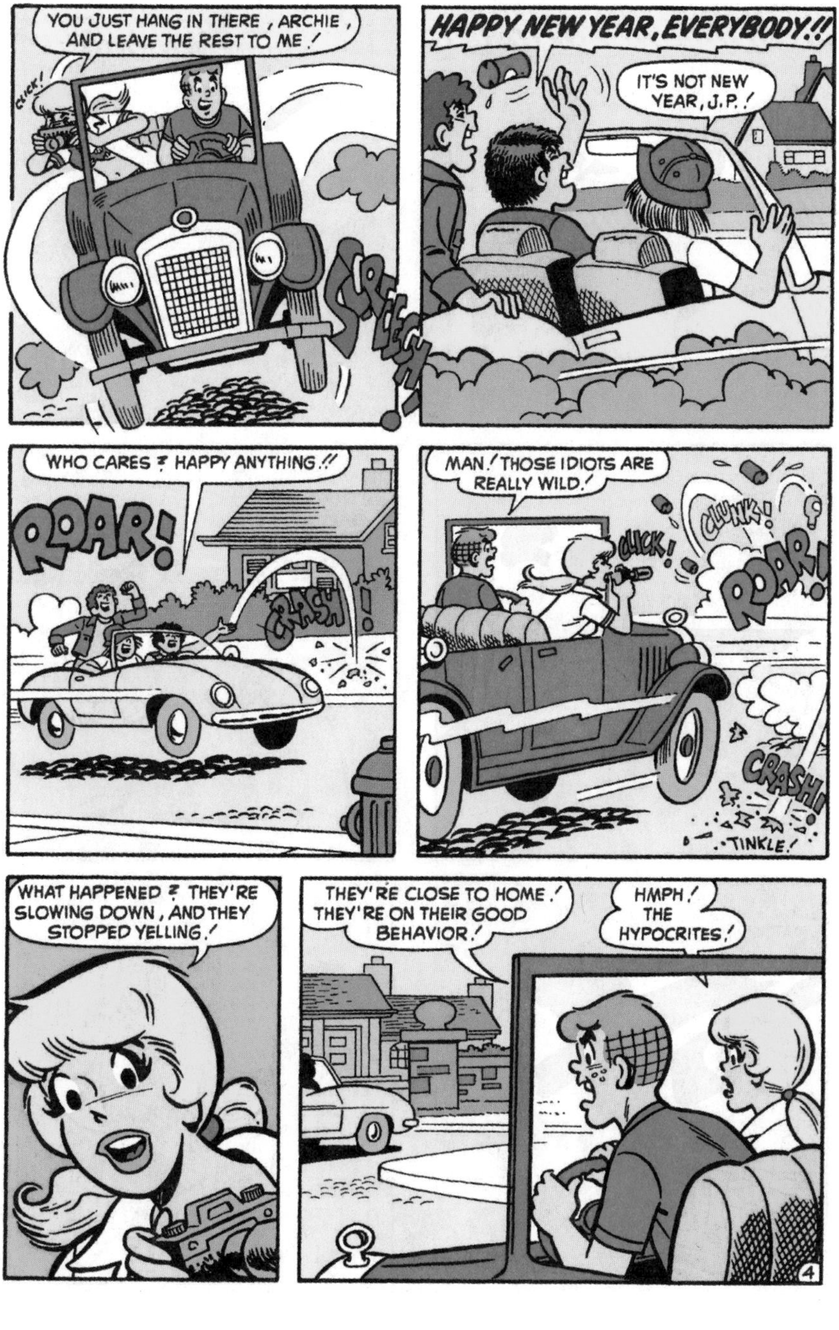
YOU JUST HANG IN THERE, ARCHIE, AND LEAVE THE REST TO ME!
CLICK!
SCREECH!
HAPPY NEW YEAR, EVERYBODY!!
IT'S NOT NEW YEAR, J.P.!
WHO CARES? HAPPY ANYTHING!!
ROAR!
CRASH!
MAN! THOSE IDIOTS ARE REALLY WILD!
CLICK!
CLUNK!
ROAR!
CRASH!
TINKLE!
WHAT HAPPENED? THEY'RE SLOWING DOWN, AND THEY STOPPED YELLING!
THEY'RE CLOSE TO HOME! THEY'RE ON THEIR GOOD BEHAVIOR!
HMPH! THE HYPOCRITES!
4

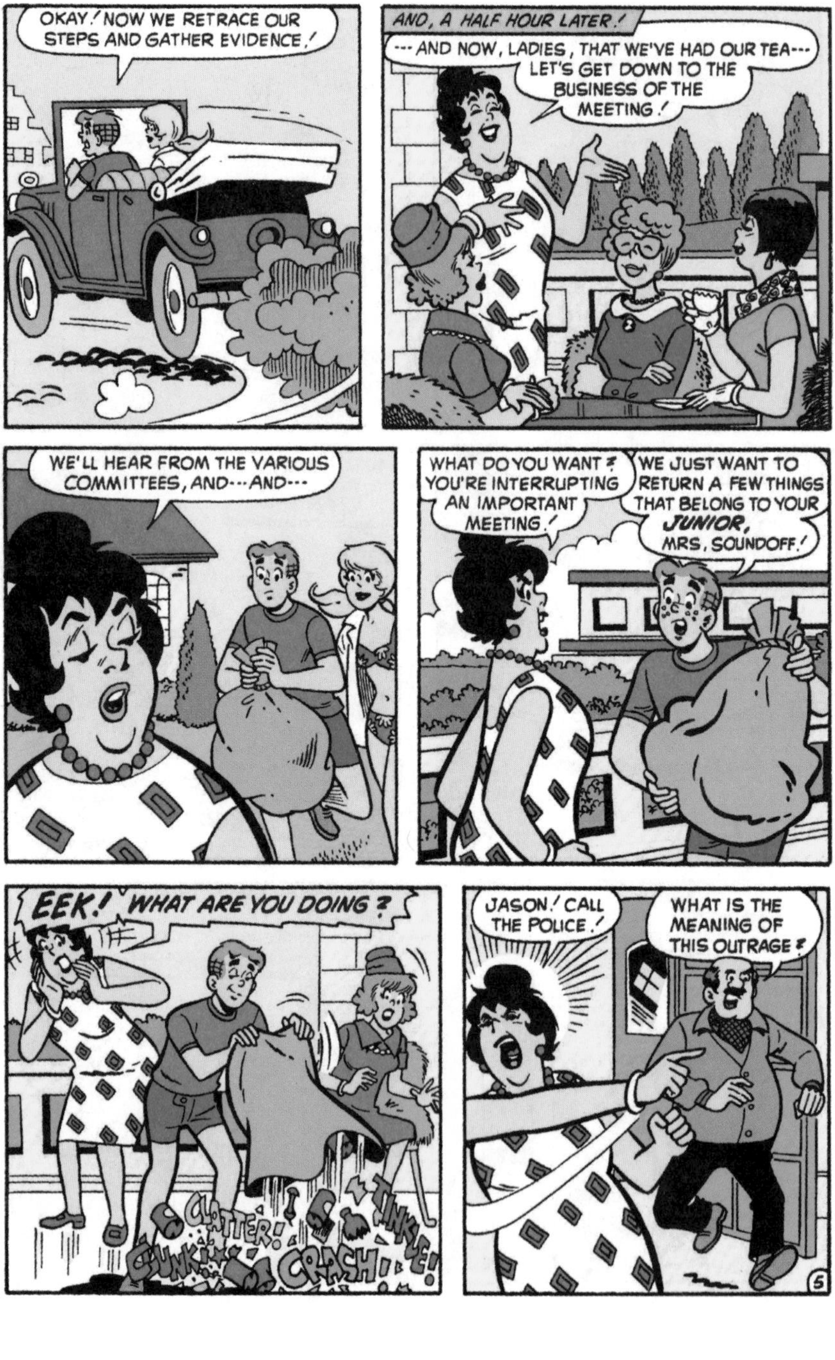
OKAY! NOW WE RETRACE OUR STEPS AND GATHER EVIDENCE!
AND, A HALF HOUR LATER!
--- AND NOW, LADIES, THAT WE'VE HAD OUR TEA--- LET'S GET DOWN TO THE BUSINESS OF THE MEETING!
WE'LL HEAR FROM THE VARIOUS COMMITTEES, AND---AND---
WHAT DO YOU WANT? YOU'RE INTERRUPTING AN IMPORTANT MEETING!
WE JUST WANT TO RETURN A FEW THINGS THAT BELONG TO YOUR JUNIOR, MRS. SOUNDOFF!
EEK! WHAT ARE YOU DOING?
CLATTER! TINKLE! CLUNK! CRASH!
JASON! CALL THE POLICE!
WHAT IS THE MEANING OF THIS OUTRAGE?
5

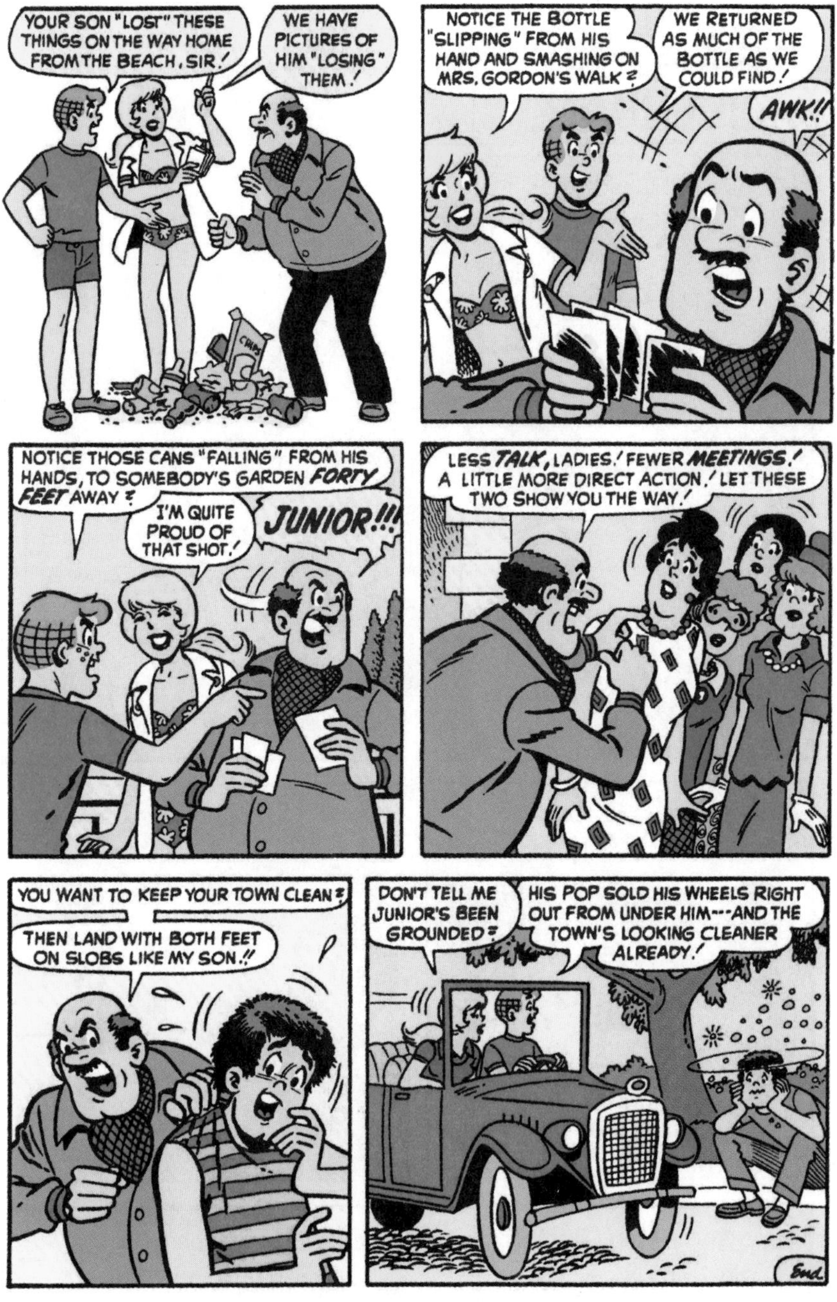
YOUR SON "LOST" THESE THINGS ON THE WAY HOME FROM THE BEACH, SIR!
WE HAVE PICTURES OF HIM "LOSING" THEM!
NOTICE THE BOTTLE "SLIPPING" FROM HIS HAND AND SMASHING ON MRS. GORDON'S WALK?
WE RETURNED AS MUCH OF THE BOTTLE AS WE COULD FIND!
AWK!!
NOTICE THOSE CANS "FALLING" FROM HIS HANDS, TO SOMEBODY'S GARDEN FORTY FEET AWAY?
I'M QUITE PROUD OF THAT SHOT!
JUNIOR!!!
LESS TALK, LADIES! FEWER MEETINGS! A LITTLE MORE DIRECT ACTION! LET THESE TWO SHOW YOU THE WAY!
YOU WANT TO KEEP YOUR TOWN CLEAN?
THEN LAND WITH BOTH FEET ON SLOBS LIKE MY SON!!
DON'T TELL ME JUNIOR'S BEEN GROUNDED?
HIS POP SOLD HIS WHEELS RIGHT OUT FROM UNDER HIM---AND THE TOWN'S LOOKING CLEANER ALREADY!
End

Archie at Riverdale in "The Beazly Ban"

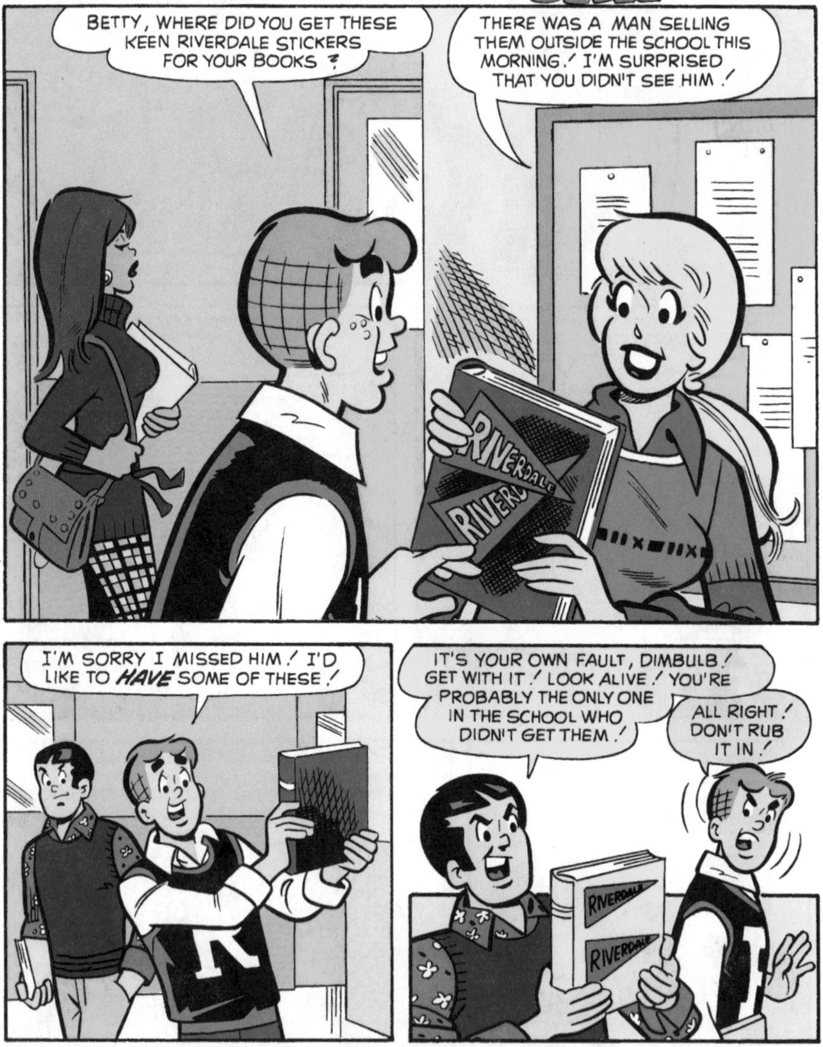
BETTY, WHERE DID YOU GET THESE KEEN RIVERDALE STICKERS FOR YOUR BOOKS ?
THERE WAS A MAN SELLING THEM OUTSIDE THE SCHOOL THIS MORNING! I'M SURPRISED THAT YOU DIDN'T SEE HIM!
RIVERDALE
RIVERD
I'M SORRY I MISSED HIM! I'D LIKE TO *HAVE* SOME OF THESE!
IT'S YOUR OWN FAULT, DIMBULB! GET WITH IT! LOOK ALIVE! YOU'RE PROBABLY THE ONLY ONE IN THE SCHOOL WHO DIDN'T GET THEM!
ALL RIGHT! DON'T RUB IT IN!
RIVERDALE
RIVERDALE

Story: Frank Doyle **Pencils:** Stan Goldberg

Inks: Rudy Lapick **Letters:** Bill Yoshida

Originally printed in ARCHIE AT RIVERDALE HIGH #23, March 1975

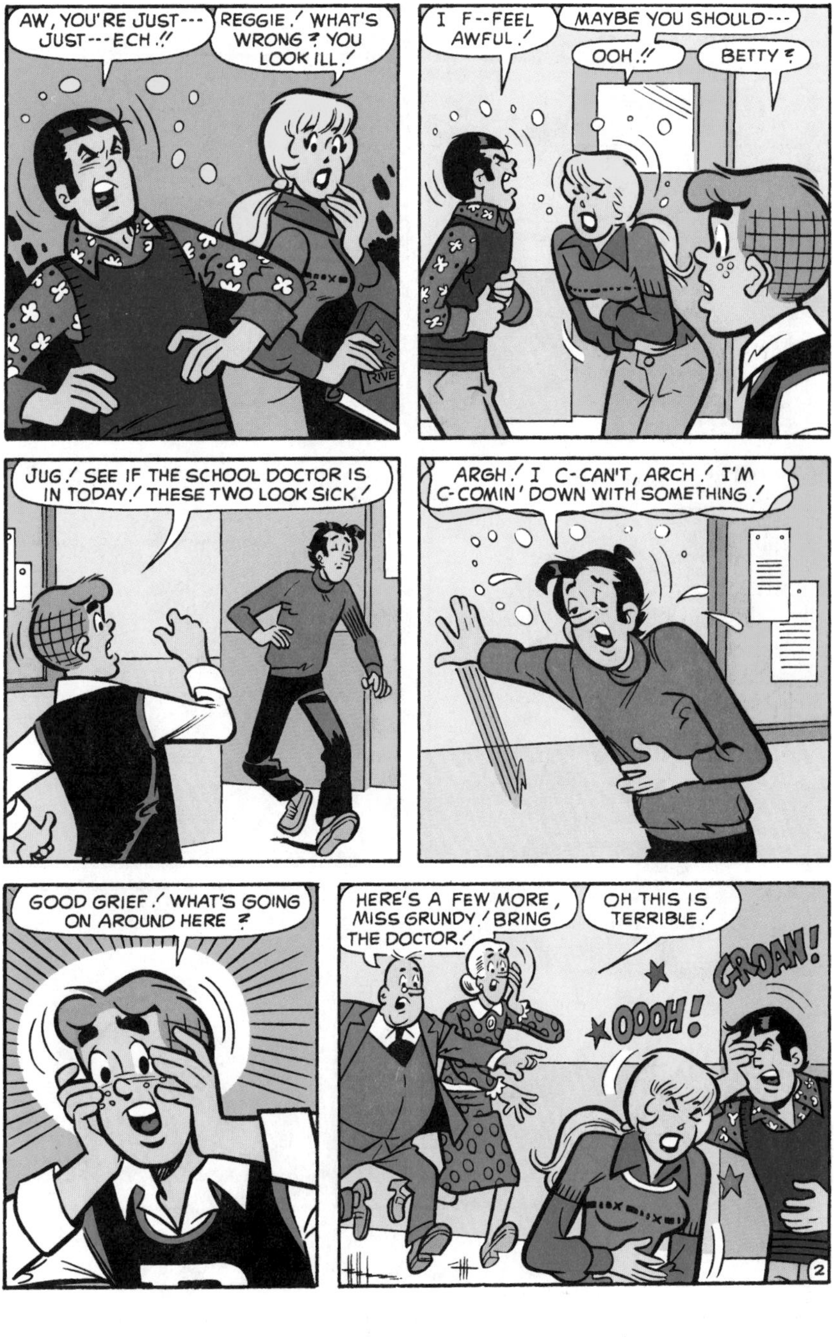
AW, YOU'RE JUST--- JUST---ECH.!!
REGGIE.! WHAT'S WRONG? YOU LOOK ILL.!
I F--FEEL AWFUL.!
MAYBE YOU SHOULD---
OOH.!!
BETTY?
JUG.! SEE IF THE SCHOOL DOCTOR IS IN TODAY.! THESE TWO LOOK SICK.!
ARGH.! I C-CAN'T, ARCH.! I'M C-COMIN' DOWN WITH SOMETHING.!
GOOD GRIEF.! WHAT'S GOING ON AROUND HERE?
HERE'S A FEW MORE, MISS GRUNDY.! BRING THE DOCTOR.!
OH THIS IS TERRIBLE.!
GROAN!
OOOH!
2

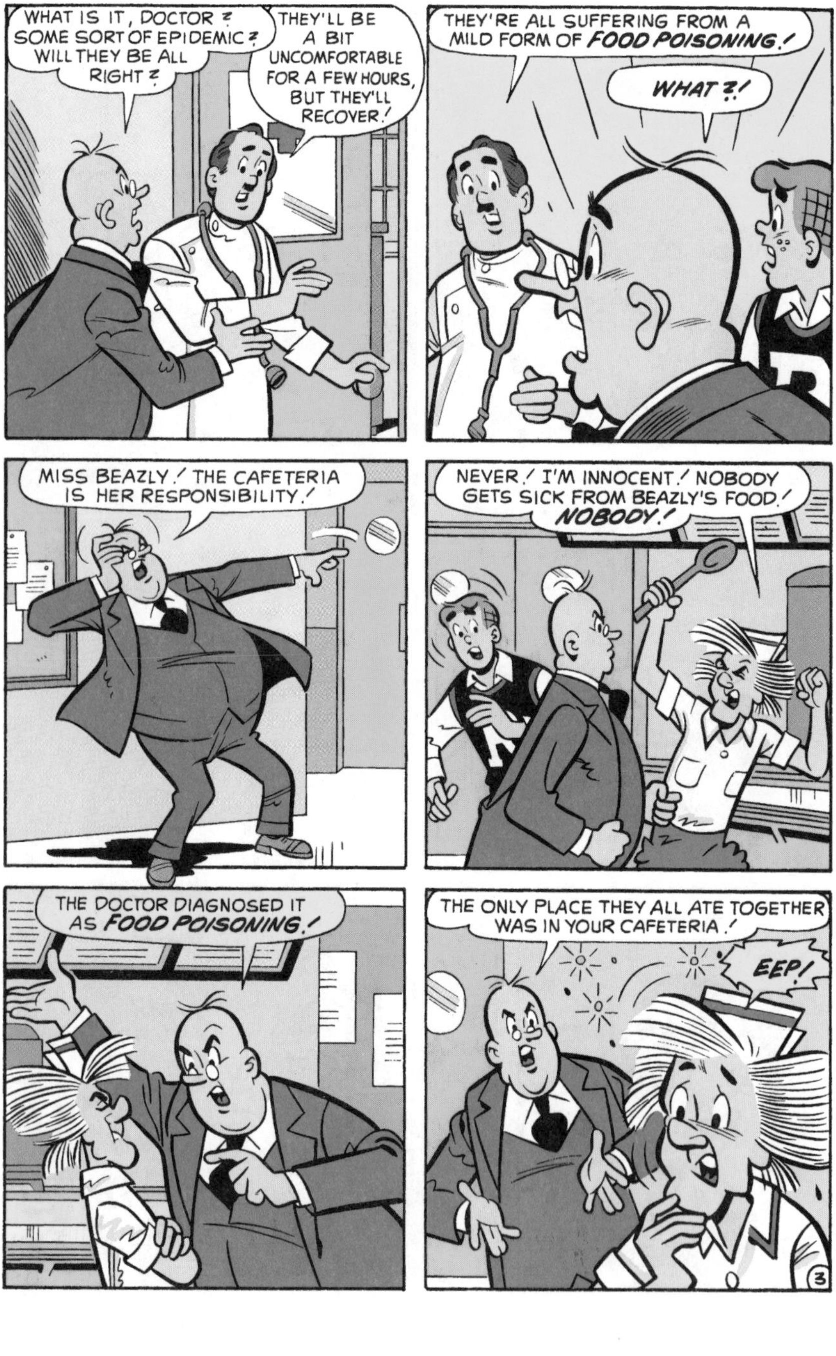
WHAT IS IT, DOCTOR? SOME SORT OF EPIDEMIC? WILL THEY BE ALL RIGHT?
THEY'LL BE A BIT UNCOMFORTABLE FOR A FEW HOURS, BUT THEY'LL RECOVER!
THEY'RE ALL SUFFERING FROM A MILD FORM OF FOOD POISONING!
WHAT?!
MISS BEAZLY! THE CAFETERIA IS HER RESPONSIBILITY!
NEVER! I'M INNOCENT! NOBODY GETS SICK FROM BEAZLY'S FOOD! NOBODY!
THE DOCTOR DIAGNOSED IT AS FOOD POISONING!
THE ONLY PLACE THEY ALL ATE TOGETHER WAS IN YOUR CAFETERIA!
EEP!
3

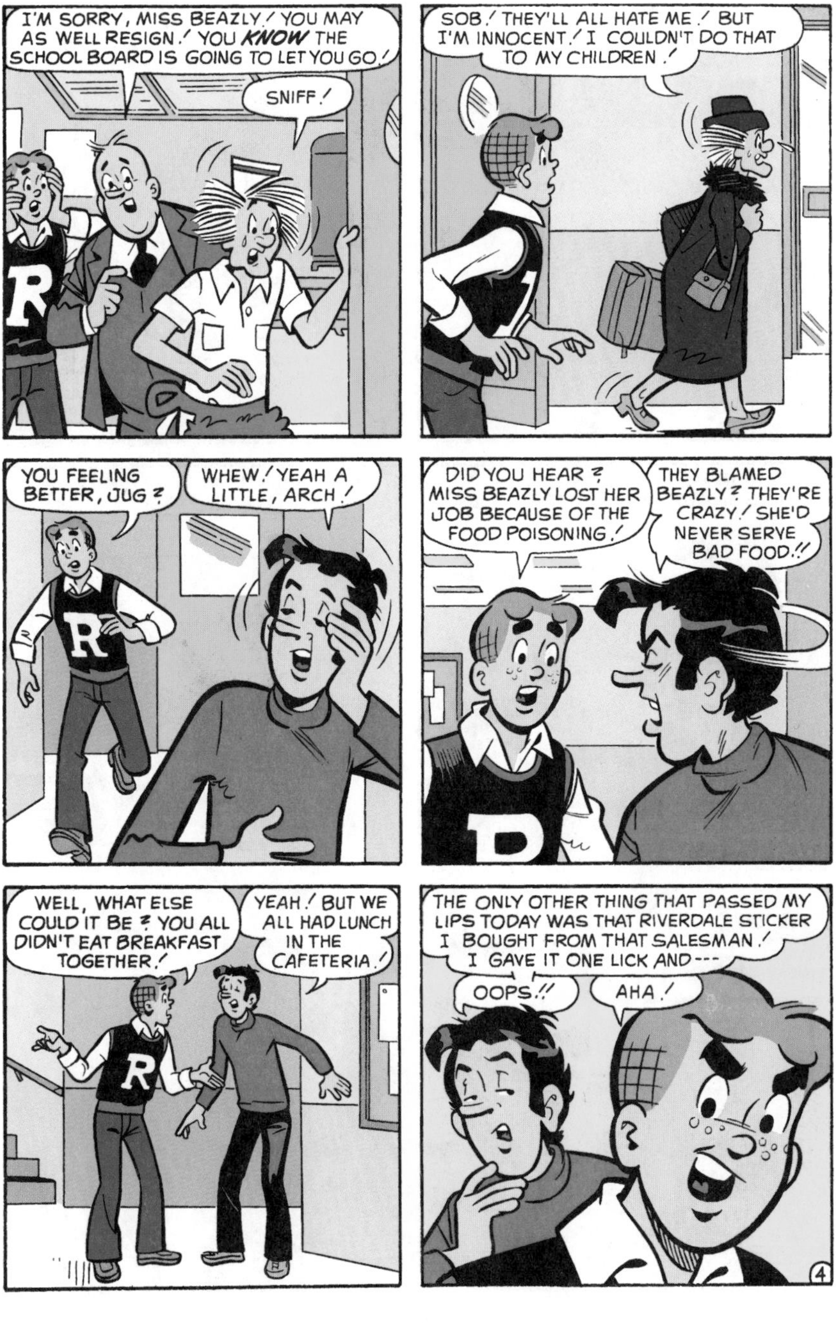
I'M SORRY, MISS BEAZLY! YOU MAY AS WELL RESIGN! YOU KNOW THE SCHOOL BOARD IS GOING TO LET YOU GO!
SNIFF!
SOB! THEY'LL ALL HATE ME! BUT I'M INNOCENT! I COULDN'T DO THAT TO MY CHILDREN!
YOU FEELING BETTER, JUG?
WHEW! YEAH A LITTLE, ARCH!
DID YOU HEAR? MISS BEAZLY LOST HER JOB BECAUSE OF THE FOOD POISONING!
THEY BLAMED BEAZLY? THEY'RE CRAZY! SHE'D NEVER SERVE BAD FOOD!!
WELL, WHAT ELSE COULD IT BE? YOU ALL DIDN'T EAT BREAKFAST TOGETHER!
YEAH! BUT WE ALL HAD LUNCH IN THE CAFETERIA!
THE ONLY OTHER THING THAT PASSED MY LIPS TODAY WAS THAT RIVERDALE STICKER I BOUGHT FROM THAT SALESMAN! I GAVE IT ONE LICK AND---
OOPS!!
AHA!
4

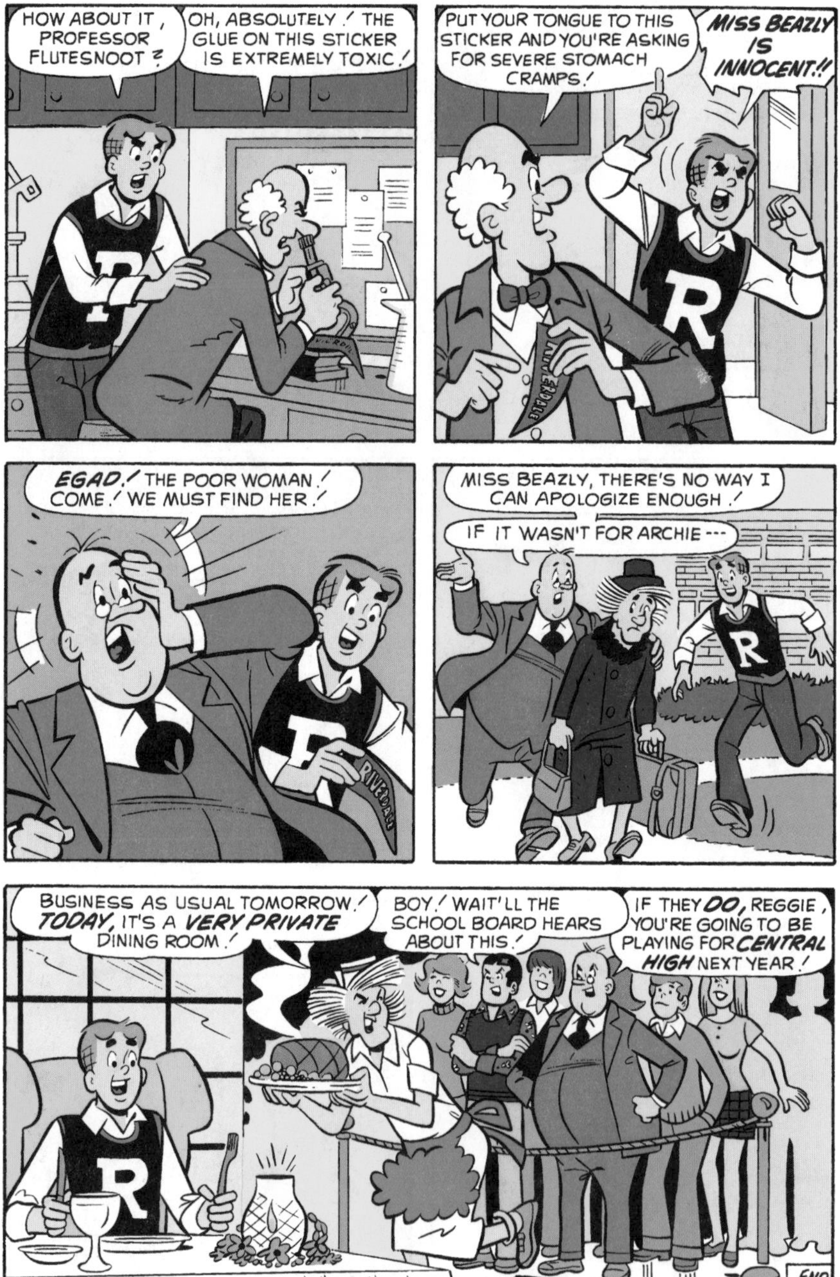
HOW ABOUT IT, PROFESSOR FLUTESNOOT?
OH, ABSOLUTELY! THE GLUE ON THIS STICKER IS EXTREMELY TOXIC!
PUT YOUR TONGUE TO THIS STICKER AND YOU'RE ASKING FOR SEVERE STOMACH CRAMPS!
MISS BEAZLY IS INNOCENT!!
EGAD! THE POOR WOMAN! COME! WE MUST FIND HER!
RIVERDALE
MISS BEAZLY, THERE'S NO WAY I CAN APOLOGIZE ENOUGH!
IF IT WASN'T FOR ARCHIE ---
BUSINESS AS USUAL TOMORROW! TODAY, IT'S A VERY PRIVATE DINING ROOM!
BOY! WAIT'LL THE SCHOOL BOARD HEARS ABOUT THIS!
IF THEY DO, REGGIE, YOU'RE GOING TO BE PLAYING FOR CENTRAL HIGH NEXT YEAR!
END

Archie AT RIVERDALE IN "SNOWBOUND" PART I

Story: Frank Doyle	Pencils: Dan DeCarlo
Inks: Rudy Lapick	Letters: Bill Yoshida

Originally printed in ARCHIE AT RIVERDALE HIGH #23, March 1975

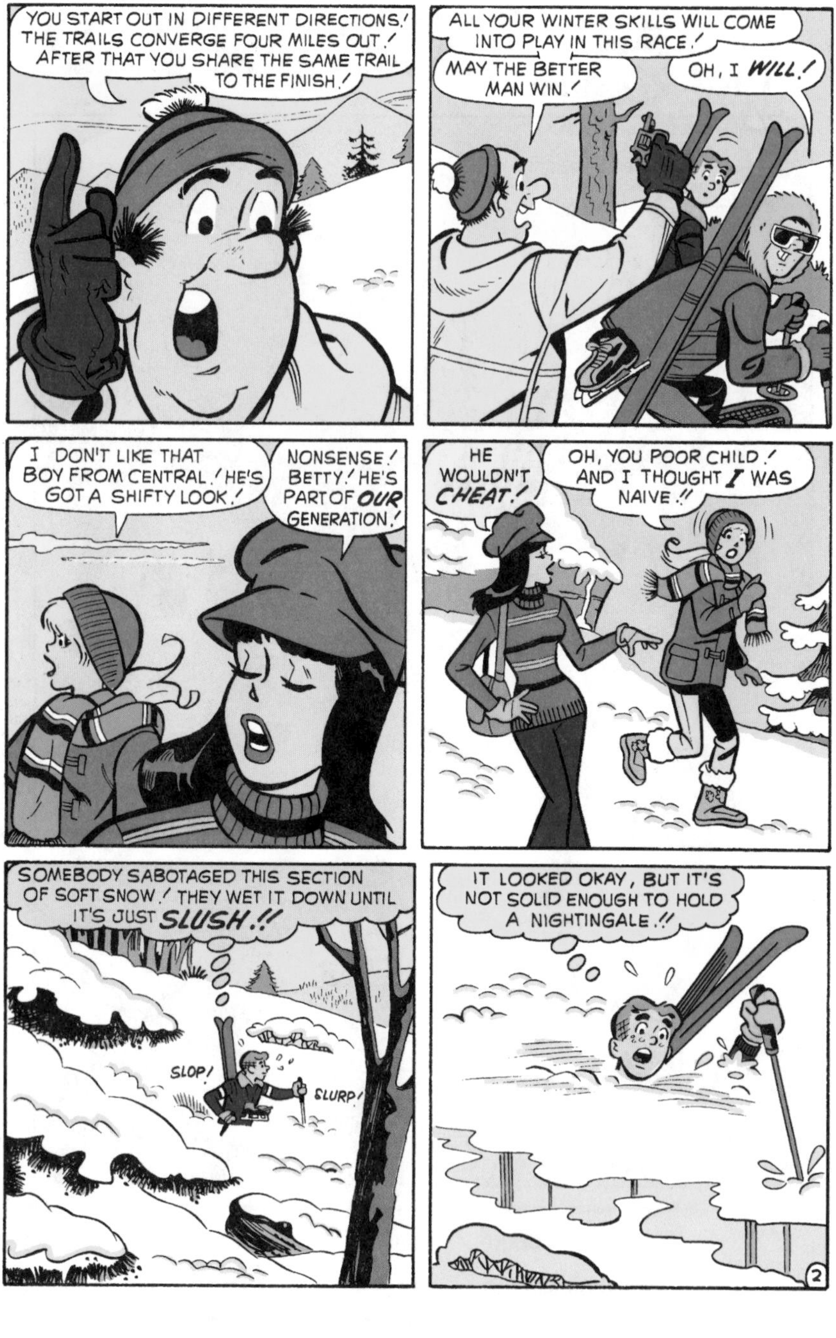
YOU START OUT IN DIFFERENT DIRECTIONS! THE TRAILS CONVERGE FOUR MILES OUT! AFTER THAT YOU SHARE THE SAME TRAIL TO THE FINISH!
ALL YOUR WINTER SKILLS WILL COME INTO PLAY IN THIS RACE!
MAY THE BETTER MAN WIN!
OH, I WILL!
I DON'T LIKE THAT BOY FROM CENTRAL! HE'S GOT A SHIFTY LOOK!
NONSENSE! BETTY! HE'S PART OF OUR GENERATION!
HE WOULDN'T CHEAT!
OH, YOU POOR CHILD! AND I THOUGHT I WAS NAIVE!!
SOMEBODY SABOTAGED THIS SECTION OF SOFT SNOW! THEY WET IT DOWN UNTIL IT'S JUST SLUSH!!
SLOP!
SLURP!
IT LOOKED OKAY, BUT IT'S NOT SOLID ENOUGH TO HOLD A NIGHTINGALE!!
2

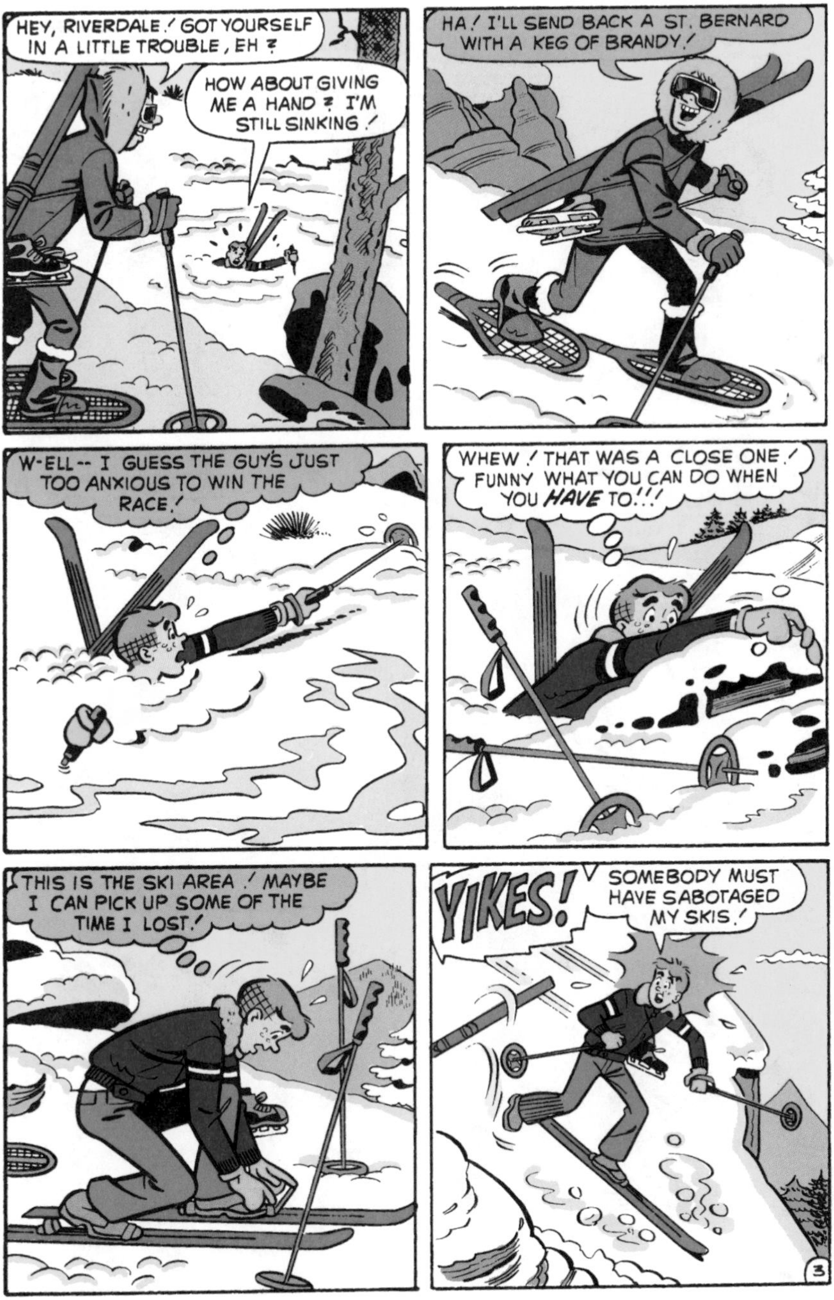
HEY, RIVERDALE! GOT YOURSELF IN A LITTLE TROUBLE, EH?
HOW ABOUT GIVING ME A HAND? I'M STILL SINKING!
HA! I'LL SEND BACK A ST. BERNARD WITH A KEG OF BRANDY!
W-ELL-- I GUESS THE GUY'S JUST TOO ANXIOUS TO WIN THE RACE!
WHEW! THAT WAS A CLOSE ONE! FUNNY WHAT YOU CAN DO WHEN YOU HAVE TO!!!
THIS IS THE SKI AREA! MAYBE I CAN PICK UP SOME OF THE TIME I LOST!
YIKES!
SOMEBODY MUST HAVE SABOTAGED MY SKIS!
3

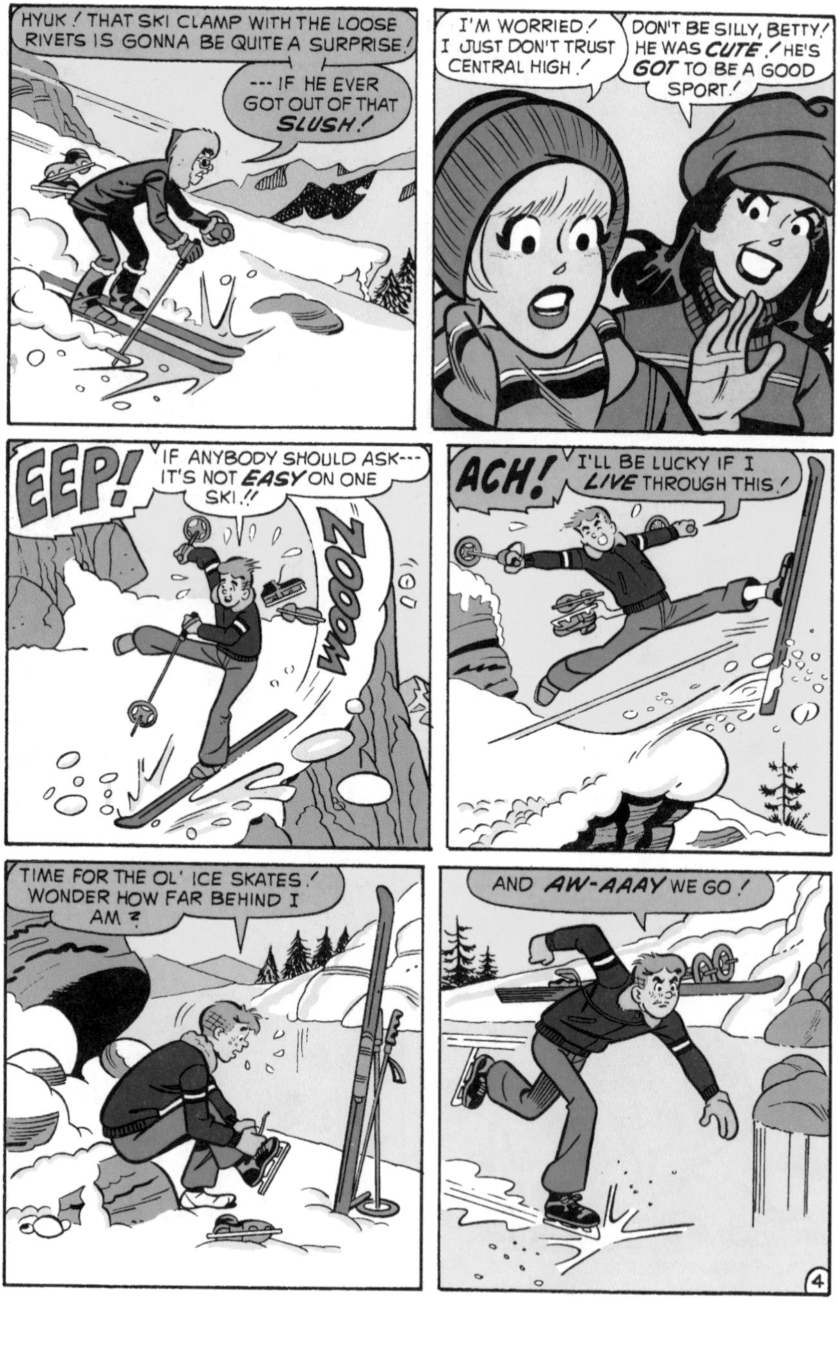
HYUK! THAT SKI CLAMP WITH THE LOOSE RIVETS IS GONNA BE QUITE A SURPRISE!
--- IF HE EVER GOT OUT OF THAT SLUSH!
I'M WORRIED! I JUST DON'T TRUST CENTRAL HIGH!
DON'T BE SILLY, BETTY! HE WAS CUTE! HE'S GOT TO BE A GOOD SPORT!
EEP!
IF ANYBODY SHOULD ASK--- IT'S NOT EASY ON ONE SKI!!
ZOOOOOM
ACH!
I'LL BE LUCKY IF I LIVE THROUGH THIS!
TIME FOR THE OL' ICE SKATES! WONDER HOW FAR BEHIND I AM?
AND AW-AAAY WE GO!
4

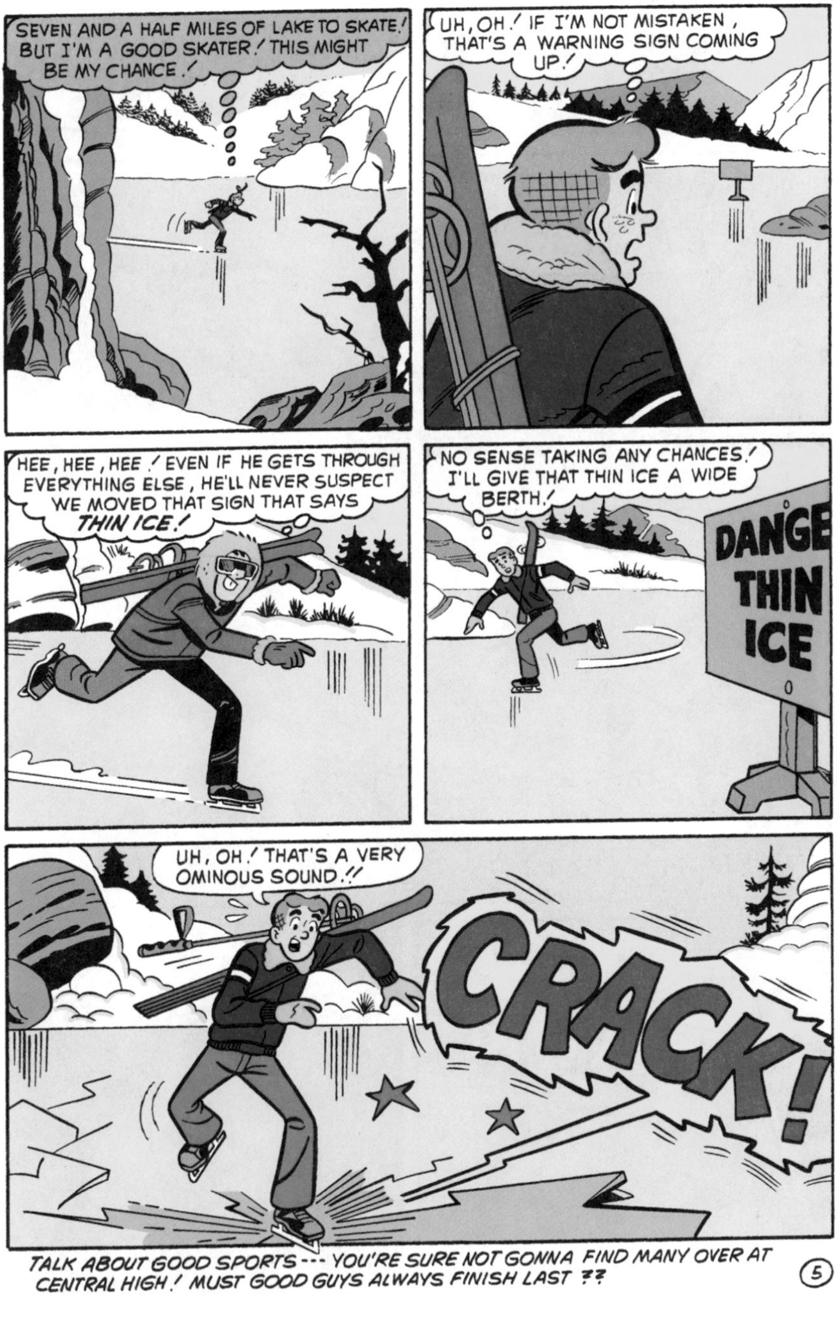
SEVEN AND A HALF MILES OF LAKE TO SKATE! BUT I'M A GOOD SKATER! THIS MIGHT BE MY CHANCE!
UH, OH! IF I'M NOT MISTAKEN, THAT'S A WARNING SIGN COMING UP!
HEE, HEE, HEE! EVEN IF HE GETS THROUGH EVERYTHING ELSE, HE'LL NEVER SUSPECT WE MOVED THAT SIGN THAT SAYS THIN ICE!
NO SENSE TAKING ANY CHANCES! I'LL GIVE THAT THIN ICE A WIDE BERTH!
DANGE
THIN
ICE
UH, OH! THAT'S A VERY OMINOUS SOUND!!
CRACK!

TALK ABOUT GOOD SPORTS--- YOU'RE SURE NOT GONNA FIND MANY OVER AT CENTRAL HIGH! MUST GOOD GUYS ALWAYS FINISH LAST ??

Archie at Riverdale
Snowbound
Part II

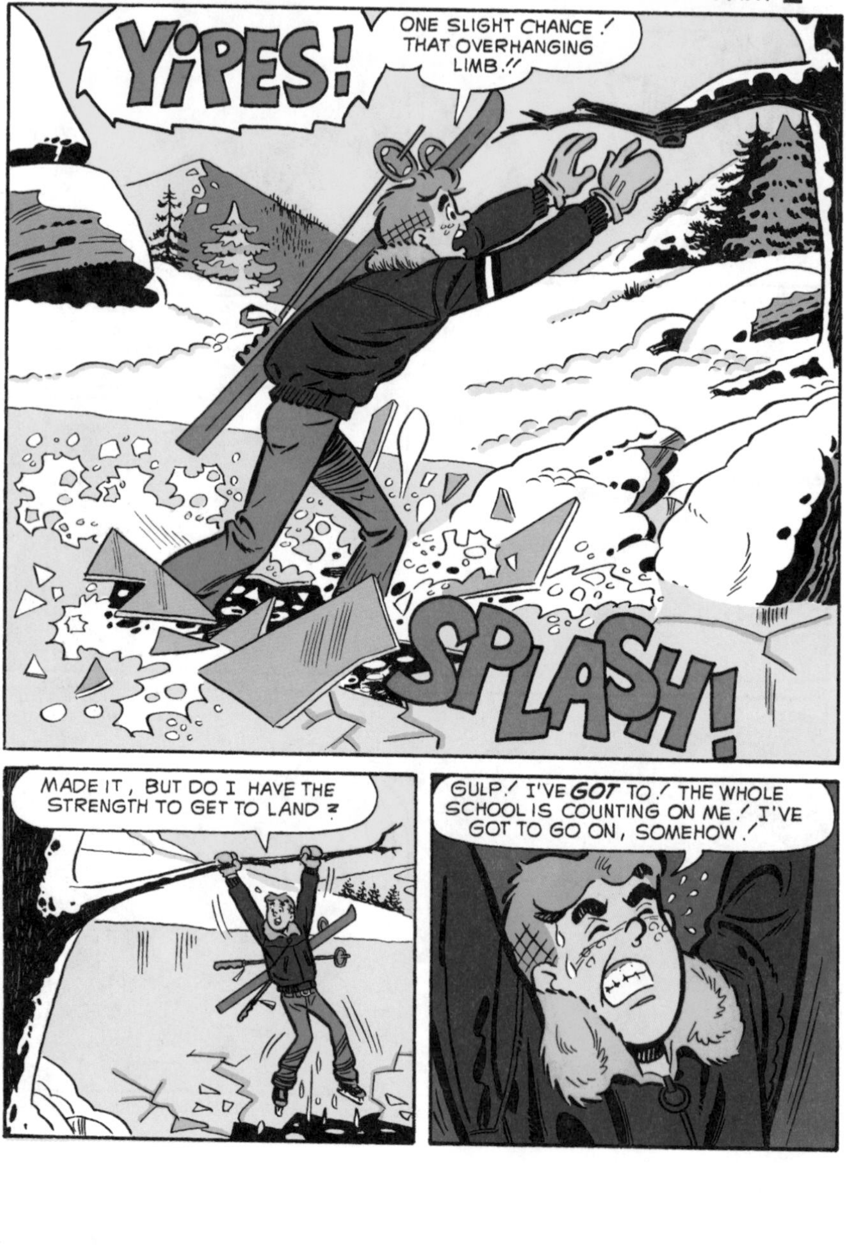
YIPES!
ONE SLIGHT CHANCE! THAT OVERHANGING LIMB.!!
SPLASH!
MADE IT, BUT DO I HAVE THE STRENGTH TO GET TO LAND?
GULP! I'VE GOT TO! THE WHOLE SCHOOL IS COUNTING ON ME! I'VE GOT TO GO ON, SOMEHOW!

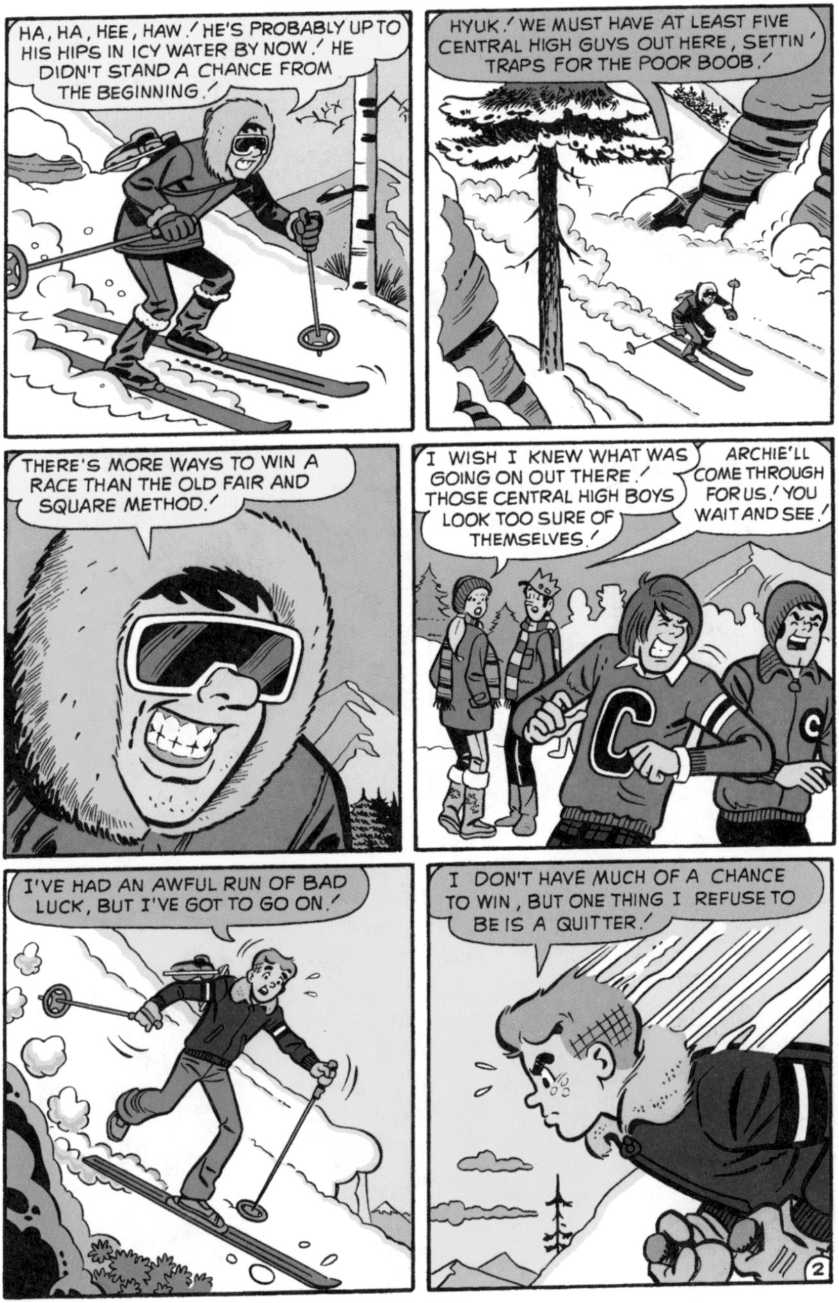
HA, HA, HEE, HAW.! HE'S PROBABLY UP TO HIS HIPS IN ICY WATER BY NOW.! HE DIDN'T STAND A CHANCE FROM THE BEGINNING.!
HYUK.! WE MUST HAVE AT LEAST FIVE CENTRAL HIGH GUYS OUT HERE, SETTIN' TRAPS FOR THE POOR BOOB.!
THERE'S MORE WAYS TO WIN A RACE THAN THE OLD FAIR AND SQUARE METHOD.!
I WISH I KNEW WHAT WAS GOING ON OUT THERE.! THOSE CENTRAL HIGH BOYS LOOK TOO SURE OF THEMSELVES.!
ARCHIE'LL COME THROUGH FOR US.! YOU WAIT AND SEE.!
I'VE HAD AN AWFUL RUN OF BAD LUCK, BUT I'VE GOT TO GO ON.!
I DON'T HAVE MUCH OF A CHANCE TO WIN, BUT ONE THING I REFUSE TO BE IS A QUITTER.!
2

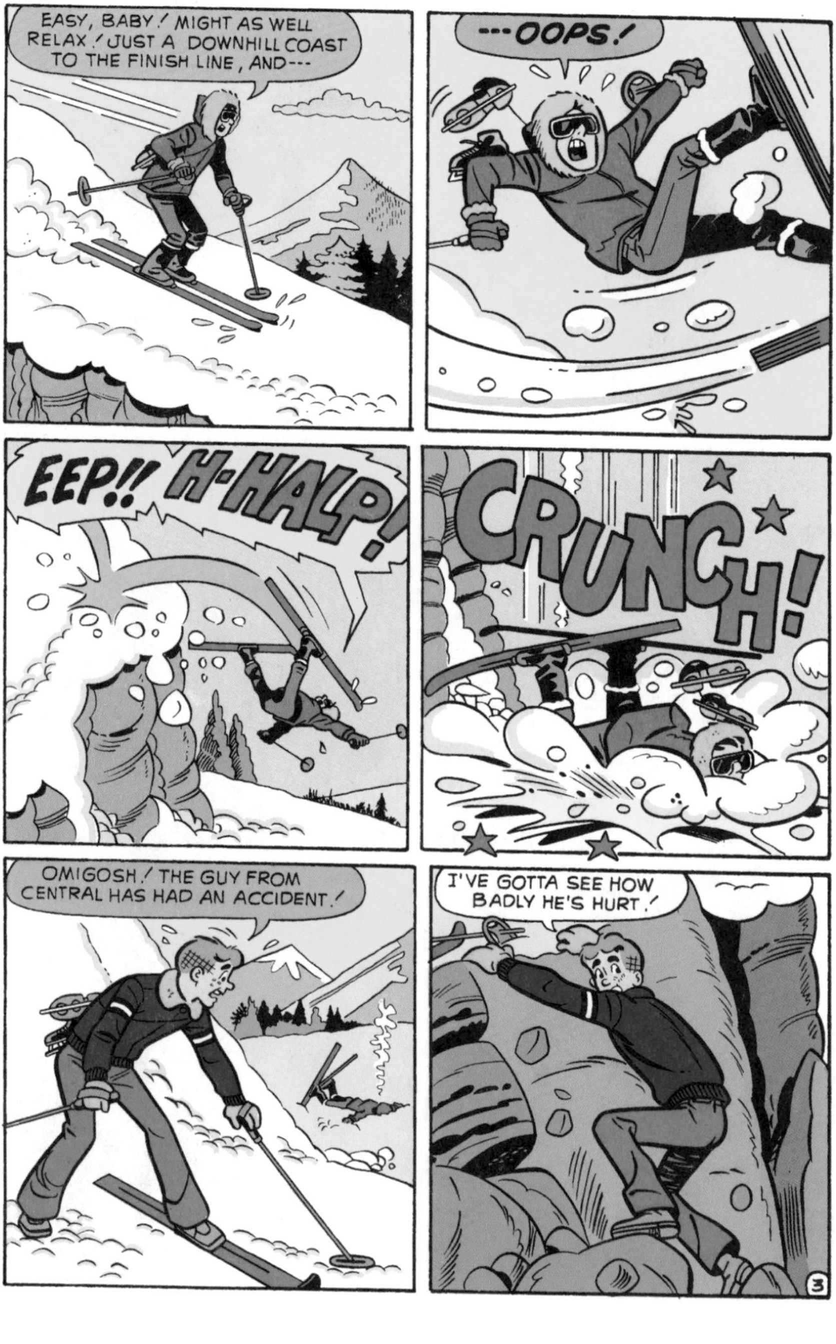
EASY, BABY! MIGHT AS WELL RELAX! JUST A DOWNHILL COAST TO THE FINISH LINE, AND---
---OOPS!
EEP!! H-HALP!
CRUNCH!
OMIGOSH! THE GUY FROM CENTRAL HAS HAD AN ACCIDENT!
I'VE GOTTA SEE HOW BADLY HE'S HURT!
3

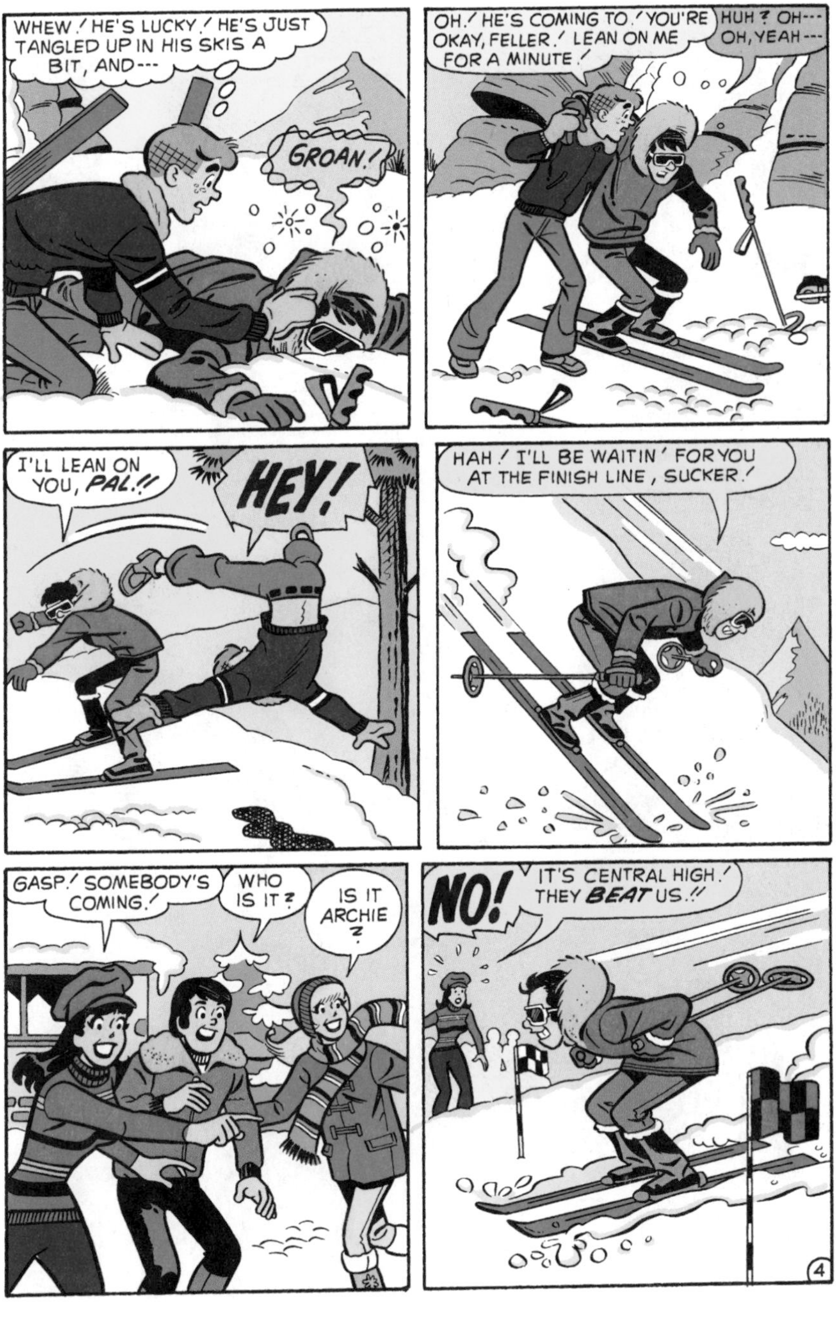
WHEW! HE'S LUCKY! HE'S JUST TANGLED UP IN HIS SKIS A BIT, AND---
GROAN!
OH! HE'S COMING TO! YOU'RE OKAY, FELLER! LEAN ON ME FOR A MINUTE!
HUH? OH--- OH, YEAH---
I'LL LEAN ON YOU, PAL!!
HEY!
HAH! I'LL BE WAITIN' FOR YOU AT THE FINISH LINE, SUCKER!
GASP! SOMEBODY'S COMING!
WHO IS IT?
IS IT ARCHIE?
NO!
IT'S CENTRAL HIGH! THEY BEAT US!!
4

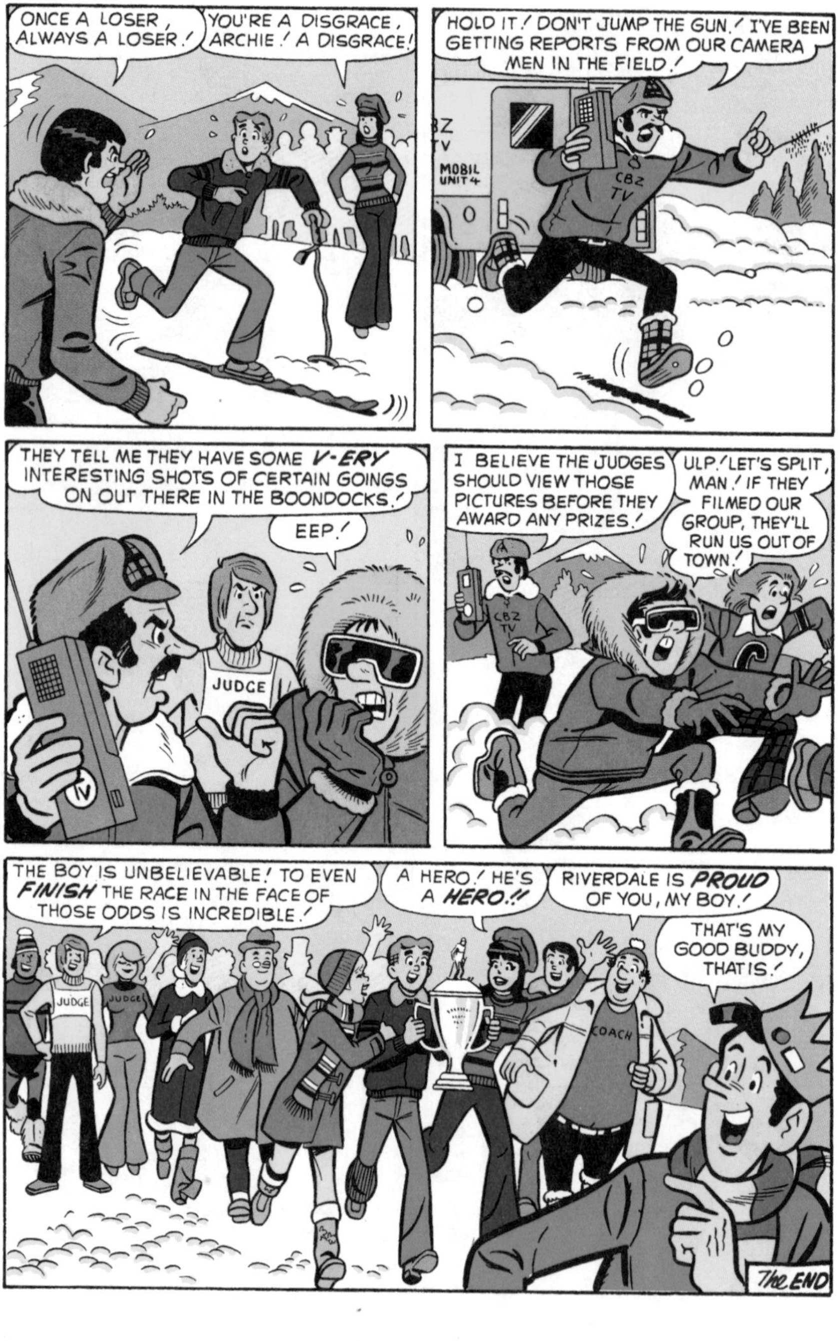
ONCE A LOSER, ALWAYS A LOSER!
YOU'RE A DISGRACE, ARCHIE! A DISGRACE!
HOLD IT! DON'T JUMP THE GUN! I'VE BEEN GETTING REPORTS FROM OUR CAMERA MEN IN THE FIELD!
MOBIL UNIT 4
CBZ TV
THEY TELL ME THEY HAVE SOME V-ERY INTERESTING SHOTS OF CERTAIN GOINGS ON OUT THERE IN THE BOONDOCKS!
EEP!
JUDGE
I BELIEVE THE JUDGES SHOULD VIEW THOSE PICTURES BEFORE THEY AWARD ANY PRIZES!
ULP! LET'S SPLIT, MAN! IF THEY FILMED OUR GROUP, THEY'LL RUN US OUT OF TOWN!
CBZ TV
THE BOY IS UNBELIEVABLE! TO EVEN FINISH THE RACE IN THE FACE OF THOSE ODDS IS INCREDIBLE!
A HERO! HE'S A HERO!!
RIVERDALE IS PROUD OF YOU, MY BOY!
THAT'S MY GOOD BUDDY, THAT IS!
JUDGE
JUDGE
COACH
The END

Archie & friends IN ICE FOLLIES

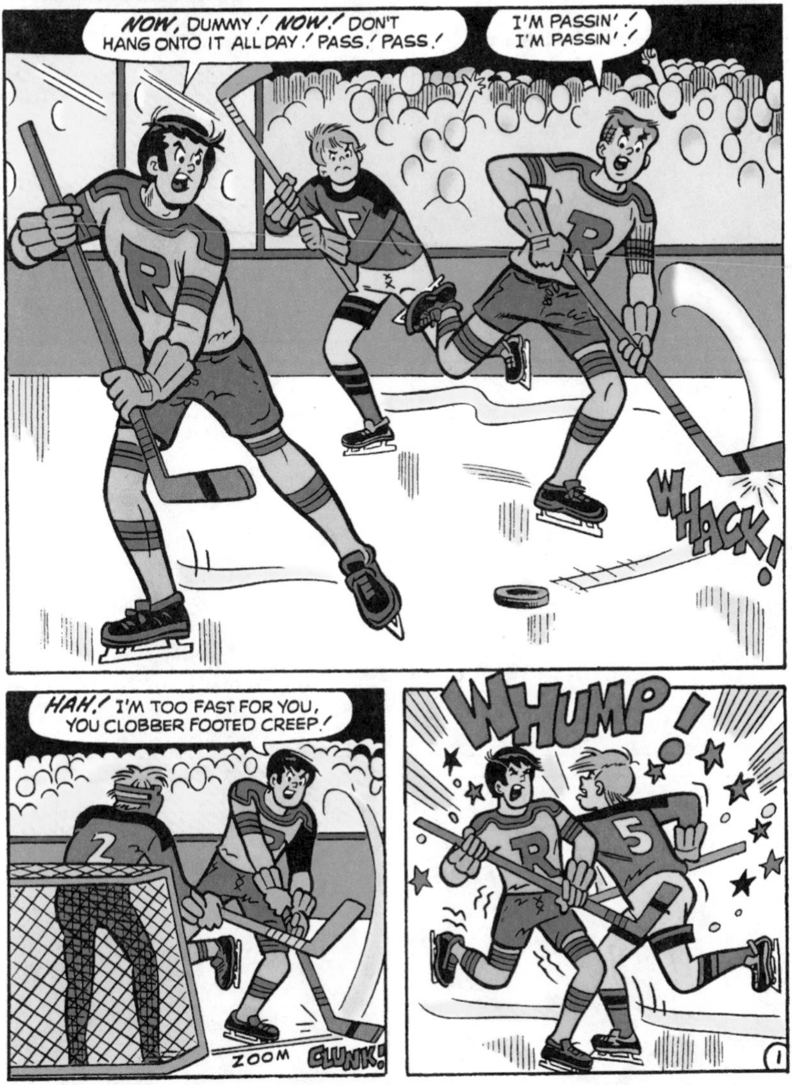
NOW, DUMMY! NOW! DON'T HANG ONTO IT ALL DAY! PASS! PASS!
I'M PASSIN'! I'M PASSIN'!
WHACK!
HAH! I'M TOO FAST FOR YOU, YOU CLOBBER FOOTED CREEP!
ZOOM
CLUNK!
WHUMP!

Story: George Gladir Pencils: Stan Goldberg

Inks: Henry Scarpelli Letters: Bill Yoshida Colors: Barry Grossman

Originally printed in ARCHIE AT RIVERDALE HIGH #24, April 1975

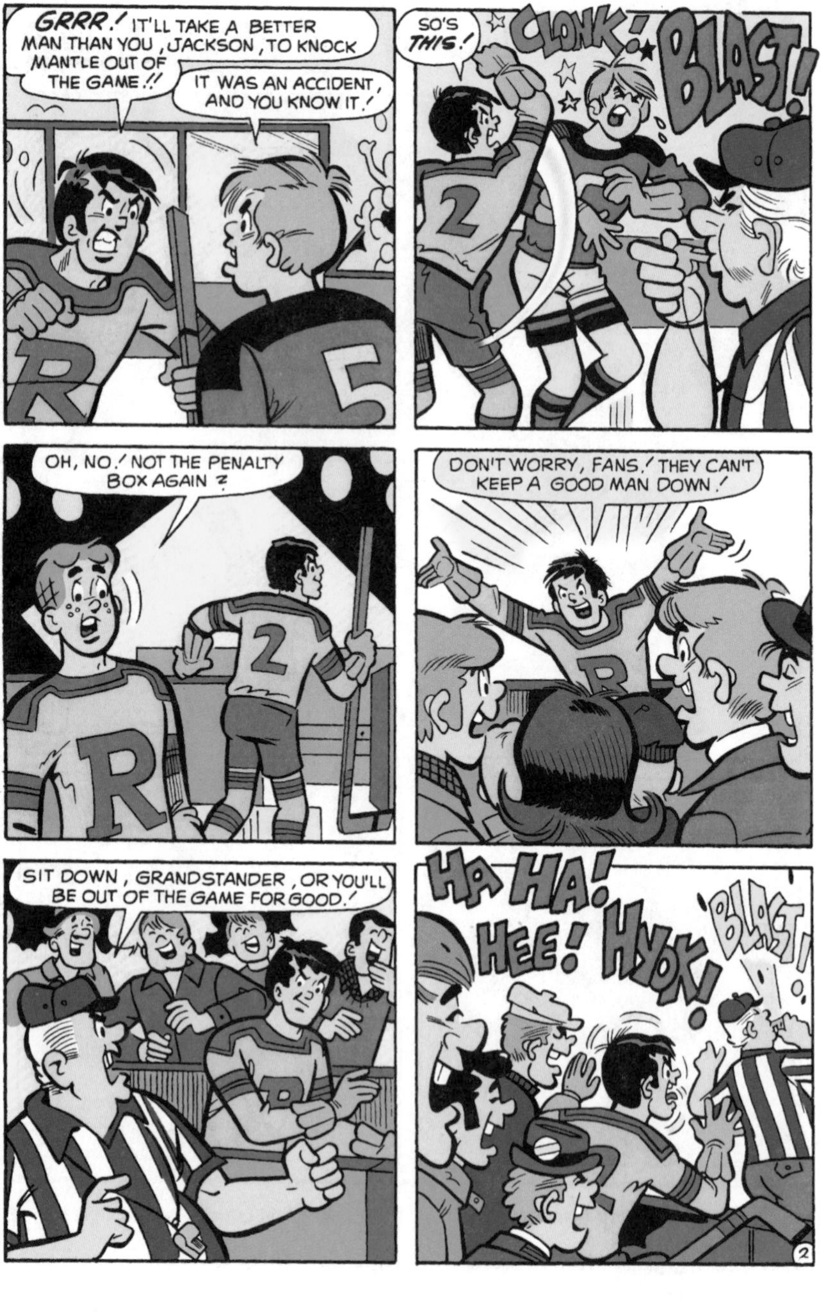
GRRR! IT'LL TAKE A BETTER MAN THAN YOU, JACKSON, TO KNOCK MANTLE OUT OF THE GAME!!
IT WAS AN ACCIDENT, AND YOU KNOW IT!
SO'S THIS!
CLONK!
BLAST!
OH, NO! NOT THE PENALTY BOX AGAIN?
DON'T WORRY, FANS! THEY CAN'T KEEP A GOOD MAN DOWN!
SIT DOWN, GRANDSTANDER, OR YOU'LL BE OUT OF THE GAME FOR GOOD!
HA HA!
HEE! HYOK!
BLAST!
2

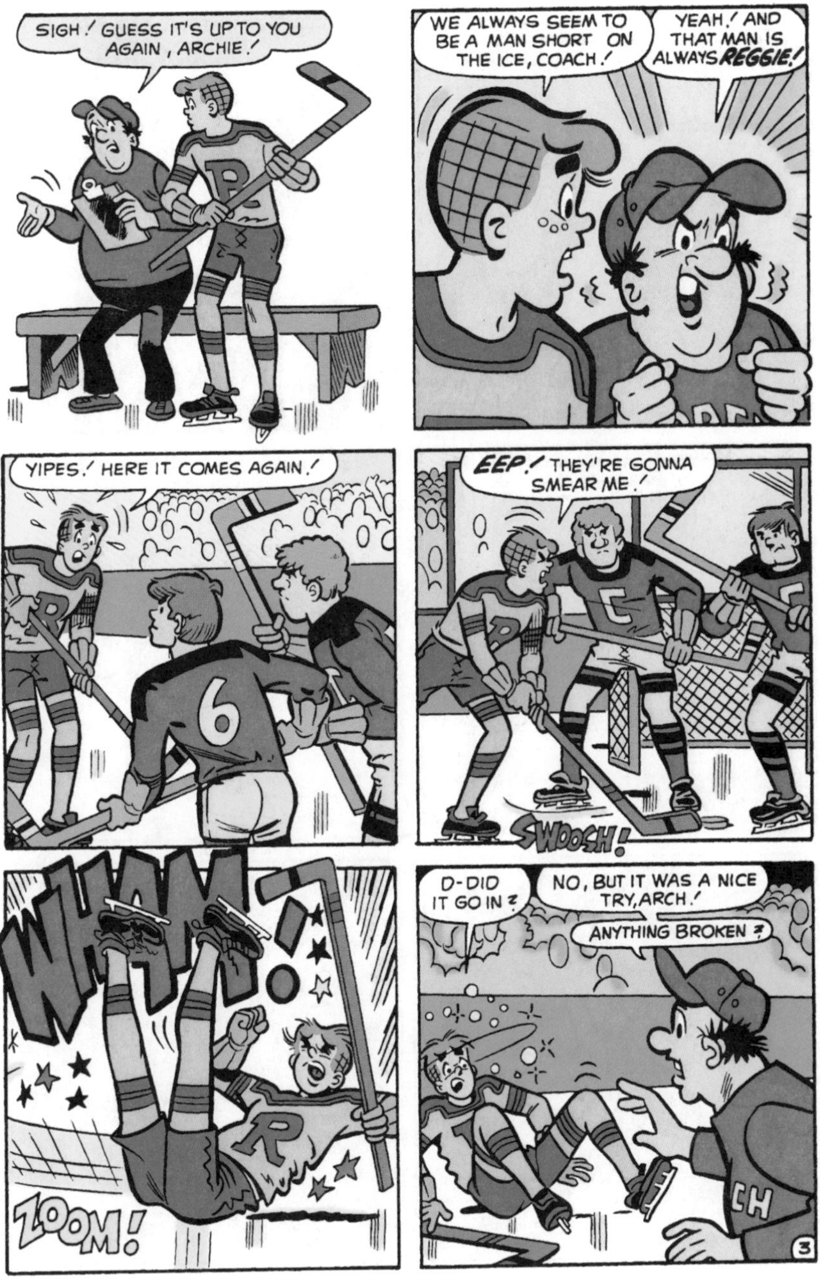
SIGH! GUESS IT'S UP TO YOU AGAIN, ARCHIE!
WE ALWAYS SEEM TO BE A MAN SHORT ON THE ICE, COACH!
YEAH! AND THAT MAN IS ALWAYS REGGIE!
YIPES! HERE IT COMES AGAIN!
6
EEP! THEY'RE GONNA SMEAR ME!
SWOOSH!
WHAM!
ZOOM!
D-DID IT GO IN?
NO, BUT IT WAS A NICE TRY, ARCH!
ANYTHING BROKEN?
3

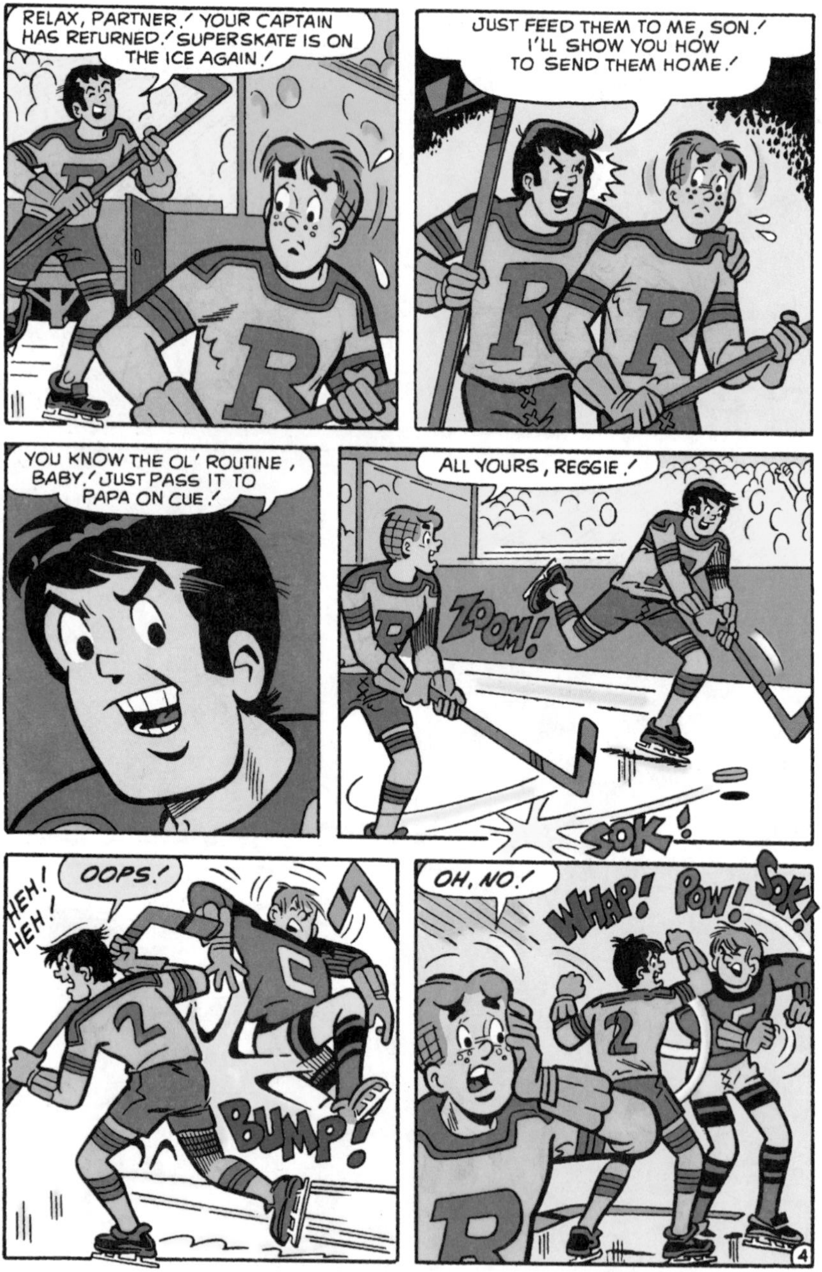
RELAX, PARTNER! YOUR CAPTAIN HAS RETURNED! SUPERSKATE IS ON THE ICE AGAIN!
JUST FEED THEM TO ME, SON! I'LL SHOW YOU HOW TO SEND THEM HOME!
YOU KNOW THE OL' ROUTINE, BABY! JUST PASS IT TO PAPA ON CUE!
ALL YOURS, REGGIE!
ZOOM!
SOK!
HEH! HEH!
OOPS!
BUMP!
OH, NO!
WHAP!
POW!
SOK!
4

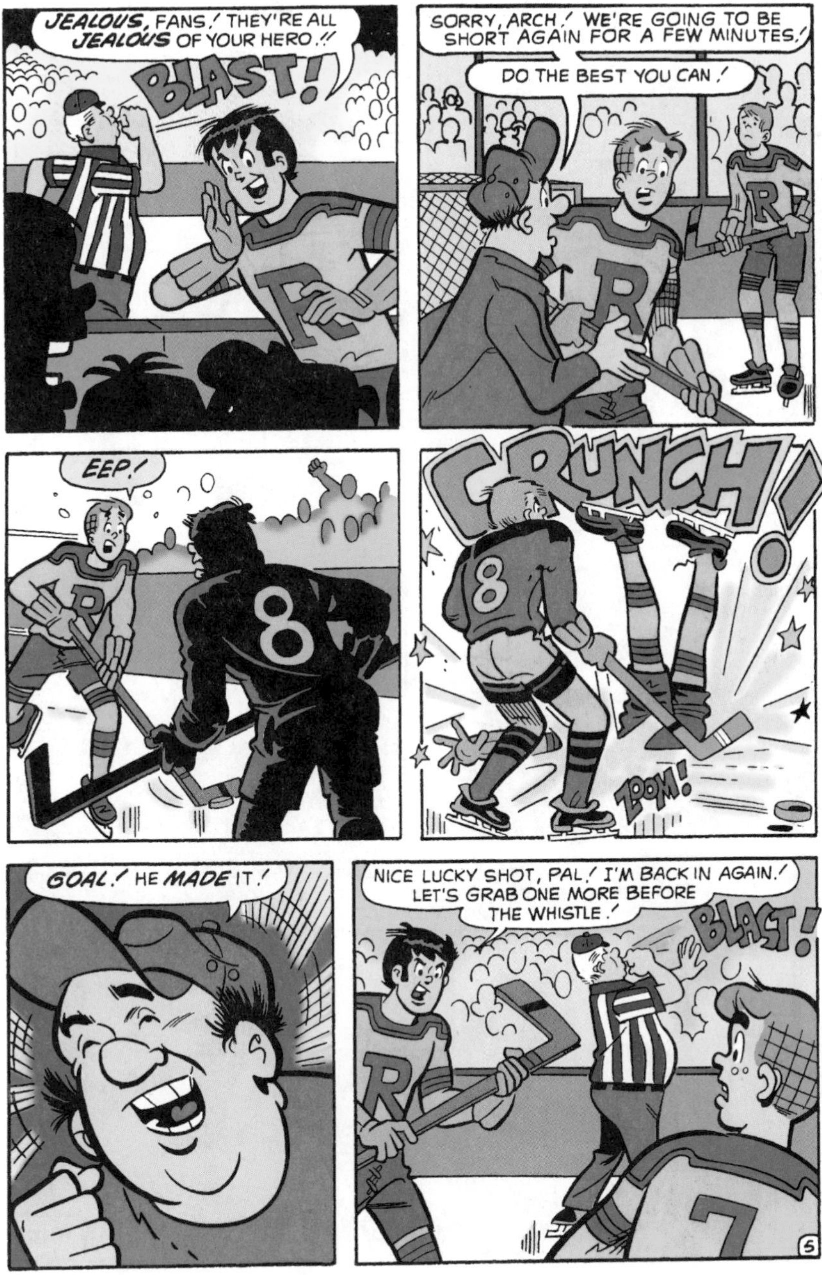
JEALOUS, FANS! THEY'RE ALL JEALOUS OF YOUR HERO!!
BLAST!
SORRY, ARCH! WE'RE GOING TO BE SHORT AGAIN FOR A FEW MINUTES!
DO THE BEST YOU CAN!
EEP!
CRUNCH!
ZOOM!
GOAL! HE MADE IT!
NICE LUCKY SHOT, PAL! I'M BACK IN AGAIN! LET'S GRAB ONE MORE BEFORE THE WHISTLE!
BLAST!
5

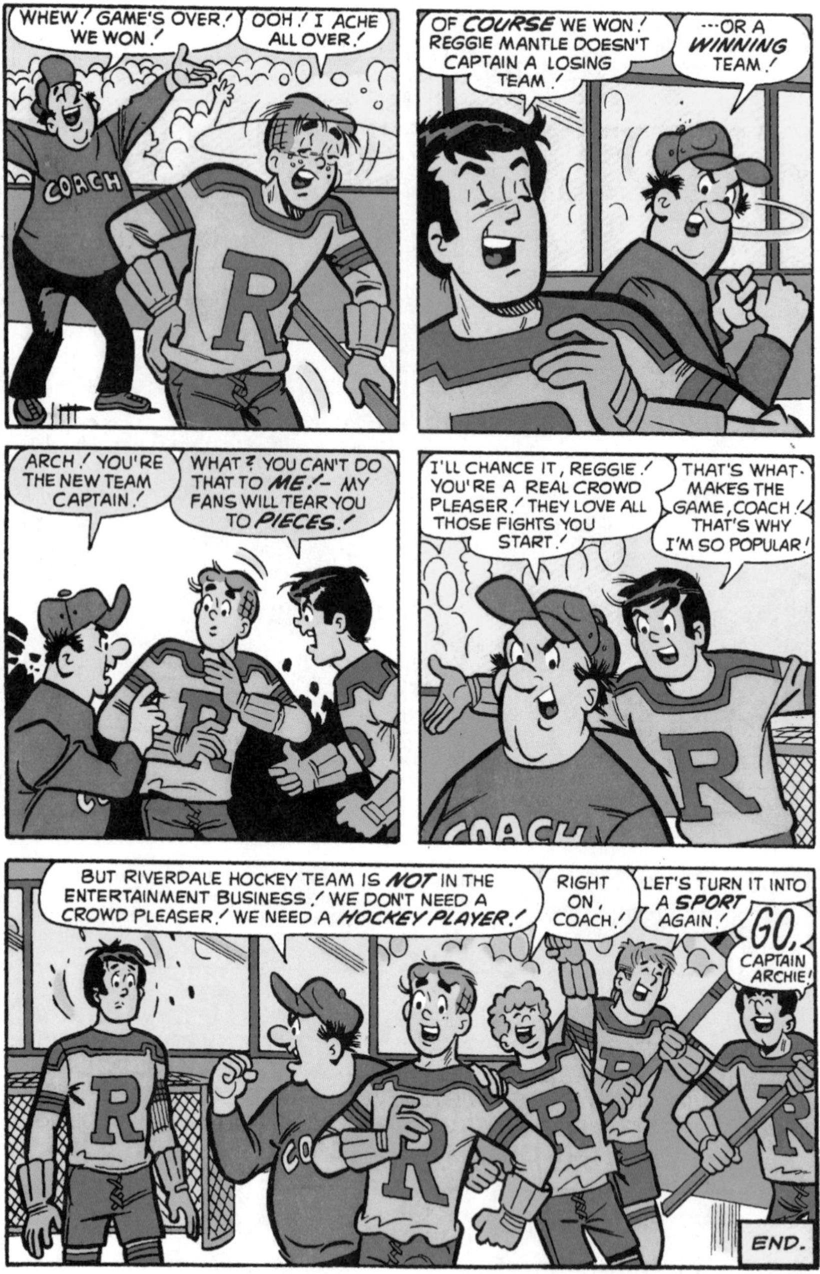
WHEW! GAME'S OVER! WE WON!
OOH! I ACHE ALL OVER!
OF COURSE WE WON! REGGIE MANTLE DOESN'T CAPTAIN A LOSING TEAM!
---OR A WINNING TEAM!
ARCH! YOU'RE THE NEW TEAM CAPTAIN!
WHAT? YOU CAN'T DO THAT TO ME!– MY FANS WILL TEAR YOU TO PIECES!
I'LL CHANCE IT, REGGIE! YOU'RE A REAL CROWD PLEASER! THEY LOVE ALL THOSE FIGHTS YOU START!
THAT'S WHAT MAKES THE GAME, COACH! THAT'S WHY I'M SO POPULAR!
BUT RIVERDALE HOCKEY TEAM IS NOT IN THE ENTERTAINMENT BUSINESS! WE DON'T NEED A CROWD PLEASER! WE NEED A HOCKEY PLAYER!
RIGHT ON, COACH!
LET'S TURN IT INTO A SPORT AGAIN!
GO, CAPTAIN ARCHIE!
END.

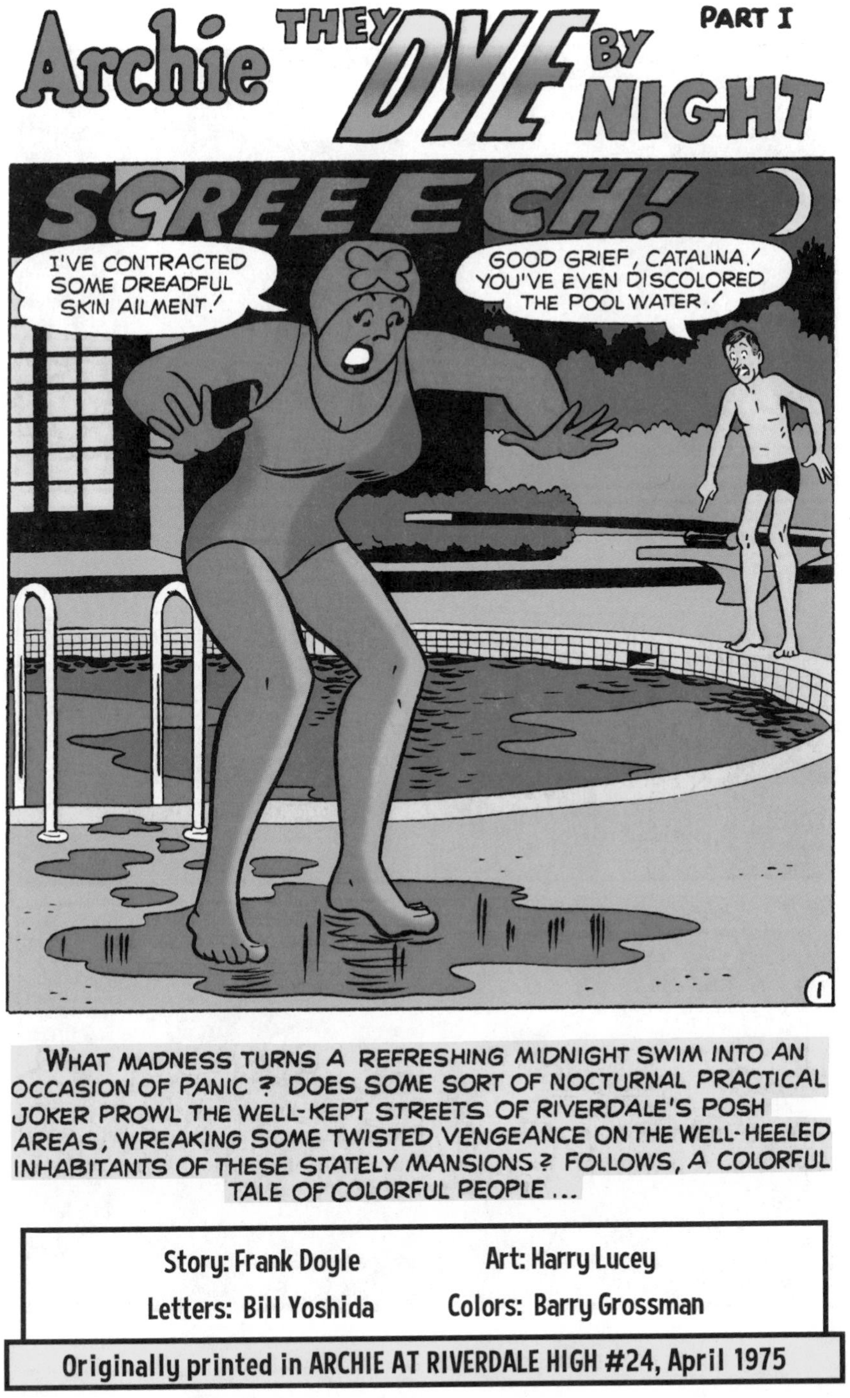
Archie
THEY DYE BY NIGHT
PART I
SCREEECH!
I'VE CONTRACTED SOME DREADFUL SKIN AILMENT!
GOOD GRIEF, CATALINA! YOU'VE EVEN DISCOLORED THE POOL WATER!

WHAT MADNESS TURNS A REFRESHING MIDNIGHT SWIM INTO AN OCCASION OF PANIC? DOES SOME SORT OF NOCTURNAL PRACTICAL JOKER PROWL THE WELL-KEPT STREETS OF RIVERDALE'S POSH AREAS, WREAKING SOME TWISTED VENGEANCE ON THE WELL-HEELED INHABITANTS OF THESE STATELY MANSIONS? FOLLOWS, A COLORFUL TALE OF COLORFUL PEOPLE ...

Story: Frank Doyle — Art: Harry Lucey

Letters: Bill Yoshida — Colors: Barry Grossman

Originally printed in ARCHIE AT RIVERDALE HIGH #24, April 1975

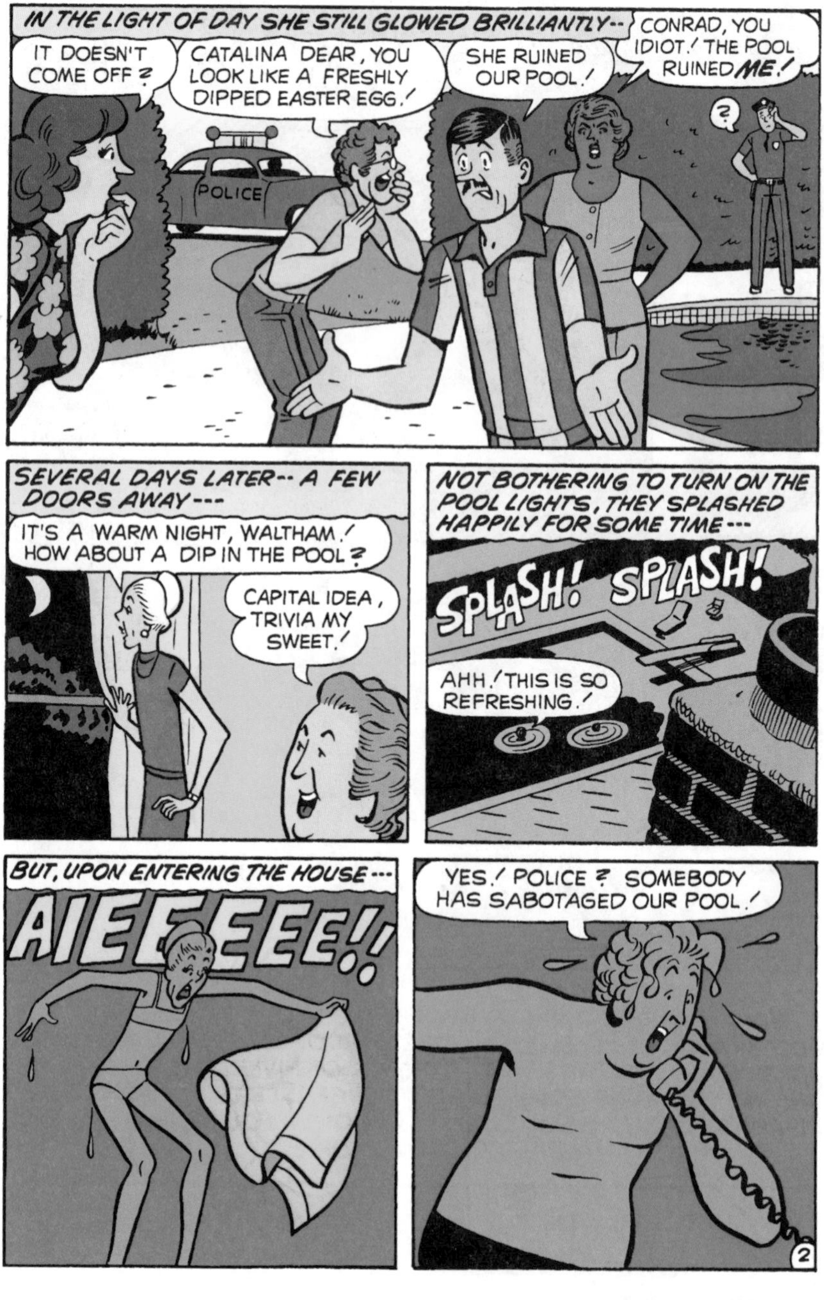
IN THE LIGHT OF DAY SHE STILL GLOWED BRILLIANTLY--
IT DOESN'T COME OFF ?
CATALINA DEAR, YOU LOOK LIKE A FRESHLY DIPPED EASTER EGG!
SHE RUINED OUR POOL!
CONRAD, YOU IDIOT! THE POOL RUINED ME!
?
POLICE
SEVERAL DAYS LATER-- A FEW DOORS AWAY---
IT'S A WARM NIGHT, WALTHAM! HOW ABOUT A DIP IN THE POOL?
CAPITAL IDEA, TRIVIA MY SWEET!
NOT BOTHERING TO TURN ON THE POOL LIGHTS, THEY SPLASHED HAPPILY FOR SOME TIME---
SPLASH! SPLASH!
AHH! THIS IS SO REFRESHING!
BUT, UPON ENTERING THE HOUSE---
AIEEEEEE!!
YES! POLICE? SOMEBODY HAS SABOTAGED OUR POOL!
2

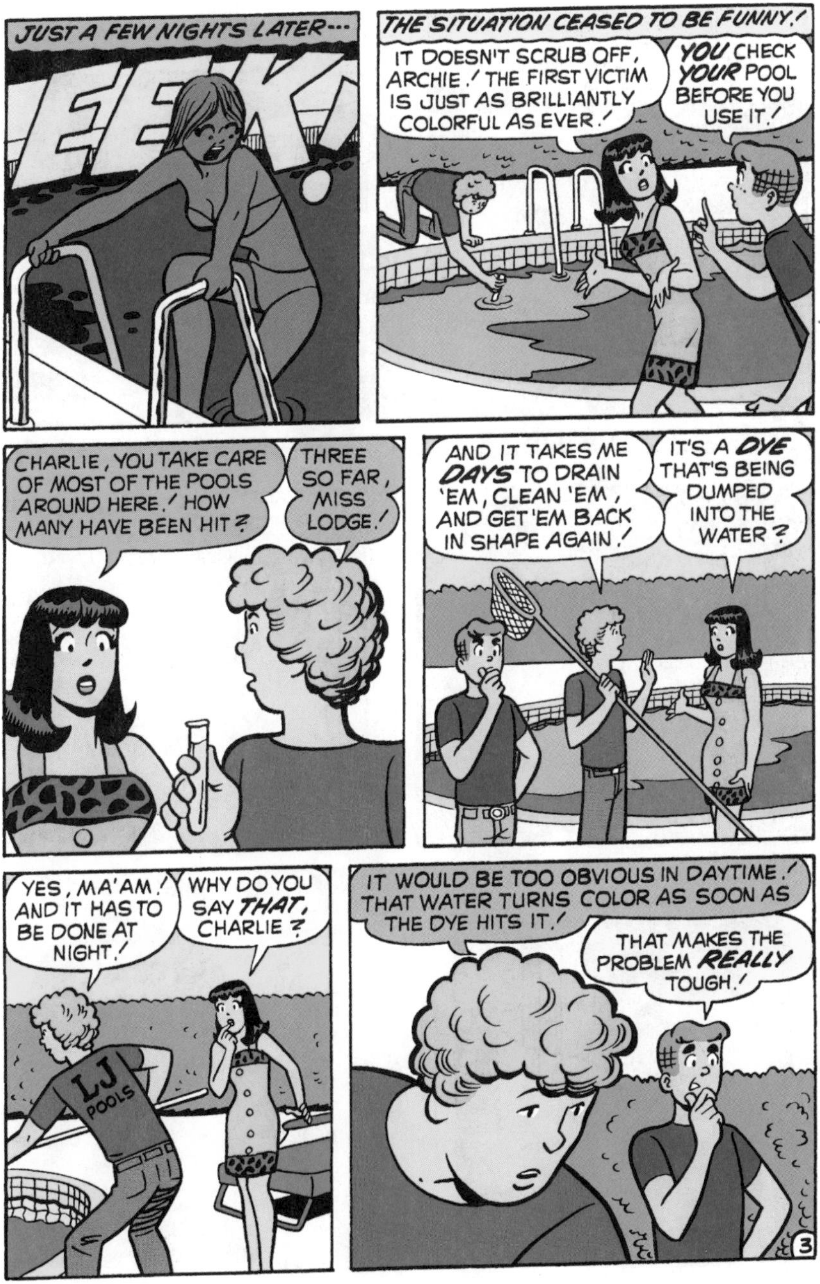
JUST A FEW NIGHTS LATER---
EEK!
THE SITUATION CEASED TO BE FUNNY!
IT DOESN'T SCRUB OFF, ARCHIE! THE FIRST VICTIM IS JUST AS BRILLIANTLY COLORFUL AS EVER!
YOU CHECK YOUR POOL BEFORE YOU USE IT!
CHARLIE, YOU TAKE CARE OF MOST OF THE POOLS AROUND HERE! HOW MANY HAVE BEEN HIT?
THREE SO FAR, MISS LODGE!
AND IT TAKES ME DAYS TO DRAIN 'EM, CLEAN 'EM, AND GET 'EM BACK IN SHAPE AGAIN!
IT'S A DYE THAT'S BEING DUMPED INTO THE WATER?
YES, MA'AM! AND IT HAS TO BE DONE AT NIGHT!
WHY DO YOU SAY THAT, CHARLIE?
LJ POOLS
IT WOULD BE TOO OBVIOUS IN DAYTIME! THAT WATER TURNS COLOR AS SOON AS THE DYE HITS IT!
THAT MAKES THE PROBLEM REALLY TOUGH!
3

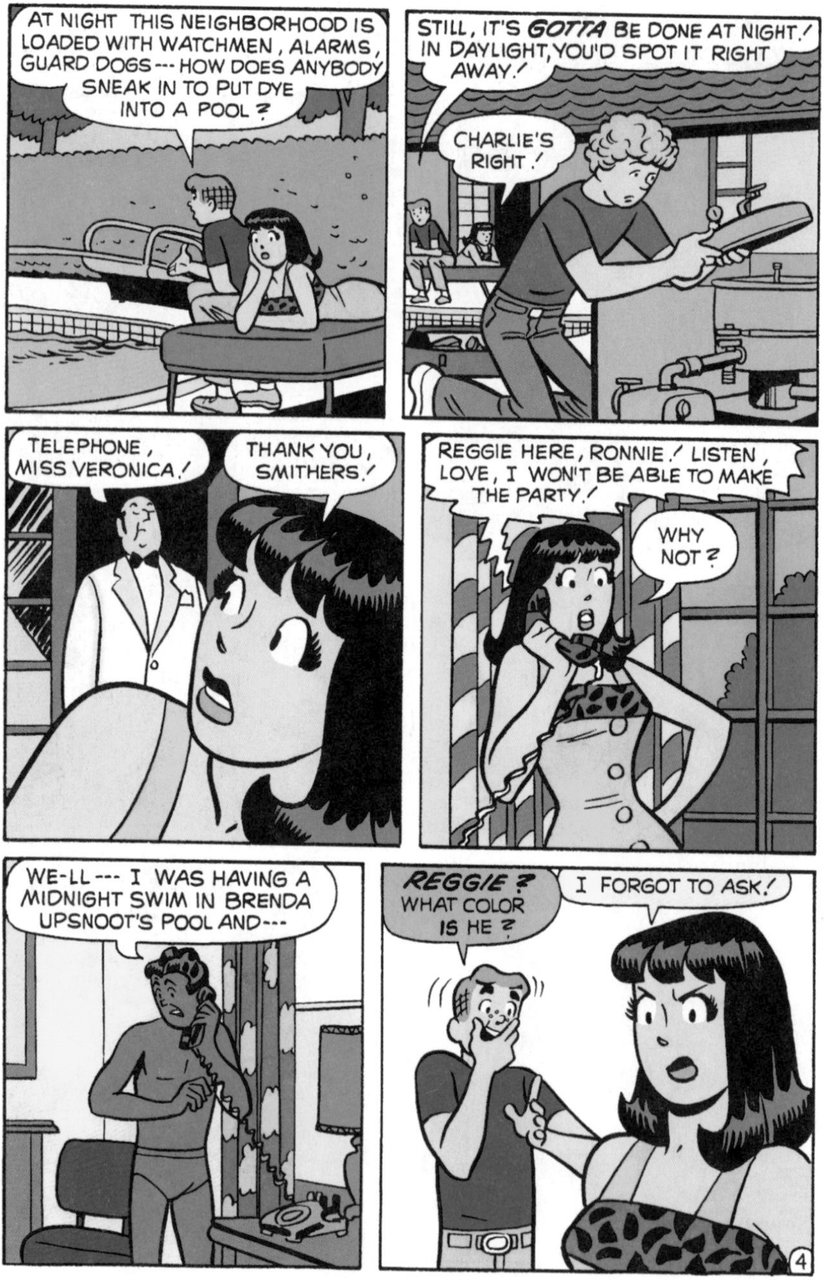
AT NIGHT THIS NEIGHBORHOOD IS LOADED WITH WATCHMEN, ALARMS, GUARD DOGS --- HOW DOES ANYBODY SNEAK IN TO PUT DYE INTO A POOL?
STILL, IT'S GOTTA BE DONE AT NIGHT! IN DAYLIGHT, YOU'D SPOT IT RIGHT AWAY!
CHARLIE'S RIGHT!
TELEPHONE, MISS VERONICA!
THANK YOU, SMITHERS!
REGGIE HERE, RONNIE! LISTEN, LOVE, I WON'T BE ABLE TO MAKE THE PARTY!
WHY NOT?
WE-LL --- I WAS HAVING A MIDNIGHT SWIM IN BRENDA UPSNOOT'S POOL AND---
REGGIE? WHAT COLOR IS HE?
I FORGOT TO ASK!
4

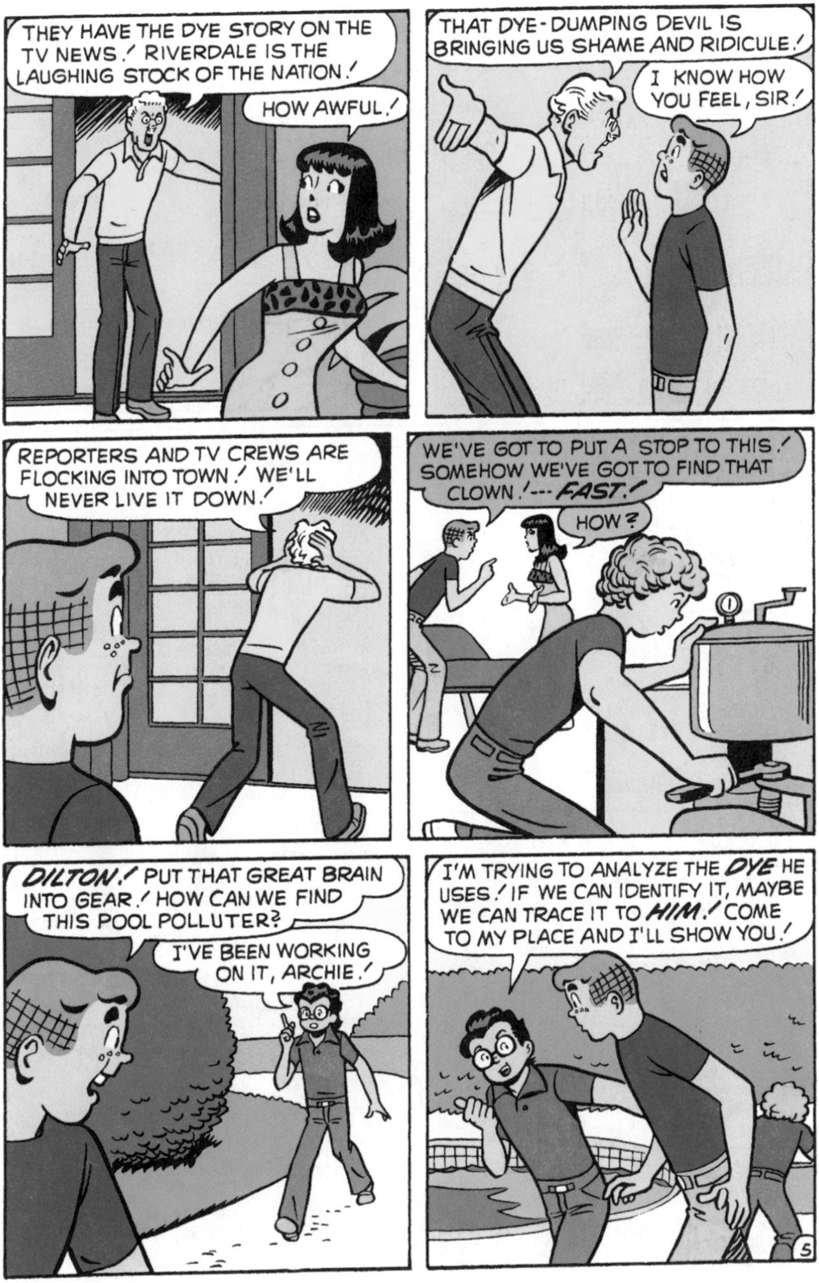
THEY HAVE THE DYE STORY ON THE TV NEWS.! RIVERDALE IS THE LAUGHING STOCK OF THE NATION.!
HOW AWFUL.!
THAT DYE-DUMPING DEVIL IS BRINGING US SHAME AND RIDICULE.!
I KNOW HOW YOU FEEL, SIR.!
REPORTERS AND TV CREWS ARE FLOCKING INTO TOWN.! WE'LL NEVER LIVE IT DOWN.!
WE'VE GOT TO PUT A STOP TO THIS.! SOMEHOW WE'VE GOT TO FIND THAT CLOWN.!--- FAST.!
HOW?
DILTON.! PUT THAT GREAT BRAIN INTO GEAR.! HOW CAN WE FIND THIS POOL POLLUTER?
I'VE BEEN WORKING ON IT, ARCHIE.!
I'M TRYING TO ANALYZE THE DYE HE USES.! IF WE CAN IDENTIFY IT, MAYBE WE CAN TRACE IT TO HIM.! COME TO MY PLACE AND I'LL SHOW YOU.!
5

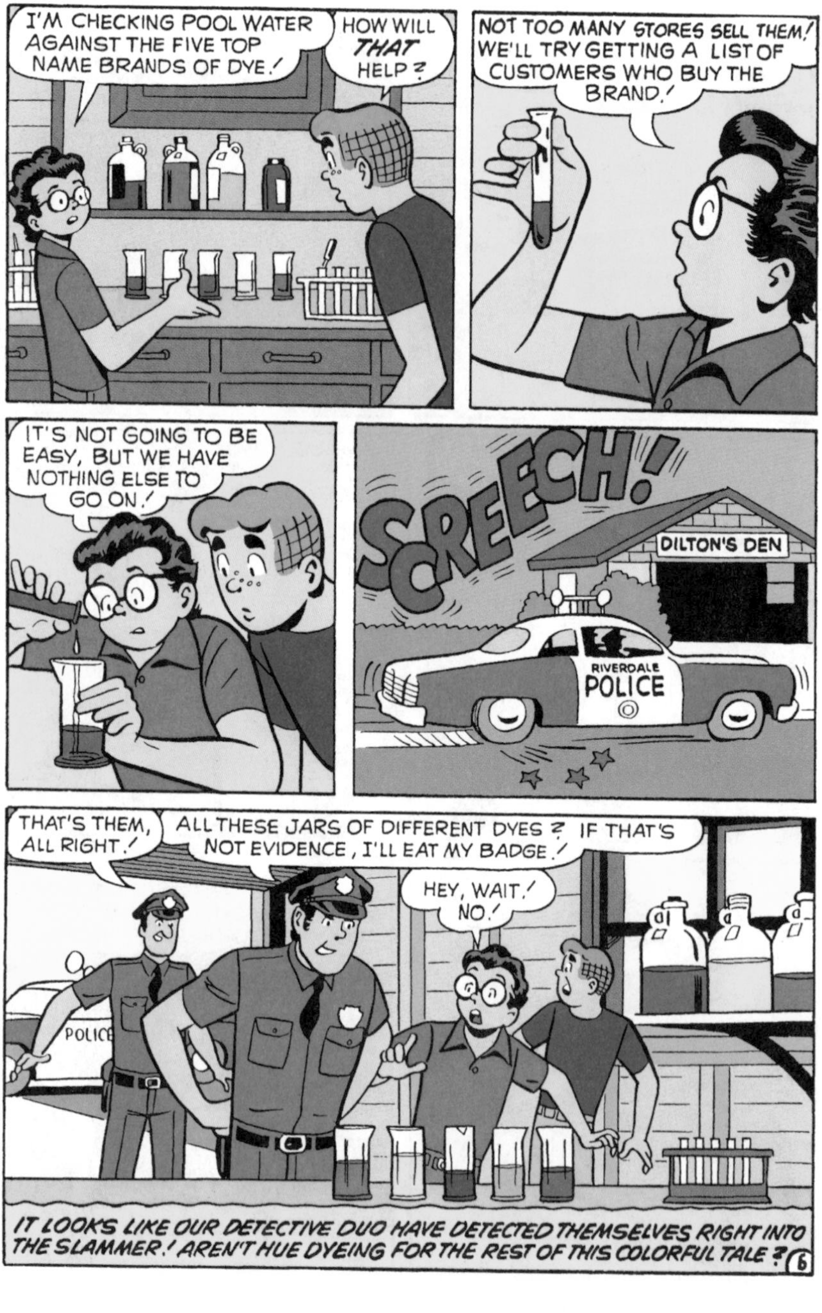
I'M CHECKING POOL WATER AGAINST THE FIVE TOP NAME BRANDS OF DYE!
HOW WILL THAT HELP?
NOT TOO MANY STORES SELL THEM! WE'LL TRY GETTING A LIST OF CUSTOMERS WHO BUY THE BRAND!
IT'S NOT GOING TO BE EASY, BUT WE HAVE NOTHING ELSE TO GO ON!
SCREECH!
DILTON'S DEN
RIVERDALE POLICE
THAT'S THEM, ALL RIGHT!
ALL THESE JARS OF DIFFERENT DYES? IF THAT'S NOT EVIDENCE, I'LL EAT MY BADGE!
HEY, WAIT! NO!
POLICE
IT LOOKS LIKE OUR DETECTIVE DUO HAVE DETECTED THEMSELVES RIGHT INTO THE SLAMMER! AREN'T HUE DYEING FOR THE REST OF THIS COLORFUL TALE?
6

Archie THEY DYE BY NIGHT PART II

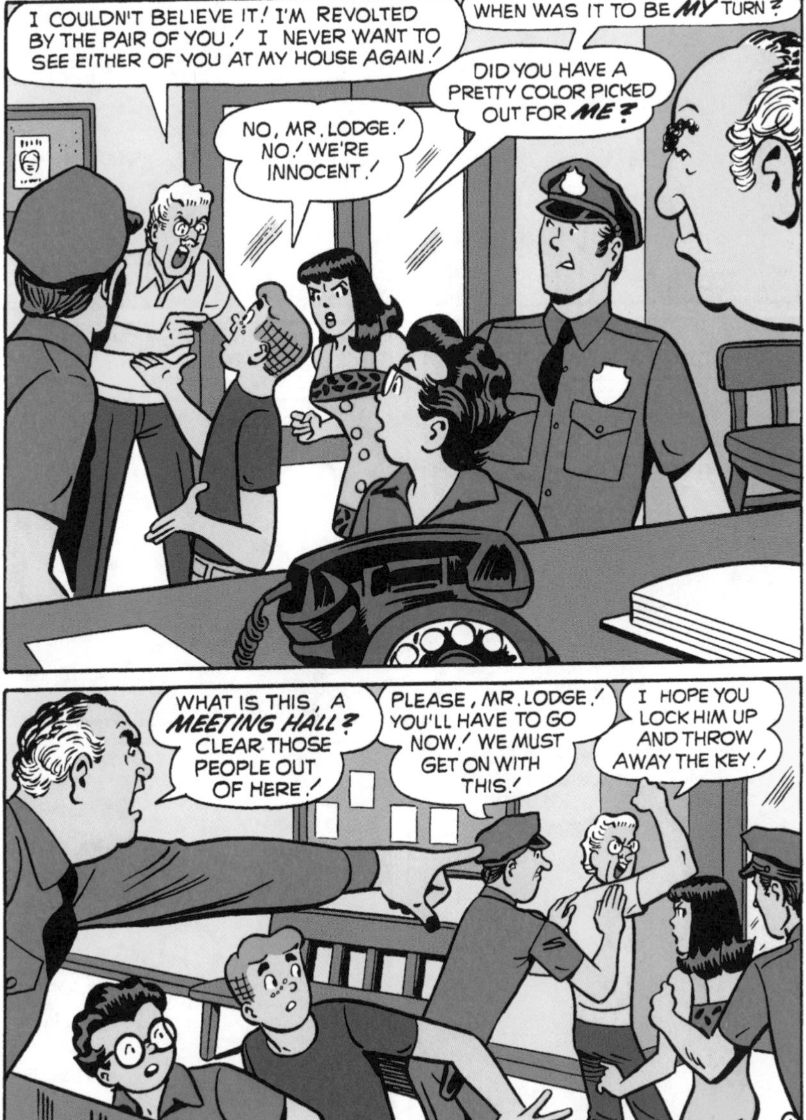
I COULDN'T BELIEVE IT! I'M REVOLTED BY THE PAIR OF YOU! I NEVER WANT TO SEE EITHER OF YOU AT MY HOUSE AGAIN!
NO, MR. LODGE! NO! WE'RE INNOCENT!
WHEN WAS IT TO BE MY TURN?
DID YOU HAVE A PRETTY COLOR PICKED OUT FOR ME?
WHAT IS THIS, A MEETING HALL? CLEAR THOSE PEOPLE OUT OF HERE!
PLEASE, MR. LODGE! YOU'LL HAVE TO GO NOW! WE MUST GET ON WITH THIS!
I HOPE YOU LOCK HIM UP AND THROW AWAY THE KEY!
1

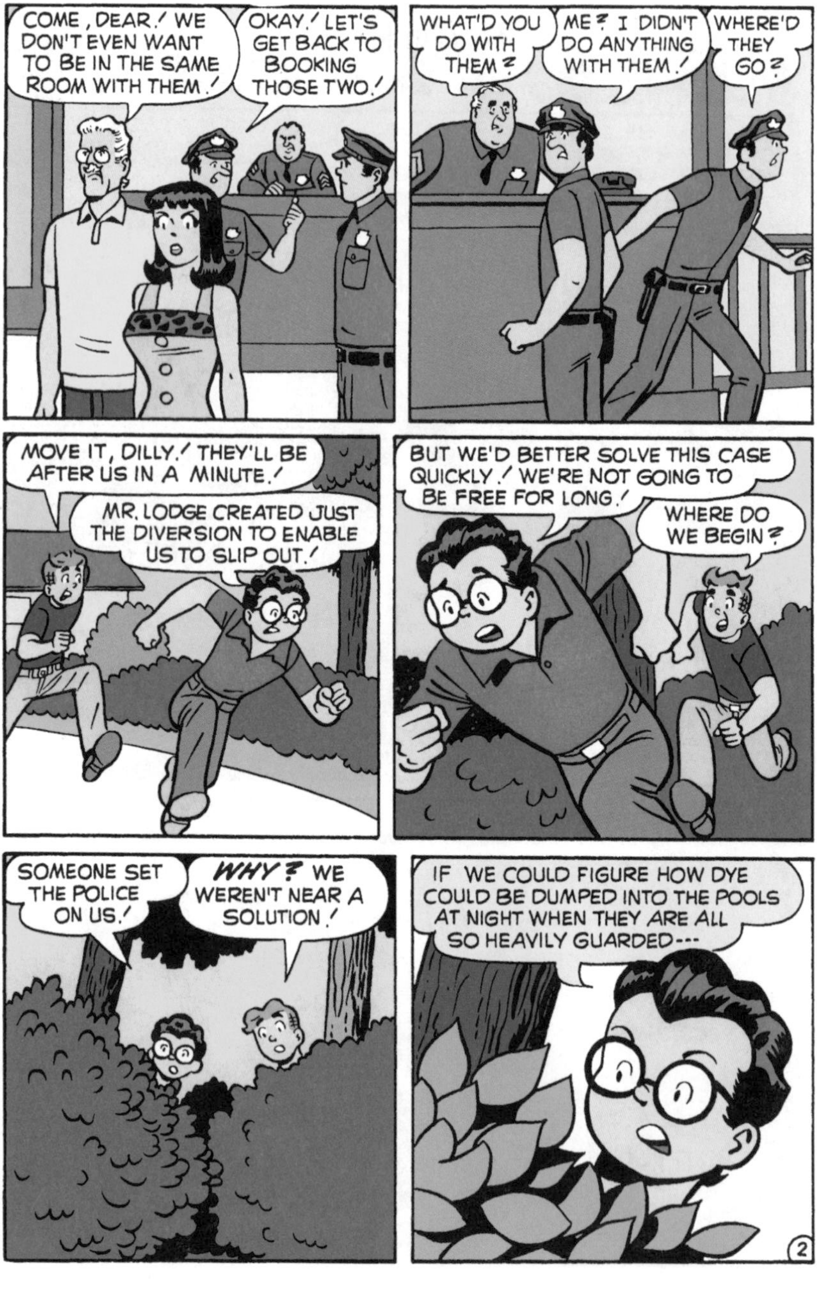
COME, DEAR! WE DON'T EVEN WANT TO BE IN THE SAME ROOM WITH THEM!
OKAY! LET'S GET BACK TO BOOKING THOSE TWO!
WHAT'D YOU DO WITH THEM?
ME? I DIDN'T DO ANYTHING WITH THEM!
WHERE'D THEY GO?
MOVE IT, DILLY! THEY'LL BE AFTER US IN A MINUTE!
MR. LODGE CREATED JUST THE DIVERSION TO ENABLE US TO SLIP OUT!
BUT WE'D BETTER SOLVE THIS CASE QUICKLY! WE'RE NOT GOING TO BE FREE FOR LONG!
WHERE DO WE BEGIN?
SOMEONE SET THE POLICE ON US!
WHY? WE WEREN'T NEAR A SOLUTION!
IF WE COULD FIGURE HOW DYE COULD BE DUMPED INTO THE POOLS AT NIGHT WHEN THEY ARE ALL SO HEAVILY GUARDED---
2

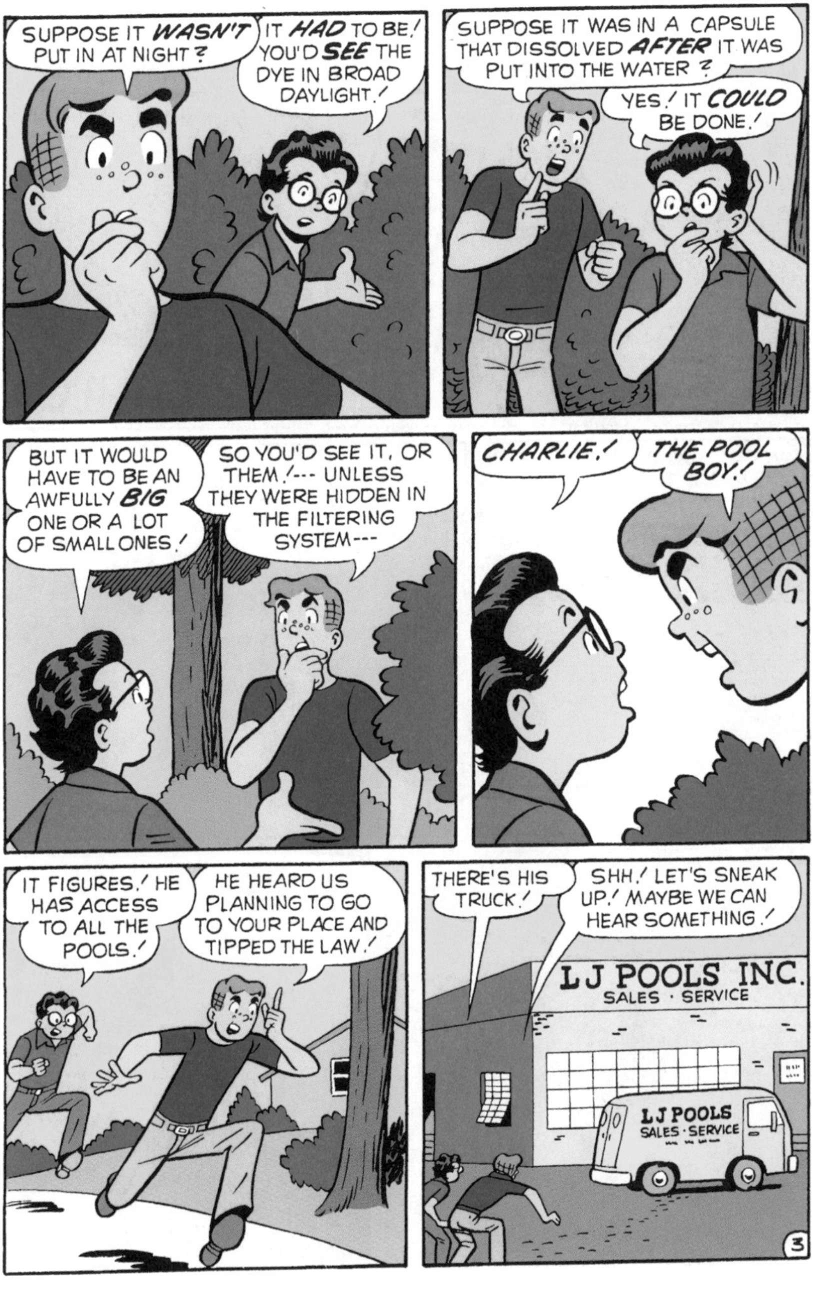
SUPPOSE IT WASN'T PUT IN AT NIGHT?
IT HAD TO BE! YOU'D SEE THE DYE IN BROAD DAYLIGHT!
SUPPOSE IT WAS IN A CAPSULE THAT DISSOLVED AFTER IT WAS PUT INTO THE WATER?
YES! IT COULD BE DONE!
BUT IT WOULD HAVE TO BE AN AWFULLY BIG ONE OR A LOT OF SMALL ONES!
SO YOU'D SEE IT, OR THEM!--- UNLESS THEY WERE HIDDEN IN THE FILTERING SYSTEM---
CHARLIE!
THE POOL BOY!
IT FIGURES! HE HAS ACCESS TO ALL THE POOLS!
HE HEARD US PLANNING TO GO TO YOUR PLACE AND TIPPED THE LAW!
THERE'S HIS TRUCK!
SHH! LET'S SNEAK UP! MAYBE WE CAN HEAR SOMETHING!
LJ POOLS INC.
SALES · SERVICE
LJ POOLS
SALES · SERVICE
3

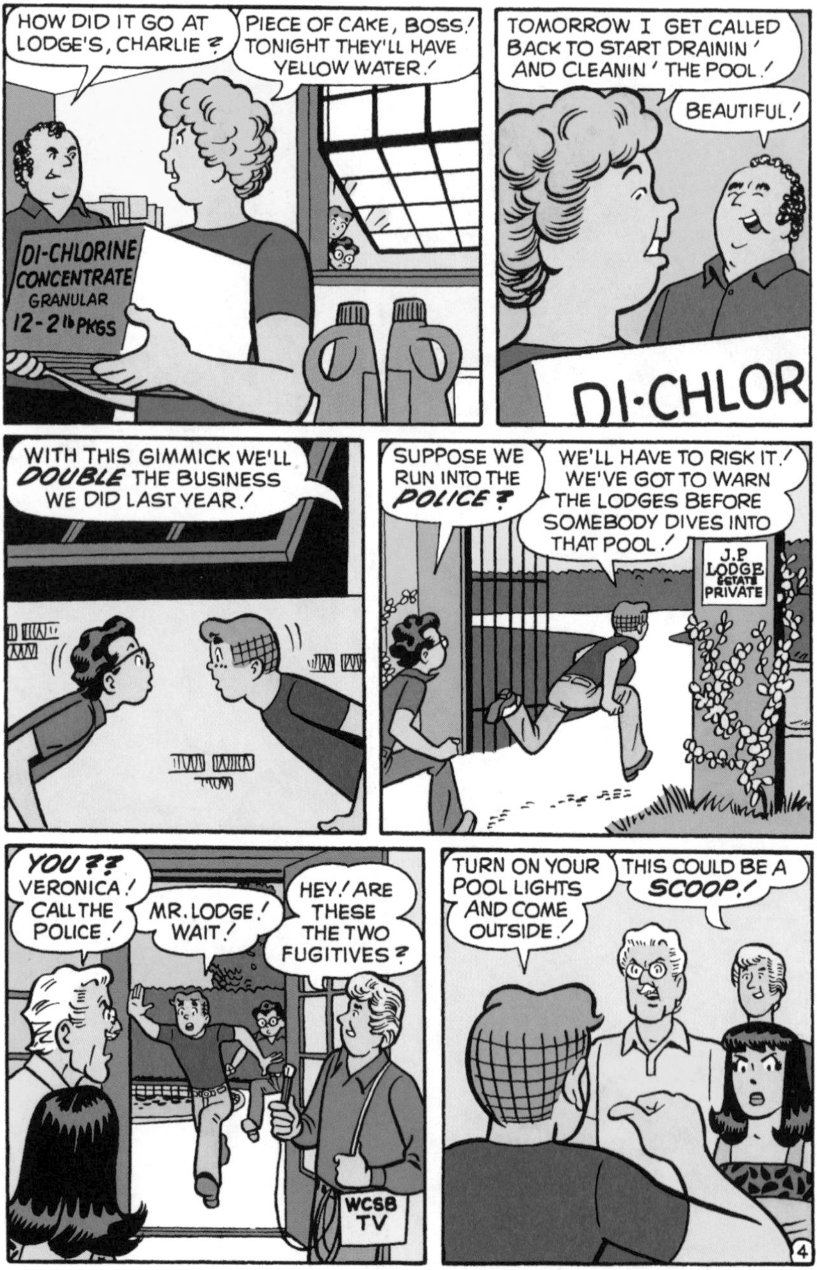
HOW DID IT GO AT LODGE'S, CHARLIE?
PIECE OF CAKE, BOSS! TONIGHT THEY'LL HAVE YELLOW WATER!
DI-CHLORINE CONCENTRATE GRANULAR 12-2 lb PKGS
TOMORROW I GET CALLED BACK TO START DRAININ' AND CLEANIN' THE POOL!
BEAUTIFUL!
DI-CHLOR
WITH THIS GIMMICK WE'LL DOUBLE THE BUSINESS WE DID LAST YEAR!
SUPPOSE WE RUN INTO THE POLICE?
WE'LL HAVE TO RISK IT! WE'VE GOT TO WARN THE LODGES BEFORE SOMEBODY DIVES INTO THAT POOL!
J.P LODGE ESTATE PRIVATE
YOU?? VERONICA! CALL THE POLICE!
MR. LODGE! WAIT!
HEY! ARE THESE THE TWO FUGITIVES?
WCSB TV
TURN ON YOUR POOL LIGHTS AND COME OUTSIDE!
THIS COULD BE A SCOOP!
4

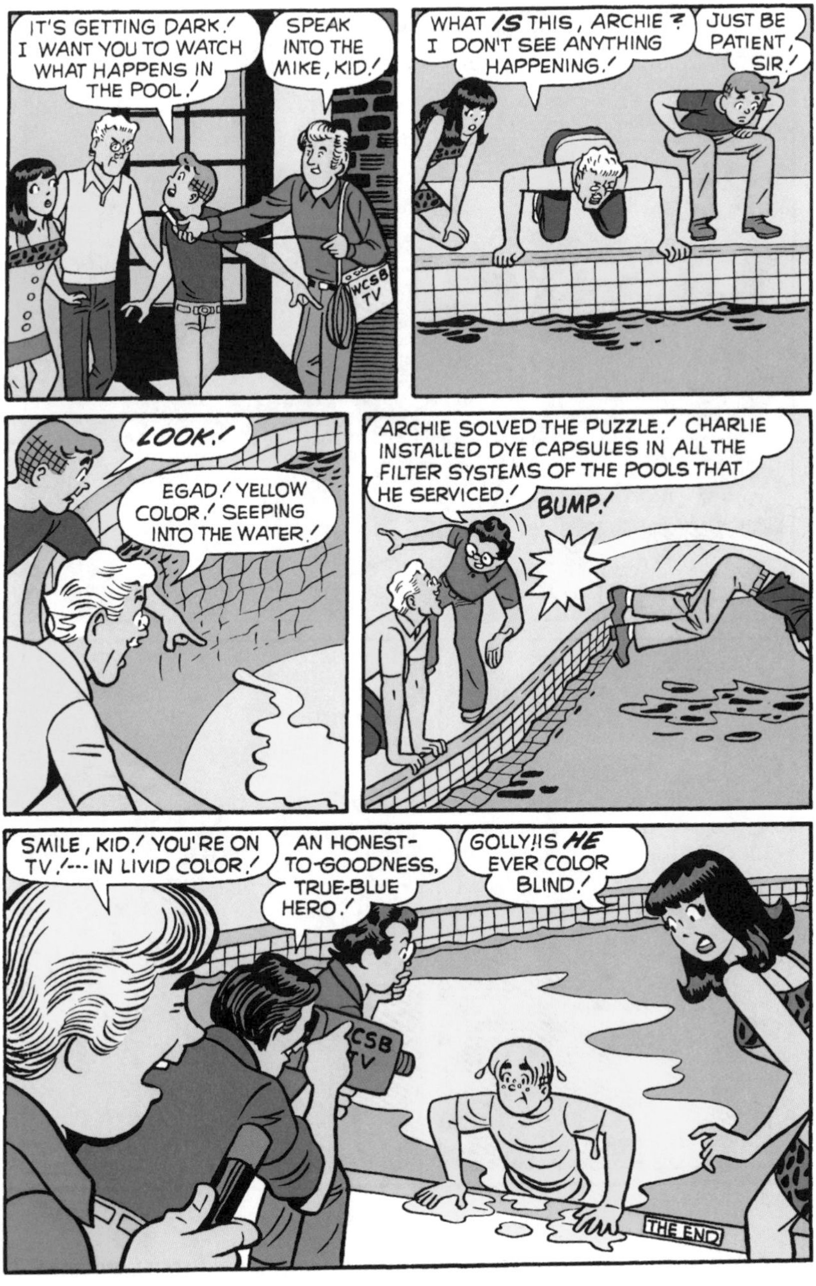
IT'S GETTING DARK! I WANT YOU TO WATCH WHAT HAPPENS IN THE POOL!
SPEAK INTO THE MIKE, KID!
WCSB TV
WHAT IS THIS, ARCHIE? I DON'T SEE ANYTHING HAPPENING!
JUST BE PATIENT, SIR!
LOOK!
EGAD! YELLOW COLOR! SEEPING INTO THE WATER!
ARCHIE SOLVED THE PUZZLE! CHARLIE INSTALLED DYE CAPSULES IN ALL THE FILTER SYSTEMS OF THE POOLS THAT HE SERVICED!
BUMP!
SMILE, KID! YOU'RE ON TV!--- IN LIVID COLOR!
AN HONEST-TO-GOODNESS, TRUE-BLUE HERO!
GOLLY! IS HE EVER COLOR BLIND!
CSB TV
THE END

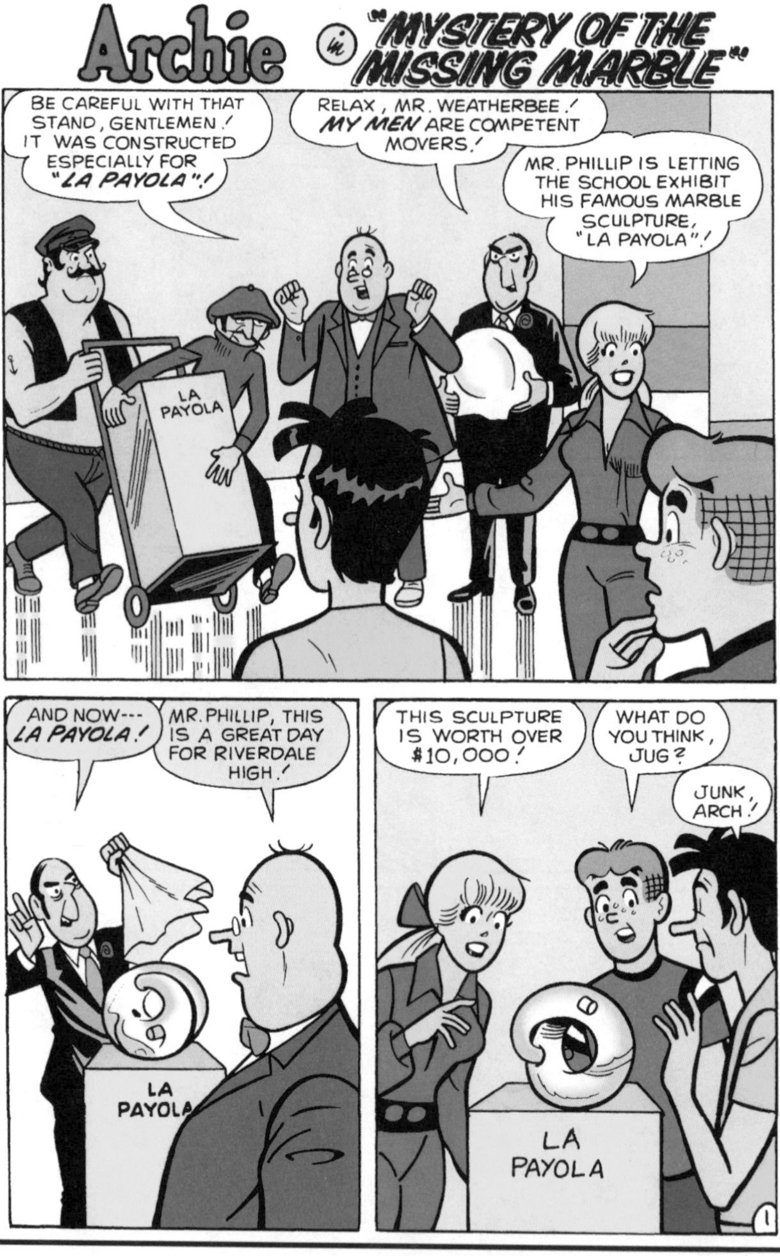
Archie in "MYSTERY OF THE MISSING MARBLE"
BE CAREFUL WITH THAT STAND, GENTLEMEN! IT WAS CONSTRUCTED ESPECIALLY FOR "LA PAYOLA"!
RELAX, MR. WEATHERBEE! MY MEN ARE COMPETENT MOVERS!
MR. PHILLIP IS LETTING THE SCHOOL EXHIBIT HIS FAMOUS MARBLE SCULPTURE, "LA PAYOLA"!
LA PAYOLA
AND NOW--- LA PAYOLA!
MR. PHILLIP, THIS IS A GREAT DAY FOR RIVERDALE HIGH!
LA PAYOLA
THIS SCULPTURE IS WORTH OVER $10,000!
WHAT DO YOU THINK, JUG?
JUNK, ARCH!
LA PAYOLA
1

Story & Pencils: Bob Bolling

Inks: Chic Stone Letters: Bill Yoshida Colors: Barry Grossman

Originally printed in ARCHIE AT RIVERDALE HIGH #30, November 1975

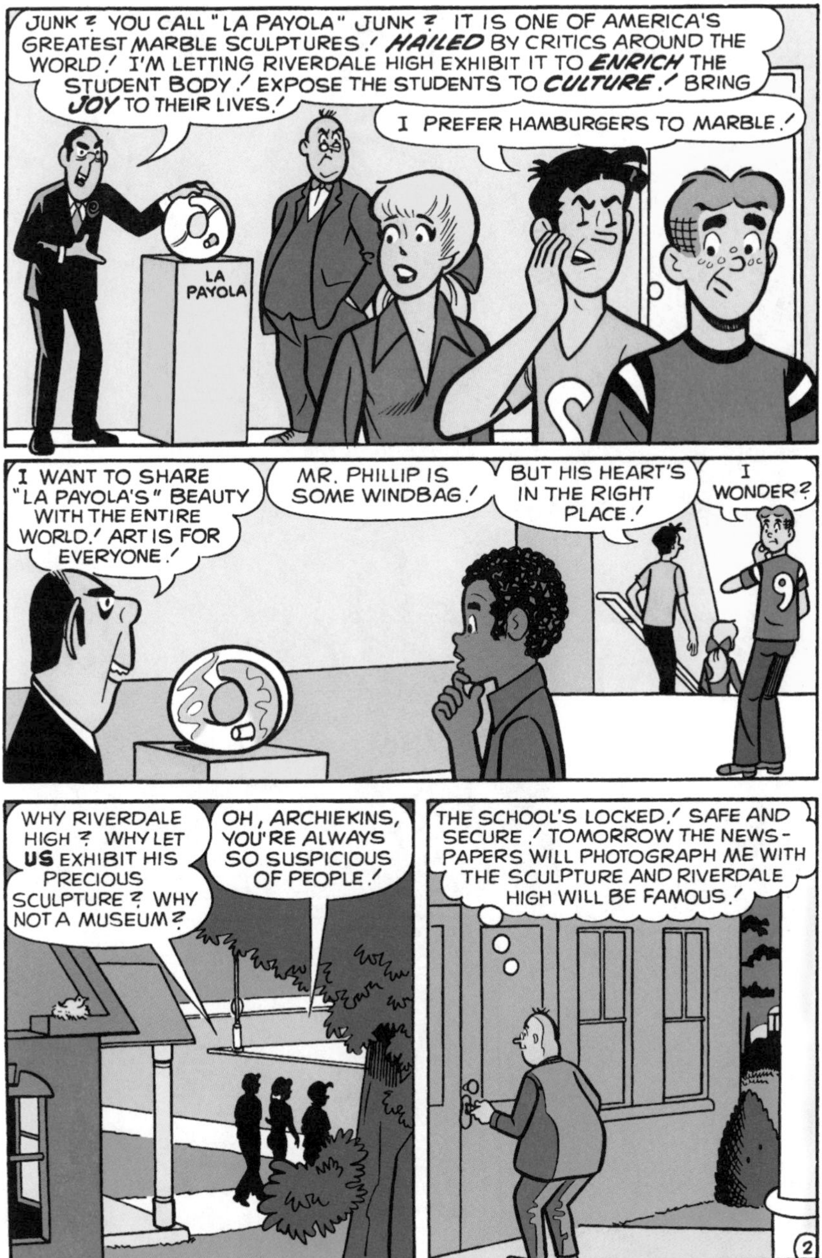
JUNK? YOU CALL "LA PAYOLA" JUNK? IT IS ONE OF AMERICA'S GREATEST MARBLE SCULPTURES! HAILED BY CRITICS AROUND THE WORLD! I'M LETTING RIVERDALE HIGH EXHIBIT IT TO ENRICH THE STUDENT BODY! EXPOSE THE STUDENTS TO CULTURE! BRING JOY TO THEIR LIVES!
I PREFER HAMBURGERS TO MARBLE!
LA PAYOLA
I WANT TO SHARE "LA PAYOLA'S" BEAUTY WITH THE ENTIRE WORLD! ART IS FOR EVERYONE!
MR. PHILLIP IS SOME WINDBAG!
BUT HIS HEART'S IN THE RIGHT PLACE!
I WONDER?
WHY RIVERDALE HIGH? WHY LET US EXHIBIT HIS PRECIOUS SCULPTURE? WHY NOT A MUSEUM?
OH, ARCHIEKINS, YOU'RE ALWAYS SO SUSPICIOUS OF PEOPLE!
THE SCHOOL'S LOCKED! SAFE AND SECURE! TOMORROW THE NEWSPAPERS WILL PHOTOGRAPH ME WITH THE SCULPTURE AND RIVERDALE HIGH WILL BE FAMOUS!
2

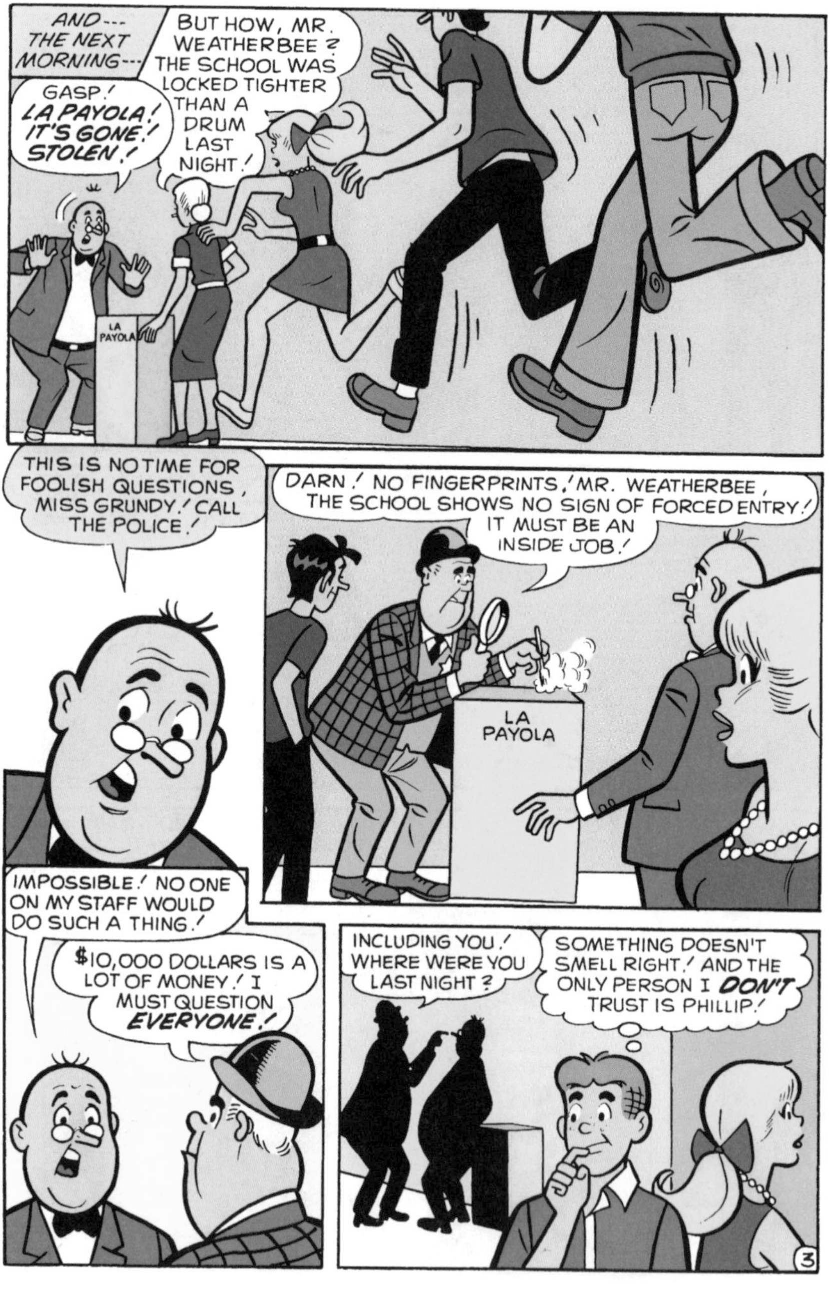
AND--- THE NEXT MORNING---
GASP! LA PAYOLA! IT'S GONE! STOLEN!
BUT HOW, MR. WEATHERBEE? THE SCHOOL WAS LOCKED TIGHTER THAN A DRUM LAST NIGHT!
LA PAYOLA
THIS IS NO TIME FOR FOOLISH QUESTIONS, MISS GRUNDY! CALL THE POLICE!
DARN! NO FINGERPRINTS! MR. WEATHERBEE, THE SCHOOL SHOWS NO SIGN OF FORCED ENTRY!
IT MUST BE AN INSIDE JOB!
LA PAYOLA
IMPOSSIBLE! NO ONE ON MY STAFF WOULD DO SUCH A THING!
$10,000 DOLLARS IS A LOT OF MONEY! I MUST QUESTION EVERYONE!
INCLUDING YOU! WHERE WERE YOU LAST NIGHT?
SOMETHING DOESN'T SMELL RIGHT! AND THE ONLY PERSON I DON'T TRUST IS PHILLIP!
3

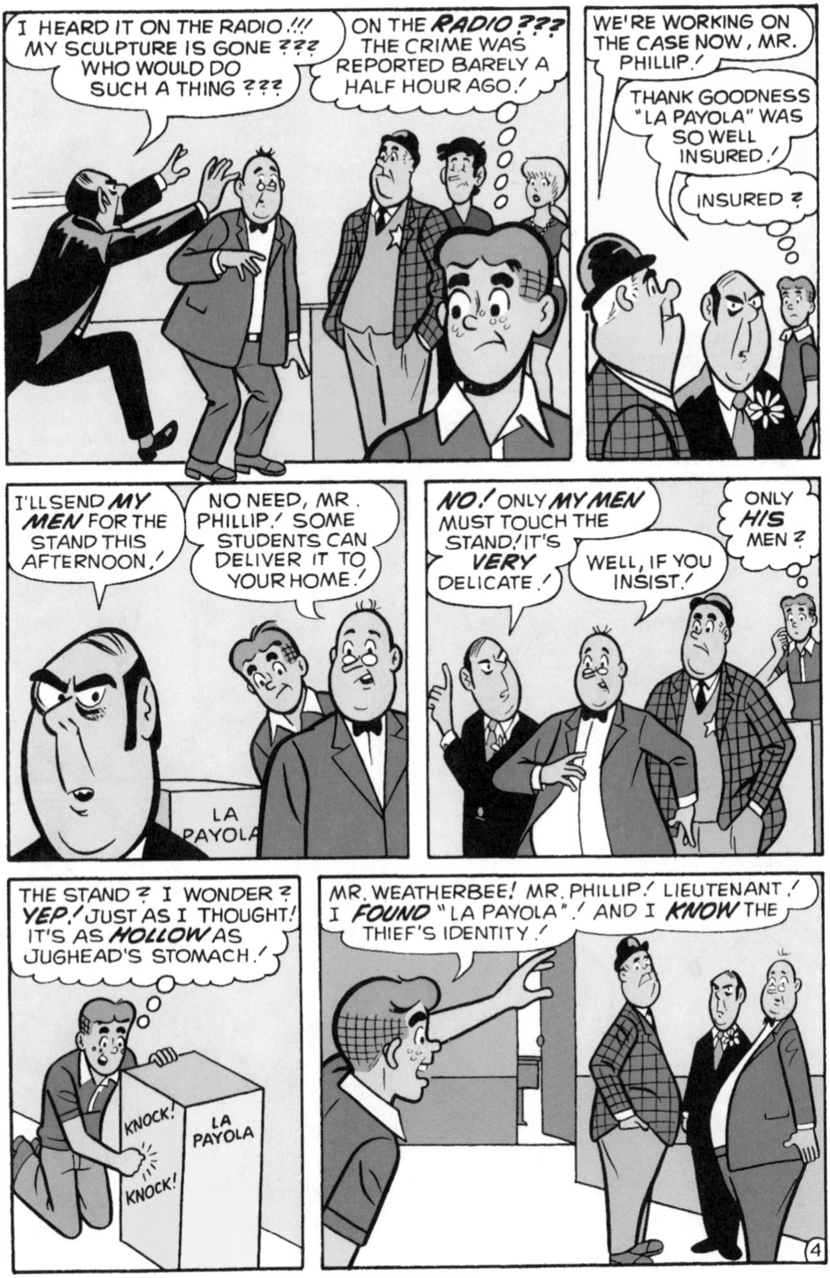
I HEARD IT ON THE RADIO !!! MY SCULPTURE IS GONE ??? WHO WOULD DO SUCH A THING ???
ON THE RADIO ??? THE CRIME WAS REPORTED BARELY A HALF HOUR AGO!
WE'RE WORKING ON THE CASE NOW, MR. PHILLIP!
THANK GOODNESS "LA PAYOLA" WAS SO WELL INSURED!
INSURED ?
I'LL SEND MY MEN FOR THE STAND THIS AFTERNOON!
NO NEED, MR. PHILLIP! SOME STUDENTS CAN DELIVER IT TO YOUR HOME!
LA PAYOLA
NO! ONLY MY MEN MUST TOUCH THE STAND! IT'S VERY DELICATE!
WELL, IF YOU INSIST!
ONLY HIS MEN ?
THE STAND ? I WONDER ? YEP! JUST AS I THOUGHT! IT'S AS HOLLOW AS JUGHEAD'S STOMACH!
KNOCK!
KNOCK!
LA PAYOLA
MR. WEATHERBEE! MR. PHILLIP! LIEUTENANT! I FOUND "LA PAYOLA"! AND I KNOW THE THIEF'S IDENTITY!
4

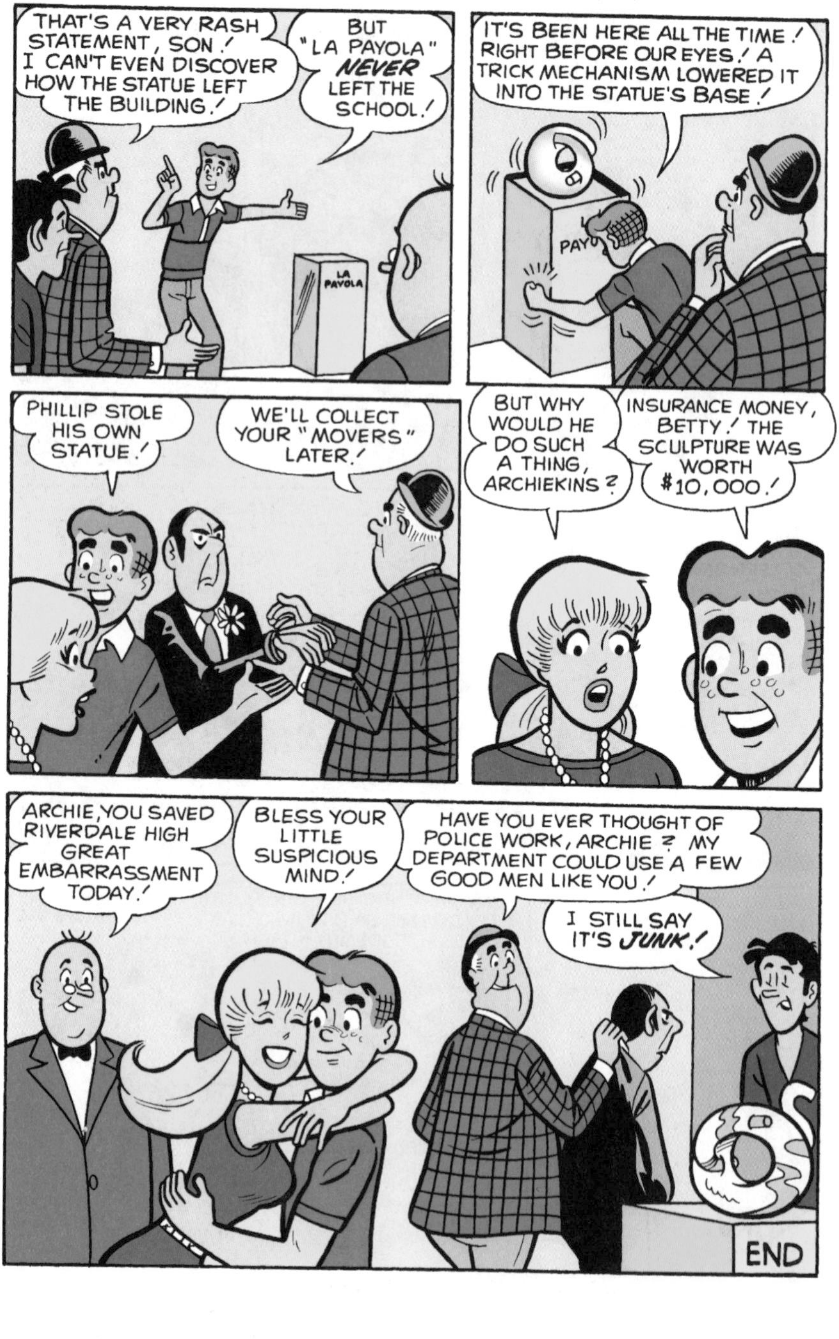
THAT'S A VERY RASH STATEMENT, SON! I CAN'T EVEN DISCOVER HOW THE STATUE LEFT THE BUILDING!
BUT "LA PAYOLA" NEVER LEFT THE SCHOOL!
LA PAYOLA
IT'S BEEN HERE ALL THE TIME! RIGHT BEFORE OUR EYES! A TRICK MECHANISM LOWERED IT INTO THE STATUE'S BASE!
PAY
PHILLIP STOLE HIS OWN STATUE!
WE'LL COLLECT YOUR "MOVERS" LATER!
BUT WHY WOULD HE DO SUCH A THING, ARCHIEKINS?
INSURANCE MONEY, BETTY! THE SCULPTURE WAS WORTH $10,000!
ARCHIE, YOU SAVED RIVERDALE HIGH GREAT EMBARRASSMENT TODAY!
BLESS YOUR LITTLE SUSPICIOUS MIND!
HAVE YOU EVER THOUGHT OF POLICE WORK, ARCHIE? MY DEPARTMENT COULD USE A FEW GOOD MEN LIKE YOU!
I STILL SAY IT'S JUNK!
END

Archie at Riverdale in Where There's Smoke---

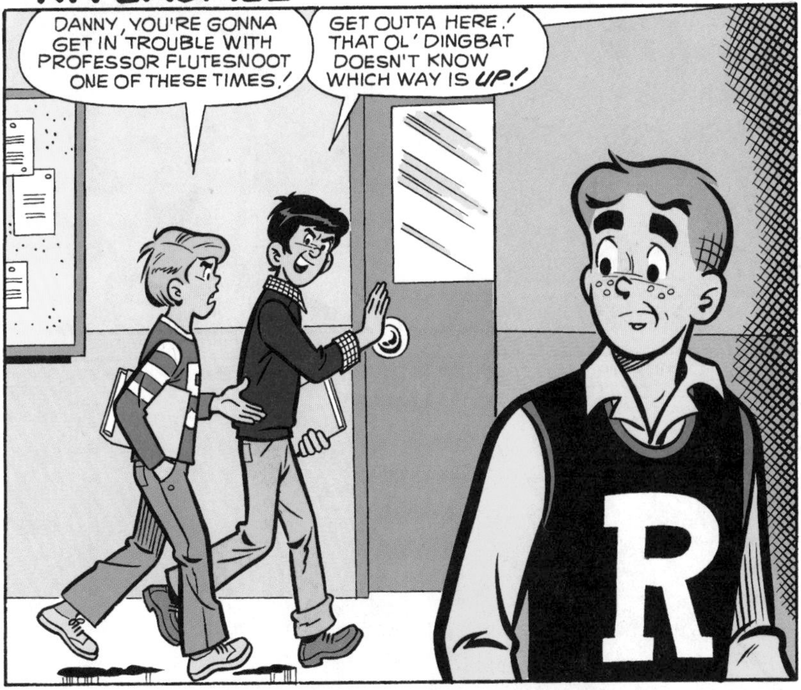
DANNY, YOU'RE GONNA GET IN TROUBLE WITH PROFESSOR FLUTESNOOT ONE OF THESE TIMES!
GET OUTTA HERE! THAT OL' DINGBAT DOESN'T KNOW WHICH WAY IS UP!

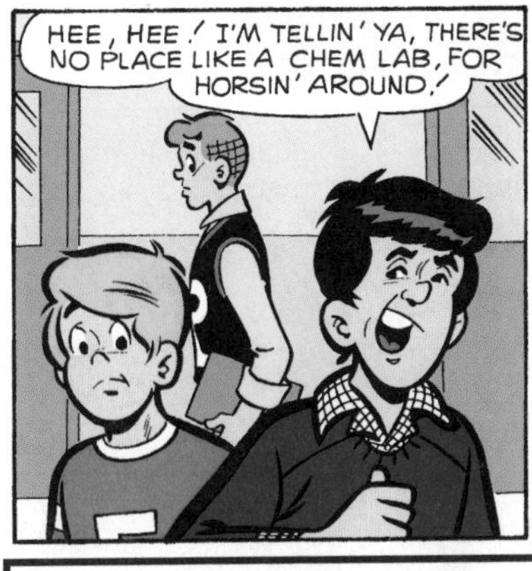
HEE, HEE! I'M TELLIN' YA, THERE'S NO PLACE LIKE A CHEM LAB, FOR HORSIN' AROUND!

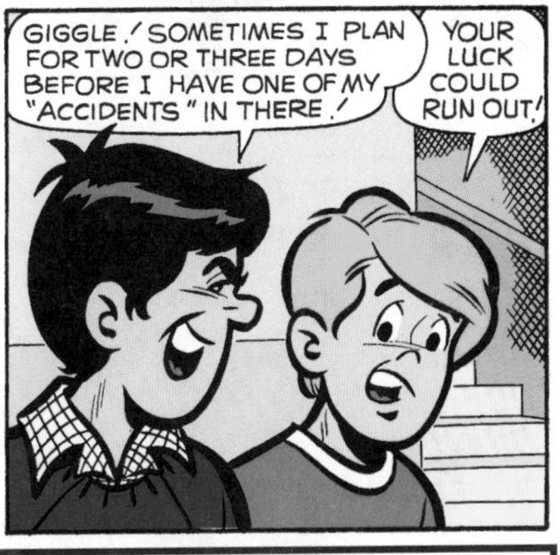
GIGGLE! SOMETIMES I PLAN FOR TWO OR THREE DAYS BEFORE I HAVE ONE OF MY "ACCIDENTS" IN THERE!
YOUR LUCK COULD RUN OUT!

Story: Frank Doyle Pencils: Stan Goldberg
Inks: Jon D'Agostino Letters: Bill Yoshida

Originally printed in ARCHIE AT RIVERDALE HIGH #31, December 1975

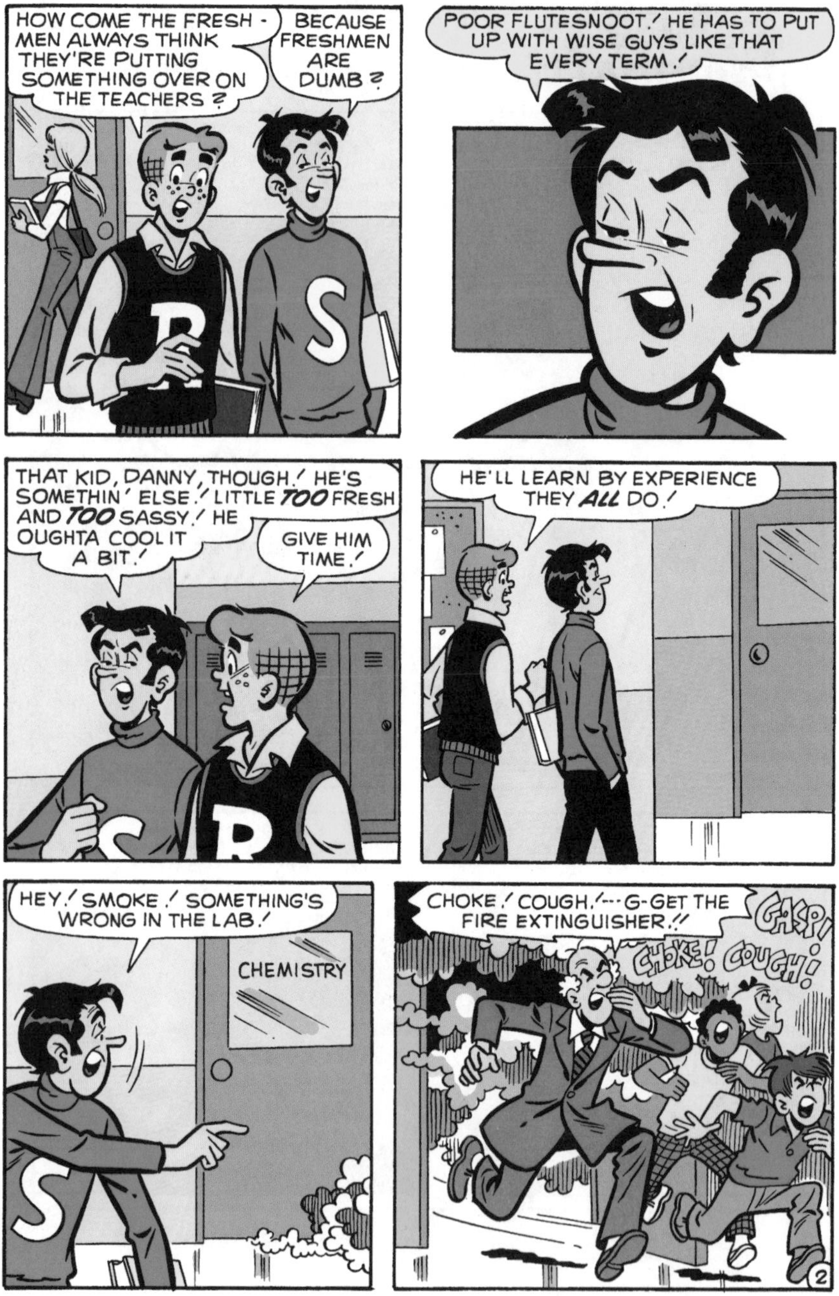
HOW COME THE FRESH-MEN ALWAYS THINK THEY'RE PUTTING SOMETHING OVER ON THE TEACHERS?
BECAUSE FRESHMEN ARE DUMB?
POOR FLUTESNOOT! HE HAS TO PUT UP WITH WISE GUYS LIKE THAT EVERY TERM!
THAT KID, DANNY, THOUGH! HE'S SOMETHIN' ELSE! LITTLE TOO FRESH AND TOO SASSY! HE OUGHTA COOL IT A BIT!
GIVE HIM TIME!
HE'LL LEARN BY EXPERIENCE THEY ALL DO!
HEY! SMOKE! SOMETHING'S WRONG IN THE LAB!
CHEMISTRY
CHOKE! COUGH!--- G-GET THE FIRE EXTINGUISHER!!
GASP!
CHOKE! COUGH!
2

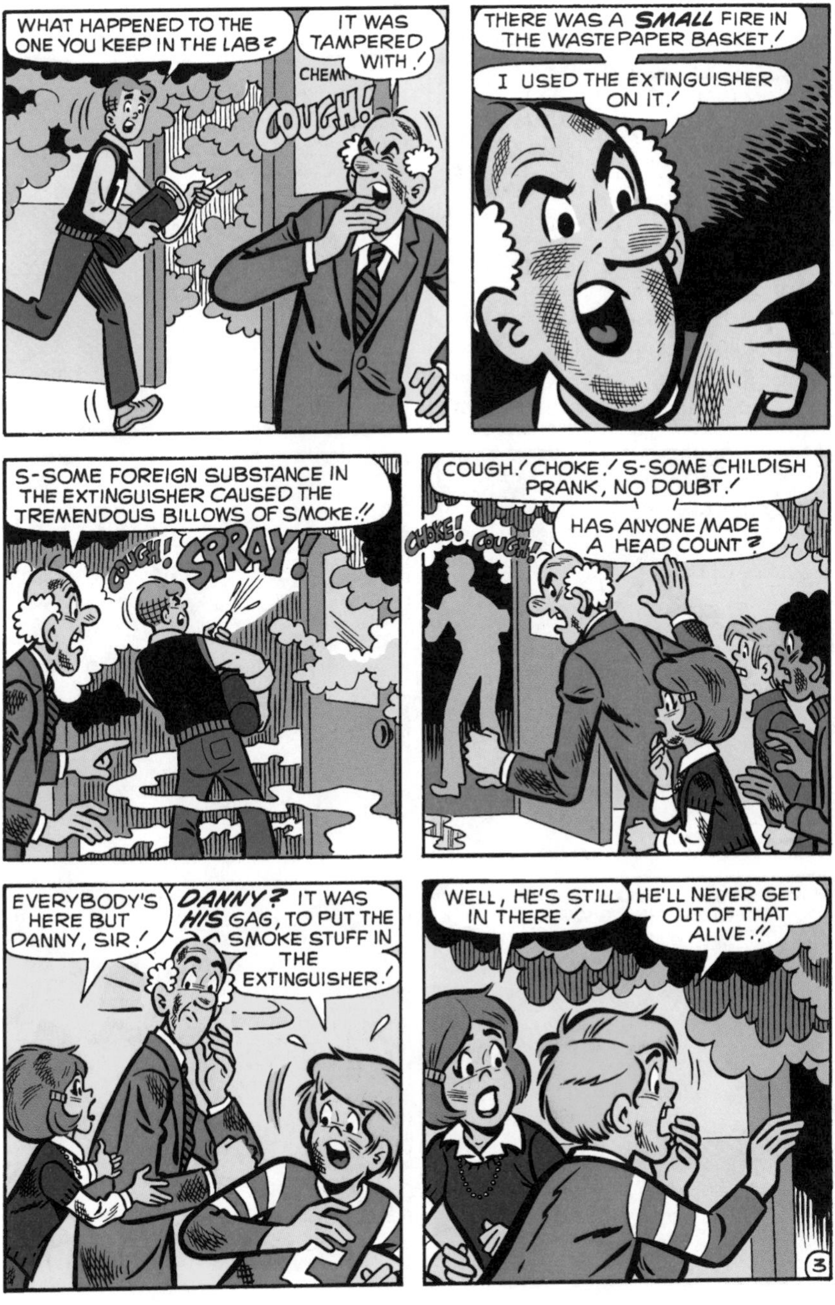
WHAT HAPPENED TO THE ONE YOU KEEP IN THE LAB?
IT WAS TAMPERED WITH!
CHEM
COUGH!
THERE WAS A SMALL FIRE IN THE WASTEPAPER BASKET!
I USED THE EXTINGUISHER ON IT!
S-SOME FOREIGN SUBSTANCE IN THE EXTINGUISHER CAUSED THE TREMENDOUS BILLOWS OF SMOKE!!
COUGH!
SPRAY!
COUGH! CHOKE! S-SOME CHILDISH PRANK, NO DOUBT!
HAS ANYONE MADE A HEAD COUNT?
CHOKE!
COUGH!
EVERYBODY'S HERE BUT DANNY, SIR!
DANNY? IT WAS HIS GAG, TO PUT THE SMOKE STUFF IN THE EXTINGUISHER!
WELL, HE'S STILL IN THERE!
HE'LL NEVER GET OUT OF THAT ALIVE!!
3

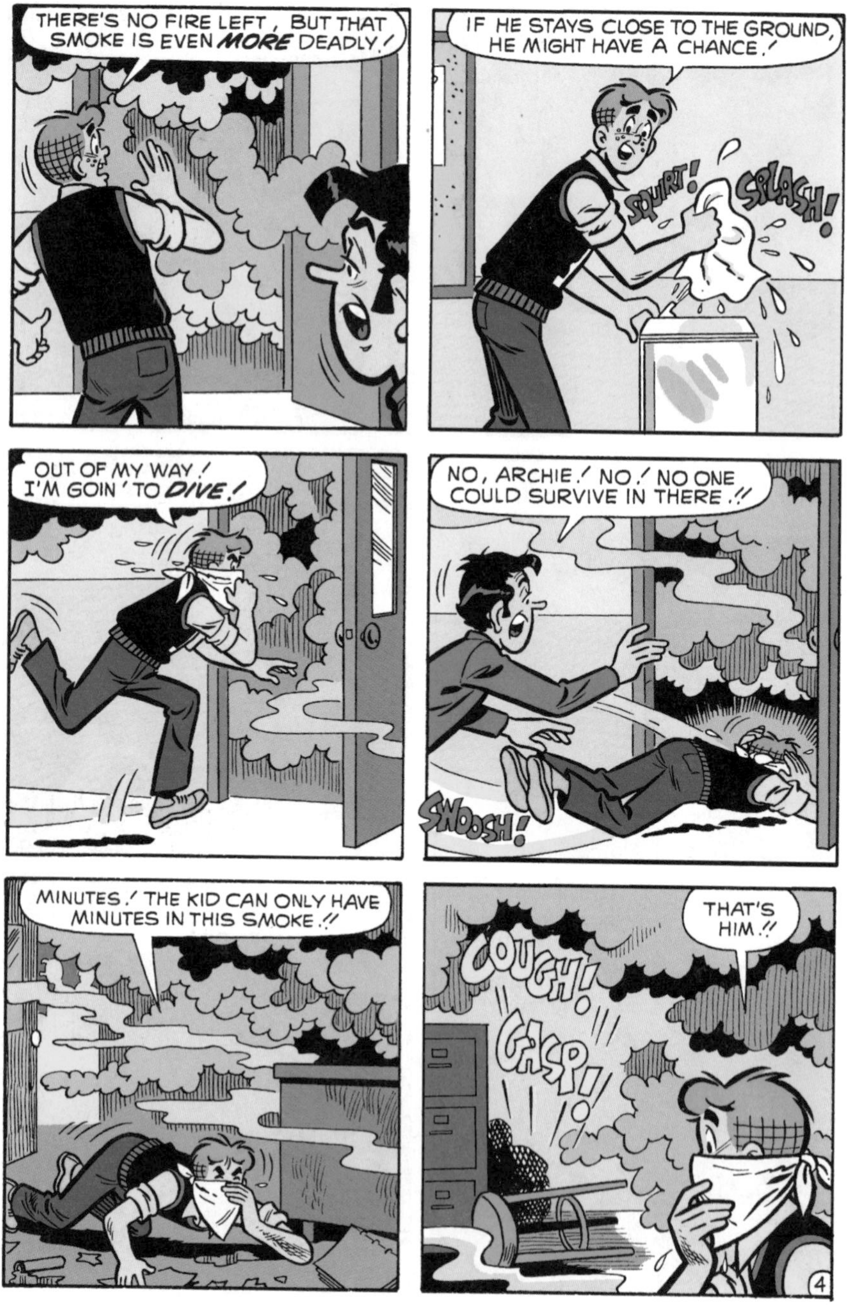
THERE'S NO FIRE LEFT, BUT THAT SMOKE IS EVEN MORE DEADLY!
IF HE STAYS CLOSE TO THE GROUND, HE MIGHT HAVE A CHANCE!
SQUIRT!
SPLASH!
OUT OF MY WAY! I'M GOIN' TO DIVE!
NO, ARCHIE! NO! NO ONE COULD SURVIVE IN THERE!!
SWOOSH!
MINUTES! THE KID CAN ONLY HAVE MINUTES IN THIS SMOKE!!
THAT'S HIM!!
COUGH!
GASP!
4

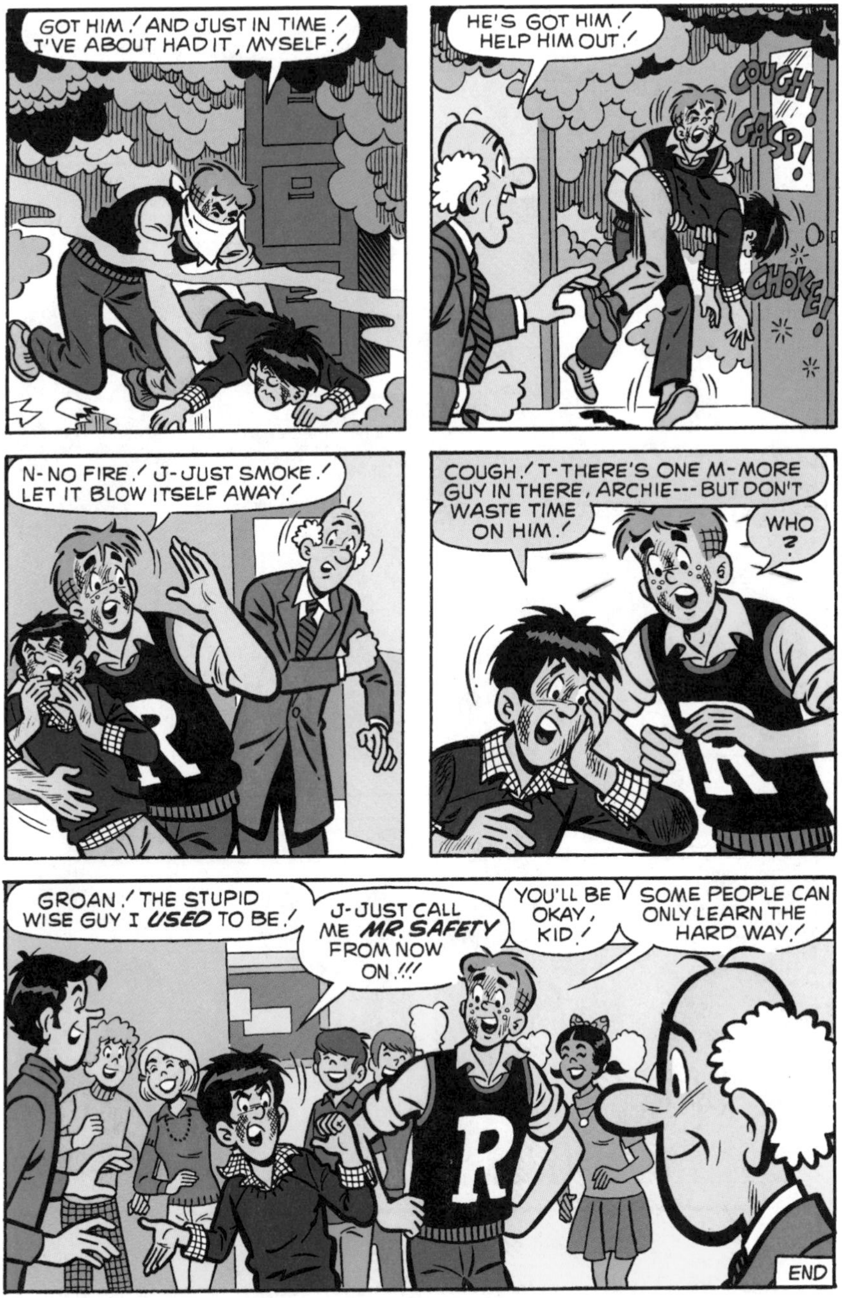
GOT HIM! AND JUST IN TIME! I'VE ABOUT HAD IT, MYSELF!
HE'S GOT HIM! HELP HIM OUT!
COUGH! GASP!
CHOKE!
N-NO FIRE! J-JUST SMOKE! LET IT BLOW ITSELF AWAY!
COUGH! T-THERE'S ONE M-MORE GUY IN THERE, ARCHIE--- BUT DON'T WASTE TIME ON HIM!
WHO?
GROAN! THE STUPID WISE GUY I USED TO BE!
J-JUST CALL ME MR. SAFETY FROM NOW ON!!!
YOU'LL BE OKAY, KID!
SOME PEOPLE CAN ONLY LEARN THE HARD WAY!
END

Archie in The FABULOUS FOUR

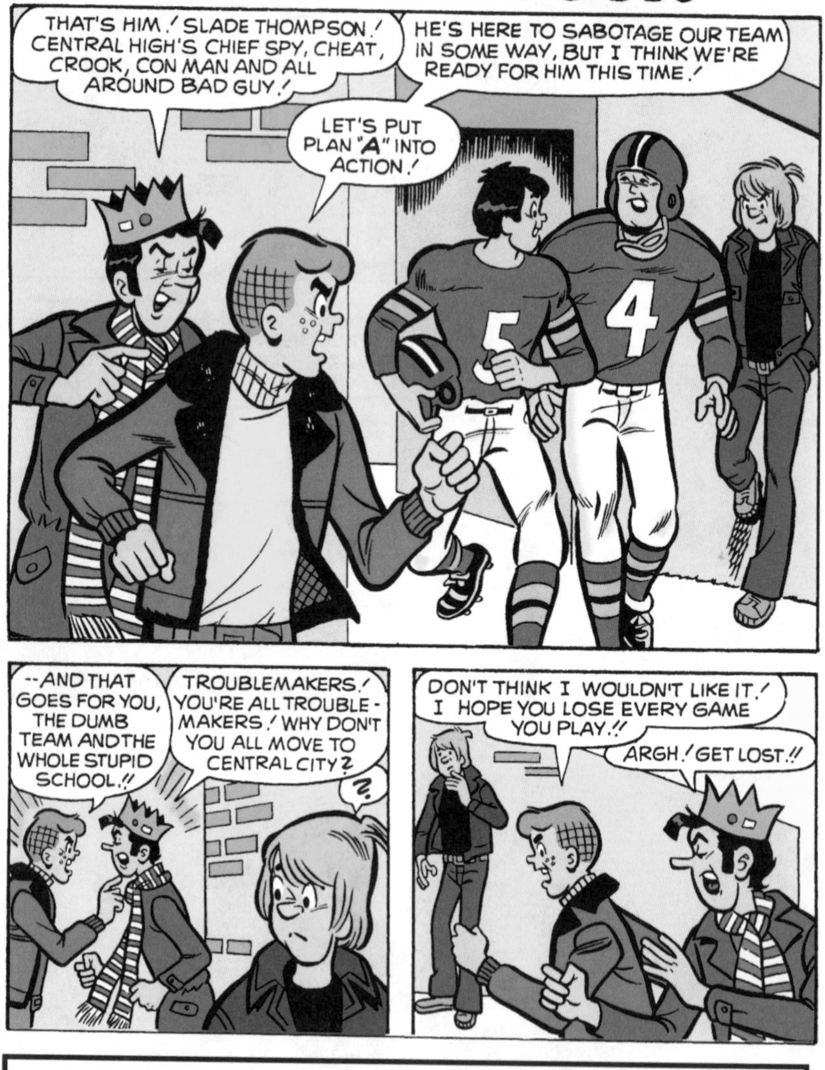
THAT'S HIM.! SLADE THOMPSON.! CENTRAL HIGH'S CHIEF SPY, CHEAT, CROOK, CON MAN AND ALL AROUND BAD GUY.!
HE'S HERE TO SABOTAGE OUR TEAM IN SOME WAY, BUT I THINK WE'RE READY FOR HIM THIS TIME.!
LET'S PUT PLAN "A" INTO ACTION.!
4
--AND THAT GOES FOR YOU, THE DUMB TEAM AND THE WHOLE STUPID SCHOOL.!!
TROUBLEMAKERS.! YOU'RE ALL TROUBLE-MAKERS.! WHY DON'T YOU ALL MOVE TO CENTRAL CITY?
?
DON'T THINK I WOULDN'T LIKE IT.! I HOPE YOU LOSE EVERY GAME YOU PLAY.!!
ARGH.! GET LOST.!!

Story: Frank Doyle Pencils: Stan Goldberg

Inks: Rudy Lapick Letters: Bill Yoshida Colors: Barry Grossman

Originally printed in ARCHIE AT RIVERDALE HIGH #32, January 1976

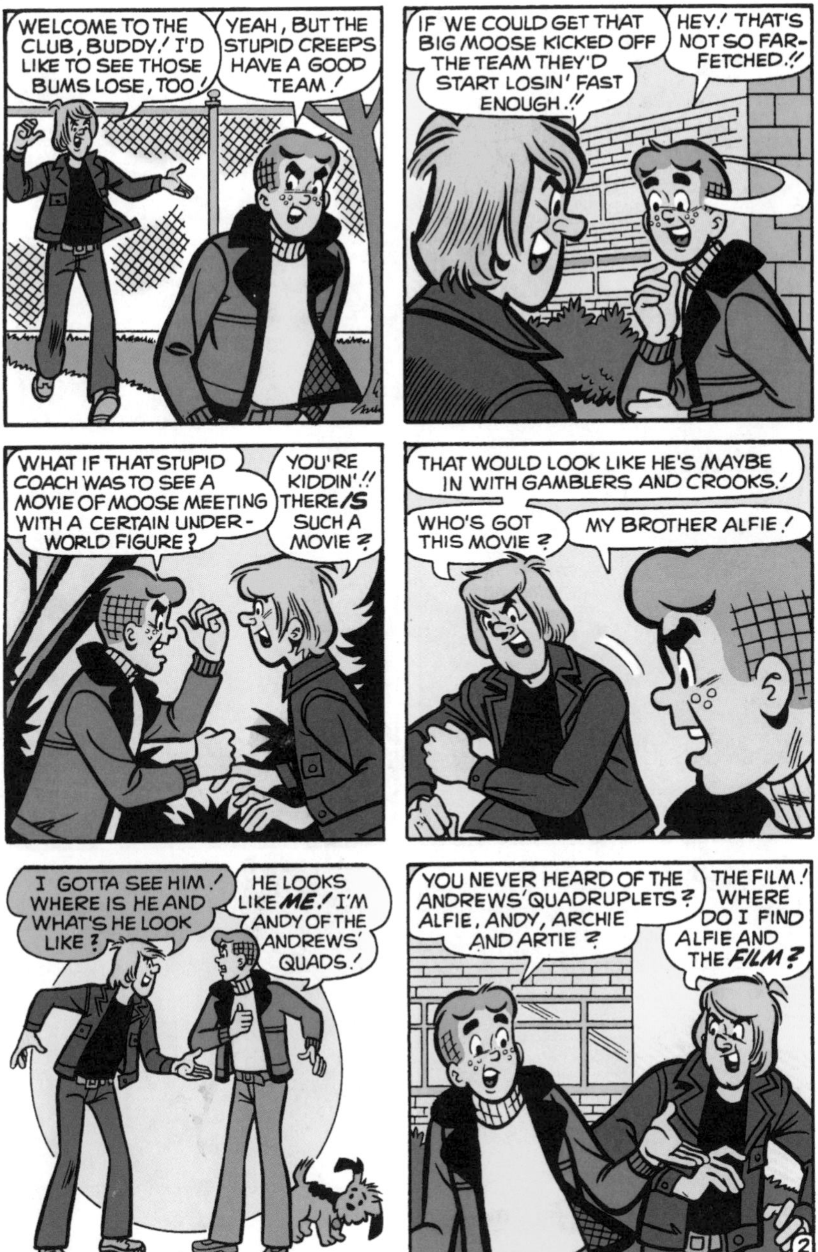
WELCOME TO THE CLUB, BUDDY! I'D LIKE TO SEE THOSE BUMS LOSE, TOO!
YEAH, BUT THE STUPID CREEPS HAVE A GOOD TEAM!
IF WE COULD GET THAT BIG MOOSE KICKED OFF THE TEAM THEY'D START LOSIN' FAST ENOUGH!!
HEY! THAT'S NOT SO FAR-FETCHED!!
WHAT IF THAT STUPID COACH WAS TO SEE A MOVIE OF MOOSE MEETING WITH A CERTAIN UNDER-WORLD FIGURE?
YOU'RE KIDDIN'!! THERE IS SUCH A MOVIE?
THAT WOULD LOOK LIKE HE'S MAYBE IN WITH GAMBLERS AND CROOKS!
WHO'S GOT THIS MOVIE?
MY BROTHER ALFIE!
I GOTTA SEE HIM! WHERE IS HE AND WHAT'S HE LOOK LIKE?
HE LOOKS LIKE ME! I'M ANDY OF THE ANDREWS' QUADS!
YOU NEVER HEARD OF THE ANDREWS' QUADRUPLETS? ALFIE, ANDY, ARCHIE AND ARTIE?
THE FILM! WHERE DO I FIND ALFIE AND THE FILM?
2

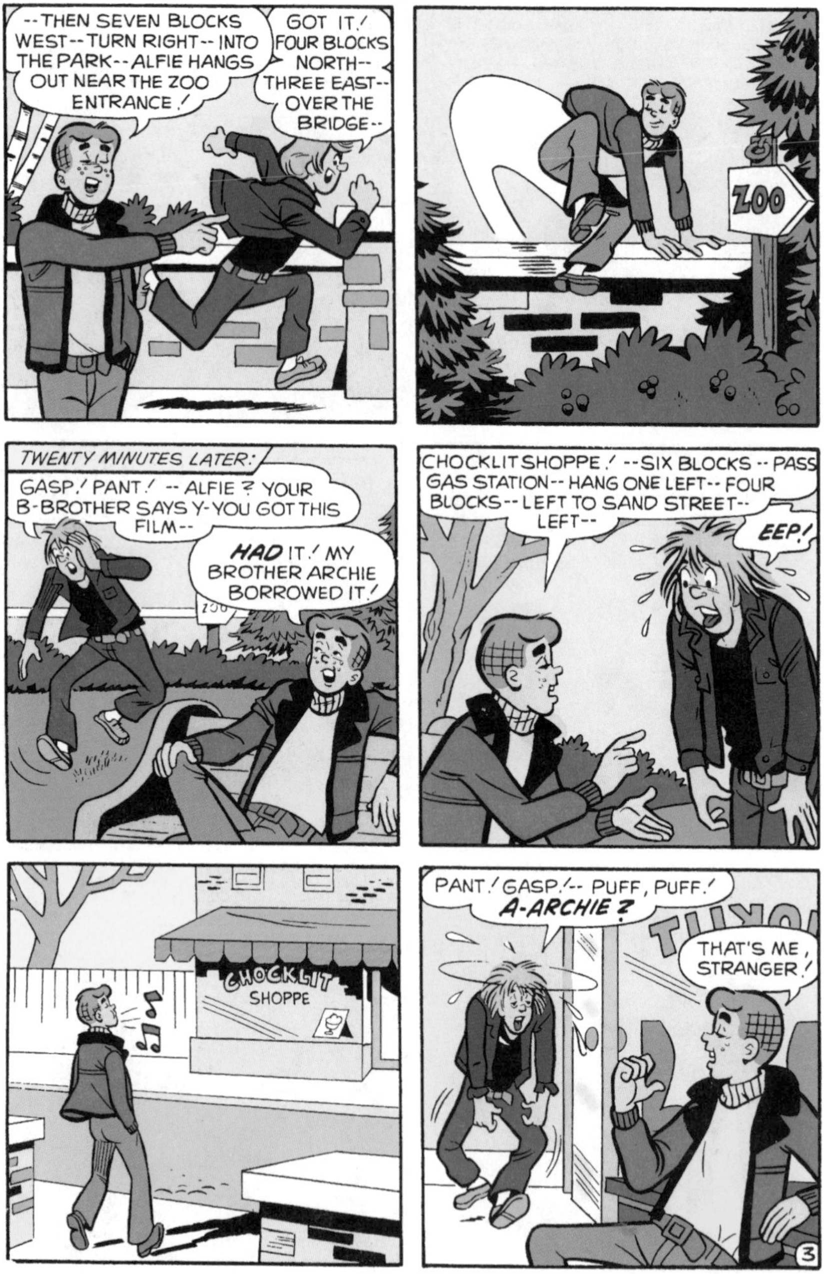
--THEN SEVEN BLOCKS WEST--TURN RIGHT--INTO THE PARK--ALFIE HANGS OUT NEAR THE ZOO ENTRANCE!
GOT IT! FOUR BLOCKS NORTH--THREE EAST--OVER THE BRIDGE--
ZOO
TWENTY MINUTES LATER:
GASP! PANT! --ALFIE? YOUR B-BROTHER SAYS Y-YOU GOT THIS FILM--
HAD IT! MY BROTHER ARCHIE BORROWED IT!
CHOCKLIT SHOPPE! --SIX BLOCKS--PASS GAS STATION--HANG ONE LEFT--FOUR BLOCKS--LEFT TO SAND STREET--LEFT--
EEP!
CHOCKLIT SHOPPE
PANT! GASP!--PUFF, PUFF! A-ARCHIE?
THAT'S ME, STRANGER!
3

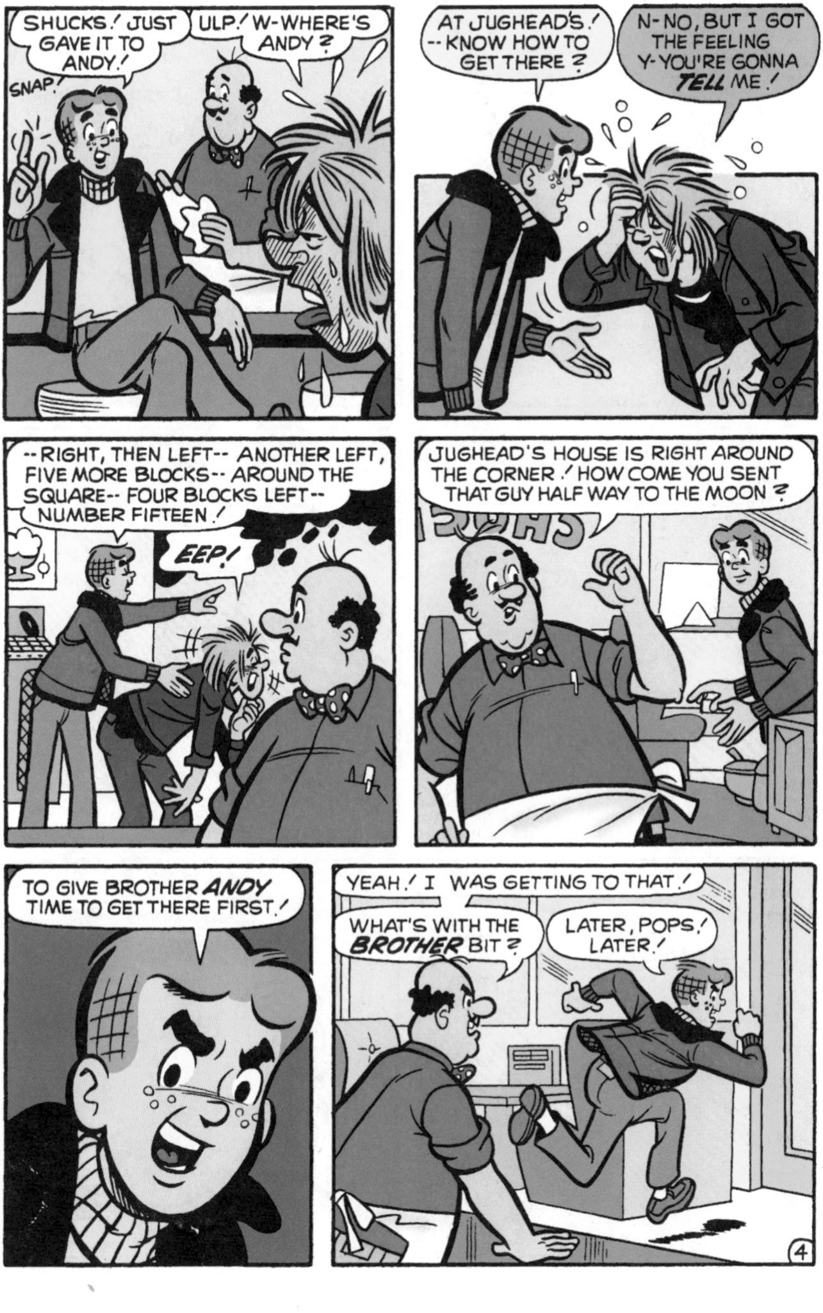
SHUCKS! JUST GAVE IT TO ANDY!
SNAP!
ULP! W-WHERE'S ANDY?
AT JUGHEAD'S! --KNOW HOW TO GET THERE?
N-NO, BUT I GOT THE FEELING Y-YOU'RE GONNA TELL ME!
--RIGHT, THEN LEFT-- ANOTHER LEFT, FIVE MORE BLOCKS-- AROUND THE SQUARE-- FOUR BLOCKS LEFT-- NUMBER FIFTEEN!
EEP!
JUGHEAD'S HOUSE IS RIGHT AROUND THE CORNER! HOW COME YOU SENT THAT GUY HALF WAY TO THE MOON?
TO GIVE BROTHER ANDY TIME TO GET THERE FIRST!
YEAH! I WAS GETTING TO THAT!
WHAT'S WITH THE BROTHER BIT?
LATER, POPS! LATER!
4

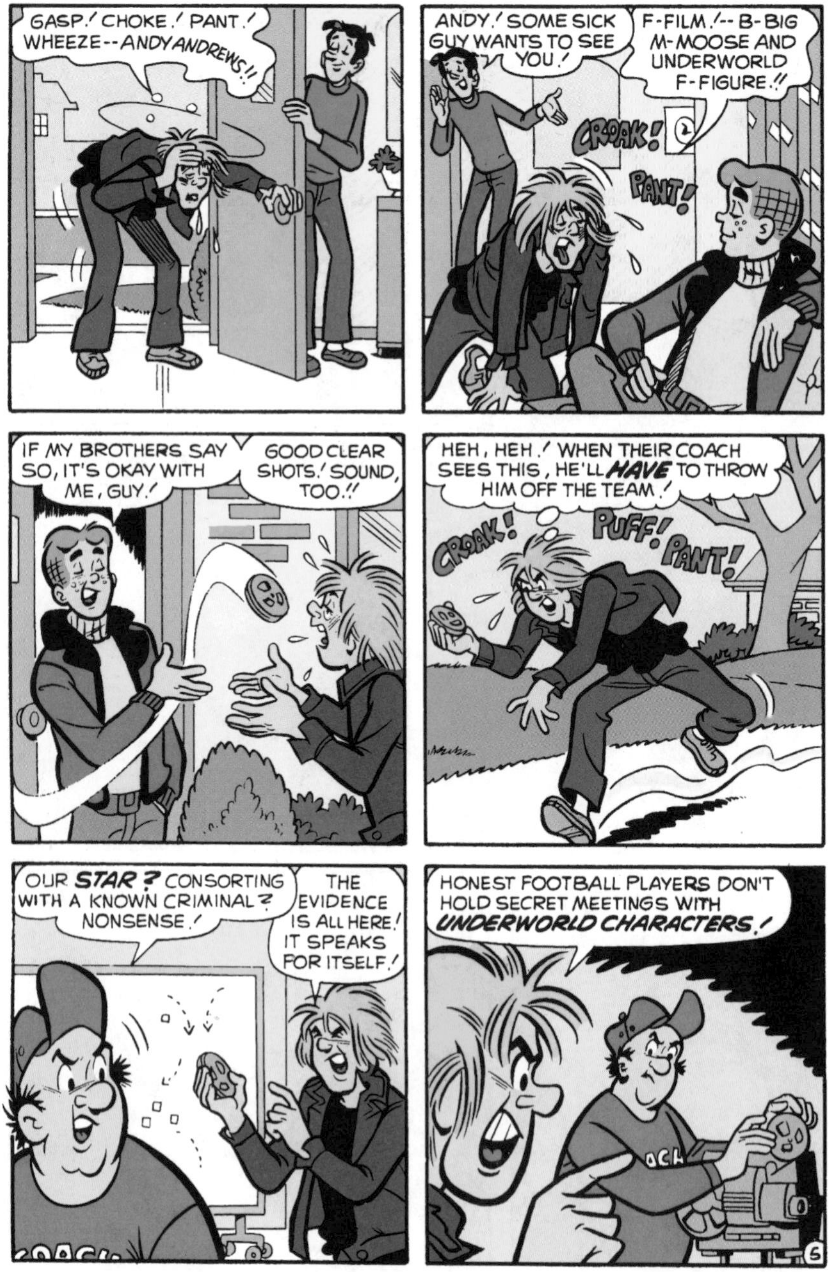
GASP.! CHOKE.! PANT.! WHEEZE--ANDY ANDREWS!!
ANDY.! SOME SICK GUY WANTS TO SEE YOU.!
F-FILM.!-- B-BIG M-MOOSE AND UNDERWORLD F-FIGURE.!!
CROAK!
PANT!
IF MY BROTHERS SAY SO, IT'S OKAY WITH ME, GUY.!
GOOD CLEAR SHOTS.! SOUND, TOO.!!
HEH, HEH.! WHEN THEIR COACH SEES THIS, HE'LL HAVE TO THROW HIM OFF THE TEAM.!
CROAK!
PUFF!
PANT!
OUR STAR? CONSORTING WITH A KNOWN CRIMINAL? NONSENSE.!
THE EVIDENCE IS ALL HERE.! IT SPEAKS FOR ITSELF.!
HONEST FOOTBALL PLAYERS DON'T HOLD SECRET MEETINGS WITH UNDERWORLD CHARACTERS.!
5

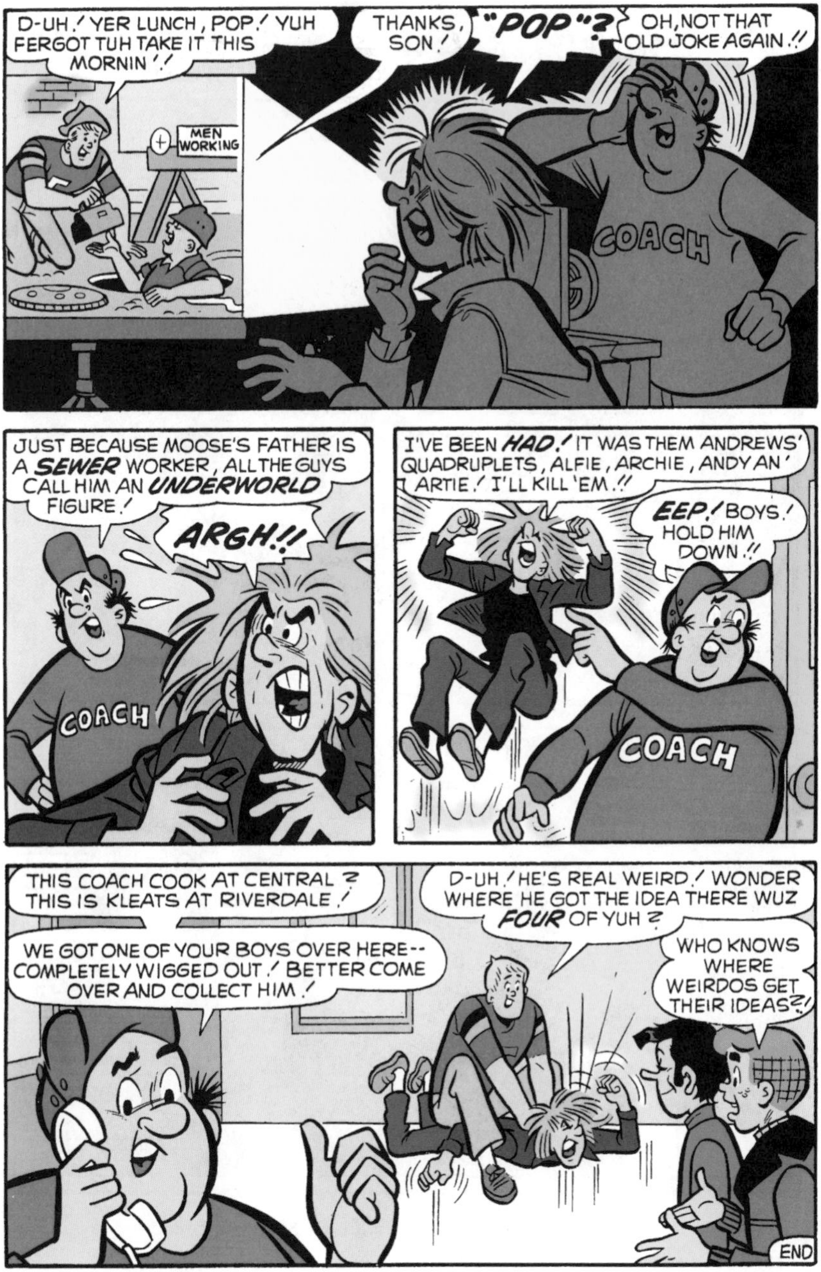
D-UH! YER LUNCH, POP! YUH FERGOT TUH TAKE IT THIS MORNIN'!
MEN WORKING
THANKS, SON!
"POP"?
OH, NOT THAT OLD JOKE AGAIN!!
COACH
JUST BECAUSE MOOSE'S FATHER IS A SEWER WORKER, ALL THE GUYS CALL HIM AN UNDERWORLD FIGURE!
ARGH!!
COACH
I'VE BEEN HAD! IT WAS THEM ANDREWS' QUADRUPLETS, ALFIE, ARCHIE, ANDY AN' ARTIE! I'LL KILL 'EM!!
EEP! BOYS! HOLD HIM DOWN!!
COACH
THIS COACH COOK AT CENTRAL? THIS IS KLEATS AT RIVERDALE!
WE GOT ONE OF YOUR BOYS OVER HERE-- COMPLETELY WIGGED OUT! BETTER COME OVER AND COLLECT HIM!
D-UH! HE'S REAL WEIRD! WONDER WHERE HE GOT THE IDEA THERE WUZ FOUR OF YUH?
WHO KNOWS WHERE WEIRDOS GET THEIR IDEAS?!
END

Archie in "Scandal Sheet" Part I

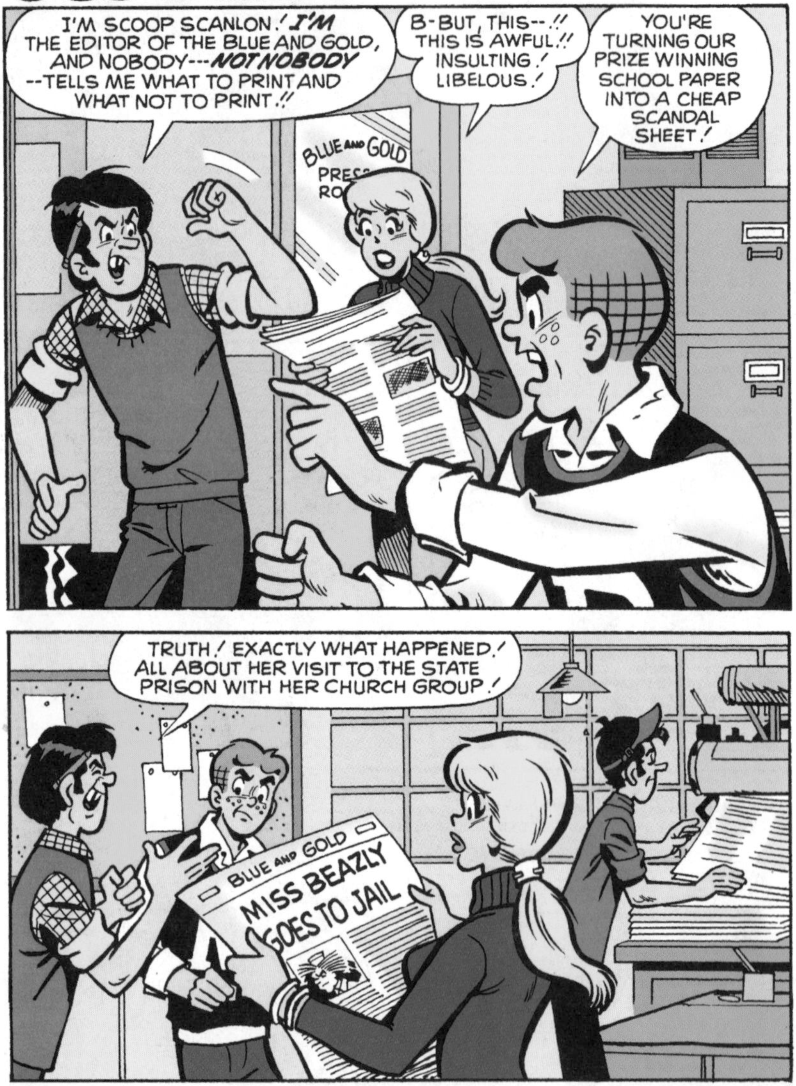
I'M SCOOP SCANLON! I'M THE EDITOR OF THE BLUE AND GOLD, AND NOBODY---NOT NOBODY--TELLS ME WHAT TO PRINT AND WHAT NOT TO PRINT!!
B-BUT, THIS--!! THIS IS AWFUL!! INSULTING! LIBELOUS!
YOU'RE TURNING OUR PRIZE WINNING SCHOOL PAPER INTO A CHEAP SCANDAL SHEET!
BLUE AND GOLD
TRUTH! EXACTLY WHAT HAPPENED! ALL ABOUT HER VISIT TO THE STATE PRISON WITH HER CHURCH GROUP!
BLUE AND GOLD
MISS BEAZLY GOES TO JAIL

Story: Frank Doyle Pencils: Stan Goldberg

Inks: Jon D'Agostino Letters: Bill Yoshida Colors: Barry Grossman

Originally printed in ARCHIE AT RIVERDALE HIGH #33, February 1976

SO NOBODY CAN SUE ME FOR LIBEL, 'CAUSE THAT'S WHAT HAPPENED, AND I CAN *PROVE* IT!

BUT THAT'S NOT THE IMPRESSION YOUR HEADLINES GIVE!

HEADLINES SELL PAPERS, BUDDY!

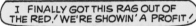

I FINALLY GOT THIS RAG OUT OF THE RED! WE'RE SHOWIN' A PROFIT!

AND MY HEADLINES ARE DOIN' IT!

NOW I'VE GOT AN INTERVIEW WITH MISS GRUNDY! YOU KIDS RAP BY YOURSELF! I'M BUSY!

CHEAP SENSATIONALISM! THAT'S ALL IT IS! IT GIVES THE NEWSPAPER GAME A BAD NAME!

HE'S NOTHING BUT AN OPPORTUNIST! BUILDING A SUCCESS ON *SCARE HEADLINES!*

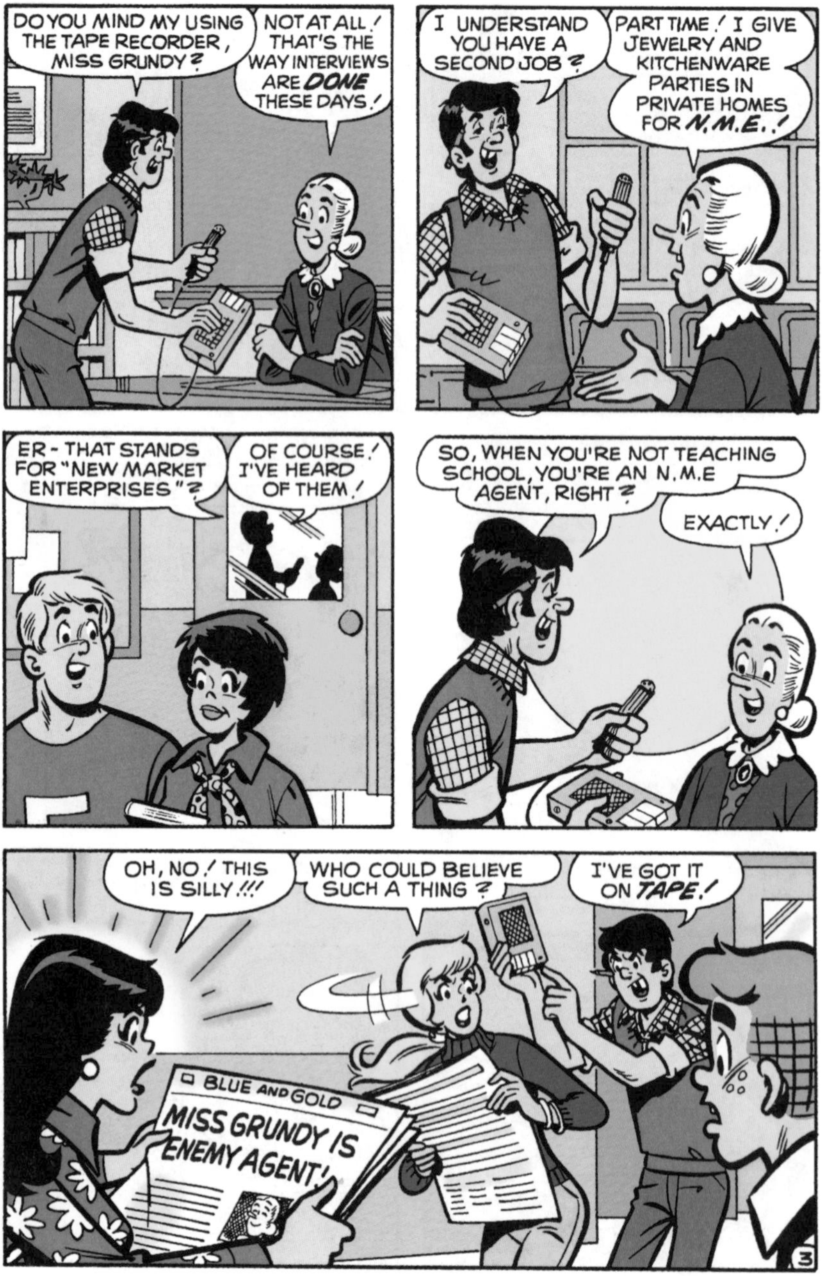
DO YOU MIND MY USING THE TAPE RECORDER, MISS GRUNDY?
NOT AT ALL! THAT'S THE WAY INTERVIEWS ARE DONE THESE DAYS!
I UNDERSTAND YOU HAVE A SECOND JOB?
PART TIME! I GIVE JEWELRY AND KITCHENWARE PARTIES IN PRIVATE HOMES FOR N.M.E.!
ER- THAT STANDS FOR "NEW MARKET ENTERPRISES"?
OF COURSE! I'VE HEARD OF THEM!
SO, WHEN YOU'RE NOT TEACHING SCHOOL, YOU'RE AN N.M.E AGENT, RIGHT?
EXACTLY!
OH, NO! THIS IS SILLY!!!
WHO COULD BELIEVE SUCH A THING?
I'VE GOT IT ON TAPE!
BLUE AND GOLD
MISS GRUNDY IS ENEMY AGENT!
3

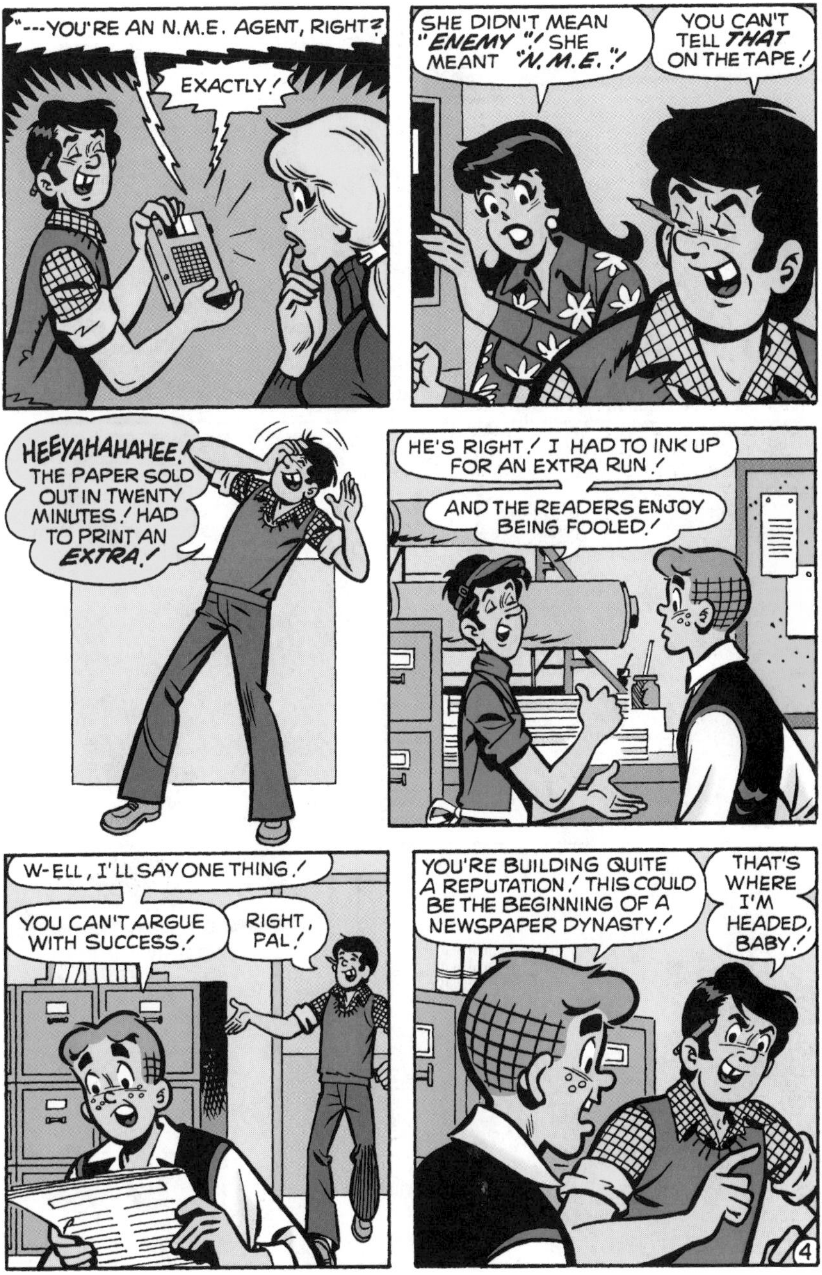
"---YOU'RE AN N.M.E. AGENT, RIGHT?
EXACTLY!
SHE DIDN'T MEAN "ENEMY"! SHE MEANT "N.M.E."!
YOU CAN'T TELL THAT ON THE TAPE!
HEEYAHAHAHEE! THE PAPER SOLD OUT IN TWENTY MINUTES! HAD TO PRINT AN EXTRA!
HE'S RIGHT! I HAD TO INK UP FOR AN EXTRA RUN!
AND THE READERS ENJOY BEING FOOLED!
W-ELL, I'LL SAY ONE THING!
YOU CAN'T ARGUE WITH SUCCESS!
RIGHT, PAL!
YOU'RE BUILDING QUITE A REPUTATION! THIS COULD BE THE BEGINNING OF A NEWSPAPER DYNASTY!
THAT'S WHERE I'M HEADED, BABY!
4

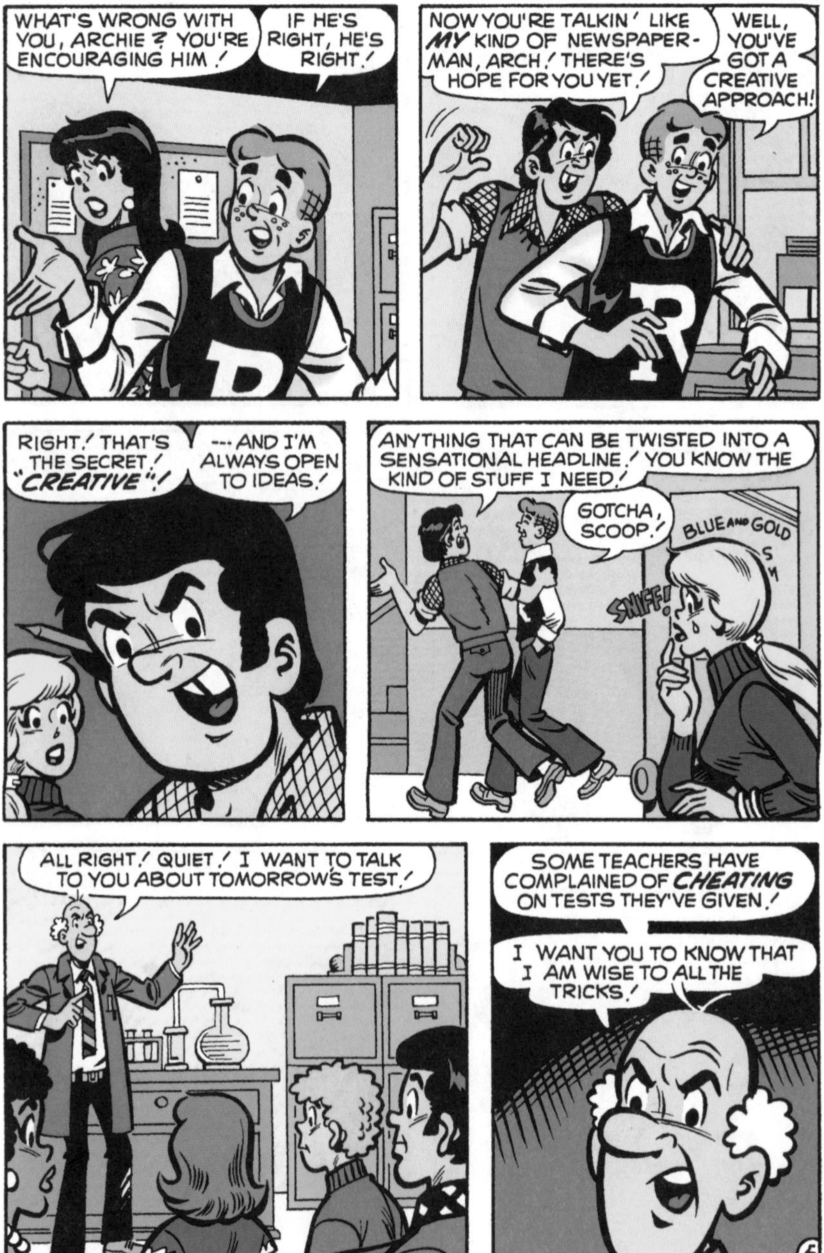
WHAT'S WRONG WITH YOU, ARCHIE? YOU'RE ENCOURAGING HIM!
IF HE'S RIGHT, HE'S RIGHT!
NOW YOU'RE TALKIN' LIKE *MY* KIND OF NEWSPAPER-MAN, ARCH! THERE'S HOPE FOR YOU YET!
WELL, YOU'VE GOT A CREATIVE APPROACH!
RIGHT! THAT'S THE SECRET! "*CREATIVE*"!
--- AND I'M ALWAYS OPEN TO IDEAS!
ANYTHING THAT CAN BE TWISTED INTO A SENSATIONAL HEADLINE! YOU KNOW THE KIND OF STUFF I NEED!
GOTCHA, SCOOP!
BLUE AND GOLD
SNIFF!
ALL RIGHT! QUIET! I WANT TO TALK TO YOU ABOUT TOMORROW'S TEST!
SOME TEACHERS HAVE COMPLAINED OF *CHEATING* ON TESTS THEY'VE GIVEN!
I WANT YOU TO KNOW THAT I AM WISE TO ALL THE TRICKS!
5

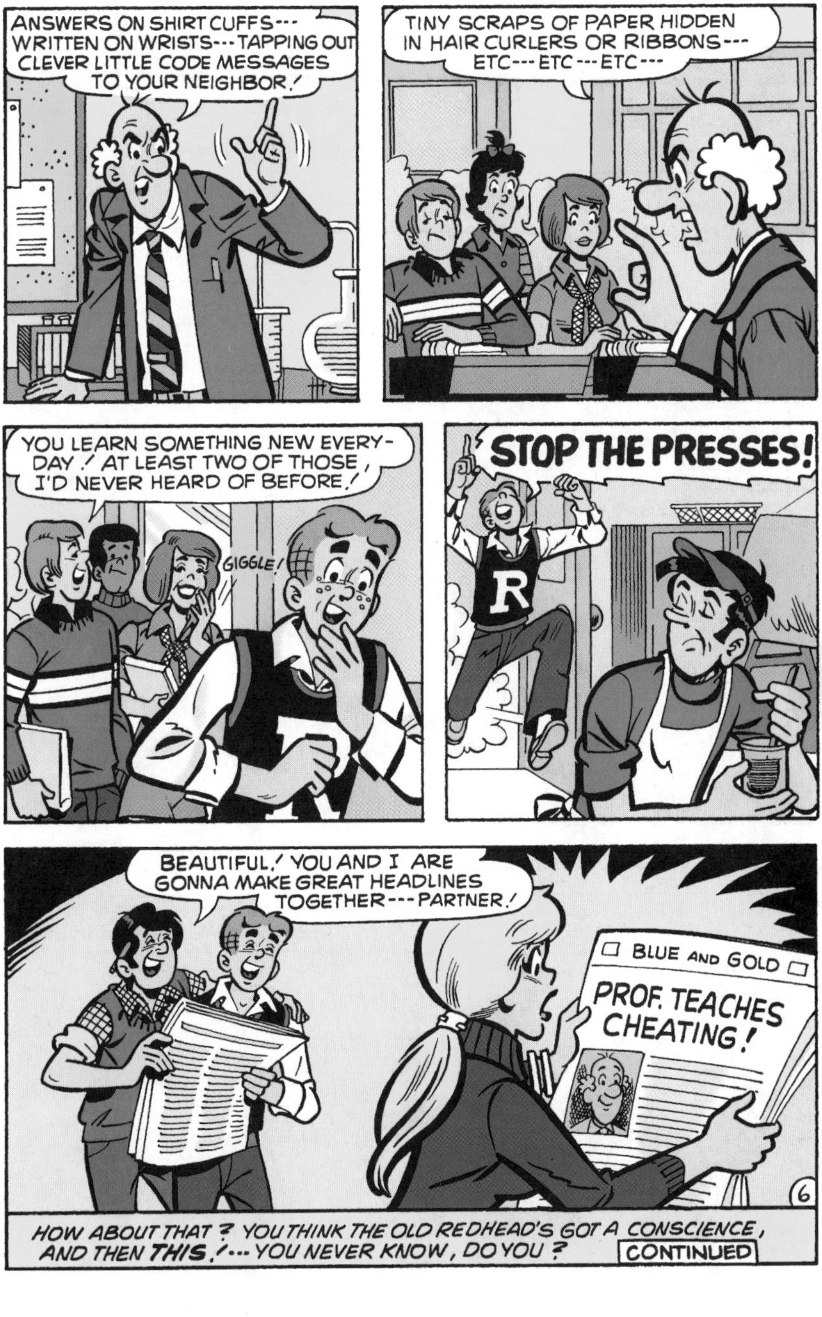
ANSWERS ON SHIRT CUFFS--- WRITTEN ON WRISTS---TAPPING OUT CLEVER LITTLE CODE MESSAGES TO YOUR NEIGHBOR!
TINY SCRAPS OF PAPER HIDDEN IN HAIR CURLERS OR RIBBONS--- ETC---ETC---ETC---
YOU LEARN SOMETHING NEW EVERY-DAY! AT LEAST TWO OF THOSE, I'D NEVER HEARD OF BEFORE!
GIGGLE!
STOP THE PRESSES!
R
BEAUTIFUL! YOU AND I ARE GONNA MAKE GREAT HEADLINES TOGETHER---PARTNER!
BLUE AND GOLD
PROF. TEACHES CHEATING!
6
HOW ABOUT THAT? YOU THINK THE OLD REDHEAD'S GOT A CONSCIENCE, AND THEN THIS!--- YOU NEVER KNOW, DO YOU?
CONTINUED

Archie in SCANDAL SHEET PART II

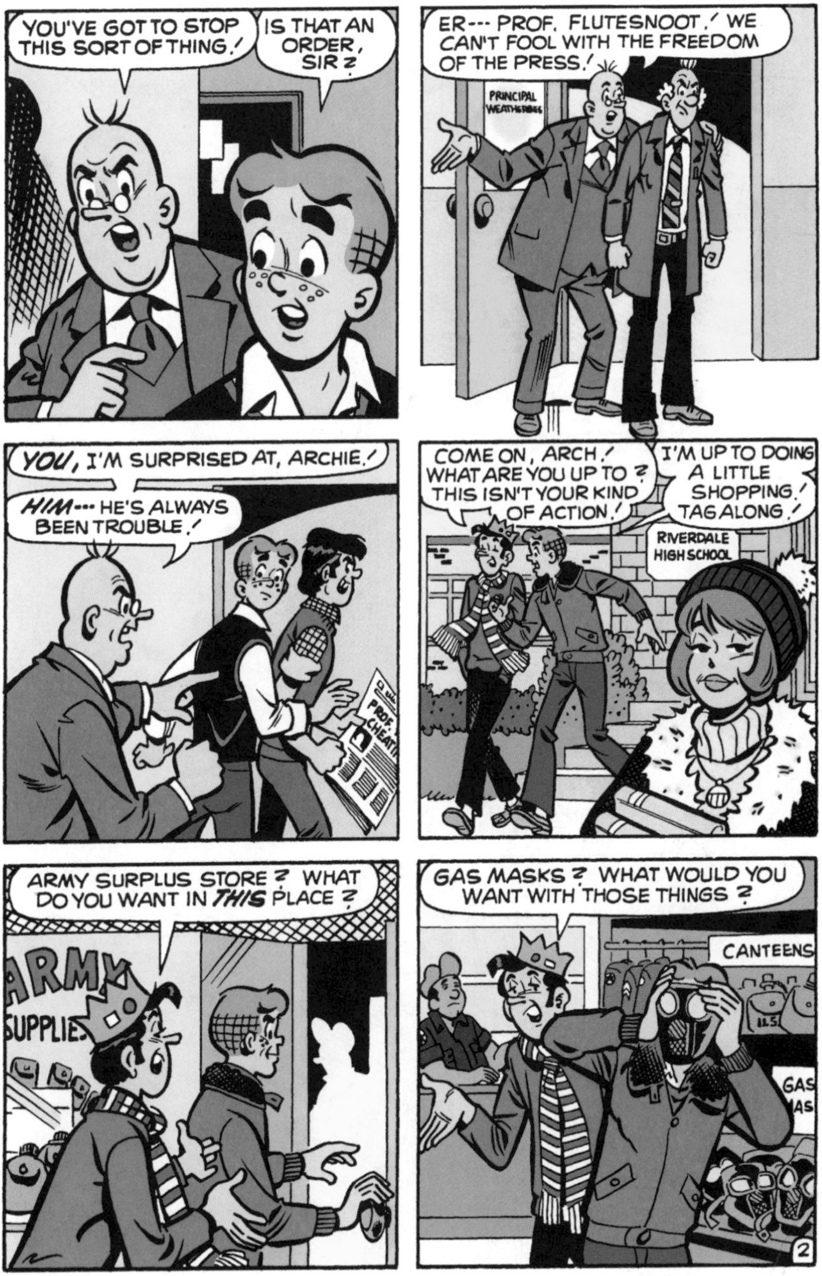

YOU'VE GOT TO STOP THIS SORT OF THING!
IS THAT AN ORDER, SIR?
ER--- PROF. FLUTESNOOT! WE CAN'T FOOL WITH THE FREEDOM OF THE PRESS!
PRINCIPAL WEATHERBEE
YOU, I'M SURPRISED AT, ARCHIE!
HIM--- HE'S ALWAYS BEEN TROUBLE!
PROF. CHEATI
COME ON, ARCH! WHAT ARE YOU UP TO? THIS ISN'T YOUR KIND OF ACTION!
I'M UP TO DOING A LITTLE SHOPPING! TAG ALONG!
RIVERDALE HIGH SCHOOL
ARMY SURPLUS STORE? WHAT DO YOU WANT IN THIS PLACE?
ARMY
SUPPLIES
GAS MASKS? WHAT WOULD YOU WANT WITH THOSE THINGS?
CANTEENS
GAS
2

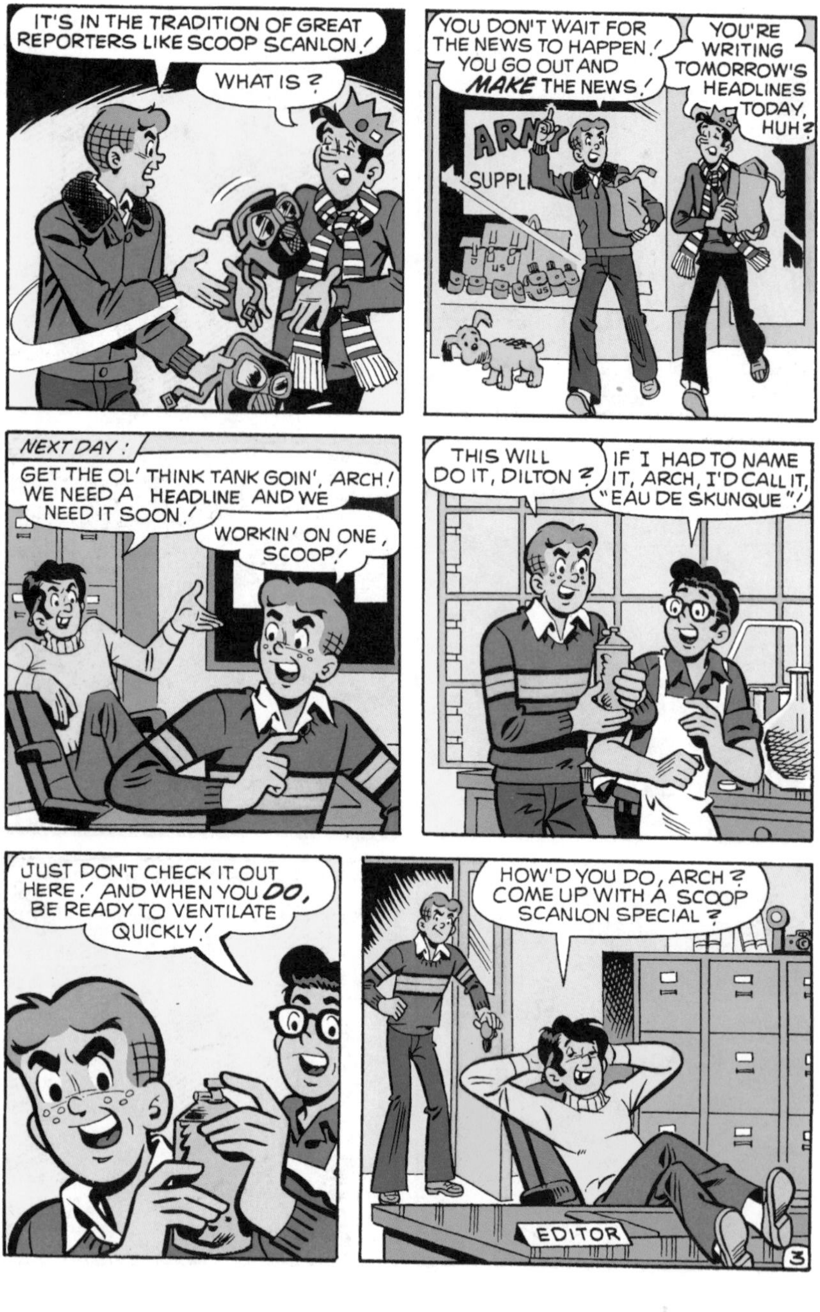
IT'S IN THE TRADITION OF GREAT REPORTERS LIKE SCOOP SCANLON!
WHAT IS?
YOU DON'T WAIT FOR THE NEWS TO HAPPEN! YOU GO OUT AND MAKE THE NEWS!
YOU'RE WRITING TOMORROW'S HEADLINES TODAY, HUH?
ARMY SUPPL
US
NEXT DAY:
GET THE OL' THINK TANK GOIN', ARCH! WE NEED A HEADLINE AND WE NEED IT SOON!
WORKIN' ON ONE, SCOOP!
THIS WILL DO IT, DILTON?
IF I HAD TO NAME IT, ARCH, I'D CALL IT, "EAU DE SKUNQUE"!
JUST DON'T CHECK IT OUT HERE! AND WHEN YOU DO, BE READY TO VENTILATE QUICKLY!
HOW'D YOU DO, ARCH? COME UP WITH A SCOOP SCANLON SPECIAL?
EDITOR
3

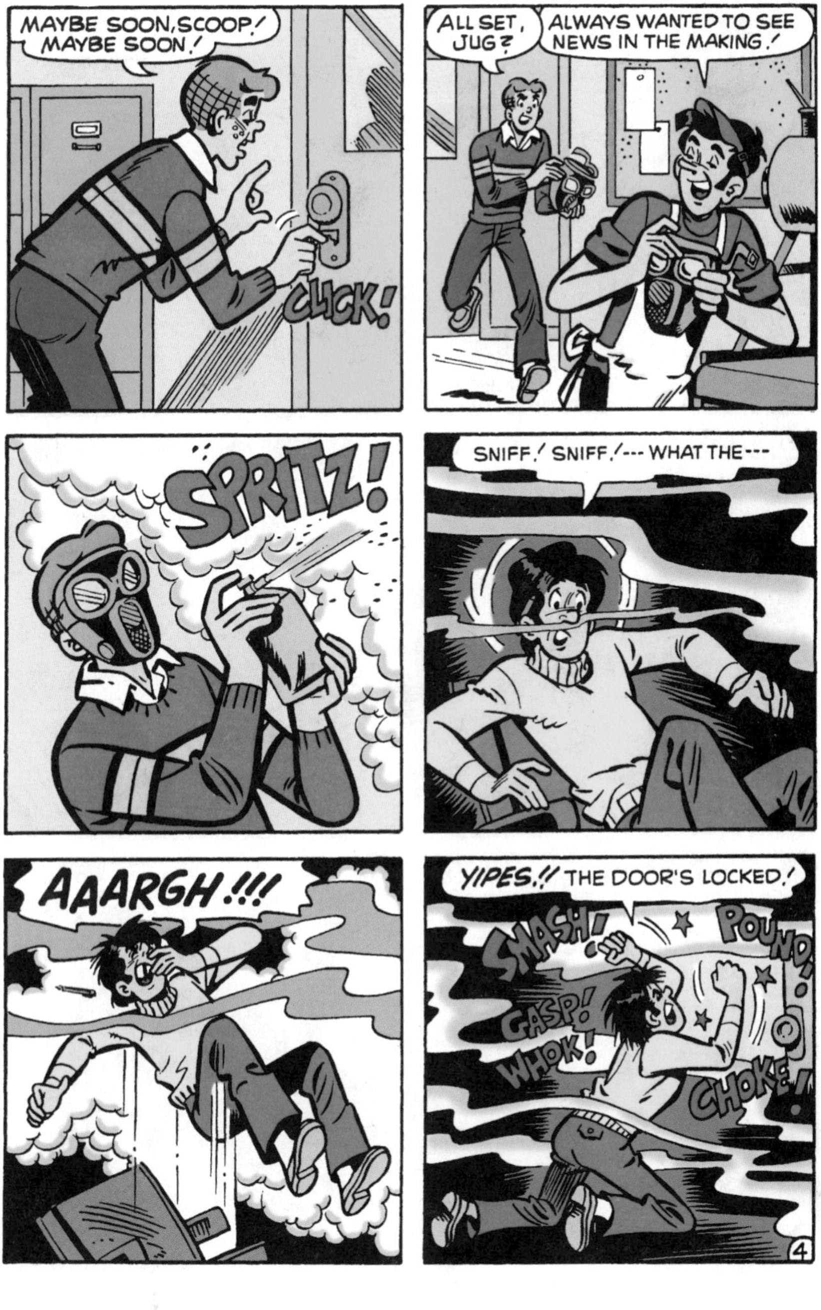
MAYBE SOON, SCOOP! MAYBE SOON!
CLICK!
ALL SET, JUG?
ALWAYS WANTED TO SEE NEWS IN THE MAKING!
SPRITZ!
SNIFF! SNIFF!--- WHAT THE---
AAARGH!!!
YIPES!! THE DOOR'S LOCKED!
SMASH!
POUND!
GASP!
WHOK!
CHOKE!
4

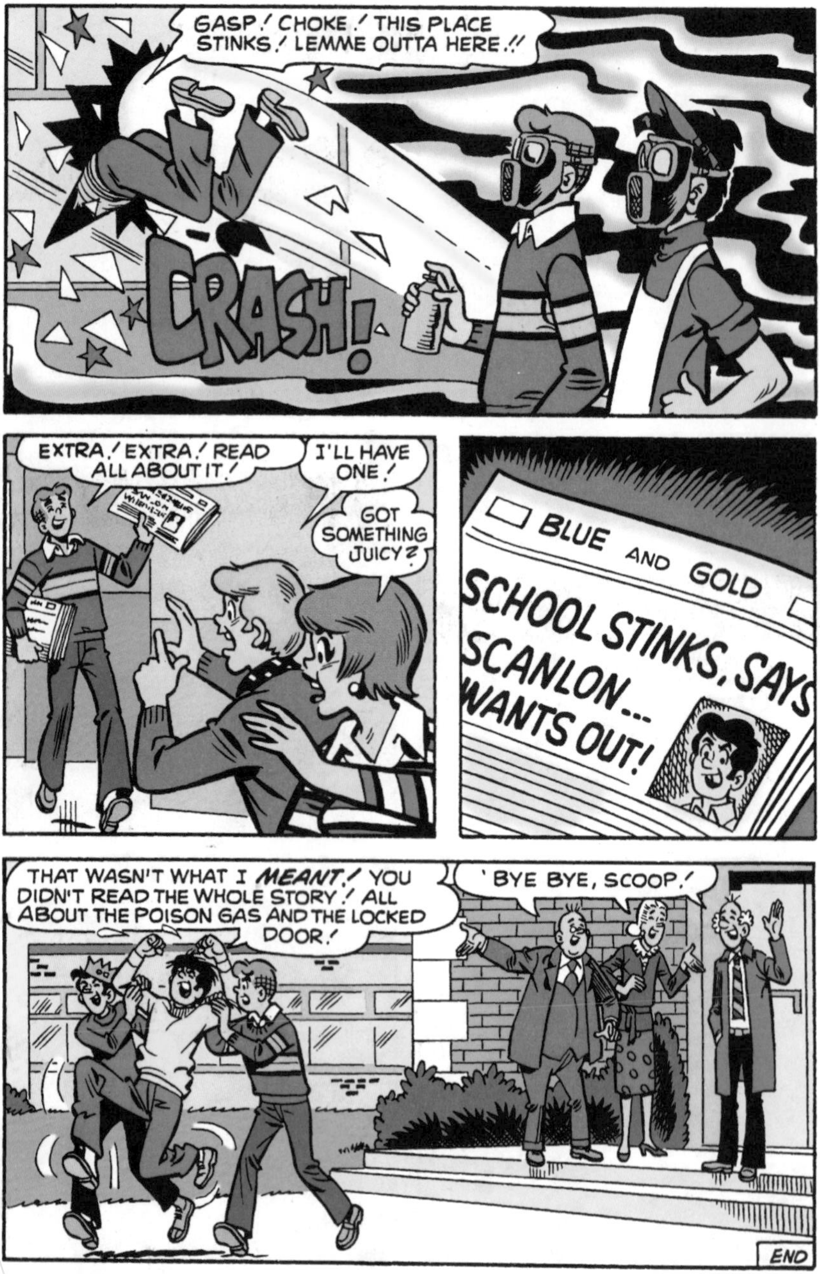
GASP! CHOKE! THIS PLACE STINKS! LEMME OUTTA HERE!!
CRASH!
EXTRA! EXTRA! READ ALL ABOUT IT!
I'LL HAVE ONE!
GOT SOMETHING JUICY?
BLUE AND GOLD
SCHOOL STINKS, SAYS SCANLON... WANTS OUT!
THAT WASN'T WHAT I MEANT! YOU DIDN'T READ THE WHOLE STORY! ALL ABOUT THE POISON GAS AND THE LOCKED DOOR!
'BYE BYE, SCOOP!
END